Orname

7

1808 – 1918

Chris Fogg is a creative producer, writer, director and dramaturg, who has written and directed for the theatre for many years, as well as collaborating artistically with choreographers and contemporary dance companies.

Ornaments of Grace is a chronicle of ten novels. *Victor* is the seventh in the sequence.

He has previously written more than thirty works for the stage as well as four collections of poems, stories and essays. These are*: Special Relationships, Northern Songs, Painting by Numbers* and *Dawn Chorus* (with woodcut illustrations by Chris Waters), all published by Mudlark Press.

Several of Chris's poems have appeared in International Psychoanalysis (IP), a US online journal, as well as in *Climate of Opinion*, a selection of verse in response to the work of Sigmund Freud edited by Irene Willis, and *What They Bring: The Poetry of Migration & Immigration*, co-edited by Irene Willis and Jim Haba, each published by IP, in 2017 and 2020.

Ornaments of Grace

(or *Unhistoric Acts*)

7

Laurel

Vol. 2: Victor

by

Chris Fogg

flaxbooks

First published 2020
© Chris Fogg 2020

Chris Fogg has asserted his rights under Copyright Designs & Patents Act 1988
to be identified as the author of this book

ISBN Number: 9781709867729

Cover and design by: Kama Glover

Cover Image: John Kay, Inventor of the Fly Shuttle, one of the Manchester
Murals by Ford Madox Brown, reprinted by kind permission of Manchester
Libraries, Information & Archives

Printed in Poland by Amazon

Although some of the people featured in this book are real,
and several of the events depicted actually happened,
Ornaments of Grace remains a work of fiction.

For Amanda and Tim

dedicated to the memory

of my parents and grandparents

Ornaments of Grace (*or Unhistoric Acts*) is a sequence of ten novels set in Manchester between 1760 and 2020. Collectively they tell the story of a city in four elements.

Victor is the seventh book in the sequence.

The full list of titles is:

1. Pomona (Water)

2. Tulip (Earth)
    Vol 1: Enclave
    Vol 2: Nymphs & Shepherds
    Vol 3: The Spindle Tree
    Vol 4: Return

3. Laurel (Air)
    Vol 1: Kettle
    Vol 2: Victor
    Vol 3: Victrix
    Vol 4: Scuttle

4. Moth (Fire)

Each book can be read independently or as part of the sequence.

"It's always too soon to go home. And it's always too soon to calculate effect... Cause-and-effect assumes that history marches forward, but history is not an army. It is a crab scuttling sideways, a drip of soft water wearing away stone, an earthquake breaking centuries of tension."

Rebecca Solnit: Hope in the Dark
(*Untold Histories, Wild Possibilities*)

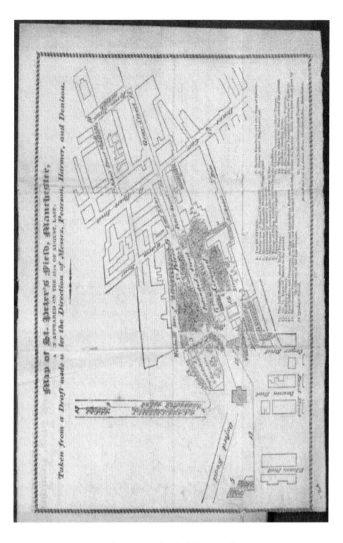

Map of St Peter's Field, Manchester
16th August 1819

Contents

ONE

A Rehearsal

1808 – 1809

in which three different futures are tried and tested –
in a court of law, a public place and a new kind of playhouse –
while a family wanders in search of a home

TWO

Ophelia

1813 – 1814

in which a lover's quarrel leads to tragedy –
a river freezes over –
and the piece of cloth becomes temporarily lost

THREE

The Year Without Summer

1817

*in which a group of young men attempt to walk to London
and back –
while another young man returns alone from war –
and a Queen welcomes migrants from afar
and invites them to make a new home*

FOUR

Weave A Gay Garland

1819

*in which many thousands gather on a great field
with sprigs of laurel in their hair to listen to some speeches –
but are prevented from doing so
by the actions of a powerful few –
a lost baby is found –
and two brothers meet for the first time*

EPILOGUE

1919

in which a vote is finally cast

Ornaments of Grace

"Wisdom is the principal thing. Therefore get wisdom and within all thy getting get understanding. Exalt her and she shall promote thee. She shall bring thee to honour when thou dost embrace her. She shall give to thine head an ornament of grace. A crown of glory shall she deliver to thee."

Proverbs: 4, verses 7 – 9

written around the domed ceiling of the Great Hall Reading Room Central
Reference Library, St Peter's Square, Manchester

"Fecisti patriam diversis de gentibus unam..."
"From differing peoples you have made one homeland..."

Rutilius Claudius Namatianus:
De Redito Suo, verse 63

"To be hopeful in bad times is not just foolishly romantic. It is based on the fact that human history is a history not only of cruelty, but also of compassion, sacrifice, courage, kindness. What we choose to emphasise in this complex history will determine our lives. If we see only the worst, it destroys our capacity to do something. If we remember those times and places—and there are so many—where people have behaved magnificently, this gives us the energy to act, and at least the possibility of sending this spinning top of a world in a different direction. And if we do act, in however small a way, we don't have to wait for some grand utopian future. The future is an infinite succession of presents, and to live now as we think human beings should live, in defiance of all that is bad around us, is itself a marvellous victory."

Howard Zinn: A Power Governments Cannot Suppress

Laurel (ii)

*"The bay-trees in our country all are wither'd
And meteors fright the fixed stars of heaven;
The pale-fac'd moon looks bloody on the earth
And lean-look'd prophets whisper fearful change;
Rich men look sad and ruffians dance and leap,
The one in fear to lose what they enjoy,
The other to enjoy by rage and war..."*

(Shakespeare: Richard II)

Air (ii)

*"It's easy to go down to Hell, night and day the gates of dark
death stand wide;
but to climb back up again, to retrace one's steps to the upper
air –
there's the rub..."*

(Virgil: The Aeneid, Book VI)

ONE

A Rehearsal

1808 – 1809

in which three different futures are tried and tested –
in a court of law, a public place and
a new kind of playhouse –
while a family wanders in search of a home

1

1808

25ᵗʰ May

Manchester Morning Post

26ᵗʰ May 1808

UNLAWFUL ASSEMBLY IN ST GEORGE'S FIELDS

ONE DEATH, MANY INJURED

EX-COLONEL ARRESTED

Three days of angry, but relatively peaceful protest by Manchester's weavers yesterday erupted into ugly violence when a crowd of three thousand unruly labourers, who had unlawfully assembled on St George's Fields, to the north of Angel Meadow, ran amok, terrorising local residents and shopkeepers.

Passions, which had been simmering ever since news broke that the Weavers' Petition to Parliament for a basic minimum wage had been rejected – a petition this newspaper had already dismissed as groundless – were further stoked by the sudden appearance among the crowds of Mr Joseph Hanson. This once well-loved, popular former Colonel of the Stockport & Salford Independent Rifles and ex-Commanding Officer of the Manchester Volunteer Home Guard, rode out into St George's Fields on a fine white stallion, from which he gave a series of inflammatory speeches. At one point he took off his hat and bowed his head, whereupon he was loudly cheered with many huzzahs by the tumultuous mob, actions which serve only to further besmirch Mr Hanson's erstwhile fine reputation.

The Boroughreeve, together with local Magistrates, calmly but decisively ordered in separate units of the 4th Dragoon Guards and Deputy Joseph Nadin's Special Constables to establish equanimity. The Riot Act was read by Mr Matthew Oldham, JP, but to no avail, and serious disturbances broke out, no doubt further fanned by Mr Hanson's intemperate intervention.

The Dragoon Guards, mounted upon horseback, rode through the crowds in a brave attempt to restore order, driving them into the adjoining St George's Lane. It was here where the day's tragic incident occurred. In a moment all turned to consternation and chaos. The Guards, galloping boldly through the ground in all directions, attempted to disperse the now angry mob, unavoidably wounding many of the more hot-headed fellows among them with their swords.

One of the men quite wilfully threw a brick and hit one of the horses' heads. The rider levelled his pistol and shot the perpetrator dead. The horse, too, later had to be put down.

The Boroughreeve declared the man's shooting as "regrettable but justifiable homicide".

In an act considered by this newspaper of extraordinary generosity, members of the 4th Dragoons have each freely and willingly donated a day's wages into a fund for the dead man's poor widow. This demonstrates, we believe, that their actions in dealing with the disturbances on St George's Fields were motivated by only the most benevolent feelings of humanity, while carrying out their painful, though necessary, duty.

Mr Hanson has been charged with incitement

and will stand trial at the County Assizes in Lancaster in due course.

Meanwhile, the Manchester Weavers must return to work, chastened and thankful for the generosity of their employers in these difficult days for our country, who, despite still being denied access to overseas markets by our enemy, the French, who continue to blockade ports across the Channel, nevertheless strive to produce the highest quality goods at the lowest possible prices.

As the esteemed Justice of the Peace and Magistrate Mr Matthew Oldham has so ably expressed it: "It is necessary that the weavers should receive a fair and living profit. But if they receive *more* than is equal, it so very often promotes intemperance and idleness."

Hear, hear to that, say all sensible Mancastrians.

Let us pray for more peaceful and more prosperous times.

*

"It's hard when folks can't find their work
Where they've been bred and born
When I was young I always thought
I'd bide amidst fruits and corn
But I've been forced to work in town
So here's my litany
From Heywood, Hooley, Heap and Hell
Good Lord, deliver me..."

Ten years have passed since Amos and Agnes made their midnight flight from the Moravians in Fairfield. Ten years since they exchanged vows beside the black poplar on the banks of Elton Brook, beneath the shooting stars of the Andromedids blazing in the night sky. Ten years since Amos placed the iron ring he had forged upon Agnes's wedding finger, and ten years since Agnes had given Amos the Roman coin she had found many years before by these same waters.

Ten years of turning the kaleidoscope.

Ten years of cat's cradle.

Cradle to Diamond. Diamond to Six-Pointed Star. Six-Pointed Star to Bird's Nest.

Bird's Nest.

Ten years since they ran with such hope towards the cottage of Cousin Silas to begin to build the first of these nests.

But things have not turned out as they hoped. Events have conspired against them. An inexorable downward spiral, which has seen their bird's nests unravelling, each one more flimsy than the one before, with fewer mosses, grasses, twigs or sticks to bind them together, until ten years finds them back beside the Irk, no more than a spit away from where Agnes first pulled Amos out of those waters when they were both just eight years old, waters which now are rank and fetid, static and stagnant, dyed and defiled by impurities of every kind.

They live in a mean, damp cellar in Dimity Court, a foul and evil place – a row of ramshackle houses built nearly forty feet below the level of the Irk for the workers of the nearby Oldham's Felt Works, where Amos has recently started as a mule-spinner on one of the newly-installed, semi-automated power looms. To reach the Court, which directly adjoins a Glue Factory, where Agnes works at stripping the horse flesh from the dead and decomposed carcasses and boiling the glutinous bones all day, they have to descend through a steep, dark, narrow passage via slime-corroded stone steps, till they find themselves at the bottom of an earthen pit, suffocated for want of air and half-poisoned by the effluvia arising from the single privy in the middle of the yard, which serves all forty houses. A tripe works stands on the far side, opposite a cat-gut factory.

Everywhere is piled high with rotting cow hooves and pig offal. When it rains, liquid filth runs right through the centre of it. The mud is so deep that it is not possible, even in the driest of weathers, to walk without sinking in it ankle deep at every step. Colonies of pigs are penned in small sties, which invariably they break out of and wander through the Court unchecked. Dead dogs are frequently to be found floating by, belly up and bloated, feasted on by crows and kites. The chimney pots at the top of each row are situated just below the river's edge so that when it floods, which is often, it will disgorge its filth directly into the houses, flushing out every kind of vermin imaginable, which will then make their way back inside as soon as the overflow has retreated.

At night, when Amos and Agnes try to snatch what sleep they can, against the constant clamour of screams and howls that reverberate through the Court, the cries of souls in torment trampling over each other to be heard, they dream of the Eden they fled from at Fairfield, the ruin that they found at Elton, and all the roads they have travelled down since that have led them to this impasse, trapped in the heart of this cess pool, which sucks them ever deeper, where each new spin of the kaleidoscope reveals nothing but darkness, and the threads of the cat's cradle unravel from their fingers. A drowning leveret's haunted cry.

And in that blanket of darkness they search for pinprick holes of light, evidence that out there somewhere, the Andromedids, those vengeful Daughters of Cassiopeia, may return, and point the way towards a second chance. A second lamb waiting to be born. Filling its lungs with a desperate gulp for air, before a defiant, pitiful bleat.

*

*"When I was courting my own pretty maid
The Elders to me they did say*

23

We've got no room for wedded folk
Choose whether to go or to stay
I could not give up the girl I loved
So to town I was forced to flee
From Heywood, Hooley, Heap and Hell
Good Lord, deliver me ... "

Ten years earlier.

Agnes grabbed Amos by the hand and ran him towards the old stone cottage across the next field. It was just after daybreak and they had been walking all night. All was silent as they approached it.

"Wait here," whispered Agnes, leaving Amos standing on the step outside the front door, while she peered in through the curtain-less, glass-less wind-eye to the side.

It was exactly as she remembered it. The black-leaded grate along one wall. The old woodwormed settle opposite, where she and her mother had slept when they first arrived there more than eighteen years ago. And there, in the centre, the giant loom, which dominated the entire room.

But as she looked closer, she began to notice things that were different. There was no fire in the grate, and it looked as though there hadn't been for some time. The ashes were cold and unraked. An old rat poked its way among them, slowly taking its time, as if it was long accustomed to being permitted to roam undisturbed. There were what looked like mouse droppings on the settle. The loom was festooned with cobwebs. It had clearly not been used for weeks.

Frowning, Agnes turned back towards Amos.

"Summat's wrong," she said. "Let's try round t' back."

As she expected the door there was not locked. She lifted the latch and stepped inside. What before had always been a hive of noise and activity, with Ham and Shem running in and out, Cousin Meg busy baking over the hearth, and the constant clickety-clack of the loom, was now as silent as a tomb. There were dried leaves and grasses on the stone floor, which floated up as Amos and Agnes entered and walked through them, before settling around their feet in drifts.

She called out tentatively. "Cousin Silas…?"

No reply.

Then again, more loudly. "Cousin Silas…?"

She placed her foot gingerly upon the first step of the narrow stairs which led to the single room above. As she did so, she heard a faint wheezy voice answer her.

"Who is it?"

The sound was little more than an exhalation of breath, causing barely a ripple or movement of air within the quiet house. But it was enough. Agnes ran at once to the top of the stairs. The shock of seeing Silas, shrunk and shivering beneath a damp sheet, alone on the narrow cot he had once shared with Meg, distressing though it was, caused her hardly to break stride. In an instant she was kneeling beside him.

"Amos," she called out, "light a fire, while I get as much water as I can from t' pump at t' back. He's freezin' up 'ere."

She covered Silas with her coat, ran downstairs to rummage for whatever she could find in the settle by way of old blankets, took Amos's coat as well, then hurried back up to add more layers of warmth and protection to her cousin's half-starved frame.

"Whatever's happened?" she asked. "How long hast tha' been like this? Where's Cousin Meg an' t' boys?"

But before he could answer she was gone again, back downstairs fetching the water and filling the kettles.

A week later Silas was back on his feet. Agnes had somehow cobbled together a pan of rabbit and root vegetable stew, which eventually Silas had managed to keep down. As his strength and colour began to return, the story of what had happened gradually emerged.

Meg had died, quite suddenly, a year ago. She'd been complaining of pains in her chest for several weeks, then one morning she simply didn't wake up. Silas had started to unravel almost immediately. It was true, Agnes told Amos afterwards. When she was little, he had always seemed a giant of a man, an old shire horse, strong and indestructible. Now he was diminished. His cheeks were gaunt, his chest was hollowed out. He had grown so thin that when, on that first day she found him, wasting away upstairs, and she had washed him, she was shocked to see the frame of his ribs showing through the skin. They reminded her of the broken struts of his now unused loom.

Amos was entranced by it. He had always loved them at Fairfield, those that were kept on the upper floor of the three-storey workshops there. He enjoyed the complicated cross-rhythms of them, the way they each syncopated and reacted to each other. He remembered the men singing along:

"The loom goes click and the loom goes clack…"

And then the women answering:

"The shuttle flies forward and then flies back…"

When the looms were dismantled and taken out, just over a year ago, no one was especially sorry. Except Amos. But the Moravians were, in that as in all matters, unsentimentally pragmatic. "Handloom weaving may have a long and noble tradition," they said, "but its time has passed. Now is the age of the machine, the age of steam." And many of those who had been occupied in weaving and spinning found better paid employment in the mechanised powered mills in nearby Droylsden, bringing much needed extra wealth to the community.

But Amos sensed even then that there was something irreplaceable about the loss of a skill, a craft stretching back centuries, passed down from father to son, producing something unique, handmade, that represented more than the mere exchange of coins. He understood the economics, but in the new mills and factories, the dignity of labour had disappeared. Now a worker merely operated a machine, rather than actually creating a product he could be proud of.

"The trouble with you, Amos Lees," Agnes would say, wrapping her arms around him in bed at night, "is you're too much of a romantic. But that's why I love you. So don't go changing on me, will you?"

"I don't intend to," he'd reply, pulling her closer to him.

"Hey – not so fast, lover boy," she'd answer, playfully keeping him at arm's length. "What about all the reasons why *you* love *me*?"

"Hmm, that's a tough one," he'd say, scratching his head, and she'd punch him playfully, and they'd laugh. Then there'd be no more words, just kisses, as they slid towards each other.

So – while Agnes nursed Silas back to health, Amos applied the same devotion to the loom downstairs. He swept away the cobwebs, restrung the frame, tightened and repaired the joints, cleaned and oiled all its separate components, until it was back in near pristine working order again. Towards the base of the frame, he discovered a carving that had been etched there. It was now so worn that what it represented was no longer clear.

"I put that there." It was Silas, who had been allowed downstairs for the first time. He was still very weak but he was improving every day. "It's a laurel. They grow wild in t' fields round about."

"Aye. I've seen 'em."

"Tha's doin' a grand job wi' that loom, lad."

27

Amos nodded his thanks, then carried on the work of the repairs. The last job he did was to re-carve the laurel, so that its outlines were sharp and clear.

When he had finished, he let his hand rub along all its surfaces. It seemed as he did so to waken to his touch, to come alive, to be impatient to be set in motion once more, rather like a horse when it has been set to the plough, its tackle and harness gleaming in the sun, eager to hear the click of its master's tongue, the signal for it to start. Then it would measure the ground, patiently plodding the field, up and down, up and down, breaking the soil as a shuttle weaves cloth, tying the ends together, till the pattern was complete.

Amos held the fly shuttle up to the light, turning it over in his hands, and in that moment he saw how the whole system worked. By jerking the picking stick in one hand, the weaver could propel this shuttle across the loom with the other, by means of a series of sliding hammers. "Them's pickers, lad," said Silas, enjoying the evident pleasure Amos was taking in his discovery of it all. The clickety-clack of its movement, like the jingling of the plough horse's harness, or the tiny, intricately carved wheels in the casement of a clock, would set the motion of the day. Not just for work, but for school, for play, for meal times and prayer, with people fitting their conversation to those easy, natural rhythms. Now, in the mighty mechanised mills, which Amos had never yet visited, but which he had heard about from others, the machines set the rhythm, not the weaver, and the noise was so deafening it was impossible to speak above them. People would mouth their words in order to be understood, so that all human discourse was reduced to a series of orders and commands.

"Aye," said Ham, who Agnes had rooted out from Ramsbottom and persuaded to visit a few days later, "that's about t' truth of it. We're nobbut cogs."

Ham worked as a mule-spinner in one of Peel's factories. He lived in one of the mill houses there, the rent for which was deducted directly from his wages, the rest of which was paid in tallies, which could only be used to purchase basic provisions from the mill shop, or exchanged for ale in the mill pub. He was bitter and taciturn. As was Shem, who came the following Sunday. Gone from both of them was the mischief and banter Agnes remembered from when they were all children together there. Ham was married with two children. Shem's wife was expecting their first. They saw their whole futures mapped out and privately thought Agnes and Amos had been naïve to leave Fairfield, where, from the way they heard it described to them, things were so much better.

"Tha' can mek a life for thyself there, wi' no overseer crackin' t' whip. Tha' still 'as a choice about what tha' might do."

"Except about who you can marry," cut in Agnes sharply.

"Aye, well..." said Ham darkly. "Marriage in't all it's cracked up to be, if tha' asks me."

"Which we're not," said Silas, sitting on the settle with a blanket round his shoulders. He was getting stronger each day.

"An' they don't hold wi' t' Unions," added Amos. "They're against Combinations of all kinds, even t' Benevolent Societies set up by t' Methodists an' t' Unitarians."

"Why's that then?" asked Shem. "That dun't mek sense. I thought tha' said t' Moravians were all about self-help?"

"They are," said Agnes wearily. "But they're also very loyal to t' Crown."

"I don't follow," said Shem.

"They're grateful they were granted freedom to worship in their own way, which had always been forbidden to 'em for centuries. I s'pose they reckon they can't 'ave it both ways."

"They're right in that," said Ham, plunging back to the heart of his black mood again.

"That'll do, lad," said Silas. "There's two sides to every argument."

"Aye," replied Ham, "Tha's either wi' us or agin' us."

"I don't think it's as easy as that," said Amos, lifting his hand from the loom, which he was still regarding with a reverence normally associated with a sacred relic.

"An' tha' wouldst know, I s'pose?" asked Ham, squaring up to Amos.

"Now then, our kid," said Shem, "there's no need for any o' that. Let's 'ear what the lad 'as to say."

"I've done nowt but listen to t' masters these last five years," snarled Ham, "and what've we got to show for it? Nowt. They mek promise after promise, but they still pay us a pittance. First they pulled t' rug from under t' likes o' me feyther, mekkin' it impossible to earn a livin' as a weaver, so we've no choice but to work in their factories an' live in them rabbit 'utches they puts us in. Then, when they flood t' markets wi' cheaper an' cheaper cloth, rather than tekkin' a small drop in their profits, which they could easily afford, they cut our wages, which are lousy to begin with. So why shouldn't I be angry? I reckon I've got ev'ry right."

Amos nodded, sensing it would be best for him to say nothing, but Ham was now wound up so tight, there was no stopping him, like the Irwell in full spate.

"Come on then, Mr Clever Clogs, what's tha' got to say for tha'self?"

Agnes shot Amos a warning look, not to get drawn in any further, but Amos felt that Ham was giving him no choice. He had to say *some*thing.

"You're right. I don't know nowt. I've 'ad it easy. Ever since Agnes pulled me out o' t'river. Up till now. Agnes an' me, we've made our bed, and we're going to 'ave to lie in't, but I don't see 'ow wreckin' machines, or burnin' down mills is going to 'elp solve owt."

"Mebbe. Mebbe not. At least it shows they can't just walk all over us."

"It's playin' right into their 'ands – canst tha' not see that? If we behave like a mob, then they can treat us like one. They can send in t' soldiers an' claim they 'ad no choice. Then if we try an' resist more, stand our ground, throw stones at th' horses an t' like…"

"Aye, that's reet – gi' 'em a tast o' their own medicine…"

"Then they'll accuse us not just o' causin' affray, but *sedition*. Which is nobbut a step away from treason. An' that's a hangin' offence. That's what t' folk at Fairfield are afear'd of."

"Tha's startin' to sound like one o' t' bosses' lackeys wi' talk like that."

Ham made another sudden lunge at Amos, which Shem tried to intercept, but Amos just stood his ground.

"I don't like t' way things are any better than thee, our kid," said Shem, "but we've got a wife an' bairns to think of now, not just us."

"Dost tha' not think I don't know that?" yelled Ham, wheeling round on his brother. "What's this all about if it's not to mek things better for *them*?"

"Listen," said Amos, spanning the loom with his outstretched arms, "I reckon this is all some kind of trial. The Factory Owners, the Magistrates, the Special Constables, the Soldiers, Parliament, even the Crown, they're all desperately holdin' on to what they've got. They can see change is comin', but they're tryin' to put it off for as long as they can. Things've never been so good for 'em as they are reet now, so is it any wonder they're squeezin' us as 'ard as they can? I'm not sayin' we should just lie down an' let 'em walk all over us, but violence won't change their minds. It'll only stiffen their resolve. They'll just say that we can't be trusted wi' t' reforms we're demandin', like a minimum wage an' t' right to vote for an MP who'll represent us in t' House o' Commons, an' they don't want any o' that, so they're changin' the script, rehearsin' a new play, wi' a different ending, which shows that we're nobbut traitors, tryin' to bring down t' Government…"

"Kick 'em *all* out's what I say…"

"That'll get us nowhere, Ham. That's just throwin' out t' baby wi' t' bath water. An' tha's already said, it's for tha' bairns that tha's doin' this…"

Ham looked hard at Amos. Then, after a time, he stepped back and turned away. Shem released the hold he had been keeping all the while on his brother's jacket.

" 'Appen there's summat in what tha' says," said Ham reluctantly.

Amos smoothed his hands along the polished frame of the loom. "There's no substitute for quality," he said. "They can modernise an' mechanise, but they can't wipe out t' past altogether." He patted the loom with an air of satisfaction. "It'll come back, I'm tellin' thee. There'll always be a demand for summat hand made."

Silas nodded from the settle.

In his mind Amos began to picture a different future, one in which it would be he who sat at this loom and worked to craft something new, something original, something that people would want, that they would be prepared to pay for. Not a fortune. But enough to get by. And that was all he wanted.

This, too, was a kind of rehearsal, an idea forming in his brain, whose hour had not yet come, but which would, in time.

His fingers searched out the outline of the laurel leaves carved near the base of the frame.

"She's a beauty, in't she?" said Silas in between coughs.

Amos nodded, still too much in thrall to her to bring himself to speak, as if to do so might in some way break the spell she had cast upon him.

"She belonged to a man by t' name o' Edwin Stone afore me."

Amos tried to imagine another set of hands upon her, apart from Silas's, but couldn't.

"A real craftsman, 'e were. 'E could mek this old girl sing wi' just t' slightest tweak of 'is fingers. 'E told me 'is father'd built 'er. Edwin could remember as a lad watchin' 'er come to life, so that she felt like she were 'is sister. 'E'd wanted 'is own son, Henry, to carry on wi' t' trade after 'im, but 'e 'ad 'is mind set on another maid, a factory lass, one o' flesh an' blood an' bone, what took 'im away from 'ere, to Manchester, where 'e got 'isself a job at a Brick Works, while *'is* son went to work at Arkwright's Mill. Broke old Edwin's 'eart, it did."

A memory of the mill stirs within Amos, of how he'd watched it rise from the earth, up into the clouds, it seemed like, through the high window at the House of Correction when he was a child.

"I were prenticed to owd Edwin, "continued Silas. "That were over in Norden, an' I must've done summat right, for when t' time came for 'im to pass on 'is shuttle, 'e chose me. I brought it 'ere, carved that laurel on t' base, an' I've not budged since."

Amos nodded. He understood. And a tiny seed was planted in his brain. Before Silas had told him the loom's history, he had not been able to imagine anyone but Silas ever working her, but now that possibility existed. It floated somewhere just beyond his reach, the way a tree might dance and shimmer upon the far horizon in the heat of the day. He knew not to approach it too hastily, for if he did so, it would be certain to disappear right before his eyes. But if he took his time, approached it with a circuitous caution and slowness, he might just catch it off guard and it would fall within his grasp. Not yet, though. He knew that. Now was too soon. But one day. He wrapped the idea of it into a tiny bundle of cloth that he could fold within his hand and keep safe in his pocket, alongside the old Roman coin he always kept there.

A week later Amos whispered to Agnes in the narrow bed, which had formerly been Silas and Meg's.

"It's time we left. We can't impose on your cousin any longer. And besides, I need to find work."

"I know," said Agnes sadly. Once again she was leaving against her will.

"We'll be back," said Amos.

"Will we?"

"Yes. I promise."

"Don't," said Agnes sharply, "make promises tha' can't be sure to keep."

Amos held her to him. "I'm sure we'll return one day."

She turned over. He nestled towards her. Like spoons. She took his arm and wrapped it around her waist. She felt his breathing adapt itself to hers until he fell asleep. But Agnes did not sleep. She stared dry-eyed at the blankness of the night, which seemed as unreadable as their future. Another layer of dried twigs in the bird's nest crumbled and fell away.

*

"I've worked in Ancoats, Accrington
And I've earned some honest brass
In Mossley, Moston, Middleton
I've kept my bairn and my lass
I've travelled all three rivers round
In spite of injury
From forges, factories, mills and mines,
Good Lord, deliver me…"

The spiral.

The whirlpool.

With the monster lurking just below the surface. They never see it. But they know it's there.

Scylla and Charibdis.

The double helix.

Sucking them in towards the vortex that is Manchester as surely as water emptying into a drain.

Surely but sluggishly, so that they are always aware of their slow, inexorable slide.

To be dragged under like the dead babies of their dreams.

One that survives is Jack. Jack. Named for both Agnes's father and her lost brother. John James. Known as Jack.

He is born in Rochdale. Just nine months after they leave Cousin Silas. So that Agnes knows that the cottage in Elton is where he was conceived. She likes that thought. A new life made in love in a place where once – twice – she has been happy. Where Amos has promised they will return. One day.

But now they are in the middle of their wandering. Their odyssey. But if Amos is her Ulysses, who is she? Not Penelope, for she has not been left behind. Not Calypso, for she is not there to tempt Amos away from whatever dream he is pursuing. Though the purpose of his quest now seems lost and hidden, even from him. Circe then? For at times their fortunes sink so low it seems they fare no better than pigs, rooting in the mud, panning, if not for gold, then nuggets of something other. She can't now remember what. No. Not Circe. For it is not she singing a siren song that keeps calling Amos on to uproot and try for fresher, greener pastures elsewhere, but something deep within Amos himself.

Or perhaps it is just Manchester itself, exerting its unstoppable force, a magnet whose pull grows stronger by the day. Opposites attract. Likes repel.

After Rochdale, Radcliffe. Each successive town rolls by, much like the one before, so that they begin to merge into one. She is reminded of when her father first transplanted them from Dukinfield, journeying anti-clockwise around the outer rings of Manchester as if it were Saturn, until they alighted on the distant moon of Elton. Now it seems as though they make that journey in reverse, the reel of cotton thread unspooled before now being wound back in more tightly than ever round the bobbin of her body, so that she feels squeezed and breathless.

The names of each town sound like a litany, as if a leper is ringing a bell before them. Bring out your dead, bring out your dead.

Bagslate, Bardsley, Birtle, Busk
Cutgate, Crimble, Clover, Clegg
Morley, Milnrow, Mattley, Mudd.
Slattocks, Sudden, Starling, Stand.
Simister, Summit, Stone Breaks, Strine.
Pimhole, Daub Hole, Gravel Hole, Goat.
Dobcross, Diggle, Dacres, Delph.

A year there, a quarter here, a month some place else.

Now they are in the brickfields of Colleyhurst, to the north of
Tinker's Hollow. No longer a Pleasure Garden from where hot
air balloons take flight, but the desolate, treeless wastes of
Harpurhey, treading the clay, trudging knee-deep in the pink
granite mud, like the inside of an old woman's mouth, bleeding
and raw, pitted with occasional rotting stumps of burnt and
blackened tree roots.

In summer the sun beats down on them, merciless and hard,
baking them like the clay Amos must fashion into bricks to
feed the ever-hungry maw of Manchester's building boom. In
winter they freeze, trying to break the ice-packed earth with
bare, torn fingers. But mostly it rains. Fat, horizontal rain that
drives across the unprotected land, drenching them so that they
and the clay become an indistinguishable sodden grey.

Jack is eight years old now, and he and Agnes walk these
killing fields day after day, while Amos feeds the clay gifts and
offerings to the gods of fire, the ovens that must always be kept
lit, which bake the precious bars of pink gold, to build the
Palaces of Power and Temples of Trade.

Jack has a sister, Daisy, who is six. Together she and Jack
tread the fields from dawn till dusk. Yoked together as one.
Agnes can hardly bear to look upon them. Two children

hauling pails of mud, carrying each like afterbirth to the waiting kilns, there to incinerate. Swung in sacks of jute they straddle the clogged stream, flies buzzing round open sores. Bowed beneath the weight of what they carry, they sink back into the earth, becoming their own clay baby.

It is Amos who sees it first. He calls to Agnes. She drops her bucket and races towards them, her bare feet slapping the wet mud like frantic wing beats. She is screaming, a blackbird scooting low across the earth, while up above the crows are circling already. She and Amos reach the pair together. Amos shoves his fingers down the throat of his son, whose arms thrash and flail as he fights for breath, scooping out handfuls of dirt from the back of his throat. Jack chokes himself back into life, coughing up great gobs of clay, spluttering, wheezing, eyes streaming.

But it is too late for Daisy. She flops in Agnes's arms, a limp rag doll, the life oozing from her like a flapping trout, her eyes, ears and nostrils stoppered.

Agnes will not believe she is dead. Not even when Daisy's grey, cold body is taken from her, slithering from her grasp, to be tossed in an unmarked grave in the pauper's pit in a far corner of Angel Meadow.

It was rumoured that grave robbers lurked there. Since Parliament had passed *The Anatomy Act*, which permitted unclaimed bodies from workhouses, prisons and hospitals *only* to be removed for dissection, there was always a shortage, a need for more and more, and medical students would pay a princely sum for a fresh cadaver, to be thrown upon a slab and be subjected to even further humiliations now that their wretched lives had come to an end. They were worth more dead than they had been when they were alive, folk would complain angrily over a pint of gin in *The Crown & Kettle* afterwards, then smash their empty glasses down.

Amos, Agnes and Jack packed their few meagre possessions and left the same night.

Their odyssey continued.

*

"I've walked at night through Hanging Ditch
T'was just like being in hell
Where furnaces thrust out tongues of fire
And roared like the wind on the fell
I've slammed up coals in Bradford Pit
With muck up to my knee
From Clayton, Crumpsall, Colleyhurst
Good Lord, deliver me…"

"I want to go home," said Agnes.

"Where's that?" asked Jack.

"Ask your father," she said, then clamped her mouth tight shut.

Amos said nothing.

They followed the course of the Ashton Canal, trudging the tow path.

For two hours they walked in silence. Jack struggled to keep up with his mother's furious pace. He began to lag behind. Amos hoisted him onto his shoulders, at the same time carrying a cotton bundle containing their few paltry possessions in each hand.

"Here," said Agnes. "Let *me*." she took one of the bundles from her husband and tied it to the other two already strapped on her back. These were the first three words she had spoken since a weak sun had begun to poke through the pale bandage of cloud.

But nothing further was forthcoming.

She twisted the iron ring that Amos had wrought and given her round and round her wedding finger. It felt heavy and stuck. Like being on a treadmill.

Instinctively, as it always did in times of stress, Amos's hand sought out the Roman coin Agnes had given him in exchange for the ring, which he kept always in his right side pocket. It felt less reassuring this cold, grey morning. More like a debt he could never repay. A burden. Duty. Guilt.

They reached Fairfield just before ten o' clock. In the distance they heard the sound of musical instruments announcing the call to prayer. They had forgotten it was a Sunday. Jack caught sight of the sackbuts and trombones glinting in the watery sun from the cupola on the roof of the Church and pointed. Agnes began to quicken her pace.

"Is this home?" asked Jack.

"Yes," said Agnes.

"No," said Amos.

Simultaneously.

Jack looked from one to the other anxiously.

"A place that refuses to let people marry for love is not a home," said Amos, and he stopped walking. "I'll go no farther."

"You may continue or not as you choose," said Agnes. "It matters not to me."

They faced each other in silence for what seemed to Jack a lifetime.

"As you wish," said Amos at last. He promptly turned on his heel and began to walk back in the direction from which they had just come.

Jack began to panic. He shouted to be set down and began to wriggle himself down from his father's shoulders. The moment his feet touched the ground he was off. But not before Amos had placed a restraining hand upon his arm. Jack tried to wrench himself free but to no avail. His father was too strong for him.

"Stop it," cried Agnes. "Can't you see you're hurting him?"

Amos relaxed his grip. At once Jack scurried towards the waiting arms of his mother. Amos set down the one remaining bundle he was holding, then turned and left without a word. He had nothing.

Agnes watched his back retreating from her until he became just a dot, a monochrome blur beside the dark waters of the canal beneath a steel grey sky. She picked up the bundle he had left and held it out for Jack to carry. The two of them, laden with ghosts, marched together through the iron gates that marked the entrance to the Moravian Settlement, their familiarity a caress, keeping the world away.

Six months pass.

Agnes grieves.

She has grieved before but nothing comes close to the loss of a child.

John and Caroline, her parents, recognise she needs time. Time and space.

They mostly leave her alone. Fairfield is a good place to recuperate. It holds a special value on quietness. Put your faith in God, they tell her. Prayer is a comfort and a solace. In every minute of every day there is always someone offering up a prayer for the strength and support to carry on. Agnes is included in these prayers. And Jack, whose cheeks begin to lose their pallor in the fresh air, who attends school, who begins to make cautious friends, but who never quite shakes off his fear and distrust of the world, which manifests itself in a nervous stammer whenever his teacher asks him a question. And the soul of Daisy, which can be saved, even if her body is lost. And

Amos too. Though silently. For fear of upsetting Agnes further.

But little by little she is invited back into the daily rituals she remembers when she lived there. Work, says John, uncurling his long body each morning in a series of painful, protracted clicks as each of his bones separately cracks and settles, so that he can resume his customary crow-like stance. Work is the great healer.

And Agnes fills her days with it, helping her mother and the other women on the farm, milking the cows, mucking out the byres, scrubbing the yard, so that by the time she climbs upstairs to bed each night, she is so tired physically that sleep comes easily.

The dreams of Daisy drowning in the mud and clay of the brickfields at last begin to subside.

After a month John asks her during supper, "But what of Amos?"

"What of him?" she asks back.

"A boy needs 'is father," he says.

"'E 'as plenty o' fathers 'ere," she says.

"That's not what I mean, an' tha' knows it."

She looks down.

"An' a father needs to see 'is son."

Agnes nods imperceptibly, then hurriedly leaves the table.

John tries to call her back, but Caroline lays a hand upon his arm. "Let 'er be," she says. "She's not ready yet."

"But when will she be?" he asks. "If I put a plant in t' cellar, it will perish for want o' light an' air."

"But it'll recover when tha' brings it back into th' open," she says. "She needs a little longer in t' cellar first."

After two months, he asks again.

"I don't wish to speak of him, Father," she says.

"But…"

"Wait," says Caroline, once again intervening.

After three months he can hold his patience no longer, but this time she is ready for him.

"If we'd stayed wi' Cousin Silas, things might've turned out different."

"Tha' cannot know that for certain."

"We'd probably be still together. I'd not be so bitter. Jack'd not be so anxious, an' Daisy'd not be dead."

"Only God knows these things."

"But Amos – 'e would not be beholden."

"A fine quality, surely? Every man wants independence. To carve a niche for 'isself that's 'is an' 'is alone. That 'e can earn enough to feed an' clothe 'is family. Provide 'em wi' warmth an' shelter."

"Like *you* did?"

"Look around thee. We want for nowt 'ere."

"I mean before. When you abandoned Mother an' me. Uprooted us from where we were happy. Forced us to live on t' road, not knowin' from one week to t' next a place we might call home. Then foisting us on Cousin Silas, who had no room for us, but who welcomed us nevertheless, before abandonin' us again, in pursuit o' tha' lofty dreams an' callin'. Does any of this sound familiar?"

"Everything comes to those who wait."

"Like t' death of a child?"

"The loss of James was God's punishment on me for those sins of omission thou hast accused me of."

"But *we* had to suffer too, Mother an' me, for those sins o' thine."

"And I'm truly sorry for it."

"And now it's 'appened all over again."

"What can I say? History 'as a habit o' repeatin' itself."

"Only if we don't learn from it first time around."

"In that case, then," he says in a voice as gentle as he could muster, "mebbe tha' should've heeded t' words o' t' Lot."

Agnes avoids having to speak directly with her father after that. They edge around each other warily. She hears him approach long before she sees him, the cracking of his joints betraying him, his shadow rising up the wall of a building like a raven in the tower, so that she has time to catch her breath and change direction.

But she can't prevent the way Jack has grown to idolise him. Where she goes out of her way to miss him, he actively seeks him out. He dogs his footsteps from the moment he finishes school each day. His grandfather is a hero to him, the way he can fix anything that's broken. Except for what matters most, thinks Agnes ruefully.

"The boy needs his father," she overhears John pronounce again to Caroline one night, when he thinks she cannot hear them. "And his father needs to see him."

"Any news?" asks Caroline, folding away the washed and ironed bed linen.

John shakes his head. "I've asked around, but nothing yet."

Amos is less than three miles away. Back west along the Ashton Canal. He found work at Bradford Pit, where he inhabits a twilight world of perpetual shadows. He works what's known as the graveyard stint. He lives in a makeshift tent pegged out on a piece of slightly higher ground, down which he scrambles before dawn each day, descending underground just as the first light of day streaks the sky, returning back to the upper air an hour or so after sunset. It's hardly surprising that no one knows where he is. He barely knows himself.

He works to excavate the new Charlotte seam, some seventy feet below the surface, along with a hundred other moles, which will eventually stretch out several miles in different directions, every yard dug out by hand. The earth is pocked with countless bell pits, narrow holes sunk to wherever the coal can be found, from where it is winched back to the surface in buckets. The bottom of each shaft has been widened to incorporate a sloping roof as the coal is removed, giving the pits their name because of their distinctive bell-like shape. No supports have been used in their construction, so that as the mining extends outwards, they are prone to collapse. Then, typically, another will be built alongside. There is no drainage system so frequently they flood.

But most of these lie abandoned now. Whatever trees there once were here have long since disappeared, either cut down to clear the ground, or reduced to charred, black stumps. No grass grows, so that a lunar landscape now prevails. In the dark it would be easy to fall down any number of these unguarded shafts, but Amos knows them all. He can walk between them blindfold if he has to, which is just as well, for most nights are moonless, starless.

The new Charlotte seam slopes underground in a steep, unforgiving one-in-three gradient. It has a maximum height of just three feet nine inches, so that Amos can spend up to twelve hours at a stretch bent almost double. But the seam is rich, yielding high quality coal, ideal for powering the new steam mills, which daily proliferate, poking their way through the dead ground up towards the sky, where their mighty brick chimneys disgorge their plumes of black smoke, which hang above them like a shroud.

But however rich the seam, there is never enough coal to stoke these fires of Hades, to feed those beasts of Tartarus, to sate the appetite of Cronos. The tentacles of Scylla extend deeper underground, probing, worming their way towards fresh morsels to suck into the ever-hungry maw of her twin sister Charibdis.

Amos descends to the lowest depths armed with his tools looped around a leather belt – auger, hammer, pricker, stemmer, black powder and match cord, a slow burning twist of braided twine. He carries a pick-axe in one hand, a candle in the other. The deeper he goes, the thicker the air. The heat is intense. While he works he wears no other clothes apart from the belt and a pair of old boots. The rest – threadbare shirt, worn trousers, patched jacket – he leaves in a rough pile in a low recess along with everyone else's. The unmistakeable reek of methane catches at the back of his throat. He places the augur against the solid coal face, lit only by the candle he carries down with him. He strikes it hard, with a practised aim, until he has penetrated the rock sufficiently for him to insert the black powder. This is a mixture which Amos has made up himself beforehand, comprising seventy-three parts saltpeter to sixteen parts wood charcoal and eleven parts sulphur. He packs this tightly with his stemmer, surrounding the powder with wet clay, before inserting the match cord with the aid of the pricker, a narrow copper rod three feet six inches long with a diameter of just one inch. He lights the cord with the end of his candle, then retreats as fast and as far as he can.

He feels, more than he hears the blast, which sends shock waves shuddering through him. Thick black clouds of dust collect in the tunnel, settling on his unprotected body like a second skin. They never quite clear, these clouds. Instead they dissipate just enough for him to see his way back to where the coal has been released from its wall of rock, which he piles into wicker tubs. Those pieces that are still too large to lift he attacks with his pick-axe, breaking them into more manageable lumps. When the tub is full he ties the flat hemp winding rope attached to the front of it to his belt, then crawls back up to the surface on hands and knees, hauling the coal behind him. This is removed from him by women working up above, who will place the tub onto rails, which will transport it down the slope towards the Ashton Canal below, where it will be tipped directly onto the waiting coal barges. At the same time, Amos will be handed another empty tub to pull back down below with him to the coal face and repeat the whole process again.

He will do this five times every hour for twelve hours every day, six days every week, for the next six months. He will not see Agnes or Jack once during that time. Each Sunday he tells himself he will wash the worst of the coal dust from his aching body in the nearby canal. Then he will try to straighten his bent back and walk the two and three quarter miles to Fairfield. If only to catch a distant glimpse of his wife and son. But each Sunday he is defeated. His weariness is bone deep, and he does not wish to present himself so defeated to them. The situation is only temporary, he tells himself. Agnes needs time to grieve, Jack needs space to grow. Something better will turn up soon. Something with a future. There is no future for them at Fairfield. Only a past. Something else will present itself.

Meanwhile he burrows deeper underground, feeding the faceless twins of Scylla and Charibdis, starving himself. No light penetrates the kaleidoscope where now he dwells. Except the diamond glint of a six-pointed star mocking him from the coal face, ignited for the briefest moment in the spark from the black powder which, as it flashes, blinds him.

At the end of each shift he puts back on his clothes, numb with fatigue. The first thing he does is feel inside his right-hand trouser pocket for the Roman coin given to him by Agnes in lieu of a wedding ring. He closes his fingers tightly round its thin, worn surface and trudges back up the shaft towards the last dregs of daylight as they drain from the sky. The coin tethers him. To Agnes, to Jack, to himself. These mines have been worked for centuries. His feet are just the latest in an endless procession. Head bent, he notes the marks they make on the land, fitting inside the footsteps of those who have walked there before him, serving as templates for those that will follow, when his own will become scuffed and indistinguishable, lost and buried.

The tent he crawls under to sleep away the twilight hours is little more than a square of calico, tied at two ends to a gnarled hawthorn tree growing through the bones of an old dry stone wall first put up as a sheep fold a hundred years before, when the land around was still part of the Mosley Estate, still grazed. Now it serves as a low shelter to keep out the worst of the wind and the rain. The other two ends of the cloth are staked into the ground, so that it forms a kind of lean-to, open at each side to the elements. Amos shares this billet with five or six others. Even in the few months he has been there, the faces of these sleeping companions are constantly changing. No one stays for long. Except for Adam. Adam was there when Amos first arrived. He showed him the ropes. He watched his back. Now they look out for each other.

It is only a matter of time. Amos and Adam know this but it is not something they ever speak of. If you keep on cutting the cards, eventually you will turn up the ace of spades. The black powder is a wilful and capricious muse.

It is a raw January day. An iron frost has gripped the ground. Neither Amos nor Adam has slept much the previous night and both are shaking with the cold. The palest of grey dawns painfully tries to peel back the sky. It will be one of those days when it hardly gets light, the kind that is barely distinguishable from the night that preceded it or the one that will follow it. Not that this matters to Amos or Adam as they make their way between the abandoned bell pits towards the entrance to Charlotte Mine, for they will see none of it.

Charlotte Mine. Named for the Queen. Amos finds himself wondering sometimes whether she would mind having such a place named after her, if she knew what horrors took place there. Does she even know of its existence? He doubts it. Just as she is equally unaware of *his*? Of Manchester's even. Closer to home Agnes knows nothing of his whereabouts either. Nor Jack. He has still not made it to Fairfield. Christmas has come and gone. Just another working day in the belly of the monster.

Whereas at Fairfield, Amos knows, they will have held a special service of thanksgiving, with musicians summoning the faithful to prayer from the cupola on the roof of the church. There will have been a Lovefeast, with prayers for those friends and family members far away, in other missions, across the country, overseas. They will have asked for the strength to do the Lord's will. Is that what he is doing now, thinks Amos, the Lord's will, as he mines the earth of its riches, to feed the coffers of merchant, king and country? God bless our Sovereign Majesty, King George III, and his consort, Queen Charlotte, he hears Brother Swertner declare, his sonorous voice intoning the benediction.

He must swallow his pride and return there. He knows this. If he does not do it soon, his son will have forgotten him, and Agnes will think he has abandoned them. Yes. It is January 6th, he realises, with no little irony. The Feast of Epiphany. He must act.

But first he must work. He cannot just walk away. Not if he wants to be paid. He will see the Overseer tonight. When his shift has finished. Inform him of his decision. His intention to leave at the week's end. But first he must work.

He and Adam stoop in silence down the long, steep descent to the seam. When they reach the coal face, they take off their clothes, stow them away as usual in their separate recesses, begin the back-breaking grind of hammering the augur deep into the bare rock. He rams in the black powder, wads it tightly with the wet clay, inserts the slow fuse of the match cord, lights it, is just about to retreat to a place of safety, when it fizzes, sizzles, glows a moment, before pitifully going out. The flame of his candle putters and dies also. He feels the acrid reek of methane burn his throat. Cursing, for this is not that unusual an occurrence, he leans in to relight it.

He knows at once something is not right. In the fraction of a second between striking the tinder and applying the spark to the fuse, he knows. The powder is not packed tightly enough. The

48

cord ignites too quickly. The flame travels too rapidly. When the blast occurs, the force of it, and his proximity to it, blows him off his feet, sends him hurtling through the air, back along the tunnel several yards, knocking all the air out of him, hitting his head, hard, against the unsupported roof, which, just before he slips into unconsciousness, Amos sees begin to buckle, split, break apart, then come crashing down around him, burying him beneath the rock and rubble.

It is hours before Amos wakes. When he finally does, it is only his eyes he can move. He forces each one open a crack. The air is thick with dust. Each particle orbits around him in a slow motion dance. As his eyes focus and adjust he begins to make out each separate particle as a single entity, unique and complete in itself, its own universe. Beyond the dust he can make out nothing. He closes them once again. Perhaps he sleeps...

More hours pass. When he wakes a second time he grows aware of different parts of himself. His skin. His body. His head. Every inch of him hurts. He supposes this is a good thing. It means he must not yet be dead after all. He had begun to wonder if perhaps he was. But now every muscle, every sinew, every joint, screams with pain. He senses he is lying at an unusual angle, his limbs splayed, his neck twisted. He tries to move. But he cannot. The weight of the rockfall upon him is simply too great. Breathing is particularly painful. He imagines he has broken several ribs...

He continues to drift in and out of sleep. When next he wakes he is aware, more than anything else, of the silence. The immensity of it deep within the belly of the earth. He begins to realise he can hear nothing of the usual, familiar sounds he normally would tune out. The repeated tapping of hammers against rock. The scraping away by pick-axes of the exposed coal. The frequent shouts of warning from the other men that a blast is about to be set off. The distant booms of explosions. The skittering of loose stones and scree cascading like hail everywhere in the mine. But now there are none of these. Just the deep smothering blanket of silence, which muffles his ears and makes him feel that, although he is almost a hundred feet below the ground, surrounded by a network of similar tunnels radiating off in all directions, he also occupies no more space than that filled by his twisted, broken skeleton. A cocoon. Invisible. Unknowable. Unreachable...

Time becomes elastic. He feels like he has become nothing but a fragment, a tiny shard of himself, mingling with those other pieces of broken glass that he would look at through the kaleidoscope. Tumbling, spiralling, settling. Like the constellations wheeling above him in the night skies, refracting colours. Except here, far below the earth, from where the sky is never visible, there are no colours. Just a never ending darkness. An absence of light.

But the longer he remains there, encased, diminishing, the more he realises this is not true. There are, he perceives, an uncountable number of different shades of black. He begins to recognise and identify different ones among them. Even here, he thinks, there is wonder. He tries, in the rough hewn shapes of the rock which entombs him, to conjure the faces of Agnes, Jack, John, Caroline, the different people at Fairfield who came and went over the years, Ham and Shem and Silas, poor innocent, lost Daisy, the other children in the House of Correction, and someone else, someone whose features he does not recognise, who is young and old simultaneously, who is lifting him up from a piece of white cloth, and staring intently into his face…

The air grows thicker. Breathing is not only painful, it is difficult. It becomes shallow and rasping. He becomes aware of the sound it makes, like when the picking stick of a fly shuttle gets stuck and snags in the loom and the weaver must take great care not to snap the threads on the fragile, rickety loom…

He *hears* them first. An insistent scuttling beyond the rockfall. Wherever men go, they will not be far behind. Sometimes they sound far away, sometimes right up close. Scraping. Gnawing.

Next he feels them. A delicate fluttering across his face. Then a not so delicate nibbling at his fingers and toes. A scratching along his arms and legs. The sudden pinch of needle-sharp teeth puncturing the skin.

They are becoming bolder. Their numbers are increasing, sensing his weakness.

Finally he sees them. One runs up his chest, using his rib cage like a ladder, till it latches onto his face. In a desperate lunge Amos manages to shake his head to one side, surprising the rat, so that it loosens its grip and lets go. All around him he sees the imprint of their feet in the black coal dust. Each foot has five toes. The inner toes are opposable. They look like a human thumb. The rear tracks resemble those an infant child might make. If, years later, they have remained undisturbed and are then lighted upon by the next generation to dig and delve these lower depths, might they be mistaken for lost children, wonders Amos?

His eyes begin to droop once more. He digs what's left of his fingernails into the palms of his hands to try and keep awake…

He hears, or thinks he hears, a shout. Then another. Then

another.

He tries to answer. But no sound comes out.

He pushes, with every last ounce of strength he has, his upper arm from where his stiff, immobile body lies useless and twisted, until eventually he manages to disturb a minuscule shower of dust. Encouraged, he pushes again. He strains so hard that he feels a blood vessel pop and burst behind his eye. The effort releases a second shower of dust, this time accompanied by a scattering of a few small loose stones. Inside this empty chamber, this black and airless tomb, it sounds like thunder.

The shouts cease at once.

A long, held pause.

Then a voice he recognises. Adam. "Over there," it says.

Then lots of things happen at once. Stones are pulled away, roughly and rapidly. "Careful," says the voice, Adam's voice. "We don't want to set off another rockfall."

The removal of stones slows down, becomes more measured, more methodical. As more and more are lifted from him, Amos feels the lightness of the space created by their absence. He experiences a sensation of floating. It rises him up to the roof of the shaft, not so very high, but enough for him to be able to look down. To look down and see this flurry of arms removing the rocks and stones and lumps of coal, piece by piece, passed along the line of them one after another, an army of ants moving and thinking as one.

"Not long now," he hears Adam's voice say. "We've almost reached him."

Then, when they do, and he feels human hands brush his skin, Amos crashes down from the roof of the shaft, back inside his own body once again, and the pain of his release shoots through him.

"We'll need a stretcher," urges Amos.

One is passed along. Two hawthorn branches and a thick piece of calico slung between them. They remind Amos of the makeshift tent he has been sleeping in when not at work down the mine. Perhaps it is.

"Careful," he hears Adam urge, as he is awkwardly manoeuvred onto the stretcher.

"How bad is 'e?" says another, older voice.

"We'll need to get 'im back up to t' light before we'll be able to tell," says Adam.

Amos can't remember when he last saw daylight.

"There's a fair few bones broken, I'd wager," continues Adam, running his lit candle quickly up and down Amos's body. "Legs, arms, ribs."

Between them the column of ants drags the stretcher back up to the surface. The passage is so painful to Amos that he winces with every shudder and jolt. It takes more than two hours. When he reaches the upper air, Amos is seized with a fit of shivering so severe he cannot stop it. Adam throws a blanket across his nakedness. He sees the sores on his body, and blood seeping from his mouth. He gently turns his head to the side. As soon as this is done, Amos is violently sick.

A doctor is summoned. The broken bones are set and splinted. His chest and ribs are tightly bound. Some clothes are found for him. He is encouraged to try a little soup.

After a few days he is to be found sitting up, leaning his back against the old dry stone wall in the field, where his tent used to be, which has now been moved somewhere else, feeling the weak rays of a pale sun beginning to warm him up. Adam comes to sit with him whenever he can.

"What happened to my clothes?" asks Amos.

If Adam is surprised by the oddness of the question, he doesn't show it. Instead he shrugs matter-of-factly. "Gone," he says. "Buried under t' roof fall, along wi' all tha' tools, I expect. Tha' was lucky. We knew where tha'd been. Even so it took us best part of a week to reach thee. We wasn't lookin' for no clothes."

Amos nods in gratitude. "No. 'Course not. It's just that…"

"What?"

"There was summat there that meant a lot to me."

Adam says nothing. They all of them have their keepsakes. He understands. Things that get lost in the fire.

Amos tries to reconstruct the Roman coin in his imagination. The shape and feel of it. The way it nestled in his hand. The heft of it. No more than a moth that has now alighted elsewhere. Gone. Yet his fingers still retain the memory of its imprint. The freight of all its years. He tries to console himself with the thought that it was only lent to him. That perhaps one day it will fall into another's keeping. But for now it will simply wait in the dark, as patient as the rock that covers it, till its time will come again.

"Can you send word to Agnes?" says Amos, after another week has passed.

Adam nods his head. "I thought tha'd never ask."

"I must go to him," says Agnes, already starting to pack a few necessities into a cotton sheet.

"Must thee?" asks her father.

"Of course I must. He's my husband."

"Not in God's eyes."

"And what's that supposed to mean?"

"Tha' knows very well."

"He needs me."

" '*Hast thou not seen that which the unmarried woman hath done? She is gone upon every mountain, and under every green tree, and there she has played the harlot?*' Jeremiah, chapter 3, verse 6."

Agnes regards her father darkly. Her eyes are slits.

"What would you have me do then? '*Go only after those that give me my bread and my water, my wool and my flax, my oil and my drink'*? Hosea, chapter 2, verse 5. Stay here wi' thee? Then indeed I shall *'hath played the harlot'*."

"If tha' leaves a second time, there'll be no returning a third."

"Then tha' can set tha' mind at rest. I'll not be coming back."

"I pray thee not to act in haste. Where will tha' go? The world is such a fearful, dangerous place. Tha'll be so much safer if tha' stays here."

Agnes looks at John keenly.

"Might I bring Amos back here then?"

"Aye, lass. He'd be well looked after. He'd get well and strong again in no time."

"As my husband?"

John pauses, but he does not relent. He shakes his head. "The Lot has spoken."

"Then tha' gives me no other choice. Kindly fetch Jack. Bid 'im be ready to leave wi' me directly."

"But where will tha' go?" asks John a second time.

"Wherever I am needed."

" *'How the city has itself become a harlot! Once righteousness lodged there. Now evil walks abroad…'* "

"Isaiah."

"Chapter 1…"

"Verse 21, I know."

Agnes ties up the corners of the sheet, hoists the bundle onto her shoulders, then makes to go past her father, who steps across the doorway to intercept her.

" *'Love not the world, neither the things that are in the world. If any love the world, the love of the Father is not in him'*."

" *'The Lord is not slack concerning His promise, as some men count slackness, but is longsuffering and patient towards us, not willing that any should perish, but that all should come to repentance'*."

" *'One that is weak in the faith, receive ye, but not to doubtful disputations'.*"

" *'One believeth that he may eat all things; another, who is weak, eateth only herbs and grasses. Let not him that eateth despise him that eateth not; and let him which eateth not judge him that eateth. For God hath received them both'.*"

Agnes lowers the bundle to the front of her waist and waits for John to step aside. Father and daughter eye one another sorrowfully. They hold the other's gaze, each equally fervent, each equally determined. Neither of them moves.

Caroline arrives with a tearful Jack.

"I don't want to go," he says.

Agnes lowers herself to his level and places her hands gently on each side of his face. "Don't you want to see your Daddy?" she says softly.

Jack nods. He wipes his eyes with the back of his hand, then shakes his head sheepishly. Agnes bites her lower lip which is beginning to tremble. She gets up and moves to one side. She must not let Jack see her cry, she thinks. Caroline kisses the top of Jack's head, then goes across to her daughter.

"Why dun't tha' leave Jack here wi' us?" she says.

Agnes turns to her sharply.

"Just till things become clearer," adds Caroline quickly. "Tha' dun't know what tha'll find till tha' gets there. But it's bound to be difficult. At first. Get tha'selves sorted, then Jack can join thee later. Once tha's more settled."

Agnes can see the sense in this. She understands how happy Jack is here at Fairfield. But John has made it abundantly clear that there's no place for Amos once he recovers, not as her husband. She may not like the life he's pursuing, but it's his, and she's pledged to live it with him.

"Aye," she says. "I'll do that. Thank you."

She lowers herself once more to Jack's eye level, kisses his still wet cheeks and whispers her goodbyes to him.

"Be good," she says. "Do as tha'rt bid."

"I will, Mother," he says.

"I'll be back as soon as I can. I promise," she adds, little knowing that almost a year will pass before she can return to fulfil it.

*

"I've seen fog creep across Bailey Bridge
As thick as the Bastille soup
I've lived where folks were stowed away
Like rabbits in a coop
I've seen snow float down Shooter's Brook
As black as ebony
From Besses, Broughton, Boggart Hole Clough,
Good Lord, deliver me…"

Dimity Court. Dimity Court.

The very name sounds like a death knell to Agnes if ever it happens to pass her lips. In answer to a question perhaps. Where do you live? Or if someone stops to ask for directions. All roads seem to lead there, have always been leading there. From when she and Amos first made their midnight flight from Fairfield. Or before that. From when she hauled him as an eight-year-old boy from the foaming waters of the Irk, the same river whose stagnant sludge they now live beneath.

Dimity Court. Built on the very spot where the two of them first clapped eyes on one another, where now they barely have time for anything more than a cursory glance.

Dimity Court. Where the sun never reaches. Not even on a Sunday, when the great engines of the mills and factories cease to rumble. But when the smoke and fumes belched from their blackened brick chimneys still hang like a pall over the town, from where it funnels down into the yards and cellars of Angel Meadow and never shifts.

Dimity Court. Dimity Court.

But even as foul as it is, Agnes knows that the whirlpool of Charibdis, which has sucked them down this far, has still further depths into which it can drag those who get caught in its relentless eddies, those who give up all hope of ever breaking free of her many-tentacled, vice-like grip. When she returns there each night from the Glue Factory, every pore of her oozing with putrescence, the stench of rotting flesh in her skin and hair, the first thing she does is to check the rats' nest beneath the rusting iron pipe disgorging effluent from Matthew Oldham's Felt Factory in the far corner opposite their cellar. Every night there are new born pups. She watches them as they start to open their eyes after ten to twelve days or so, the way they take in their surroundings, look to strike out on their own, find a way out of Dimity Court, even though there is plenty of what they need to be found there, curious for new horizons. If *they* can survive here, and afterwards escape, then so will *she*. But for now she finds herself stuck between that rock and a hard place that is the whirlpool of Charibdis and the unyielding figure of Scylla, who is her father, stern and implacable, four miles and a world away, in far off Fairfield. A distance she and Amos walk each Sunday to visit Jack, but they both know that Dimity Court is no place for a young boy to grow up in, so it is with a heavy heart they trudge their way back there without him as night falls.

Dimity Court.

Dimity – a rough and serviceable cotton, sometimes woven with stripes or checks.

Agnes supposes that while it is unquestionably rough, it just about serves. For the time being. But she also knows that they must not let too much more time elapse before they join the young rats in their hopeful exodus, or, just as the pups' eyes start to open, theirs will begin to close. She does not think that Amos has begun to open his yet. It is as if he still dwells in the subterranean passages of the Charlotte Mine, beneath the rockfall, in the absolute dark of the tunnels he had dug and delved himself. His bones have mended, the broken legs and arms and ribs, but the body has not healed, nor has the spirit. Both still bear the dimity stripes, keeping him in check.

He goes uncomplainingly to work each day at the Felt Factory, where he climbs inside the great engines, to oil and lubricate each cog and mechanism, to keep the wheels turning that power the looms that spin the cotton. The dimity cotton.

It is May, 1808. They have lived in Dimity Court for fifteen months.

Almost ten years since they plighted their troth beneath the black poplar tree by Elton Brook, less than a stone's throw from the cottage of Cousin Silas, the handloom weaver. Ten years since they saw the kingcups, columbines, forget-me-nots and other wild flowers growing in the hedges there. Agnes wonders if Silas is still alive, if Ham and Shem have managed to curb their tempers and stay out of trouble. She hopes so. But she admires their passion, their belief in fighting for something bigger than them.

Amos does not think of the wild flowers. Nor does he speculate about whether Silas still sits at the loom. But what he does see, frequently rising up before him in his broken, troubled dreams, is the loom itself. The curve and feel of it. The warmth of its wood to the touch. The smoothness of the grain, which he had polished so attentively when he had repaired and restored it, the pattern of the laurel leaf at its base, which he had recovered and re-carved, and which he had been so reluctant to let go of and leave. But while he brought it back to life, rethreaded and revived it, so Agnes had nursed Silas back to health. The shuttle flies forward, the shuttle flies back.

Silas sat with the picking stick in his right hand and retook possession of it, so that Amos knew the time had come for him and Agnes to leave. To begin their odyssey. Which is still continuing. In his dreams he is always on the point of returning to it, of sitting behind the loom himself, but he always wakes up before he manages it.

Although Amos hardly remembers Ham's temper now, he is surrounded by other firebrands. His friend Adam is not one of them. It was Adam who had got him the job at the Felt Factory to begin with. He stayed with Amos in the first weeks after his accident and looked after him till Agnes arrived from Fairfield. It was Adam who had made his way there first to ask her if she would come. Then, after she arrived, it was Adam who promised to find them somewhere to live. He headed back the one and three quarter miles from Bradford Colliery to Manchester, heard that there were jobs going at the Felt Factory, secured one for himself, then found the cellar on Dimity Court.

"It's not much," he told Agnes when he went back to tell them the news. "But it's got a roof and four walls."

That was the end of January. Agnes and Amos arrived a couple of weeks later. Amos still couldn't walk but Adam fixed it for them to be conveyed by coal barge along the Ashton Canal to its terminal in Ducie Street, where Adam met them with a handcart he'd somehow managed to 'borrow', on which Amos was painfully pushed.

Agnes realised it would be up to her to find a job that would at least provide them with the money they would need to pay their half of the rent with Adam, so she got the first thing she could find, which was at the Glue Factory, where she's been ever since. Three more months would pass before Amos was ready, and even then every bone of his body still ached. Breathing, after all those broken ribs, was especially painful. But on Monday 2nd May 1807 he walked with Adam through the gates of Matthew Oldham's Felt Factory to start his new job there.

"What's 'e like?" he asks, looking up at the large hand

painted sign above the entrance.

"The owner?"

Amos nods.

"Fair to middlin', I s'pose. Better 'n some, worse 'n others. We never see 'im. 'E spends most of 'is time up at t' Bench."

"Best not to cross 'im then?"

"Aye. Tha's learnin'. Folk say 'is feyther were summat real special. Treated t' workers like family. But this 'un's different. It's all about t' bottom line wi' 'im. 'E even looks different. Tha' can't see any likeness twixt 'im an' t' first Mr Oldham. Why, 'e looks more like *thee* than 'e does 'is feyther."

A year later he is still there.

But he and Matthew never meet. Once, after about six months, Amos sees him on a rare tour of the factory. He glimpses him only from behind, and briefly, wearing one of the felt top hats produced by their sister mill in Ramsbottom.

The Firebrands mutter darkly. The Factory is doing well. Mr Oldham is expanding, so they say, gone into partnership with the Peels from Lancashire. Connections in Parliament. Government contracts. Making money hand over fist. "But do *we* see any of it?" they rail. "Do we buggery! Our wages go down instead of up."

And it's true. Even in the twelve months Amos has been there, his pay has declined from fifteen to just twelve shillings a week, and half of this is deducted at source to pay the rent on their single-roomed cellar, and the other half is paid in tallies, which can only be redeemed in shops under license from Mr Oldham, who creams off *their* profits too. Yet they're busier than ever. Production levels increase. The overseers urge them to work faster, harder, longer, but still their pay stays low.

"It's the cost of raw materials," they say.

"Transport."

"Dearer, imported cotton."

"From India, America, Jamaica."

"It's the war with France."

"The blockade of the Channel ports."

"The failed harvests."

"The unreliable weather."

"Too wet, too dry, too hot, too cold."

They should be grateful to have a job at all, they are told.

The Firebrands talk about walk-outs, the owners retaliate with pay-cuts. The Firebrands call for strikes, the owners threaten lock-outs. The Firebrands organise meetings, the owners read the Riot Act.

The Firebrands get together with other, calmer, more restrained voices, who are also lobbying for change, advocating for greater representation. Together they put forward a petition, signed by many thousands of workers from across Manchester, which is submitted to Parliament, requesting the implementation by law of a minimum wage, to which all employers must agree to be bound.

Ten years before, to clamp down on what it sees as the danger of popular unrest at a time of political uncertainty, following the French Revolution and the beginning of the Napoleonic Wars, the Government of William Pitt (the Younger) passes the punitive Combinations Act, the *Act to Prevent the Unlawful Combinations of British Workmen*, prohibiting all forms of Trade Unions or acts of collective bargaining attempted by any group or association of labourers. Fearful of the rise in Jacobin sympathies, the Bill receives Royal Assent in 1799. But the more moderate of employers, especially those with Non-Conformist sympathies, the Methodists and Unitarians, turn a blind eye to the formation by their Chapels of the so-called Benevolent Societies, which get round the law by stating that their aims are purely altruistic, focusing on coming to the aid of those members who become sick, unable to work for whatever reason, or on improving the safety of conditions inside their mills and factories, providing Sunday School and Evening Classes to teach people basic skills in reading and writing, and acting as social support groups. In this capacity they also on occasion act as the official voice of protest when matters of grievance need to be raised.

Matthew Oldham, unlike his father before him, discourages any association with these Benevolent Societies, refusing to acknowledge, or even recognise their right to represent his workforce in any capacity, official or otherwise. In this he is at one with the Moravians, muses Amos ruefully, who, as loyal subjects of the Crown, eschew all such Combinations.

The murmurings of the Firebrands grow to a clamour. Their cries ricochet from every rooftop, every ledge and chimney pot, as the starlings wheel overhead in ever greater numbers, before roosting uncomfortably and impatiently, increasingly cramped and overcrowded, their voices demanding to be heard.

Twice the petition is sent to Parliament and twice it is ignored. On the third time it is, at last, debated, but rejected out of hand.

The Firebrands call for direct action, the Benevolent Societies for calm.

A compromise is reached. The following is proposed.

A MEETING
of the
FRIENDS OF REFORM
WILL BE HELD AT
ST GEORGE'S FIELDS
MANCHESTER
On Wednesday 25th May 1808 at 12 Noon
to take into consideration
the
Distressed State
of the
Spinners & Weavers

Posted alongside this on walls and lamp posts are to be found more detailed announcements of the meeting's purpose.

IT IS UNANIMOUSLY PROPOSED

That the Friends of Liberal Opinions, Members of the recently formed Hampden Clubs
(who meet severally in Oldham, Royton, Middleton and Manchester)
deeply regret that so many of our Townspeople have suffered greatly from their Adherence to the Cause of Reform, whereby they are still not in receipt of
A Fair Day's Pay for a Fair Day's Work.

These same Friends do now pledge themselves for the future to support and countenance all who have been, or who hereafter may be VICTIMS of the System of Unfair Dealing practised by
The Enemies of Reform.

It is to be put to this Meeting that, in order to promote and protect the Interests of Reform & the Daily Needs of the Labouring Man, it is necessary that AN ASSOCIATION for that purpose be now commenced, to be called:

THE MANCHESTER & SALFORD SPINNERS & WEAVERS ASSOCIATION

People attending are cordially requested to comport themselves in an orderly and law-abiding manner throughout the Meeting so as not to incur in any way the risk of being charged with unseemly, unbecoming or unlawful behaviour

Signed: pp The Committee
Samuel Bamford, John Knight
Dr Healey, John Cartwright
William Fitton, Joseph Johnson
John Thacker Saxton

As quickly as these are printed and distributed, so they are countered by ripostes from the owners and manufacturers, multiplied ten fold.

NOTICE

We, the undersigned,
COTTON MANUFACTURERS of Manchester,
believing that our Work People have been compelled
UNWILLINGLY
to leave their Employment by the
INTIMIDATION
OF A LAWLESS MOB
Hereby Give Notice that
We Shall Open Our Mills for Work
AT THE USUAL HOUR
ON WEDNESDAY MORNING
and that
PROTECTION WILL BE PROVIDED
TO ALL THOSE WHO ARE
Desirous to Return to their Employment

Matthew Oldham, Laurence Peel
Nathaniel Phillips, Jonathan Haworth
William & Daniel Grant, William Yates

PUBLIC NOTICE
The Magistrates of the Court Leet of Manchester
having received Communications from Divers Trades in the Town
that many of their Labourers are both
Desirous and Willing
To Return to their Work
Hereby Give This Instruction
THAT ANY MEASURES TAKEN TO SUPPRESS
ANY ATTEMPTED RESISTANCE
TO THEIR GOING TO WORK
WILL BE PROSECUTED
and that
Any Persons Desirous of Pursuing their Usual Employments
WILL BE PROTECTED

MR WILLIAM STARKIE
BOUROUGHREEVE of MANCHESTER

When former Lieutenant-Colonel Joseph Hanson, ex-Commanding Officer of The Manchester Volunteer Home Guard, reads these handbills, posted everywhere throughout the town, he is deeply alarmed. He goes at once to his father.

"It's a trap," he says. "They mean to kettle the protesters."

"Kettle?" queries his father,

"It is an effective but brutal form of crowd control. They corral the people into especially narrow confined spaces, where they may be harried and contained."

Joseph's father frowns. He knits his bushily wayward eyebrows together as he finishes his usual rushed breakfast of a boiled egg and coffee before departing for work at his own mill. His name is a notable absentee from the signatories at the foot of the notice posted by those differently alarmed cotton manufacturers.

"You have experience of this, I take it?"

"Yes, Father. These were the tactics so cruelly deployed at the Shude Hill Potato Riots of four years ago."

His father sighs. "You must not blame yourself for what happened there. You acted under orders from the authorities. You were a soldier. Doing your duty."

Joseph shakes his head.

"And you did the honourable thing," continues his father, picking up his hat and cane, "by resigning your commission post haste."

"I shudder to think of the consequences if there is to be a repeat at next week's public meeting. I know St George's Fields. I have in the past reconnoitred the lie of the land there. I know exactly what the Military will do, should the authorities summon them – as summon them they surely will. They will drive the protesters back towards the adjoining lane."

Mr Hanson Senior shudders at the thought. "It will be like herding recalcitrant cattle."

"It will be worse than that."

Joseph's father contorts his eyebrows still further. "How

so?"

"It could be a massacre."

Mr Hanson Senior sighs deeply. "What do you propose to do about it?"

"I've been considering the possibility of approaching the other owners who have signed that damned inflammatory Notice guaranteeing protection for any labourer choosing to turn up for work rather than attend the Public Meeting, and speaking to them individually."

"Aye, lad, there's sense in that. Though I must say that I have some sympathy with supporting folk who want to do an honest day's work."

"That's a smoke shield, Father, and you know it. The authorities are itching for a confrontation, which they can hold up as a precedent, a warning, to stave off any subsequent copycat strikes. 'This is what awaits you,' they want to be able to say. They fear this Public Meeting next week may be just the beginning of a whole wave of protests, for it's not only a minimum wage the Radicals seek – that is merely the tip of the iceberg. It's a whole raft of reforms they are pressing for, right up to universal suffrage."

"They'll not get that," buts in his father, "however hard they try. We'll not see that in our lifetime."

"Maybe not, Father. But representation at Westminster, an elected Member of Parliament for Manchester – surely *that* is not too much to hope for?"

"Nay, lad, it's not. But I can't see the Boroughreeve willingly ceding any of his power or authority, can you? Nor the rest of his cronies who ride on his coat tails – the Magistrates, Justices of the Peace, Deputy Constables and the like. They run Manchester like their own personal bailiwick. But change is coming, son, I'm certain of it. Manchester's a Dissenting town, a Non-Conformist town, a Modern town. Out wi' th' old, in wi' t' new. Why, there's nobbut a week goes by wi'out a dozen new patents being granted for all manner of inventions and improvements. I reckon it's only a matter of time before a new form of government comes along that's more suited to our needs, that reflects more accurately the kind of place we've become. A New Jerusalem."

"I hope you're right, Father, but the spinners and weavers today don't have time to wait for that New Jerusalem. They don't have the luxury of being able to let history run its course. They're starving, many of them. They can't afford to live on the wages they're currently being paid as it is, and there's every likelihood these wages may be cut further."

"Not in *our* factory."

"No, Father, but I'm not talking about ours. That's why I thought about going to speak to those other owners to try and persuade them to let this Public Meeting pass off peaceably. Then, when everyone's had a chance to calm down and the temperature's started to cool a little, I thought perhaps *you*, Father, might convene a Meeting of the Owners to see if an agreement might be reached for you *all* to pay your workers the same, right across the town."

"You'll be lucky."

"The Government may have rejected the Petition for a legally binding minimum wage, but surely it's not beyond the ken of the Manchester Mill Owners to come to a more informal arrangement?"

"No, lad, it's not. It could be done as quick and easy as that." He snaps his fingers for emphasis. "But first there's got to be a will, a desire, to do it. And that's where I think this notion of yours comes unstuck, son. We're all in competition wi' each other. Why would anyone in their right mind want to give an advantage to their rivals by agreeing to pay their workers more than they currently do and thereby lessen their profits?"

"Because it's the right thing to do."

"Right's got nowt to do wi' it, not where Business is concerned."

"*You* manage it, Father."

A silence falls between them. It is Mr Hanson Senior who breaks it.

"Aye, lad, 'appen so. But I'm not a member of their little club, am I? I don't sit on t' Court Leet, or dispense justice from their Magistrates' benches. I don't go to St Philip's Anglican Church. But they all do. I tell thee, son, they'll be more than 'appy to come to some kind of informal arrangement between 'em – I reckon they already 'ave – but to keep t' workers' wages *down*, not consider puttin' 'em up. That's why they'll never listen to any of these demands for Reform."

Joseph breathes deeply and nods. "I daresay, Father. But I'm still going to try."

"Good for you, lad. Tha'd be no son o' mine if tha' didn't."

The two men smile warmly at one another.

"So," continues Joseph, "what can you tell me about the first name on this list? Matthew Oldham?"

"Ah," replies Mr Hanson Senior, his language reverting more and more towards the dialect of his own parents, "he's a queer 'un, an' no mistake. Nothing like 'is feyther. Old Andrew Oldham were a truly great man, a visionary, an' modest wi' it. He were not one o' those grasping, avaricious types o' bosses, wantin' to move out o' t' town into t' country at th' earliest opportunity. He knew every single one of 'is employees by name, plus those o' their husbands, wives, childer an' sweethearts. 'E made a lot o' money, to be sure, but 'e gave away as much as 'e kept for 'isself. But the son – Matthew – 'e's a different kettle o' fish an' no mistake, a cold 'un an' all. I tell thee, lad, I can't fathom 'im. Tha'll 'ave tha' work cut out wi' 'im, that's for certain."

"I can only do my best, Father."

"Aye, lad, that's all any of us can do. But what wilt tha' do if tha' gets no joy wi' 'im, or any o' t'others?"

"I shall go along to the Public Meeting myself and try and persuade the protesters to stay calm, to offer no possible excuse or justification that might induce the Boroughreeve to call in the Military."

Joseph's father nods grimly, then shakes his son by the hand. "Good luck," he says. "Tha'll need it."

Afterwards Amos is not able to explain it. Not to the Constables, not to Agnes, not to himself. Except for one thing. The kindness of Joseph Hanson the moment before his arrest.

He had not wanted to attend the Meeting. It was not that he was unsympathetic towards the men's cause. Heaven knows he understood their plight, for it was his too. If it were not for the pitiful few shillings Agnes earned boiling bones in the Glue Factory the two of them would have starved. It was more that he liked to keep his head down, not draw attention to himself, just be one of the crowd.

"Then why not be one of *this* crowd?" Adam had argued. "Don't let others fight tha' battles for thee."

Amos saw the wisdom and justice in Adam's words but he couldn't quite bring himself to break the law, which was how he knew he would feel if he joined the strike. But when he turned up for work as usual on that Wednesday morning, there were so few who did – less than a handful – that the Overseer noted their names, thanked them for their loyalty, then sent them on their way. Oldham's Felt Factory would remain shut for the day, he was told. Not possessing Joseph Hanson's political insight, he did not see this as a calculated ploy on Matthew's part. Draw the enemy out into the open, refuse to accede to any of their demands, declare the Meeting unlawful, read them the Riot Act, then, when they do not disperse, call in the Military, thereby justifying whatever punitive measures are brought in next. No – Amos had no such suspicions, took the Overseer's words at face value, had not heard of Joseph Hanson, though all of that, and so much more, would change by day's end...

He intends to use this unexpected gift of free daylight hours to walk to Fairfield and visit Jack. He will surprise him, then take pleasure in recounting it all to Agnes when he returns home at night, as if from a usual shift at the mill.

But as soon as he steps out of the factory gates he is at once swept up by the enormous crowds making their way towards St George's Fields. He spots Adam and threads his way between the transverse weft of marching men and women to reach him.

"Eh up?" says Adam cheerfully. "Tha's changed tha' mind then?"

Amos nods, not wishing to disappoint his friend, and soon he is caught up in the mood of buoyant excitement and hope that infuses the marching throng.

"You Englishmen of each degree
One moment listen unto me
From day to day you all may see
The poor are frowned upon by degree
To please you all I do intend
So listen to these lines I've penned
By them you'll know you never can
Do without the labouring man..."

By the time he reaches St George's Field, Amos hears himself singing as loudly as all the rest.

"In former days, you all do know
A poor man cheerfully used to go
Quite neat and clean, upon my life
With his children and his darling wife
And for his labour it was said
A fair day's wages he was paid
But now to live he hardly can
May God protect the labouring man..."

But just as quickly, the moment they arrive at St George's Fields, this camaraderie dissipates. Because no official permission has been granted for the Meeting, there has correspondingly been no kind of organisation. There are no marching bands, no hustings, no rallying point, no raised platforms for the speakers, Mr Samuel Bamford and Mr John Knight, who, as a consequence, can neither be seen nor heard.

Amos and Adam have no sense of what is happening. They are not alone in this. The crowds grow restless and impatient. Voices are raised, grievances aired. There is pushing, then shoving, as different sections of the crowd try to make their way towards where they think the speakers might be gathered, only to find they have been surging in the wrong direction. Scuffles break out. Some people are thrown to the ground, others nearly trampled on. Then a great roar goes up and everyone is pointing. On a slightly raised piece of ground in the north-eastern corner of the field a man on a white stallion appears., like St George about to take on the dragon. He rears up on the horse's back legs, the sun at his back. He takes off his hat and waves it triumphantly above his head. A wave of huzzahs fills the air.

"It's Colonel Hanson," Amos hears one of the people cry out.

"He's not a Colonel any more," shouts another.

"Not these four years," calls a third.

"He's still the People's Champion," declares the first. "Three cheers for Colonel Hanson!"

More huzzahs follow. Amos does not know who they speak of. The name Hanson means nothing to him. But he senses the excitement, the optimism, the hope, in the atmosphere around him, which is no longer fractious and divided, but united as one, with everyone clamouring to get as close to the Man on the White Horse as they can.

Then another shout goes up, this time from behind them, from the south-west entrance to the field.

"It's the Military," cries one.

"Wi' t' Boroughreeve at th' head of it," shouts another.

"And there's Joe Nadin," points a third, and a deep-throated booing spreads through the crowd.

Amos knows who Nadin is. The Deputy Constable. Everyone in Manchester knows Joe Nadin. And fears him. He is not noted for observing the finer points of the law when it comes to making arrests, interrogating suspects and beating confessions out of them, even for crimes they have not committed. Especially those, some say.

The boos grow, transmuting into guttural pig noises.

"Joe Nadin and his big, bold hogs
As you will plainly see," they sing.
And on the other side
Stand the bloody cavalry..."

One of the soldiers gallops towards Mr Hanson. They appear to know one another and exchange salutes. Amos later learns that this is Lieutenant Trafford, Commanding Officer of the 4th Dragoon Guards. In the jostling, frightened crowd, Amos can just make out the two of them talking to one another. The soldier appears to be asking Mr Hanson something, to stand aside maybe. Meanwhile, the Constables on one side and the Cavalry on the other begin to press the crowds tighter and tighter together.

The kettling has begun.

Seeing this, or so it appears to Amos, Mr Hanson kicks his heels into the flanks of his white stallion and charges directly towards where the crowds are now being herded, Amos and Adam among them. It is impossible for anyone to stand their ground. With a click of their tongues, the riders from the Constabulary and Cavalry on either side of them gradually quicken their pace, forcing Amos and Adam and everyone not just to move in the direction they are being forced, but to run there.

It is not clear what the former Colonel Hanson is attempting to do. Perhaps he is trying to reach the crowd before either Nadin's or Trafford's men, and, once there, hold the ground for them, to enable them to leave the field in a safer and more orderly fashion. Perhaps he is trying to confuse both sets of riders and divert them away from the now panicking men and women, so that they will not fall beneath the thundering hooves of the oncoming horses. Or perhaps, as the authorities will subsequently claim, he is merely attempting to effect his own escape, having been ordered to leave by the Boroughreeve.

What, amid the ensuing chaos, remains certain to Amos, no matter how the different reports will try to twist it later, is this.

He sees one of the soldiers in the Cavalry raise his musket and fire a warning shot directly over the head of Mr Hanson as he gallops past. The noise resounds like thunder in St George's Fields. The white horse that Mr Hanson rides upon is immediately spooked. It throws back its head in a startled whinny, rears up on its back legs and unseats Mr Hanson, who is in immediate danger of being trampled on by the arrival of the Dragoon Guards, outriders of whom begin driving the crowds into the adjoining St George's Lane, which is narrow, and from which there is no escape. The terrified crowd, screaming with panic, turn and run in every direction at once, trampling and crushing each other indiscriminately in the process.

Amos and Adam, attempting to force their way against the flow, two shuttles weaving their way through the relentlessly unstoppable human warp, somehow manoeuvre their way past and reach Mr Hanson, hauling him from the path of an oncoming Constabulary horse at the very last moment.

Amos stoops to attend to Mr Hanson, not aware that a Cavalry Officer is charging towards him from a different direction.

Adam, in desperation, picks up a stone that he finds lying

close to hand and hurls it at the oncoming Guard, hitting the horse full square in the head, felling it with a single blow. Its legs buckle from under it and it rolls across its rider.

The Officer who had previously discharged the warning shot above Mr Hanson's head now reloads his musket and fires directly at Adam, killing him outright. He dies without a word in Amos's arms. His open eyes are fixed on something only he, it seems, can witness, while his bruised, cracked lips are slightly parted, as if they had been on the point of issuing some dire warning of what it was he saw approaching.

It has all happened so fast. In less than a heartbeat Adam's lifeless body is unceremonially dragged away, while Deputy Nadin is giving orders for the immediate arrest of Mr Hanson.

Just before he is taken away, he turns to Amos and says, "Thank you."

Without knowing how he might honour the promise he is about to make, Amos replies, "If I can be a witness at tha' trial, tha' need only to ask."

Hanson makes as if to shake Amos by the hand, but is restrained by the cuffs clamped to his wrists. "I am most sorry about your friend," he says, before he is led away by the Constables.

Amos watches him go, then turns back towards St George's Lane, which is strewn with the injured bodies of scores of protesters, many of them suffering severe sabre wounds and gashes.

It is some hours before he finally makes it back to Dimity Court.

Over the coming weeks the Authorities rehearse their arguments, while the 'official' version of the events, which took place on St George's Fields on 25th May 1808, is written, recorded, revised and rewritten. In the run up to Hanson's trial they are determined to make an example of him, to demonstrate to those who would argue for Reform that this way lies sedition and treason, for which there can only be one outcome – further repression and a tightening of the ever stricter measures brought in by the Court Leet. They will have a state of Martial Law. But if Amos's employer, Matthew Oldham, Magistrate and Justice of the Peace for the Town of Manchester within the Hundred of Salford, believes that these will serve as a deterrent, he is mistaken. They will serve only to politicise and radicalise Amos, along with thousands of others, still further. He will seek to become a member of Samuel Bamford's Hampden Club.

Amos, uncharacteristically decisive, turns to Agnes one evening in June and says, "We're leaving."

"When?" she asks, hardly daring to breathe.

"Now," he says. "At once."

"Where are we going?" she asks again, now barely daring to hope.

"Home," he says and pulls her tightly to him.

After they have kissed, Agnes opens her eyes. A procession of young rats is climbing up the mended pipe towards the upper air.

2

25th November

Nine years earlier.

The scene is *The Bull's Head* at Shude Hill. A meeting is to be held. The landlord is no longer Mr John Raffald, who has succumbed to that most common of publican's ailments – excess through overindulgence, caused by imbibing too freely of the products intended more for his customers. He has been replaced by Mr Capswick Shawe, an equally genial individual, with a large red nose indicative that he too is partial to the occasional quart of ale, or claret, or both, but one which is equally accustomed to being tapped on the side by a crooked forefinger, signalling that other important characteristic of one undertaking his current profession – of knowing when and where there are lines to be drawn, lines which must not be crossed, and when it is advisable to emulate Sir John Hume in Shakespeare's Henry IV, part 2, to "*seal up the lips and give no words but mum*".

The meeting, notices for which have been posted liberally throughout the town, is '*intended to be holden at the aforesaid house of Mr Shawe, on Monday, the twentieth day of this instant September, at eleven of the clock in the forenoon*', at which '*surveys, plans, levels, estimates and proposals will be presented for an extension of the river transport afforded by the Mersey & Irwell Navigation, to incorporate a new waterway, to be named the Manchester, Bolton & Bury Canal.*'

It is the height of Canal Mania, which is gripping Great Britain as a whole and Manchester in particular. Following the quite literally groundbreaking achievement of James Brindley in constructing the Duke's Cut, the world's first industrial canal, named for Lord Francis Egerton, the 3rd Earl of Bridgewater, which arrived in the town in the summer of 1761, having made its elegant way from Worsley via the Barton Aqueduct without recourse to a single lock in its entire length of forty-one miles, Manchester has experienced an especially febrile strain of the mania, witnessing the opening of the Rochdale, Ashton and Peak Forest Canals, each of them bringing their daily cargoes to the town from all points of the compass, together with the various smaller Junction Canals, connecting them to the Rivers Irwell, Irk and Medlock, linking them all into an ever-expanding spiderweb, serving the scores of mills, mines and factories springing up almost hourly, it seems, along their banks, so that they serve as the veins and arteries of the town, providing the necessary blood supply to its rapidly beating heart. This latest proposed addition, the Manchester, Bolton & Bury, will take advantage of the Irwell's upper course, flowing north-westwards out of the town, bringing the goods of men like Matthew's friend Laurence Peel's older brother, Robert, now the Member of Parliament for Tamworth, having successfully purchased the seat from the lapsed estates of Lord Bath, to many more customers, for, contained within the initial plans for the Canal, as outlined by the celebrated engineer Hugh Henshall, who even now is to be found in full flow addressing the meeting in the upstairs room of *The Bull's Head*, are proposals to extend the canal from Bury through Littleborough to connect with the Rochdale Canal at Sladen, with additional extensions suggested to Sowerby Bridge and thence to the Leeds-Liverpool Canal, thereby opening up considerable opportunities for increased trade across the Pennines, adding yet further radial strands to that ever-growing spider's web, spun by the merchants of Manchester, who are at this very moment hanging onto every word of what Mr Henshall has to tell them.

Among this most attentive audience is Sir Ashton Lever, still in pursuit of any get-rich-quick scheme which might serve to finance his ever-declining *Holophusicon*, unaware that in less than fortnight he will succumb to a heart attack in this very room, while in pursuit of yet more funds to stave off his impending bankruptcy. He thinks of the genus *erigoninae*, a sub-family of *linyphiidae*, of the order of *araneae*, in the class of *arachnida*, the common money spider, who secretes mile upon mile of silk during its lifetime from its spinneret glands at the tip of its abdomen. Each gland produces a different type of thread, each with a specific purpose – hunting, guiding, signalling – a trailed safety line for navigating to and from the heart of the web, a stickier silk for trapping prey, and a finer silk for wrapping it. Its properties are infinite. It possesses countless admirable qualities. The tensile strength of spider silk is greater than the equivalent weight in steel yet has substantially more elasticity. Although it cannot be denied that the cost of construction is high, especially in terms of energy loss and the large amount of protein required, there is no shortage of supply to offset these costs, and allowing for the fact that, after a time, the silk may lose some of its adhesiveness and therefore become less efficient at capturing and storing prey, the spider compensates for this through the habit of daily eating its own web in order to recoup some of the energy used up in the spinning of it. Thus it renews and recycles itself and production continues unabated.

Sir Ashton is not interested in the specifics of Mr Henshall's plan, only the hoped-for outcome, and so he does not listen quite so attentively as his fellow attendees. Instead he amuses himself by doodling different sketches of the busy and, he hopes, lucky *erigoninae*.

Among those others present, who continue to listen to Mr Henshall almost as a congregation of new converts might to the minister of some new denomination, are: Lord Grey de Wilton of Heaton House, representing also the Earl of Derby, who between them will pledge five thousand pounds towards the scheme; Sir John Edensor Heathcote, a supporter of Sir Robert

Peel in his Staffordshire constituency, who will pledge three thousand pounds to Sir Robert's somewhat parsimonious three hundred; Mr Matthew Fletcher, a mine owner and engineer from Bolton, together with fellow Boltonians Mr Peter Drinkwater and his son Mr John; Mr Thomas Hatfield and his son Mr Walter; Mr Fletcher's own son, another John, as well as his cousin, Mr Nathaniel Heywood, a right family affair, who collectively promise to put up a further four and a half thousand pounds. Yet to commit and still keeping their powder dry are Mr Thomas Butterworth Baley of Hope in the Hundred of Salford, Mr Robert Andrews of Rivington, and Messrs Marsden, McNiven, Pilkington and Wareing, Gentlemen of Manchester.

It is not the first such meeting. Preliminary sessions have already been held in *The Eagle & Child* in Bury, where a Management Committee was formed, which subsequently met at the home of Mr Alexander Patton, the brother-in-law of Sir Edensor Heathcote, where the important resolution was passed dispatching Mr McNiven to procure 'one hundred wheelbarrows' and 'as many planks as he shall think necessary' for the 'use and accommodation of the canal navigation'. Mr Henshall was instructed to 'survey the line of the canal' beginning 'within the estate of Sir Robert Peel' and ending at 'the southern extremity of the Reverend Dauntesey's estate', beside his elegant 15th century Tudor Mansion in Agecroft, which the Reverend, duly giving his apologies for this evening's meeting, will, over the course of the next ten years, uproot stone by stone, transport across the Atlantic and rebuild, exactly as it originally stood, on his family's plantation in Richmond, Virginia. It is the report on this survey that Mr Henshall is now delivering which holds those present so rapt in their attention. They do not have long to wait for those items which are most demanding of their interest.

"Gentlemen," he declares, "it gives me great pleasure to be able to confirm to you this evening that, following the

Parliamentary Survey, Government approval has been granted and the Bill has now received Royal Assent."

This remark is greeted with a great rapping of fists upon tables by all those assembled as they voice their approval at this news.

"Furthermore," continues Mr Henshall, "the Manchester, Bury & Bolton Canal Company are empowered to purchase land for a breadth of twenty-two yards, that is one chain, on level ground for the purpose of construction, and wider up to two chains where required for a cutting or embankment."

"Hear, hear!"

"And finally, the Act allows the Company to raise an initial forty-seven thousand pounds through an issue of one hundred pound shares at a dividend of five percent – modest, I admit, Gentlemen, to begin with, but not to be sneezed at neither, with a further provision for ten percent subsequently."

This is what the assembled company have been wishing to hear and the news is greeted with a further thunderous fist-rapping, which Sir Ashton too now joins in with considerable enthusiasm, screwing his doodled sketch of the money spider into a tight ball that he tosses into the air, catches, then deposits in his waistcoat pocket, as if neatly completing a conjuring trick. Money – now you see it, now you don't.

"The Bill entitles us," concludes Mr Henshall, "to take water from any brook within a thousand yards of the passage of the canal, and up to three miles from the twin summits of Bolton and Bury."

The Gentlemen frown at this last second codicil. They are perturbed by the possible consequences of its inclusion.

"However," interjects Sir Robert Peel, sensing their discomfort, "I have secured an agreement with the House that this scheme cannot with propriety be ascertained until such time as it has been certified from whence, and in what proportion, the proprietors – namely ourselves, Gentlemen – of the intended Navigation expect to draw their resources of water."

"Thank you, Sir Robert. My report makes it quite clear that our plan – should you approve it – will not require water from the Irwell in times of drought, but that floods and rivulets will supply the reservoirs that I propose to build…" And at this point he pauses to produce a map which he unrolls on the table in front of him, pointing as he continues.

"… here, at Clifton; here, at Smithy Bridge, and here, the largest of the three, at Elton."

"With an additional clause I insisted was included when the Bill came up for its third reading in the House," pronounces Sir Robert once again, with an air of suitably grandiose self-importance, causing all in the Upstairs Function Room of *The Bull's Head Inn* to switch their attention from Mr Henshall back to him, as he reads directly from the Act. " '*That all mill and mine owners, whose factories will now find themselves situated along the proposed route of the Navigation, be not in any way disadvantaged in terms of having their own water supplies interrupted, rather that outflows should be linked directly into the Canal, and that the owners' rights are hereby guaranteed and enshrined in the new legislation*'. I insisted upon it, Gentlemen, and this clause is now included."

A great round of applause spontaneously greets this announcement, after which the Gentlemen happily gather round the table to peruse the plans Mr Henshall now sets before them. Eight meticulous drawings outline the proposed route, with its two branches, fifteen locks, seven wharfs and basins, and two tunnels. They nod sagely, some of them clapping him on the back, some shaking him by the hand, others even going so far as to offer him a cigar.

A cigar that is not offered that same morning to Amos, when Agnes gives birth to their son John James, to be known as Jack, after a difficult all night labour, just a few miles to the north, at Brindle Heath, where Amos's itinerant work has at the time taken him, which will be close to the Cock Robin Bridge that will span the canal there once it is built.

Nine years later, had he the means, Amos might well have been lighting up another of those cigars, as he stood beside the now fully constructed canal with Agnes and Jack, to celebrate their long dreamt of return to Elton, home to the great reservoir that provided water for the Navigation, as well as the prospect of sanctuary, and an unlikely salvation.

> *"But now that we're together again*
> *To the country we've come back*
> *There's many a mile o' heathery moor*
> *Twixt us and the coal-pit stack*
> *And so I sit by the fire each night*
> *With my wife and son at my knee*
> *From Heywood, Hooley, Heap and Hell*
> *The Good Lord has delivered me..."*

When, a week after the tragic events of St George's Field, Amos had taken Agnes in his arms and promised to take her home, he meant every word of it. What he had not fully considered was how he might make it happen. But he knew with a certainty whose fierceness surprised him that he could no longer merely drift, casting their lives like broken nets upon the choking waters of the Irk or the Irwell and somehow expecting to haul in a huge catch. No – he must first attend to those broken nets and then seek out less polluted waters.

In the end it took him six months but during that time Agnes could see the change in him, witness the efforts he was now making, and so this new-found hope never quite left her, not even when an early winter gripped Manchester, freezing the surface of the canals, so that the barges had to deploy ice-breakers to clear a passage through.

One Sunday in early November, the two of them walked

beside the frozen Ashton Canal to Fairfield. A thick fog rose from its surface, swirling around their ankles and waists, clinging to their faces and hair, so that they had to cover their mouths with grey cotton rags to avoid breathing in its noxious fumes, which never fully cleared. They could barely see ten yards ahead of them, and it seemed to Agnes that the whole world had shrunk to this smothering sheet of mist, that there was never an end to it, but somehow Amos strode tall. His spirits were not dampened by it, unlike hers. "Have faith," he said simply. "In what?" replied Agnes. "Each other," he said, taking her hand in his. Together they walked the final mile to Fairfield.

When they arrived, Caroline was waiting for them at the gates. They could tell at once from the expression on her face that something was wrong.

"What is it?" asked Agnes. "What's happened?"

"Here," answered her mother, "read this." And she thrust a creased and folded letter into her hands.

Dear Cousin John & Caroline,

I write with sad news. Last month our father, Silas, passed away. Truth to tell, it were a blessing. He'd not been well these five years. We laid him out back, along with Meg and young James.

I would've written sooner but there's been much to do.

Please can you let Amos and Agnes know. I don't know where they live these days and we have lost touch, which I'm sad about.

Our father's last wish was that Amos should have the loom. Shem and I will look after it for him till he comes.

Your cousin,

Ham

As soon as she had finished reading it, Agnes passed it across to Amos. The two of them looked at each other and nodded. They didn't need to speak. The palest of pale suns was trying to chisel its way through the dense wall of cloud, almost as if it were chipping away with a weak but determined hammer, much as Amos had done day after day down the Charlotte Mine, a sound he fancied he heard that moment as a first finger of light tapped him on the forehead.

"Can tha' fetch Jack please?" he said. "Please ask 'im to be ready to leave in less than an hour."

Caroline's mouth opened, like a gaping fish coming up for air from beneath the surface of the Ashton Canal, but no words came out, only wraiths of silver mist that coiled around her like frozen shackles. She looked at her daughter, but if she was hoping for a reprieve, for her daughter to produce a key to unlock these chains, she was at once disappointed.

"Tha's heard my husband," she said. "We've come for our son."

Now the three of them, Amos, Agnes and Jack, stand on the quayside of the Manchester, Bolton & Bury Canal, each of them carrying a small bundle over their shoulders, containing everything they own, which hardly amounts to a bean. They have handed over a sixpence each, the last three coins they had, to purchase tickets aboard the packet boat which conveys passengers as well as coal along the canal.

They are all of them quiet, each lost in their own thoughts, Amos especially. He is remembering back to those days as a child, roughly the same age his son Jack is now, when he was incarcerated in the House of Correction on New Bridge Street, how he would climb up on an old barrel to reach towards the tiny barred window in the dormitory where he slept with forty other boys so that he might look out onto the River Irwell below. Its waters were cleaner then, faster flowing than they are now. All manner of barges and boats sailed upon it, bringing in the raw materials the many mills and factories devoured, before sending out the goods they spat out afterwards, to every corner of the globe. Or so it had seemed to Amos as a boy. Here was the crossroads of the world, with people from all nations arriving, while he dreamed about departing.

Now he was fulfilling that childhood dream.

"Penny for 'em," says Agnes, smiling.

"Tha's not got a penny," says Amos, smiling back.

"But *I* have," says Jack, darting suddenly into the path of an oncoming cart, then returning triumphant, holding aloft a worn and misshaped coin, which had just been rolled and flattened by the wheels of the cart.

"Best keep that, eh?" says Amos, remembering the Roman coin he had lost in the Charlotte Mine. "For luck?"

Jack nods seriously and bestows his new found treasure deep into his pocket, where he holds it tightly, balled up in his tiny fist for added protection.

The skipper rings his bell and Amos, Agnes and Jack, along with the other passengers waiting on the canal steps, all proceed to board. The barge is long and narrow. The central section is filled with rows of wooden tubs. These are used for carrying the coal. Each tub has a strong base fitted with two halves, hinged and held shut with chains. At every drop-off point these tubs are lifted out of the barge by a crane positioned over a bunker or cart and emptied by releasing the chains at the base. Simple but ingenious, these tubs are what helps keep the Canal Company competitive, increasing the speed with which loading and unloading can take place, thereby raising the dividend those original investors continue to recoup. The passengers must squeeze themselves at either end of the barge, away from the hold containing the tubs. *Their* access on and off is a much slower and more cumbersome affair, for they are not as precious as the cargo, involving a nerve-jangling walk across a wooden plank connecting the barge with the quay. Amos,

Agnes and Jack skip along it, without once looking back.

It is the 25th of November, 1808. The winter grips the town even tighter. Great slabs of ice have formed across the rivers and canals. Here on the Irwell, at the start of the Manchester, Bolton & Bury Canal, the icebreaker *Sarah Lansdale* is attempting to clear a passage. Owned by the James Crompton Paper Works, but leased out to the Canal Company at times like these, it is towed by a team of heavy horses. The crew stands astride the deck, secured by ropes to the hand rails, rocking the boat wildly from side to side, thereby breaking the ice in the process.

Jack watches this enthralled. He had not wanted to leave Fairfield. He loved it there, especially the times he spent each day with his Grandpa John, who was more like a father to him than Amos, who he hardly knows. But he had missed his mother and she had won him round with promises of fish to be caught in the Elton Brook. It would be an adventure, she had said, and now it seems that after all she is right.

Once they reach the point where the Canal leaves the river and follows its own Navigation, by the Ordsall Basin, they are free of ice and can say their farewells to the *Sarah Lansdale*. Progress is now smoother but still slow, for they have to make their way through six locks as they climb towards the Gaythorn Wharf and the junction with the Rochdale. There is much to see in this short stretch and Jack is allowed by the skipper to help the crew tie off the ropes at each lock.

Through Salford it begins to quieten and, by the time they have reached Pendleton, they briefly rejoin the Irwell itself for a while, passing under several bridges – Bedlam Bridge, Broughton Bridge, Indigo Bridge and Cock Robin Bridge, by Brindle Heath, which Agnes points out to Jack.

"This is where you were born," she says.

"Where? On t' shores o' t' river? Like Moses?"

Agnes and Amos laugh. It is a long time, she realises, since they have both laughed so freely. Jack regards them curiously.

"No," she says, but she does not tell him where exactly. She has long since buried the memory of that awful night in the cold, damp cellar in the lee of the Indigo Mill, where the water ran blue – still does, she thinks, looking over the side of the boat – of how, in those first few frightful months she had indeed been tempted to set him adrift in a basket to float away towards what she dreamed might be a better, safer, freer life. Instead she had plucked a handful of wild flowers from the wayside and cast their petals onto the surface, watching them be carried away by the current, beyond sight. Back then they were moving inexorably with that current, away from Elton and towards Manchester. Now they are retracing their steps, heading back to those first hopeful beginnings.

She rummages inside her bundle till she finds what she is looking for.

"Here," she says to Jack. "Look through this and tell me what you see." She hands him the kaleidoscope.

Jack holds it at once to his eye and turns it.

"Lost treasure," he says excitedly.

Agnes smiles. "Let's hope we find it." She takes it back from her son and turns it over reverently in her hands. "Your father made this when he wasn't much older than you are now."

"Really?" Jack looks over towards his father with a new respect.

The hours flow. The water barely ripples. The mist thins a little. Rooks call defiantly from the leafless trees. They pass under more bridges. Lumb's, Hogg's, Pack Saddle. Clifton, Kilcoby and Ham Pee, where a heron stands to attention for so long Jack wonders if it might be a statue. It reminds him of a soldier standing guard outside the Castlefield Barracks, which they had seen earlier that morning on their way to the quayside. But then it takes off, unexpectedly, without warning, its long, slow wing beats lifting it with difficulty into the still, heavy air. Once airborne it assumes its element. It rapiers the sky, passing swiftly beyond sight, an echo in the thrumming air, a shadow, a memory.

Swinging by the arm to Fletcher's Canal they make their way through the Giant's Seat Locks, which take them past the Tram Road out to the Colliery Basin by Ringley Fold Bridge, then through the Ringley Locks, past Stoneclough to the Appleyard Bridge just before the Prestolee Aqueduct, which carries the canal over the River Irwell once more at Nob End, where the skipper skilfully manoeuvres them through the tricky Waters Meet onto the Bury Branch close by Little Lever.

Amos sees many landmarks he does not at first recognise, seen as they are now from this new perspective, but which gradually resurface as the route reels him back in, the wanderer returning. But to what? Not to Penelope, for she is standing by his side, which she has done through most of his seemingly purposeless odyssey, the different spindles unspooling him randomly, so that the thread became hopelessly tangled. Only now is it beginning to wind him back, the deep, straight cut of the canal untying each separate knot and snag as the miles roll by. It's the loom – he knows this now – that is calling him. He understands more clearly what he failed to see the last time he was there, when his pride compelled him to seek his own path, rather than walk in another's footsteps. The loom belonged to Silas. And before that, to Edwin. All Amos had done was to borrow it for a time, to repair and restore it while Silas himself was mended back to health. But something about the way it had sat in his hands, had responded to his touch, had sang its clickety-clack rhythms while his fingers had danced across it, had stayed with him. Nothing else he had done had come close. Silas must have seen this, must have heard it while Agnes nursed his ailing body, and itched to go downstairs once more to pick up the shuttle one last time, knowing, even before Amos did himself, that he was not ready for it yet, but that one day he would be.

And now, it seems, that day has come.

"It's not about the money," he tells Agnes. "We'll probably earn less than we did before, at t' Felt an' Glue Factories. The bottom's dropped right out of th' handloom woven products. It's about having a trade to call me own, a craft to master, a skill to keep working at, an' then summat to show for it afterwards, summat to hold in me hands, an' say, 'I made this'."

Agnes understands. She doesn't need to say so, but she does anyway. "Summat that's ours," she says.

Once they join the Bury arm of the Canal, the miles begin to ravel more quickly. The Steam Crane at Ladyshore Colliery pounds into the earth, the winding gear of the headstocks hauling up the men and coal from underground, a mechanised world away from how it was for Amos in the Charlotte Mine.

Then more bridges – Mount Sion, Nickerhole, Scotson Fold. Within's, Bank Top, Daisyfield, which their lost daughter was named for, where they alight, running together the last mile beside the Elton Reservoir, to Silas's empty cottage. It remains glassless. The wind whispers through the empty casements. Agnes fancies she can hear words within its many voices.

"You're back then," she hears them say. "We thought you would."

"We hoped."

"We dreamed."

"But we never really believed it."

"I did," says Agnes out loud, then turns towards her two boys. "We're here," she says.

Later that evening, as the sky, which never grew fully light all day, becomes truly dark, Agnes, Amos and Jack, each in their separate thoughts, in a separate space in what is now their new

90

home, look back over the events that have led them there.

Agnes, outside, looks up at the sky. The fog has lifted and she can see the Milky Way arching clear and cold overhead. By the light of the North Star, the Pole Star, the *Stella Maris*, she makes her way to the patch of land at the back of the house, where the bodies are buried. Silas, Meg, her brother James. She makes a cairn of small stones. Into it she thrusts a cross she has tied together with a snag of old yarn and two sticks of ash she has found, on which she has carved the name of Daisy.

From inside the cottage, standing at a narrow wind-eye, an opening in the wall to let in light and the wind, Jack watches his mother go through this private ritual. When she has finished, she starts to sing. He can't hear the words. He supposes it must be some kind of hymn. Or a lullaby perhaps. One by one the words rise up towards him, carried by the smoke of a small fire his mother has lit.

> *"When the marigold no longer blooms*
> *When summer sun is turned to gloom*
> *See the forecast winter snow*
> *See the evergreen that lonely grows*
> *Move close to the fireplace*
> *Neglect the garden*
> *See the ground harden*
> *At a ghostly place…"*

He doesn't really remember his sister. He looks beyond his mother towards the empty field. He sees a patch of reflected moonlight glinting from the Reservoir. He's already feeling lonely. What is he going to do here? He strains to see as far as he can across the night sky. A shower of shooting stars rains down from the eastern quadrant. They remind him of the patterns he has seen in the kaleidoscope his mother showed him earlier in the day. He wonders about going out to join her and asking her if she might let him look into it once again, but he decides against it. His mother is still singing, and in any case the shooting stars have all gone now.

Agnes does not notice the meteor shower. She is too engrossed in remembering her daughter, her lost flower.

"*The golden summer sun is silver now*
The fruit has fallen from the bough…"

She breaks off her quiet singing a moment, sensing she is being watched perhaps. She looks quickly over her shoulder, is aware of Jack's shadow darting from her in the upstairs window. This must all be very strange for him, she thinks. Perhaps she should have brought him out with her for this memorial. No. It would only confuse or upset him. She needs this time to herself.

"*You wrap around you*
But the cold confounds you
On an autumn day…"

Back inside the house, in the large downstairs room, Amos has finished cleaning and polishing the loom. He has lit a fire in the hearth. Now he sits at the frame, letting his hands reacquaint themselves with the feel and touch of it. He cannot wait to set the shuttle back in motion, flying forward and back across the weft. But wait he must. He will not begin this night. It is too late. Instead he watches the sparks from the flames taking hold on the few pieces of coal he found lying outside, almost as if they had been waiting for them to arrive. He watches them dance up the chimney and out into the night sky to join the last embers of a shower of shooting stars he catches a final sight of before they fade. He is at once transported back to when he and Agnes first came here, almost ten years to the day, after their night time escape from Fairfield. He looks up and sees the Pole Star shining cold and clear, almost directly above where Agnes still sits and croons for their dead daughter. He would like to join her, but fears to disturb the private intensity of her grief.

He looks back down at the loom, places his hands reverently upon it, reaches down for the carved laurel. He will start tomorrow. Early. Before daybreak. He dares to imagine a future.

Six-Pointed Star to Bird's Nest.

"Stout and strong the walls of home and hearth
Curtains drawn against the draught
The rake has reaped, the blade has mown
Nights draw in to call the harvest home
The quiet of a heart at rest
In peace abounded
By love surrounded
Here the home is blessed..."

They have been at Elton for more than a month now. Christmas has come and gone. Twelfth Night approaches. Each has found their rhythm. Amos works the loom from dawn till dusk. It is long, tiring, back-breaking work, but Amos has never felt happier, never surer that this is what all his wanderings have been leading towards.

Agnes roams the lanes and hedgerows looking for plants for new dyes. She lays out the finished cloth that Amos gives her in the field behind the cottage to be naturally bleached by the action of the sun and water before applying the different dyes.

Jack is pretty much left to fend for himself. At first he revels in the freedom. He climbs trees, he fords streams, he traps rabbits, he catches fish. But soon he begins to grow restless. There must be more to the world than what is bounded by these few fields. His parents, he suspects, are retreating from the world, trying to keep it at bay. Whereas he would like to run fast towards it and dive headlong into it. Treasure, the kaleidoscope had shown him. Lost treasure, which he would like to try and find. Treasure and adventure.

Then, on the morning of Twelfth Night, he wanders down towards the Turnpike Road.

He hears them before he sees them, and he feels them before he hears them. The horses. Their hooves drumming up from under the earth. Then they appear over the rim of Harcles Hill. A platoon of soldiers. Jack catches a glint of sharp winter sun bouncing off their helmets and sabres, from the highly polished bits and bridles, spurs and stirrups. He is entranced. He watches them the full half hour it takes for them to reach him, then the subsequent half hour for them to march past him. One of them gives him a salute, which he returns with as much fervour as he can, for which he is rewarded with a smile and the light tap of a sabre on his shoulder.

He learns they are escorting a prisoner, all the way from Manchester to Lancaster, where he is to stand trial. He is being made to walk the entire way. His wrists and ankles are not chained. He walks freely and almost proudly, thinks, Jack, as if defiantly convinced of his innocence. Jack wonders what he must have done. He must ask his father about him when he gets home. He hears one of the soldiers address him by his name. Hanson, he calls him. Mr Hanson. Jack determines to remember that when he speaks to his father. He too has a salute for Jack as he passes, which Jack happily returns, but then worries that he might in some way be betraying his King and Country by saluting a prisoner under guarded escort. But then, he asks himself, aren't all men presumed innocent until proven otherwise? It feels complicated and confusing, when what he desires more than anything, he realises, is clarity and certainty.

Watching the soldiers now march away from him towards the ancient hill fort at Castlesteads that he can just make out on the horizon, one thing he is absolutely clear and certain about is that he would like to be marching along with them. The reds and whites of their uniforms, the golden plumes and tassels dancing from their helmets, the jangle of the reins upon the horses, they seem so perfect, so familiar, as if he has always known them, even though he has never seen them before. And then he realises that of course he has. These are the colours he has glimpsed in the kaleidoscope. He has found the lost treasure.

Bird's Nest to Soldier's Bed.

3

1809

22nd – 24th February

Lancaster Spring Assizes

Rex vs Hanson

TRANSCRIPT OF THE PROCEEDINGS IN THE CASE OF ONE JOSEPH HANSON, ESQ., FORMERLY LIEUTENANT-COLONEL, SALFORD & STOCKPORT INDEPENDENT RIFLES, ON AN INDICTMENT FOR A SERIOUS MISDEMEANOUR, IN AIDING AND ABETTING THE SPINNERS & WEAVERS OF MANCHESTER IN A CONSPIRACY TO RAISE THEIR WAGES.

The case is tried before the Hon. Sir Simon Goose, a Judge of His Majesty's Court of the King's Bench, and a Special Jury, at Lancaster Spring Assizes, the 49th year of the reign of our Most Sovereign King George III.

Counsel for the Crown

Mr Cockell, *Attorney-General for the Duchy of Lancaster*
Mr Park (*afterwards Judge of the Common Pleas*)
Mr Topping
Mr Wardley (*afterwards Judge of the King's Bench*)
Mr Scarlett Mr Cross
Mr Yeats Mr Richardson

Attornies

Mr Litchfield, *Solicitor to the Treasury*
Messrs Sergeant & Milne

Counsel for the Defendant

Mr Raine Mr Williams
Mr Littledale Mr Ambrose

William Fitzherbert Brockholes, *of Clayton*
Edmund Leigh, *of Chorley*
John Harrison, *of the same place*
Robert Lightollers, *of the same place*
James Orrell, *of Parr Stocks*
John Hodson, *of Smithy Brook*
John Jackson, *of Middleton*
John Adams, *of Kirkdale*
George Grundy, *of the same place*
John Whittle, *of the same place*
William Tarbuck, *of Sutton*
Joseph Armstrong, *of Manchester*

Day 1: Wednesday 22nd February

The INDICTMENT is opened by Mr Richardson. This is his first appearance before the King's Bench and he is so filled with the gravitas and importance of the occasion that his nerves have begun to master him. He is both simultaneously pale and perspiring, so that his face resembles that of a rather unattractive, desiccated prune, while his voice rises and swoops the octaves, a motion mirrored by the erratic bobbing of his most protuberant Adam's apple, the sight of which so distracts the Defendant, the former Colonel, now plain Mister, Hanson, (although for the purpose of the trial he has elected to wear his old military uniform), that he fails as a consequence properly to listen to the words being set against him.

MR RICHARDSON:
May it please the Court.
The Defendant, Mr Joseph Hanson, stands before you accused of incitement of others to disturb the peace in pursuance of an unjust and unlawful cause.

He now unrolls a scroll from which he reads, having first cleared his throat, a sound somewhere between a bark and a honk, in a single breath.

Be here apprised that before and at the time of committing the offences hereinafter-mentioned, (to wit, on the 25th day of May, in the 48th year of the reign of our Sovereign Lord George III, by the Grace of God, of the United Kingdom of Great Britain and Ireland, King, Defender of the Faith), at Manchester, in the County Palatine of Lancaster, divers evil-disposed persons, (to the number of one thousand and more, whose names to the jurors aforesaid are yet unknown, being workmen and journeymen in the art, mystery, and manual occupation of weavers, not being content to labour in that art, mystery, and manual occupation at the several rates and prices at which they and other such workmen and journeymen had been wont and accustomed to receive, but oppressively devising to exact and extort unwarranted increases in the sums of money for their labour and hire from the masters who employed them therein), did unlawfully, unjustly, and corruptly combine, conspire and consent to demand, procure and obtain for themselves and other workmen and journeymen in the said art, mystery, and manual occupation, from the masters who employed them therein, *greater* wages, hire, and reward than the customary wages, hire, and reward then usually paid for their labour and work.

Mr Richardson deposits the first of the writs on the bench of Sir Simon Goose, takes a sip of water, mops his lips extravagantly with a handkerchief, then continues in a second single breath.

And that, in pursuance of the said conspiracy, combination and agreement, and in order to carry their said unlawful intentions into effect, divers and very many of the said evil-disposed workmen and journeymen, (whose names are to the jurors aforesaid as yet unknown), had, then and there, for a long space of time before, desisted, and did then and there continue to desist from, and totally leave and refuse to continue, their labour and work, as such workmen, and journeymen. And that, in further pursuance of the said conspiracy, on the 25th day of May, in the 48th year of the reign aforesaid, at Manchester, in the County Palatine of Lancaster, they did unlawfully, riotously and tumultuously assemble and gather themselves together, to the great breach and disturbance of the peace of our said Lord the King.

Mr Richardson's face is becoming redder and redder. He delivers the following final section of the Indictment in a third, even more rapid single breath, so that at the end it appears he might almost burst, spraying the Court with a mixture of spittle and sweat.

Nevertheless, the defendant, Mr Joseph Hanson, (well knowing all and singular the premises and unlawful proceedings aforesaid, but being an evil-disposed person himself and disturber of the peace of our said Lord the King, and unlawfully and maliciously devising and intending to promote and encourage those aforesaid unlawful actions, that is, to urge and promote the said conspiracy and combination, and to aid, abet, and support the said conspirators in their said conspiracy and combination, heretofore, and whilst the said unlawful combination and conspiracy was prosecuted and undertaken, to wit, on the 25th day of May, in the 48th year of the reign aforesaid, with force and arms, at Manchester, in the County Palatine of Lancaster), did go to and, (amongst the said evil-disposed persons so assembled and gathered together, as aforesaid, and by speeches addressed to those same persons), incite, encourage, and endeavour to move and thereto persuade the said evil-disposed persons so assembled and gathered together, to persevere and persist in refusing to work in the said art, mystery, and manual occupation, and to persevere and persist in striving to accomplish and bring to effect the said unlawful conspiracy and combination, (and the unlawful designs and intentions aforesaid), and did then and there (also unlawfully and maliciously for the unlawful purpose aforesaid), speak, utter, and publish, to, and in the hearing of, divers of the said evil-disposed persons, so assembled and gathered as aforesaid, a series of malicious and inflammatory words.

Mr Richardson's Adam's apple at last ceases its wayward peregrinations. Exhausted, he looks around the Court, hoping for some sign or recognition of approval. On receiving none, he withdraws backwards towards his seat, overwhelmed with a mixture of relief and anti-climax, before sitting himself down upon his allotted chair, his hands trembling, his countenance perspiring and his eyes watering.

Mr Cockell, Attorney-General to the Duchy of Lancaster and Chief Prosecutor in the case, now takes to the floor. He strides confidently towards the Jurors, his imposing figure further enhanced by the magnificence of his robes – ivory black damask trimmed with white ermine – so that he appears to swoop towards them like an apocalyptic angel, or rather, he would do, were it not for the fact that he is somewhat hampered by the portly size of his girth, which is not afraid to display the effects of much fine dining, further evidenced by the ruddiness of his complexion, which matches perfectly the shade of his preferred libation, a bottle of the finest French claret.

MR. COCKELL:
  May it please your Lordship, Gentlemen of the Jury, I represent Counsel against the Defendant in this prosecution, which is certainly of a very grave and serious nature. I shall rejoice if the Defendant can deliver himself from this heavy charge by proof of his innocence before you this day; but if

the evidence which I am now about to adduce shall be as forcible as I conceive it will be, I do not know how you can discharge your duty but by convicting him; and if this should be the case, the former Colonel Hanson has only himself to thank for his misfortune.

He throws an amused glance in the direction of the Defendant, almost as if he might be considering him as a minor tid-bit, an appetising morsel to be consumed later, between courses.

Gentlemen, in prosecuting this case, I shall not endeavour to inflame your passions, or to excite your indignation against the Defendant. All expressions of this sort shall be avoided; and if you have out of Court heard anything of the transaction, which is the subject of the present indictment, I beseech you to dismiss from your minds every impression which such a circumstance may have occasioned, for every British subject is assumed to be innocent until his guilt is established by evidence. In conducting this prosecution, I shall endeavour to do my duty to the public, and at the same time to behave with the utmost moderation towards the Defendant. I have no malice to gratify; nor do I entertain any personal woe against the former Colonel Hanson, and nor do I wish for his conviction unless the charge shall be satisfactorily proved to your own minds. Do you, on the other hand, *your* duty, whatsoever consequence may ensue.

He looms magisterially over the Jurors at this point, before sweeping his robes dramatically behind him as he reverts to a more central position in the Court Room. He assumes a strong theatrical pose, one he has seen Mr Garrick adopt on the stage at Drury Lane to most winning effect and, accompanied by a series of grand gestures, he proceeds to outline his case.

I shall now begin to describe the conduct of the Defendant

on the 25th of May last.

The former Colonel Hanson, who henceforward I shall refer to as plain *Mr* Hanson, is, I understand, a man of fortune. I believe he has been in trade. He stands before us today in the uniform of an Officer of the Realm, but he certainly was not carrying out either function at the time this offence is alleged to have been committed. Indeed, he had, I understand, already resigned his commission before being summoned to appear before this Court today. I believe he possesses an ample fortune by inheritance. I mention this only for the purpose of stating that Mr Hanson, having himself been, or his father having been, in trade, must have known what consequences would ensue from inflaming so discontented a body of men, who, though they had always received from their employers a just recompense for their labour, were striving by force to augment their wages.

He looks in the direction of the Gallery, where several prominent Manchester merchants are seated, who rap as one the wooden balustrade in front of them, a sound reminiscent of a kettle of kites alighting on their prey.

On the 24th of May last, the day before the offences of which the Defendant stands accused allegedly were committed, the Spinners and Weavers of Manchester, in the Hundred of Salford, had considerable difficulties to contend with. The depression of trade bore hard upon them, as upon all, and every one of them must have been subjected to a certain portion of the common pressure of the times. I believe these Spinners and Weavers were much to be pitied. Their distresses were very great. The high price of provisions would have made it difficult for them to procure a livelihood. But, the greater their grievances were in reality, the less ought Mr Hanson to have concerned himself

102

with these misguided people, especially at a time when they were assembled to the number of thousands, and meditating most destructive measures unless their wishes were complied with. His appearance could only contrive to make matters more inflamed, as I now intend to show.

Mr Cockell sighs heavily and shakes his head sorrowfully.

On the 24th of May, as I have said, a very large body of workers assembled in St. George's Fields at eleven in the morning. They were most resolute. They had assembled there for the purpose of raising their wages, and were determined that their employers should comply with their demands, and furthermore, that they would not leave that spot until their demands were satisfied.

He raises a somewhat rueful eyebrow, a gesture much practised before the gilt mirror in his Chambers.

Gentlemen, some of the Police (who have been most diligent and to whom the public are deeply indebted for taking it upon themselves to act so selflessly and courageously in the services of the Magistracy, with no thought as to their own safety) having received intelligence of this meeting, arrived directly at twelve noon, the appointed hour of commencement. The Boroughreeve followed hard upon their heels, and, like the very honest and conscientious gentleman he is, told the assembled workers that, if they had grievances, they should be redressed. "But," added he, "this is not the way in which you ought to act. You will bring upon yourselves and your families great calamities. You are an unlawful mob. You are come here to disturb the peace and alarm the neighbourhood, and I beg you to disperse."

He looks towards the Boroughreeve, who is seated toward the back of the Court, awaiting his time to be called as a Witness, and inclines his head in a dignified bow. The Boroughreeve gravely returns the compliment with a gesture of his own.

But no – they would not disperse, they would not return, they thought they had better remain there and be shot, than go home and see their families in want. The Boroughreeve, finding his arguments were all in vain, went to the Magistrates and told them the situation in which they now found themselves was a grave one. The Military were consequently summoned, in order that the mob might be safely dispersed. The Magistrates then confirmed that they would do what they could for the Spinners and Weavers. They would undertake to advocate their cause as far as it was proper for them to do so. With these assurances the mob dispersed, I think at about four in the afternoon, and it was hoped that, by these prompt and wise actions, tranquillity was now restored.

Here Mr Cockell rises on demi-pointe, an action he carries out with surprising grace and control when one considers the nature of his build, holds up four fingers of his left hand in turn, as if counting down the hours, and pauses for further dramatic effect, a moment he clearly relishes.

Alas, it was not so.

On the morrow, at the same hour of twelve o' the clock, a terrible number of these Spinners and Weavers assembled – to what amount you will hear from the various witnesses, but be assured there were many thousands of them. Many of you know what the town of Manchester is composed of, what a number of persons of other descriptions there are to be found mingling with those who meet unlawfully for these purposes. Women, children, respectable persons such as yourselves, Gentlemen of the Jury. The town was alarmed. Mr Nadin, the Deputy-Constable of Manchester, went among the aforementioned Spinners and Weavers, told them the likely consequences of their conduct, was shamefully laughed at, and treated with contempt. The Boroughreeve appeared once more, argued with them most reasonably, did every thing he could to exhort them to return quietly home. He was told:

"This is not the language to hold out to us to-day. Did you not say yesterday our grievances should be redressed ?"

Whereupon they showed a very strong disposition to become yet more riotous. The Boroughreeve was then informed that they had appointed Delegates: "which Delegates," said they, "are now at the Magistrates' Court. Go you to them, see what can be done, and we will wait here." Accordingly, despite the rudeness of their manner, the coarseness of their speech, nevertheless the Boroughreeve went straight to the Magistrates, and reported what he had heard from the mob to the aforesaid Delegates, whose representations proved fruitless, and I think the note I am going to read to you next did great honour to the head and heart of Mr. Matthew Oldham, a most active and conscientious Magistrate in the town of Manchester, who wrote this answer:

He holds out his right hand to the side of him and slightly behind, the palm facing upwards. Into this open palm is thrust a piece of paper by one of his assistants, a Mr Topping, who completes the action with the élan of a magician's assistant. With his left hand Mr Cockell takes a pair of spectacles from his waistcoat pocket. These he does not place upon his nose; rather he holds them before his eyes, merely for the duration of what he now reads.

'It is the opinion of the Magistrates that, under the existing circumstances, we cannot treat with men deputed from a large body of other men assembled in a tumultuous and unlawful manner. If they disperse, and go peaceably and quietly back to their homes, we will take their situation into consideration, and we are ready to attend to any representation which may be made in a proper and peaceable manner.'

He holds out the piece of paper back to his right, which is similarly removed from him by Mr Topping with the same showman's flourish as before, while returning the spectacles to his waistcoat pocket. Having thus relieved himself of his theatrical props, he marches towards where Matthew is sitting in the Court and places his hand warmly and firmly upon his shoulder.

There is no man living who, on such an emergency, could possibly have acted with more dignity than Mr Oldham.

He now steps away from Matthew and directs his attention back to the Jurors.

This paper was then put into the hands of the Boroughreeve. He handed it over to the Delegates, and it was read by them in turn to the large number of persons still unlawfully assembled on St George's Fields. Instead, Gentlemen, of showing any disposition to act under the advice of these Magistrates, they became even more tumultuous. There was no time then to deliberate. The Military were once again sent for. Mr. Nadin and several officers had been there during the whole time of this assembly, but, without the additional support of the Military, they had waited patiently, acted cautiously and with the utmost restraint, knowing they could do nothing. Any precipitous actions they may have undertaken might, they correctly assumed, have only served to exacerbate an already tense situation and rendered it even more dangerous.

He now returns to the centre of his stage to address his entire audience.

And now I call your attention to the conduct of this Defendant, than which I cannot, if I prove my case, imagine anything more calculatedly wicked.

About half-past three, or thereabout, Mr Hanson came upon the ground. He had at this time neither a civil nor a military uniform. He is not a Magistrate, neither is he a Keeper of the Peace, nor had he any longer the command of a military company. Therefore he had no business there, unless to suppress a riot, to endeavour to assist the peace-officers in sending these unhappy men back to their homes. If he had come with *this* purpose, it would have been well. And here I must make this observation: that soon after he came on to the ground, he boasted of his influence over the mob, that it was in his power to make them disperse and go quietly home. If he had that power, why did he not use it? If he was a good subject of the country, why did he not go to the Magistracy? Why not join the Police, and by the power he had over these people, occasion them to disperse? Let us rather look at what he did do.

He proceeds to act out what he now describes, walking between Mr Hanson and Lieutenant Trafford, seated in the Assizes, as required. He is evidently enjoying every moment.

He came to the ground on horseback, in order that he might

have the command and view of the people. Thus mounted, he rode up to an officer, Lieutenant Trafford, who had been detached to see what was going forward, and if possible to disperse the multitude. Mr Hanson approached that officer, who was not unknown to him from that time when he himself was Colonel of the Salford & Stockport Independent Rifles—and that I may not do Mr Hanson an injustice, or misrepresent what passed between him and Lieutenant Trafford, I shall now read what is given to me as his testimony.

He once again produces the pair of spectacles, which he holds before him as he reads the following.

Lieutenant Trafford of the 4th Dragoon Guards, says that, 'as part of the regiment was proceeding to St. George's Fields, I was detached in order to undertake the command of the same, and to ascertain the condition of the rioters.'

Mr Cockell momentarily lowers his spectacles.

No gentleman could have acted with more prudence than did Lieutenant Trafford on this occasion, and I think that when I have read the whole of his account of this transaction, you will say the same. He continues.

He then raises the spectacles once more in front of his eyes.

'On coming on the ground, I had not been above a few minutes before Mr Hanson came up to me, and asked me if I would allow him to address the populace, and he added that he had much influence over them, and that whatever he desired them to do, it would be done immediately. When I then found he was the commander of this vast meeting, that he was the very principle on which it acted, I told him I could not allow him to address the people. He then most insidiously answered me that he *hoped* they would go quietly home, but he could not *guarantee* it.'

Having completed his re-enactment, Mr Cockell sadly shakes his head.

Gentlemen, this compounds Mr Hanson's guilt. Lieutenant Trafford replied that he could not allow him to harangue the people, that it would exasperate them the more. Whereupon, following this most sound of judgements from the good Lieutenant, Mr Hanson went a short distance away from him towards the assembled mob. He addressed the populace, *pulling off his hat to them, huzzahing and bowing before them!* Men who had come to that place so riotous, so inflamed, so determined! With actions so designed as to inflame them further!

Mr Hanson then addressed the people in the way I have described to you a second time. The people then cheered him further, and, thus encouraged, he shouted again with more loud huzzahs. Lieutenant Trafford, on seeing this, rode up to Mr Hanson and said he "would be particularly obliged to him," – observe, Gentlemen, "would be *obliged* to him," – "to go off the ground. The people do press so much upon the Military that it is impossible to maintain order, and it is your presence that induces the people to be so tumultuous."

Good God, Gentlemen, in the face of such a reasonable request, what would an honourable man and good subject have done? Would he not have said, "Of course, Officer. I will leave the ground this moment rather than stay here inflaming such an angry mob"?

But no. Mr Hanson instead asked Lieutenant Trafford if he *ordered* him off the ground. We know, Gentlemen, he had not. He said, he "would be *obliged* to him to go off."

Mr Hanson then replied, "Do you *order* me off the ground? If so I will go off." The good Lieutenant replied that he could not order him off, but that no gentleman well-disposed would appear in that manner at the head of a people so inflamed.

Whereupon Lieutenant Trafford, finding Mr Hanson would not go, very properly sent for a Constable. At which point Mr Hanson went to another part of the ground, bowing and pulling off his hat, further inflaming the already angry mob and, from the exertion he made, Lieutenant Trafford had no doubt he must be using the most violent and inciting language. What passed precisely he could not tell, but he could collect what effect it had upon the people. They huzzahed, and became a very tumultuous assembly indeed. The Defendant then proceeded to a small elevation, and there harangued the mob for a considerably longer time – six or seven minutes will amount to that in such an assembly.

Now, mark what the Defendant did next. He saw the Magistrates arrive. Then he slunk away. He did not disappear till he found the Magistrates approaching, and probably thought that he should be the first victim of their power. If he had been a good subject he would have said, "I will join the Magistrates. I will endeavour as far as I can to assist in dispersing the people." No, Gentlemen, Mr Hanson knew if mischief did ensue, it would be well for him to be out of the way, and so he chose to proceed in a most cowardly and shameful manner, not befitting a gentleman and former officer of His Majesty's forces.

Mr Cockell has by this point reached the place where the Jurors are seated once more and has been looking each and every one of them in the eye in turn. Now, with a predetermined suddenness, he wheels away from them.

Gentlemen, I will now turn to the actual words he spoke in different parts of the field.

On one occasion he excited the mob to such a degree that his horse reared up, and he tumbled backwards. However, having been so thrown, he mounted once more, and with a persevering malignity began again to stir the people further. I will read to you what he said to different parts of the mob.

The same pantomime as before, involving Mr Topping, a piece of paper and a pair of spectacles, is repeated, but with even greater rapidity.

'Your cause is good. I will support you as far as three thousand pounds. Stick to your cause.' That cause was, to stand out and not work till their demands were complied with by their employers. 'Stick to your cause,' he says again, 'and you will certainly succeed. Neither Nadin nor any of his faction shall put you off the field today.'

Mr Cockell lets both his hands fall to his sides, the piece of paper in one, the pair of spectacles in the other. He shakes his head and sighs.

Gentlemen, I ask you, what are the principles of such a man? Are they the principles of an honest man, or those of a disaffected and disloyal subject? He tells these men *not* that Mr. Nadin is an Officer of Justice, that the Magistrates are the preservers of good order. No, instead of treating the names of these gentlemen with respect, he impudently, dishonestly, and disloyally, designates them as a *faction*. I cannot, after this, say that Mr Hanson is either a loyal subject or a good man; and in this I do no injustice to Mr Hanson.

Furthermore, he says, 'Stick together, and you shall gain your ends.' Is not this an incitement to further tumult? But is he content to stop at this? No, Gentlemen. He goes on – and this is the most abominable part of the whole – he says, 'Gentlemen, you cannot live by your labour alone. There is room on the employers' part for an increase of six shillings in every pound. I should know. I have made my own fortune in the weaving trade. And if you cannot obtain that from them, *I* will advance you six shillings in the pound.'

Good God! How profligate is this? He tells them they ought to have so much, and that if they cannot obtain it, he will advance them the same? But does he end there? No, Gentlemen, he does not. He continues still further.

'My father was a weaver,' he says, (which is true). 'I understand your situation. I am your real friend,' (which is not). 'I would advise you to be steady and stick to your purpose. Stick to your purpose and you will gain your ends. Stick to your purpose but do not disturb the tranquillity of the country.'

This again aggravates his guilt, because he was endeavouring to do all the mischief he could. It proceeds from an artful and wicked disposition to desire them not to disturb the tranquillity of the country, when he has but just told them not to regard Deputy Nadin or his fellow Officers of the Law, exhorting that they should not put them off the field that day. This, Gentlemen, I say, was a shallow artifice, proceeding from a wicked mind, qualifications which would go but a little way in checking the effects his words were calculated to produce. Gentlemen, if I prove all this, to comment upon it further would be to insult your undoubted intelligences, for there is not a man living who, upon hearing it proved, will not consider Mr Hanson as guilty of the charge.

With a self-satisfied smugness he turns away from the Jurors, affording the slightest of winks towards the other members of his prosecuting team, a gesture reserved for their sight only, then faces the Court directly, immediately altering his expression to one of grave sadness. He places his right hand upon his heart and slowly bows his head.

I am sorry to tell you that the exertions of the Magistrates and the kindness shown by them to the populace availed nothing. All arguments urged by them proved fruitless. The mob was not dispersed till a melancholy catastrophe closed the scene.

He points dramatically and censoriously towards Mr Hanson.

Inflamed, no doubt by the violent conduct of the Defendant – for nothing of the sort had been done till *he* appeared on the scene – a man threw a brick at one of the soldiers, fatally injuring the poor, faithful horse on which he rode. The soldier fired. The man was shot, and afterwards died.

Mr Cockell has acted out each of these moments as he describes them.

What Mr. Hanson's feelings may be I could not say, but I would not have his feelings for all his wealth. When I hear Mr Hanson's defence, if his cause be well defended, I shall reply. If it be not, in the discharge of my duty, I certainly shall take an opportunity of making my observations upon it. To convict men in humble situations will effect but little good. But when I have brought before you a man of wealth, of great property, and you find him one who would carry every single thing he does to the last extremity – if such a man is consigned to punishment by the justice of his country, such an example will be of real use. It will do more good than the conviction of ten thousand poor. And so, Gentlemen, when you behold this man coming into such an assembly with the view of exciting riot and mischief, you see the guilty character, who ought, if the charge is brought home to him, which I am most confident it will be, to be consigned to legal and (what will necessarily attend him) absolute infamy.

Mr Cockell holds the moment, before bowing solemnly to the Bench. Several Members of the Public, seated above in the Gallery, spontaneously begin to applaud, which Mr Justice Goose is rapidly required to quell with three sharp raps of his gavel.

MR JUSTICE GOOSE:
Order! We shall have no such disturbances in my Court. If there are any further interruptions of this nature, I shall be obliged to ask Officers to remove the transgressors forthwith.

May I remind you, Mr Cockell, that this is a Court of Law, not a Public Playhouse.

MR COCKELL: (*inclining his head*):
My Lord.

Mr William Starkie is then sworn in and examined by Mr Cockell's Chief Assistant, Mr Park, who is as tall and thin as

114

Mr Cockell is wide and round. Where Mr Cockell's complexion is akin to a glass of claret, Mr Park's more closely resembles liquid lead. While Mr Cockell favoured an actor's method, Mr Park adopts that of a scholarly academic, or more precisely perhaps, a cadaverous surgeon, the quill he holds in his hand, and with which he makes occasional marks upon the parchment weighted down upon his desk on each corner with four pewter ink wells fashioned in the shape of skulls, standing in for a scalpel.

Mr Starkie, the Boroughreeve, is equally tall, but much more languid than his interrogator. He holds a white handkerchief in his left hand, onto which he has sprinkled a few drops of lavender, which he has a habit of raising to his nose while Mr Park asks him each successive question. When he speaks, it is with extremely elongated vowels, as if he means to distance himself in his speech as far away as possible from the accent of the common northern people whom he governs. He appears to regard the entire proceedings as somewhat beneath him and so, when he does bring himself to answer the questions that are put to him, he does so with as few words as possible.

MR PARK:
You are the Boroughreeve of Manchester?

MR STARKIE:
I am.

MR PARK:
And you were the Boroughreeve of Manchester last year?

MR STARKIE:
I was.

MR PARK:

Do you recollect anything particular happening on Tuesday, the 24th of May?

MR STARKIE:

I do.

MR PARK:

What was the circumstance that attracted your attention on that day?

MR STARKIE:

I was informed of several assemblies on that day.

MR PARK:

In consequence of such information, did you proceed to St. George's Fields?

MR STARKIE:

I did.

MR PARK:

Did you find any number of persons assembled there, as you had been informed there would be?

MR STARKIE:

I did.

MR. JUSTICE GOOSE: (*leaning forward to intervene*):

How near to Manchester do you suppose St. George's Fields to be?

MR STARKIE:

They are *in* Manchester.

MR JUSTICE GOOSE:

Whereabouts in Manchester?

MR STARKIE:

At the far end of Newton's Lane.

MR PARK:

I'm obliged, Your Lordship. Mr Starkie, did you find any persons assembled there?

MR STARKIE:

I did.

MR PARK:

Yes, I see. How many – in your opinion?

MR STARKIE:

Five or six hundred were assembled in St. George's Lane, adjoining to St. George's Fields, before a public-house.

MR PARK:

Were they so assembled in a quiet and peaceable, or in a riotous manner?

MR STARKIE:

They were peaceable at the time we got there.

MR PARK:

How long did you stay there at that time; when you first went?

MR STARKIE:

About an hour and a half.

MR PARK:

Did you learn from the people assembled there, what was their object in being so assembled?

MR STARKIE:

I did.

MR PARK:

And what was it?

MR STARKIE:

They said they were waiting for a report from their Delegates, who were then sitting in the House.

MR PARK:

Did they state upon what subject this report was to be made?

MR STARKIE:

They did.

MR PARK:

And...?

MR STARKIE:

I heard some of them say, it was in consequence of their Bill being thrown out of Parliament.

MR JUSTICE GOOSE: (*once again intervening*):

What Bill is that?

MR STARKIE:

A request for the implementation of a minimum wage.

MR JUSTICE GOOSE:

And this Bill was defeated, you say?

MR STARKIE:

It was.

Mr Justice Goose leans back, satisfied.

MR PARK:

What more did you hear?

MR STARKIE:

I heard them say nothing more.

MR PARK:

During the hour and a half you were there, was there any other disposition manifested than what you have described?

MR STARKIE:

There was not.

MR PARK:

What time of the day was it when you first went there?

MR STARKIE:

About eleven o'clock.

MR PARK:

Did you hear any of the gentlemen who were with you desire to see those Delegates ?

MR STARKIE:

Colonel Sylvester desired to speak with them.

MR JUSTICE GOOSE:
Colonel Sylvester?

MR PARK:
Commanding Officer of the 4th Dragoon Guards, Your Lordship.

Mr Justice Goose nods and makes a note on his papers.

MR PARK: (*turning back to Mr Starkie*):
Did you hear any person say any thing to the mob at that time?

MR STARKIE:
He addressed them.

MR PARK:
He?

MR STARKIE:
Colonel Sylvester.

MR PARK:
What did he say?

MR STARKIE:
He told them to go quietly home, and the consequences of remaining where they then were if they did not.

MR PARK:
Did they obey him?

MR STARKIE:
They did not.

MR PARK:

Was it at that time, and before you quitted the place, that the Riot Act was read?

MR STARKIE:

It was.

MR PARK:

By whom?

MR STARKIE:

Mr Matthew Oldham.

MR PARK:

A Justice of the Peace and Local Magistrate?

MR STARKIE:

Correct.

MR PARK:

Did the reading of the Riot Act, in your judgement, from your observation at the time, produce any effect?

MR STARKIE:

It did not.

MR PARK:

In consequence of information so received about others coming down, was there any message sent for the Military?

MR STARKIE:

I was requested to do so by Colonel Sylvester.

MR PARK:

Were you on the field yourself when they arrived?

MR STARKIE:

I was.

MR PARK:

What time did they come?

MR STARKIE:

It might have been one o'clock.

MR PARK:

I will shortly go on to the Wednesday, but first – they were on the Tuesday dispersed?

MR STARKIE:

Yes, about four o'clock, and all was then quiet.

MR PARK:

Now, on the following day, Wednesday the 25th of May, did you go again to St. George's Fields?

MR STARKIE:

I did.

MR PARK:

At what o'clock?

MR STARKIE:

About twelve.

MR PARK:

Were there any number of persons then assembled?

MR STARKIE:

There was a very considerable number.

MR PARK:

What is your estimate of the numbers?

MR STARKIE:

Speaking moderately, I think from three to four thousand.

MR PARK:

Three to four thousand?

MR STARKIE:

That is what I said, yes.

MR PARK:

In consequence of your observation of the numbers, did you give any information to the Magistrates?

MR STARKIE: (*barely concealing his growing disdain*):

It was in consequence of the request of the Magistrates that I went to the ground in the first place.

MR PARK:

Yes, I see.
Did you ask the mob any questions?

MR STARKIE:

I did. I asked them the cause of their meeting there in such numbers. They told me I could not be ignorant of their situation, that their families were in the most distressed state, that they could not live by their wages, and that it was now time to endeavour to get them mended.

MR PARK:

I take it for granted then, Mr. Starkie, you knew their situation?

MR STARKIE:

You may not take it for granted, sir, but I did.

MR PARK:

What did you say to them in consequence of their having told you this?

MR STARKIE:

I told them, I thought that they had taken a wrong method to obtain their ends. I recommended them to go home quietly, but if they remained where they were, I should consider them as a mob, and treat them as such.

MR PARK:

Did you say any thing to them about the Military, Mr. Starkie?

MR STARKIE:

Not at that time. They were not then come up.

MR PARK:

Did you say any thing more to them but what you have mentioned at that time?

MR STARKIE

I entreated them to disperse. They then asked me if four of their people, their... Delegates, had not been with me that morning; and I told them they had. The reason for their waiting on me was to require my interference with their masters.

MR PARK:

The factory owners?

MR STARKIE:

Correct.

MR PARK:

And had you seen their Delegates by this time?

MR STARKIE:

I had not.

MR PARK:

Why was that?

MR STARKIE:

I should have thought that was transparent. I was at St George's Fields. Even a Boroughreeve cannot be at two places at once.

MR PARK:

Quite.

Did those persons on the field remind you of the purpose of their waiting on you?

MR STARKIE:

I told them, *if* they would go quietly home, I would go down and meet their Delegates at the New Bailey, as I had fixed, at half past twelve.

MR PARK:

Did they go, sir, in consequence of your advice?

MR STARKIE:

They did not.

MR PARK:

You did, I believe, go to the Magistrates?

MR STARKIE:

They said, if I would allow them to remain till their Delegates returned, they then would go home quietly. I said, "My lads, may I depend upon you?" They said that I might, and that they would not move from their places until my return.

MR PARK:

You went immediately, I take for granted, to where you said you would be?

MR STARKIE:

You may *not* take it for granted, sir, but I did.

MR PARK:

Do you happen to know, in point of fact, whether a message was returned by the Magistrates on the subject?

MR STARKIE:

It was. We have that message in writing.

MR PARK:

Have you seen this before, sir? (*He points to a paper which is handed to the witness*). Will you be so good as to look at it, and say whether it is the answer?

MR STARKIE: (*barely glancing at it*):

I make no doubt of it.

MR PARK:

That is the paper, is it?

MR STARKIE:

It is.

MR. JUSTICE GOOSE:

Are you sure it is the same piece of paper?

MR STARKIE:

I have no doubt of it. (*In exasperation he now addresses the Judge directly*). Though I might add, My Lord, that I cannot vouch for which of the Magistrates was responsible for it, for I am not familiar with their separate handwriting.

MR JUSTICE GOOSE:

Quite so.

The paper is here read as follows:

MR RICHARDSON: (*his Adam's apple pursuing its now customary erratic motion*):

'May 25, 1808, a quarter before 3pm. It is the opinion of the Magistrates, that under the existing circumstances they cannot treat with men deputed from a large body of men, assembled in a tumultuous and unlawful manner. If they disperse, and go peaceably and quietly to their homes, the Magistrates will then take their situation into consideration, and be ready to attend to any representation which may be made in a proper and peaceable manner.'

Mr Richardson hands the paper to Mr Justice Goose, who then instructs it to be shown to the Jurors.

MR PARK:

Before that answer was given, Mr. Starkie, did you see any of the persons who were called Delegates, with the Magistrates ?

MR STARKIE:

I did. Three of them.

MR PARK:

And was what they had to say heard by the Magistrates, before that opinion was written?

MR STARKIE:

It was.

MR PARK:

After that, did you return to St. George's Fields?

MR STARKIE:

I did. Immediately.

MR PARK:

Did you find any difference, as to the numbers? Were they less, or the same?

MR STARKIE:

I thought the numbers were then greater.

MR PARK:

Was that paper, or that opinion of the Magistrates, read to those who were so assembled?

MR STARKIE:

It was.

MR PARK:

By whom?

MR STARKIE:

First by Mr Oldham, next by their own Delegates. I requested, as they were pressing forward, that they would keep on their own ground, and tried to persuade the people to go towards the high road.

MR PARK:

Did they obey you?

MR STARKIE:

On the contrary, they did not. For the first time I heard a murmuring run through the assembly. I must confess I began to feel anxious.

MR PARK:

Did you yourself say anything to them as to any promise they had made to you?

MR STARKIE:

I did. I reminded them of the promise they had made to me that they would disperse, if I would obtain an interview of their Delegates with the Magistrates.

MR PARK:

Did your advice or remonstrance to them appear to produce any effects on the mob in dispersing them?

MR STARKIE:

It did not.

MR PARK:

Was there anything said by any of them about dispersing?

MR STARKIE:

I think not at that time.

MR PARK:

Or at any point before the time Mr Hanson came to the field?

Mr Park stretches out a reptilian arm to indicate the

Defendant. Mr Starkie follows the direction of the arm with his own gaze before returning his attention back to Mr Park.

MR STARKIE:
I again urged them to go home, and told them the consequences of remaining there.

MR PARK:
Having stated these consequences to them, what was said or done by the mob?

MR STARKIE:
They said they would not go. They might as well remain there and be killed, they added, as go home.

MR PARK:
Did all your kind remonstrances produce any effect?

MR STARKIE: (*sighing heavily*):
None.

MR PARK:
In consequence of that, what did you yourself do?

MR STARKIE:
I then said, "My lads, I can stay here no longer. I must go and inform the Magistrates."

MR PARK:
In consequence of *that*, I take it for granted, you did so?

MR STARKIE:
Once again, sir, you presume too much. You may not take for granted what I did, or did not do, unless I so inform you. But yes, I did.

MR PARK: (*revealing as little as possible of his growing frustration with this witness who is meant to be endorsing their case*):

Did you return to the field with the Magistrates?

MR STARKIE:

I did.

MR PARK:

About what o'clock did you come back?

MR STARKIE:

I think it was near night.

MR JUSTICE GOOSE:

What distance is this field from where the Magistrates sat at the New Bailey?

MR STARKIE:

About a mile, My Lord.

MR JUSTICE GOOSE:

How many Magistrates went up with you?

MR STARKIE:

Three. Mr Nathaniel Philips, Mr Laurence Peel, and Mr Matthew Oldham.

MR PARK: (*coldly acknowledging the intervention of the Judge with a thin lipless smile, stiffly, as if his facial muscles have never till that instant carried out such an action, before continuing to cross-examine*):

Did they take any Military with them?

MR STARKIE:
  They did.

MR PARK:
  Do you remember what number of soldiers?

MR STARKIE:
  I do not.

MR PARK: (*narrowing his hooded eyes with barely concealed impatience*):
  The Cavalry were there?

MR STARKIE:
  They were.

MR PARK:
  Was Colonel Sylvester present?

MR STARKIE:
  He was.

MR PARK:
  Was Lieutenant Trafford there at that time?

MR STARKIE:
  I cannot say. But the regiment of which he is Lieutenant most certainly was.

MR PARK: (*flares his nostrils, before scrutinising his immaculately trimmed fingernails*):
  When you got back to the fields, did the Magistrates, or any other Officers of the Police, use any means to induce the mob to return home?

MR STARKIE:

> They did. Mr. Nadin addressed them. He told them to go, and what would be the consequences of their remaining there.

MR PARK:

> In many parts of the field?

MR STARKIE:

> Yes.

MR PARK:

> Did *he* mention anything to them about the Military?

MR STARKIE: (*witheringly*):

> I really cannot say.

MR PARK: (*becoming increasingly exasperated*):

> Did you hear any directions given by Mr Nadin, or any other Officers of the Police to the Military at that time?

MR STARKIE:

> I did not.

MR PARK:

> I believe, sir, they were dispersed finally by the Military?

MR STARKIE:

> I believe so.

MR PARK: (*insinuating a hope that his witness may be a little more forthcoming, presses on*):

> Sir, did you remain on the field yourself till they were dispersed?

MR STARKIE: (*looks down his nose at his inquisitor as if he has just become aware of the source of the rather unpleasant smell which he has been attempting to stave off with his scented handkerchief throughout his questioning*):
I did.

MR PARK:
What time in the evening was that?

MR STARKIE:
I did not come off the field till ten at night.

MR PARK: (*realising that he is not going to obtain any further useful information, yields the floor*): Thank you, Mr Starkie. (*He turns towards Mr Raine, whom he cannot bring himself to acknowledge directly*). Your witness.

MR JUSTICE GOOSE:
Mr Raine, you are acting for the Defendant, I take it?

MR RAINE: (*rising to his feet*):
I am, Your Lordship.

Mr Raine is a young, idealistic lawyer. He affects, when not in the Court Room, a somewhat dandyish appearance, though even here he has contrived to wear a buttonhole of a white lily on a bed of green laurel. His hair, beneath his wig, is fashionably long and curled, in the manner of a Shelley or a Byron, and he has allowed a lock or two of it to escape the confines of his horse hair wig and tumble, most becomingly in the opinion of the few females in the Public Gallery, onto his forehead.

MR JUSTICE GOOSE: (*with a somewhat supercilious air*):
Very well. You may proceed.

MR RAINE:

I'm obliged, Your Lordship.

Mr Raine now turns his attention to Mr Starkie.

MR RAINE:

At what point did you first become aware of the Defendant?

MR STARKIE:

I did not see Mr Hanson on the Field at all.

There is a gasp from the Court Room. Mr Justice Goose raps his gavel sharply, restoring order at once.

MR RAINE:

Not at all?

MR STARKIE:

I did not.

MR RAINE:

I see. Was any mischief actually done by the mob?

MR STARKIE:

One poor fellow lost his life.

MR RAINE:

Yes, but that was not in the Field, was it?

MR STARKIE:

No, it was not. It was in the lane adjoining.

MR JUSTICE GOOSE:

A most lamentable incident and evidence enough, I should have thought, Mr Raine, of more than mere mischief?

MR RAINE:

I am grateful, Your Lordship. And yet the witness states that at no time did he see the Defendant in the Field at all, therefore calling into question whether he might in any way be held responsible for any mischief, or worse, that occurred.

MR JUSTICE GOOSE:

That is for the Jury to decide, Mr Raine.

MR RAINE:

Indeed it is, Your Lordship.

Mr Starkie, I shall trouble you with very few further questions. You appear to be very direct and proper in your evidence.

Mr Starkie inclines his head slightly.

MR RAINE:

You stated, if I understood you correctly, that the representatives of the Spinners and Weavers complained of their Bill having been lost when heard in the House?

MR STARKIE:

They did.

MR RAINE:

If you remember aright, Mr Starkie, this intelligence first reached Manchester on the Sunday?

MR STARKIE:

It did.

MR RAINE:

That was May the 22nd?

MR STARKIE:

It was.

MR RAINE:

And it was thrown out of the House of Commons on Thursday the 19th?

MR STARKIE:

So I understand.

MR RAINE:

The Bill was an application to fix the price of the wages of the Spinners and Weavers, below which they should never sink, was it not?

MR STARKIE:

I believe so.

MR RAINE:

You believe so?

MR STARKIE:

I do.

MR RAINE:

And this was not the first time such an application had been submitted, was it?

MR STARKIE:

I cannot say.

MR RAINE:

You cannot say?

MR STARKIE:

> I cannot.

MR RAINE:

> Then let me refresh your memory. It was but thirteen months before.

MR STARKIE:

> Yes.

MR RAINE:

> Were you not Boroughreeve at the time?

MR STARKIE:

> I was.

MR RAINE:

> In effect, Chief Magistrate over all of Manchester?

MR STARKIE:

> Yes.

MR RAINE:

> And yet you appear to be insensible to the likely effect this rejection of their Bill might have had upon the Spinners and Weavers?

MR STARKIE:

> I resent the implication, sir.

Mr Raine smiles. He deliberately pauses while he partakes of a sip of water, then flicks back one of the unruly forelocks from his brow, before proceeding with this cross-examination.

MR RAINE:

Let us turn our attention to the Monday, the day after the news of the Bill's rejection in the House reached the town. Was there not a number of persons assembled on that day also?

MR STARKIE:

In Manchester?

MR RAINE:

In Manchester, yes.

MR STARKIE:

I did not hear.

MR RAINE:

You did not hear?

MR STARKIE:

I did not.

MR RAINE:

And were you not aware either of the great interest the Defendant, Mr Hanson, had already displayed in the cause of the Spinners and Weavers?

MR STARKIE:

I do not follow you, Sir.

MR RAINE:

Then allow me to try and assist you. It was common knowledge, was it not, that Mr Hanson had on many occasions most strenuously advocated for this Bill?

MR STARKIE:

I could not say.

MR RAINE:

Not even when he stood for candidate to Parliament in Preston, making this the central platform of his campaign?

At this point Mr Cockell rises languidly to his feet.

MR COCKELL:

My Lord, what has Preston to do with the matter? I understood we were here to examine what happened in Manchester?

MR JUSTICE GOOSE:

I thank you, Mr Cockell. I was beginning to wonder myself. Mr Raine, kindly confine yourself to the case in question.

MR RAINE:

Forgive me, Your Lordship. I was merely attempting to establish that Mr Hanson's history in championing the Spinners and Weavers and their cause makes his presence at St George's Fields on the day these alleged events took place all the more plausible.

MR JUSTICE GOOSE:

I believe that that is exactly what you have now done.

MR RAINE:

And that he was merely exercising his lawful right to speak on their behalf.

MR JUSTICE GOOSE:

That is what we are here to determine.

MR RAINE:

I am once again obliged, Your Lordship.

MR JUSTICE GOOSE:

Do you have any further questions for the Boroughreeve?

MR RAINE:

I do not, My Lord. I fear he would only continue to treat the Court to the same diet of monosyllabic reluctance we have been forced to endure thus far.

MR JUSTICE GOOSE:

In which case, he may stand down. (*He now turns towards Mr Starkie*). I should like to take this opportunity of thanking you, sir, for your patience and dignity while having to endure what has been a thinly disguised attempt to undermine the unambiguous clarity of your answers this morning and for the orderly, conscientious and sympathetic handling of the disturbances in St George's Fields.

MR STARKIE:

Thank you, My Lord.

MR JUSTICE GOOSE:

Mr Cockell, do you have any further witnesses you intend to bring before this Court?

MR COCKELL:

I do, My Lord. Deputy Joseph Nadin. I refer you to my esteemed colleague, Mr Wardley.

Mr Wardley, an older advocate, rises to his feet. His face is so deeply lined – forehead, cheeks, chin and jowls – that he resembles nothing less than an ageing bloodhound, who wears a permanently anxious and troubled expression.

MR JUSTICE GOOSE: (*smiling*):
Ah yes, Mr Wardley and I have long been sparring partners on the King's Bench.

Mr Wardley bows politely, all the cracks and crevices of his face constantly re-configuring themselves, as water might when it gurgles and overflows, coursing into ever-changing channels.

MR WARDLEY:
My Lord.

Joseph Nadin takes the stand. He is a large bull of a man with deep, sunken, bloodshot eyes and a potato-shaped, veined and bulbous nose, which, after taking the oath, he blows noisily. He is known as a man of action rather than of words.

MR WARDLEY:
Mr Nadin, you are the Deputy Constable of Manchester?

MR NADIN:
I am.

MR WARDLEY:
Were you present at St. George's Fields, or, Lane, on Tuesday the 24th of May?

MR NADIN:
I was.

MR WARDLEY:
Were you present there on the Wednesday, when the journeymen Spinners and Weavers were assembled again?

MR NADIN:
I was.

MR WARDLEY:

What time of the day was it when you first went there?

MR NADIN:

About twelve. I went with Mr Starkie and Mr Oldham.

MR WARDLEY:

Did you go round amongst the people there and say anything to them?

MR NADIN:

I did.

MR WARDLEY:

What was the subject of your discourse to them?

MR NADIN:

To persuade them to go home. Peaceably.

MR WARDLEY:

And what answer made they to your 'peaceable' persuasions? Did they accede to them?

MR NADIN: (*sneering*):

They said they would not go home. They said they would rather be shot in the field than go home and see their families starved.

MR WARDLEY:

I see. Did you go amongst them to different parts of the field, using the same persuasions?

MR NADIN:

I did.

MR WARDLEY:
And?

MR NADIN:
They also said they would rather die on the field, for they could not live on the wages they had.

MR WARDLEY:
I believe you went about to the different spinning and weaving shops in the town, and found them all shut up?

MR NADIN:
Beforehand, yes.

MR WARDLEY:
Did you find any of them at work?

MR NADIN:
I was not inside the shops, but the shutters were shut, and there was no sign of any at work.

MR WARDLEY:
Did you make any inquiry amongst them as to the cause of their being off work?

MR NADIN:
Some said that others came and fetched away their shuttles, so they could not work.

MR WARDLEY:
Was it to those so assembled you put this question ?

MR NADIN:
They appeared to be Spinners or Weavers, yes.

MR WARDLEY:
And were they among the mob?

MR NADIN:
No. (*Mr Wardley looks up, the lines on his face a river of surprise and concern*). They were five or six together. On Ancoats Lane.

Mr. Raine springs to his feet.

MR RAINE:
Then I object to that question, for it was not in the Field.

MR JUSTICE GOOSE:
Sustained.

MR WARDLEY: (*acknowledging this ruling with a wobbly nod*):
Did you make a like inquiry of those who *were* assembled in the field?

MR NADIN:
I did not.

Mr Wardley is momentarily put off his stroke, the myriad lines on his face converging into a single, compressed knot. He absently shuffles his papers before him, while regaining his composure, until the knot unties itself, the different threads uncoiling themselves once more.

MR WARDLEY:
You know Mr Hanson, the Defendant?

MR NADIN: (*not bothering to conceal his contempt*):
Oh yes. Very well.

MR WARDLEY:

Did you see Mr Hanson in St. George's Fields, or Lane, on Wednesday 25th May?

MR NADIN:

I saw him in St. George's Lane.

MR WARDLEY:

What time of the day was it when you first saw him there?

MR NADIN:

It was when the Military came on the ground.

MR WARDLEY:

Was he on horseback or foot?

MR NADIN:

He was on horseback.

MR WARDLEY:

What time of day was that?

MR NADIN:

About four o'clock. There was a shout, and then I saw Mr Hanson ride on into the Lane.

MR WARDLEY:

What did he do, or say, then?

MR NADIN:

He had his hat off then, and when he pulled his hat off, they shouted.

MR WARDLEY:

They shouted?

MR NADIN:

They did.

MR WARDLEY:

Did you hear him say anything?

MR NADIN:

It was such a distance I could not tell. But I could guess easily enough.

MR RAINE:

Objection.

MR JUSTICE GOOSE:

Sustained. Really Deputy Constable, a man in your position should know better than to offer this Court your guesses. It is only the facts that interest us here.

Mr Wardley?

MR WARDLEY: (*clearly dissatisfied*):

That is all, My Lord.

MR JUSTICE GOOSE:

Mr Raine?

MR RAINE:

Then all you can say as to the actions of the Defendant, is his bowing to them with his hat off?

MR NADIN: (*with a hint of a smirk*):

Yes. That is all. But it was enough.

MR RAINE:

Enough? For what, sir?

MR NADIN:

To raise my suspicions.

MR RAINE:

And these 'suspicions' appertained to what exactly?

MR NADIN:

That the Defendant was out to make mischief.

MR RAINE:

I put it to you, Deputy Constable, that it is *you* who is out to make mischief?

MR NADIN:

You may do so if it pleases you, sir.

MR RAINE:

It does indeed please me.

MR NADIN:

Then know this – I've got my 'suspicions' of *your* motives too.

MR JUSTICE GOOSE: (*intervening*):

That is quite enough, Mr Nadin. You are in danger of being in contempt of Court, but I am inclined to be lenient, for I do believe you have been unnecessarily goaded by Mr Raine.

MR RAINE:

Your Lordship, I must protest!

MR JUSTICE GOOSE:

You may protest all you wish, Mr Raine, but you will desist from using this Court as the setting for your own personal gratification. The Assizes hold up a mirror to society, within which it may view its faults magnified for our greater scrutiny. That mirror is not intended for any narcissistic pursuits of your own. Do I make myself clear?

MR RAINE:
Perfectly, Your Lordship.

MR JUSTICE GOOSE: (*turning towards Mr Nadin*):
The witness may stand down. The Court thanks you as ever, Mr Nadin, for the clarity and concision of your answers.

Mr Raine bites the insides of his cheeks but cannot fully conceal his smile, which he directs towards the Jurors, as Mr Nadin, smirking more openly, steps down.

Lieutenant Trafford is then sworn in and examined by Mr Yeats.

Where Mr Wardley has been a bloodhound, meticulous but ponderous, Mr Yeats is more of a springer spaniel, and a puppy to boot, who bounces to his feet.

The Lieutenant, by contrast, stands ramrod still and stiffly to attention at all times. He does not once look at Mr Yeats. Rather, he addresses all of his answers directly to Mr Justice Goose, as though to his Superior Officer. He has dark, closely cut hair, no wig, and a finely chiselled, pointed chin, within which lies a clearly delineated neat cleft, into which, when considering what he is to say, he occasionally places the sharp fingernail of his left hand. His right hand holds his helmet, tucked under his arm, at all times.

MR YEATS:
Lieutenant Trafford, I believe you are in the 4th Dragoon

Guards?

LT TRAFFORD:
I am, sir.

MR YEATS:
Do you remember receiving any orders on the 25th of May last?

LT TRAFFORD:
The regiment received orders to turn out immediately. It was then about two o'clock, as the men were going to their dinners. They were in the Barracks, ready to turn out, when we proceeded as far as Oldham Street, forty file of men, of which I was the head, having orders to proceed by the nearest way to St. George's Fields, where the riot was unfolding.

MR RAINE:
Objection. My Lord, we have yet to establish that there was in fact any kind of riot taking place.

MR JUSTICE GOOSE: (*wearily*):
Sustained. Do be more fastidious as to the facts, Mr Yeats.

MR YEATS: (*cowering, big-eyed and sorrowful*):
I apologise, My Lord.
Upon your arrival at St. George's Fields, what did you see?

LT TRAFFORD:
A large crowd of people assembled together.

MR YEATS:
Can you form any guess at their number?

LT TRAFFORD:

I should think there were six or seven thousand at least. They were greatly increasing by the hour.

MR YEATS:

I understand. Did you go with your men amongst them?

LT TRAFFORD:

I did, sir.

MR YEATS:

Had you any difficulty in going amongst them?

LT TRAFFORD:

Great difficulty, especially without hurting the people.

MR YEATS:

Which you wanted to avoid at all costs?

LT TRAFFORD:

Naturally.

MR YEATS:

When did you first see Mr Hanson on the ground?

LT TRAFFORD:

After I had been there a few minutes. Mr Hanson addressed himself to me directly, sir.

MR JUSTICE GOOSE: (*interrupting with particular intensity*): Did he come up to you, sir? By which I mean, did *he* approach *you*?

LT TRAFFORD:

He did, My Lord.

MR JUSTICE GOOSE:
Was he on horseback?

LT TRAFFORD:
He was, My Lord.

MR JUSTICE GOOSE:
The Jury will please note that.

MR. YEATS:
Thank you, My Lord.
Was anyone with him?

LT TRAFFORD:
Not that I know of at that time, no.

MR YEATS:
What did he say?

LT TRAFFORD:
He looked about him at first, and then asked me not to hurt
the people by any means, and he begged me leave to
harangue them. He said, "Would you allow me, sir, to speak
to the people? For then they will go quietly home." That
was the expression, My Lord, "Then they will go quietly
home." He continued saying, in the same breath, "I have
much influence over them."

MR YEATS: (*scarcely able to contain his excitement*):
Much influence over them?

LT TRAFFORD:
Yes, sir.

MR YEATS:

And what did you reply?

LT TRAFFORD:

I replied that I would *not* allow him to speak to them.

MR YEATS:

What then passed?

LT TRAFFORD:

He rode off a little distance to the left.

MR YEATS:

Did you see him do or say anything thereafter?

LT TRAFFORD:

He was speaking, bowing, and huzzahing to the people – at the last, with his hat off.

MR YEATS:

With his hat off?

LT TRAFFORD:

Yes, sir.

With tongue panting, Mr Yeats surveys the Court, allowing time for the significance of this observation to sink in before continuing.

MR YEATS:

What did he say?

LT TRAFFORD:

I could hear him speak, but could only collect a few words, sir, for the noise was so great.

MR YEATS:
What was the nature of the noise?

LT TRAFFORD:
Sir?

MR YEATS: (*bouncing on his heels*):
Was he doing anything else besides speaking to the mob with his hat off?

LT TRAFFORD:
Huzzahing.

MR YEATS: (*almost cheering himself*):
Huzzahing?

LT TRAFFORD:
Yes, sir. One time particularly, there was a great huzzah, and he went... (*He describes the manner with his hand in a clockwise circular motion*).

MR YEATS:
Like so? (*He copies the Lieutenant's gesture, who is still carrying on with it*).

LT TRAFFORD:
Yes, sir. Like so.

The two of them continue to wave their arms in the air, as if accompanying a huzzah, which Mr Yeats cannot help himself from encouraging members of the Public Gallery to take up also, forcing Mr Justice Goose to intervene.

MR JUSTICE GOOSE:
Thank you, Mr Yeats. I believe we all get the picture.

MR YEATS (*his tail between his legs*):
I apologise to the Court, Your Lordship.

MR JUSTICE GOOSE:
Accepted.

MR YEATS:
Lieutenant, when you saw this going forward, what did you do?

LT TRAFFORD:
I at once rode up to him, and requested him not to speak to them any more.

MR YEATS:
Would you be so good as to repeat the exact words you said for the benefit of the Jurors?

LT TRAFFORD:
I said, "I will be particularly obliged to you, Mr Hanson, not to speak to the people. It is by your presence that they are so exasperated."

MR YEATS:
Thank you. (*He repeats two of Lt Trafford's words again with a slow, heavy emphasis*). So exasperated.

After you had urged him not to speak to the people, did you desire him not to do any thing else?

LT TRAFFORD:
I particularly wished he would leave. I said, "I shall be obliged to you, Mr Hanson, to go off the ground."

MR YEATS:

What answer did Mr Hanson make to your request ?

LT TRAFFORD:

He went a little to one side, and there, I believe, he was thrown off his horse. (*He is unable to conceal a sneer at the memory of this*).

MR YEATS:

When you desired Mr Hanson to go off the ground, did he make any reply?

LT TRAFFORD: (*regards his own reflection in his helmet, which he still carries by his side*):

He said *some*thing, but I could not exactly hear what it was.

MR YEATS:

Was anything further said at that time before Mr Hanson rode off?

LT TRAFFORD:

I said that I could not allow him to harangue the people, and that I must insist he go off the ground directly.

MR JUSTICE GOOSE:

Do you recollect what he said to that?

LT TRAFFORD:

I do not, My Lord. I rode away back towards my men.

MR YEATS:

Did you observe Mr Hanson again?

LT TRAFFORD:

I did, sir.

MR YEATS:

What was he doing when you observed him afterwards?

LT TRAFFORD:

He was getting back the saddle of his horse. Somebody else was leading it.

MR YEATS:

Where was he going?

LT TRAFFORD:

Towards the rear of the men.

MR YEATS:

What do you mean by "the men"?

LT TRAFFORD:

The rear of our own men. The 4th Dragoon Guards. I said again, "I will be particularly obliged to you if you will immediately go off the ground," for he seemed dilatory in doing it.

MR YEATS: (*insistently, as a puppy with a bone*):

You said you desired him to go immediately off? What said he to that?

LT TRAFFORD:

He did not make me any other answer but that he hoped the populace would be quiet.

MR YEATS:

Did you see him, afterwards, amongst the populace?

LT TRAFFORD:

I saw him then proceeding in St George's Lane by the sign

of *The Gaping Goose.*

MR YEATS:
Did you see what he was doing there?

LT TRAFFORD:
I saw him a little elevated, and speaking to the people, and doing as he was before, bowing to them with his hat off.

MR YEATS:
With his hat off again, note.
Soon afterwards, I believe, the rest of the troops came. Was he still elevated from the ground?

LT TRAFFORD:
There was a mound upon which he stood, the better to command the crowd.

MR YEATS:
Where was this?

LT TRAFFORD:
I cannot tell whether it was the Lane side or the Field side.

MR YEATS:
Was he on horseback or on foot then?

LT TRAFFORD:
On horseback.

MR YEATS:
How soon after this did the remainder of the troops come up?

LT TRAFFORD:

I suppose, from the time I first saw Mr Hanson on the ground, it might have been twenty minutes before the rest of the troops came up.

MR YEATS:

What did Mr Hanson do after the troops came up?

LT TRAFFORD:

He rode off. Though I cannot say whether he saw them or not. He was a little further off than I was myself.

MR YEATS:

In which direction did he ride?

LT TRAFFORD:

I think he rode towards the left, towards *The Gaping Goose*, after which I saw no more of him.

MR YEATS:

As Mr Hanson was going off, did you observe anything particular among the populace?

LT TRAFFORD:

Many of them followed him.

MR YEATS: (*in extreme excitement*):

The mob followed him? In what way?

LT TRAFFORD:

Running after him.

MR YEATS: (*now practically chasing his own tail*):

And doing anything?

LT TRAFFORD:
Shouting.

MR YEATS: (*round and round*):
And Mr Hanson had his hat off part of the time?

LT TRAFFORD: (*caught up in the excitement, shouting*):
He did!

MR YEATS:
Your witness.

He sits down, breathlessly panting.

Mr Raine smilingly runs his little finger around the rim of his buttonhole, gently caressing the laurel, lifting the lily to inhale its aroma.

MR RAINE:
Towards *The Gaping Goose* was his road to Manchester, was it not?

LT TRAFFORD:
I did not know.

MR RAINE:
Come, Lieutenenant. The 4th Dragoons are stationed in Manchester, are they not?

LT TRAFFORD:
They are, sir.

MR RAINE:
In which case I put it to you, sir, that you must perforce know that the road towards *The Gaping Goose* is in the

direction of the town?

Lieutenant Trafford looks down and away.

MR JUSTICE GOOSE:
You must answer the question, Lieutenant, however distasteful that may seem to you.

LT TRAFFORD:
Yes, My Lord.

MR RAINE:
Is that a 'yes' to His Lordship or to my previous question?

LT TRAFFORD: (*reluctantly*)
To both, sir.

MR RAINE:
I thank you.
Mr Hanson lived at Strangeways, I believe?

LT TRAFFORD:
I did not know that either.

MR RAINE:
You did not?

LT TRAFFORD: (*barely maintaining his temper*):
No, sir. I did not.

MR RAINE:
Is not the road towards *The Gaping Goose* also the way to Strangeways?

LT TRAFFORD:

I believe it may be.

MR RAINE:

Come, man – either it is or it isn't.

LT TRAFFORD:

It is.

MR RAINE:

It is indeed. (*He lets the weight of this sentence hang in the air before continuing*). You would concede, therefore, that it was quite possible that Mr Hanson may merely have been attempting to return to his home when he mounted back upon his horse and rode along the Lane?

LT TRAFFORD:

It is possible, yes.

MR RAINE:

Now – when he was elevated in the way you described, did you see any other person or persons with him?

LT TRAFFORD:

I was too far off to distinguish.

MR RAINE:

Were there, or were there not, other gentlemen on horseback besides Mr Hanson?

LT TRAFFORD:

Yes.

MR RAINE:

How many?

LT TRAFFORD:
I could not say with any accuracy.

MR RAINE:
Try.

Lieutenant Trafford eases his collar, which has suddenly grown tight around his neck, with the fingers of his left hand, which he then proceeds to press more sharply than he intended into the cleft in his chin, drawing a distinctly discernible pinprick of blood.

LT TRAFFORD:
I saw more than one.

MR RAINE:
More than one?

LT TRAFFORD:
Yes. But they did not speak.

MR RAINE:
You're sure about that?

LT TRAFFORD opens his mouth to answer, but before he can do so Mr Raine continues.

How can you be when you are so uncertain about everything else?

No more questions.

MR JUSTICE GOOSE:
The witness may stand down. I am sure I speak for all here present, Lieutenant Trafford, for addressing us so

eloquently this morning, and for the meritorious way in which you and all fellow officers and men of the 4th Dragoon Guards carried out your duties on the day in question under such provoking circumstances.

Corporal William Wrighton is next sworn in. He approaches the stand with a cocky bravado, accompanied by several exhortations of support from a number of his comrades in the Public Gallery, to whom he offers a reciprocal wink and thumbs up. In his swagger he knocks into a chair. A small, but nevertheless instantly recognisable hip flask falls from his pocket, which he bends to retrieve and replace without once breaking his stride.

Another member of Mr Cockell's team, Mr Scarlett, steps up to examine him. He is one of the younger barristers present, with, appropriately considering his name, a shock of red hair, which persists in escaping from beneath his wig, which frames a face so freckled and cratered as to resemble the surface of a strawberry moon.

MR SCARLETT:
  I believe you are a Corporal in the 4th Dragoon Guards?

CORPORAL WRIGHTON:
  Yes, sir.

MR SCARLETT:
  Were you out in St. George's Fields, in Manchester, on the 25th of May last?

CORPORAL WRIGHTON:
  I was.

MR SCARLETT:

On what occasion did you go?

CORPORAL WRIGHTON:

I was ordered out to quell a riotous mob that was said to be in St. George's Fields that day.

MR RAINE (*rising upon the instant*):

Objection, My Lord. The presence of a riotous mob has yet to be established.

MR JUSTICE GOOSE: (*shaking his head*):

Yes, yes. Sustained. Really, Mr Scarlett, you must do better than this.

MR SCARLETT: (*his face reddening to match his hair*):

I beg your pardon, My Lord.

Corporal Wrighton, when you arrived at St George's Fields, did you find many persons there?

CORPORAL WRIGHTON:

Several thousands, sir.

MR SCARLETT:

Did you hear these persons declare what their purposes were?

CORPORAL WRIGHTON:

I heard some of them say they would rather be slain on the field than go home and see their families starved...

MR RAINE: (*once more rising to his feet*):

Objection, My Lord.

MR JUSTICE GOOSE:
On what grounds?

MR RAINE:
The Corporal's words sound remarkably similar to those already uttered by my learned friend, Mr Cockell – *he inclines his head towards his adversary, who graciously half rises from his seat to return the compliment* – almost as if his answer is coached.

MR JUSTICE GOOSE: (*with barely concealed, incredulous contempt*):
Over-ruled. You may continue with your answer, Corporal.

CORPORAL WRIGHTON: (*his face screwed in concentration as if remembering what he must say*):
… but they expected there was somebody coming that would do them justice.

MR SCARLETT:
Was that said by one or several?

CORPORAL WRIGHTON:
By several.

MR SCARLETT:
How long was that before the Defendant, Mr Hanson, came on to the ground?

CORPORAL WRIGHTON:
It was about two minutes before I perceived him.

MR SCARLETT:
Had they said anything to the Military?

CORPORAL WRIGHTON:

At the time I came on the field, they said they hoped I was
not come to hurt them…

MR SCARLETT:

Yes?

CORPORAL WRIGHTON:

… but after Mr Hanson had come, and paid his obedience to
them, they said we might come and cut and be damn'd.

*Mr Raine glances at once towards the Defendant, who shakes
his head.*

MR SCARLETT:

Did you hear anything particular that Mr Hanson said?

CORPORAL WRIGHTON:

I did, sir. At the time they cheered him, he took off his hat
and said, "Stick to the cause that you are now on. I will
support you as far as three thousand pounds will go. I
gained my fortune by Spinners and Weavers, and I will
support you."

*There is a general uproar around the Court upon hearing these
words reported, which Mr Justice Goose noticeably allows to
rumble for several moments before half-heartedly rapping his
gavel and calling for order.*

*Encouraged by a gesture from Mr Cockell, Mr Scarlett seeks to
press his advantage further.*

MR SCARLETT:

Strong words indeed, Corporal. Do you recall anything else
the Defendant spoke to the people?

CORPORAL WRIGHTON: (*beginning to relish his time in the limelight*):

I do, sir. He addressed them thus: (*He clears his throat, then delivers in a loud, clear voice*): "And if that won't do, my friends, I will go further." The rioters then cheered him again, so loudly his horse reared up, and he fell off him. (*He chortles at the memory and his laughter is taken up by several in the Public Gallery*).

MR SCARLETT:

In what way did they cheer him?

CORPORAL WRIGHTON:

They took off their hats with loud huzzahs. His servant, or some person else, took hold of his horse, and he walked across the field, discoursing with several of the rioters.

MR RAINE:

Objection.

MR JUSTICE GOOSE:

Over-ruled. The witness is quite legitimately expressing his opinion from what he observed on the ground.

CORPORAL WRIGHTON:

There was one of them made answer to him, and said…

MR SCARLETT:

Yes?

CORPORAL WRIGHTON:

… that the Constable was coming into the field.

MR SCARLETT:

By which you took him to mean who exactly?

CORPORAL WRIGHTON:

Why – Joe Nadin, of course.

MR SCARLETT:

Deputy Chief Constable Joseph Nadin?

CORPORAL WRIGHTON:

Like I said, and Mr Hanson did make reply that, "Neither Nadin nor none of his faction shall put us off the ground this day."

MR SCARLETT:

That word again – *faction*.
Now, tell us in what manner the mob cheered him?

CORPORAL WRIGHTON:

Why in this manner it was – they took off their hats, and cheered him, that he was their friend and their champion.

MR SCARLETT: (*addressing the Jurors directly, he repeats*):
"Their friend and their champion."
Now, Corporal Wrighton, think very carefully before you answer my next question. Did you observe any, and what, difference in the behaviour of the rioters, as you have called them, after Mr Hanson had so spoken to them?

CORPORAL WRIGHTON: (*rubs his chin thoughtfully*):
They seemed to be inclined to quit the field before Mr. Hanson came, but afterwards they became very riotous, and told us, like I said, we might come and cut away, and be damn'd.

MR SCARLETT:

Did you observe any difference in the behaviour of the mob, after Mr Hanson had left the field?

CORPORAL WRIGHTON:

A great deal of difference, sir. They were much rougher, and said they would not quit the field that night, or any night, till their demands were met.

MR SCARLETT:

How long in fact did the rioters remain on the field?

CORPORAL WRIGHTON:

I think it was between four and five when they were finally dispersed.

MR SCARLETT:

This was after Mr Hanson went away?

CORPORAL WRIGHTON:

Yes, sir.

MR SCARLETT:

About four or five o'clock, you say?

CORPORAL WRIGHTON:

Yes, sir. After the Riot Act had been read, and we were obliged to clear the ground.

MR SCARLETT:

Yes. I see. And how soon after Mr Hanson went away was the Riot Act read?

CORPORAL WRIGHTON:

Very soon.

MR SCARLETT:

How soon?

CORPORAL WRIGHTON:

Almost at once. His speeches had so enflamed them.

MR SCARLETT:

Thank you, Corporal. I have no further questions.

MR RAINE: (*standing gravely*):

But *I* have.

MR JUSTICE GOOSE:

Very well, Mr Raine. You may cross examine.

Mr Scarlett resumes his seat to a fatherly pat on the back from Mr Cockell, while Mr Raine moves towards Corporal Wrighton.

MR RAINE:

You have an excellent memory, Corporal.

CORPORAL WRIGHTON: (*beaming as he continues to bask in the plaudits from the Gallery*):

I believe I have, thank God.

MR RAINE: (*smiling insidiously*):

Can you recollect all other words as well as these?

CORPORAL WRIGHTON:

Any words that I hear, I can recollect; but what I do not hear, I cannot recollect.

MR RAINE:

Did you hear the Attorney-General, Mr. Cockell's opening speech, earlier this day?

Corporal Wrighton replies with a puzzled frown.

MR RAINE: (*continuing*):

Did you hear that gentleman, who is sitting at the table, just now speak?

He points towards Mr Cockell.

CORPORAL WRIGHTON:

I heard him, I suppose.

MR RAINE:

You suppose? Have you not been in court all morning?

CORPORAL WRIGHTON: (*starting to feel uncomfortable*):

No, not all morning.

MR RAINE:

Have you been in court since the trial began? (*The Corporal frowns once more*). Have you been in court since that gentleman – *Mr Raine once more points towards Mr Cockell* – began his speech?

CORPORAL WRIGHTON:

Er – I do not know.

MR RAINE:

Do you mean that you were not in the Court at that time, or that you are not quite sure whether you heard him or not?

CORPORAL WRIGHTON:

I did not take particular notice.

MR RAINE:

You did not take notice? Mr Cockell will be most disappointed, for he spoke just as passionately, just as eloquently as you claim for the words you say you heard spoken by the Defendant.

CORPORAL WRIGHTON: (*becoming increasingly flustered*):
I – er…

MR RAINE:
I put this to you, sir, whether you will speak to the Jurors and say you have, or have not, been in Court since Mr Cockell addressed them on this offence.

CORPORAL WRIGHTON:
I have.

MR RAINE:
Are you able to mention any words he spoke to the Jurors?

CORPORAL WRIGHTON: (*sullenly*):
I heard him speak.

MR RAINE:
And you have already testified for us, under oath, that – and here I quote – "any words that I hear, I can recollect."

CORPORAL WRIGHTON:
Well…

MR RAINE:
"Any words that I hear, I can recollect."

CORPORAL WRIGHTON: (*hanging his head, speaks almost inaudibly*): Yes.

MR RAINE:
How does it happen, then, that your memory will not serve you on this occasion?

CORPORAL WRIGHTON:
I don't follow, sir…

MR RAINE: (*with sarcastic relish*):
Repeat these words after me: "I have fought a good fight, I have told a good story, but I am somewhat afraid the Jury will not believe me."

Corproal Wrighton looks towards the Bench in serious discomfort.

MR JUSTICE GOOSE: (*intervening*):
Really, Mr Raine, you should know better. The witness cannot be called upon to invalidate his own testimony.

MR RAINE:
Your Lordship is, as ever, correct. The witness has invalidated himself.

Mr Cockell rises to his feet.

MR COCKELL:
Might I crave Your Lordship's indulgence and put one final question to the witness before he is released?

MR JUSTICE GOOSE:
By all means, Mr Cockell.

MR COCKELL: (*with great care and gentleness*):
Corporal Wrighton, are you quite sure the words you repeated today were those that were uttered by Mr Hanson?

CORPORAL WRIGHTON: (*with evident relief*):
Yes, sir. I am certain. On the 25th of May last.

MR COCKELL:

Thank you, Corporal. You may stand down.

Constable Thomas Bickerson is now sworn in. He is a stocky individual with thick shaving brush moustaches, which cover much of his mouth, so that the words he speaks appear to emanate from somewhere within them. He has large protruding eyes that fix whomever he is addressing with a rather intimidating, accusatory stare.

MR JUSTICE GOOSE:

Mr Cockell, am I to understand that the Constable is your final witness?

MR COCKELL:

He is, My Lord.

MR JUSTICE GOOSE:

In that case, I propose we shall adjourn for the day after you have finished with the Constable. Unless, that is, Mr Raine has any objection?

MR RAINE:

None, My Lord.

MR JUSTICE GOOSE: (*bowing his head to Mr Cockell*):

Very well. You may so proceed.

MR COCKELL:

I am most grateful to Your Lordship. My colleague Mr Cross will examine Mr Bickerson.

Mr Cross, who has been waiting patiently throughout what has been a long day for his opportunity, now takes to his feet. He is a short person, wiry and upright in stature. A former military man himself, he speaks in short, clipped sentences. Before he begins, he briskly, and as discreetly as possible, combs the ends of his own moustache, which is a mere pencil to Constable Bickerson's shaving brush. But for all their differences in upbringing, background and education, these are two gentlemen cut from very much the same length of cloth. Each prefers to speak plainly, seeing little to be gained from unnecessary verbiage.

MR CROSS:
You are one of the Constables of Manchester, I believe?

CONSTABLE BICKERSON:
I am, sir.

MR CROSS:
Were you at St George's Fields on 25th May last?

CONSTABLE BICKERSON:
I was, sir.

MR CROSS:
Did you see Mr Hanson come upon the Field?

CONSTABLE BICKERSON:
I saw him *on* the Field, sir, not coming *into* the Field.

MR CROSS:
Quite so. Did you hear any noise?

CONSTABLE BICKERSON:
I heard the mob shout several times.

MR CROSS:
Could you discern what they said?

CONSTABLE BICKERSON:
Yes, sir.

MR CROSS:
Pray, enlighten the Court.

CONSTABLE BICKERSON: (*wets the tip of his finger and flicks open his policeman's notebook*):
They wished to have an advance of wages, for they could not support their families.

MR CROSS:
Quite. When you first saw the Defendant, was he on horseback or on foot?

CONSTABLE BICKERSON:
On horseback, sir. A fine white stallion.

MR CROSS:
The more clearly to be seen, would you say?

CONSTABLE BICKERSON:
You could not miss him, sir.

MR CROSS:
Did you hear him say anything?

CONSTABLE BICKERSON:
I did, sir.

MR CROSS:
What did he say?

The Constable refers once more to his notebook.

CONSTABLE BICKERSON:

He took off his hat and addressed the assembled populace, styling them 'his friends'.

MR CROSS:

I see. Now, have the goodness to repeat as near as you can the actual words he said, without reference to 'he said so', or 'he then made mention of', but just the words themselves *verbatim*.

CONSTABLE BICKERSON:

I made a memorandum of it, sir, which, with your permission, I can read from directly.

MR JUSTICE GOOSE:

You made this memorandum at the time?

CONSTABLE BICKERSON:

Yes, My Lord.

MR JUSTICE GOOSE:

Then the Court so permits.

MR CROSS:

I'm obliged, My Lord.
Constable?

CONSTABLE BICKERSON:

'Friends, my Father was a Weaver. I was taught the weaving trade myself. I am the Weaver's friend. I desire you to be steady and stick to your purpose. I have no doubt you will obtain your end. I desire you will be peaceable and not disturb the tranquillity of the country.' He said something more afterward, which I could not retain.

MR CROSS:

Thank you, Constable. Now, what became of him after you heard him make this speech which you have repeated?

CONSTABLE BICKERSON:

His horse reared up and he fell to the ground.

MR CROSS:

What happened next?

CONSTABLE BICKERSON:

There was considerable consternation. Some of the Spinners and Weavers helped him to his feet.

MR CROSS:

And how did they answer him, these Spinners and Weavers?

CONSTABLE BICKERSTAFF:

They shouted, "Hanson for ever! Hanson for ever!" as one man.

MR CROSS:

What did the Defendant do next?

CONSTABLE BICKERSON:

He went away to St George's Lane.

MR CROSS:

And did you follow him?

CONSTABLE BICKERSON:

No, sir, I did not.

MR CROSS:

Then you had no opportunity of hearing what he said further?

CONSTABLE BICKERSTON:

I cannot honestly say whether he said anything further or not, sir.

Mr Cross frowns and agitatedly brushes the ends of his moustache with the tip of the middle finger of his left hand. He sees in the Constable a man after his own heart, who will report only what he has seen or heard, nothing more, nothing less. In fact, were their positions reversed, Mr Cross believes he would wish to emulate the Constable's eminent succinctness, but the sight of his mentor Mr Cockell's fingers discontentedly drumming the top of his desk, while his foot taps impatiently underneath, makes him wish the Constable might be tempted to become a little more expansive and loquacious. He will try a different tack and he twists the ends of his moustache a final time.

MR CROSS:

Tell us, Constable, did you observe whether what Mr Hanson said had any effect upon the people, making them more quiet or otherwise?

CONSTABLE BICKERSON:

They shouted. They took off their hats. They huzzahed and they cheered him.

MR CROSS:

Were they more quiet and peaceable *after* he said this than they were before?

CONSTABLE BICKERSON:

No, rather more *unruly*, I would say.

MR CROSS:

Yes, I see. (*He appears to walk back to his desk, only to turn once more to face the witness, just as he is about to sit down, a trick he has learned from Mr Cockell, who he has observed carry out this ploy successfully on several occasions*). One last question. When the mob, as you say, cheered him, did he do anything? Anything at all?

CONSTABLE BICKERSON:

He bowed to them several times.

MR CROSS:

With his hat upon his head?

CONSTABLE BICKERSON:

His hat in his hand.

MR CROSS:

Thank you, Constable. No More questions. (*To Mr Raine*): Your witness.

MR RAINE:

I too, Constable, would like to echo my learned friend Mr Cross's vote of gratitude for your conscientiousness of duty and accuracy of memory.

CONSTABLE BICKERSON:

The Constable's best friend is his notebook, sir. (*He taps it reverently*).

MR RAINE:

Quite so. Would you mind reading to the Court once more

the last words you heard Mr Hanson say to the people before he left the ground, just to refresh our own *less* than perfect memories?

CONSTABLE BICKERSON:
Certainly, sir. (*He opens his notebook once again and reads*): 'I desire you will be peaceable and not disturb the tranquillity of the country.'

MR RAINE: (*he repeats the sentence once more*):
'I desire you will be peaceable and not disturb the tranquillity of the country.' Thank you, Constable. I have no more questions.

MR JUSTICE GOOSE:
In which case, Court is now adjourned until ten of the clock tomorrow morning.

CLERK OF THE COURT:
All rise.

As soon as Mr Justice Goose has left the Court, Mr Cockell quickly summons all of his associates to him, where they gather in an anxious, secretive huddle. Mr Raine looks across towards his Defendant, Mr Hanson, who quietly nods before being led away by one of the Court Attendants.

*

A month before the trial began, once the date had been set, an advertisement appeared in all of the Manchester newspapers requesting witnesses to come forward who might be prepared to speak in defence of ex-Colonel Joseph Hanson and make themselves known, either by letter or in person, to one Mr Ambrose, who was the local Attorney acting on behalf of Mr Raine in the case.

It was Ham who showed it to Amos. Since Amos, Agnes and Jack had returned to the cottage in Elton, Ham had been a regular visitor. The years had calmed him a little. He was still as outspoken as ever, but less inclined these days to advocate machine-wrecking as he had formerly done.

"What's brought this change on?" Agnes had asked him teasingly one Sunday afternoon.

Ham had smiled and pointed. Running across the fields towards them was young Ned, Ham's son, a couple of years older than Jack, who idolised him, and a definite chip off the old block. He was frequently to be found fearlessly climbing trees, leaping from rock to rock across the Elton Brook, showing Jack where to catch the best eels or birds' eggs, how to spot a wasp's nest or where an adder might be basking in the gorse. It amused Agnes to see the way her once firebrand of a cousin would step in to warn his fearless son from climbing too high or wading in too deep.

"Don't get us wrong, Cousin," he said to her, "I still think all t' bosses are bastards, but smashin' up t' factories dun't do nobody any good in th'end, do it?"

"I think things are changin'," said Agnes, "little by little, bit by bit." She was thinking of the mill nearby in Summerseat, where Jack had started as a little piecer, and where she worked too as a dyer now, as well as bleaching and finishing the cotton Amos produced by hand on Silas's loom. The owner, Sir Robert Peel, was advocating in Parliament to bring in a Bill that would reduce the number of hours children could work in a factory.

"Mebbe," said Ham, "but I reckon 'e's still got one eye on t' bottom line. Childer get tired after too many hours and don't produce as efficiently as when they're fresh, that's all it amounts to."

"Well I have hope, Ham, that we might appeal to t' best in people…"

The two of them walked in reflective silence a while.

After a few moments he fetched a creased and crumpled page of a newspaper from out of his pocket.

"Oh aye, I almost forgot. Read this. P'raps show it to Amos, eh?"

Agnes read the advertisement asking for witnesses and a shadow fell across her face.

"Aye," she said, " 'e'll want to answer this."

"I thought 'e might," said Ham.

"That were a terrible day," said Agnes. "Amos lost his best pal that day. Adam."

"The lad who pulled 'im out o' t' pit?"

Agnes nodded.

"The day after Adam were kill't was when Amos decided to bring us all back 'ere. 'E'll want to 'elp Mr Hanson any way 'e can."

"Then tell 'im best not build 'is 'opes up. They mean to make an example out of Hanson as a means of stoppin' t' likes o' thee an' me from seekin' further Reform."

"Little by little," was all that Agnes offered by way of reply.

After he had answered the advertisement, Amos heard nothing for almost four weeks. He hadn't known what to expect. He imagined there must have been scores of better qualified witnesses than he, people with greater social standing, whose words might carry more weight in a Court of Law than those of a lowly handloom weaver. Yet wasn't it precisely for the plight of people like him that Mr Hanson had ridden into St George's Fields that fateful afternoon to defend? And the fact that he had come so swiftly and immediately to the aid of Adam after he had been shot, asking only how he might lend assistance, and that he, Amos, had spoken to him directly, seen at first hand the depth and sincerity of his feelings for those less fortunate than he, whose sorrows and suffering he sought to ameliorate, might that not make any testimony Amos could offer all the more affecting and helpful to Mr Hanson's cause?

So, when he did not hear back, he put it out of his mind and turned all his thoughts once more to the demands of each day, working Silas's Loom from dawn till dusk. He still thought of it as Silas's Loom – they all did – that had somehow been passed on to him as a gift, which he in turn hoped to pass on to Jack when the time came. Although Jack had so far shown little interest in it, preferring instead to run off across the fields to Bury, to the fort at Castlesteads, to watch the soldiers. Still, he was young yet, thought Amos charitably. There would be plenty of time before he would need to inculcate him into the art, mystery and manual occupation of it.

Then, when he had ceased to think about the trial altogether, he received a letter, late on the afternoon of Monday 17th February, from Mr Ambrose's Chambers.

14th February 1809

Dear Mr Lees,

I am instructed by my learned friend, the Most Honourable Mr Raine, Attorney at Law, who requests the pleasure of your attendance at Lancaster County Assizes three days hence, upon the 19th inst at the hour of ten of the clock, when he will be most obliged if you may present yourself as a witness for the Defence in the Trial of Mr Joseph Hanson.

He will endeavour to speak to you before giving evidence but cannot guarantee that this will be possible, given the uncertainties arising in any case heard before the King's Bench. Upon arrival at the Assizes please report to the

Office of the Clerk of the Court, where you will await
instructions, either from myself, or Mr Raine.

I am
Your most obedient servant etc
Everton Ambrose Esq, Solicitor
pp Mr Charles Raine, Attorney at Law

Amos was, to put it mildly, both surprised and puzzled. Surprised to be summoned so late in the day and puzzled that there had been no prior communication, no pre-arranged meeting at which Mr Raine, or Mr Ambrose on his behalf, might have asked him about his encounter with Joseph Hanson in St George's Lane and gone over what questions to expect during the trial.

But there was little time to wonder about such things now, for if he was to be there on time, he would need to leave almost immediately. They calculated that it would take him between fourteen and eighteen hours to walk the nearly fifty miles from Bury to Lancaster. There was no other way for him to get there and none of them knew what the state of the roads was between the two towns.

"Best get some sleep now," urged Agnes, "then set off while it's still dark in t' mornin'."

At a little before five on the 18th Amos set off. He walked across the local fields towards the Brandlesholme Moss Gate in Elton, where he followed a local road to Haslingden, little more than a cart track, from where he could pick up the Turnpike through Whalley to Blackburn. By the time he reached Blackburn it was almost noon, but the sky had only just started to lighten. There was a hard frost and the world showed itself to him in differing shades of grey – the ground, the stone walls, the leafless trees, the frozen air, the blanket of low cloud. At Blackburn he paused briefly at a cross roads to eat a crust of bread before heading off once more. He was now on the Preston Road, following the course of the River Ribble for much of the way. A couple of miles south-east of the town he crossed the river by the Bamber Bridge, close to the village of Walton-le-Dale, from where the old Roman Road from Manchester to Carlisle now served as his route. By the time he finally reached Preston it was already once again growing dark.

Preston. The Priests' Town. Named for the priory of St Wilfrid's near the Ribble's lowest ford, whose Paschal lamb on its crest was the same as that of Preston's. There was still bunting hanging in the town as Amos arrived, tattered and streaming from the Guild of the previous summer. Even Amos, who had never before been this far from Manchester, knew of the Preston Guild. Held only once every twenty years it had entered the lexicon to describe something that happened only rarely. He had just missed it, but the debris of it still rolled through the fast-emptying streets as night fell. Tradition had it that each Guild would begin on the first Monday after the Feast of the Beheading of St John the Baptist, which presaged what? Amos had always found that difficult to answer while growing up at Fairfield. Victory or defeat? Everlasting light or never-ending darkness? Or would they always hover somewhere in between? A limbo of permanent grey, travelling always from one place to another, never arriving, like this day had been? Which of these would his eventual arrival in Lancaster mean for Joseph Hanson? Was he following the path of the donkey into Jerusalem or the cross into Calvary? He sincerely hoped the former and, instead of palm leaves to lay before him, he picked a few branches of laurel to make a bed for the night in Colley's Garden, a tract of open ground behind the Market Place, where Fisher Gate, Church Gate and Friar Gate all converged, close by the outer wall of the House of Correction, under whose lee Amos ruefully tried to snatch a couple of hours sleep away from the worst of the winter wind, glad, in spite of it, to be on the outside, rather than the inside of those high, forbidding walls.

The clock on the tower of the Church of St John the Evangelist tolled midnight. If Amos was to reach Lancaster by the appointed hour of ten the next morning he must leave at once. The milestone by Pattenfield on the edge of the town signalled nineteen miles still to cover.

St John the Baptist or St John the Evangelist. Which one would he be? The bringer of good news or a voice crying in the wilderness?

As the miles passed he began to persuade himself that it must be one or the other, or why else, at this eleventh hour, had he been summoned to speak in defence of Mr Hanson? They must be mustering all the witnesses they could to testify in his favour, to emphasise his integrity, his honesty, his resoluteness of character, so that a Jury would find they had no alternative but to dismiss the charges against him.

But what if the Crown were doing likewise, which no doubt they were? Amos had for the most part been far removed from the action in St George's Fields on that terrible day, unable to hear anything of what any of the speakers said, including Mr Hanson. Only when the Dragoon Guards drove through the crowds and kettled them into the narrow adjoining St George's Lane, and his friend Adam had so catastrophically thrown a brick at one of the advancing horses, had he been, briefly, at the heart of things, when Mr Hanson had come so sympathetically to his side. He was certain that the Crown would be bringing in all manner of people to put a quite different complexion on the events for consideration by the Jury, people such as Magistrates, Police Officers, Soldiers. How would *his* word count against such as them?

Still the miles rolled by and still he vacillated between hope and doubt. St John the Baptist, St John the Evangelist. St John the Baptist, St John the Evangelist.

Or perhaps it would be neither?

Six hours later, he arrived in Lancaster, footsore, travel-soiled and weary. He climbed the steep incline of Castle Hill towards the Castle itself, which housed both the Shire and the Crown Courts of the County Assizes. He decided to rest just outside the Castle Gates until they opened an hour and a half later, and perhaps take a short nap. He had barely positioned himself there, however, when his eyes began to droop and he fell into a much deeper sleep than he intended, only to be rudely awoken by a sharp kick in the ribs and a rough rebuke from a Constable to move on.

"If th'art lookin' for a place to rest thy 'ead, my lad, we've plenty o' room in yon Gaol. I'd get a move on if I were thee."

A passer-by, taking pity on him in his wretched-looking state, pressed a penny into his hand and told him where he might get something hot to drink.

He brushed himself down as best as he could, then walked back down the Castle Hill a short way to recover himself and wait until the Constable who had threatened to arrest him had moved on. Now that it was starting to get light, Amos tried to get a sense of where he was, to check his bearings and work out what his next move might be. The Hill was lined on both sides with grand houses, as well as many inns and taverns. It was clearly a prosperous neighbourhood. He saw stable lads hitching immaculately groomed horses with plaited manes and braided tails to a row of ornately carved and polished carriages, which, even on this bitterly cold, steel-grey morning, glittered brightly. The horses stamped and snorted, their breath coiling in fluted stone columns around them. Amos knew that Lancaster held the only Right of Assize for the whole County of Lancashire, a right the town guarded jealously, for the regular income generated by the twice-yearly influx of lawyers to the town each time the Assizes sat brought much welcome income to its traders and shopkeepers. It was something he remembered his adoptive father telling him when he was a boy, how he had had to apply for certain permissions there to be granted before he could begin the building work for the

Moravians at Fairfield. But that had been in the Shire Court. Amos had been summoned to the Crown Court. There was nothing for it. He must walk back up the Hill towards the Castle Gate and present himself.

He had barely walked ten yards when he became aware of a flurry of activity by one of the carriages. A man roughly the same age as he, though much more finely dressed, rushed out of one of the fine houses towards a waiting cab. Perhaps he's one of the lawyers, thought Amos as he hurried to get out of his way.

"Watch where you're going, damn you!" shouted the man. "Can't you see I'm in a hurry. I'm to try another case in Manchester this afternoon."

And with that he was gone. The whole incident had lasted less than a few seconds. Neither had had time nor opportunity to see the other's face. As Amos hunkered deeper into his threadbare jacket for warmth, Matthew burrowed down in his seat inside the carriage and stared gloomily across the frozen landscape.

Another near miss.

Amos watched the carriage disappear down the bottom of the Hill, then turned to walk back up towards the Castle. A different Constable blocked his path as he reached the Gates. Amos fished around in his pocket for the letter from Mr Ambrose, which he presented, somewhat creased and grubby, to the Constable for inspection. After scrutinising this rather unsavoury scrap of paper intently for several seconds, he eventually let Amos through, who, now that it had started to become a reality, began to wonder just exactly what it was he would be asked and what it was he would reply.

Would he be listened to? Would he be ignored? Would his words carry weight? Or would they just vanish into air, as the breath of the horses on the hill had done? St John the Baptist or St John the Evangelist?

Whereas outside he had felt awkward and conspicuous, now

that he was inside the Castle itself, with its towering stone walls and all the centuries of history held within them, the pleas of countless witnesses imprisoned within them, he felt voiceless and invisible.

*

Day 2: Thursday 23rd February

CLERK OF THE COURT:
　All rise.

MR JUSTICE GOOSE:
　Mr Raine, are you ready to begin your Defence?

MR RAINE:
　I am, Your Lordship.

MR JUSTICE GOOSE:
　Then pray, proceed.

Mr Raine takes to the floor. The locks of his hair protrude even more prominently this morning in a distinctively Napoleonic style, a look not guaranteed to curry favour among the Jurors, but one which satisfies his own vanity. He sports a fresh lily in his buttonhole, which rests against the same bed of laurel as from the previous day. He allows himself a brief pause while he inhales its fragrance before embarking upon his opening speech.

MR. RAINE:
　Gentlemen of the Jury, in rising to discharge the important duty which has fallen upon me to-day, I assure you I feel an anxiety and solicitude far beyond any I have experienced previously in the course of my professional life. And, you will not be surprised when I say so, called upon as I am, to

meet, on the part of this gentleman, the Defendant, the former Colonel Joseph Hanson, a charge of so serious a nature. Such a charge would be serious if applied to any individual subject of this realm, but most particularly so, perhaps, when applied to a gentleman holding such a situation in life as the Defendant, Mr Hanson, and still more so, Gentlemen, when we see that this cause is brought forward with all the weight and gravity that can attend a prosecution conducted under the immediate direction of the Government. But notwithstanding every defect under which I most sensibly feel myself labouring in this respect, notwithstanding all these circumstances of disadvantage, under which I am now called upon to address you, I approach the discussion of this great and important case undismayed.

Let me not be misunderstood, Gentlemen, when I say that – I trust you will not, none who know me will. I mean 'undismayed' from any vain confidence in my own strength, of which I assure you sincerely, I entertain a becoming *dis*trust, but it is from a confidence in the truth and justice of the cause in which I am engaged, that I feel thus encouraged, a confidence so absolute that, if I have the good fortune to convey to your minds but half of what I myself feel most strongly, my client will, I am sure, have no reason to dread the verdict, which it will shortly be your duty to pronounce. If I have but the good fortune, Gentlemen, to present in a clear and perspicuous light the view, or even a faint glimpse of the view *I* have of this case, then my client is already acquitted.

He gracefully clicks his heels together, offers a small bow in the direction of the Bench, permits himself a further inhalation of his buttonhole, then performs a gracious pirouette, before striding purposefully towards the Jurors.

Gentlemen, contemplating this prosecution, carried on as it is under the immediate direction of Government, I would say a word or two to obviate any prejudice that might arise in your breasts against my client. We are but too apt to conclude, when Government have directed a prosecution to be set on foot, that they must have good grounds for doing so, and that they would not raise their arm against an individual without some adequate cause. But – you must never forget that it is with Government as with private persons, in making inquiries after evidence, that they as well as others have this to seek for, and are, in the search of it, equally liable to imposition and mistake. And if I wanted a precedent for this, Gentlemen, the history of the proceedings that have taken place on this great and important subject – I mean in respect to Riots in this country – would afford me an ample and convincing proof. Because, out of no less than twenty-five men tried for this offence at the last Assizes, eight only were convicted. Eight. And here again, let me guard against any misconstruction of my words. Do not imagine that I wish to force upon your minds any unfair conclusion. Do not suppose I would have you think that because many other persons indicted for offences somewhat similar to this have been acquitted, Mr Hanson must needs be innocent also, and so entitled to your verdict. God forbid! I mean no more than this: that if Government have, in so many instances, been unsuccessful, it is possible – I do not offend, I think, when I say it is possible – that in this case also, they may have been misled in their information. Even without my expressing to you the anxiety which I too deeply feel, you might naturally conclude from the appearance of the case, that I, on this occasion, deserve some little indulgence.

Emboldened by several smiles he detects among members in the Public Gallery, he executes a neat cabriole before positioning himself alongside Mr Cockell and his team of lawyers.

But what, Gentlemen, are the facts? You see here what a formidable host in rank and talents, in learning and experience, has been called into the field by Government, and put in battle array against me. Here, for instance, is my learned friend the Attorney-General, Mr Cockell; Mr. Park also; and Mr. Topping, all three of His Majesty's Counsel and, to speak of them with sincerity, undoubtedly stars of the first magnitude. To these are added (*he counts them on his fingers*) five lesser, yet still most bright stars, and forming, in the whole, a cluster of glittering northern lights, sufficient to dazzle poor weak eyes like mine into perfect blindness.

He closes his outstretched fingers to form a fist.

Be this as it may, feeling as I do the unequal conflict in which I am engaged, I shall address myself to your candour, and if I have the good fortune to possess that, I do flatter myself that I shall, in the sequel, be able to convince you – aye, even after the formidable reply with which we have been threatened shall have been delivered – of the innocence of Mr Hanson.

He pounds that enclosed fist into the open palm of his other hand.

Gentlemen, my learned friend, in the early part of his opening of this case, pledged himself to a line of moderation with respect to Mr Hanson. Now, I think – and my learned friend must not take this as an offence – but I think it happened to him, that in the warmth of argument he forgot the moderation upon which he had professed to act.

This at least struck my mind when I heard the many epithets with which he thought proper to characterise Mr Hanson, even before any evidence was heard. And even though I allow my learned friend's right to use such characteristics, yet I must aver in terms of their veracity. I think them calculated to produce improper prejudices, especially when their applicability is not made out in a satisfactory manner.

What are these epithets which my learned friend, in his mildness and forbearance, has thought fit, on this occasion, to use, with a view to degrade my client? Let us examine them.

He has called him: "impudent", "malicious", "abominable", "disloyal", "mischievous", "wicked", and "about to be consigned to absolute infamy". These are just a sample of them, which I wrote down at the time with great concern, and which indeed, I am sorry to say, form but a small part of his invective. This is inflaming the accusation a little too much, methinks. That there may be in tumultuous assemblies individuals to whom these expressions might without injustice be applied, I can readily admit, but are we therefore at liberty to put Mr Hanson on a footing with such as them, merely because he happened to be present at such a meeting on a particular occasion? I do not believe so, and I trust that you will not do so either. But even if we suppose him to be *somewhat* to blame, is he accountable for every act of outrage which may have been committed by *other* persons? No, gentlemen, this is too much for any advocate to hope to convince you of. Even one as distinguished as Mr Cockell.

He places his right hand across his heart.

In order to enable you to form a full and proper judgement

of the case, and that you may have every information that is calculated to satisfy your minds upon it, I shall proceed to describe to you the circumstances relating to these transactions, so far as Mr Hanson was concerned.

He bows low, as if on a stage.

You have it already in evidence that the Spinners and Weavers were at the time reduced to a state of extreme distress. This was owing to the pressure of the very portentous War against our enemy, the French, in which we were, and still are, engaged, which has had such lamentable and disastrous consequences on the wages of the labouring man, who is no longer able to afford the ever-rising costs of even the most basic of daily necessities. Do not imagine that it is my wish, in stating this, to excite discontent. God forbid I should do this at any time, much less at a crisis like the present, when we are told by those who know, or ought to know, that we shall be called upon in all probability shortly to fight, on British ground, battles for our country with an inveterate foe. And if it be so, is there a British bosom, within which the heart does not burn for the fight, to add one more to the noble army of martyrs? For without profaneness we may be permitted to say, not only they who fight and die in the cause of religion, but they also who fall in defence of their country, are martyrs. And if this battle is to be fought, confident I am that the country will not find within its shores a more zealous defender, nor one more faithful to its dearest interests than Mr Hanson. No, Gentlemen, it is not unknown to you, how much of his time, aye, and of his fortune too, he has devoted to the service of his country, in training up to arms a Regiment of Riflemen, and that to a state of discipline, which may be fairly set in competition with that which any of the Volunteers of this realm can boast to have attained to. I feel a little personal pride in mentioning this circumstance, because I myself belong to that description of individuals, and therefore you will pardon me, if I have gone a little out of the way, in speaking on this subject.

Gentlemen, it was, if I recollect right, towards the close of the year 1807, and the commencement of the year 1808, when the pressure to which I have alluded fell with most peculiar hardship and severity on the Spinners and Weavers, and for this most obvious reason. Because our inveterate enemy had shut the ports of Europe against our trade, thus depriving our manufacturers of the power of exporting their goods, and consequently the Spinners and Weavers of their employment, were these hard-pressed labouring men thus reduced to the state of extreme distress already described, and that that distress they sought to relieve by an humble representation to the British House of Commons, beseeching them to pass a Bill, a Bill which would fix a standard for their wages, under which they should not thereafter sink. In that application, Gentlemen, they had the misfortune to fail, but at that time, and ever since, these matters have been canvassed by political economists, by many of whom the measure has been deemed essential to the welfare of those classes of the community, who are not as yet represented in Parliament, such as is still the case for the people of Manchester.

He strikes up a pose, as if speaking in the House of Commons itself, his feet placed apart to the width of his shoulders, one slightly in advance of the other, while he points the index finger of his right hand skywards.

Gentlemen, you will please to recollect, for it is in evidence, that the intelligence concerning the fate with which the Bill had met in the House of Commons reached Manchester on

197

Sunday the 22nd of May. A communication of this event having taken place was made to that highly respectable gentleman, Mr. Starkie, the Boroughreeve, who gave his evidence in a manner that has no doubt done him credit among his peers.

At this point Mr Raine pauses briefly, but long enough to indicate that though Mr Starkie may indeed have done himself credit among his peers, he may not have achieved the same credit elsewhere.

Now, what was the consequence of the communication of this crucial intelligence? What, I would ask, might one have expected to ensue, when this failure was announced? The first application to Parliament, some months before, had been unsuccessful, but the thing had then undergone but little discussion. On this, the second, it was discussed more fully, and expectations were more strongly raised. Why, then, is it a matter of great surprise that, at this moment, smarting as they were under their distresses, unable to express their feelings, can it, I say, be thought astonishing, that at such a time, the communication of such an event should operate as a violent shock, and make these loyal, conscientious, diligent and hard-working labourers almost despair of any improvement in their condition?

He lowers his right hand and looks up towards the Public Gallery, which he addresses directly.

We have been told, in no less reliable a source as the Book of Proverbs, that 'hope deferred makes the heart sick'. If this be the case, what is hope completely defeated and disappointed likely to produce? But what *was*, in point of fact, the consequence resulting from this intelligence? What effects *did* it occasion? Why, Gentlemen, all that it

198

occasioned was a meeting of a *small* number of persons who assembled together, and *conversed* upon the subject of their late disappointment during a spring afternoon.

He now signals to his assistant, Mr Littledale, to remove a piece of cloth which has been draped over a small table, which the latter does to great effect with much flamboyance, as a conjuror might to entertain crowds at a Fair. He reveals a scale model of St George's Fields, complete with toy figures to represent separately the crowds, the Magistrates, the Dragoons, the Special Constables, Mr Hanson on his white charger. Mr Raine strides enthusiastically towards it and begins to move several of the figures around the table as he describes his version of what took place, rather like pieces on a chess board, speaking with increasing rapidity as he does so.

On the following day, namely, on Tuesday the 24th, they did indeed assemble in larger numbers in St. George's Fields, and that for the purpose of coming to some satisfactory arrangements respecting their moderate demands on their employers. And in what way did they proceed? They had, it seems, appointed Delegates, on which step my learned friend has laid some stress. I do not know on what account this mode of proceeding can be deemed improper. Rather, I would argue that it was most *proper*. If the whole body had gone, it would have presented at once the appearance of a Riot. They, therefore, in my opinion, judged wisely in deputing a few persons to represent their grievances. These Delegates, so appointed, went to the Magistrates, and begged some means might be hit upon for relieving their distresses. This application, however, it seems, had not the effect expected. Here, Gentlemen, I wish it to be understood, that I am not imputing blame to the Magistrates. I believe they were disposed to render every assistance in their power, but I merely state the fact, that it so happened that the application of the Spinners and Weavers was not, or could not, for whatever reason the Magistrates so decided, be complied with. Then, on their return, you will find, that after some further conversation, they all left the field together.

Mr Raine continues enthusiastically to manipulate the model figures as he further describes the events of the day.

On the following day after, the 25th, they unfortunately assembled on the same spot, in still greater numbers. Here I ought to mention one circumstance which is already in evidence, and it is this: five or six hundred persons assembled in St. George's Fields on Tuesday, the 24th. They were quite peaceable, and were awaiting the report of their Delegates. Colonel Sylvester, Commanding Officer of the 4th Dragoon Guards, addressed them, and told them to go quietly home, exerting, much to his honour, all the address he was master of, to prevent riot and disturbance. But then, Gentlemen, he ordered, and I think it very odd, the Riot Act to be read, which it was, by Justice of the Peace Mr Matthew Oldham, who, mysteriously, is not in Court with us today. I intend no dishonour upon that gentleman, nor upon Colonel Sylvester. I merely re-state the facts. Why? Why adopt so harsh a step? We are told, forsooth, that it is not proper so large a number of persons should be together; that it *may* lead to Riot; that it was desirable they should disperse, and so on. Well, but when we are also told, that there was *no* disposition to tumult, that the men were peaceable and quiet, that they conducted themselves in an orderly and sober manner. I cannot help regretting, therefore, that they should have been so rigidly treated. I say again, I cannot but regret that this step was adopted, because it appears to me calculated to produce the very effect they were endeavouring to prevent. It would irritate the minds, and add fuel to those heated passions, which, I have no manner of doubt, it was Colonel Sylvester's wish to check.

Having picked up the figure representing Colonel Sylvester in order to give a certain emphasis while describing the particular incident appertaining to him, he now replaces it, selecting instead, the one of Mr Hanson upon his white horse.

We come now once more to the afternoon of the 25th, but before I enter upon the transactions of that day, it is but just that I should say a word or two about my client.

Here Mr Raine temporarily leaves the display to walk towards Mr Hanson, behind whom he now stands, a hand upon his shoulder, as he gives his eulogy of him. Mr Hanson attempts to put on a brave face throughout. This moment is clearly a source of considerable embarrassment to him. He looks distinctly uncomfortable, an impression heightened by the way his uniform now hangs so loosely upon his shoulders. He presents a much reduced, shrunken form to the Court compared to the heroic figure he cut upon St George's Fields. It is clear he has been subject to the close attentions of Mr Nadin's more imaginative ministrations while awaiting the trial. He winces as Mr Raine places his hand upon his shoulder. He starts at every loud noise. His lower lip appears to be almost permanently trembling.

Mr. Hanson is the son of a most excellent man, of whom you must have heard, and who advanced himself to a state of considerable wealth by his industry in this county. Nothing more honourable can be said of any man. He had the good fortune to recommend himself to all around him. His whole life was a continued series of charitable and benevolent actions. And, not to tire you with an over-zealous account of the virtues of this excellent man, I will say at once that he lived his entire life respected, esteemed, and beloved by all who knew him. When the time came for the Good Lord to judge that he had lived his allotted span of years among us, a fate that awaits us all, he died no less extolled, and, in the language of that most elegant living author, Mr Thomas Brinsley Sheridan, 'when he died, he left not a more benevolent heart behind him to lament his loss,' than his son, who sits before you this day. For Mr Hanson Junior is likewise what the inestimable Mr Milton would deem 'of virtuous father, virtuous son.' He has been early trained to habits of business by his late father, from the influence of whose precepts, added to the weight and dignity of his example, Mr Hanson has imbibed, interwoven, as it were, in his very habits, a spirit of benevolent concern for the sufferings of the poor. To them he has never failed to administer well-timed and seasonable relief on every suitable occasion. I am sorry that I should have to say this in his presence. I know it will give pain to his most fine feelings, but, Gentlemen, painful as it is, the case appears to demand from me that I should pay this tribute of justice to Mr Hanson and his virtues. I will only remind you of one other circumstance: Mr Hanson, having been long acquainted with the Spinners and Weavers in this county, offered himself, when the last Dissolution of Parliament took place, as a candidate for the representation of Preston. He would have preferred to stand for Manchester, but as yet no such representation is afforded that great metropolis. A large body of Spinners and Weavers then thought it right to exact a pledge from their favourite, that he would support their Bill in Parliament. What was the former Colonel Hanson to do on this occasion? He must not rashly sign this pledge. "No," said he, "show me your Bill, and I will consider it carefully." They did show him the Bill, and he did approve of it, as many others have likewise done. He accordingly pledged his support, in the event of his being elected. Unluckily, however, Mr Hanson was a little too late in starting, and therefore did not succeed in this honourable object of his ambition. But his commitment to the Bill, to the cause it represented for the downtrodden Spinners and Weavers, of whom he was their champion, has never wavered.

With a barely concealed choke in his voice, Mr Raine moves slowly away from his client, back towards the table with its diorama of St George's Fields and reverently places the model of Mr Hanson on his horse back into what he considers to be its heroic position.

We can now begin to examine more closely the transactions of the day alluded to. It is a most remarkable circumstance if Mr Hanson be guilty of the offence charged upon him, that not a tittle of evidence can be adduced to prove that any conspiracy or meeting of the Spinners or Weavers with Mr Hanson existed previous to the 25th of May. Did he, if concerned in a conspiracy for the subversion of the peace of his country, league with five or six thousand men, to enable him to prosecute it with success? Gentlemen, if he were guilty of the conspiracy charged upon him, I appeal to your own good sense, whether you have not a right to expect from the Crown, that they should produce evidence of at least one of these men having gone to his house, and conferred with him on the subject. But what is the fact? The 25th of May is the *first* day, in which it is attempted to connect Mr Hanson with this conspiracy.

MR JUSTICE GOOSE: (*interrupting*):
The Indictment does not charge the Defendant with a conspiracy.

MR. RAINE:

Gentlemen, it is charged as a conspiracy on these rioters, and the conspiracy in respect to them was an attempt, on their part, to exact an increase of wages.

Mr. Raine here reads that part of the indictment relative to Mr. Hanson's aiding and promoting the conspiracy of the rioters.

"The Defendant, Mr Joseph Hanson – *et cetera, et cetera* – to urge and promote the said conspiracy – *et cetera, et cetra* – did incite, encourage, and endeavour – *et cetera, et cetera* – to bring to effect the said unlawful conspiracy."

He strikes the paper containing the Indictment with the back of his hand for extra emphasis.

My observation (and I am sure His Lordship will not deny it) applies with equal strength to this part of the case. I most strongly feel that it has very great weight, and that it would have been satisfactory to the Jurors' minds, if the Crown could have shown him leagued with any of these so-called Rioters previously to the 25th of May. This defect, Gentlemen, does not arise from any lack of zeal in searching for the evidence. No, you may depend upon it, that if the fact I speak of had existed, evidence of it would no doubt have come out this day.

Mr Justice Goose, with seeming reluctance, concedes the point.

We come now to what occurred on the 25th. It is chiefly charged against Mr Hanson that he aided and abetted, by speeches, these so-called Rioters. To this I humbly crave your attention. I do think, however strange it may appear, that the Indictment furnishes an answer to this charge. The following is from the speeches which it charges upon him, as having been made by him when he came into the field.

Mr Littledale hands Mr Raine a transcript of these speeches, from which he now reads.

'My father was a weaver, and I myself was brought up to that trade, I am your real friend. I would advise you to be steady. Stick to your purpose, and you will gain your ends. But, for God's sake, do not disturb the tranquillity of the country.'

He returns the papers to Mr Littledale, then turns back towards the Jurors.

'Do not disturb the tranquillity of the country.' Does that sound like aiding and abetting Rioters? That, however, is part of the charge, that is his departing speech, and I need not remind you, Gentlemen, that persons in general are apt to remember the last words they hear. These are commonly the most strongly impressed on their minds. These then are his parting words, 'For God's sake do not disturb the tranquillity of the country.' Now upon this, Mr. Cockell, the Attorney-General no less, has thought fit to make an observation in his opening speech.

Mr Raine at this point scampers back to his desk, where he theatrically rummages through more papers till he finds what he has been looking for, which he now holds up for the Court to see, referring to Mr Cockell as he continues.

Says my learned friend, "This is a colour." He is referring to a use of language in which the tone in which a thing is expressed goes contrary to the literal meaning of it. What? When I am addressing a large body of persons, if I say, "Stick to your cause, but do not for God's sake disturb the tranquillity of the country", is that a *colour*? But how, I would ask my learned friend, would these persons understand such words? Will he say that men not brought up to Letters, as he is, would put such a forced construction on what they heard? I cannot doubt but you will agree with me that it is much more natural that they would take it as it was said, and understand plain common words in a plain common way. The very last words which he used, according to the charge itself are, 'I entreat you not to disturb the tranquillity of the country.' What man in his senses, then, can apply these words in the way they would have you think they were intended to be used by Mr Hanson, namely, the opposite of their true meaning, with a view to excite these men to tumult? Still, my learned friend will have it, that it is all *colouring* on the part of Mr Hanson. Cunning and guile, Gentlemen, cunning and guile never found their way into Mr Hanson's heart. No, where the heart is warm, as his is, you seldom find either.

Mr Raine places his right hand upon his own heart, lets his left hand fall to his side, allowing the papers he has been holding to fall and scatter where they lie, then bows his head.

So much for that particular art of the charge.

After a suitable pause, he picks up the thread once more and addresses the Jurors.

And now, Gentlemen, with respect to Mr. Hanson's arrival at the scene of action, let us continue to explore the events as they unfolded.

He returns to the diorama.

You will recollect that his house is about a mile and a half from St George's Fields. Mr Hanson had heard that there was a considerable number of persons there assembled. He had heard of the rejection of their Bill being announced, and that this large meeting was owing to that circumstance. In short, he heard on the Wednesday, that they had assembled again. He likewise knew from the course of his life – and I have no hesitation in saying it, that he was a favourite with the Spinners and Weavers – that no man can by mere profession procure to himself that respect, or enjoy that satisfaction which arises from acts of beneficence to the world. You may preach as long as you please, but so long as you do not accompany it with the necessary *deeds*, it will have no effect.

Mr Raine now somewhat mischievously turns to address the whole court once more as if he were back in his Gentleman's Club.

And this reminds me of a story of an Archbishop, who was one day accosted by an half-starved beggar, who asked him for a piece of gold. The Archbishop, astonished at the impertinence of the demand, replied, "No, sir, not a *sou*." "Then, Father," said the beggar, "will you give me your blessing?" To which the Archbishop said, "Aye, kneel down, my son." "Hold, hold, Good Father," says the beggar, "if your blessing is not worth a *sou*, it is not worth having!" And, Gentlemen, I am perfectly sure you will agree with me, that the beggar bested the Archbishop.

Mr Cockell rises languidly to his feet, an amused expression on his face.

MR COCKELL:
My Lord, entertaining as my learned friend undoubtedly is, I fail to see the relevance of this to the matter in hand.

MR JUSTICE GOOSE:

I am inclined to agree with you, sir. Mr Raine, from now on please confine yourself to facts appertaining to the case.

MR RAINE:

As Your Lordship pleases.

MR JUSTICE GOOSE:

I do indeed. And might I remind you that this is a Court of Law, not some disreputable London Playhouse.

Mr Raine signals quickly to Mr Littledale, who unfurls the piece of cloth once more and allows it to settle slowly and gently across the diorama, with all the panache of a curtain falling in a theatre at the end of an Act.

MR RAINE:

To return to Mr Hanson.

He, Gentlemen, not with a view to recommend himself – for he purposely concealed his name – having heard of the great distress prevailing in the county, resolved to distribute a number of loaves, as being, in his opinion, the most suitable way of relieving it. Loaves, you will note. Not fishes. Mr Hanson pretends no airs or graces. Accordingly the servant is sent with a strict charge not to make it known who is the donor behind these gifts, and a number of loaves are distributed. He does the same thing with respect to the parish of Middleton, and the township of Pendlebury. He knew, therefore, that by these acts of benevolence and charity, he had contributed some small crumb of comfort to the well-being of the poor, and it naturally occurred to him, that he might be doing great service to his King and his Country, if he strenuously advised those assembled upon St George's Fields to be peaceable and orderly. With this view he went, and in that spirit addressed them, telling them that if they were sufferers, so were the manufacturers, and entreating them for God's sake to be quiet and orderly. He previously informed some of his friends, that it was his intention to go, because he felt it his duty to do so. My learned friend says that Mr Hanson, having been unsuccessful in his bid to become a Member of Parliament, and having some years before resigned his commission from His Majesty's Armed Forces, had no civil or military character, and would therefore persuade you, he had no business there. Gentlemen, I deny it, on the authority no less, of the Earl of Mansfield, our most esteemed late Solicitor-General, and Sir John Scott, the incumbent Lord High Chancellor of England.

Mr Raine pauses to let the weight of these names sink in with everyone there present, the impact of which brings its immediate reward, for both Mr Cockell and Mr Goose lean forward in their seats with the utmost concentration, not to say consternation, apparent in their demeanour.

Lord Mansfield said, when speaking of Riots, that it was the duty of every good subject to exert himself to the utmost of his power in quelling them, and that it is highly praiseworthy and meritorious so to do.

So says Lord Mansfield.

But, Gentlemen, I have another, even more remarkable authority for Mr. Hanson's being justified in taking the course he did, and it is not only important in showing you that he was well justified in so doing, but inasmuch as it will show how very careful witnesses should be in ascertaining the precise words they claim they have heard, where words misrepresented may produce such great mistakes. You will recollect the recent Shude Hill riots? The so-called Potato Riots, in which crowds assembled to protest about the extreme high prices in food? The Defendant had the misfortune to witness first hand these distressing incidents while still a Colonel with the Manchester Home Guard. You recollect the circumstance, Gentlemen, no doubt? It was a matter of notoriety in the country at large, not just in Manchester.

A noble Lord and Honourable Baronet, whom, out of respect of his most notable personage, we shall not name, exerted himself to quell that Riot. I am speaking now of an historical fact. This noble and unnamed Lord and Honourable Baronet composed a hand-bill, in which he styled the Rioters, 'Friends and fellow-churchmen,' but concluded by entreating them to respect the laws of their country.

Now, Gentlemen, this is, on the face of it, extremely suspicious. 'Friends and fellow-churchmen?' Why, in reality they were neither the one nor the other. But it was the duty of this person, this noble and unnamed Lord and Honourable Baronet, to soothe and compose the inflamed mob, and therefore he used this stratagem for that very purpose.

Some time after, the conduct of this gentleman was called into question in the House of Commons. His 'conduct', I say, was 'called into question'. It did appear to be 'blameworthy', and it was taken up as a 'matter of censure', insinuated that he had 'assisted' the Rioters on this occasion by his actions and his words. The proceedings of this noble and unnamed Lord and Honourable Baronet being thus brought before the House, another Honourable Gentleman expressed himself to the following effect – and here I shall read directly from his speech to Parliament, where he expressed his position thus:

'After the most impartial consideration, I am of the opinion that no evidence ought to be received with more caution than that which relates to certain facts, which took place at a time when men's minds were agitated with fear, and I must protest against any proceedings founded on expressions at such a moment of alarm.'

Now, Gentlemen, who is the person that uses this language? Not a factious demagogue. No indeed, Gentlemen, no such person. The person who uses this argument, so precisely in point with respect to the present business, is no less a personage than the Attorney-General of that day, Sir John Scott, now Lord High Chancellor of Great Britain.

It appears to me that there can be no more decisive pronouncement on this subject than that delivered by the Lord High Chancellor of Great Britain, who maintains, in this pronouncement, that, in a moment of danger, a person must endeavour to soothe the people, and for a person speaking on such an occasion, the greatest possible allowance is to be made.

During this last argument, Mr Raine has worked himself into a high state of emotion. He pauses, takes a sip of water, mops his brow with a white silk handkerchief. Then, certain that he is once more quite restored, he resumes his normal smiling demeanour as he turns his attention fully back to the Jurors.

What, then, will you say, Gentlemen, when I shall prove to your entire satisfaction – and I am enabled to do so – that Colonel Hanson so addressed himself to his friends? That he clearly and positively told them what his motive was in

211

going to this assembly, and that this motive was no other than to use his influence with the Spinners and Weavers, to induce them to be peaceable, and to retire? By three respectable persons who dined at his house – from whom you shall hear later by way of several *affidavits* – I shall prove he then renewed the subject, addressing them in the following manner:

He strides across to where Mr Hanson is seated and speaks the following from his side.

"I think I have some influence with them, and I will use it to the best of my power to prevent disturbance." One of his friends attempted to dissuade him from his purpose, but Mr. Hanson thought he could not satisfy his conscience as a good subject, if he did not use his best exertions accordingly.

Mr Raine places an affectionate hand once more upon the shoulder of the Defendant before returning to the centre of the Court.

He was further stimulated to his purpose by the knowledge that no less a figure than Colonel Sylvester had addressed himself to them, unfortunately without effect, and Colonel Sylvester was a person of much consideration in the county, so that Mr Hanson said, "If Colonel Sylvester is to address them, for God's sake why, then, cannot I?" This, therefore, assisted him further in persuading him to make his speech.

Mr Raine feigns to turn away, then smartly swivels back to face the Court.

Well, but he went on horseback, I hear you say? And why not? If he was to go at all, it was a mile and a half from his abode. There were many others on horseback; so why should not he?

He tosses aside this remark with the back of a hand, an affecting gesture he has observed the actors adopt on several stages, and is pleased to find his attempt rewarded with some laughter from the Public Gallery.

Now, let us attend to his expressions, which you have heard commented upon with so much vigour. No doubt some awkward expressions have been introduced by some of the witnesses, but mark, Gentlemen, how they contradict each other, and that in some most material circumstances.

He lets his gaze linger upon each of Mr Cockell's assistants who, one by one, discover they have something of intense interest in front of them on their desks, which requires their urgent attention, rather than undergo the prolonged scrutiny of Mr Raine.

On the part of Mr Hanson, I shall call many witnesses, and every one of them will tell you that they were so near to Mr Hanson from the beginning to the end of this affair, that it was impossible for him to have used these expressions without their hearing them, and which they will have no hesitation in saying was *not* the case. They will tell you, however, that so far from using expressions likely to lead to Riot, the whole of Mr. Hanson's conduct was calculated to have a *contrary* effect, and that in short the meeting did disperse. I believe some of my witnesses will tell you that at the end of his speech, there was an effusion of loyalty. Yes, to Mr Hanson, who, I repeat, had been urging those displaying their loyalty towards him not to disturb the tranquillity of the country. Now, all of the soldiers, who testified for the Crown, have sworn to certain expressions of an opposing nature. If you are satisfied of the veracity of the witnesses *I* shall produce – and they are such as I feel confident you will have no reason to discredit – you must of necessity disbelieve the others.

Having finished his opening statement, he now formally bows towards the Bench, before returning one last time to address the Jurors.

I thank you, however, most cordially for the patience and attention, with which you have heard me. I have only to entreat you to bestow the same attention upon the evidence I am now about to produce for you relative to the purpose and effect of Mr Hanson's conduct and actions on the day in question. I sit down satisfied that you will deliver Mr Hanson from this most serious charge and pronounce a verdict of Not Guilty.

Mr Raine, with the aid of his assistants Messrs Littledale, Wilson and Ambrose, then proceeds to examine the following witnesses in turn:

Mr Thomas Appleton, Calico Printer, Manchester
Mr John Carey, Schoolmaster, Pendlebury
Mr William Gaskell, Book Keeper, Manchester
Mr James Moss, Special Constable, Manchester
Mr John Sneddon, Groom to Mr Hanson, Strangeways
Mr George Bluntson, Excise Officer, Salford
Mr Edward Shepley, Clock & Watch Maker, London Road, Manchester
Mr C.B. Stennett, Property Holder, Manchester
Mr John Carr, Tax Collector, Manchester Division
Mr Charles Satterthwaite, Visiting Businessman
Mr Joseph Oliver, Commercial Traveller, Hollins Green, near Warrington

Mr Robert Norris, Resident, Manchester

Mr Thomas Kearsley, Fustian Cutter, Ancoats, Manchester

Mr John Speerit, Porter, Manchester

Mr James Brocklehurst, Cotton Spinner, Hayfield, Derbyshire

Mr John Brierley, Upholsterer, Swinton

Mr Alexander Patterson, Keeper of The Bridgewater Arms, Manchester

and

Mr Amos Lees, Weaver, Elton

A full account of the cross examination of each of these witnesses cannot now be given. After the case was concluded, the papers were filed away, but not as respectfully perhaps as they should have been. Insufficient care was given either to the binding of them, or to their security, not being filed, stored, or locked away as befits such important matters of justice. When, several years later, they were unearthed, upon the request perhaps of some academic scholar hunting down the minutiae of the case in the hope of establishing future precedent, it was discovered that the records had fallen victim to the nibblings of Mus Musculus, or Rattus Rattus perhaps, and so large portions are now missing. What follows, therefore, is a collection of fragments painstakingly reconstructed with the judicious use of scissors and glue.

......

Thomas Appleton is sworn in. He strikes a somewhat formidable presence as he takes the stand, for he has only one eye, the left, which is large and protuberant, seemingly revolving on its axis with a will of its own, while where his right eye must once have been is now just a patch of scarred, sewn-up skin.

MR RAINE:

Mr. Appleton, you live in Salford, I believe?

MR APPLETON:

I do, sir.

MR RAINE:

You are a calico printer there, I believe?

MR APPLETON:

I am, sir.

MR RAINE:

I believe you were formerly a member of the Rifle Corps once commanded by Mr Hanson?

MR APPLETON:

Yes, sir.

MR RAINE:

You have been acquainted with him from the time you were very young, since being a child, in fact?

MR APPLETON:

I have, sir.

MR RAINE:

Do you remember on the twenty-fifth of May last, Mr Hanson calling at your house?

MR APPLETON:

Yes, sir.

MR RAINE:

What time was it when he called?

MR APPLETON:

Betwixt eleven and twelve.

MR RAINE:

Do you remember his saying…?

Mr Cockell rises rapidly to his feet, a movement in stark contrast to his more customary languid demeanour.

MR COCKELL:

I fear I must object, My Lord.

MR JUSTICE GOOSE: (*wearily*):

Yes. I had a feeling you might. Really, Mr Raine, you should know better than this. You are about to subject the Jurors to what can only be described as…

MR COCKELL: (*interjecting*):

Hear say, My Lord.

MR JUSTICE GOOSE:

Quite so, Mr Cockell. Hear say.

MR RAINE:

I submit to Your Lordship that this is evidence as part of the *res gestae* and goes to the very heart of the matter.

MR COCKELL:

Hear say.

MR RAINE:

Res gestae. The things done. The only question that can arise is, whether these conversations about to be described by the witness can be considered, for if they be, a most significant consequence naturally follows: that this is what was said at the commencement of the Defendant's purpose, and it is impossible to confine the transaction to one precise spot, or point of time.

MR COCKELL:

It is supposition at best, My Lord, and therefore must be deemed inadmissible.

MR RAINE:

On the contrary, My Lord, I consider this as highly admissible evidence since it is directly explanatory of the intent, which is what is at issue here. The intent, or otherwise, of my client. Both the speaking of the words, *and the intent*, charged by the Indictment, must be proved, or the Defendant is entitled to an acquittal.

Before Mr Justice Goose can stop him, Mr Raine now distances himself from the Bench, where hitherto this academic disagreement was been being prosecuted, so that he might address the entire Court, thereby ensuring that, whether he is successful in his plea to continue to question Mr Appleton further about alleged conversations taking place between him and Mr Hanson before the events which occurred later on St George's Fields or not, his arguments may be clearly heard by all.

Now, that being so, let us consider what would undoubtedly be evidence against him.

Suppose the Defendant had, before he left his house, delivered inflammatory speeches in *favour* of General Riot and Disorder. Suppose it had been proposed to show by evidence that the Defendant had put a pair of pistols into his pocket, can it be doubted that such facts and such language would be admissible evidence against the Defendant? I think not. If so, why are not facts of a *contrary* tendency equally admissible for him? Moreover, this is not a singular case. In ordinary prosecutions for uttering, let us say, counterfeit notes or money, acts done, and payments made at distant periods of time, are routinely received to explain the purpose. If so, why may not the same explanation be allowed, not from remote, but recent and almost contemporary expressions and conduct, such as Mr Appleby will be able to furnish us with, if the Court so approves?

MR JUSTICE GOOSE: (*rapping his gavel upon the Bench as he tries to restore order*):
I am of the opinion that you cannot give in evidence any words but such as were spoken on the field.

MR COCKELL:
I'm much obliged, My Lord.

Mr Raine shakes his head in disbelief and Mr Appleton is instructed to step down.

......

John Gray is now sworn in. His face and hands have a rather disconcerting blueish pallor, as if they have been permanently stained with ink, which will not satisfactorily ever submit to the administrations of washing or scrubbing, however assiduously they are applied.

Mr Raine hands the reins of the Defence to his colleague, Mr Littledale. The contrast between the two could not be more marked. Where Mr Raine is expansive, Mr Littledale is brief. Where Mr Raine is theatrical, Mr Littledale is academic. Where Mr Raine is at times free with the facts, Mr Littledale is punctilious. And where Mr Raine plays to the Gallery, Mr Littledale addresses himself exclusively to the witness.

MR LITTLEDALE:
You are a schoolmaster, I believe?

MR GRAY:

Yes, sir.

MR LITTLEDALE:

And your address?

MR GRAY:

Ancoats Lane, Manchester.

MR LITTLEDALE:

Do you remember a meeting of the Spinners and Weavers in St. George's Fields, in the afternoon of the 25th May last?

MR GRAY:

Yes, sir.

MR LITTLEDALE:

Did you see Mr Hanson and his servant there?

MR GRAY:

I saw them come up into the Fields.

MR LITTLEDALE:

What time of the day was it?

MR GRAY:

About ten minutes after four.

MR LITTLEDALE:

Where did he appear to be coming from?

MR GRAY:

From Manchester.

MR LITTLEDALE:

That is the same road as from his own house at Strangeways?

MR GRAY:

Yes.

MR LITTLEDALE:

Were the Cavalry coming up at that time also?

MR GRAY:

Yes, they were.

MR LITTLEDALE:

Were they coming up on the same side that Mr Hanson was, or on the opposite side?

MR GRAY:

On the opposite side.

MR LITTLEDALE:

Where did Mr Hanson ride up to?

MR GRAY:

He rode into the centre of the Fields.

MR LITTLEDALE:

He rode near the Spinners and Weavers?

MR GRAY:

He did.

MR LITTLEDALE:

Was he between where the Cavalry were forming and where the Spinners and Weavers were already assembled, or were the Spinners and Weavers between him and the Cavalry?

MR GRAY:

The latter.

MR LITTLEDALE:

When he came up, were you near Mr Hanson?

MR GRAY:

Yes, sir, I was about three yards only from his horse.

MR LITTLEDALE:

Was Mr Hanson on foot or on horseback?

MR GRAY:

On horseback, sir.

MR LITTLEDALE:

Was his servant with him?

MR GRAY:

I did not see his servant at that time, for I think he was a little way off.

MR LITTLEDALE:

What happened next?

MR GRAY:

A great shout ensued amongst the people, and the horse raised himself on his hind legs.

MR LITTLEDALE:

What effect did that produce on Mr. Hanson?

MR GRAY:

He slid off backward.

MR LITTLEDALE:

Did you observe what became of his horse then?

MR GRAY:

I do not know who got hold of it, for Mr Hanson was walking away then, and my attention was fixed on *him*, not the horse.

MR LITTLEDALE:

Which way did he appear to be going?

MR GRAY:

Towards the Lane.

MR LITTLEDALE:

Was that in the road towards his own house?

MR GRAY.

St George's Lane, yes.

MR LITTLEDALE:

Was he able to get forwards?

MR GRAY:

He was not.

MR LITTLEDALE:

What prevented him?

MR GRAY:

The crowds of people.

MR LITTLEDALE:

Did Mr Hanson continue on foot, or did he mount his horse again?

MR GRAY:

He mounted his horse.

MR LITTLEDALE:

How near were you to him when he mounted his horse?

MR GRAY:

I was just by the hedge backward, I might be four or five yards off by that time.

MR LITTLEDALE:

Where was the horse when he mounted again?

MR GRAY:

In the Lane.

MR LITTLEDALE:

Did you hear him say any thing to the people after he mounted his horse?

MR GRAY:

He said he himself had been ordered out of the Fields, and that he had obeyed that order. He said he desired them to be peaceable and quiet likewise.

MR LITTLEDALE:

Did he say anything more at that time?

MR GRAY:

God bless the King! God bless the King!

MR LITTLEDALE:

Did he say any thing else at all, sir?

MR GRAY:

I did not hear him say any thing else. He rode off.

MR LITTLEDALE:

Which way did he ride off?

MR GRAY:

Towards Manchester. Down St George's Lane.

MR LITTLEDALE:

Was it towards Strangeways?

MR GRAY:

Yes, that way.

MR LITTLEDALE:

Which is where Mr Hanson's home is to be found?

MR GRAY:

I believe so.

MR LITTLEDALE:

Did you in the course of the time you were on the ground hear him say any thing of supporting the Spinners and Weavers with three thousand pounds, or any like money?

MR GRAY:

Never.

MR LITTLEDALE:

Did you hear him say anything about Nadin and his 'faction'?

MR GRAY:

Never, sir.

MR LITTLEDALE:

Did you hear him desire the people to 'stick to their cause'?

MR GRAY:

Never, sir.

MR LITTLEDALE:

Did you hear him say any thing about 'six shillings in the cut', or 'six shillings in the pound'?

MR GRAY:

Never such a word.

MR LITTLEDALE:

Were you so attentive to what he said, that if he had made use of these words while you were near him, you must have heard him?

MR GRAY:

I am certain I should.

MR LITTLEDALE:

Now, I would just ask you during the time you were on the ground, what was his conduct?

MR GRAY:

He desired them for God's sake to be peaceable and quiet.

……..

Mr Gaskell is sworn in. He wears a pair of fingerless woollen gloves, at which it would appear the moths have been gnawing, for there are loose threads threatening to unravel the entire garment at the slightest pull.

MR LITTLEDALE:

Of what occupation are you, sir?

MR GASKELL:

Bookkeeper.

MR LITTLEDALE:

Do you remember being in St. George's Fields on Wednesday the 25th of May last?

MR GASKELL:

Yes, sir.

MR LITTLEDALE:

Do you remember the Defendant being dismounted, his being off his horse?

MR GASKELL:

I do.

MR LITTLEDALE:

Now during the time he was walking along the road-side, how near were you to him?

MR GASKELL:

About five yards from him only.

MR LITTLEDALE:

Did you hear him say anything while walking along the road-side?

MR GASKELL:

I heard him speak to Lieutenant Trafford

MR LITTLEDALE:

Lieutenant. Trafford told him that he 'came there to breed a Riot'. What said Mr Hanson to that?

MR GASKELL:

He said: "Mr. Trafford, I know your family, and you know mine, and I thought you had known me better than to suppose I should come here to breed a Riot. I am come to prevent one, if possible."

MR LITTLEDALE: (*to the Jurors, repeated with emphasis*):

"Come to prevent one…"

He now turns back to Mr Gaskell.

During the time you were on the field, what was the conduct of the Defendant?

MR GASKELL:

He was as peaceable as possible, sir.

MR LITTLEDALE:

How did the people conduct themselves after Mr Hanson had gone in the direction you speak of?

MR GASKELL:

As peaceably as possible.

……

James Moss is sworn. He is a big man with fair hair and extremely red cheeks. He beams as he takes the oath, an expression which he appears to wear permanently.

MR LITTLEDALE:

Do you remember being in St. George's Fields on Wednesday the 25th of May last?

MR MOSS:

I do.

MR LITTLEDALE:

How came you there?

MR MOSS:

I am a Special Constable of the town of Manchester.

A ripple runs round the Court. It is of considerable surprise that a man in Mr Moss's position should be testifying for the Defence. Mr Justice Goose raises his spectacles through which to inspect the Special Constable with an expression of barely concealed mistrust. Mr Moss appears blithely unaware of the commotion he is creating. He continues to beam affably and disarmingly upon the entire Court.

MR LITTELDALE:

And where do you live?

MR MOSS:

Up on Mount Zion, close by Irlams o' th' Heights.

MR LITTLEDALE:

And pray what brought you from Mount Zion there?

MR MOSS:

I heard, during luncheon, that a great number of people were gathered there. Being a Special Constable, I put my truncheon in my pocket and went there also.

MR LITTLEDALE:

Having been at your work in the morning and being a responsible man, hearing that this large meeting were assembled, you, like a prudent Special Constable, went, after luncheon, with a truncheon in your pocket?

MR MOSS:
Yes, sir.

MR LITTLEDALE:
Pray, did you take any other persons with you?

MR MOSS:
I went by myself.

MR LITTLEDALE:
Did you see an assembly of people there?

MR MOSS:
I did.

MR LITTLEDALE:
Did you see Mr Hanson?

MR MOSS:
I did.

MR LITTLEDALE:
Did you see him come on the field?

MR MOSS:
I did.

MR LITTLEDALE:
Were you near him?

MR MOSS:
I was not far off.

MR LITTLEDALE:
Did you hear Mr Hanson address the people that were collected there?

MR MOSS:
I did.

MR LITTLEDALE:
What did he say?

MR MOSS: (*refers now to his notebook*):
He said he "desired them to disperse and go peaceably and quietly home to their families".

MR LITTLEDALE:
Did you hear him say anything more?

MR MOSS: (*closing his notebook*):
I did not.

MR LITTLEDALE:
What opinion did you form upon the Defendant's conduct?

MR MOSS: (*turning to address the Jurors directly*):
I considered his conduct to be of the very highest, in advising the men assembled there to disperse and go quietly home.

Mr Littledale allows a slight pause to let the weight of the Special Constable's last remark to sink in before continuing.

MR LITTLEDALE:
Pray, did you see him go off the field?

MR MOSS:

I did not. I never stirred from my place.

MR LITTLEDALE:

During the time you were near enough to hear Mr Hanson speak, did you hear him say any thing about supporting the Spinners and Weavers with three thousand pounds?

MR MOSS:

I did not.

MR LITTLEDALE:

About Nadin and his 'faction'?

MR MOSS:

I did not.

MR LITTLEDALE:

Did you hear him say that, if they would stick to their cause, they would gain their ends, or to that effect?

MR MOSS:

No.

MR LITTLEDALE:

Did you hear him say any thing about six shillings in the cut, or that there was room for it?

MR MOSS:

I did not.

MR LITTLEDALE:

Or, any thing about six shillings in the pound?

MR MOSS:
I did not.

MR LITTLEDALE:
Now, if such words had been used, do you think you should have heard them?

MR MOSS:
I could not have missed to have done so.

MR LITTLEDALE:
If you had heard them, you would have remembered?

MR MOSS: (*tapping his notebook*):
Yes.

Still beaming, Mr Moss stands down.

......

Mr John Seddon is sworn in. He is of a small and wiry build, with narrow pointed features, not unlike a Jack Russell terrier, an impression further strengthened when he speaks, his voice resembling a series of short, sharp barks.

MR LITTLEDALE:
You are Mr Hanson's groom, are you not?

MR SEDDON:
Yes, sir.

MR LITTLEDALE:
How long have you lived in his service ?

MR SEDDON:
From nine to ten years, sir.

MR LITTLEDALE:

When you reached St George's Fields with your master, there were a great number of persons assembled there?

MR SEDDON:

There were.

MR LITTLEDALE:

Were they armed with any weapons?

MR SEDDON:

I did not see any, sir.

MR LITTLEDALE:

Do you remember seeing the Cavalry?

MR SEDDON:

I do.

MR LITTLEDALE:

Were *they* armed?

MR SEDDON:

Yes, sir. They carried sabres and some of 'em had pistols or muskets.

MR LITTLEDALE:

Were they formed in a line?

MR SEDDON:

Yes, sir. In a line, and my master rode up to speak to them.

MR LITTLEDALE:

What did your master say to them?

MR SEDDON:

He asked where the Commanding Officer was.

MR LITTLEDALE:

Did the soldier tell him?

MR SEDDON:

He told him he was in the rear.

MR LITTLEDALE:

What said your master to the Officer in Charge?

MR SEDDON:

He bowed to him, but I cannot say what was the first word he spoke. I heard him ask him, if he would allow him to speak to the people, but the Officer said he would not and my master was ordered out of the Fields. A large quantity of people gathered round him. They seemed to wish to hear what he had to say.

MR LITTLEDALE:

Did your master then address them?

MR SEDDON:

He did.

MR LITTLEDALE:

What did he say?

MR SEDDON:

He said, "If they had any regard for their king, any regard for their country, any regard for themselves, or for him," they would "disperse quietly and go home."

MR LITTLEDALE:
Did the people make any answer to that?

MR SEDDON:
They said they would.

......

George Bluntson is sworn in. He wears a dark coat, whose shoulders are dusted with flakes of dandruff, rather like a less than pristine snowfall. This less than pleasant aura enveloping him is further exacerbated by regular bouts of violent sneezing which threaten to overwhelm both him and the Court.

MR LITTLEDALE:
Mr Bluntson, where do you reside?

MR BLUNTSON: (*sneezing*):
In Salford.

MR LITTLEDALE:
What are you?

MR BLUNTSON: (*sneezing a second time*):
An Officer of Excise.

MR LITTLEDALE:
How long have you been such?

MR BLUNTSON:
For twenty-five years.

MR LITTLEDALE:
Do you remember, on the twenty-fifth of May, being in St. George's Fields?

Mr Bluntson threatens to sneeze a third time. The entire Court holds its collective breath in anticipation, only for Mr Bluntson to avert the eruption at the last moment with a smile of relief that radiates across his face in a way reminiscent of a pale winter sun breaking through a cloudy sky for a moment - the Court breathes a cautious sigh of relief - only for darker thicker clouds to scud across it once more.

MR BLUNTSON:
> I do. I met with a friend, who asked me to go, out of mere curiosity.

The postponed third sneeze now explodes, louder than the first two combined.

MR LITTLEDALE:
> What time did you get there?

MR BLUNTSON:
> A little past three o'clock.

MR LITTLEDALE:
> Did you see Mr Hanson come on the ground?

MR BLUNTSON:
> I did, sir.

MR LITTLEDALE:
> Where did Mr Hanson first go, when you saw him?

MR BLUNTSON:
> Opposite the ring, where the Delegates and Magistrates were together.

MR LITTLEDALE:

Did you lose sight of him?

MR BLUNTSON:

I did. I lost sight of him for about five minutes.

MR LITTLEDALE:

What was he doing when you saw him again?

MR BLUNTSON:

When I saw him again, he was come up towards the road, and the people surrounded him.

MR LITTLEDALE:

What did you hear him say, then?

MR BLUNTSON:

As soon as I got up, I could not understand what he was about. The first thing I heard him say, was that he "felt for the Spinners' and Weavers' sufferings as much as any man", and then he said that he "hoped they would consider the badness of the times", for he was "sure the manufacturers were suffering a little", as well as they were. Therefore he had to beg they would "do nothing against the laws of the country", and "put confidence in their Delegates", who he was "sure would do everything in their power" to get their "distresses relieved". He begged they would go to their respective homes. He then had further to observe that his "father was a Weaver", and he too "a Weaver born", and that the property he enjoyed had "come from the Weavers", therefore he was "in duty bound to be their friend", which they might depend upon it he "always would be", whenever it was in his power. There was then a loud huzzah!

Mr Bluntson finishes his oration with a loud "huzzah" of his own, which action causes yet more clouds of dandruff to rise about him, so that for a moment the Court resembles more a Mill, the air being choked with cotton dust, requiring not just Mr Bluntson but members of the Jurors and Public Gallery to sneeze in chorus.

......

Mr. Edward Shepley is sworn in.

MR LITTLEDALE:
Where do you reside?

MR SHEPLEY:
On London Road, Manchester.

MR LITTLEDALE:
What are you, pray ?

MR SHEPLEY:
A clock and watchmaker.

MR LITTLEDALE:
Did you in the course of the day see Mr Hanson in St George's Fields?

MR SHEPLEY:
Yes, I did.

MR LITTLEDALE:
You were there all day?

MR SHEPLEY: *(checking his pocket watch as he answers)*:
I was. Between the hours of eleven and four. Excepting the time I left to get dinner, which was between twelve-thirty and one.

MR LITTLEDALE (*suppressing a tiny smile*):
Did you see him come onto the Fields?

MR SHEPLEY:
I did not, sir.

MR LITTLEDALE:
But you did see him there?

MR SHEPLEY:
I did. That would have been a little after a quarter of three of the clock, sir.

MR LITTLEDALE:
Did you hear him address the people in the Fields?

MR SHEPLEY:
I heard the noise, sir, and I turned my head, and I saw a quantity of people drawing towards the Lane, I went towards them, and Mr Hanson, who began to address the people.

MR LITTLEDALE:
Were you near him then?

MR SHEPLEY:
Yes, sir, within ten or twenty yards.

MR LITTLEDALE:
Did you *hear* him address the Weavers?

MR SHEPLEY:
Spinners and Weavers, yes.

MR LITTLEDALE:
  Yes. On horseback?

MR SHEPLEY:
  Yes. He said, "I have been ordered out of the Fields, and I have obeyed that order." He said he was exceedingly sorry for them, sorry their bill was thrown out, but he begged they would continue to be peaceable and quiet, and he begged they would disperse, and go quietly home. He endeavoured to convince them that that was the most proper of ways to attain their ends.

Mr Cockell rises to cross-examine.

MR COCKELL:
  What was your business there?

MR SHEPLEY:
  I went, seeing a parcel of Weavers pass from Stockport.

MR COCKELL: (*in a kindly if perplexed tone*):
  But you are not a Weaver yourself. What had you to do with the Delegates raising their wages?

MR SHEPLEY:
  I had nothing at all to do with it.

MR COCKELL: (*shaking his head*):
  I admire your candour, sir.

......

Mr. C.B. Stennett is next sworn in. He takes the stand furtively looking over his shoulder, almost as if he fears he is being followed. His eyes dart this way, then that. His discomfort is extreme. He would clearly rather be anywhere other than where he now is.

MR LITTLEDALE:

I understand you live upon your own property in Manchester?

MR STENNETT:

I… I do, sir.

MR LITTLEDALE:

Do you remember Lieutenant Trafford coming up to Mr Hanson?

MR STENNETT:

I do, sir.

MR LITTLEDALE:

I believe, Mr. Stennett, you did not happen to hear what Lieutenant Trafford said?

MR STENNETT:

I did not, sir.

MR LITTLEDALE:

But you did see him address himself to Mr Hanson?

MR STENNETT:

I did, sir.

MR LITTLEDALE:

But you did not hear what he said?

MR STENNETT:

I did not, sir.

MR LITTLEDALE: (*trying his best not to display any exasperation, for trying to extract answers from this witness is proving more difficult than pulling teeth*):
Did you hear what *Mr. Hanson* said in reply?

MR STENNETT: (*reluctantly*):
I did, sir.

MR LITTLEDALE:
Would you mind relating to the Court what it was you heard Mr Hanson say in reply to Lieutenant Trafford?

Mr Stennett pauses, screwing his eyes tightly shut in an effort to recreate the scene in his memory. He pauses for what seems an inordinate length of time. Eventually Mr Littledale is impelled to give a small cough.

MR LITTLEDALE:
Well, Mr Stennett?

MR STENNETT: (*in a single rushed breath*):
Mr Hanson said, "I thought you had known me better – I respect, you know, your family much – than to suppose I should come here for such a purpose as to breed a Riot."

(He exhales loudly with relief).

MR LITTLEDALE:
Did Mr Hanson at that time say any thing more to Lieutenant Trafford?

A look of great pain passes across Mr Stennett's face, which is suddenly replaced with a relieved smile as he remembers.

MR STENNETT: (*practically shouting*):
Yes! He said, "I came here to assist in *quelling* one!"

……

Mr John Carr is sworn in.

MR LITTLEDALE:
Mr. Carr, you are Collector of Excise for the Division of Manchester, are you not?

MR CARR:
I am, sir.

MR LITTLEDALE:
Had you the curiosity to go into St. George's Fields, on the twenty-fifth of May last?

MR CARR:
Yes, sir, I was there.

MR LITTLEDALE:
Now, when you got there, how did you find things?

MR CARR:
There were a great number of people there. They appeared to me of many different classes. (*He turns directly towards Mr Justice Goose, whom he addresses with confidence*). The people, My Lord, whom I took to be Spinners or Weavers, were on what is called St. George's Lane, the road to Shude Hill.

MR LITTLEDALE:
How did they appear to be, quiet or tumultuous?

MR CARR:

They were standing still, all of them.

......

Charles Satterthwaite, Esq. is sworn in.

Mr Littledale is now replaced by Mr Williams to put the case for the Defence. Where Mr Littledale was precise, Mr Williams appears distracted and bumbling. He has a habit of misplacing important papers – or seeming to – and forgetting where he has put his spectacles, which are invariably on the top of his head. He has even been seen apparently asleep at his desk. However, the witness who mistakes this absent-mindedness for vagueness of mind would be unwise to do so, as many in the past have found to their cost, as indeed have opposing Counsel. This disarming tendency always to desire to put his witnesses at their ease conceals a razor-sharp ruthlessness when required, not unlike a fisherman, who sits immobile at the riverside for hours at a stretch, only to spear his unwitting victim, who believes he is swimming safely beneath the surface unseen, with no threatening shadow looming on the horizon, with a sudden, nerveless precision.

MR WILLIAMS:

Mr. Satterthwaite, you, I believe, were in Manchester on the 25th of May last?

MR SATTERTHWAITE:

I was.

MR WILLIAMS: (*as if surprised almost*):

Excellent. State as nearly as you can, what you heard Mr Hanson say?

MR SATTERTHWAITE: (*clearing his throat, then declaiming in a booming voice*):

"I have one request to make, which I hope you will not refuse."

MR WILLIAMS (*in a mock recoil*):

My word, Mr Satterthwaite, one might almost imagine you are on St George's Fields at this minute and are trying to make us hear you all the way from there to here in Lancaster. Perhaps you might confine yourself to a description of events, rather than attempt a re-enactment of them. Pray, continue.

MR SATTERTHWAITE: (*sotto voce*):

He seemed to be playing with the people, to bring them into good humour.

MR WILLIAMS: (*now cups his ear with his hand*):

Alas, we appear to have veered from one extreme to the other. A metaphor indeed for this troublesome case. Perhaps we may now adopt a happy medium?

MR SATTERTHWAITE: (*at last assuming a much more acceptable volume*):

There were some females present, scattered among the men. As a consequence he said, "The ladies, I am sure, will grant my request, for I have always found them more polite than the gentlemen," at which remark there was a deal of laughter, "and I have most particularly to request, that you will all go home. Your remaining here can answer no purpose whatsoever, and I beg and entreat you to disperse." He then rode away.

MR WILLIAMS:

Thank you. I am sure the Jurors will agree with me – hardly

the words or tone of one who stands accused of inflaming passions or inciting tumult.

......

Mr Joseph Oliver is sworn in. He is a Commercial Traveller. He carries a large bag with him to the stand, almost as if he hopes he might get occasion to display his wares to the assembled company.

MR WILLIAMS:
Where do you live, pray?

MR OLIVER:
Hollins Green.

MR WILLIAMS:
Near Warrington?

MR OLIVER:
The same, sir.

MR WILLIAMS:
Ah – a delightful spot. Know you *The Eagle & Child*, a most splendid Inn? I recall a particularly pleasant afternoon there one summer with Mrs Williams...

Mr Justice Goose coughs somewhat querulously, raising an arched eyebrow in the direction of Mr Williams.

MR WILLIAMS:
I beg your pardon, My Lord. Now – where were we?

MR OLIVER:
Hollins Green.

MR WILLIAMS:
Quite. What is your profession, Mr Oliver?

MR OLIVER:
A Commercial Traveller, sir.

MR WILLIAMS: (*observing the bag*):
Yes, so I see. Now, Mr Oliver, will you please be so kind as to travel your way to St George's Fields on 25th of May last. What was Mr Hanson's conduct in the field as far as you saw or heard?

MR OLIVER:
It was that of a gentleman, and a good subject to his King and Country.

MR WILLIAMS: (*echoing*):
A good subject to King and Country.

……

Mr. Norris is sworn in. He is extremely nervous and is visibly shaking.

MR WILLIAMS:
Please do not be agitated, Mr Norris. We are all friends here, I do assure you. You live in Manchester, do you not?

MR NORRIS:
Y-yes, sir.

MR WILLIAMS:
Do you remember seeing Mr Hanson come into St. George's Fields?

MR NORRIS:
I do.

MR WILLIAMS:
Whereabouts did you see him first?

Mr Williams does not answer.

MR WILLIAMS: (*encouraging a response with a circular hand gesture*):
When you were near him…?

Still Mr Norris does not answer.

MR WILLIAMS: (*repeating the gesture*):
Mr. Norris…?

MR NORRIS: (*his reply bursting out in an embarrassed rush*):
I never saw him till he was out in the Lane.

MR WILLIAMS:
Yes, I see. But that will do nicely. Now, so far as you had an opportunity of observing, what did Mr. Hanson's conduct appear to be?

MR NORRIS:
It appeared…

MR WILLIAMS:
Yes…?

MR NORRIS:
It appeared…. that of a friendly adviser.

MR WILLIAMS:
A friendly adviser?

MR NORRIS:
Yes.

MR WILLIAMS:
Advising whom? And to do what?

Mr Norris thinks a moment – a long, agonising moment – before finally answering.

MR NORRIS:
For the people to go about their business and go home.

MR WILLIAMS: (*repeating this last phrase*):
To go about their business and go home.
Now, after Mr Hanson went away, did any of the Spinners and Weavers go too?

MR NORRIS:
A good many went.

MR WILLIAMS:
Are you sure, Mr Norris?

MR NORRIS: (*smiling and nodding vigorously*):
I am confident of it.

MR WILLIAMS: (*smiling and nodding back*):
Thank you. Your witness.

Mr Cockell signals to the reptilian Mr Park, who slithers to his feet and approaches Mr Norris, coldly rubbing his hands together.

MR PARK:
You perceived them to go, you say, these Spinners and

Weavers? Did you perceive them also to throw brick-bats at the soldiers?

MR NORRIS:
  N-no.

MR PARK:
  Did you see *any* misfortune happen?

MR NORRIS: (*so vehemently that his voice threatens to crack*):
  I did not!

Mr Park regards Mr Norris for what seems an eternity through his hooded, slitted eyes before finally sliding back to his seat.

MR WILLIAMS: (*turning to address the Jurors*):
  There was much misfortune that happened that day. But none, I put to you, Gentlemen, caused by the Defendant.

MR JUSTICE GOOSE;
  Might I remind you, Mr Williams, to reserve all your questions and comments for the witness and the witness alone? Kindly refrain from directing any remarks which might be considered prejudicial to members of the Jury, who will ignore and strike out from their memories what you have just so mischievously delivered to them. We have not yet reached Summation, I trust, Mr Raine?

MR RAINE: (*rising hastily*):
  We have not, Your Lordship.

He turns sharply, affording Mr Williams an approving wink as he does so.

......

Mr Kearsley is now sworn in. Mr Littledale, upon a signal from Mr Raine, now resumes his role as Cross Examiner, with his familiar efficiency.

MR LITTLEDALE:
You are a fustian-cutter, I believe?

MR KEARSLEY:
Yes.

MR LITTLEDALE:
Did you go to St. George's Fields on Wednesday the 25th of May?

MR KEARSLEY:
I did.

MR LITTLEDALE:
What made you go there?

MR KEARSLEY:
I went to get a view of my fellow workmen.

MR LITTLEDALE:
I see. When Mr Hanson came up, were there any Spinners or Weavers near him?

MR KEARSLEY: (*proudly*):
Yes, sir. I did see him come into the field, and some did come around him.

MR LITTLEDALE:
Did you hear him say anything to them?

MR KEARSLEY: (*even more proudly*):

Yes, sir. He said, "My father was a Weaver, and he was a well-wisher to the Weavers. As am I. And, as a well-wisher to you all, I urge you to go home."

MR LITTLEDALE:

Was anything else said?

MR KEARSLEY:

Yes, sir. The last words I heard him say were, "And if you are well-wishers to your King and Country, Gentlemen, as I am, disperse and go to your own homes."

......

Mr John Speerit is next sworn in. As he makes his way to the stand, he carries with him the distinct – and somewhat overpowering – aroma of rotting fish. Mr Justice Goose cannot disguise his displeasure or disgust, visibly wrinkling his nose and turning his back upon him.

MR LITTLEDALE:

You live in Manchester, I believe?

MR SPEERIT:

I do.

MR LITTLEDALE:

What are you?

MR SPEERIT:

A porter.

MR LITTLEDALE:

In the markets?

MR SPEERIT:

Yes, sir – fish, fowl, vegetable, fruit, wherever there's call.

MR LITTLEDALE:

How near were you to Mr Hanson, when he came upon the field?

MR SPEERIT:

He rode right past me. I was standing on the road side.

MR LITTLEDALE:

Were there people about you?

MR SPEERIT:

There was a large ring of people.

MR LITTLEDALE:

Did Mr Hanson stop there, or did he ride on?

MR SPEERIT:

He rode on towards the Cavalry.

MR LITTLEDALE:

How near were you to him then?

MR SPEERIT:

I touched him at the time. On the shoulder and the back.

Mr Justice Goose once more visibly shudders as he imagines this outrage upon his own person.

MR LITTLEDALE:

Was he upon his horse at the time?

MR SPEERIT:
  He was.

MR LITTLEDALE:
  What did he say on this occasion?

MR SPEERIT: (*leaning forward, the Jurors simultaneously reeling backwards*):
  He particularly requested the people to attend to what the Magistrates said, as they were the only people to apply to. He particularly requested them to be peaceable and quiet, if they persisted in meeting.

MR LITTLEDALE:
  Did you hear him say any thing else then?

MR SPEERIT:
  No, I cannot recollect that I did.

MR LITTLEDALE:
  Were you close to him the whole of this time?

MR SPEERIT:
  I was very nigh unto him.

MR LITTLEDALE:
  What was Mr. Hanson's conduct on the ground during the time you were there?

MR SPEERIT:
  Very fine, sir, as far as I judged.

As Mr Speerit leaves the Court, one of the Attendants opens as many windows as he can, which, even on this cold February day, does not draw a single contrary comment.

......

Mr James Brocklehurst is sworn in. He has grey hair, is softly spoken, with a quiet dignity.

MR LITTLEDALE:
Where do you reside?

MR BROCKLEHURST:
At Hayfield in Derbyshire.

MR LITTLEDALE:
What are you ?

MR BROCKLEHURST:
I was lately a Cotton Spinner, but am now in no business at all. I have retired since last May.

MR LITTLEDALE: (*inclining his head in a small bow of acknowledgement of this fact*):
Did you hear Mr Hanson address the people?

MR BROCKLEHURST:
Yes, sir, I did.

MR LITTLEDALE:
What did he say to them?

MR BROCKLEHURST:
To the best of my recollection, sir, he addressed the Spinners and Weavers and said that he looked upon them to be a distressed people, whose claims he believed to be just. He had not a doubt but there would be something done for them. He exhorted them to conduct themselves peaceably and quietly, and as long as that was the case he, Mr Hanson, was their friend.

MR LITTLEDALE:

> The Court is most grateful, Mr Brocklehurst. May you have a safe journey back to Derbyshire and there may you enjoy many years to come of peaceful retirement.

......

Mr John Brierley is sworn in. He has a tape measure loosely draped around his neck, with several pins attached to the lapels of his jacket.

MR LITTLEDALE:

> Mr. Brierley, I understand you are an upholsterer residing in Manchester?

MR BRIERLEY:

> I am, sir.

MR LITTLEDALE:

> Did you hear the Defendant address the people? If you did, will you be so good as to tell us accurately what you heard him say?

MR BRIERLEY:

> He was speaking at the time when I arrived. He was saying, "Gentlemen, I respect you and I have a right to do so." He then mentioned something of his father having accumulated a property by the endeavours of the Spinners and Weavers. He next said, or the next I could understand, for the people who surrounded him were moving from place to place, he said, "I am sorry you have lost your Bill, but, for God's sake, let not that precipitate you to any acts of violence." After that he had got into the rear of the crowd and I was not able to ascertain anything exactly as to what he particularly said, but I heard him frequently say, I am sure, "For God's sake be peaceable."

MR LITTLEDALE: (*endeavouring to intervene and cut the witness short*):

Did you hear him say anything about their going home?

MR BRIERLEY:

I do recollect him saying something as to their dispersing. I do believe he said so…

Mr Littledale gestures somewhat helplessly towards Mr Cockell, who smiles back indulgently, benignly rising to his feet.

MR COCKELL:

I am sure the Court is most entertained by the evidence you have just purported to have given us, Mr Brierley, although I use the word 'evidence' with a certain elasticity, for there is much embroidery in the telling of it, sir. "You believe," you say. "To the best of my recollection," you add. "Not able to ascertain exactly," you protest. "But I heard him frequently, I am sure," you speculate. "You do recollect him saying something or other," you conclude. Come, come, Mr Brierley, this will not do. I am sure your measurements when carrying out your occupation of upholstery are much more precise than this. Otherwise you would cease to retain a single customer. Now please, I entreat you, did or did not what you say you think might have occurred actually take place or not?

MR BRIERLEY: (*somewhat lamely*):

To the best of my recollection, yes, sir. I believe it may.

……

Alexander Patterson is sworn. The amiable Mr Williams takes over once again from Mr Littledale.

MR WILLIAMS: (*smiling*):

Mr. Patterson, you keep *The Bridgewater Arms*, in

Manchester, I understand, a hostelry with a fine reputation?

MR PATTERSON:
Yes…

MR WILLIAMS:
Mrs Williams and I once had the great pleasure of sampling one of your excellent steak and ale pies…

Unfortunately, the remainder of Mr Patterson's testimony has succumbed to the ravages of Mus Musculus or Rattus Rattus.

……

MR JUSTICE GOOSE: (*pointedly looking at his watch*):
Do you have any more witnesses, Mr Raine? *Tempus fugit,* does it not?

MR RAINE:
Just one, Your Lordhip, with your indulgence.

MR JUSTICE GOOSE:
Very well. After which we may adjourn for the day.

MR RAINE:
Your Lordhip is, as ever, in the right of it.

Call Amos Lees.

CLERK OF THE COURT:
Call Amos Lees…

Amos has been waiting outside the Court throughout the entire day, the roughness of his appearance having dissuaded the Attendant from granting him entry, who, even when confronted with the irrefutable evidence of Mr Ambrose's Letter of

Invitation to Amos to attend, has been so discomfited by its creased and grubby aspect that he is still reluctant to accept the right of Amos to be there at all. Accordingly, he has been instructed to wait until his 'credentials' have been verified. He has been waiting all day.

Now, as his name is called, he feels fear and apprehension. He has not eaten or drunk in more than two days and is feeling faint with fatigue. The high interior walls of the Crown Court within the imposing grounds of Lancaster Castle tower above him, threatening to close in and topple down upon him at any moment. The various heraldic beasts on the dozens of shields and escutcheons and coats of arms, the lions, leopards and eagles, gryphons, wyverns and unicorns, seem to be rearing up and snarling all around him, their eyes aflame, their nostrils breathing fire. His mouth is dry, his lips parched, his head pounding, and his skin grey with a cold sweat, He cannot think what he is doing there. He simply does not belong...

Amos is sworn in. Mr Raine now resumes his role as Cross-Examiner, referring to notes hastily assembled for him by Mr Ambrose.

MR RAINE:

You are Mr Amos Lees, now a handloom weaver of Elton, formerly a worker at Oldham's Felt Factory, and before that an itinerant labourer?

AMOS:

I am, sir.

MR RAINE:

And on the 25th of May last, you were present at a meeting held on St George's Fields to petition for a basic minimum wage?

AMOS:

That is correct, sir.

MR RAINE:

Did you see the Defendant, Mr Hanson, at this meeting?

AMOS:

I did, sir.

MR RAINE:

Did you hear him speak to the assembled masses, of which you were one?

AMOS:

I did not, sir.

Mr Raine raises a surprised eyebrow.

MR RAINE:

Explain.

AMOS:

There was too much noise, sir, and I were too far away to make out what any o' t' speakers might be saying.

MR RAINE:

Was this because there was a riotous tumult occurring which prevented you?

AMOS:

No, sir. There were no tumult, sir. Just a lot o' people shoutin' that they could not hear but that they wished they might.

MR RAINE:

I see. At what point, then, did you see Mr Hanson and what was it that you saw him do?

AMOS:

It were after t' soldiers had driven us down t' Lane, sir.

MR RAINE:

St George's Lane?

AMOS:

Yes, sir.

MR RAINE:

And why were they thus driving you?

AMOS:

I couldn't say, sir. One moment we were all tryin' to get nearer to t' speakers, an' t' next there were horses chargin' towards us.

MR RAINE:

Did the soldiers draw weapons?

AMOS:

They did, sir. They carried sabers, which they whirled above their 'eads, sir, an' which they then aimed directly at us.

MR RAINE:

Do you know why the soldiers rode towards you in this war-like manner?

AMOS:

I do not, sir. Someone must've ordered 'em.

MR RAINE:

And who do you suppose that might have been?

AMOS:

I couldn't say, sir.

MR RAINE:

Had the Riot Act been read before they so charged?

AMOS:

I don't know, sir. But if it were, I din't hear it. I'm sure nob'dy did.

MR RAINE:

And the Defendant? It was at this time you say you saw him?

AMOS:

Yes, sir.

MR RAINE:

Please, Mr Lees, in your own words, tell the Court exactly what happened next?

AMOS:

The people were panicking, sir. We were bein' kettled into t' narrow lane alongside t' Fields, an' there were just too many of us, so that some people fell an' were trampled on. Then Mr Hanson, 'e rode out from a different direction, tryin' to head off t' soldiers, make 'em turn round an' go back, so we could all leave more freely, wi'out bein' pressed an' harried so.

MR RAINE:

What happened next?

AMOS:

It were no use, sir. For all 'is efforts, there were just too many of 'em. 'Is 'orse reared up an' 'e were thrown off, but 'e were up again in a flash, goin' among us, helpin' those 'e could. It were then that I saw 'im close up, sir, assistin' me wi' Adam, another weaver, who were dyin' in me arms…

Mr Raine allows a suitable pause before continuing.

MR RAINE:

How would you describe Mr Hanson and the actions you saw him carry out that afternoon, Mr Lees?

Amos thinks a moment before answering.

AMOS:

A kind-hearted gentleman, sir, who was looking out for t' labouring man, an' tryin' to 'elp us, sir.

MR RAINE: (*turning towards the Jurors*):

A kind-hearted gentleman. So kind, in fact, Gentleman, that at great risk to his own personal safety, he strode into the path of the oncoming Dragoon Guards who, sabres raised, were charging towards him, in order to assist a dying man caught up in the chaos and confusion. Do these sound like the actions of a man inciting a mob to violence, or to those of a Good Samaritan, trying to bring succour and aid where it was most needed?

Thank you, Mr Lees. Your witness.

Mr Cockell rises languidly from his seat, rubbing his chin thoughtfully.

MR COCKELL:

I am sure the Court would wish me to extend its sympathies

towards the loss of your friend, Mr Lees.

AMOS:
Thank you, sir.

MR COCKELL:
I say "*would* wish me to" under advisement, for is it not also the case, Mr Lees, that this friend you describe died, not because he was somehow caught up in a panicking crowd and accidentally crushed, but because he was shot, quite deliberately, by one of these charging soldiers – these 'war-like' soldiers, to borrow an epithet from my learned friend, one more true than he could have realised when first he coined it, for this is a War, Gentlemen of the Jury, between the forces of Law and Order and those of Treachery and Sedition, between those who would seek to bring about peace and harmony in society, working towards the common good, and those who seek only to bring about its ruin and destruction?

There is a collective gasp around the Court. Amos looks anxiously towards Mr Raine, then Mr Hanson.

MR COCKELL:
Come now, man, you must answer the question.

AMOS: (*inaudible, bowing his head*):
Yes, sir.

MR COCKELL:
You will need to speak louder, Mr Lees, for the Court cannot hear you.

AMOS: (*raising both his head and his voice*):
Yes, sir.

MR COCKELL:

And why was he shot?

AMOS:

I couldn't say, sir.

MR COCKELL:

Really? You couldn't say?

AMOS:

No, sir.

MR COCKELL:

Could it perhaps have been because this same man had some seconds earlier hurled a large brick at the oncoming soldier – an officer who was merely doing his duty to try and bring about a peaceable dispersal of this unruly mob of which you, Mr Lees, and your friend were a part – and that this same brick – this missile, this projectile – did kill the valiant, innocent horse upon which this most diligent and conscientious officer was riding?

Amos lowers his head once more.

MR COCKELL:

The Jurors will note that the witness says nothing by way of refutation. For there is nothing he *can* say. It is the truth. Inflamed by the words and actions of this so-called 'kind hearted gentleman' – *he gestures witheringly towards the Defendant* – this witness's co-conspirator acted with malice aforethought in a deliberate and treasonous attempt to deal a murderous death to one of His Majesty's loyal and obedient officers and almost succeeded. This is the true nature of the man who stands before you, Gentlemen, and this – *he now points contemptuously back towards Amos* – is his legacy, his spawn, his brood.

I have no more questions.

Amos stands shaking in the dock and he has to be led away by one of the Court Attendants. Mr Raine puts his head in his hands. Mr Hanson attempts to catch the eye of Amos before he leaves, to offer him a look of reassurance and gratitude, but is unable to do so.

MR RAINE: (*trying to put on a brave and dignified face*):
My Lord, that concludes the case for the Defence.

MR JUSTICE GOOSE:
Which, as I hinted earlier, I take to be a most convenient point at which we might adjourn proceedings till tomorrow, when we shall hear final summings-up from Counsel. Unless you have any objections, Mr Cockell?

MR COCKELL:
None, Your Lordship.

MR JUSTICE GOOSE:
Till tomorrow then. At ten o'clock. (*He raps his gavel smartly*).

CLERK OF THE COURT:
All rise.

On this occasion it is Mr Raine, who anxiously gathers his Assistants to him, while Mr Cockell walks serenely from the Court.

*

Day 3: Friday 24th February

CLERK OF THE COURT:
  All rise.

MR JUSTICE GOOSE:
  Mr Cockell, are you ready to submit your reply to Mr Raine?

MR COCKELL:
  I am, Your Lordship.

MR JUSTICE GOOSE:
  Pray, proceed.

Mr Cockell faces the Jurors, beaming his most avuncular smile upon them.

MR COCKELL:
  Gentlemen of the Jury, although this case has occupied a very considerable portion of your time, and although my learned friend has produced a great many witnesses on behalf of his client, it appears to me that at this moment the case substantiated against the Defendant is as clear as the sun, and, if I do not very much mistake, I declare that the testimony which has been delivered by the several witnesses who have been adduced on behalf of Mr Hanson, instead of tending even in the least degree to prove his innocence, shows manifestly his guilt, and that he is an artful and designing man, who, having found himself detected in one character, was, by the assumption of another, attempting to screen himself from observation.

Mr Cockell complacently places the fingers of each hand beneath the lapels of his robe – a characteristic gesture of his, much recognised by those who follow his cases, and occasionally imitated by those of his assistants wishing to ingratiate themselves into his favour – and proceeds to pace up and down the Court.

Gentlemen, it has been stated that Mr Hanson is one of the most amiable men in the world, that his character is that of the benevolent kind Christian, who pities and alleviates the distresses of his fellow-creatures; nay, that he is one of the most loyal subjects in the country, and that if the time arrives when his assistance shall be required, you will see this daring, valiant man advancing at the head of His Majesty's troops to vanquish the foes of his country. If Mr Hanson ever held these sentiments, I am sorry he has abandoned them. I am sorry my learned friend referred to acts of former times. If Mr Hanson has performed any services to his country heretofore, he has certainly by his present misconduct consigned them to oblivion.

He turns from the Jurors to indicate Mr Raine with his right arm outstretched.

My friend passed an high *eulogium* on Mr Hanson's father, who, I dare say, might well deserve it. I lament that such a father has had so degenerate a son, and that that son has forgotten his former virtues, and has become so disaffected and dangerous a subject to his country.

With a neat one-hundred-and-eighty-degree swivel, he now stretches out his left arm towards the Defendant.

It has been said that Mr Hanson has not been well treated, that he deserved a better fate. But, if Government had suffered Mr Hanson to escape without inquiry, it might be charged upon them that they were only singling out *poor* individuals for punishment, while they permitted a great and daring offender to violate the laws of his country with impunity. This prosecution of Mr Hanson, therefore, in its effects, will be worth ten thousand such, of men of a lower order. If Mr. Hanson at any time deserved the *eulogium* my learned friend gave him, I must take it that some disappointment has rankled in Mr Hanson's heart, and that whatever his affection at one time was towards Government, when he fell from his proud eminence, his mind changed with his situation, and that though once his country's determined friend, he has now become its determined foe.

He returns to the centre of the Court, speaking to the Public Gallery as well as the Jurors, numbering off in turn each of the points he now makes.

Let us now see what has been charged against Mr. Hanson. That a number of the unlawfully striking labourers had unfortunately conspired in times of distress and misery in order to raise their wages; that they assembled, as we have heard, to the amount of many thousands, and determined to have their demands complied with, or to remain on the place where they were then met, and be shot to death.

It is said, that Mr. Hanson endeavoured to quell the mob; that he endeavoured to disperse them; that he came from his home with that laudable view and purpose – a friend to his King and Country, a foe to Misrule and Riot – and that he conscientiously set out with a view to quell the disturbance, to assist in dispersing the people, and to tell them it was best to defer their deliberations to a future period. The evidence, however, contradicts this view, evidence which the Defence have not in any credible way been able to produce. Oh, there have been many fine words spoken, but these do not signify one farthing, for there is not one tittle of evidence to disprove the charge on which the Indictment stands. And it is through *evidence*, Gentlemen, and evidence alone, that you must reach your verdict, a verdict which can be nothing other than Guilty.

He walks purposefully towards the Jurors and faces them directly.

Gentlemen, I have done my duty, and a painful one it has been. But it is a duty which has been imposed upon me, and I felt myself bound to discharge it. If Mr Hanson could have manifested his innocence, I should have been the first man to have rejoiced at it. But the laws of England, as it has been well said, are like the sun. 'They shine alike on rich and poor.' Mr Hanson, from his rank in life, ought to have known better than to have plunged himself into this transaction. Most serious mischief might have been the result of his interference, and, if mischief had followed, Mr Hanson must have considered himself the author of it. The present is a case of peculiar importance in this great county, and if men of power come forward and lend their support for the purpose of fomenting Riot, they ought to be the first to suffer the consequences.

He points an unyielding finger in the direction of the Defendant, fixing him with a fierce glare, before softening his tone, turning back to the Jurors, leaning intimately upon the rail behind which they sit.

Gentlemen, I think I have made out the case, and I do not now retract the expressions I used at the onset. I am unknown to Mr Hanson, and he is unknown to me. I have no motive in what I have offered to you but to discharge my duty between the King and the Defendant. Feeling, as I do, that the case on the part of the prosecution suffers no imputation from the evidence that Mr Hanson has adduced, I sit down with perfect confidence, and in the most ardent expectation, of receiving your verdict that Mr Hanson is Guilty as Charged.

Mr Cockell bows formally to the Bench before resuming his seat with supreme slowness.

MR. JUSTICE GOOSE:
Gentlemen of the Jury, this is an Indictment against Mr Joseph Hanson, charging him with a misdemeanor. The Indictment states – *and here he refers to the official papers* – 'that certain evil-disposed persons having assembled in a riotous and tumultuous manner, in great numbers, for the purpose of compelling their masters to advance their wages, the Defendant, Mr Joseph Hanson, did unlawfully and wickedly encourage them in that Conspiracy, Riot, and Tumultuous Meeting, which they had been guilty of, by using certain expressions to them, encouraging them to proceed in that illegal manner, and in prosecution of their unlawful purpose'.

He puts down the papers and speaks directly to the Jurors with painstaking deliberateness, as if to reluctant pupils in a school room.

This, Gentlemen, is the nature of the charge. It is undoubtedly a most serious charge, because if the Defendant attended for the purpose of assisting these rioters, there can be no doubt that he is highly culpable, and it will be for you to consider, upon comparing the evidence which has been delivered, whether you are convinced that charge has been brought home satisfactorily.

That a very great number of persons did assemble on the twenty-fourth and twenty-fifth of May, there can be no doubt; and that they were so collected together for the purpose of procuring an advance of wages, which they said at that time were not sufficient, is equally indisputable. It is also clearly proved in evidence, that the situation in which they were on the twenty-fourth and twenty-fifth of May, was considered by the Magistrates at that time in Manchester to be so serious as to call for the interposition of the Military, and that they had consequently attended on the twenty-fourth and again on the twenty-fifth, the twenty-fifth being the day upon which Mr Hanson is charged with having conducted himself in the manner stated in the Indictment.

The question then for your consideration will be whether he did so encourage them or not; whether he was, as the Defence claims, persuading them to disperse; or whether he was, as the Crown avers, encouraging them to persevere in their illegal conduct. For the purpose of making it clear to you which of the evidence is permissible and which you therefore may consider, and which of it is not and which you shall therefore disregard, I shall now re-state what I believe to be the salient points of the case.

Here Mr Justice Goose repeats in summary the evidence presented by both sides, in which he is at pains to point out the discrepancies in status of those witnesses brought by the Crown with those presented by the Defence.

Gentlemen of the Jury, you must now compare the evidence and, upon taking the whole into consideration, say whether you are satisfied that Mr Hanson addressed the people for the purpose of encouraging them to continue in that state of tumult. If you are, the charge is made out, and you must find him guilty. If, on the contrary, you think the expressions he uttered were not of that nature, and that he did not use any with the intention to encourage them in rioting, and if you think you can fairly ascribe the words to another motive, you will acquit him.

You have heard from a great number of witnesses over the course of the last two days. Those called by Mr Cockell have offered one version of events, those called by Mr Raine another. Each has been consistent with the perspective they separately represent. However, I put it to you to consider the rank and position of those who have testified before you. For the Crown you have heard from a Boroughreeve, a Deputy-Constable, a Magistrate, a Lieutenant of the Dragoon Guards, while from the Defence you have heard from a Fustian Cutter, a Fish Market Porter, a Commercial Traveller, an Upholsterer, a Groom and a Publican. I leave you to draw your own conclusions.

Mr Justice Goose shakes his head querulously at this thought, takes a deep breath, then addresses the Jurors once more with undisguised directness.

One final question, I feel, is incumbent upon me to put to you, and I would be failing in my duty if I did not do so.
If a gentleman of Mr Hanson's rank wanted to do all that he could to abate the tumult, we must be surprised, must we not, that he seems never to have joined with the Magistrates in concerting proper measures for that end? This observation is made for your consideration, and you will find Mr Hanson either guilty, or not guilty, as you are satisfied his conduct was intended to allay or *encourage* the disturbance.

*

After less than one hour, the Jurors return.

274

CLERK OF THE COURT:

Gentleman of the Jury, have you reached a verdict on which you all agree?

WILLIAM FITZHERBERT BROCKHOLES (*Jury Foreman*):

We have.

CLERK OF THE COURT:

Do you find the Defendant guilty or not guilty?

MR BROCKHOLES:

Guilty.

There is a gasp from the Court, followed by a mixture of cheers and boos, from the different sets of supporters, which Mr Justice Goose immediately quells with several sharp raps of his gavel upon the bench.

MR JUSTICE GOOSE:

Thank you, Gentlemen. May I take this opportunity to thank you for your loyalty to His Majesty. It is a verdict with which I concur completely.

He now turns his attention towards the convicted man.

Mr Joseph Hanson, you have been found guilty of the charges as set out in the Indictment. It now befalls me to pass sentence. I have been advised by your Counsel, Mr Raine, of several *affidavits* from respectable gentlemen in Manchester, all of them testifying to your good character over a period of many years: Mr Francis Astley, a former military officer from Dukinfield; Messrs William Nabb, Joseph Kershaw and William Shaw, gentlemen; Mr John Whitehead, calico dyer, Mr Edward Rushton, wine merchant, Mr Gavin Hamilton, surgeon, Messrs Richard

Hancock and Thomas Millington, cotton merchants, and Mr William Cowdrey, printer, all from Manchester. However, these can in no way mitigate the extent of your guilt, as pronounced by a jury of your peers.

These affidavits, which he has been holding up for the Court to see, he now lets drop to the Bench.

When we contemplate what is stated on these *affidavits*, the story is hardly credible that a respectable person in society, as your witnesses represent you to have been, the friend of Trade, brought up to it, and a friend to the Spinners and Weavers, as you represent yourself to be, should be so disposed to encourage such a tumultuous assembly of discontented men, the attainment of whose object must in the end be pernicious to themselves, to their employers, and to society at large.

He now turns his attention to the whole Court for the following part of his address. Journalists from several newspapers, including The Times, can be seen furiously scribbling his every word.

It is a material benefit to every rank of society, that manufactured goods should be sold at as reasonable prices as are consistent with enabling those who produce them to purchase provisions by their manual labour; because if by his labour the artificer cannot earn what is sufficient for the daily support of himself and family, he will cease to labour in that line of commerce, and will resort to another. It is necessary that he should receive what is called a fair living profit. I am not the first to say this. Nor shall I be the last. But if they receive *more* than that, it very often promotes intemperance and idleness, and prevents that quantity of goods from being produced, which otherwise would have been.

This last remark is greeted with a mixture of cries of "Hear, hear!" and "Shame!" from various factions within the Public Gallery. Mr Justice Goose is forced to wait until the brouhaha has died down before he can continue.

It is advantageous to *all* ranks of persons that commodities should be brought to market in as *great plenty* as possible, and that, once they have been brought there, they should be sold as *cheaply* as possible. But if the manufacturer be forced to pay unreasonable wages, he must sell the commodity at an enhanced price. And when this is effected by numbers of men assembled in breach of the peace, in a great manufacturing town like Manchester, it leads to the destruction of the trade of the Spinners and Weavers, of those very men who hope to be enriched by it. It is in breach of the peace, and in violation of those laws, which, being necessary for the support of society, must be sustained.

He here raps his gavel several times for emphasis and to forestall any subsequent possible outburst, whereupon he turns his attention back solely towards Mr Hanson.

Your rank and situation in life is an *aggravation* of your offence, for you must have known what the consequences of such proceedings by you were likely to be. It is our duty to check this by example, to enforce the law, and to teach men, while their lives may be supported by the law, that it is improper to support an assembly in violation of that law, and that he who has done so must be punished. In order therefore to prevent the repetition of such crimes, this Court, taking all the circumstances of your case into our consideration, doth order and adjudge, that for this offence

277

you do pay a fine to the King of One Thousand Pounds; and that you be henceforth committed to the custody of the Marshal of this Court, escorted to the New Bailey Prison in Manchester, and there imprisoned for Six Calendar Months' Hard Labour.

He brings down his gavel one last time.

Having so heard the sentence of the Court, is there anything you now wish to say?

MR HANSON: *(whose countenance is pale and trembling, rises to his feet)*:
My Lord, the consciousness of my innocence will support me under the present judgement, or any other that Your Lordship might have been pleased to pronounce.

MR JUSTICE GOOSE: *(contemptuously)*:
Take him down.

CLERK OF THE COURT:
All rise.

Mr Raine shakes the hand of Mr Cockell and then proceeds in the direction of Mr Hanson, who stands with head bowed. On his Counsel's approach, he merely shrugs and spreads his hands. Mr Raine detaches his buttonhole of the lily and the laurel leaves, which he duly fastens into the top coat of Mr Hanson, who is then led away.

4

Manchester Observer

30th September 1809

DISGRACED EX-COLONEL RELEASED

GRATEFUL CROWDS LINE STREETS TO GREET HIM

Hundreds of supporters and well-wishers gathered outside the New Bailey Prison yesterday to welcome Mr Joseph Hanson on his release from a sentence of six months with hard labour for his alleged role in inciting the crowds of striking Cotton Spinners and Weavers in St George's Fields in May of last year.

This newspaper has always believed Mr Hanson to be innocent of such charges and maintains that our esteemed Authorities set out to make an example of the former Colonel of the Salford & Stockport Independent Rifles as a means to deter the populace from mounting any similar such demonstrations in pursuit of the much-needed Reforms that this newspaper will continue to campaign for.

Mr Hanson emerged from his ordeal much diminished physically. His face and form appeared harried and gaunt, as well they might, given the cruelties imposed upon him, and other prisoners alike, confined within the New Bailey's notorious dungeons. But his visage and demeanour were surely heartened by the rousing reception on his re-entry into society as a free man. Representatives of the Spinners and Weavers, whose cause he has so valiantly espoused, were on hand to present Mr Hanson with a commemorative service of glasses upon a silver salver, purchased from moneys raised by public subscription.

Upon receiving this magnificent token of just how highly he is held within the affections of the Common Man, who have shown through the generosity of this gift the gratitude they feel for his brave and selfless acts of valour and heroism on their behalf, Mr Hanson thanked the assembled crowd in a dignified and moving address, after which he was given three hearty cheers. We at *The Manchester Observer* now add a resounding fourth!

It is perhaps not insignificant that Mr Hanson's release should coincide with St Michael's Day – or, to give it its full title and nomenclature, The Feast of St Michael & All Angels – commemorating those highest, most revered servants of our Lord, the Archangels, who fought against Lucifer and those other rebellious angels who sought to supplant the Ruler of Heaven, but who found themselves cast down into the everlasting flames of that other place.

If the Boroughreeve and Magistrates thought to make a comparison here with the actions of Mr Hanson and his supporters, in attempting to subvert and overthrow the current *status quo*, perhaps they would do well to remember that other important tradition associated with St Michael's Day, hitherto known as a Holy Day of Obligation, when, after the time of the harvest, the Bailiff or Reeve of the Manor would be making out the Accounts of the Year. Such accounts, this newspaper believes, would make for interesting reading, and we would remind the Authorities that the Feast of St Michael & All Angels is the day when all outstanding accounts must be settled, for it is also then, traditionally, that the Peasants would elect the Boroughreeve's successor.

Among the crowd that day, adding his own voice to the three loud and long cheers that greeted Joseph Hanson upon his release, is Amos. He has not spoken to Hanson since the day Adam died in his arms, but Hanson spots him in the throng, seeks him out directly, puts his hand in his.

"I have not forgotten your kindness in offering to speak for me as a witness," he says.

Amos thanks him, but adds, "All I did were to make matters worse, for which I am most truly sorry."

Hanson shakes his head. "Not at all. They're slippery fellows, these lawyers. Too tricky for the likes of you and me. I'm grateful to you for taking the trouble you did."

"And I for you for trying to come to Adam's aid."

"Adam? He was your friend?"

Amos nods.

"A terrible thing."

Amos agrees but says nothing, for what is there that he could add?

"Do you have work?" asks Hanson.

Amos replies that he does.

"Good," he says. "That's good. We all of us need to work. It will be our salvation. What is it Monsieur Voltaire says?"

Amos shrugs that he doesn't know.

"*Il faut cultiver notre jardin*," Hanson adds with a thin smile, but before he can translate this for Amos, he is swept away by more of his admiring supporters, after which he will withdraw completely from the world, his spirit broken, to tend his garden.

Also present in the crowd that morning is Mr Carlton Whiteley, who has been invited by Mrs Sophia Hanson, to "present something suitable for the importance of the occasion". Never one to turn down a challenge, Carlton has pressed Mrs Hanson for further details.

"Something to remind the world of my son's innocence."

Carlton immediately warms to the theme. "If it is something to stir the blood, set the pulse a-racing, fire the spirit of indignation in the hearts of the people, move the ladies to tears, then look no further than the Bard, Madam. He has something for every occasion and I, Mr Carlton Whiteley, am your man to present it. 'If you have tears, prepare to shed them now'," he booms, and this at once gives him an idea.

"Whatever you think best, Mr Whiteley. We must let the Authorities know that we are not beaten just yet."

While at the same time not risking arrest ourselves, thinks Carlton, bowing low before his new benefactress and kissing her gloved hand. We are not as young as once we were, and we know we could not survive a term of hard labour in the New Bailey. "We must choose something that the Authorities cannot take exception to," he says aloud, straightening himself back up again not without difficulty, each bone in his back complaining noisily, "yet at the same time be clear to every person present exactly where our sympathies lie."

"Quite so, Mr Whiteley. I am not as educated as you are. I do not know my Shakespeare. But I do know this. It will catch the Boroughreeve off his guard. He will not be expecting something like this. And he can hardly arrest an actor, can he? For the words he speaks are not his own."

Carlton inclines his head modestly. Little does she know, he thinks. We actors have ever been harried as rogues and vagabonds. Many has been the night he has spent in a County Gaol in his younger days as a Strolling Player.

"Nor Mr Shakespeare," Mrs Hanson continues, "who's been dead nigh on two centuries."

With that the two part company amicably, satisfied that a bargain has been struck. A fee has been agreed – one which Carlton might, in former times, have haggled over, but these days beggars can't be choosers.

The truth is, reflects Carlton, these past five years have not been kind to those pursuing the dramatic arts. Mrs Whiteley abandoned him directly after they had finished their *Romeo & Juliet*, fleeing to the fleshpots of London in a barouche with that damned lothario, Ponsonby, taking with her not only the takings for the week's run, but the remainder of her inheritance too, so that Carlton has found himself both cuckolded and bankrupted at a single stroke, the latter weighing far more heavily with him than the former, while his *protegée*, Miss Appleby, too, has deserted him, for the more lucrative but less artistically fulfilling roles to be found at the new *Theatre Royale* on Fountain Street, managed by that upstart Macready.

> *"And many strokes, though with a little axe,*
> *Hew down and fell the hardest-timbered oak…"*

Carlton smiles, in spite of himself, in remembrance at this, his first spoken lines upon the stage, as the Messenger in the Opening Scene of *Henry VI, part 3*, when but a callow youth. How many more strokes has he been forced to endure since then? Yet still this oak survives, he thinks, hard-timbered and much ravaged by many blows of axes great as well as little. He is not ready to surrender the field just yet, for even *"the smallest worm will turn, being trodden on,"* he declares, narrowing an eye and clenching a fist. He had uttered these words too, in that same production, as Lord Clifford, the Lancastrian military leader during the Wars of the Roses and the killer of Rutland, the 3rd Duke of York – this had been a touring production, with actors taking on multiple roles. He had worn a patch, he recalls as the embattled Lord, to distinguish him from the earlier Messenger…

He finds himself drifting off into reminiscence mode. Were he in a tavern now, with the younger actors sitting at his feet like acolytes, Miss Appleby among them, hanging off his every word, the ale flowing freely, he might have been tempted to launch into more stories of his own first forays wherein he has "*suited the action to the word, the word to the action, with such special observance that he o'erstepped not the modesty of nature*". But such days are over now, his company disbanded, scattered to the four winds, which do indeed "*shake those darling buds of May*", while the early onset of a troubling gout perforce must curb his liking for a good claret.

"You must try to live a more temperate life," his Doctor had scolded.

Carlton had smiled back politely, immediately tempted to riposte. " *'Good wine is a good familiar creature'*," he had said, " *'if it be well used'*."

"Quite possibly," his Doctor had replied, "but I fear you have not been using it well."

"Why sir, for my part I say, this gentleman '*hath not yet drunk himself out of his five senses'*."

"But he shall if he does not desist soon."

"What? Dost thou not think '*because thou art virtuous there shall be no more cakes and ale'*?"

" *'Drink, sir, is a great promoter of three things – nose-painting, sleep and urine…'* "

"And lechery, sir. Let us not forget lechery. '*It provokes and it unprovokes. It provokes the desire but takes away the performance…'* "

"You speak, sir, as if from experience."

Sadly this was something with which Carlton had had to concur. He cannot now recall the last time he did the act of darkness. Is it not strange that desire should so many years outlive the performance? He has been persuaded but disheartened, been made to stand to and not stand to. Yet still he is driven on by the flesh and finds he must go where the devil drives. But what's his offence? Groping for trouts in a peculiar river? No – for that is but the pleasure of a moment.

" *'Thus momentary joy breeds months of pain.*

Thus hot desire converts to cold disdain'."

"In that case, sir, I suggest you have answered your own question, diagnosed your own malaise."

"Sir?"

"Work, sir. Work for some is a distraction. But for others, like one of your disposition, for whom work is a calling…"

"… an art –"

"– quite… it is their means of salvation."

"Thou'rt i' th' right of it, sir!"

" *'A quarter pound of reason, a half a pound of sense, a small sprig of time, and as much of prudence…'* "

" *'No sooner knew the reason but they sought the remedy'.*"

It is his art that will cure him of his malady, that will give him far more lasting satisfaction and fulfilment than the glance of a pretty girl, her shapely ankle or her comely hip, the thought of resting his head upon her snow white breast, the meeting of their lips – no, these are but the fleeting pleasures of the moment, the shallow fripperies of those comedies now being offered by Mr Macready at his *Theatre Royale*.

Daily he walks about the town, surreptitiously tearing down the playbills for Mr Macready's new theatre, with its silly comedies, like *Rosina*, by Miss Frances Brooke – in which Miss Appleby no doubt excels, with her sighs and simpers, but will be forgotten in a moment – or lavish spectacles designed to keep the populace amused.

Bread and circuses.

Like the playbill he now sees before him pasted to a lamp post, which he contemptuously tremoves. Back in his meagrely furnished lodgings above the Riding School he unfolds where he has scrunched and torn it, smoothing out its creases to study it more closely.

THEATRE ROYALE
Fountain Street, Manchester

All the New Favourite Pieces
(Now performing in the London Theatres)
are in preparation
and
will be brought forward with all possible Expedition

This present FRIDAY 29th September 1809
Their Majesties' Servants will act Mr Sheridan's Tragic Play

PIZARRO & THE PERUVIANS
With Battles – Executions – Scenes of Human Sacrifice

To which will be added Mrs Inchbald's Polite Comedy
THE WEDDING DAY

Featuring Manchester's Sweetheart
Miss Appleby
In the role of Hannah

" *'Thus conscience doth make cowards of us all',"* he muses somewhat ruefully. "There but for the grace of God go we all."

If this request to present something to the people by Mrs Hanson to coincide with the release of her son is indeed to be Carlton's final performance, his swan song, let it be something worthy of the name of it, something to go down in the annals, something that will linger long in the hearts of all who are present to witness it, something that will propel them '*to take arms against a sea of troubles, and by opposing end them…*'

His instinct tells him it needs to be something classical. He thinks of Thespis first stepping out of the chorus to provide the people with a voice, brandishing his staff decorated with a branch of laurel. Yes, that is who he will emulate, somebody timeless, universal. He thinks how often he has longed to

286

present *Coriolanus*. Could this finally be its moment? Has its hour come at last? Something apocalyptic, revelatory?

"And the temple of God was opened in heaven, and there was seen in his temple the ark of his testament: and there were lightnings, and voices, and thunderings, and an earthquake, and a great hailstorm…"

Alas, no. He is too old to play the great warrior, and he is now but a company of one. If not Coriolanus, what then? Another Roman play?

And there, by the light of his last candle in the bare room above the Riding School, in the lee of the Actor's Bridge, at the foot of the twenty-nine wooden steps leading down from the *Ring o' Bells Tavern*, Carlton Whiteley has his Damascene moment of Epiphany. For once he will not be trying to tempt the people to enter his theatre, he will not have to stoop to base spectacle, as Mr Macready does. Instead he will be taking the theatre to the people. They will already be there, a captive audience. He will present his *Julius Caesar*, or rather, an extract of it. The steps leading up to the Outer Gates of the New Bailey Prison will be his Capitol. The crowds awaiting the release of their hero will be citizens of Rome, Mr Hanson will be their Pompey, and he, Mr Carlton Whiteley, will be Marullus.

Now, as the crowd calls for those three rousing cheers for Joseph Hanson, Carlton prepares to make his entry. Standing beside one of the four radiating arms of the New Bailey Prison's octagonal design, he throws a toga over the respectable fashions of the day – brown knee-length breeches worn over white stockings, a darker brown tailcoat cut high over the breeches, a white collar turned up with a blue ruffled cravat tied at the neck, leather shoes with a gold brass buckle and a felt top hat – to his mind perfectly capturing both the classical heritage of the play combined with its contemporary message.

At precisely the moment that the echoes from the final cheer are dying away, he strides purposefully forward, mounts the steps of the Capitol in his imagination, directs his gaze firmly in the direction of the Boroughreeve, the Deputy-Constable, the Magistrates and the Soldiers all in anxious attendance, and delivers the beginning of his oration directly to them.

"You blocks, you stones, you worse than senseless things!
O you hard hearts, you cruel men of Rome,
Knew you not Pompey?"

Here Carlton gestures towards Hanson, a graceful sweeping action with a pleasingly elegant line. He is relieved to discover that his craft has not deserted him, nor the power of his voice to command an audience as great as this, in an amphitheatre as vast.

"Many and time and oft
Have you climbed up to walls and battlements,
To tow'rs and windows, yea, to chimney tops,
Your infants in your arms, and there have sat
The livelong day, with patient expectation,
To see great Pompey pass the streets of Rome..."

He has them now, his years of experience tell him this, and he is able to speak almost in a whisper, as if in private intimacy with each individual present, as he parades a bewildered Joseph Hanson through the Square towards where the Authorities are stonily mustered.

"And when you saw his chariot but appear,
Have you not made an universal shout,
That Tiber trembled underneath her banks
To hear the replication of their sounds
Made in her concave shores...?"

At this point, the crowds, which must number in their thousands, answer as one, with a mighty roar, echoing their approval for Carlton-Marullus, as they stand beside the teeming Irwell which, in their imagination, has now transformed into the Tiber.

Encouraged by their response, Carlton walks directly up towards the Boroughreeve and Magistrates, even at times plucking them by the sleeves of their garments as he proceeds to mock and berate them.

"And do you now put on your best attire?
And do you now cull out a holiday...?

He turns suddenly to the crowds below him –

"And do you now strew flowers in his way..."

– then just as swiftly wheels back towards the Magistrates.

"... that comes in triumph over Pompey's blood?
Be gone!"

He senses a restlessness among the Soldiers mounted on horseback, itching to receive orders to ride amongst the people and disperse them. The horses stamp and snort, shaking their huge heads from side to side and up and down. The sunlight bounces off their riders' helmets, spurs and sabres. For the moment the Boroughreeve stays his hand, but Carlton knows when a house is on the edge of a riot, he has played to such audiences before, and he knows that in times such as these it is best to quit while he's ahead. He must quicken his pace, and so he builds towards his pre-planned climax.

Turning away from the Authorities and hurrying down the Prison-Capitol steps back towards the People of Manchester-Citizens of Rome, he delivers his final lines as a defiant call to arms.

> *"Run to your houses, fall upon your knees,*
> *Pray to the gods to intermit the plague*
> *That needs must light on this ingratitude."*

Although no order appears to have been given, the Cavalry now begins to advance as one, slowly but menacingly towards where Carlton still speaks, his tone even quicker and more urgent than before.

> *"Go, go, good countrymen, and, for this fault,*
> *Assemble all the poor men of your sort;*
> *Draw them to Tiber's banks and weep your tears*
> *Into the channel, till the lowest stream*
> *Do kiss the most exalted shores of all."*

With that, he runs directly into the arms of the crowd, who hoist him onto their shoulders, at the same time several others lifting Joseph Hanson likewise, so that the two of them are borne aloft around the perimeter of the New Bailey Prison, to the joyous accompaniment of *'For He's a Jolly Good Fellow'*, the origins of the song, though perhaps not known by those who sing it so loud and lustily, not lost upon the classically educated Mr William Starkie, Boroughreeve of Manchester, who knows it was first sung by the French peasantry as an attack upon the British Crown after the Battle of Malplaquet.

> *"Marlborough s'en va-t'en guerre*
> *Marlborough s'en va-t'en guerre…"*

"Why did you not give the order for the Cavalry to charge?" demands Nadin after the crowds have all dispersed. "We could have arrested Hanson a second time."

The Boroughreeve merely smiles.

"Think of this as but a dress rehearsal," he says. "The final act is yet to be played out. When it is, we must be ready."

"Don't worry," replies Nadin. "We shall be."

"Of that I have no doubt," says the Boroughreeve. "Nor need you concern yourself with Hanson. That man is finished. He shall not trouble us again. Now – there is just one more thing. That actor…"

"Carlton Whiteley."

"Revoke his licence."

"No sooner said than done, sir."

Well, thinks, Carlton afterwards, when news of the Boroughreeve's decision reaches him, if indeed our revels now are ended and that is to be my final performance, then so be it. He stands alone before the mirror in this bare room, empty except for memories, which serves as salon, bed chamber, dressing room and cell, and makes a much practised, deep bow before it.

> *"As you from crimes would pardon'd be*
> *Let your indulgence set me free."*

He pours himself a glass of less than fine claret – a sacrifice, but needs must – and drinks a toast to his disapproving Doctor, who hovers always on the edge of his vision.

" *'Good wine is a good familiar creature'*," he whispers to his reflection in the glass, then adds with a wink, " *'if it be well used'*." And he downs it in a single draught.

The lines drawn between theatre and life, the playhouse and the world, have grown so blurred as to become practically indistinguishable. Mr Shakespeare has once again been the perfect teacher, holding up a mirror to life, as he has always done, while he, Mr Carlton Whiteley – his humble talent "*an ill favoured thing, but mine own*" – has been his ever obedient pupil.

> *"A poor player that struts his hour upon the stage*
> *And then is heard no more…"*

TWO

Ophelia

1813 – 1814

in which a lover's quarrel leads to tragedy –
a river freezes over –
and the piece of cloth becomes temporarily lost

5

1813

16th December

'Lord, we know what we are, but not what we may be…'
(Ophelia, *Hamlet*: Act IV, scene 5)

An unnatural dark lay over the town. A low, heavy sky smothered it like a shroud. Snow had been falling in a thick sludge for days. Black as coal, it froze where it fell. Great slabs of ice clogged the Rivers Irk and Irwell, which not even the *Sarah Lansdale* could force a way through. People slithered and skittered across the greasy streets, clutching at walls and railings as they edged their slow, treacherous way towards their different destinations. If they needed to venture into an open square, they would cling to each other instead. They sought hand- and finger-holds in every nook and crevice, as if attempting to scale the most vicious of mountain peaks, rather than merely trying to cross a near-deserted street.

Three individuals looked out at the frozen world that late Thursday afternoon simultaneously from three separate rooms. Each of them felt something crackle in the air around them, as three different clocks tolled four of the clock on a day that had never properly grown light. They involuntarily shivered, as though a ghost had walked across their graves.

Matthew, Robin, Lavinia.

*

Matthew put on his coat and hat, wrapped a thick scarf around his throat, wrested from its stand in the hallway his silver-topped walking cane and stepped outside. Even though the chances of seeing her were slim on such an afternoon as this, he dared not risk missing her. Just in case. This recent daily ritual had quickly become a compulsion, a pattern he knew he must on no account break, like the willow pattern dishes and plates that hung on the dresser in the hall, which had been his mother's pride and joy, and which one day, shortly after Fanny had announced her intention to be married, he had snatched one of and hurled it against the wall in his fury, smashing it into a thousand tiny pieces. He had been made by his father to collect every single one of those pieces, fit them all together like a jigsaw, till the plate was complete. Then his father had paid a ceramicist to glue the pieces back together, expertly, so that the plate had become whole again, but the cracks were still there if you knew where to look, and Matthew saw them everywhere.

The plate may have been his mother's heirloom to him – an heirloom he chose not to recognise, for his mother was not his mother, just as his father was not his father, he was nobody's child, a foundling, a bastard – but it was Fanny who had explained its meaning to him. Fanny, whom he idolised above all others, but who had, like his false parents, betrayed him too, when she had left to marry that upstart of a surveyor. It was Fanny who had helped him put the broken pieces back together.

"It's a story," she had said. "Look – canst tha' not see? There's a big house, a palace, wi' a high wall all around it. It belongs to a wealthy gentleman, a merchant and magistrate, called a Mandarin…"

"Man-da-rin…" Matthew had rolled the unfamiliar word around his tongue. He liked the sound of it.

"He built this high wall," continued Fanny as she found the appropriate shard of pot, "because he had a daughter he wanted to protect. She'd fallen in love wi' a young man who worked on 'er father's estate, who 'er father did not think was suitable, so 'e built the wall…"

"To keep him out?" Matthew had interrupted.

"Aye," said Fanny, "and to keep her in. The Mandarin 'ad planned for 'er to marry someone of 'is own choosing, a rich Duke, who were travellin' by boat for t' wedding, which were to take place just as t' blossom fell from t' willow tree."

She now held up a piece of the plate depicting the tree. Matthew studied it, engrossed.

"The young man sneaked 'is way into t' palace disguised as one o' t' Duke's servants," she continued. "He an' t' daughter then stole away, over this bridge – dost tha' see…?"

Matthew nodded that he did.

"The Mandarin chased after 'em wi' a big whip, but they escaped in t' Duke's boat, to a secluded island, where no one could find 'em…"

"And lived happily ever after, I suppose," sneered Matthew. "I'd have preferred it if the Mandarin and the Duke had followed them to the island, arrested and executed them with a cross-bow." He mimed pulling back an invisible draw-string and letting loose an imaginary arrow, making a whooshing noise as he did so, then pretending to die a grisly death.

"Don't be cruel," scolded Fanny. "That's like pulling t' wings off a moth."

The corner of Matthew's mouth drooped. Nothing mattered more to him than winning Fanny's approval.

"As it 'appens," she said, "tha's not far wrong. In some versions o' t' story, they do catch up wi' 'em, an' kill 'em just like tha' showed, but t' Gods take pity on 'em and turn 'em into love birds – see?" And she held up two fragments of the broken plate which she had joined together, depicting a pair of doves cooing in the willow tree. "They even wrote a nursery rhyme about 'em." She looked down upon her crestfallen charge. "Wouldst tha' like to 'ear it?"

Matthew nodded.

"Right then," she said. " 'Ere goes…"

She proceeded to sing the rhyme, complete with actions made with her hands.

"Two birds flying high
A stately ship sailing by
A bridge, a girl, two men who love her
A willow tree, whose leaves hang over
They cast a shadow on the lake
The two must escape before it does break…"

Before opening the front door, Matthew made himself go back upstairs, retrace his footsteps to his bedroom, draw back the curtained recess beside the fireplace and gaze upon the portrait of Mercy. He had not looked upon it in almost a decade, and in truth he did not need to. Every brush mark was etched as finely into his mind as they were into the canvas, but the expression in her eyes still had the power to stop him in his tracks, to torment him, fixed upon the caged bird, yearning to escape. He drew the curtain roughly across to cover it once more and hastened back downstairs, past the mended willow pattern plate, which had not been taken from its cupboard for even longer than it had been since Matthew had looked upon Mercy's portrait. Not since his false mother had died more than a decade and a half ago. These daily walks to catch a glimpse of his new obsession – Lavinia, whose name he had learned from certain enquiries he had made, discreetly, in such a way that might arouse no suspicious thoughts in those he asked – he saw as a path towards exorcism, towards redemption.

He stepped outside. The cold knifed through him instantly. The icy chill clutched his heart. He welcomed it. This 'big freeze', as the newspapers were calling it, which had sent the population of Manchester scurrying indoors like frightened mice, had woken him up. He pulled the scarf from his mouth and breathed deeply the contaminated air. He strode boldly out onto the ice, not caring whether he slipped or not.

Lavinia.

"Big Sister, Little Mother,
Faithful Daughter, Friend and Lover…"

So goes the nursery rhyme that has danced around Lavinia's head ever since she can remember. Today she plays the role of Schoolteacher.

"Good afternoon, children."

"Good afternoon, Miss Robinson. Good afternoon, everybody."

"Today is the last day of term before the Christmas holiday. Hush now, children. Fingers on lips. Before you leave, I want you all to make sure you have tidied your desks, handed in your compositions, and finished your drawings of the pressed flowers we collected during Nature Studies last autumn – the pansies, violets, rosemary and rue. Good. Now – who would like to read their selected Bible verse to the rest of the class?"

A forest of hands shoots up. Lavinia smiles down upon their eager, shining faces, seeing in them a mirror image of herself when she was their age, just a few years before.

"Very well." She closes her eyes, spins gracefully round once, then points. "Harriet," she says, opening her eyes once more.

Those who have not been picked briefly murmur their disappointment, but only for a moment. The slightest of furrowed brows from Lavinia is enough to quell them instantly and they settle at once to listen to Harriet, the oldest of the children, whose last day at school this is, who will be leaving to begin work in Jacob's Milliners the following week, and who is loved almost as much as Lavinia – Miss Robinson – herself.

"It is taken from Isaiah, Chapter 43, Verse 19," says Harriet. " *'Behold, I will do a new thing; now it shall spring forth; shall ye not know it? I will even make a way in the wilderness, and rivers in the desert'.*"

"Thank you, Harriet. That's a good lesson for us all – to think about how we might do a new thing every day and try to make the world a better place. Let us all say together the words of our school motto." She points with a ruler towards a plaque beside the blackboard where the words have been stitched into a sampler, by Lavinia herself, when she was just eight years old and had not long arrived at the Moravian Settlement in Fairfield, which she had hung upon the classroom wall on her return, with the help of Billy, her older brother, who fixed it with the aid of the nail his late father, Zachary, had left to him, that first nail made by Zachary's grandfather, Caleb, and passed down the generations since.

"Wisdom is the principal thing. Therefore get wisdom and within all thy getting get understanding. Exalt her and she shall promote thee. She shall bring thee to honour when thou dost embrace her. She shall give to thine head an ornament of grace. A crown of glory shall she deliver to thee."

After the children have dutifully recited the words, they stand in readiness for another ritual they go through at the end of each day. Lavinia moves to the piano to play the school hymn by Charles Wesley, and the children open their mouths wide like baby sparrows in their nest, waiting to be fed.

"Father, I stretch my hands to Thee
No other help I know
If Thou withdraw Thyself from me
Ah, whither shall I go…?"

Their innocent voices rise up into the air just as the first snowflakes begin to fall outside.

"Now off you go, children. Quietly please. Fingers on lips. I shall see you all again at the start of our next term. Until then, a very Merry Christmas."

"Merry Christmas, Miss Robinson."

Lavinia waits until the last child has gone, briefly savouring the silence which has descended upon the now empty classroom…

Ever since her mother died, nine Christmases ago, Lavinia has tried to hold true to the promise she made to her, to be a little mother to her seven brothers and sisters, even though she was not the oldest of them. Both Billy and Susannah were older, but they had other, different strengths. She did not return to Fairfield, but she never forgot the deep pleasure and satisfaction she had derived from the school for girls there, the first such anywhere in England, which taught her, as well as her reading, writing and arithmetic, that girls should expect no less than boys when it came to receiving a proper education, and that they should set their sights no less high. She is reminded of this again now, as she sits among the quiet of the school room, pondering another verse from Isaiah, which she had first learned at Fairfield.

" *'For I the Lord thy God will hold thy right hand, saying unto thee, Fear not; I will help thee'.*"

And He had held her hand, and she had felt helped, and, by and large, she feared nothing.

When, four Christmases later, Zachary, her father, followed his beloved Fanny, their mother, to the grave as inevitably and certainly as water will find its way through the most solid of rocks, it was Lavinia's older sister, Susannah, the practical one, who first came up with the idea.

"We need to find a way of earning more money," she had said. "Billy gladly tips up all his postman's salary, and Lemuel does the same, but he's still only prenticed to Mr Byrom, Father's old boss at the Surveyors' Office, so he doesn't bring home that much. Richard and Paul are still too young, as is Jemma, while Ginny…"

"… lives in as a maid at Ordsall Hall and gets no other pay than her keep. I know this, Su. What are you saying?"

Susannah eyed her sister squarely. "You're clever. You always have been. That's why Mother and Father sent you away to the Moravian School at Fairfield."

Lavinia blushed and looked down.

"You loved that school. I know you did. And I know how hard you found it when you had to leave. So – what I'm saying is: why don't we open one ourselves?"

"Where?"

"Right here."

Lavinia's jaw dropped, but before she could say anything, Susannah ploughed straight through any possible objections she might have tried to raise. "I've already thought how we might rearrange the rooms in the house to create the space. I can picture exactly how it might be. *'The Robinson Academy for Young Girls'*. Principal and Head Teacher: Miss Lavinia Robinson."

Lavinia's amazement had turned to excitement and in no time at all the two sisters were giggling in each other's arms, delighted by the prospect of it.

Now, four years later, that gleam in Susannah's eye had become a reality. What's more, it had become a success. They had eighteen pupils, all of them girls, each paying a modest sixpence a day for the privilege. This amounted to half a crown a week per pupil, which in turn added up to two pounds and five shillings regularly coming into the household for forty weeks a year. This brought the family an extra ninety pounds income per annum. They were not rich, but they were comfortable. Susannah managed the house, Lavinia the school, while Ginny was able to hand in her notice at Ordsall Hall and assist both as required. Lemuel completed his apprenticeship and set out along the same road his father had done, even using the same surveyor's instruments of theodolite, compass and tripod he had inherited from him, completely at ease with talk of triangulation, parallactic angles and meridian arcs, while Jemma enrolled as a pupil in the school, where she happily endured the close and rigorous attention applied to her by her two older sisters in their capacity of teacher and classroom assistant, neither one of whom displayed any outward sign of favouritism towards her, but who glowed with pride inside at her hard-earned progress.

On Sundays, after the whole tribe of them returned from the Chapel on Mosley Street, they sat down to a meal of roast pork and vegetables, presided over by Billy, recently promoted to Deputy Post Master at the service's depot on Spring Gardens. In less than twenty years the Manchester Postal Office had come a long way. Back then, at the start of 1793, the entire service had been managed by one old woman, Mrs Sarah Willatt, together with her daughter and a solitary letter carrier, the first such anywhere in England, decades before the Uniform Penny Post. Now an ever growing web of deliveries and collections was carried out by an army of spiders, people like Billy, who scurried their way across the whole of the town and its outlying villages and hamlets. James Harrop, the son of the printer of *The Manchester Mercury*, now headed the service, at the same time ensuring that the denizens of Manchester could readily avail themselves of that organ's increasingly pro-Establishment, anti-Reform views. Billy did not concern himself with politics. He saw what he did in much simpler terms, enabling more and more people to keep in touch with one another. He enjoyed being a welcome and recognised figure in other people's lives. At the same time he was growing more comfortable with each passing month in his role as Head of the Robinson Household, hardly crediting their rise in good fortune, and wondering just what their absent parents would have made of their unexpected prosperity.

"Maybe they wouldn't regard it as that unexpected," Susannah would say as Billy carved the meat. "Maybe they would simply see it as a promise fulfilled."

"Mebbe," replied Billy, whose talk was less refined than his sisters had become. "Any road up, I wish they were 'ere now to witness it an' share in't."

"Oh, but I think they are," said Ginny earnestly, her eyes shining, "don't you? I feel them sitting here beside us this very minute."

Jemma looked anxiously over her shoulder as her sister said this. She wished more than ever her mother and father were back with them – especially her father, whom she missed so much it hurt her sometimes simply to breathe, while she didn't really remember her mother, she was too young, and this would always make her feel guilty – but the thought of ghosts hovering behind her while she tried to eat her Sunday lunch filled her with alarm. Richard and Paul, the twins, teased her mercilessly. They'd started to do this more and more since they became Bluecoat Boys at Humphrey Chetham's School a few months ago, and they began to make a series of phantom shrieks and moans, until Lavinia gave them her sternest schoolmistress look, which silenced them instantly.

Susannah watched her sister carefully. She was not her usual self these days, she thought, and she suspected she knew the reason for it.

"Will Mr Holroyd be coming to pay a call this afternoon, Lavinia?"

The twins giggled behind the backs of their hands.

"I really couldn't say," said Lavinia, pulling herself out of her reveries. "Perhaps. Perhaps not…"

Lavinia is thinking about Mr Holroyd now in the silence of the school room. Robin. He has been paying her closer and closer attention lately. He has asked if he might call on her this very evening, when he finishes his work at the Lying-In Hospital, where he is an *accoucheur*. He has enquired as to whether Billy might also be at home, and if not, at what time he might be expected.

"Why do you wish to know?" she had said when he first raised this, half guessing what the answer might be.

"I need to ask him a question," he had said, and then added, stammering somewhat over his words, "b-but I sh-shall n-need to ask y-you something f-first…"

Lavinia had blushed when he said that and looked shyly away. She finds she is blushing again now, just in remembering it. Not that she requires Billy's permission for anything, least of all something like this. For today marks not only the end of the school term, but the occasion of her twenty-first birthday. Today, she thinks with a smile that dimples her cheeks, I come of age. Though in reality she knows that she came of age the night her mother died nine years before. When she was just twelve. All she is doing today is switching the numbers around.

Matthew had first noticed her following a routine visit to the New Bailey Prison to check on the release date for a particularly troublesome felon on whom it had been his not unpleasant duty to pronounce a term of twelve months' hard labour, a sentence universally deemed too lenient by his fellow Magistrates at the Court Leet and the public at large, but, as he had been at pains to point out at the time, legislation prohibited him from committing him for longer for this particular type of offence – relieving a gentleman of his pocket watch – the tariff stipulated the maximum, by which Matthew's hands had been tied. He could, he supposed, have ordered him for transportation to Van Diemen's Land, but while the War with Bonaparte continued to rage, the Navy needed all the ships it could lay its hands on.

Accordingly he had visited the Prison in the hope that the aforesaid felon, a violent, unsavoury cutpurse by the name of Eli Cross, might perhaps have committed a new misdemeanour while serving at His Majesty's pleasure. Happily, the Prison

Warden informed Matthew, he had only that week been apprehended peddling wipes to the Lady Visitors of a local Penal Reform group. In the normal course of events Matthew had neither time nor sympathy for the causes of the various do-gooders who besieged his office weekly with their letters and petitions, but on this occasion he rejoiced in their reporting of Mr Cross's clumsy attempts to earn some dishonest shillings by exploiting their silly, weak-minded gullibility. He had, as a consequence, been able to post a further six months' extension to the man's sentence and was almost to be found dancing his way along Bridge Street when the sight of Lavinia stopped him quite literally in his tracks.

It was the particular angle of her head, inclined forward as she stooped to attend to one of her charges. She was, he noted, seemingly at the head of an orderly crocodile of almost twenty young girls, all lined up behind her in pairs, walking across the New Bailey Bridge, the smallest at the front, the tallest at the rear. With their hands clasped demurely in front of them as they walked, their neatly beribboned hair bobbed and bouncing, they made a most pleasing sight, almost as if one of the paintings depicting children that were currently all the rage in the courts and salons of Europe had sprung to life before him – Hogarth's depiction of the Graham children perhaps, the daughters of the apothecary to King George II, or John Hoppner's portrayal of the Sackville children, belonging to the 3rd Duke of Dorset, but perhaps the celebrated portrait by Thomas Lawrence, Painter-in-Ordinary to the present King George III, of the eleven-year-old Sarah Moulton, more widely known as *Pinkie*, a copy of which hung in the Drawing Room of the *Manchester Lit & Phil*, where something about the loose, energetic brushwork, combined with the direct gaze of the girl, had given it a vibrant immediacy which had stirred in Matthew a memory of deep loss and longing. Lavinia was at that very moment attending to a young girl who was not unlike Pinkie in complexion and form. She appeared to have lost something and was on the verge of tears. Lavinia, Matthew observed, was both kind and firm in equal measure. She reminded him at once of how Fanny had acted towards *him*, when he had been inconsolable over the loss of his pet cat, Smokey.

Smokey.

Matthew hadn't thought of him in years. Not since he had encountered his feisty, independent offspring in the home of his good friend Laurence Peel. Having survived the balloon flight of Mr Sadler, Smokey had established a new territory among the farms and factories between Holcombe and Summerseat, where now his brood roamed uncontested. Laurence's brother had made quite a name for himself in Westminster. Now a Baronet of Drayton Manor in the County of Stafford, as well as of Bury in the County Palatine of Lancaster, he had successfully introduced the *Health & Morals of Apprentices Act* in Parliament. This, much to the chagrin of men like Laurence and Matthew, required cotton mills and factories to be more properly ventilated (at not inconsiderable expense to the owners), and that apprentices were to be guaranteed a basic education, assisted in attending a religious service at least once a month, and, in addition, were to be provided with free clothing and their working hours limited to a maximum of twelve hours a day. Publicly Matthew supported such enlightened improvements but, following advice from the Brothers William and Daniel Grant, circumvented these strictures by not designating the children they employed as apprentices, thereby avoiding the legal need for compliance.

Matthew pulled himself away from such concerns and focused his attention once more upon the delightful scene still being played out in front of him on the New Bailey Bridge.

The young girl – now entirely congruent in Matthew's mind with Pinkie – appeared consoled. Lavinia stood up and adjusted the shawl which was hung about her shoulders. Matthew's eyes widened in near disbelief. The shawl was the very article that Fanny had worn on her wedding day, that she had taken away with her when she broke her promise and abandoned him.

Lavinia could not have been more than a few feet away from Matthew at this point and so there was no possibility he might be mistaken. She looked at him directly now and apologised if the children had been in any way blocking his path. He was momentarily lost for words. He could not take his eyes away from the shawl, from the fluttering moths caught in the leaves of a laurel.

"Sir?" she said, observing his confusion. "Are you quite well?"

Her voice roused Matthew from his temporary mania.

"Yes. Thank you. It is I who should be apologising, not you, for behaving so oddly and discourteously. Please forgive me."

He raised his silver-topped walking cane to the brim of his beaver felt hat. She made a demure, polite curtsey in return.

"I was," he said, "distracted by your shawl. Such an unusual woven design."

She smiled. It lit up her whole face. She had the most beguiling dimples, Matthew saw. "It belonged to my mother," she replied, "so yes, it is very special to me."

They bade each other a formal "Good day", and Matthew watched her lead her crocodile of young girls along Bridge Street to a house into which they now followed her. Upon further enquiries Matthew learned that this was the premises of a School for Young Ladies and that its proprietress and schoolmistress was a Miss Lavinia Robinson.

Robinson. Yes. That was the name of that damned surveyor, Matthew recalled. I must make further enquiries. He walked back towards Oldham Street swinging his cane like a Dandy and whistling *Lilliburlero*.

Robin.

Robin first saw Lavinia in Acresfield – or St Ann's Square

as the Court Leet insisted it should now be called, though the old name still stuck with most people – on the occasion of the Annual Whitsuntide Fair. It was a case of history repeating itself, though Robin was not to know that. It was only later he learned this, when Lavinia told him, after they had properly met and were out walking together for the first time. On that Whit Monday morning, after Robin had emerged bleary and fatigued from an all night lying-in, she appeared before him like an angel. Dressed from head to toe in white, a garland of spring flowers interwoven with leaves of laurel around her long fair hair, which fell in plaits and braids below her shoulders, she danced with a dozen other similarly clad young women around the maypole in the centre of the green, just like her mother had done more than a quarter of a century before, when Zachary had first spied her through his theodolite from the top of St Ann's church tower. Robin was not in such an elevated position. Rather he was in the middle of the crowds encircling the dancers, pressing to obtain a closer view. And when he caught that first glimpse of her, it was as though scales had been lifted from his eyes and he could only now begin to see.

'Forswear it, sight!
I ne'er saw true beauty till this night...'

Except that it was no longer night, but midday, when the sun was at its highest. Perhaps I am blinded, he thought. But if I am, I do not care.

For the most part Robin inhabited a near permanent twilit world. He was an *accoucheur*, a male midwife, though he preferred the term 'obstetrician', yet if, at awkward social occasions, he was asked about his profession, this last word was barely recognised, so that he found he must resort to what was more readily understood – midwife – at which point an audible frisson would ripple around the room, and he would receive a mixture of expressions from all who were present, ranging from piqued curiosity through visible discomfort to scarcely disguised contempt, especially from the ladies, who would wrinkle their noses at the thought of a man being present at such a frankly intimate transaction, immediately and squeamishly dismissing him as a suitable marriage prospect for any daughter of theirs, so he would rarely be invited a second time. When asked, therefore, he would adopt the French term – *accoucheur* – which was suitably vague, less directly associated with female body parts, and introduce himself as Dr Charles White's assistant at St Mary's Hospital, which had the dual advantage of being both true and more socially acceptable. Now that Dr White had died, however, just a few months before in February, his position was less secure and therefore less clear, and would remain so until a successor was appointed, which was proving troublesome. Dr White had left behind very large shoes to fill.

In truth Robin enjoyed his work for the most part. What could be more rewarding, he thought, than to be the instrument of ushering new life into the world?

"And his skills will certainly prove useful when your own time comes," Susannah had remarked in her usual pragmatic manner, when he and Lavinia had first become more closely attached, just a few short months after this first sighting at the Whitsuntide Fair.

"Let's not rush things," said Lavinia, trying to avoid further discussion of it.

"He was most capable for me when Baby Emma was born last year," continued Susannah, cheerfully unconcerned, while rinsing out her freshly-boiled sanitary rags. The thought of her future husband's hands having been inside her sister's vagina caused Lavinia a momentary unease.

Yet the unease Robin's position caused *him* still rankled and so he had begun to set his sights on becoming a more general surgeon. He hoped such a position might yet open up for him at the Infirmary, but for now he would continue in this twilit role of the *accoucheur*, on hand to deliver babies at all hours of the day and night, for which he received a fee of half a crown per birth. This provided him with a decent enough living of fifty pounds a year, sufficient for him to afford lodgings on Bridge Street, just a five minute walk away from the Lying-In Hospital on nearby Stanley Street.

And now, as he stood enraptured by Lavinia dancing in a ring, he realised he had seen her before. She was a neighbour of his on Bridge Street. He was normally so tired as he traversed its length, returning home after a late night's lying-in, or setting off early the following morning to attend yet another, that he normally walked head bent, with his hat pulled low upon his brow, that he scarcely took in any of his surroundings. But, now that he found himself thus transfixed by her, he recalled an occasion when he had quite literally almost bumped into her as she was directing a group of children across the street and he had been so preoccupied with the events of the previous night, when a baby had been still-born in a damp, mean cellar in Dimity Court, and he had lamented the fact that had they been able to persuade the young mother to have come to them earlier, to the hospital where conditions were so much more hygienic than the appalling windowless, airless black hole she was forced to call home, the baby might have been saved. But now that he could study Lavinia's face in such close proximity as she continued to dance before him, a face illuminated with such radiant happiness, he was certain that this was the same face he had so hurriedly glimpsed on that other occasion.

A neighbour! What fortune!

He found his spirits soaring even higher, and he imagined that, if he were one of the swallows wheeling overhead after their six thousand mile migration from Africa, he would swoop down low over the heads of the young women dancing, single out Lavinia in a heartbeat, fly directly in front of her face, try to attract the attention of those sky-blue eyes of hers and steer their gaze directly towards his, so that she would see and know the fervour they contained in their steadfast regarding of her.

And, as if by heavenly intercession, at that very instant a swallow duly obliges. It briefly forsakes its trawl of catching and devouring the winged insects of the air to dive towards the earth, where it circles the garland of laurel around Lavinia's head, just as she is ascending the dais in the centre of St Ann's Square to be crowned Queen of the May, an accolade afforded to one of the young maypole princesses each year at the start of the Whitsuntide Fair. Robin sees her through this vortex of motion, the whirling of the ribbons, the patterns made by the feet of the dancers, the applauding hands of the crowd, the throwing of hats into the air, and the soaring, swooping, mazy flight of the swallow. In the midst of all this movement her eyes somehow fix on his through the lifted arms of the gathered throng and remain there, fused. It is how he will view her ever afterwards, the radiant smile, the dimpled cheeks, the flowers in her hair, raised upon a pedestal.

Matthew has amassed an entire Manila folder of information about Lavinia. In this, as in all things, he has been meticulous. He knows her weekly schedule by heart, down to the *minutiae* of each hour of each day. He has a chart showing her family tree, as far back as he has been able to trace it. He knows the names, ages and dates of birth of each one of her siblings. He has seen Employment Records for her two brothers currently in work. He has obtained references for the sister from when she was a maid in Ordsall Hall. He has spoken to the parents of some of the young ladies attending her school, under the pretence of considering the establishment as a possible place for a distant relative, and has received nothing but the most glowing of recommendations. He has followed her to the Independent Chapel on Mosley Street – though he has drawn the line at crossing its threshold, its reputation for Radicalism has seen to that – and he has observed her comings and goings from her house on Bridge Street. He has taken great care never to establish a regular pattern or routine about his followings, lest his presence is detected. He does not believe she is aware of his presence even as the faintest shadow of a rook's wing passing across the roof of a building, or the surface of a river or canal, and he intends to keep it that way, at least until he is ready to reveal himself. She has, he has noted, not once since that first accidental first meeting near the New Bailey Prison, worn the white cotton shawl with the moths and the laurel. He wonders why. He duly records what she wears after each occasion he has followed her in the notebook he keeps along with all the other miscellaneous facts and details he has accumulated about her in the Manila folder, which he places under lock and key in the desk in his study, opposite the curtained recess where the portrait of Mercy hangs.

His latest focus of interest lies with her brother-in-law, Mr James Bentley, a successful cotton manufacturer, not unknown to Matthew. They have on occasion had cause to raise their canes to the brims of their hats in mutual acknowledgement outside The Exchange on Penniless Hill. Mr James Bentley, who is married to Susannah, Lavinia's elder sister, on whom, Matthew knows, she leans heavily for guidance and advice. This is where he will concentrate the next moves of his campaign. Tactics, he muses. Strategy. He is quite prepared to play the long game. Knight to Queen's pawn. An exchange of Castles if necessary. The sacrifice of a Bishop even. Check.

It was James who formally introduced them.

Lavinia was helping Susannah with Baby Emma. Susannah had had a difficult time at the birth and was only just, after nearly six months, beginning to regain her colour and her strength. Lavinia would come round most evenings after supper to her sister's home just a few doors away. James never seemed to mind.

"If anything," he would say, "I'm grateful. She needs the distraction, and I'm not much use with either girls or babies. They're like china plates. I'm always frightened I might drop her."

Lavinia smiled. She took Emma from Susannah as she recomposed herself after a feed, the two of them exchanging a warm, mischievous glance between them.

"He means well," said Susannah fondly after James had left them to it, "but he's right. He's perfectly hopeless. He hasn't the foggiest notion what to do with Emma, or how to be. Whenever he tries to talk baby language, it just sounds ridiculous coming from his mouth. Doesn't it, my little sausage?" she cooed as Lavinia handed her back. "Maybe the next one will be a boy," she continued with a sigh.

"The next one?" said Lavinia. "Already?"

Susannah nodded. "I think so. Don't say anything to James, though. I haven't told him yet."

Lavinia shook her head. "How will you manage?" she said.

"I don't know, but somehow I will. I always do, don't I?"

"Yes," agreed Lavinia vigorously. "You do."

"Always the practical one, eh?"

"Perhaps Ginny might help as well as me."

"We'll work something out, don't worry."

The ghost of their mother hovered over them. Both of them sensed her, though neither said anything.

It was then that James burst back in on them.

"Shh!" they both hissed simultaneously. "She's almost asleep."

"Oops, sorry," he whispered. "There I go again, putting my foot in it. Can you leave her a minute? We have a visitor."

"You two go," mouthed Susannah carefully. "I'll join you later. Let me make sure she's fully settled first."

James proceeded to exit the way he had come extravagantly on tiptoe, lifting his knees high into the air with each step, his finger clamped to his lips. Intrigued and amused in equal measure, Lavinia followed him out of the sitting room into the hallway.

Once there, James exhaled loudly with relief and turned to his guest, who was waiting patiently, nervously rotating his hat by the brim between his fingers.

It was Robin.

He too had been doing his homework and had engineered this apparently chance encounter quite deliberately, but now that she stood before him, less than a month since she had so hypnotised him at the Whitsuntide Fair, he felt himself threatening to unravel. James, with his punctiliousness for formality, came to his rescue just in time.

"Robin, may I present my sister-in-law? Mr Holroyd, Miss Robinson."

Robin and Lavinia bowed and curtseyed to each other as custom and good manners dictated, silently and awkwardly.

"Forgive the intrusion," he said. "I had just called to check on the progress of my patient." He gave a self-conscious cough. "My *former* patient, I mean to say."

"Are you a doctor?" asked Lavinia somewhat superfluously.

"An *accoucheur*," he replied, with yet another polite inclination of the head.

Lavinia said nothing by way of reply, but could not prevent the raising of a curious eyebrow, which she covered with a second, equally modest curtsey.

"But as I am a neighbour," he continued, "living just a few doors away, I took it upon myself to call unannounced."

"A neighbour?" replied Lavinia before she could check herself. "I thought your face was familiar."

"Actually," he said, stepping a little closer to her, "we have met before – fleetingly – in St Ann's Square, when you were crowned Queen of the May." He immediately stepped back. He was blushing, he could feel it. He sensed he had said too much and too quickly. But this time it was Lavinia who saved him, with her directness.

315

"Yes," she said. "I remember now."

And she did. The memory of a swallow wheeling about her. A face in the crowd. A look passing between them. Then both the swallow and the young man gone. Until now. Standing before her.

Even James, who as a rule never noticed such things, not even when they had been pointed out to him and were as plain as the nose on his face, could not fail to see the sparks fly between them. He raised a hand to his mouth and coughed in order to suppress the grin he was certain must be spreading across his face.

"She's through here," he said, gesturing towards the sitting room. "Your patient," he added to Robin's confused expression.

"Ah yes," said Robin, reluctantly tearing himself away from further study of Lavinia's face.

"Through here," added James.

"Of course. Mother and baby doing well, I trust?"

"See for yourself," said James, opening the door and ushering him in.

"Miss Robinson," said Robin, with a final bow.

"Mr Holroyd," replied Lavinia, with the tiniest of curtseys.

"An admirable young man," said James to Lavinia, once the two of them were alone in the hall. "With prospects. He aims to be a surgeon one day." He tapped the side of his nose and winked exaggeratedly.

"Does he?" said Lavinia, looking back towards the closed door of the sitting room, behind which the object of their conversation now stood, or sat, then turned back to address her brother-in-law directly. "Though what concern that should be of mine I cannot conceive," she said, immediately regretting her choice of words. "Good night, James," she added, wrapping the white cotton shawl around her as she stepped through the front door. For an instant the moths fluttered about her ears before settling once more among the safety of the laurel leaves.

316

A fine filly, thought James, as he watched her make her way the dozen yards or so back to the schoolroom and the family house above it, but like all fillies, he could not fathom her. One of life's unsolvable mysteries. "I'm damned if we chaps will ever understand 'em, but we can't do without 'em, what?" He closed the door chortling to himself before retreating to the Smoking Room, where he decided he'd earned himself a cigar. He relished these now rare quiet moments to himself and took extra pleasure in all the rituals that accompanied the smoking of a cigar. The trimming of it, the rolling it between his fingers, the breathing in of the fragrance of the tobacco leaf, the precise method required to light it, to let it completely catch, then that first delicious taste of it as he inhaled deeply into his lungs, before the delayed gratification of the very slow blowing out of the smoke. He decided to dedicate the next thirty minutes to the execution of the perfectly formed smoke ring while he pondered how best to engineer a second meeting between the *accoucheur* and his sister-in-law.

But it was Matthew who unexpectedly provided the opportunity. He arranged to bump into James outside The Exchange just after the day's trading was finishing at around noon, seemingly by chance, on the steps leading down onto Penniless Hill. After their now customary wordless greeting – the tipping of their canes against the brims of their hats – Matthew waited until James had passed him, performed a neat *tour en face*, then gently tapped him on the shoulder with the silvered top of his cane.

"I say – it's Mr Bentley, is it not?"

"The same, sir."

"Yes, I thought so. Pardon me for detaining you in this unconventional manner, but we pass each other so frequently these days, either here on the steps of The Exchange, or in other parts of the town, that I thought we should properly introduce ourselves to one another. Mr Matthew Oldham," he said, producing a monogrammed card from his waistcoat pocket, which he offered to James with an elegant flourish and a click of his heeled boots. "At your service."

"Ah – Mr Oldham. Delighted to make your acquaintance at last. I know of your reputation of course. Your father's too…" Here he allowed a respectful pause, which Matthew acknowledged with an appreciative bow of his head. "It's a wonder you can still find time for trade, sir, when your duties at the Bench must keep you so busily occupied."

"One does one's best," said Matthew, spreading his hands, "but what can one do? The town is growing, more and more flock to take advantage of what she has to offer, and with them, alas, must follow in their wake those less desirable elements which, as you say, do exercise my time so. Still, it is a civic duty and one tries to do what one can."

"Quite so, sir. Nevertheless I marvel at how you manage to juggle so many balls in the air."

"Unlike you, sir," replied Matthew, "I do not have the good fortune to be blessed with a wife, and so I am a man of relative leisure."

"Ah – footloose and fancy free still?" quipped James. He momentarily felt a pang for those former days of few responsibilities but quickly dismissed them. He knew which side his bread was buttered. He would be lost without Susannah.

"We always envy what the other man has that we ourselves lack, I believe," remarked Matthew, scarcely crediting that he was actually hearing such vapid nonsense usher from his own lips, but the game was afoot now, and he could scent the closeness of his prey. He did not have much longer to wait. It duly arrived with Mr Bentley's very next utterance.

"I expect you are much in demand, Mr Oldham, an eligible bachelor such as yourself, always receiving invitations from the ladies desirous of palming you off with their unmarried daughters."

Matthew once more spread his hands, as if confiding in a fellow man of the world. "One does one's best," he said again.

"It's a long time since I was last at a ball or supper party," mused James, speaking aloud thoughts he would have preferred to remain unspoken.

"Come, come," joked Matthew. "You speak like an old gentleman. Yet there cannot be more than a year between us. I wager you cut quite a caper in *The Assembly Rooms*?"

"I did, sir!" beamed James, remembering.

"I thought as much," laughed Matthew, while cringing inside at the thought of such an exhibition. "How would you like to revisit those days?"

"I don't follow, sir."

"It just so happens that only this morning I received an invitation to attend some new debutante's twenty-first from a person I hardly know. Part of me would like to attend but another part feels a certain anxiety about going alone. If *you* would do the honour of accompanying me, sir, offering me your advice and expertise, I would be for ever in your debt."

"Well…" blustered James, somewhat taken aback. "I'm really not sure."

"Dear me," replied Matthew, "what can I be thinking? You have a wife. You are no longer able to attend such a ball simply on the whim of a poor unattached bachelor such as myself."

"You flatter me, sir, but…"

"Wait – I have it. The perfect solution." Matthew clapped his hands together and performed a passable *pirouette*. "You must bring Mrs Bentley along too!"

"Well, I… I really don't know… It's true that Mrs Bentley might indeed enjoy such an occasion, a rare evening's break from looking after the baby…" Matthew was already beginning to grow bored as James stumbled his way forward. "Though I'm sure her sister might be persuaded to stand in for a night. She adores her niece."

"Her sister?" oozed Matthew, his voice dripping with as much unaffected casualness as he could pretend to muster.

"Yes. Lavinia. A schoolmistress."

"Perhaps she might like to come too?"

James looked up sharply.

"To keep your wife company, you know, while you and I... partake of a little brandy perhaps...?"

"Ah yes, I see. I take your meaning. Most thoughtful. I daresay it could be arranged. There is another sister – Ginny – most capable. I'm sure she could be trusted with the baby."

"Excellent."

"Yes, I'm certain of it."

"Then it is all arranged."

"Yes, sir, by Jove. Let us shake hands on it."

After this effusive display of affection between them, which was almost more than Matthew could endure, James became suddenly thoughtful.

"The sister," he began.

"The schoolmistress?"

"Yes."

"Miss Lavinia, you said?"

"Indeed. I do not believe she has ever attended a ball before. She will be nervous."

"But excited too, like all young ladies at the prospect of an evening at *The Assembly Rooms*?"

"Yes, yes, no doubt, but..."

"Yes?"

"She's a serious girl, not silly like so many of them are these days..."

I like her even more, thought Matthew.

"I wonder... might you do her the honour of promising her at least one dance, sir, and making sure she receives no kind of unwanted attention from less trustworthy types?"

"Your wife, surely, will act as a most worthy chaperone, being her sister. She will look out for her, I have no doubt. But yes, James – may I call you James? – you may depend upon it. I shall see she comes to no harm. And I promise to escort her onto the floor for her first dance. You have my word on it. Come – let us shake hands once more."

Matthew watched James descend The Exchange steps and make his way down Penniless Hill towards the Dean's Gate with a mirthless smile upon his lips, swallowing the bile that had formed in the back of his throat.

When, later that evening, James informed Susannah of the idea, she smiled at her husband with fond indulgence.

"What a gull you are," she said. "Mr Oldham is as transparent as a window pane."

"What do you mean, my love?" asked James. He felt like a deflated balloon with all the air escaping from him at once.

"It is not *you* he wishes to accompany to the ball, you noodle, but Lavinia," she laughed. The sound, like a carillon of small hand bells ringing, filled him with joy, quite dispelling the disappointment of a few moments ago. "But he's too late."

Once again James feels himself being outflanked. "Is he? He would make the most suitable match, don't you think? He has money, position, a fine standing in the town."

"But ˙she has begun walking out with Mr Holroyd – a situation *you* engineered, if you remember?"

"Really?" he asked, his eyebrows dancing a veritable jig upon his brow. "I'd no idea. No one tells me anything."

"But I see no reason why she should not attend this ball."

Once again James's eyebrows turned somersaults, knitting themselves into a tangle of knots. "But you just said…?"

"Why, he shall take *your* place of course. You will come down with a heavy cold at the last minute, and I shall take Robin as my protector in your stead."

"A heavy cold? But I've never felt better in all my…" But James was prevented from finishing this sentence by a well aimed pin-cushion, flung by Susannah, hitting him full square on the nose.

A month after meeting formally in Susannah's house, two months after their eyes had fused at the Whitsuntide Fair, Robin and Lavinia strolled happily through the crowds gathered on St Peter's Field for Lammas Day. It was a hot, unforgiving sun that beat down upon them, encouraging them to seek the shade of Cooper's Garden, beside the windmill which gave the adjoining street its name. The huge sails turned slowly, slicing the air between them into sharp delineations of sunlight and shadow, heat and cold.

"I've only ever known two Robins," she said.

"Hmm?" he said, not really listening. He held a blade of false brome grass between his fingers, with which he was delicately tracing the outline of her face.

"Robin Hood," she said, brushing away the grass which tickled. "Would you rob the rich to give to the poor?" she asked, teasingly.

"If you were my Maid Marion I might," he answered.

"*Might*?" she scoffed. "That's rather equivocal, isn't it?"

"I'm not equivocal about you," he said, suddenly serious.

"Hmm." She eyed him playfully. "And the other is Robin Goodfellow," she continued. "Are you a good fellow?"

"I hope so," he said. "I try to be." He tossed his cane from one hand to the other.

"Wilt thou put a girdle round the earth in forty minutes?"

"If you asked me to." He tossed the cane back again.

"I don't."

"What do you ask?"

"Nothing," she said. "Just this." She put her arms around his neck and kissed him.

They leant back against the windmill for a long time looking up at the sky. The sails continued to turn the same *chiaroscuro* slice.

After a while Robin said, "I wish things could stay like this for ever. Here. Now. Always. Never changing."

"But that's not possible," said Lavinia. "It's in the nature of things to change. Look around you. Manchester's for ever changing. From one day to the next. The years turn. Like this windmill."

"If I could, I'd stop it," he said vehemently. "I just want to remain here, gazing up at you like this."

"Like what? A statue?"

"An angel."

She shook her head, smiling tenderly at him. "Then you're going to have to get used to being disappointed."

"You could never disappoint me," he said.

"Don't say that," she said. "Come here." She put her arms around him once more. "Let's not spoil the day." Just as she drew him towards her, to allow him to kiss her again, the sails of the windmill stopped turning. As if someone had thrust in a hand to a clock face to hold back time. "Oh!" she exclaimed. "Look – you've got your wish." The pair stood in a wedge of bright light between the hard-edged shadows of the sails. "Who will grind the miller's corn?" she said, taking in the strolling crowds in a single sweeping gesture. "Who will feed the hungry masses?"

Robin pulled her roughly out of the sunlight into the shadow.

"I want you all to myself," he said.

'The best-laid schemes o' mice an' men
Gang aft agley…'

Susannah's plan was thwarted at the last moment by nature's intervention, or rather man's, specifically woman's.

"He can't come," said James, blundering into their bedroom

323

while Susannah was still dressing.

"Who can't?"

"Mr Holroyd. Robin. There's a woman in Angel Meadow in desperate need of his services."

Susannah sat heavily on the edge of the bed.

" *'I'm truly sorry man's dominion*
Has broken nature's social union...' "

James shook his head in bewilderment. "I don't follow you, my dear."

"Never mind," she said, rousing herself to stand once more. "You shall have to take his place."

"But don't I have a heavy cold?"

"Not any more. Mr Oldham is expecting you in any case still, and we can't disappoint Lavinia. She's been looking forward to this evening for weeks. Do me up at the back, will you, dear?"

Susannah, James and Lavinia took a carriage James had arranged to convey them the half mile from their home on Bridge Street to *The Assembly Rooms* on Mosley Street. They could have walked it easily but a light rain had begun to fall. In less than no time the streets would have been awash with puddles in the deep pot holes, which would have been sure to splash and spoil the two ladies' dresses.

Lavinia had never before ridden in a carriage. Although she was disappointed that Robin had been called away to assist with a birth, she was excited by the prospect of her first ball. He had insisted she still go without him.

" *'Give me your hands if we be friends'*," he had gallantly said.

" *'And Robin shall restore amends...'* "

The gaslights, which were now everywhere throughout Manchester, gave an almost fairy-tale glow to the town. Lavinia was all too aware of the suffering of those less fortunate than she, who were forced to make the streets their home, but passing them now, as the carriage crossed the Dean's Gate, into King Street, passing the late Dr White's house, before turning briefly down Red Croft, into Tib Lane, along North Street, towards Fountain Street, where they were for a short time held up by the crowds milling around the *Theatre Royale*, which was that night presenting Mrs Inchbald's 'petite comedy', *The Wedding Day*, billed as 'the latest London favourite, being brought forward with all possible expedition', featuring Mr Browne as Lord Rakeland and Mr Davis as Sir Adam Contest, who must literally compete for the hand of the heroine, Hannah, played by Miss Appleby, before finally turning into Mosley Street itself, the warm amber of the gas lights in which those poor pathetic, homeless creatures were bathed lent them an almost picturesque aura. It was only when the carriage was once more forced to halt outside the theatre and one of those wretches thrust a gaunt hand inside, grasping Lavinia's wrist so tightly it left its mark upon her skin, that she roused herself out of this shameful reverie.

Mosley Street was no longer the demesne of the Lord of the Manor. Nor was it a boulevard of grand mansion houses as it had been still but a quarter of a century before. Now it was the home of Manchester's growing commercial empire, with several banks and warehouses. As well it contained *The Portico Library, The Royal Manchester Institution*, (later to become the city's art gallery), *The Union Gentlemen's Club House*, and *The Assembly Rooms*, where their carriage now deposited them.

Matthew was waiting on the steps to greet them, smilingly unaware of the subterfuge that had been plotted by Susannah, to whom he now formally bowed and kissed her proffered hand, as was permissible with a married lady accompanied by her husband. 'Kissed' would be a misleading verb to use to describe the way he allowed his dry lips to brush against Susanna's gloved fingers with the barest of actual physical contact. Susannah coolly observed this thinly disguised revulsion. She was reminded of an adder she had once surprised, hiding under a stone, its eyes narrow slits recoiling from the sharpness of the light, its tongue flicking drily from its mouth.

But she did not have long to dwell on this comparison, for once he had seen the two ladies comfortably settled in chairs along the walls of the main ballroom, from where she and Lavinia might watch the dancing and listen to the orchestra, he whisked James away with him in search of punch. He had not, Susannah noticed with some surprise, looked at Lavinia once, except for the briefest of moments when they were introduced.

The evening passed pleasantly enough. Susannah and Lavinia knew no people who were there and so they were not invited to dance, except by one or two older gentlemen, who took pity on them and accompanied them rather slowly and decorously around the floor for some of the less hectic dances. Neither of them minded. They were quite content to be spectators, enjoying the sumptuous surroundings, the array of fine gowns, the stirring pieces of music for the various different dances – the cotillons, the reels, the minuets and quadrilles, the gavottes, écossoises and espagnoles, and even, most daringly, the new sensation, the waltz, in which couples publicly embraced upon the dance floor – all rendered dazzlingly romantic under the crystal chandeliers and silver candelabra, which illuminated the ornate ceilings and wall hangings. Susannah and Lavinia secretly hid their faces, giggling behind fans, as they sought out who appeared to be the most handsome young men there, like characters in the sentimental comedies they sometimes read from the Circulating Libraries. None, they decided, measured up to either James or Robin.

It was almost an hour before Matthew and James returned, James looking decidedly red-faced, either with embarrassment or a surfeit of drink. Probably both, thought Susannah indulgently, as he nobly offered to partner her in a quadrille. This left Matthew and Lavinia awkward and tongue-tied alone together for the first time. Unlike James, who was continuing to perspire, desperately trying to loosen his cravat, while at the same time gallantly attempting to give at least a passable rendition of the dance, Matthew appeared cool and collected. His hair, Lavinia noted, was short and curled in the latest Napoleonic fashion, while he carried about him the not unpleasant aroma of Albany and Bay Rum. Here was a gentleman of studied fastidiousness, of scrupulous manners, but of few words. Either he was cripplingly shy, or he merely disdained unnecessary small talk. Lavinia rather hoped it was the latter, for she too had little patience and even less admiration for the braying repartee of the fops and dandies who were each trying to outdo the other in their supposed quips and witticisms designed to flatter and impress the ladies they danced with. Perhaps they had detected this in her manner and bearing, which might have explained why none approached her now, when the Master of Ceremonies announced another waltz. Perhaps Matthew sensed it too, for, rather than enquiring whether she might be free to take to the floor with him, he offered her his arm instead and said, "It's rather warm, don't you find? Shall we take some air? There's a balcony overlooking the garden just through here, which has been lit to produce a most pleasing effect. Would you do me the honour of accompanying me there?"

Lavinia wondered whether he had been privately rehearsing this little speech in the silence which preceded it, for it was most elegantly expressed and, although she did not find Mr Oldham remotely attractive, she thought it would be churlish of her to refuse him. But her most over-riding emotion was curiosity. He intrigued her, the way he appeared to make no effort at all to be witty or charming, quite content to remain silent. A quality she too preferred.

Outside the air was unusually fragrant. The scent of lavender masked the customary Manchester smells that now pervaded the town day and night. Matthew's bay rum pomade mingled pleasantly with the evening air. She breathed it all in deeply, admiring the illuminated gardens below where they stood.

"Thank you," she said.

"For what?"

"For inviting my sister and brother-in-law this evening." He inclined his head modestly. "And for inviting me too."

"Are you enjoying yourself?"

"Very much."

"I am delighted to hear it. But you do not mind missing the dancing?"

She shook her head. "I have no partner."

"And I am not someone who could fill that role for you, I'm afraid."

"You do not dance?"

"I do, if pressed. But dreadfully."

"Then I shall not press you."

"Your toes will be eternally grateful."

She laughed warmly at his joke.

"You would not think we were in the centre of the fastest growing metropolis in all of Europe," he said, spreading an arm towards the garden, from which they could hear an unseen owl hooting.

"It's like an oasis here," she said.

"Then you'd best make the most of it."

"Why?"

Matthew turned to face her. "Because all this," he once again indicated the garden behind him, "is about to disappear. Dug up, paved over, and a new warehouse constructed."

"What a shame," said Lavinia, looking anxiously back towards it, almost as if it might disappear right then and there before her eyes.

"But necessary. We produce more and more cotton goods year upon year. We must have somewhere to store them."

"Yes, I suppose. But there are other places, surely?"

"All of Manchester was like this once – fields, woods, meadows – but the people starved. There was no work. Then the fly shuttle was invented, then the spinning mule and jenny, then the powered looms were built, then there was work for everyone. People flocked here from all over the world. They still do. Change, Miss Robinson, it's not only inevitable, it's necessary. Without it where would we be?"

Lavinia thought back to the conversation she had had with Robin when she had said much the same thing that Matthew was saying now, only not quite so forcefully, and she was talking about people rather than places.

"You're very quiet," he said, edging a little closer to her.

"I'm sorry. I was thinking about what you said. Do people make places or do places make people?"

The owl hooted a second time.

"I don't know," he said, smiling. "It's a conundrum. Like when you draw a circle. You have to put your pencil to the paper somewhere, in order to begin it, but once you've drawn it, if you've drawn it well, you then can't see where you started from."

"This place was here first, though, wasn't it? Before it was ever called Manchester. Then people arrived and began to leave their mark upon it."

"But the nature of those marks they made, they were influenced by what they found here."

"Which now they're covering up. Like this garden."

"I suppose. Though something new will take its place."

"But will it be better?"

Matthew shrugged. "I believe so."

"Believe?"

"We must try to have faith."

"In what?"

"Ourselves."

Lavinia looked away.

"Anyway," she said, "it's not a circle. It's more of a helix, a

329

Catherine wheel, spinning out wider and wider, like the Milky Way up there above us, an uncountable number of stars and constellations."

"And if we had bigger, more powerful telescopes, which we will do one day, we'll see even more."

"But never count them all."

"It's exhilarating, is it not?"

"What?"

"The future. The absolute unknowableness of it…"

The owl hooted a third time. They each felt the rush of its wings disturb the air, before it swooped past them into the dark unseen and beyond sight.

Matthew leaned in closer to Lavinia and whispered in her ear.

"… except that it will come."

Lavinia felt her skin go cold.

"When a painter begins a portrait," he continued, "the lines he puts on the canvas at first appear to make no sense. They have neither shape, nor meaning. Just dots and splashes of colour, daubs and streaks of paint, resembling nothing. Then gradually the likeness emerges, slowly at first, then more quickly, until you can see the very image of the subject, caught in a single moment, but preserved for all time."

"I thought you were an advocate of change, Mr Oldham," said Lavinia warily.

"You misunderstand me, Miss Robinson. A portrait is never finished. The painter has merely put down his brushes until he is ready to pick them up again."

No, thought Lavinia, I do not misunderstand you at all. She became aware that there was now nobody else but the two of them out here on the balcony, overlooking the garden that was shortly to disappear. She felt his breath upon her face. The scent of bay rum seemed suddenly overpowering.

"I fear I must inform you," she ventured carefully, "that I… am already spoken for."

In the days that followed Matthew brooded. He did not leave his house on Oldham Street unless he had to. This had been a most unexpected setback. Unexpected because unpredicted. He thought he had planned for every contingency. His planning had been painstaking, his research meticulous. But nowhere had he found evidence of a rival. Perhaps, he speculated, in the colder light of day, because he had not been looking for one.

Now he found himself drawn back to the portrait of Mercy. He had not looked upon it for a long time. He sat in front of it, with the curtain still drawn across the recess, concealing it from view, forcing himself to resist the temptation to open it, willing himself not to look directly upon its mocking gaze. Not that he needed to. He knew every brushstroke by heart, almost as if the marks upon the canvas had been scored directly upon his own skin.

Although the nights grew chilly, with the threat of an autumn frost licking the air, he did not light a fire. He let the ashes stay where they were, cold and unraked. A mouse scrabbled undisturbed among them.

He sat and he thought.

He sat for three nights, thinking.

Thinking, scheming, planning.

Then he had it.

He stood up from the chair he had placed before the hidden portrait and flung open the curtain. "Do your worst," the look upon his face appeared to show. "I defy you."

If *he* could not have her, then nobody would.

Outside the window it was still dark. "I'll start first thing tomorrow," he said to himself. "I shall begin with the young man, the rival, the *accoucheur*."

And with that thought, he threw himself fully clothed upon his bed and at once fell into a deep, untroubled sleep, the pale ghost of a smile upon his thin, bloodless lips.

*

331

Robin and Lavinia stood on the New Bailey Bridge, their favoured trysting place, watching the barges laden with cotton and coal making their way up and down the Irwell. At times there were so many of them, jostling for position, trying to force their way through a gap that wasn't there, that the river itself almost disappeared beneath the surge and swarm of them. They reminded Lavinia of when she once looked into a beehive. So many thousands of workers clamouring to leave, while an even greater number tried to squeeze and force their way back in, their *corbiculae*, those hairy receptacles on their hind legs, bursting with pollen, which they emptied into the waiting cells. A worker bee will typically carry half her own body weight of it with each journey she makes. Her stomach, gorged with nectar, she will empty into the mouth of a neighbour, who will in turn expel it to the next, until all the water has left it, leaving only the pure honey remaining, which is stored and stockpiled in the royal cells. The Queen, for whom all this unpaid, unrewarded toil is spent, is rarely seen. Once, and once only, she will take to the air for her nuptial flight. Then, after she has mated, she will return to the hive, to be fed and pampered, cushioned and served. Sometimes, if the hive becomes too overcrowded, or if a rival appears on the scene, the Queen will rouse herself one last time and leave the nest, a bloated, puffed-up popinjay, followed by a swarm of her most loyal subjects. But for the most part she is invisible, a vengeful goddess demanding unquestioned obedience and servitude from her followers.

Lavinia, looking down upon the heaving river and teeming waterfront was reminded of this hive she had seen as a girl and shuddered. Robin appeared not to notice it. He had eyes only for Lavinia, for she was his queen, and he her patient drone. He pressed himself against her. She held up a hand in passive resistance.

"Later," she said. "Ask me later. In December. When I'm twenty-one."

This reply brought Robin immense relief and satisfaction. He breathed out deeply, tossing his cane from one hand to the other. His shoulders relaxed. An autumn moon rose up above them. Silhouetted swallows were lining the rooftops, preparing themselves for their long journey south. They looked around them, surveying the town, as if storing a memory of it, for when they would return.

Ten miles to the west, as the swallow flies, skimming above the log-jammed Irwell to where the Medlock empties its muddy waters into it, by the Castlefield Basin at the entrance to the Bridgewater Canal, then following the Duke's Cut back to its beginnings in Worsley, behind the Old Hall, on the edge of Bittern Wood, an army of estate workers is preparing for the annual bird trapping. The wood is a major crossing point for the migrating swallows. Not just swallows. Finches of all varieties – gold, green, bull, chaff; rose, haw, crested, long-tailed – siskin and serin, brambling and twite; redwing, redpoll, redshank, redstart; waxwing, wheatear, whitethroat, wigeon; linnet and lark, pintail and plover. Giant nets are slung between branches, stretched across fields, more than a mile wide and a hundred feet high. Mist nets, cannon nets, funnel traps, noose traps. Lures and lanterns, quicklime and glue. More than a million plucked from the skies, their feathers and plumes, wings and tails, stitched and trimmed to adorn dresses and hats.

"Whoop-whoop-whoo!" goes the cry, as the first great flocks of them appear on the horizon, blotting out the sun. "Whoop-whoop-whoo!" Up it goes again.

The trappers release their lures.

Matthew uses a different type of lure. He writes a letter.

Dear Mr Holroyd,

I hear wonderful reports of your work at the Lying-In Hospital and the outer districts of the town. Would you do me the great honour of meeting me in my chambers at the Court Leet on Monday next at midday? I have a matter to discuss which may be to our mutual advantage.

Yours etc

Matthew Oldham, Esq.
Justice of the Peace

Robin is intrigued. He replies by return that he would be delighted to attend. Blithely unaware of the significance of its contents, Billy delivers the letter later the same day, whistling like a songbird.

"I thought we'd lunch at *The White Bear*," says Matthew before Robin has even had time to remove his hat. "Do you know it?"

"Er – no, I…"

"Oh? I thought you would. It's opposite the Infirmary, and you being a medical man…"

Robin shakes his head.

Excellent, thinks Matthew. The fool's already on the back foot.

"Not wishing to split hairs, it's closer to the Lunatic Asylum," he adds. "I imagine your duties must have taken you there?"

"No, actually…"

"Splendid," says Matthew, picking up Robin's cane and tossing it towards him, enjoying his guest's further discomfort as he fumbles and drops it. "I recommend their pork chops."

"Now," he said again, after their plates had been cleared away, Robin's toyed with, Matthew's picked clean as if by a scalpel. "I understand you have ambitions to become a surgeon?"

Robin's eyes widened in amazement. "Why yes, but how could you possibly know that?"

Matthew tapped the side of his nose with the forefinger of his right hand and winked. "I have my sources," he said, "my moles, my spies." He laughed – a sound so unpractised in him that it sounded false and strained, rather like an orchestra tuning up before embarking upon a difficult piece of music, it rang a warning note inside him. Not unlike the din emanating at regular intervals from the Asylum across the way, which, Matthew noted with considerable relish, was causing his guest to wince and start with increasing alarm.

"Thank you for the lunch," said Robin, attempting to get to his feet. "Most generous. But I really should be getting back…"

"Nonsense," said Matthew, sitting Robin down again, "we've oceans of time. I expect the female population of Manchester can wait a little longer before they pop their next brood, don't you? Besides, I've ordered coffee. Shall we take it in the lounge downstairs? I've a proposal to put to you." And with that he was on his feet and walking away from the table, leaving Robin to flounder once more in his wake.

"That will be all, Charles," said Matthew curtly to the young waiter who had just brought in their coffee. "You may leave us now. We can pour for ourselves. Thank you." He dismissed the boy with a wave of his hand, then immediately called him back, rather like the way a cat plays with a mouse, or a fisherman reels in his catch, not too rapidly, so as not to snag the line. "Here." He rolled a sixpence quickly and casually back and forth between each finger across the knuckles of his right hand, before tossing it deftly towards Charles, who caught and pocketed the coin with practiced ease. "Please see to it that my guest and I are not disturbed."

"Yes, sir. No, sir. Thank you, sir."

"Now," said Matthew once they were alone, "where were we?"

Robin's mouth opened and closed like a cod fish.

"Cigar?"

Robin shook his head.

"Good for you. Filthy things. Never smoke 'em myself either. Except on special occasions. Like today." And he proceeded to light one, from which he blew a satisfied smoke ring that expanded and grew until it framed Robin's face perfectly.

Robin felt the corona of smoke settle around him, growing thicker and thicker, until it seemed as though it blotted out his peripheral vision completely, so that all he could now see was his host's inscrutable face.

"Mr Oldham," he began.

"Matthew – please."

"Matthew… I'm most grateful for your time and hospitality, but I am still at a loss as to understand the purpose of our meeting. You said in your letter," which he now produced from his waistcoat pocket, "that you had 'a matter to discuss which may be to our mutual advantage'. And yet you say nothing." He placed the letter on the table between them.

Matthew continued to regard the discomfort of his guest with considerable pleasure, but he had played out the line long enough. Now it was time to begin reeling him in.

"You are an *accoucheur*, are you not?"

Robin replied that he was.

"A somewhat unconventional profession for a man, wouldn't you say?"

Robin supposed that this was probably true.

"There's nothing 'probable' about it. It's a fact. A male midwife is a most *im*probable occupation for a man. Less than one in more than a hundred females carrying out the same

336

function. I have looked into it, I have discovered this to be so, and so I am intrigued, Mr Holroyd…" Suddenly, the 'Robin' had been dropped. "What on earth induced you to take up such a disgusting practice?"

Robin could feel himself shaking. "I was a protégé of the late Dr White. It was he who encouraged me."

"Ah yes. Dr White. We have much, it seems, to be thankful to him for. The Infirmary across the way," he said languidly, gesturing towards the window with his now half-smoked cigar. "And its adjoining Asylum, whose inmates have been keeping us so entertained during our lunch of pork chops and roasted mushrooms, which you, I perceived, left for the most part untouched. Tell me, Mr Holroyd, do you retain a similar admiration for all of Dr White's teachings?"

"I don't quite follow you, sir. He was a man of enormous prestige and reputation. He was held in the highest esteem by the entire medical profession of Great Britain. He was a Fellow of the Royal Society." Robin was becoming hotter and crosser by the second.

"Yes, yes, no doubt," replied Matthew, "I was referring to his less scientific views concerning polygenism."

Robin could feel the skin on his face and neck begin to grow crimson. "No. That was not an opinion I shared."

Matthew ignored this last remark and wafted away another cloud of cigar smoke with the back of his hand. "He had a penchant for comparing different parts of a woman's anatomy most unfavourably with edible *légumes*, did he not?"

Robin bowed his head.

"Her *pudenda*, for example, he likened to a *porcini* mushroom, I believe? No wonder, then, you found your luncheon so unappetising."

Robin wanted nothing more than the floor to open up and swallow him. He should have simply stood and left several minutes ago, but something about Matthew Oldham held and compelled him to remain.

"I imagine you must have seen enough *porcini* mushroom to last you a lifetime."

Robin looked up appalled.

"I refer of course to your work, Mr Holroyd, your professional practice. Little wonder you seek pastures new. The fish farm of surgery instead of the weed-choked allotment. Where you might gut and fillet to your heart's content, rather than wallow up to the elbow in rotting vegetable matter, or thrust in your snout like a pig snuffling to reach that prize truffle."

"Why are you talking like this?" asked Robin, at last finding his tongue and his courage to speak. "What possible purpose might you have?"

Matthew spread his hands. "I hear excellent reports of your successes in the field, Robin." His tone had reverted once more to a friendly *bonhomie*, the conspiratorial sharing of confidences, the nudge, the wink, the use again of the first name. "The wife of a colleague of mine on the Bench might have died in parturition but for your most skilled and timely intervention. She herself has supplied me with further examples of your excellent care, ministered with sensitivity and tact. I subsequently learned of your aspiration to become a surgeon and I thought perhaps I could help." He closed his hands so that the fingers of each interlocked with a calm finality.

"I don't understand. Why should you want to help *me* – someone who, until today, you have never met?"

Matthew now leaned forward. He was ready to play his trump card, which he had been saving until the precise moment arrived. He judged that to be now.

"Because," he said, carefully measuring out his words like an angler slowly spooling in the fly before casting it once more onto the surface of a river, "I believe we have a mutual acquaintance."

Robin shot Matthew an anxious glance, his senses on even higher alert. He had a second question to ask but that would have to wait, for already Matthew was addressing him again.

"Although in your case the word 'acquaintance' does not do justice to the precise nature of the relationship. I speak of Miss Robinson."

"What do you know of Lavinia?" barked Robin unguardedly.

Matthew preened inside at the nakedness of this response. Reeling him in was going to be easier than he could have imagined. "I met her – briefly – at *The Assembly Rooms* last month."

"You danced with her?" choked Robin.

"No, no, no. No one, as far as I am aware, danced with her apart from one or two gallant, old married gentlemen who took pity on a single, unattached young lady sitting by herself on the sidelines. I am a business associate of her brother-in-law – Mr Bentley – we are both cotton manufacturers, don't you know, who meet from time to time at The Exchange. He and Mrs Bentley were my guests. They brought Miss Robinson – Lavinia, did you say? – along with them. I understand you were meant to have been accompanying her, but you had a cold. Or was that Mr Bentley? I forget now. I trust you are quite recovered?"

Robin seethed, but at the same time he was relieved to learn that his slippery-tongued host had not danced with Lavinia. The thought of those serpent hands touching his darling's waist was almost too much to bear.

"I did not have a cold. I was called away."

"On a professional duty, I expect."

"Yes, as a matter of fact. To a young expectant mother in Angel Meadow."

"Angel Meadow?" Matthew's eyebrows arched knowingly. "A consequence of her profession, no doubt. Oh, don't get me wrong. I make no judgement. We are all of us, are we not, engaged in one sort of trade or another? I expect she paid you for your services, if only in kind."

Robin exploded to his feet and launched himself across the table at Matthew, who remained quite still, unflinching. At the very last moment, he spoke in a voice little more than an urgent whisper. "I shouldn't do that if I were you."

The remark stopped Robin in his tracks.

"Something told you to obey me then, didn't it?" he continued, still speaking quietly, but commandingly. "Something buried deep inside you. Treasure it. That instinct is worth more than anything that might be bought or sold at The Exchange. Now listen to me very carefully. This is a public place. You do not wish to cause a scene here. It would reflect much worse on you than it would on me, Mr Holroyd. For look at the conjunction of the two of us. You stand aggressively over me, with your fists clenched, having earlier raised your voice. While I... I just sit here quietly, talking to you as if to an old friend. Just think how the newspapers might interpret it. 'Male Midwife Assaults Respected Magistrate in Unprovoked Attack'. You would not come out of such a mauling too well, would you? Those lofty ambitions of yours to become a surgeon would fly right out of this window behind me, would they not?"

Robin said nothing.

"Would they not?" Matthew repeated.

"Yes," said Robin at last. "I dare say they would."

"Good. Then we understand one another. So – what is going to happen next is this. You are going to lean in even closer to me and whisper in my ear, and I am going to laugh, quite loudly, as if you have just uttered the most comical remark. Then I am going to clap you on the back and you are going to resume your seat opposite me. As soon as you have sat down, you will attract the attention of Charles standing over there looking quite concerned, as if contemplating whether or not to fetch the Manager of this most excellent establishment, which serves luncheons to men of business, men of substance, and which has its reputation to consider, and you will ask him for two more coffees. Do I make myself clear? Are you a man of business, Robin, a man of substance?"

Robin leant in closer and answered in Matthew's ear. "Yes."

"Then we understand one another," replied Matthew, a cruel smile creeping across his mouth, and then he laughed extremely noisily.

After the waiter, Charles, had brought the two additional coffees and received yet another sixpence from Matthew, once again rolled rapidly across the back of his hand – "No, my dear chap," effusively to Robin, "I couldn't possibly allow you to. Let me, I insist." – Robin waited till he was sure they were no longer being overheard before asking him his second question.

"How?" he said simply. One word. "How could you arrange this?"

"I have contacts," said Matthew straightforwardly. "Don't pretend to be surprised."

"I wasn't."

"Good. You're beginning to understand the rules of the game."

"Game?"

"Of course. All business is a game. And the first rule is not *what* you know, but...?"

"*Who* you know," replied Robin glumly.

"And *I* know everyone."

"You scratch their back and they'll scratch yours."

"Exactly. You're beginning to catch on fast."

"And whose backs are we talking about?"

"Yours actually. I shall expect something in return for the service I am about to render you. But that's not what you meant, is it?"

Robin shook his head. He could feel the fish hook dig deeper into his skin.

"I have a business associate," said Matthew airily, "who also happens to be a friend. He has family connections in the highest places. Westminster. A Baronetcy, no less."

Robin looked up despite himself. "A Baronetcy?"

Matthew smiled. "Yes. I am always amused at the power of a title to impress and enthrall. This particular one, whose name we need not mention at this point, also happens to be on the Boards of several charities, including a hospital, where he takes a special interest in the appointment of new surgeons. I happen to know that a vacancy has recently arisen there. It could be a wonderful position for the right candidate. With excellent prospects. Now, if I were to suggest a certain person whom I deemed suitable for this vacant position, I know that my recommendation would be listened to most attentively."

"I should be for ever in your debt."

"Indeed you would."

"Then I should be obliged to you, Mr Oldham, if you might put my name forward for consideration for this position. Most obliged."

"No sooner said than done, Mr Holroyd. Shall we shake hands on it?"

"Yes indeed, sir. Let us do so."

The two men shook hands vigorously for several seconds, a gesture which Matthew made sure was witnessed by all those still present in the lounge of *The White Bear Hotel*.

After they had sat down again, Robin asked, as casually as he could, "Where *is* the hospital?"

"Oh?" said Matthew. "Didn't I say? In the Baronet's Seat. Tamworth."

"Tamworth in Staffordshire?"

"I know no other."

Robin went pale.

"My dear sir," said Matthew in affected concern, "whatever's the matter? Charles – a glass of water for my friend. He is suddenly unwell."

342

"I apologise most profusely," said Robin, after he had drunk not one, but two glasses of water from the ever-attentive Charles. "And now I must take my leave, for I have embarrassed you enough. Forgive me."

He rose unsteadily to his feet, whereupon Matthew immediately put a hand upon his shoulder and gently, but firmly, steered his guest back to a seat.

"Not until you have fully recovered, my friend, and explained to me the cause of this most extreme reaction. You have an objection to Tamworth?" he asked, trying hard to conceal the amused expression he was certain must be playing across his lips.

"No. None. Far from it. I do not know the place."

"Then I do not understand."

"It is the thought of leaving Manchester that so unhinges me."

"Well – she is a fine town," responded Matthew, still playing the game of cat and mouse, deftly patting his victim back and forth between his as yet sheathed paws, "and in time will be a great one, but not sufficient cause to hold a young man back when a new horizon beckons?"

"I have ties, sir."

"Really? You surprise me. To whom, sir, or to what? You live alone, I understand? Both your parents are sadly passed away. You have no younger siblings who might call on you for succour or aid. You are young, footloose and fancy free. What could be possibly holding you back? Unless it is some noble but needless sense of obligation towards your patients, who would, I can assure you, be well cared for by your successor."

"I am not, as you so carelessly put it, free."

"Ah," said Matthew, coming around to sit by Robin's side and place a manly arm about his shoulder. "I think we understand one another. *Cherchez la femme.*"

343

Robin looked up miserably, his face transparent and naked.

"You are engaged, I take it?"

"Not officially, no, not yet, but we have an understanding. I am to formally ask her next month, when she turns twenty-one."

"And you have hopes that she will accept?"

"Yes. Most high hopes. She has given me every encouragement to think so."

"Then why so glum? This is cause for celebration. Charles – a bottle of your finest champagne. Now that you have this offer of an improved position as a surgeon, an occupation with respect, dignity and standing, she will have even more cause to accept your proposal. I am certain a fine house will come with the post..." He dangled this additional tid-bit before his hapless victim, tossing him lightly into the air with it, before watching him continue to squirm on the ground when he landed.

"The thing is," said Robin as Matthew instructed Charles to pour the first two glasses of champagne, "I do not believe she would follow me there."

"Come, come, my friend," said Matthew raising his glass, "it is a wife's duty to follow her husband wherever he bids her."

"She is a schoolmistress."

"Then she'll be intelligent enough to see the logic and advantages of what you would be proposing."

"No, you don't understand. She has her own school here. On Bridge Street. It thrives, it prospers."

"Then she could open a new school in Tamworth, which would equally thrive and prosper."

"Yes, I'm certain of it," replied Robin distractedly, "but then there's the question of her family."

Matthew raised an arched eyebrow.

"Her mother died when Lavinia – Miss Robinson, my intended – was not yet twelve years old. She made Lavinia promise to look after all of her brothers and sisters..."

"A promise she has fulfilled many times over from what you say of her," interrupted Matthew. He had no desire for further details of death-bed partings.

"Yes indeed, but she would be reluctant to leave any of them behind, especially her sister Susannah."

"Mrs Bentley?"

Robin nodded. "They are especially close."

"I could perhaps have a word with Mr Bentley, if you wish? He'd be sure to persuade his wife not to stand in the way of her sister's future happiness."

"Would he?"

"If I asked him to."

Robin's fragile hopes, momentarily raised, then collapsed before him like a house of cards. "But then there's the twins, and the two younger sisters, not to mention the older brother…"

"… who will assume the responsibility of providing for the others once Miss Robinson has left to follow you."

"Yes, but…"

"You remain unconvinced, I see?" said Matthew, deciding that the time had come to change tack. He slowly unsheathed his claws. "I believe that what is troubling you more is the nagging doubt that perhaps she does not love you after all? That she will use these 'obligations', as you call them, as excuses to turn you down?"

Robin hangs his head.

"Ah-ha! Now we come to it, I see. *'Frailty, thy name is woman'*."

"I will not hear a word said against Miss Robinson. She is a paragon."

"If so she be, why do you fear her rejection so acutely?"

"Because I am not worthy of her. No man could be."

" '*There's none so foul and foolish thereunto
But does foul pranks which fair and wise ones do'*."

"Foul pranks?"

345

"Let us not be coy, Mr Holroyd. We are both men of the world. You know of what I speak."

"I do not!"

"The beast with two backs."

"You will take that back, sir. You dishonour her most heinously. She is without blemish, without stain. She is a *nonpareille*."

"Such passion does you credit, Robin," replied Matthew with maddening calmness, "but empty vessels, they say, make the most noise, do they not?"

"What are you inferring?"

"I infer nothing. But I will wager you this: that before the month is out, I shall bring you proof of an indiscretion."

"Name your sum, sir."

"I admire your confidence, Robin. Are you so sure that I will fail?"

"She is chastity personified."

"*A Chaste Maid in Cheapside*, eh?"

"There is nothing cheap about Miss Robinson."

"All women stray, Mr Holroyd. Does the moon rise as the sun sets? Does the earth turn on its axis? It's in their nature. Like a bitch on heat. They itch, they scratch."

"I resent your tone, sir. Miss Robinson, I tell you, is as pure as the driven snow."

"Untrodden and clean?"

"Virginal."

"Do you know what snow is, Mr Holroyd? Shall I tell you? It occurs when vapour in the air freezes before it can turn into water. The flakes when they fall are crystals of ice that have formed around granules of dirt in the air. The snow may melt in time, but the dirt persists. It lingers. It settles like a veneer upon every surface it touches."

"Very well. I accept your wager, but you shall eat your words, I warrant you."

"Let time be the judge."

"What do you propose?"

Matthew smiled. He had reached that final moment of the catch. When the lure has been cast and the bait has been taken. When the unwary fish has bitten the hook and the reeling in has begun. When the final struggle has all but ceased, the thrashing and flailing at the end of the line all but spent, and the fish gapes and flaps helplessly on the shore.

"One month from today, on Friday the 16th of December, the day Miss Robinson turns twenty-one, when it has been agreed that you shall ask for her hand in marriage, I invite you to deposit yourself behind a lamp post upon the New Bailey Bridge, at a little after five o' clock in the afternoon, an hour before you and she are due to meet there yourselves, and to wait. While you are waiting, you are to listen and to observe. That is all. If, after so doing for no more than a quarter hour, you are still satisfied that your intended is as you believe her to be, a Diana, a Daphne, then I shall submit to you a written apology, to do with what you will. If, however, events prove otherwise and you discover a truth you would rather not know, then I require nothing in return from you, nothing whatsoever, except that you take up my offer of the position of surgeon in Tamworth Hospital and quit Manchester forthwith. In either scenario you come away with something – a most favourable set of terms, I would suggest."

"And what is in this for you? What do you gain from this one-sided arrangement?"

Matthew characteristically spread his hands wide once more and smiled. "The satisfaction of having been proved right."

"Agreed," said Robin roughly. "Prepare to be disappointed. I have a higher opinion, it would seem, of the fairer sex than do you, and my faith, I believe, will be vindicated."

"Believe what you will. Faith is a fickle mistress."

"But Miss Robinson will be steadfast."

"One month from today…"

Matthew holds out his hand. After a sharp pause, Robin

347

takes it in his own and grasps it firmly.

"I accept the wager," he says, "and your terms. One month from today." Then he leaves.

Matthew watches him go. He picks up a napkin from the table where they have been sitting and wipes his mouth with it, like a cat licking the last of the cream from his lips. Bored with the sport, he lets his victim go – his bird, his mouse – and sheathes his untested claws, until they are needed another time.

"One month from today," he whispers quietly under his breath.

*

The clock in the hallway strikes five. He will be here in an hour, thinks Lavinia, rousing herself. I must go upstairs and change. I must be sure to look my best for when he arrives. It is not every day a girl is proposed to.

Susannah, ever the practical one, has asked her outright. "Well?" she has said. "Have you decided how you will answer him?"

Lavinia looks at her sister and smiles. "Yes," she says, nodding her head quickly, "I shall accept."

The two sisters embrace warmly.

"And I shall not be far away," adds Lavinia, "for Robin lives just a few doors from us. I shall see you all every day."

"We shall hardly notice a change," agrees Susannah. "It will be just as it was when I married my James," she adds. " 'I shall still be needed to attend my duties here,' I told him, and he agreed in an instant. 'Of course, my dear,' he replied – you know how he dotes on me, Sister, and will do anything to please me – 'your resourcefulness has made it possible for you to remain within the circle of acquaintances you enjoyed while your father was alive.' 'And Lavinia's too,' I corrected him. 'Quite so, Lavinia's too, yes,' he conceded, right gladly might I add, 'and together you have managed,' he continued, 'to protect the younger members of the family from all the harms and dangers that lurk within the world.' 'Aye, that we have,' I said, allowing him to put his arm about my waist, 'and so naturally you must maintain a regular presence there.' 'Which I intend to,' I replied smiling. 'So long as,' he added, with a mischievous glint in his eye, 'you do not forget where your prime duty now lies.' He pulled me closer as he said that and I let him kiss me, for, bless me, he's not a bad soul, not really, not when you get to know him."

"I know that, Sister, and I couldn't be happier for you, nor more grateful for all the help and assistance you still give us here. I don't know how we'd have managed without you."

"You'd have managed just fine, but it just wouldn't've seemed right not coming and seeing all my brothers and sisters each day. Now – to sensible matters, what of the school? What's to become of it after you marry?"

"He hasn't asked me yet."

"But we both know he shall – probably tonight – so don't be coy, it doesn't become you. Let us be practical. These things have to be thought about."

"Oh," says Lavinia with passionate certainty, "I shall continue to run it. I have no intention of giving up my role as schoolmistress here. The children will just have to get used to calling me Mrs Holroyd instead of Miss Robinson."

"Good for you," replies Susannah, her hands and arms dusted in flour from where she has been preparing the pastry for a rook pie for supper. It rises in a white sieved shower catching the last of the winter sun as it slants through the kitchen window before it falls around them like dust motes of snow.

Their celebrations are interrupted by a knocking on the front door, puncturing their high spirits like a pin in a balloon, all of the air escaping in a rush. It continues, louder and more determined.

"You answer it," says Susannah. "I need to continue getting the supper ready."

Lavinia makes her way along the hallway, wondering what this prolonged and insistent knocking can mean. When she opens it, a blast of cold air blows into the house, revealing a small ragamuffin of a boy, noisily sniffing, who thrusts a piece of paper towards her.

"The man says," repeats the boy, screwing up his face as he tries to recall the message he must impart word for word, "The man says, 'Come at once. It's a matter of life and death'."

Lavinia takes the creased and crumpled note from the boy who, with an extra loud sniff, runs off down Bridge Street as if the hounds of hell were after him.

"Wait," she calls, fetching a penny from her purse, but he has already fled from sight.

Shaking her head with a puzzled frown, she closes the door, shutting out at least some of the cold air, but not before she feels a shiver travel up and down her spine. She pauses before unfolding the piece of paper to read the message it contains. She has a sudden, sharp sense of foreboding, which forces her to sit down on the oak settle in the hall to compose herself. This is not the first occasion she has experienced such feelings. They have been occurring more frequently than she would care to admit, even to herself, especially recently, when she has had the distinct impression of being watched, of being followed whenever she has been abroad in the town, but each time she has stopped to look over her shoulder, there has been nobody there. It must be nerves, she has thought, her imagination playing tricks with her, working overtime as her twenty-first birthday approaches and, with it, the prospect of a proposal of marriage.

Taking a deep breath, she smoothes out the creases on the note, written, she cannot help but noticing, on what was once a fine linen paper – before the young messenger boy got his grubby fingers all over it, that is. She does not recognise the hand. She has assumed it must be from Robin, but she realises that she has in fact never seen anything before that he has written. It has not been an issue until now. Living just a few doors away from her further down Bridge Street has meant there has been no need for letters. The message she now reads, however, could not be clearer.

"Meet me in half an hour upon the New Bailey Bridge. What I have to say to you is of the greatest urgency."

It is unsigned and, although the words suggest they must have been written in extreme haste, the penmanship is clear, bold, assured and steady. If the hand which wrote them shook as it did so, it is not apparent in their appearance on the page.

Not wishing to delay a moment longer, she hurriedly fastens her finest green mantle over her fawn gown, ties a pink and yellow silk handkerchief around her neck and places a black beaver felt hat firmly upon her head. At the last moment she takes the white cotton shawl with the pattern of moths interwoven into leaves of laurel, given to her by her dying mother, and places it around her shoulders over the mantle, before rushing out of the house towards the New Bailey Bridge. It is already early evening and the temperature bitterly cold. A hard frost has covered the ground, which is slippery underfoot. Several times, in her anxiety not to keep her fiancé waiting a moment longer than she can help, she skids and nearly falls, grabbing at a railing or a lamp post to save her. The recently installed gas lamps in the town cast a sickly orange glow, throwing sinister shadows which climb the walls of the nearby prison.

Matthew, Robin, Lavinia.

At last the three protagonists find themselves in the same location upon the same instant. Matthew waits on the bridge, his back turned, facing away from the direction that Lavinia will come. Robin has positioned himself, as instructed, lurking unseen in one of the eerie shadows cast by the flickering gaslights, behind a lamp post, from where he will be able to witness and eavesdrop upon what takes place when Lavinia arrives. Lavinia is even now running towards the bridge, heedless of the treacherous surface beneath her feet.

She sees a man at the far end of the bridge. In the dusk of the evening she is not certain who it is. He wears clothes that are similar to those she has seen Robin wear but his bearing is different, stiller, stronger. He is familiar to her, but she cannot think from where. As she gets nearer, he tosses his cane nervously from one hand to the other, a gesture she has seen Robin perform many times before, especially when he has something important he wants to say. Perhaps she is mistaken and it is him after all.

Robin watches her approach from his concealed position in the shadows. He sees her running as fast as she can, without thought to her personal safety, or that of others on the bridge, whom she brushes aside in her unseemly haste. Is she so desperate not to be late for her rendezvous? He does not recall her ever running so eagerly to meet *him*.

Matthew turns at the very moment her footsteps are almost upon him. He raises his hat to greet her, but she is running so quickly she cannot stop herself in time and slips. He puts out a hand to save her from falling. The evening could not have begun better, he thinks.

Robin watches in horror as she appears to swoon in his arms. He sees Matthew's hands linger upon her body for longer than is seemly or necessary in lifting her back to her feet. She makes no effort to prevent him. He raises his hat. He kisses her gloved hand. She drops a curtsey. Her cheeks colour, even on so cold a night as this. It is clear to Robin that the two are more than merely acquainted, as clear as the bells of St John's Church which begin to peal loudly through the dark from further down the Dean's Gate.

Lavinia is mortified. Each peal of the bells appears to strike right through her. The only thing which saves her from further embarrassment is the thought that at least Robin has not been here to witness what has just occurred, for he would be certain to misconstrue its meaning.

"Forgive me," she says to Matthew as she tries to regain her composure. "I was in haste. I mistook you for someone else. I received an urgent note…" She begins to move past him.

"A note sent by me," said Matthew, catching her elbow to prevent her from leaving.

Lavinia's eyes widen in surprise. "From you?" She pauses mid-stride. She can feel the pressure of his grip upon her arm but is too thrown to free herself from it.

"You sound surprised. Please don't be." He releases his hold on her sleeve and turns her round to face him. "I thought I had made my feelings for you quite plain when we spoke at *The Assembly Rooms*."

"As I made my own completely clear to you also."

"Alone together, on the balcony, looking out over the illuminated garden. Such a romantic setting."

Robin hears all this and is felled by the words. "Feelings completely clear… Alone together… Romantic…" He sees Matthew reach across towards her, place his hand upon her shoulder, then turns away. He cannot watch more of this.

In that instant, when he turns away, he does not see Lavinia flinch in revulsion, shrug Matthew's icy hands from her, their cold penetrating right through her mantle to her skin. Nor does he hear the words that follow this.

"I told you at the time I was already spoken for. Still am. It is he I rushed to meet here on the bridge. Not you."

"But he is not here, is he?" says Matthew, turning his head from side to side, as if Robin might somehow materialise out of the night air right in front of them. "Whereas I am."

"I cannot think what you hope to gain from this subterfuge, Mr Oldham, but say what you have to, for he may arrive at any moment."

Robin hears her raised voice – "say what you have to… he may arrive any moment" – and forces himself to turn back, watch and listen further.

"He's not coming," says Matthew, so quietly that Robin cannot catch what he says. "Not now, not ever."

All he can see are his lips moving, pressing themselves closer to Lavinia's ears, so that only she may hear his words, secret words, honeyed words, a lover's words, meant only for each other. Now he understands the game that Matthew has been playing, how he has been duped by him, lured into trusting him, when all along his intention has been to expose him to this cruel joke, of overhearing him swapping dalliances with the woman he had dreamed to marry, exchanging tokens and caresses with her.

Lavinia listens to the words Matthew whispers in her ear like poison, paying no care to the way his fingers paw at her hair, or fondle the moths in her cotton shawl.

"It's not true," she gasps.

"But he told me himself," wheedles Matthew. "She will hold me back. I have offers of positions in reputable hospitals. A Baronet in Staffordshire, no less, has requested my services personally. But she will not leave her school or her family. She thinks to remain on Bridge Street for ever, expecting me to wait upon her like a lap dog."

A tear slowly slides down her cheek. "I don't believe you," she whispers.

"Then you must ask him yourself," he says, raising his voice, "for I think I see him coming even now."

Robin hears this last exhortation and knows this to be his cue to emerge from behind the lamp post and confront them, but it is as if the extreme cold has turned his muscles to stone, to ice, and he finds he cannot move. Instead he is forced to endure more humiliation. He looks on as Lavinia throws herself at her seducer.

"Then you must go at once," she pleads. "He must not see us together. He will not understand. He will not believe me, no matter what I might say, how ever many times I deny it."

Her fingers cling to the lapels of Matthew's jacket as she desperately tries to solicit him to assist her. He disentangles them from him, gripping her wrists firmly, the expression on his face a mixture of triumph and disgust.

" *'Methinks the lady doth protest too much'*."

Robin finally propels himself into action and leaps from his sanctuary in the shadows and rushes headlong across the bridge towards the wrestling pair.

"Don't worry," he hears Matthew call, extricating himself from Lavinia's clutches, "your secret is safe with me." And then he is gone.

Lavinia slumps to the ground just as a breathless Robin arrives at her side.

He looks bitterly down on her. He makes no effort to help her to her feet. He thinks only of how she has betrayed him.

She becomes aware of a shadow falling across her. She knows it must be Robin. She waits for him to speak, or to act.

But Robin says and does nothing. He remains looking down at her, as one might a beggar, or a fallen woman, for a long time, time which hangs suspended between them, like the snow which has now begun again to fall, those minuscule pieces of dirt wrapped in daggers of ice.

Lavinia is dimly aware of the shadow of a small bird hovering around her face, a swallow that has somehow been left behind for the winter. It grows weaker with each trembling wing beat until it is plucked out of the air by something larger, darker, stronger.

Robin makes a sudden lunge towards her, hauling her to her feet.

"What secret?" he hisses, bringing her face close up to his own. "What secret is it that is safe with him?"

Lavinia is shaking. She can barely speak. Eventually she whispers. It is scarcely audible. "That I am... already spoken for."

He pushes her harshly away from him towards the bridge's stone parapet. "Then there is yet another?" he cries. He pulls open his coat and tears at his hair. "Is there no end to your depravity?"

People crossing the bridge pass by on the other side, avoiding the embarrassing intimacy of this private catastrophe.

One of these is Abner Halsinger, on his way back from visiting a client in Salford on the other side of the Irwell. In addition to his duties at Heywood's Bank, where he assists his father, he also has a thriving sideline as a private accountant with a growing number of influential mill and factory owners making up the bulk of his portfolio. Among these is Matthew, whose arcane, dispersed investments he has recently taken over from his father, which he keeps track of and advises when the most auspicious time might be to shift his assets from one esoteric quarter to another. They are neither of them ones for social chit-chat, so mostly their business is conducted by letter, an arrangement which suits them both, but occasionally it is necessary for the two of them to meet, when certain documents have to be signed, for example, and so the two of them will, if they ever run into each other on one of Manchester's busy streets, raise their hats, bid the other a cordial "Good day", then proceed along their separate ways. Frequently, given his albinism, Abner will not be sure that it is Matthew until he has almost bumped into him.

And this is what happens on this particular evening. Abner, returning from his client in Salford, is almost knocked flying by a triumphantly striding Matthew. Abner is stepping onto the bridge at the very moment that Matthew is rushing from it, so that they have already passed from sight before either can acknowledge the other on this freezing December evening.

Steadying himself once more, Abner's thoughts are returning to his chief love, his astronomy. On such a night as this, he thinks, if the snow ceases, he may well behold the stars arching clear and bright over the town. He will be able to train his telescope on a dazzling Venus, the elusive Mercury, and even the Moons of Jupiter, which will all be crowding the eastern skies. So engrossed is he in the prospect of such a sighting that he barely registers the pitiful scene of a young woman sobbing on the pavement, with a stern, reproachful-looking young man standing over her. He has almost stepped off the bridge at the opposite end when a loud, impassioned cry from the woman forces him to turn round. He is just in time to catch sight of what he thinks is the young man striking her. But he cannot be certain, and he knows his sight is not to be trusted. But his hearing more than compensates and what he hears next sounds as clear as the counting of coins in the Bank.

"Please believe me, I beg you," the woman cries, "but you won't. I don't care if you murder me, if you'll only believe me."

"Never," the man replies bitterly, "I shall never forgive you."

But then it appears that the two of them are in each other's arms again and Abner departs, thinking this is nothing more than the couple beginning to make up after a routine lovers' tiff.

"I came here this night to ask you to marry me, but instead you humiliate me in a public place. Do not think, when the time comes, that I shall not seek to exact my revenge on you. I shall let it be known to all the world that you are not what you say you are. I shall proclaim it from the rooftops. When purchasing a new shirt, one should be sure to ascertain it is not shop-soiled. Likewise, when selecting a wife, it is essential to check she is not damaged goods."

"I'm innocent of all your accusations," pleads Lavinia, clinging to him desperately.

"Then go – get thee to a nunnery."

He prises her arms from around his neck and flings her to the ground, stepping over her prostrate body on the hard, unforgiving ground.

After what feels like hours, but is no more than a few moments, after she realises that Robin is not coming back, she slowly drags herself back to her feet. She leans over the stone parapet and stares down into the Irwell below. There are no boats or barges plying its water tonight. Already its surface is beginning to freeze over. Great slabs of ice knock against the base of the arches beneath the bridge, clogging the river's flow. She peers down into it for a long time. She remains so still that she might almost become a carved statue, her face etched in cold marble.

She sees no way forward, her future trapped like one of those slabs of ice forming on the river, which will doubtless melt in time but leave nothing but a stained memory behind. Her school, which she has worked so hard to build up and establish, will collapse, along with her reputation. Her family's fortunes too will suffer, and this feels even harder to bear than her own ruin.

She contemplates the dark, freezing waters below, imagines them closing over her head, but pulls away at the last. No – there must be another way. From somewhere behind her she hears a shout, followed by the sound of footsteps running towards her, then nothing.

Pity is back on her old stamping ground.

She lives quite the respectable life these days – if she discounts the fact that the man she shares that life with publicly as a brother she shares her bed with as a husband. Jem has status, a much sought-after stone and brick mason, and the reputation that accompanies that, while Pity still works in the dress and hat shop of Philip Jacob's Tailors, her nimble fingers as deft as they ever were with needle and thread. She has been there for fifteen years now, is so much a part of the fixture and fittings that her odd ways are scarcely commented on. She still rarely speaks, only if it is absolutely necessary and no other alternative presents itself. In all the years she has been there Mr Jacob cannot recall hearing more than a half-dozen words issue from her lips, and not a one of them of her own volition. Most of her co-workers, all of whom have joined the firm after her, have not heard her utter a sound. Nor do any of them comment on her singular appearance, the tiny body, more like a child's than a woman's, more like a bird's than a human's, half waif, half wizened crone. The only thing that has altered down the years is her hair. Where once it fell in a tangled, matted mass almost to her knees, now it has been cut. An accident five years before, where a knotted handful of it became caught in one of the machines, caused her, quite calmly, to shear off a chunk with a pair of eight-inch fabric scissors. Afterwards, unhurt and unperturbed, she allowed Mrs Jacob to level it off at her shoulders, since when she has kept it at more or less this length, jutting out in a red frizz. Mrs Jacob has also furnished her with one or two items of clothing, garments discarded by customers – children's skirts and dresses mostly – which Pity now wears instead of the street-grime rag she had worn like a second skin for as long as she could remember. She cuts a cleanlier figure these days, does not object to Jem's insistence on a monthly all-over wash with water from the pump in the yard at the back of where they live above the shop, all that remains of the old Fogg's Yard, whose ruin and squalor are now a dim memory.

But the old ways still call her from time to time. She still gets a yearning to wander the old haunts, especially at nights, roaming the streets in search of wherever the Hulks have relocated themselves. She seeks out the fires lit within the skeletons of unfinished, partly-constructed new buildings, or the shattered bones of half-demolished ones, where Manchester's homeless huddle, foraging with the rats for the town's scrap and discard. She looks out for the familiar figures of old and occasionally stumbles upon one, but mostly these are long gone, The Old Retainer, The Great Usurper, dead most probably, but she sees the same wary expressions on the faces of the new arrivals, the same hunched and guarded bodies, ready to lash out if their territory is threatened or invaded, hissing like a nest of feral cats, before settling back down again a few yards farther off.

Pity feels the old lure on this particular night, hears its voice wrenching her from the pit of sleep, tugging her hair, plucking her skin, so that she rises before she knows it, answering that old ancestral call, puts on one of Mrs Jacob's cast-off dresses and wanders into the night. Jem senses her stir but hardly notices these days. He turns over to fill the gap her tiny body has left in their bed, the weight of her so slight that she leaves no imprint in the sackcloth mattress, knowing that, come the dawn, she'll be back.

Outside she does not feel the cold, even though it must be several degrees below zero now. She walks beside the Irwell, sees it freezing over almost right before her eyes, the great slabs of ice sparkling like crystal under a Wolf Moon. She hears them groan and crack as if mighty forces beneath the earth's crust are straining. She feels its axis shift and tilt beneath her. She is reminded of another night, thirty-six years ago, when the earth buckled and split, the Great Quake, when she found the dying woman who gave birth to twin boys three quarters of an hour apart, whom she helped deliver and rescue, one to the House of Correction and one to the step of a fine house, wrapped in a white muslin cloth of moths caught in leaves of laurel, where he was taken in and cared for. She thinks of the times she has seen those boys over the years – not so often these days. The one from the House of Correction she has not seen in half a decade, not since the riot in St George's Fields, while the other one, not since she stood before him in the Court Leet. He's done well for himself. She likes to think she played a part in that, but something about the hard line of his mouth, the cold look in his eyes, unnerved her. She wonders what has caused such bitterness and cruelty. Though he showed her some unasked for pity, gave her this new name even, which now she answers to. It has been a long time since she was last called Whelp. She has almost forgotten it. But it comes back to her now, as she walks beside the river, seeking out the Hulks.

She stands poised on the edge of the frozen Irwell. It has frozen so hard that she feels certain it would take her weight if she chose to venture out upon it. Silhouetted against the Wolf Moon, one leg raised, head lowered as if seeking out a fish trapped beneath the glittering surface that she might spear and rescue, she resembles a white egret, of the kind once common in Manchester, but now, since the poisoning of the rivers, confined to stretches of water further upstream, but still occasionally glimpsed, solitary and alone, scudding across a bleak winter sky.

She places one foot, then the other, onto the ice. It creaks beneath her. It shifts in a kind of suspended flow, but it holds. Delicately she picks her way across it, towards the far bank, where she can see lit fires burning, smoke rising in coiled and twisted statues, and hear the spit and crack of wood splitting in the heat.

Halfway across she becomes aware of a slight flurry of movement to her left. She turns her head and sees a figure standing on the bridge. A woman. A white shawl is wrapped around her shoulders. She is leaning over the stone parapet, almost as if she is looking for a gap between the ice floes into which she might leap. Pity hurries as best she can towards her, though progress is not easy across the shifting surface. It takes her several minutes to reach her. When she does, she looks up towards her from below the bridge's central arch. The woman has spread her arms out wide, almost as if she means to jump. From where Pity stands beneath her, it looks more like she is about to fly. Her arms stretch like wings. Pity instinctively mirrors their shape, so that the woman, looking down, almost imagines she is seeing her own reflection. Startled, she raises her arms higher, a frightened flap of her wings, and the white shawl falls from her shoulders. It descends in a gentle slow motion, almost defying gravity, as if buoyed up by the moths fluttering among the laurel leaves, trying to float free. Pity holds out her arms to catch it as it drifts down towards her, dancing with the petals of ash and smoke from the nearby fires in the Hulks. She cradles it gently against her breast. There is no mistaking it. She knows it in a heartbeat. It is the very same cloth she found with the dying mother, which she wrapped around the second twin.

As if awoken from a dream, the woman above steps away from the parapet. She looks anxiously to her left. Pity hears what she hears. The sound of a man shouting, of footsteps running across the bridge, shouts and cries, an arm appearing to be raised as if to strike the woman. Pity hurries as quickly as she can towards the far bank, using the slabs of ice like stepping stones which threaten to slip from under her, until eventually she reaches it, clambers ashore, then runs round towards the bridge. The man – if indeed there was a man – is gone. The woman lies slumped upon the ground. Pity approaches her, quietly and carefully, as if she were one of the feral cats to be found in the Hulks. The young woman remains where she is, eyeing Pity unblinkingly, some deep buried instinct telling her that she presents no threat. She waits until

Pity has reached her, has stooped to help her to her feet, has wrapped the white cotton shawl back around her shoulders. They look at each other a long time. Neither of them speaks. Eventually the young woman breathes in deeply, before exhaling a long, emptying sigh. Finally she speaks.

"Pity me," she says.

Pity says nothing. She imperceptibly nods.

"Thank you," says the young woman, in a voice so low only Pity can hear it. She is not certain the sound she has heard has not been the shift and scrape of ice below them. She watches the young woman – Lavinia – walk slowly away from her.

Then, when she can no longer see her on the bridge, she turns the other way, heads in the direction of the still lit fires smouldering beside the frozen river. An owl hoots unseen from somewhere close by. She feels the rush of air as it swoops past in pursuit of its innocent prey. The bells of St John's Church toll midnight.

*

At a quarter to four the next morning Susannah woke with a start. She had forgotten to remind Lavinia about the chimney sweep, who was coming first thing. There would be much to do to get the house ready for his arrival and she was sure Lavinia would be too excited after Robin's proposal the previous evening to have given any thought to sweeping chimneys.

Making sure not to disturb a gently snoring James, she crept downstairs, opened the front door and prepared to walk the few yards to her old family house, where the rest of her brothers and sisters still lived, though for Lavinia, not for much longer. Susannah smiled at the thought of the soft words that had no doubt passed between her sister and her intended last night. She would prepare the downstairs rooms and fireplaces before Lavinia was awake and surprise her with what she had done. Then, once the chimney sweep had begun his work – he was expected at around six – the two of them would sit down to breakfast together and she would question her sister all about what Robin had said and how she had answered him and what plans had been made already for the wedding.

She barely noticed the extreme cold as she scurried the short distance between their two houses, less than two chains apart from one another along the same street. The church bells were just chiming four o'clock as she reached her old front door.

As soon as she stepped through it, she was aware that something was wrong. The white cotton shawl which had been their mother's, a gift from Mrs Oldham, which she had worn on her wedding day, and which Lavinia had inherited from her on her death bed, lay strewn upon the hall floor, creased and careless, abandoned where it had fallen. Frowning, Susannah picked it up. This was most unlike Lavinia, who was normally so scrupulous in putting things neatly away. 'A place for everything and everything in its place' was one of her favourite maxims. She hurried into the kitchen, where a lamp was still burning. Another uncharacteristic oversight on the part of Lavinia, thought Susannah with growing concern, to have retired for the night without first making sure that all the lamps had been extinguished. Perhaps, she thought with a blush, the two lovebirds had simply become too engrossed in each other to be mindful of such domestic trivialities. She pictured a scene of Robin and Lavinia running in from outside, where he has just proposed to her and she has breathlessly said yes. She has flung the shawl to the floor in her impatience to fall into her fiancé's arms and be covered with his kisses. She has not spared the lamp a second's thought as Robin has swept her up in his arms and carried her upstairs. Surely not, thinks Susannah, surprising herself with such fantasies, not before they are married! Perhaps, even now, the two of them are clasped in a lovers' embrace upstairs…

But such idle dreams were dispelled in an instant. There, lying alone and bereft in the centre of the otherwise clear kitchen table, was a note. Like an island lost in the middle of a cruel and empty ocean, it sat there, waiting for a passing ship to discover it. Susannah was that ship. She picked it up and read the two bleak sentences that were written on it.

"With my last dying breath, I attest myself innocent of the crime laid to my charge. God bless you all, I cannot outlive his suspicion."

It was unsigned. The hand was shaky but the meaning clear.

Susannah immediately sprang into action, roaring through the house like a tornado, rousing and questioning all, but no one had a single scrap of information they could add. They had seen nothing, heard nothing. Susannah's practical nature assumed instant control.

"Billy," she said, "run to the Police House and inform the Constables. Richard and Paul, go to the river. Ask anyone you come across if they've seen or heard anything. Ginny, you stay here in case Lavinia returns, and mind Jemma."

"What will *you* do?" asked a frightened Ginny.

"I shall rouse Mr Bentley and instruct him to fetch Mr Holroyd and see what light he may shed upon the situation." And with that she was already halfway out of the door when Ginny called her back.

"I don't believe this is Lavinia's hand," she said, holding up the note.

Susannah returned swiftly to examine it one more time and shook her head. "I cannot say whether it be truly her hand or not. The writing is too shaky, which is hardly surprising, given what it contains."

Within seconds the house was empty. Ginny lifted a sleepy Jemma into her arms, sat her down beside her on the bottom step of the stairs in the hallway, and waited. The silence, after the recent clamour and commotion, felt like a tomb.

Within five minutes James was up and dressed. Within five more he was banging loudly and determinedly on the front door of Robin's lodgings opposite the New Bailey Prison.

"Good God," he exclaimed as he heard James inform him of her disappearance, "is she not at home?"

"Indeed she is not. When did you last see her?"

"I cannot be certain."

"Try, man."

"I'm not sure. I think it was ten o'clock, perhaps eleven."

"Where was this? At the house?"

"No, sir. On the bridge."

"On the bridge? You left a young woman, unaccompanied and alone, at night, on the New Bailey Bridge?" James was becoming apoplectic.

"We had a most serious quarrel."

"Really? I am astonished to hear it, for a bitter word has never passed Miss Robinson's lips in all the time I have known her."

"Indeed, sir. I cannot tell. I am utterly miserable. I cannot tell what I must do."

"You can tell me the particulars of this quarrel you had to begin with."

"Very well. Mr Bentley, I believe in the circumstances all delicacy must be laid aside. I discovered…"

"Yes? What did you discover, damn you?"

"I discovered a want of chastity in Miss Robinson."

James's eyes threatened to pop out of their sockets. His face was purple with rage.

"Were it not for the extreme urgency of the situation, I would demand that you took back that remark upon the instant. I will not stand by and have the virtue of my sister-in-law besmirched, her honour impeached. She is a paragon. But if – when – we find her safe and unharmed, you will apologise for it publicly. But for now I would be obliged to you, Holroyd, to furnish me with the exact details of your movements from

366

when you and Miss Robinson first met last evening until the moment I knocked on your door."

"I have nothing further to say – except that if I do marry her, I shall not live long and be for ever miserable and unhappy."

"I don't care a fig for your feelings, man. I just want to find Miss Robinson. You will at the very least accompany me to the river to conduct a search for her?"

Robin said nothing, but nodded his head and followed James in the direction of the bridge.

When dawn finally broke on the Friday morning and Lavinia had still not returned, the whole of Manchester was agog with the news of her disappearance. The Special Constables asked for volunteers to form search parties and were overwhelmed by the response. Soon the whole town was being combed, especially alongside the banks of the rivers and canals.

Billy went to the offices of *The Manchester Mercury*, who agreed to print a notice asking if anyone had seen her, foregoing their customary fee. By mid-afternoon handbills of this notice were being posted on every street corner, on every building and on every lamp post. By evening sufficient donations had been received for a reward to be offered for any information that might lead to Lavinia's recovery.

ONE HUNDRED GUINEAS REWARD

Whereas LAVINIA ROBINSON, one of the Daughters of the late Zachary Robinson, Surveyor of Manchester, was, during the evening of THURSDAY 16TH DECEMBER LAST, in the company of a Gentleman (to whom she was on the point of marriage) in the environs of Bridge Street. When, the following morning, her sister, Mrs Susannah Bentley, arrived at the home of Miss Robinson, where she lived with her brothers and other sisters, she found her not to be at home. On the table in the kitchen there was a NOTE, purporting to be in Lavinia's handwriting, the contents of which caused her family to fear that she may no longer be living. HER FAMILY & FRIENDS have been plunged by this most UNHAPPY EVENT into the GREATEST DISTRESS. They feel the most painful anxiety to obtain any Intelligence respecting this UNFORTUNATE YOUNG LADY and, as an Inducement to Strangers to exert themselves a REWARD OF THIRTY GUINEAS (free of all expenses) is offered by the family to be paid by Mr John Redhead, Solicitor, St Ann's Church Yard, Manchester, to any Person or Persons who shall be the agents of discovering, ALIVE OR DEAD, the Lady who is the Subject of this Advertisement. She is twenty-one years of age, of a middle size and a good figure, of a fair complexion, with long, light brown hair. She had on a fawn-coloured, stout-twilled dress, a pink and yellow shot figured silk handkerchief around her neck, a green cloth mantle, a black vintage bonnet of beaver felt, and her linen is marked 'L.R.' We, the BOROUGHREEVE and CONSTABLES of Manchester, as a further stimulus and incentive to the exertion of Strangers, do hereby offer a REWARD OF SEVENTY GUINEAS in addition to the above figure.

Thomas Hardman, Boroughreeve
Roger Touchin, Chief Constable

6

1814

7th February

A week passes. Then two. Then three. In the end seven long, agonising weeks pass before there is any news.

It has been the hardest winter in more than a century. All the rivers and canals have frozen over. Trade has come to a near standstill. Food supplies have run dangerously low. The Boroughreeve places all Soldiers and Constables on high alert. Mounted troops patrol the streets in case of riots. But it is far too cold for even the most die-hard of Radicals to contemplate a riot in these Siberian temperatures. Fires have been lit on the ice on the Irwell, Irk and Medlock, but still they do not thaw. Horses draw wagons across them and their surfaces do not crack. With each day's precipitation children build snowmen, which overnight transform into Ice Warriors, mighty and unvanquishable.

Each day Billy trudges the streets putting up more handbills, searching the cellars and passages, but there is no news. Robin keeps his head down, buries himself in work. There are always babies being born, whatever the weather.

Every hour the heavy bells in tower and steeple toll across the town – at St John's, St Ann's, St Werburgh's, the Collegiate Church of St Mary, St Denys and St George – sounds like a death knell to the Robinson family, waiting hopefully for a miracle. The long-case clock in the hallway ticks away the minutes as slow and ponderous as the army of pick-axes striking the ice like an anvil when the fires in the forge have gone out.

Then, on the morning of Monday 7th February, everyone feels it. Or rather, first, they hear it. It begins with a light tinkling, tiny chimes of crystal, as the icicles hanging from gutter and pipe, rooftop and ledge begin to melt one by one. This is followed by a series of gentle cymbal rolls, the mosaic shattering of infinitesimally small fragments of glass beneath the slightest tap from a silversmith's cross-peen hammer. The high-pitched scraping of rusting metal on metal, of fingernails on a chalkboard, cuts through a thin, stinging sleet that has begun to fall, the sound of it like sharp gravel hitting a kettle, underscored by the deep timpanic boom of subterranean rumblings underneath the rivers as the thick sheets of ice upon their surface begin to shift and crack. The symphony of the thaw has begun with this slow, sad *largo*, melting into a more expressive *andante*, before breaking out into a mocking, accelerating *scherzo*, as the rivers burst their banks, sweeping away their guardian Ice Warriors with them.

Three miles downstream, at the Mode Wheel Mill in Barton, near Eccles, Mr Percy Goodier was awoken by the sharp rat-a-tat drumming of rain upon the window of his adjoining cottage, accompanied by a sound he had not heard for two months, the slow, rhythmic turning of the giant water wheel which drove the mill, its oak paddles finally able to smash their way through the splintering ice.

He hurried on his clothes and poked his nose outdoors, feeling the sting of sleet upon his face. At first he thought he must be dreaming. He rubbed his eyes, stretched them wide, rubbed them again, then focused them upon the far bank.

There, as he would later tell the Coroner, the newspapers and anyone who cared to ask him, he saw the body of the poor unfortunate Lavinia "reclining upon a frozen mud bank, environed by a tomb of ice, with icicles hanging from her hair, where there should have been orange blossom." She was perfectly preserved. The harshness of the winter and the coldness of the water had staved off any decay. She was wearing the clothes listed in the description of her in the notices hung about the town by Billy. The fawn-coloured twill gown. The green mantle. The pink and yellow silk handkerchief. The black beaver hat. All that was missing was the shoe from her left foot.

Word of the discovery being sent at once to Manchester, the police and members of her family were quickly on the scene, and the body, having been formally identified by Susannah, was conveyed by hearse to Lavinia's home on Bridge Street.

Soon the whole town was agog with the news.

"Tragic Discovery!" screamed *The Manchester Mercury*.

"Ice Maiden!" lamented *Bell's Weekly Messenger*. "Her Beauty Preserved!"

"The Manchester Ophelia!" declared *The Manchester Observer*.

Percy won praise from the press and plaudits from the public when he returned the thirty guineas reward offered by the family back to them, and tacit approval from the populace when he kept the seventy guineas put up by the Boroughreeve and the Constables.

The inquest was set for the following day in the Upstairs Room of *The Star Inn* at the junction of King Street West and the Dean's Gate, to be presided over by the Coroner, Mr Nathaniel Milne.

"It is with a sad and heavy heart that I open these formal proceedings today," he began.

The room was packed, standing room only, every available inch taken up by somebody, with hundreds more gathered outside craning their necks to hear whatever they might glean from the open windows up above. Higher up, perched along the tavern rooftop a parliament of rooks hung out their wings to catch the first of the sun's rays to reach the town for two months as the big freeze finally loosened its grip and the thaw continued to stretch its diffident fingers across the town. The birds looked down upon the people below, huddling together for warmth, stamping their feet and flapping their arms about their backs, as if recalling that primeval moment when they had first crawled from the frozen seas and their fins had grown into arms, from which time they had always looked up with envy at those creatures who had developed wings instead. The rooks cawed and crowed, cackled and croaked. They had witnessed such scenes before.

"After her parents' premature deaths," the Coroner continued, "only a few years before her own, Miss Lavinia Robinson supported her brothers and sisters by converting their home into a seminary, based upon the model she herself had known in the Moravian Settlement of Fairfield. Her resourcefulness enabled them to keep within the circle of the acquaintance they had enjoyed during their father's life, and to protect the younger branches of the family. From what I have myself learned already, Miss Robinson was a young lady possessing superior mental accomplishments, with a character as lovely as her mind, of the most fascinating manners, whose compositions in prose and in verse, breathed throughout the purest sentiments of religion and virtue, and prove her to have had a warm and affectionate heart, great vivacity, and an uncommon playfulness of disposition. In other words, ladies and gentlemen, a paragon. How this paragon came to meet with such a tragic and untimely end, it is this Court's sad duty now to ascertain if it can."

A troubled murmur ran through the Function Room of *The Star Inn*, spilling out into the street outside, where a low ripple of applause for the deceased began, which in turn spread back inside the inn and up the stairs to where the Coroner allowed it to subside in its own due course before calling upon his first witness.

"Mr Ainsworth," he said, "you are the surgeon, I believe, who has carried out the autopsy on the body of the deceased?"

"I am, sir," replied the Doctor, a scholarly gentleman, with delicate, refined fingers, which appeared more suited to the playing of the harpsichord than the internal investigations of recently discovered cadavers, and with which he now balanced a pair of spectacles upon the end of his rather long and pointed nose, in order to read from the meticulous notes those same fingers had composed, tiny crotchets, minims and quavers which danced across the page.

"Please could you tell the Court of your findings during your examination?" requested the Coroner, Mr Milne, of the musician before him.

Mr Ainsworth cleared his throat, raised his notes, rather like a conductor about to begin an overture.

"Her right temple had a crack of two inches, possibly the result of crushing in the ice. There was bruising around the neck, the causes of which are impossible to determine."

"Anything else, Mr Ainsworth?" asked the Coroner.

Mr Ainsworth cleared his throat once more, as if faced by a particularly challenging section in the music. "I carried out a thorough examination of the body. There was nothing to shake my conviction that she had passed a strictly unimpeachable and virtuous course of life."

Another ripple ran around the Court.

"In other words, Mr Ainsworth, not wishing to be indelicate at such a distressing time, you can confirm that the deceased was…?"

"A virgin, yes. Any suspicions to the contrary are completely groundless."

The ripple now grew to a roar. Heads turned, seeking out Robin, to gauge what his reaction to this pronouncement might be, but he was nowhere to be seen.

"Thank you, Mr Ainsworth. You may step down."

Mr Milne turned towards the crammed and assembled throng before him, raising his voice as he now spoke, so that those still waiting for news outside might also hear him.

"Mr Robin Holroyd, *accoucheur* to St Mary's Lying-In

Hospital, was invited to give evidence today, but he has declined my request."

Cries of "Shame" and "Outrage" threatened to bring the proceedings to an injudicious early end. It took all of Nathaniel Milne's experience to bring the Court back to order.

"However," he continued, as a kind of calm was finally restored, "he has sent this letter." He now held up a manila envelope by the corner with just the tip of his thumb and forefinger, as if to grasp any more of it might expose him to a most unpleasant, infectious disease. He handed it to the Clerk, who sliced it open with a letter opener, in a way not dissimilar to paring the pith of a bitter lemon, then handed the contents back to Mr Milne, who read aloud a brief extract from it.

" *'As I confided to Miss Robinson's brother-in-law, Mr Bentley, on the night of her disappearance, I was concerned that my fiancée suffered a want of chastity...'* "

A low hiss ran through the Court, which the Coroner elected not to quell, and over which he continued to read.

" *'I ventured upon the desperate alternative of being convinced of her virtue before marriage. On the night in question I discovered with horror that my fears were realised. I immediately taxed her with it, in answer to which, she asserted her innocence with considerable vehemence, but I would not believe her...'* "

Mr Milne handed back the letter with the same offended air to his Clerk. "I do not believe we need trouble the Court with any more of Mr Holroyd's self-serving letter, especially in the light of Mr Ainsworth's more objective analysis of the facts of this case."

Further witnesses were called.

Lavinia's sister, Ginny, repeated her assertion made to Susannah on the Friday morning that she doubted the handwriting on the note found upon the kitchen table to be Lavinia's. When pressed further by Mr Milne, however, she could not say with certainty that it was not.

Mr Bentley repeated his dealings with Holroyd after Lavinia's disappearance was discovered, but had nothing further to add, apart from his condemnation of the *accoucheur*'s now discredited accusations.

Abner volunteered the fact that he had seen a couple on the night in question matching the appearance of Miss Robinson and Mr Holroyd, who appeared to be engaged in some kind of passionate argument upon the bridge, but readily admitted that his sight was not the kind to be trusted to give evidence that could be relied upon.

At the end of two days, Mr Nathaniel Milne delivered the official verdict of the Court, which was duly printed in full in all of the town's newspapers.

"I, Nathaniel Milne, Coroner, do declare that the said Lavinia Robinson was found drowned in the River Irwell on Monday 7th February in the Year of our Lord 1814 by the Mode Wheel Mill in Barton, near Eccles, three miles from where she had last been seen, upon the New Bailey Bridge on the night of Thursday 16th December 1813, but how, or by what means, she came into the water of the said river, no evidence thereof appears to the said Coroner's Court."

In other words, an open verdict.

The rooks took off as one from *The Star Inn* roof to raucously spread the news.

Robin's reputation lay in tatters.

Bell's Weekly Messenger

11th February 1814

STONES THROWN AT WINDOWS OF ACCOUCHEUR

An unassuaged fury hangs over the people of Manchester today. Local feeling against Mr Robin Holroyd, a male midwife at St Mary's Hospital, yesterday reached fever pitch as angry crowds gathered outside his lodgings to demand his arrest. His walls and door were scrawled with all manner of lurid graffiti, the contents of which were too explicit for this newspaper to feel it is able to publish. Less offensive, though no less powerful accusations included the words, "Liar!" "Coward" and "Murderer!" daubed in red paint.

Special Constables appeared content to let the demonstration run its course until stones were thrown and windows smashed, when eventually the crowds were politely asked to disperse.

In a separate development, the Board of Trustees at the Hospital has dismissed Mr Holroyd with immediate effect. They released the following statement:

"We are sickened and disgusted by Mr Holroyd's morally craven and lily-livered behaviour."

The whereabouts of Mr Holroyd are currently not known.

Robin was bereft. Of hope and of ideas.

All his efforts to reach Matthew were thwarted. His letters were returned unopened, his requests for appointments refused. He even took to camping outside the entrance to Matthew's Chambers in the hope of catching him off guard, but in the end he was intercepted by a Special Constable, who informed him he was in danger of trespass, causing a nuisance, and disturbing the peace, and that if he knew what was good for him, he would move on and not come back.·

What happened next remains uncertain. Some say that he went in any case to Tamworth, only for news of his involvement with 'The Manchester Ophelia' case, as it had come to be known, to have arrived ahead of him, so that all doors there were politely but firmly closed against him. Rumours spread that he had committed suicide in Wolverhampton, but this proved to be a case of mistaken identity, or that he had returned to the village of his birth, Middlestown, near Thornhill, in Yorkshire, to pursue his ambition to become a surgeon there, but this too could not be substantiated. Only the rooks knew the truth of it, and they were not for telling.

'And so to 'scape the serpent's tongue
He will not make amends ere long
And so the Puck a liar call
And so goodnight unto you all...'

Matthew accompanies Mr Ainsworth to his Dissecting Room. But today the surgeon makes no cuts. He gently bathes the wound upon the corpse's right temple. He washes the hair. He delicately checks each orifice in turn, before the final one, when even Matthew finds he has to look away.

"Intact," says Mr Ainsworth. "Poor creature."

He turns back to Matthew. "You shall have a copy of my report tomorrow," he says, "after I have given evidence to the Inquest."

Matthew inclines his head respectfully. He says nothing. He looks down upon her perfectly preserved form, recalling his earlier, less respectful vow. "If I can't have her, then no one shall." Now nobody would and he finds he is sorry for it, an emotion that feels alien to him, but one which he can observe with a scintilla of legal detachment still, while Mr Ainsworth finishes the rest of his offices, finally covering her with a white cotton sheet. Matthew is reminded of that other white piece of cotton, which she was wearing the last time he saw her alive.

Once the Inquest is over and the Coroner has concluded his enquiries, Lavinia's body is released to the family for burial. The undertaking firm of Jupp & Gittings assume all responsibilities from this point onwards. Matthew visits them in the back room of their Funeral Parlour on Cateaton Street.

"I'm here on behalf of the Boroughreeve," he says.

"I assure you," replies the lugubrious Alfred Jupp, "we carry out our duties to the highest possible standards."

"I've no doubt of it," agrees Matthew.

"Then why the sudden interest from the Court Leet? We've never received such visits before, have we, Mr Gittings?"

Mr Gittings, who has just at that moment entered the room, and who is as short and round as Mr Jupp is long and thin, interlocks his fingers across his large, prominent stomach. "Indeed we have not, Mr Jupp."

"It's simply because of the high level of public interest in this case," Matthew explains. "The Boroughreeve wants to leave no stone unturned. I'm sure you understand?"

"Quite so," answers Mr Jupp, looking down on Matthew from his great height. He has the bearing and appearance of a tall long-case clock ticking slowly and dependably in the corner of the room, and his voice is equally sonorous.

"I'm sure that the Boroughreeve will not fail to show his appreciation of a job well done," adds Matthew, looking from one to the other of his two differently-sized hosts.

Mr Jupp and Mr Gittings nod gravely. They now remind Matthew of figures one might see in an even larger clock tower, one mechanically trundling out as the hour strikes, while the other rocks and rolls his way back in.

"Of course," says Mr Jupp, sensing a good business opportunity when he sees it. "What is it you wish to observe?"

Matthew looks in the direction of the coffin, on which the lid has been placed but not sealed.

"I presume the body of the deceased is inside?" he says.

"Her final resting place," says Mr Gittings.

"Such a tragedy," adds Mr Jupp.

"To have died so young," agrees Mr Gittings.

"May I see her?" asks Matthew.

Messrs Jupp and Gittings turn their differently positioned heads as one towards him.

"I must in good conscience report that Miss Robinson has indeed been placed there," says Matthew, seemingly without guile.

With an expression of distaste, Mr Jupp signals to Mr Gittings to remove the lid. Matthew approaches it, notebook in hand, and peers inside.

"Yes," he says at last, "she appears to be there."

"Appears?" says Mr Gittings.

"A figure of speech," says Matthew, his eyes still fixed upon Lavinia. She appears even more unblemished than when he last saw her, naked upon Mr Ainsworth's table. The mortician has spared none of his art in embalming the corpse.

"She quite takes one's breath away, does she not?" says Mr Gittings, as if interpreting Matthew's silence for appreciation of the craft of their profession. "Mr Jubb worked on the face, I on the hands."

Still not taking his eyes away from her, Matthew asks, "Have the family now seen her?"

"They have," replies Mr Gittings.

"For the last time?" asks Matthew again.

"Until that place where we all of us hope to be reunited," adds Mr Jupp, "yes."

"They expressed themselves quite satisfied?" asks Matthew a third time.

"They did," says Mr Jupp. "She is dressed exactly in accordance with her sister, Mrs Bentley's, instructions."

"And so they will not be viewing her here again?" Matthew's tone is naggingly insistent.

"We shall be sealing the lid as soon as you leave us, Mr Oldham," explains Mr Gittings, "in readiness for her journey to

St John's Church Yard tomorrow morning."

"I see. Thank you, gentlemen. I believe that will be all. I am certain the Boroughreeve will be entirely satisfied with the arrangements."

Once again the two gentlemen incline their very different heads.

"Might I..." ventures Matthew, uncharacteristically hesitant, feigning a cough, as if attempting to conceal a level of emotion in his voice, "might I possibly have some time alone with her?"

Messrs Jupp and Gittings simultaneously frown.

"That is somewhat irregular," observes one.

"And not something we would normally consider," says the other.

"A matter of protocol," adds the first.

"Family members only," concludes the second.

"Of course," says Matthew. "That is quite as it should be. But..." he pauses, raising a hand affectingly to his brow, then slowly massaging the side of his temple in a circular motion, in evident distress. "I knew her, you see. Her brother-in-law is a business associate of mine. We met socially too on a number of occasions."

"In which case," says Mr Gittings, gently reaching up a hand to tap his partner on the elbow, "we shall leave you alone with your thoughts."

The two gentlemen retreat backwards in step from the room, bowing slightly as they go, closing the door behind them, leaving Matthew alone.

Immediately his demeanour changes. Gone are the slow, reverential movements he has been adopting hitherto. Now he springs rapidly into action. He had hoped that a certain item of clothing might have been placed inside the coffin with her, and as soon as the lid was removed, he saw it at once. The white cotton shawl, with its repeating pattern of moths caught in leaves of laurel. Wasting not a second he darts towards her, removes the shawl quickly but carefully from around her shoulders, making sure not to disturb a single strand of her hair, before stowing it roughly in his coat pocket, then sliding the coffin lid firmly back in place..

With another forced cough, he calls out. "Thank you, gentlemen. I have finished."

Mr Jupp opens the door with one hand, while gesturing the way out with his other. Matthew sweeps hurriedly through to where Mr Gittings is waiting with a handful of business cards to present to him. Matthew takes these without comment, depositing them neatly in the other pocket of his coat.

He rarely takes risks, and so he is relieved to hear, as he stands outside the door to the Funeral Parlour's inner sanctum, about to put on his hat before stepping back into the still chilly air, in spite of the continuing thaw, Mr Gittings passing on an instruction to one of his assistants to seal up the lid directly without further delay. He just has time to hear the first of the nails being hammered into the oak lid before twirling his silver-topped cane between the fingers of his left hand, while his right feels inside his pocket for the cotton shawl, closing his fingers around the fluttering moths, then striding purposefully away.

The funeral was held in St John's Church in Byrom Street. Tens of thousands of people followed the coffin as it was carried along the Dean's Gate. Lavinia had touched the hearts of the whole town and a hastily arranged public subscription had defrayed the expenses entirely so that the family could focus instead on their grief. They walked in pairs behind the horse-drawn hearse hardly aware of the eyes of Manchester upon them.

The service was taken by the Reverend John Clowes, St John's first and, up till this point, only vicar, where he would remain for sixty-seven years. Although the church served an Anglican parish, Clowes was a follower of the Lutheran theologian Emanuel Swedenborg, who, not unlike the Unitarians, whose members were also represented at the funeral, but in sharp contrast with the Moravians from Fairfield and the Methodists from the Independent Chapel on Mosley Street, where Lavinia had herself attended, claimed there was but one true God of both heaven and earth, and He was to be found across all religions. Clowes had also preached the first sermon in the town to call on all churches to provide regular Sunday Schools, many of whose attenders crowded into the church this day to hear what he had to say about the passing of the Manchester Ophelia.

"Let us begin," he said, his voice booming with emotion, "with a hymn that was a favourite with Lavinia, one with which she ended each day at her school, some pupils of which are now going to lead us in, Charles Wesley's *Father, I Stretch My Hands To Thee*."

A clutch of half a dozen tearful school girls bravely sang the first verse.

"Father, I stretch my hands to Thee
No other help I know
If Thou withdraw Thyself from me
Ah, whither shall I go...?"

Then, at a signal from the Reverend Clowes, the rest of the congregation took up the second verse.

"Surely Thou canst not let me die
O speak and I shall live
And here I will unwearied lie
Till Thou Thy Spirit give..."

He then began to deliver the eulogy while the organ continued to play softly beneath his words. The people, wherever they were, inside the church or out, right across the town, listened to him as keenly as the birds straining to catch that slight, subtle shift in the air when the seasons turn and a wind from the west rustles through all the leaves on every different tree.

"Lavinia's was a life cruelly cut short," he declared. "She'd barely begun to make her mark upon the land, but those faint scratches she *had* made showed such a promise of what there was to come, which is why so many of us have gathered here today to mourn her passing. But not just mourn her. We are here to celebrate her short life and the difference she had made to so many already. Sister, daughter, teacher, friend. Little Mother to her younger siblings when her own mother died. Her whole future lay before her."

The organist briefly swelled in the playing of the hymn as Mr Clowes continued his eloquent panegyric.

"In so many ways we see ourselves reflected in her somewhere, our hopes, our dreams, our determination to leave the world a better place than how we found it. She reminds me of this town we all live in, where we work and worship together. Manchester. A hundred years ago we were little more than a village. Now we are the fastest growing town in all of England. A city in all but name. Exporting our goods throughout the world. And how is this made possible? By men of vision, yes, but more by the Lavinias amongst us. For what is a town but a community of souls, all bound together by the Gospel according to Matthew's simple precept – that '*whatsoever ye would that men should do to you, do ye so unto them*', that we all of us may strive to make better lives for ourselves and our children, and help this great town of ours that we all love so much to build and grow, just as Lavinia was already beginning to do with the minds of her young charges. For as we are told in Isaiah, the true servant of the Lord shall '*grow up before Him as a tender shoot, and as a root out of a dry ground. Surely she hath borne our griefs and carried our transgressions. She was wounded for our transgressions, bruised for our iniquities...*'

"Let us now cherish her memory in our hearts as we sing the final verse of her favourite hymn."

The congregation inside the Church began to sing, the words being taken up by the thousands more still lining the Dean's Gate outside, rising up into the air above the restless, teeming sprawl of Manchester, an ever-growing murmuration.

"Author of faith to Thee I lift
My weary longing eyes
O let me now receive that gift
My soul without it dies…"

Outside a pale winter sun broke through the sheet of cloud, just as the great slabs of ice upon the surface of the Irwell were melting. Its faltering rays fell defiantly upon the words on the headstone on Lavinia's grave, lain in the same ground as Zachary and Fanny.

'More lasting than in lines of art
Thy spotless character's imprest
Thy worth engrav'd on every heart
Thy loss bewail'd in every breast.'

*

Theatre Royale
Fountain Street, Manchester

Monday 14ᵗʰ February at 6pm

A Special Valentine's Day Performance
FOR ONE NIGHT ONLY

THE MANCHESTER OPHELIA

Miss Appleby will give a Timely Recitation

Proceeds to the Bereaved Family Robinson

Mr Carlton Whiteley broke the promise he had made to himself more than half a decade before, which he had kept religiously ever since, that never would he darken the doors of this populist upstart of a playhouse on Fountain Street, the one whose arrival had hastened the end of his own more modest, less ostentatious, though more classically pure enterprise at the foot of the twenty-nine steps, which once led the more refined and perceptive theatregoer through the *Ring o' Bells* entry, along the narrow passageway, and down to the Actor's Bridge, knowledge of which was the *'wing wherewith he might fly to heaven'*. Henry VI again, a failure which had almost bankrupted him, but a magnificent one.

He remembers it fondly as he makes his painful way along Spring Gardens. He needs a stout stick nowadays to navigate these ever-changing streets, which threaten to betray him with each new twist and turn, even when illuminated by these gracious gas lamps, which sprout everywhere, like Birnam Wood, across the town. He could still tackle older roles, he feels, despite his infirmity. The Old Man in *Macbeth*, perhaps, reporting portents.

> *"Threescore and ten I can remember well*
> *Within the volume of which time I have seen*
> *Hours dreadful and things strange, but this sore night*
> *Hath trifled former knowings..."*

He becomes aware of people staring at him, muttering behind the backs of their hands, steering a wide berth around him, avoiding catching his eye. Is it because they recognise him, he wonders, but have forgotten his name? Hardly surprising, for it has been many a year since last he trod the boards. Not since his Marullus on the steps outside the New Bailey Prison upon the release of Joseph Hanson. Oh, what a triumph that had been...

Or it is perhaps that he has spoken these lines out loud? He finds himself doing this more and more these days. The line between thought and word grows ever more blurred. Well, no matter. I am become '*a very foolish, fond old man*'. He chuckles. '*Like the poor cat i' th' adage*'.

He looks up at the poster advertising tonight's performance. Miss Appleby. His protégée. Come of age at last, it seems, and giving her Ophelia. He does not know when he has last felt so proud – as, it appears, does the whole of Manchester, for the 'House Full' signs are proudly displayed on the steps leading up to the theatre, the 'Sold Out' banners stuck across the handbills and posters. Such is the demand for tickets that Miss Appleby is giving three shows this evening – at six, eight and ten o'clock.

He laboriously climbs the steep, slippery, stone steps. Twice he almost falls before a gallant young blade comes to his rescue, accompanied by his equally young and equally handsome female companion, who flashes Carlton a dazzling smile.

"I'm so excited," she says to him. "This is my first visit to a theatre. I'm told she's very good."

"Oh yes," says Carlton as he catches his breath once more, "she is."

"The Manchester Ophelia. It sounds very sad. Shall it make me weep?"

"If it's good, it will," he says. "And so it should, for she serves to remind us of our past failings, so that we might not make the same mistakes again."

They escort him to his seat, where he settles himself. He begrudgingly has to admit, as he looks about him, that the décor in the auditorium is impressive, the proportions of the stage quite enviable, the sightlines most promising. At last, by means of a device he does not quite understand, the level of the gaslights is lowered, creating a most pleasing effect around the proscenium.

The curtain rises and there, quite alone in the centre of an empty stage, stands Miss Appleby. Dressed as Ophelia, with a garland of laurel leaves entwined within her hair, she carries a bunch of wild flowers in her hands. Her garment is of the purest white and is wringing wet, as if she has just been pulled from of a river. The audience gasps.

Miss Appleby, now Ophelia incarnate, in remembrance of Lavinia, steps forward, holding out her hands piteously, the flowers falling from her fingers. Everybody in the audience afterwards will swear that she was addressing them directly.

"There's a daisy. I would give you some violets,
But they wither'd all when my father died...
They say I made a good end.

(Sings)
For bonny sweet Robin is all my joy...

I hope all will be well. We must be patient; but I
Cannot choose but weep to think they would lay me
I' th' cold ground...

Indeed, la, without an oath, I'll make an end on't!

(Sings)
To-morrow is Saint Valentine's day,
All in the morning betime,
And I a maid at your window,
To be your Valentine...

No, my good lord; but, as you did command,
I did repel his letters and denied
His access to me...

(Sings)
For bonny sweet Robin is all my joy...

I shall th' effect of this good lesson keep
As watchman to my heart. But, good my brother,
Do not as some ungracious pastors do,
Show me the steep and thorny way to heaven,
Whiles, like a puff'd and reckless libertine,
Himself the primrose path of dalliance treads
And recks not his own rede…

There's rosemary, that's for remembrance.
Pray you, love, remember…
And there is pansies, that's for thoughts.
There's fennel for you, and columbines.
There's rue for you,
And here's some for me.
We may call it herb of grace o' Sundays.
O, you must wear your rue with a difference…

They say the owl was a baker's daughter.
Lord,
We know what we are, but know not what we may be…

'Tis in my memory lock'd,
And you yourself shall keep the key of it… "

When the performance has ended, there are several seconds of hushed silence before the entire audience rises to its feet and cheers. The applause lasts for several minutes. Miss Appleby makes a deep curtsey, accepting the garlands of laurel leaves that shower onto the stage around her.

The gallant and handsome young couple who escorted Carlton to his seat look over their shoulders to share their reaction with him.

"You were right," says the young woman, wreathed in smiles and tears alike. "It *was* good and I *did* cry."

Carlton has remained seated, a broken stump in a forest of taller trees. The young woman lowers herself to his side. His face is serenely still, as if it has witnessed the fulfilment of a promise. The thin trace of a smile plays across his lips, while the ghost of a tear slides down his cheek. He has taken his last bow. 'Tomorrow and tomorrow and tomorrow…'

Matthew is not at the *Theatre Royale* but the Manchester Ophelia is very much on his mind. The Ice Maiden.

He is upstairs in his private room.

He places a chair in the centre of it.

He draws back the curtain in the recess to his left, revealing the portrait of Mercy.

The expression in her eyes, which are drawn upwards towards the bird in the bamboo cage, floors him, as it always does.

He moves across to the recess on the other side of the fireplace, on the right.

A curtain has been erected there also.

He slowly draws this back too, with an even greater reverence.

Within it is a new frame, identical in size to the one confining Mercy, a perfect mirror image.

But this frame does not surround another painting.

Instead, mounted in the centre of it, is the white shawl he took from Lavinia's coffin.

He stands right up close to it, his face pressed against its freshly laundered cotton, inhaling its distinctive paper aroma, which he can't quite place.

Then it comes to him.

It is the smell of hope.

He reels away from it.

He sits on the chair and looks first at the picture of Mercy, then at the piece of cotton.

He fancies he sees the bird fluttering against the cage.

Or the moths rustling among the laurel leaves.

He hears the faint echo of laughter tripping down the years.

Fanny.

Then Mercy.

It sounds like the tinkling of tiny bells.

Or icicles melting.

Or flocks of migrating birds trapped in a mist net.

He holds out his hands to try and catch them.

But they remain empty.

He stays in the room a long time.

Looking and listening.

Looking and listening.

In the distance, in the farthest corner of his mind, he hears a rumbling, from deep underground.

The drumming of horses' hooves.

Getting nearer. Coming closer.

Soon they'll be upon him.

He knows this. He feels this.

He draws the curtains across each recess and leaves the room.

THREE

1817

The Year Without Summer

in which a group of young men
attempt a walk to London and back –
while another young man returns alone from war –
and a queen welcomes migrants from afar
and invites them to make a new home

7

1817

10th March

'For two years now we have not had what could properly be called summer. Easterly winds have prevailed throughout. The sun during that time has generally been obscured and the sky overcast with clouds. The air has been damp and uncomfortable, and frequently so chilling as to render the fireside a most desirable retreat.'

So wrote John Lees in his diary at Fairfield, which he kept religiously every day, detailing the seasons as they came and went, avoiding where possible any expression of personal feelings or opinion. But the sustained winter they were now forced to endure was testing his resolve.

'It has been another poor harvest this year, though our farmers did succeed in bringing *some* crops to maturity, but corn and other grain prices have risen dramatically. The price of oats, for example, rose from sixpence per bushel last summer to five shillings per bushel this. Good news for us, but less so for those outside the Settlement.'

The year also heralded the arrival of a new Minister at Fairfield, Brother Carl August Pohlman taking over from Brother Christian Gottfried Clemens, who had himself succeeded the still much-missed Brother John Frederick Swertner. John had inherited from Brother Swertner the picture of the Great Vine, over which the latter had laboured many years. It had now fallen to John to act as the painting's custodian. Though he was by no means the artist Brother Swertner had been, he nevertheless meticulously added to it each fresh cluster as best he could whenever a new mission was formed, either in England or abroad. Thus there was now new fruit planted in Holland and Haiti, Jamaica and Java. There was great rejoicing when a letter reached them all the way from the Spice Islands, the Dutch East Indies, from one Joost Kam, whose father Joseph, a wigmaker from the small town of Zeist, near Utrecht, had been a recent visitor in Fairfield. Joost had answered the call for new overseas missions and worked his passage to the Sunda Islands, where he hoped to plant seeds for a new Settlement in the remote region of Sumbawa.

In normal times this would have been cause for a Lovefeast, but these were not normal times, and Brother Pohlman urged caution. "Let us have a service of Thanksgiving," he counselled, "but without the accompanying feast." Many of the faithful were disappointed but Brother Pohlman reminded them of the Pharaoh's Dream in Egypt.

" *'Behold, seven ears of corn came up in one stalk, full and good. And, behold, seven ears, withered, thin, and blasted with the east wind, sprung up after them. And the thin ears devoured the seven good ears'.*"

They all knew this story, even the children, and nodded their heads in silent agreement. Seven years of plenty followed by seven years of famine. Caroline, silently watching her husband, John, continuing to labour over the painting of one more cluster of grapes for their new outpost in Sumbawa, reflected on how it had been seven years now since she had last seen her daughter Agnes, when she, Amos and Jack had left for the last time, for Elton, near Bury, which, for all the contact she now had with them, might just as well have been the Dutch East Indies. She decided she would write to them, that night after prayers had ended, while John continued his work on the Great Vine, in secret, not telling him, for he would only shake his head and say, "They rejected the wisdom of the Lot. They must learn to accept the consequence of their choice. As must we, my dear," and she knew she would not be able to bear it. So much for Pietism.

Agnes reads this letter now with a heavy heart and passes it across to Amos, who looks up briefly from his own reading matter, William Cobbett's weekly *Political Register*, or *The Tuppenny Trash*, as its detractors like to call it, tuppence which Agnes feels they cannot really spare just now in these difficult times, but she would not begrudge it him, for she knows it is only through his growing involvement with the fortnightly meetings of the Hampden Club, or Potter's Planning Parlour as it has now come to be called, in Bury, or Oldham, or Middleton, wherever they might happen to take place, listening to the likes of Samuel Bamford, John Knight, or Thomas Potter himself, after whom the Parlour is named, decry with such passion the evils of the ruling classes, hearing the heated talks and debates over what should be the best tactics to adopt in order to bring about the much needed Reform, which has gradually brought him back to the world, a world that she consistently keeps at a distance. 'No taxation without representation'. That is their watchword. Agnes is aware of this – heaven knows she's heard Ham and Shem repeat this often enough, like their equivalent of the Lord's Prayer, 'Give us this day our daily bread,' a plaintive enough plea in this year without a summer – though she cannot imagine Amos leading the call for revolution. He is just a listener. she thinks, weighing up the different arguments on his walks back home through the dark after each meeting's end. She almost envies him this outlet he has carved for himself in the two endless, dark years since Jack has left them.

Jack.

Two years gone.

Each day now, after another night without sleep in these years without sun, she walks downstairs hoping that somehow time has slipped, and that it will be that same morning two years ago, when people first began to notice the changes in the climate, and the note that she found waiting for her on the top of the loom, where it had been threaded between the slackened weft, would not be there. But time has not slipped. It is just the start of another day, another day when once again it will not grow light, the sun will not shine, and Jack will not be there.

'Gone for a soldier,' it had said. 'There's nowt for me 'ere. Wish us luck.'

He was just fifteen years old.

He'd fought at Waterloo, she supposed. But that was nearly two years ago now. And still he'd not come home. Her head told her he wouldn't be, not now, not after all this time, but her heart spoke to her otherwise, so that when Amos would ask her, as he did unfailingly every week, if she wanted to go with him to his meetings, "Lots o' t' wives do," he'd say, she would always shake her head. "No," she would reply, "what if Jack should arrive an' neither of us were 'ere to greet 'im? 'E might just walk off again…"

She had barely stepped out of doors since the day Jack had left. Only when she was sure that Amos would be there, working at his loom, in case Jack might turn up, would she walk the mile and a half into Bury Market for bread and potatoes.

But since the sun had stopped shining, there'd been less and less food to be had there. An iron frost had gripped the land unceasingly in that time. Root crops froze, stalks withered, harvests failed. The first month after Jack left, red snow fell from a black sky, covering the earth in tears of blood. A unit of soldiers, dispatched from the garrison at Bury Castle, rode out across the land while the snow fell, blowing their bugles. Agnes, rushing out to greet them, daring to hope that Jack might be among them, was almost knocked aside. As they were swallowed up by the storm, she feared they were sounding the first of the seven trumpets from the Book of Revelation, when hail and fire mingle with blood.

Amos was considerably more terse and laconic.

"It's what Sam Bamford's been sayin' all along," he said. "Ever since t' Government passed t' bloody Corn Laws. It dun't tek a prophet from t' Bible to predict a poor harvest. It's as certain as night follows day."

But not as day follows night, thought Agnes, looking up at the preternatural darkness all around them.

The kaleidoscope lies untouched on the stone hearth. It's been a long time since either of them last looked through it. In this perpetual winter they would see nothing. Nor do they gather together the broken threads from the loom to play cat's cradle. Not since before Jack left. Bird's Nest to Long Case Clock. Long Case Clock to Tea Kettle. Tea Kettle to Moth.

A moth is caught in the tangled ends of unspun cotton. Agnes reaches down to release it. It rests a while on the tip of her finger, slowly opening then closing its almost completely black wings, before flying off into the immutable night.

And so she watches Amos read the secret letter from Caroline, smuggled out of Fairfield to Audenshaw, from where she knows the post is collected, without John's knowledge, from where it has wended its slow and torturous way along rutted roads, frost-hard lanes, while showers of brown ash continue to fall. Amos reads it slowly, carefully, then folds it back along the folds and creases it arrived with, and passes it back to Agnes.

"She's always welcome to visit us here," he says. "She can stay for as long as she likes."

But that's not going to happen, is it, thinks Agnes? So she says nothing. Their fingers brush lightly against one another, as they each retreat to their own respective burrows, she to her constant vigil in case Jack should return, he to his *Tuppenny Trash*, where Cobbett is expounding further upon the evils of the newly-passed Corn Laws.

The shadow of the Corn Laws hangs over the time like a carrion crow, impatiently waiting to swoop down upon the ravaged bodies of those who suffer because of them. When Amos looks up at the blanket of dark cloud which permanently cloaks the land these days, it has assumed the shape of just such a giant version of it. This black hooded crow, hovering over the earth, biding its time, before swooping on its next victim.

Proposed in the uncertain peace when Napoleon languished on Elba before making his daring escape to freedom, the Corn Laws outlawed the import of foreign cereals until home-grown wheat had reached eighty shillings a quarter. Immediately there were riots. It was finally passed by a House of Commons ringed by troops with bayonets fixed.

"For it protects th' interests of an élite alone," boomed Bamford at one of the meetings of the Hampden Club, quoting Cobbett. "Aye, some o' t' farmers it supports need th' help, but by having a law which adversely affects everyone else is not the way to go about it."

"Hear, hear!" roared the Potter's Planners in unison, rapping the tops of tables with closed fists.

"We spinners an' weavers've long been used to tradin' our cloth overseas for grain. Now, at a stroke, we are forbid. Come t' next bad harvest an' prices'll rocket. It dun't tek a genius, nor a weathercock, to tell thee that'll be sooner rather than later. Then where will us be? Up salt creek wi'out a paddle."

"Aye," came the reply

That failed harvest had come the very next year.

Amos recalls other responses to the Bill, less predictable perhaps than the crude, if accurate, over-simplification of Samuel Bamford. Sir Hugh Hornby-Birley, the then incumbent Boroughreeve, presiding over an anti-Corn Law meeting called by various members of The Exchange, representing the position of many of the masters and owners, expressed himself in sympathy with their concerns, that the inevitable higher prices in corn that would follow would in turn lead to legitimate demands from the workers for higher wages to compensate, wages they would feel morally obliged to look upon favourably, thereby driving up costs when the price of their finished products was falling. It was not just the Non-Conformists who opposed the Bill. Even High Anglican Tories found themselves in opposition to it when its effects hit their own pockets, but they all closed ranks in the face of the upsurge in calls for Radical reforms that arrived in its wake. Shopkeepers, watchmakers, tobacconists and farriers, publicans, book-binders, saddlers and brewers, all joined forces to condemn any talk of petitions or protests.

Even in Fairfield, fearful of the rising tensions and the threat of violence upon its doorstep, funds were found to double the number of watchmen patrolling the Settlement's perimeter at all times. To mitigate this measure somewhat, Brother Pohlman urged an increase in collections to help the poor and needy of Droylsden, though some of these funds had sometimes to be diverted to support other Settlements overseas, such as Dublin, where famine was rife, Barbados, when a hurricane levelled their church to the ground, Sarepta in Russia, after a fire had reduced the entire community there to smoke and ash, or Sumbaya in the Spice Islands, where Joost Kam had perished, along with thousands of the still-to-be-converted population, as a result of the volcano which had erupted there.

No sooner had John completed his labours to add this new cluster to the Great Vine, news of the explosion reached them, claimed by some to be the mightiest visitation yet delivered to His People by God since Noah's Flood, so that John was forced to place a cross right through it.

Brother Pohlman signed an anti-Slavery petition, which shocked the Elders of the Settlement. "We do not involve ourselves in questions of social justice or human rights," they said. "We do not challenge the vested interests of Government. Non-interference is in strict accordance with prudence and with Scripture."

Brother Pohlman was obliged to write a letter to the Manchester Anti-Slavery Committee, declaring that his own personal views did not, in this matter, reflect those of the Moravian Church, which '*does not interfere in the question of Colonial Slavery.*'

When Samuel Bamford read this disavowal by the Minister, which had been reprinted in full, without comment, in *The Manchester Observer*, he asked those present in the Middleton Planning Parlour, what the Good Brother Pohlman might make of the Government's latest outrage – to suspend the right of *Habeas Corpus* in the light of alleged plots by Radicals to 'march on the capital'.

Amos did not speak his thoughts out loud, but the answer lay heavily in his heart. So much for Quietism.

"Ever since t' Glorious Revolution o' 1688," resumed Bamford, "it's been t' People's Right to be able to petition t' reigning monarch to air their grievances in person. The best way o' doing this has always been a Public Meeting, out in th' open air, wi' folk marchin' from miles around just to be there, to listen to t' speeches an' pass t' resolutions. Now this is bein' denied us an' all." He picked up his copy of *The Manchester Observer* once more, brandishing it aloft, before reading from it further. " '*The Government hereby introduces a System of Alarm, for the security of His Majesty's peaceable subjects'*," Bamford quoted mischievously, " '*the maintenance of our liberties, and the perpetuation of the blessings of the Constitution*', the vital liberty of *Habeas Corpus* excepted, that is."

Amos re-reads all of this once more in his *Tuppenny Trash* and smiles grimly. A march on the capital? Perhaps that might not be such a bad idea. He decides he will break his 'listening only' rule. At the next meeting of The Hampden Club he will speak for the first time. In this Year Without a Summer, they must let their voices be heard. He wraps a blanket around his shoulders and huddles closer to the last of the dying embers in the hearth, trying to poke more life into them. A sudden draught blows through the glassless wind-eye, sending a few brave sparks up the chimney, where they blaze briefly in imitation of stars beneath the obsidian sky. At the back of the cottage a door bangs. Agnes looks up in hope. But it is only the wind.

Abner has not explored the night skies through his Dollond & Aitcheson telescope for almost two years. It has not been able to penetrate the pall of pyroclastic clouds that have hung over the town. He first noticed something awry while attempting to measure the decline in sunspot activity in the solar cycle.

It was Galileo of course who had first observed them and coined the description, but more recently John Dalton had grown increasingly interested in a possible pattern. He mentioned this in passing once, during a lecture Abner attended at the New University, and referred his students to a recent paper by the Danish astronomer, Christian Horrebow, who wrote: 'It appears that after the course of a certain number of years, probably eleven, the appearance of the sun repeats itself with respect to the number and size of its spots.' Abner took it upon himself to see if he might test this thesis with his own observations. His mentor was interested in the study for meteorological purposes. They were, he explained, undergoing a period of lower than average temperatures. Might there be, he speculated, a link between this recent fall and the decreasing number of sunspots? Abner began to take detailed notes of the various aspects of solar activity he took it upon himself to chart, such as the stream of particles issuing outwards from the sun's corona, reminiscent of the canopies of trees being tossed in a winter storm, or the sudden intensity of solar flares erupting from the sun's surface in mass ejections.

It was while he was immersed in these observations that he began to sense that what he was seeing was growing dimmer. At first he put this down to his recent neglect in looking after his telescope as scrupulously as he normally did, and so he vigorously applied a cleaning fluid to the lenses, but to no avail. Next he wondered if perhaps he had been spending too much time staring into the sun and that his sight was being affected. Never strong at the best of times because of his albinism, he had nevertheless discovered a way of seeing through a set of delicate alterations to the telescope's specifications he himself had customised which he could usually rely upon. But once again, after a careful recalibration of the mechanism, he quickly realised that this was not the cause of the diminution in quality of what he was observing. He re-trained his scope to the southern quarter of the sky once the sun had set and sought the four Galilean moons of Jupiter, which always shone so brightly there during March.

Io, Europa, Gannymede, Callisto.

This time there was no mistaking it. A highly discernible cloud of ash, some twenty-five miles above the Earth's atmosphere he calculated, was obscuring the sky. He took his observations to Mr Dalton, who studied them with minute care.

"I can only conclude," he said after several minutes, "that a catastrophic event has occurred on the far side of the globe, a volcano perhaps in the East Indies, which has thrown up this sulphurous cloud. This will have devastating effects on the climate," he continued. "Mark my words. I predict a year, possibly two, without a summer."

Abner pats his now closed up Dollond & Aitcheson telescope fondly, as he might a faithful dog. "Patience," he whispers softly into the air. "This darkness cannot last for ever. The sun will pierce it eventually. The shroud will lift. And then we shall be able to train our eye upon the clear night skies once more and see what lies beyond the other side."

*

"I was brought up in Lancashire and before I was sixteen
I ran away to London for a soldier to be seen

With my fine cap and feather, likewise my ruffle and drum
They learnèd me to play upon the rub-a-dub-a-dum..."

Jack remembers the day he saw the soldiers escorting Joseph
Hanson along the Turnpike Road from the Bury Fort to stand
trial at the County Assizes in Lancaster like it was yesterday.
He has never forgotten it – the proud horses with their groomed
flanks, their plaited manes and braided tails, the polished boots
of their riders, so shiny he could see his face in them as they
passed, the gleaming helmets and sabres, the jangle of stirrups
and the sparks from the shod hooves striking the ground, but
most of all the soldiers themselves, their redcoats like a bright
sunrise with their promise of a golden future.

He sees no prospect of that future in the cold and draughty
cottage where he lives, his father permanently bent over his
loom, his mother constantly boiling and stirring noxious dyes,
into which she will dip the finished cloth before hauling it out
to the field at the back, where he has to help her drape it across
the hedges to dry. In the damp and dreary winters of Lancashire
all these colours seem to blend into single indeterminate mud
browns or clay greys or faded moss greens. Nothing like the
reds and golds and silvers of the soldiers.

He has no intention of following his father as a weaver. Nor
of trudging across the fields in the dark to work in Peel's
factories with Ham and Shem, then returning home bone-weary
in the middle of the night, never seeing daylight for the rest of
his life, though he must endure it for now. No – it's the
soldier's life for him. But how? He occupies his every waking
hour in wrestling with this problem. There is no standing army
in England, even with the seemingly endless War with the
French, and, unlike the Navy, there is no kind of Press. The
Recruiting Officers march up and down the land in search of
brave lads to volunteer for the different local regiments, but
you have to be seventeen. Jack is not yet fifteen. He will be
soon, but even then he knows he could not pass for older, for

he's small for his age.

Whenever he has any free time, which is not often, he will steal away and run alongside the Elton Brook till it joins the Reservoir, from where he follows the feeder channels down to the Manchester, Bury & Bolton Canal, keeping to the tow path till he reaches the first of the two tunnels, which he climbs the grass-covered roof of, before dropping down to Bury Fort, where there are always soldiers garrisoned.

It is here where he first sees the drummer boy.

Not much older than he is, and certainly no bigger.

He watches him with studied concentration. The way he goes through his repertoire of different rhythms on different types of drums – snares, tabors and, his favourite, the kettle, which is used for sending out messages across the lines of battle, he learns.

I could do that, he thinks.

He hangs around after the marches, drills and exercises have finished. He waits till he sees the drummer boy running across the Parade Ground and calls him over. Who do I need to speak to join, he asks? The boy points in the direction of the Barracks, where the tallest man Jack has ever seen is just coming out of the door. He has to fold his body almost in half just to fit through. By the time Jack has run over to him, the Captain, for that is what he is, Captain Josiah Blacker, appears even taller, for he is atop a flight of stone steps, at the bottom of which stands Jack looking dizzily up at him, dazzled by the fierce midday sun – for this is a time before the permanent shadow falls – which forms a perfect halo around the Captain's head, completed by the placing upon it of a fine cockade hat. Jack shields his eyes with his left hand against the brightness, while attempting to give a salute with his right.

"Well now, Young Master," booms the Captain, "how may I be of service?"

"I want to be a drummer boy," Jack replies breathlessly, "an' go across to France to fight Napoleon."

The Captain looks down at this sprat of a boy from his great height and smiles. "Is that right?"

Jack nods his head vigorously.

"Can you play?" asks the Captain.

"I can learn," says Jack.

The Captain laughs. His voice is as deep as his head is high.

"Then I think we should start by introducing ourselves. What's your name?"

"Jack, sir. Jack Lees."

"Pleased to make your acquaintance, Jack. I'm Captain Josiah Blacker. Son of Henry Blacker. Perhaps you've heard of him?"

"No, sir. I'm afraid not."

"Do you think I'm tall, Jack Lees?"

"Yes, sir, I do."

"Well I'm just a dwarf next to him. The British Giant, they called him. Seven feet and five inches high, he was. They used to exhibit him in fairs around the country. Along with Toby the Sapient Pig. Now surely you've heard of Toby?"

Jack again shakes his head that he has not.

"Why, you've never lived till you've seen Toby. The most celebrated of all porcine creatures. He could play cards, read books, tell the time from a pocket watch, guess a person's age and, most wondrous of all, discover a person's thoughts."

"But could 'e beat on a drum for soldiers to march to?" asks Jack with a smile.

"I couldn't say," says Captain Blacker, "but he and my father would hold highly intelligent conversations on all manner of topics – political, poetical, philosophical and spiritual – especially when they shared the same bill in London, at Mouse Lane, where the Duke of Cumberland visited him regularly, eventually persuading him to join his army. 'Just the sight of you, Mr Blacker,' said the Duke, 'will be enough to fright the enemy'. And so it proved. His appearance alone at the Convention of Klosterzeven helped the Duke to broker peace between the French and the Hanoverians and bring the Seven Years War to a satisfactory conclusion, for which the Duke did not receive the gratitude he fully deserved, and so he retired from military life to pursue a much more dangerous career in politics, helping to establish His Majesty's Rockingham Ministry. My father never left his side. At court he was a source of much curiosity among the ladies, who wished to establish whether he was a giant in every aspect of his being. I cannot report, therefore, with any reliable accuracy, as to the personage of my mother, for the Duke's dying words to my father were to 'quit the court and return to the army', which he duly did, taking me along with him. And so here you find me, my father's son, Captain of the 30th East Lancashire Regiment of Foot, at your service, Master Lees."

He solemnly removes his hat and bows so low that Jack, if he stands upon tiptoe, might reach up to tap his bald pate, on which the sun now gloriously shines, but of course he does nothing of the kind. Instead he feels himself wrapped in the warm glow of that reflected golden light, in which anything and everything seems possible.

It is the last time Jack will see the sun for many months, for even at that very moment, when he is contemplating running away to live the life of a drummer boy, seven and a half thousand miles away, on the opposite side of the globe, Mount Tambora is violently erupting on the island of Sumbawa in the Dutch East Indies.

*

"Well, Amos," says a somewhat disgruntled Samuel Bamford, "I'd not've put *thee* down for a Spencean."

He scans the assembled gathering before him on the moors at Red Lumb, midway between Bury and Rochdale, looking for support. The rising popularity of the Hampden Clubs has meant they have outgrown front parlours or back kitchens, or the upstairs rooms of public houses, and migrated outdoors.

Upwards of a hundred people huddle together on the hillside, straining to catch what the speakers have to say as a raw wind blows up from the Ashworth valley below.

"I don't 'ave thy book learnin', Mr Bamford," says Amos quietly, "so I don't rightly know what tha' means wi tha' long words. I only know that our voices aren't bein' 'eard by folk who mek decisions. An' I'm not just talkin' about t' wind drownin' us out neither. We need to *do* summat…"

"Aye," shout several others. "But what?"

"That's what we're 'ere to discuss," says Samuel again, trying to make himself heard over the growing discontent rising around him. "But we must be seen to be acting within t' Law. Else we'll not be listened to."

A chorus of boos drowns him out.

"Explain it to 'em, John, will thee?" And he yields the ground to his older associate John Knight.

Knight, though born on the Yorkshire side of the Pennines, has lived and worked in Lancashire for all but the first five of his fifty-four years. Originally a handloom weaver, like Amos and many of the others congregated before him now, he understands their concerns. He was very early on convinced that the ills of his adopted county, together with those of the country at large, stemmed from the corruption endemic in an unrepresentative Parliament. Reform, not revolt, was his watchword.

"Samuel's right," he says. "Even a meeting as innocent as this one is a risk at times like these, especially if voices are raised in support of violent action. Now I'm not saying that that's what tha's been advocating, Amos, but it could be misconstrued, an' then we'd have to run t' gauntlet o' Joe Nadin's henchmen, an' tha' wouldn't want that, I can tell thee. Samuel an' I speak from first hand experience. 'E's no respecter of niceties, is Deputy Nadin. 'E rides roughshod o'er t' lot of 'em, an' he dun't care who gets in 'is way."

The crowd quieten, shuffling uncomfortably. Tales of

Nadin and his big bold hogs, as his men are dubbed, are legion, along with his methods for extracting information from any who dare to cross him.

The speech is next taken up by William Fitton, a leading figure in The Hampden Club in Royton, a passionate believer in the Rights of Man as put forward by Thomas Paine, whom Fitton has met, about which he never tires of telling people, and from whom he has imbibed not just his ideas, but his grasp of political tactics, which tend towards the longer game. He has a mop of flame-red hair, more fiery than his rhetoric.

"Now I want change as much as t' next man," he begins, "but we 'ave to be prudent, we 'ave to be patient. I realise that that's not summat tha' might want to hear just now, wi' t' cost o' living risin' an' t' price o' finished goods fallin'. It's hard, I know, an' there's plenty o' folk 'ere who'd like nowt better than to march on t' Town Hall like they were storming t' Bastille. But that's precisely what t' Magistrates are worried about, an' it'd give 'em just th' excuse they're lookin' for to round us all up, lock us in t' New Bailey Prison, an' throw away t' key. An' I ask you – what good would that do for t' rest of us, especially our wives an' t' childer? That's what Samuel means when 'e talks o' t' Spenceans, Amos. Folk like Thomas Spence from Newcastle, who came out on t' side o' Boney. That's what t' Government's scared of most – a French Revolution startin' up right 'ere."

At this point Fitton is interrupted by a vociferous few who cry that that is exactly what they do want. First up are who Bamford uncharitably refers to as the Unholy Trinity – Messrs Johnston, Drummond and Bagguley – who, while not being Spencean in terms of directly calling for violent means to achieve their ends, make no bones about deploying the threat of it. Younger than Bamford or Fitton or Knight, they are also wilder and more daring, and their calls are for more heroic and seditious action.

"Storm the New Bailey!" cries Johnston.

"Release all t' prisoners!" urges Drummond.

"Brothers-in-arms!" calls out Bagguley.

"Let's march on t' Town Hall!" goads Johnston.

"String up t' Boroughreeve!" roars Drummond.

"Torch Th' Exchange!" suggests Bagguley.

"Make a Moscow o' Manchester!" they chant as one.

"Aye!" cry the more hot-headed members of the crowd.

"Nay!" shout the older, wiser majority, fearful lest Nadin might even at this very moment have planted his spies among them.

It takes the combined efforts of Knight, Fitton and Bamford, plus the various members of the dozens of Female Union Societies who've journeyed to Red Lumb this evening, whose instinct is always for conciliation, rather than confrontation. It was women such as Alice Kitchen and Susanna Saxton, secretary of The Manchester Female Reformers, who kept the people going earlier in the year when the spinners and weavers had gone on strike for higher wages and better conditions in response to the immediate, crushing effects of the Corn Laws.

'We relieve our own sick,' they had written in a letter to Lord Sidmouth, the Home Secretary no less, 'as well as subscribing to other casualties. Therefore, when our hours of labour, which are from five in the morning until seven in the evening (and in some mills even longer), filled with unremitting toil, in factories heated in excess of ninety degrees, are taken into consideration, we believe that the public will agree with us that no body of workers receives so inadequate a compensation for their labour.'

It was that single word 'subscribing' that the Home Secretary took particular and vehement exception to. It smacked of 'Combinations', which remained strictly illegal for any group of labourers to contemplate forming. The creation of 'Benefit Societies', especially those explicitly supported by religious denominations – Methodists, Unitarians and the like –

had partly circumvented the need for them, together with the recent upsurge in what had come to be called 'Union Societies'. Originally conceived by the Reverend Joseph Harrison of Stockport, a long time friend and associate of Johnston, Drummond and Bagguley, their maxim was the same as that selected for Lavinia Robinson's eulogy delivered by the Reverend Clowes – "*do unto others as ye would they should do unto you*". Using the number of Apostles as their guide, Stockport was divided into twelve districts, each district sub-divided into a further twelve classes. In the house, or room, or wherever these classes would meet, a leader, democratically elected by the members of each class, would hold a meeting each week, where it would explore new ways of making manifest the Union's mission – 'to promote human happiness' – and to achieve that, it declared that all men and women were born free, that sovereignty lay with the people, and that 'association' – another provocative word – was necessary to preserve human rights. These were followed by a set of twenty-four rules – two further sets of twelve – the last of which boldly stated that, with the present Government, it was impossible to uphold the Union's maxim and 'do unto them as ye would they should do unto you', and so all members were expected to 'work towards a Radical Reform of Parliament by means of Universal Suffrage', even if that meant resorting to 'Direct Acts of Provocation'. Such were the popularity of these Unions that they rapidly spread to other towns – Bury, Bolton, Rochdale, Oldham – and they began to meet more than once a week on Sundays, but on other nights too, to study reading, writing, simple arithmetic and scripture. A strong emphasis was placed on preparing people for power once it had been won. Which they were certain it would be. In these additional activities they incurred the wrath of the Non-Conformists, especially the Methodists, who furiously complained that their own mission was being usurped and their particular territory as instructors of youth trampled upon. Similarly, as the fortunes of the Union

410

Societies waxed, so those of The Hampden Clubs waned.

All of these internal rivalries and jealousies now began to surface in the open air meeting on the moor at Red Lumb, as faction shouted at faction, and splinter groups fractured further, each blaming the other for their lack of progress so far. Feelings were still running high because of the recent failure of the Spinners' Strike which, after months of holding out, had finally caved in and capitulated, their spirits broken.

Upon the urging of Lord Sidmouth, Manchester's Magistrates began randomly arresting anyone not at work under *The Rogues & Vagabonds Act.* 'By what means,' he had written, 'has so large a body of mechanics subsisted without any visible means of livelihood for so long a period?' The implication was clear. Some form of illegal Combination must surely be at work. By withdrawing their labour the spinners immediately forfeited their wages, even those so low that they had been the catalyst for their action in the first place. They were initially supported by the penny a week each paid into one of the Benefit or Union Societies. But after a period of three months these funds were depleted. The workers and their families were exhausted and starving. Donations from philanthropic sympathisers filled the gap for a short time, but it was at a very low level when spread across the many thousands in need. Amounting to little more than a shilling a week, sufficient only for a pound of potatoes, a few meat bones stewed for broth and a little bread. The failed harvests caused by the 'Year without Summer' only exacerbated their plight. With their leaders divided, without funds and without food, the spinners gave in. They returned to work in exactly the same conditions and for even less wages than when they had first gone on strike. A humiliating climb-down.

What Amos has tried modestly to suggest, just a few minutes before, is now all but forgotten, as all these old grievances rear their heads once more.

It takes several minutes for Bamford, Knight and Fitton,

together with members of the Manchester Female Reformers, to quiet and quell the rage and rancour, with the banging of pots and kettles, which sets up a steady rhythm, over which Samuel Bamford's wife, Jemima, known to all as Mima, begins defiantly to sing:

"You pull down all our wages so shamefully to tell
You go into the markets and say you cannot sell
And when that we do ask you when these bad times will mend
You quickly give for answer when the Wars are at an end..."

The Handloom Weaver's Lament. The great leveller and unifier, its chorus now ringing loud and clear across the moor.

"You tyrants of England, your race may soon be run
You may be brought unto account for what you've sorely done..."

Alice Kitchen takes up the second verse:

"When we look on our poor children it grieves our hearts full sore
Their clothing it is worn to rags while we can get no more
With little in their bellies they to their work must go
Whilst yours do dress as swanky as monkeys in a show..."

Susanna Saxton the third:

"You go to church on Sundays, I'm sure it's nowt but pride
There can be no religion where humanity's tossed aside
If there be a place in heaven, as there is in the Exchange
Our poor souls must not come near there, like lost sheep they must range..."

Sara Fitton the next:

"You say that Bonaparty has been the cause of all
And that we have good reason to pray for his downfall
Well Bonaparty's dead and gone and it is plainly shown
That we've got bigger tyrants in Boneys of our own..."

Then, for the final verse, all four of them combine in a unison of strength:

"And now, my lads, for to conclude, it's time to make an end
Let's see if we can form a plan that these bad times may mend
Then give us our old prices as we have had before
And we can live in happiness and rub off the old score..."

The entire crowd is now reunited, all differences temporarily laid aside, as they come together in a last, rousing chorus. They gather armfuls of laurel, the only thing still growing in this endless winter, from where it colonises the hidden hollows of Red Lumb, and make garlands from it that they wear in their hair, linked by an unbroken chain of evergreen leaves.

"You tyrants of England, your race will soon be run
You may be brought unto account for what you've sorely done..."

In the silence that follows the people look about them. A wind whips across the moor, carrying the fading echoes of their voices. There is solidarity here despite their differences. A common purpose that fills them with hope, even at this darkest hour. In the distance they can just make out the forest of brick towers and chimneys of the mills and factories of Manchester rising up towards the low blanket of unbroken grey above their heads. The black smoke which belches from them adds a further layer to the pall. From this distance they resemble a mighty army on the move, throwing up great clouds of dust and earth into the thickening air. Not an army of soldiers, but of men and women marching towards some half-glimpsed future, one seen only in dreams, which will come into the light once the everlasting night is vanquished and the perpetual darkness lifts.

Samuel Bamford recognises the shift in mood and seizes the moment. It is a time for concession, not reproof.

"Tell us again, Amos," he says softly, "about this idea tha's had."

Amos steps forward reluctantly. He is not one for the limelight, nor for addressing crowds in public. His life has been a litany of standing in line, of doing what he's been told, of never answering back, of not speaking unless spoken to first. In the House of Correction, where he learned fast the art of keeping his head down, his sole aim to become invisible. At Fairfield, where the creed was always to put the needs of others before his own, never to draw undue attention to himself. In the brickfields of Colleyhurst, the mines of Bradford, the cellars of Dimity Court, where for a time he lost all sense of who he was. And these last years in Elton, in what had been Cousin Silas's cottage, with no glass in the wind-eyes, through which the wind has blown night and day, as he has sat hunched over his loom, rattling in time to that constant rhythm, which might have been an extension of his own body, his arms and legs in ceaseless motion with it, his salvation and his destiny, as well as his prison and his tomb, a silent cell, where no words that either he or Agnes might speak could ever lessen the grief and pain of losing Jack, so that neither of them choose to utter a word. All these things have rendered him ill-prepared to stand before this crowd today and share with them the thought that, since it first had come to him, as unbidden as an owl at noon, he has not been able to rid himself of.

He stands upon a rock which juts out from the moor,

elevating him several feet, so that he now commands the hillside. He feels the eyes of everyone upon him. But as he looks out towards them, he begins to understand they are not hostile eyes. They are eyes that have known suffering too. And they look towards him now expectant, not judging, with a frail hope that appears to say, "Anything is better than this. Who will speak for us if not another like us, hewn from the same rock, hauled from the same earth, woven from the same cloth?" And this gives him courage.

"Well," he falters, "the way I see it is..." He pauses, reaching for the right word, like when his fingers strained to hold on to the Roman coin that Agnes had given him as a child, but which he lost in the explosion at the mine.

"Yes?" says Samuel Bamford, clutching a wreath of laurel in his large hands. "What *is* the way you see it?"

And Amos begins.

"I were at St George's Fields – nigh on nine year ago now – when Colonel Hanson rode up on 'is white stallion."

A murmur ripples through the crowd, with those who were there also that day nodding their heads in remembrance.

"A pal o' mine were killed that day. Adam. Shot wi' a soldier's musket. He died in me arms. But I were angry as much as I were sad. I remember sayin' to 'im as 'e lay there. 'You daft beggar – what did tha' go an' do that for?' 'E'd chucked a brick at t' Cavalry as they were chargin'. An' though I could understand why 'e'd done it – it were a spur o' t' moment type thing – it achieved nowt, save for gettin' 'isself killed. An' worse than that, it gave Joe Nadin just th' excuse 'e'd been lookin' for to round up all 'e could lay 'is 'ands on."

He pauses, remembering the panic and chaos of that day. Samuel Bamford, standing alongside him, grips his shoulder.

"Take tha' time, lad. We're listenin'..."

Amos breathes deeply, gathering himself.

"A woman standin' nearby gave me a blanket, which I lay across Adam's body as the 'orses galloped by." He reaches inside a sackcloth bag that has been strung across his shoulder and pulls out a folded piece of cloth. A blanket. "This is that very blanket," he says. There is a gasp from the many hundreds of people still gathered on the Red Lumb moor. "I've kept it ever since. As a reminder. Not just of Adam. But of why we were there." He proceeds to wrap it around his shoulders. "I'm a handloom weaver," he says. "An' though it's not always been my trade, it feels like summat I were born to. But lately, as this winter wi'out an end drags on an' on, I've taken to wearin' it all t' time, even while I'm sat at t' loom. An' it got me thinkin'. Folk in t' Parliament don't 'ave a clue what it's like for us up 'ere. Mr Bamford, Mr Fitton, Mr Knight an' all t' rest of 'em can speak their fine words, but they just don't seem to get listened to, do they? While t' likes of Misters Johnston, Drummond an' Bagguley urge us to tek to t' streets and storm t' New Bailey Prison. But all that'd do, as far as I can tell, is lead to more young men bein' shot at. Like Adam. Well I don't know about you, but I don't want to lose no more pals..."

"No," murmur the crowd, who by now are hanging on every word Amos struggles to deliver.

"So what I'm suggestin' is this. Why don't a whole host of us, as many of us as can, walk from Manchester to London, each of us wrapped in a blanket of our own, an' present a petition to Parliament. They say a picture paints a thousand words. Well, I reckon t' sight of a thousand cotton spinners an' weavers all mekkin' our way to th' House o' Commons, wearin' these blankets like a banner, a badge o' what we share, summat as brings us all together, would really make those politicians sit up an' tek notice, for we all need a blanket, whoever we may be, rich an' poor alike, an' what's more, it'd be a peaceful protest. No throwing o' stones. No unlawful assembly. There's nowt seditious about parading before Parliament wearin' nowt but a blanket. So what dost tha' think? Are thee wi' me? Who's walkin' to London Town?"

A great roar goes up from the crowd. "Me!" they cry. "And

me! And me!" A forest of hands shoot up into the air, hurling their leaves of laurel above their heads.

Messrs Johnston, Drummond and Bagguley, seizing the moment, mount the platform alongside Amos, raising his arm aloft.

Messrs Bamford, Fitton and Knight, sensing the way the wind is blowing, shrug their shoulders and join them.

"We shall call it 'The March o' the Blanketeers'," cries Johnston.

"An' we shall use th' Hampden Clubs an' Union Societies to spread t' word," echoes Drummond.

"Let us reconvene a month today – Monday 10th March – at St Peter's Field. To wave our brave Blanketeers on their way."

The women of the Manchester Female Reformers, led by Mima Bamford, Alice Kitchen, Susanna Saxton and Sara Fitton, lead the united crowd in a new song, which is swiftly taken up by all, as Amos is carried shoulder high towards the summit of Red Lumb.

"Beat the drum slowly
And play the fife lowly
Marching to victory as we go along
And lead us to Manchester
Where wounds no more fester
And free from arrest, sir
When we've righted each wrong…"

If anyone felt reservations or qualms about singing these words to the old traditional tune of *A Young Girl Cut Down In Her Prime*, they did not acknowledge it to themselves or reveal it to others.

*

Two years before it had been another song of love and loss that had rung out across the Lancashire hills – *The Girl I Left*

Behind Me – as Jack marched to War with the 30th Regiment of Foot proudly beating out a brisk rhythm on his drum. Many tearful girls did indeed line the route out of Bury. They threw down wild flowers to strew the way the soldiers would take. Jack gave little or no thought to the girl he was leaving behind – his distraught mother, Agnes, who, on discovering his hastily scrawled note on the edge of the loom, had immediately fled in the direction of the fort, but she was too late. When she got there, it was all but deserted, just a few old retainers who'd been left behind to maintain the garrison, and a young boy, who informed her that a boy named Jack had just taken over as drummer boy from him. He'd've liked to have gone too, he said, but his mother needed him at home. The starkness of these words left a bleak emptiness inside Agnes, where her heart had once resided. She slowly made her way back home, walking unseeing over the trodden flowers tossed there earlier by the weeping girls.

But Agnes was beyond tears. When she neared their home, she paused to look upon the makeshift graves that had been dug behind the house – Silas, Meg, her brother James, a marker for Daisy – and began to mark out in her mind the spot she felt certain would now need to be occupied by one for Jack. He would not be coming back. She felt this with a certainty that felled her as surely as if she too were a corpse upon the battlefield. From inside the cottage she heard Amos starting up the loom. Work. That was all he knew. The sound of the click and clack of its rhythm was like gunfire, each report riddling her body.

Already several miles away Jack heard only the fifes, the marching feet, and the sprightly beat of his own drum. A dozen yards in front of him, at the head of the line, he fixed his eyes upon the giant head of Captain Josiah Blacker, a beacon of hope and promise as the rains began to fall. The 30th East Lancashire Regiment of Foot would follow him to the end of the world if he asked them.

Long Case Clock to Kettle.

The end of the world proved to be a Flemish farmhouse in Hougoumont, in a grove of elm trees, at the heart of the Battle for Waterloo.

The Duke of Wellington would later describe the holding of Hougoumont as the decisive factor that swung victory away from Napoleon and towards the Coalition of forces lined up against him. 'I am happy to add that it was maintained, throughout the day, with the utmost gallantry by these brave troops,' he wrote in his diary, 'notwithstanding the repeated efforts of large bodies of the enemy to obtain possession of it.'

Major Sir John Byng from the 3rd Hanoverian Brigade, with whom Captain Blacker would link up the East Lancashire boys, was more expansive in his recollections.

'I stood about a minute to contemplate the scene,' he wrote. 'It was grand beyond description.'

This was how Jack thought it too. At first.

'The wood around Hougoumont sent up a broad flame through the dark masses of smoke that overhung the field,' the Major recalled. 'Beneath this cloud the French were indistinctly visible. Here, a waving mass of long red feathers could be seen. There, gleams as from a sheet of steel showed that their Cavalry were moving. Four hundred cannon were belching forth fire and death on every side. Bodies of Infantry and Cavalry were pouring down on us. It was time to leave contemplation. The roaring and shouting were indistinguishably commixed. Together they gave me an idea of a labouring volcano...'

They had arrived two days previously, having been marching for weeks, slogging their way through the mud of Flanders as the rain continued to fall in torrents. They were just too late to

419

engage at the Battle for the strategic cross roads of Quatre Bras, that inconclusive affair, which saw Wellington hold out against Marshall Ney, despite incurring the heavier losses, while simultaneously Napoleon blunted the advance of Blücher's Prussians at Ligny, but did not defeat him altogether.

But they could hear it and they could see it. Captain Blacker set up camp on a hilltop beside the Great Windmill of Brye, from where they could look down upon the Belgian plains below. The two opposing armies, tens of thousands of soldiers on each side, faced each other like chess pieces. Jack watched the battle unfold between the giant blades of the windmill slicing the sky and the bars of rain which fell from it like arrows, an added weapon to the massed firepower of artillery, muskets and sabres being fired and wielded below.

Captain Blacker pointed out to Jack the separate movements of the troops on either side, the way different flanks were stretched and sacrificed, each move setting off a counter move, with the opposing Generals, like Queens on the chess board, omnisciently directing it all from the rear, with drummer boys like Jack rapping out instructions in a series of precise cross-rhythms on the mighty kettle drums each regiment towed along with them wherever they marched.

Jack heard those drums threading their way through and beneath the pounding of the guns and the deep rumble of the horses' hooves coming up from the earth, resonating deep within his own as yet ungrown body, a pulse in the blood, stitched together in a single bonded cloth. The shuttle flies forward and then flies back.

Over the weeks they had been marching Jack had learned all the different calls and rhythms, and he had practised them every night, so that he knew each by heart, which, it seemed to Jack, would beat in time to all of them, even as he slept.

Night fell. The fighting stopped. A deep calm descended on the valley. The only sounds now were the rain, which continued to pour unceasingly, the occasional rustle in the undergrowth of some small nocturnal animal, the stamp and wicker of an anxious horse, the hiss and crack of twigs in the camp fires, and the snores of the soldiers sleeping beside them. Captain Blacker came to check on Jack and was not surprised to discover the boy was still wide awake, his back leaning against a tall elm tree. He pointed down to the other distant fires still smouldering on the battlefield below.

"This is the land of the Belgians," he whispered, "or, to be more accurate, the Flemish. The province of Hainault in what used to be the Netherlands but is currently part of the Empire of France. Though not for much longer if the Iron Duke has his way. Three hundred and fifty years ago a Flemish Queen, Phillipa, married King Edward III of England. While he was away fighting wars, she invited a group of weavers from her homeland, from hamlets and villages in the plain where this great battle was fought today, who were unhappy about their lives there, to come to England, as her guests, to settle and set up a linen trade there. They went to Manchester, liked what they saw, and decided to stay. And now your father's a weaver too, Jack, along with thousands and thousands of other folk in Lancashire. And here we are, back where all that began, fighting to make sure we don't lose it, to keep hold of what's been hard won. It makes you think, eh Jack?"

Jack said nothing. It made no sense to him. He hadn't thought much about the War with the French. It had been going on since before he was born. It was just always there. Like the Elton Brook and the Reservoir and the Canal. Like the graves at the back of his house. Like the loom that filled the downstairs room. That never stopped working. Like his father. Like what he couldn't wait to see the back of. Is that what the War was about? Is that what they were meant to be fighting for? For what he'd run away from? He shivered.

"Try and get some sleep," said Josiah, seeing the troubled look upon the boy's face. "You'll need it come the morning."

Jack lay down. There was a brief pause in the incessant

421

downpour. The moon prised a narrow crack through the low blanket of cloud. The windmill kept turning. Its sharp blades scissored the moon.

*

Ten thousand people gather in St Peter's Field in Manchester on the morning of Monday 10th March 1817 in support of the March of the Blanketeers. How many of these actually intend to walk to London is unclear but the mood is one of celebration as Amos, with his blanket wrapped around his shoulders, is paraded before the crowd. Samuel Bamford is not there. Neither is John Knight, but William Fitton is, having volunteered to report back on the success or otherwise of the protest.

"Let 'em have their day in t' sun," says Bamford, "should that celestial body ever deign to show its face again." He is speaking of the Unholy Trinity – Johnston, Drummond and Bagguley – whose brainchild the event has become.

His wife, Mima, attends, though, along with several other members of The Manchester Female Reformers, whose role it is to ensure that there are sufficient blankets available for those setting off for London, and to raise morale with their songs and smiles.

Agnes is not there. She has taken no interest in her husband's sudden involvement in politics.

"Why now?" she asks. "Why not before, when Jack was still at home?"

"That's exactly why," he answers.

But she turns away from him. Two children born, two children lost. One to the brickfields of Manchester, one to the lowlands of Holland, the name of the tune to which the Female Reformers sing to the growing tumult on St Peter's Field.

"It was on a Monday morning as I have heard folk say
The orders came that afternoon we were to march away.

Oh the Lancashire lads are rambling boys and they have but little pay
How can they keep a wife and child on thirteen pence a day...?"

Agnes waits at Elton. Just in case her Jack should return.

The crowd swells. Perhaps ten thousand is too low an estimate. Perhaps fifteen thousand is nearer the mark.

Sir John Byng, a veteran of the Peninsula Wars and Waterloo, who had recalled how the scene at Hougoumont had reminded him of a labouring volcano, now the Commanding Officer of the 7th Hussars (Northern District), is summoned to the Upstairs Room of the home of Sir Hugh Hornby-Birley, the Boroughreeve, on Mount Street, from where he and his fellow Magistrates are looking down upon St Peter's Field with growing alarm.

"Well?" demands Sir Hugh. "What is to be done? You have your troops in readiness, I trust, Sir John?"

"I do," replies the old soldier. "They await my orders, just as I await mine."

"Yes, yes," says the Boroughreeve impatiently, "but what do you advise?"

"For the moment, nothing," says Sir John.

A dozen jaws hit the floor upon hearing this remark.

"Did I hear you correctly, Sir John? Are you seriously suggesting that we simply let this seditious crowd continue to grow before our eyes and do nothing?"

"For the moment, yes. The mood at present is festive. There are no speeches, no agitators, just a holiday crowd enjoying a few folk songs."

"A holiday crowd?" sneers one of the Magistrates. Matthew Oldham steps away from the window and back into the room. "On a working day? I, along with everyone else here, am losing money while these ne'er-do-wells are singing their folk songs, as you so quaintly put it."

"Permit me, sir, to explain. I have witnessed many crowds in many different settings in more than one country. In my experience, too hasty an intervention, before it becomes strictly necessary, is more likely to enflame passions than to quell them."

"No intervention can be too hasty for me. What *you* term a holiday crowd, sir, *I* call a seditious mob." Matthew appeals directly to the Boroughreeve. "This is an unlawful assembly. The Riot Act should be read to them. And if they do not disperse at once, *you*, sir," he adds, turning back to face Sir John, "should make them do so with as much force as you deem necessary."

"I agree with Mr Oldham," says Sir Hugh, "whom you will kindly escort, Sir John, to the site of this illegal gathering and allow him to read from the Riot Act, after which you have your instructions."

Sir John Byng sighs, shakes his head, but answers in the affirmative. "Yes, Sir Hugh. Gentlemen, good day. If you would follow me, Mr Oldham, we shall proceed directly."

Matthew makes a beeline for a cart from which Messrs Johnston, Drummond and Bagguley are exhorting the crowd for volunteers to accompany Amos on his march to London.

"Let us present our petition to t' Prince Regent in person, so that 'e may hear directly from our lips an' see wi' 'is own eyes the desperate plight o' t' workin' folk here in Manchester."

Matthew takes no note of the man wrapped in a blanket standing by their side, nor Amos of Matthew, as he finds himself being thrust roughly aside before being swallowed up by the crowd pressing around the cart. Matthew, speaking loudly above their heads, proceeds to read the Riot Act to a chorus of whistles and boos.

"Our Sovereign Lord the King chargeth and commandeth all persons being here assembled immediately to disperse themselves, and peaceably depart to their habitations, or to their lawful business, upon the pains contained in the Act made in the first year of King George the First for preventing tumults and riotous assemblies."

The cart is immediately surrounded by Sir John Byng's Hussars. Johnston, Drummond and Bagguley are unceremoniously hauled down and hastily removed from the scene.

"This is not an unlawful assembly," cries Johnston. "We're simply here to wave goodbye to our friends, who are going on a journey to London."

Furious that the ring leaders only have been arrested, while the rest of the crowd is being allowed to voice their protests unmolested, Matthew leaves the Field and returns to Mount Street to make his dissatisfaction known. Sir John Byng, however, observes the man in the blanket walking swiftly away in the opposite direction, up Mosley Street towards the Daub Holes. He is followed by a contingent of what Sir John estimates to be at least five hundred determined young men, while The Female Reformers begin once more to sing, taunting the Hussars as they harry the crowds.

"Boney was a warrior
Way-ay-ah
A warrior, a harrier
Jean François

Boney went to Waterloo
Way-ay-ah
There he got what he was due
Jean François…"

But Sir John ignores them. There is no way he is going to allow hundreds, maybe even thousands, of disgruntled spinners and weavers to pour out of Manchester, with this man in a blanket as a figure head, a rallying point, to gather more supporters around them as they go, causing further mayhem and mischief. He instructs a small troop on horseback to follow them, with orders to head them off and round them up, rather like they would with lost sheep. They herd them down the London Road, well beyond sight of the diminishing crowds on St Peter's Field, happily singing as they leave, corralling the bulk of them at Longsight, little more than a mile away. Another batch is apprehended in Stockport a couple of hours later, just as they are setting up camp for the night. The last few stragglers make it to Macclesfield the following day, but decide to turn back, disheartened by the less than enthusiastic welcome they receive when they get there. Only a few die-hards decide to continue, Amos among them. But by the time these last few reach Ashbourne in Derbyshire, just forty-six miles from Manchester, only Amos remains.

*

No one can say for certain when the Battle of Waterloo began.

Some say as early as ten in the morning, while some say as late as midday, and there are as many other opinions as there are minutes in between. Everybody agrees, however, that it ended at precisely nine o'clock in the evening, as dusk fell and General Wellington and Marshall Blücher saluted each other as victors at a farmhouse aptly known as *La Belle Alliance*, from where Napoleon had been directing his forces, and outside which stood an abandoned carriage still containing the Emperor's annotated copy of Machiavelli's *The Prince*, while all around the cries of "*Sauve qui peut*" echoed in the warm night air.

But for Jack the opposite was true. He knew exactly when it started – with a single musket shot which felled Captain Blacker like an axe splitting an oak – but not when it finished. The battle raged all day, a close run thing, with fortunes ebbing first one way, then the other, like a neap tide after the first quarter of the moon when there is little difference between high and low water.

Without the Captain's reassuring presence Jack was in a maze. His head filled with a white noise he could not detect the source of. Sometimes it sounded like the screeching of rooks, sometimes like the agitated buzzing of a swarm of flies burrowing into his brain, or sometimes like the never-ending surge of water – the River Irwell in full spate, the ebb and flow of the tide of battle, the rain that still fell unrelentingly – so that he waded knee-deep through the churned-up mud, not knowing which way to turn, as the battle raged around him.

Beside the Chateau at Hougoumont he remembers an elm tree, whose long shadow, a pointing, spectral finger of death, circled the land like a sundial, cutting down the skirmishers with its grim scythe. He remembers the advance of the French Cavalry. A long, moving line, stretched as wide as the eye could see, glittering like a storm-tossed wave on the sea when it catches the sunlight, which here and there was poking through the blanket of cloud. On and on they came, until they got so near he could see the flecks of spittle foaming at the horses' mouths and feel the ground vibrate beneath their thundering charge.

Yet still Major Byng delayed the order to fire. "Wait," he cried. "Wait." Finally, when it appeared as though the enemy was all but upon them, he gave the command. "Fire!"

Jack beat out the signal on his drum, the sound instantly obliterated by the volley and discharge of cannon and gunfire.

Later the Major would write, 'The effect was terrible. The fusillade from every gun was followed by a fall of men and horses like that of grass before the mower's scythe. The scrape and strike of sabres against breast plates a thousand hammers upon red hot anvils.'

After that Jack remembers nothing.

When dawn broke the next morning he found himself still wandering in a daze. The rain had finally stopped. The sun, which would scarcely be visible again for almost two years after this day, rose from the east, a red wound leaking through the bandage of sky.

A scene of carnage greeted him.

Forty-seven thousand bodies heaped one upon the other. The multitude of carcasses, with mangled limbs unable to move, festering in the heat. The sound of crows and flies feasting. Pockets of smoke rising up from the smouldering earth. Mixed with the early morning mist they cover the ground like a shroud. Tattered strips of flags and banners streaming in a hot, sickly breeze. Charred embers of flaked skin falling like tiny cotton dancers daubed with ash.

For Jack the battle never ceases. The sights and sounds never leave him. They haunt him day and night, blotting out the world. When people speak to him, he cannot connect their voices with their faces. His mouth is dry, his tongue swollen. His body trembles, collapsing in on itself like a broken marionette. His feet propel him forwards in an antic parody of motion, a stuttering stumble seemingly undirected by his brain, which remains locked here, at Hougoumont, beneath the moving finger of the elm tree, which always seeks him out, and from which he always tries to hide, but which finds him in the end.

He never speaks of it to anyone. He never speaks another word at all.

The distant volcano rests. It knows it is not quite done yet.

Somewhere, far, far away, Jack hears a voice call his name.

*

Amos sets off from Macclesfield at dawn. He is alone now. The last of his supporters lost heart on the steep, rutted lanes around Alderley Edge but reluctantly agreed to accompany him as far as Macclesfield. They were already missing their families, had not realised just how far their journey would be. Amos understands. In many ways he envies them, wishing that he too might be missed at home, but he knows that Agnes is still so stricken with grief that she will barely register he is not there.

She may wonder occasionally at the unusual quiet in the cottage, with the loom lying silent, but then perhaps be glad of it, making it easier for her to hear Jack's voice calling out her name if he finally makes it home, something she hourly expects, even though logic tells her he will not be coming back.

This journey he is himself now making is in part a recompense for the guilt which never leaves him, how he might somehow have stopped Jack from running away, a guilt which stretches back to when they lost Daisy in the brickfields, earlier to when he persuaded Agnes they should leave Elton in the first place, and further back still to when they had made their midnight flight from Fairfield almost twenty years ago. It is time to make amends. Or at least try to.

They had arrived at Macclesfield the previous evening just as dusk was settling on another day which had never properly grown light. Market traders were packing away their stalls on Waters Green, which they reached via a flight of one hundred and eight steps descending into the square from St Michael's & All Angel's Church high on Kerridge Hill overlooking the town. There had been a Horse Fair that day and brisk business had been done. Amos spied a gentleman in military uniform whose face seemed familiar leading away a fine mare he had just secured after a most successful and enjoyable barter. They passed within inches of each other, but so engrossed was the Officer in his latest purchase that he failed to register Amos, or the rest of the straggle of marchers, who now wrapped their blankets round their shoulders as they hunkered down for the night by the wall of Paradise Mill. Amos learns that Bonnie Prince Charlie passed this way on his own ill-fated attempt to reach London at the height of the Jacobite Rebellion, having first set off from Manchester. He only made it as far as Derby, where Amos hopes to pass and go beyond in two more days.

He leaves the others behind before they are awake. Let them sleep, he feels. He bears them no ill will for not accompanying him further. He is relishing the time alone. Heading south he passes a milestone indicating 'Ashbourne: 29 miles'. That is where he hopes to lay his head this night.

He follows the River Dane, which by mid-morning brings him into Congleton, where he rests briefly on the steps of the Trinity Chapel on Wagg Street. A scrawny black cat wheedles his way in and out of Amos's legs.

"You've stolen his spot," says a kindly-looking woman approaching him. "He used to like to catch the morning sun that always fell on those steps," she adds, "when there was any sun to be had."

Amos smiles thinly and pulls the blanket tighter round his shoulders. The Minister's wife, for that is who the woman is, fetches him a beaker of water and a crust of bread. She asks him about the blanket he wears and listens carefully as he explains.

"We're not all godless folk here," she says, "no matter what you might've heard."

Amos shakes his head in a puzzled frown.

"Surely you've heard the rhyme?" she says.

He declares that he has not.

" *'Congleton Rare, Congleton Rare*
Sold the Bible to buy a Bear'."

Amos smiles in bewilderment.

"Well," she continues, "there used to be a great passion for bear-baiting here – not any more, I hasten to add – an' folk'd come from all over. But the bear got old an' tame. People stopped coming an' the town were losin' money. The story goes that they used the money they'd put by for a Bible to buy a younger, angrier bear instead."

Amos thinks of Johnston, Drummond and Bagguley now locked up in the New Bailey Prison. Would that curb their tempers or make them angrier still? How many times must a man – or beast – be whipped and chained before he is tamed?

"Are you all right?" asks the Minister's wife. "I think I lost you for a while back there."

430

"Yes, I'm sorry. I've been walking a long time."

"An' you've a fair way to go yet before you reach your journey's end."

He nods and stands up from the steps. He absent-mindedly picks up the cat, which he strokes beneath his chin, causing him to purr noisily.

"He likes that," says the Minister's wife, taking the cat from him, "but then which of us doesn't?"

Amos thinks back to his time as a child in the House of Correction, when the only touch he ever knew would be a cuff or a blow.

"Thank you," he says, handing her back the beaker. "I don't know your name."

"Margery," she says simply, helping him to his feet.

"I'm Amos."

"A good name," she says. "It means someone who's been carried by God and so become strong."

"I don't feel like either if I'm honest."

"But what you're doing's important. You're taking a stand. You're walking to London, to speak to the King's Regent, to tell 'im summat 'e wouldn't otherwise know. Only those in power can change the way things are, but how can they *do* that if they don't know what needs changin'? That's where *we* come in, folk like you an' me. It's us who put 'em there, an' it's our job to show 'em what needs doin'."

Amos says nothing. All very well, he thinks, if the town where you live has a Member of Parliament you can elect, which Congleton has, but which Manchester doesn't. Even though it's more than ten times the size. Which is why he's making this march in the first place, though more personal reasons have taken precedence with each mile he covers.

She continues to walk with him down Lawton Street towards the Town Hall, a somewhat dilapidated black and white half-timbered building, opposite *The White Lion*, where Margery halts again briefly. The inn has also seen better days,

431

though is in less need of attention than its civic neighbour, and is already appearing to be doing a brisk trade.

"That's where John Bradshaw served his articles," she said.

Amos looks blank.

"What? You've not heard of John Bradshaw? He became Attorney General and was appointed Lord President of the Parliamentary Commission to try King Charles. It's his signature that's first on the death warrant. He refused to let the King have any last words. 'Under English law,' he's supposed to 'ave said, 'You have been condemned to death and a condemned man is no longer alive. Therefore you have no right to speak further'." She chuckles at the thought.

Amos wonders if that is why he no longer speaks to Agnes back at Elton. Because he is in her eyes a condemned man?

What he does know is that Manchester saw the first casualty of the Civil War. When Richard Perceval of Levenshulme, a weaver like Amos, was killed outside another inn, *The Bull's Head*, on Hanging Ditch, by the Royalist Thomas Tyldesley, leading to the town coming under siege from the King's troops, which, though greatly outnumbered and against all the odds, the local volunteers, loyal to Cromwell and to Parliament, survived and defeated, when this same John Bradshaw led a heroic last ditch charge.

Since when Manchester has paid a long and heavy price. When Charles II was restored to the throne, one of his first actions as King was to rob Manchester of its Parliamentary status. Amos knows this only too well from his meetings in the Potter's Parlour and tries to articulate some of it to Margery, the need for representation, but he makes little sense, even to himself.

Margery nods in sympathy. What she doesn't tell Amos is that another of The Merry Monarch's first actions after the Restoration was to exhume Bradshaw's dead body from its tomb in Westminster Abbey, display it in chains for three days on Tyburn Hill, then publicly behead it, before tossing the body

432

into a common pit and impaling the head on a spike in Westminster Hall.

"Good luck," she says simply when they part. "It's not every day we get to meet a king, is it?"

Amos shrugs. He knows the chances of being allowed to present his petition directly to the Prince Regent are virtually nil. It's the walk alone that matters.

The cat squirms out of the Minister's wife's arms and slouches towards a gaggle of small children skipping with a rope in the street, who gather it up between them.

> " *'Pussy cat, pussy cat, where hast thou been?'*
> *'I've been to London to visit the Queen.'*
> *'Pussy cat, pussy cat, what didst thou there?'*
> *'I frightened a mouse hiding under a chair…'* "

Amos leaves Congleton more thoughtfully than when he arrived. He heads east, exchanging the county of Cheshire for that of Staffordshire. He follows the Biddulph valley, passing the busy pits of Knyperley, Black Bull and Chatterley Whitfield. He recognises the scene from his time at Bradford, the men and women toiling up the steep hillsides, hauling baskets of coal by hand from the workings near the surface, which they carry on their shoulders back down to the yards in the valley bottom. There's no canal here, not yet, so the coal has to be carried by horse and cart the five and a half miles to the one at Caldon. Nobody gives him a second glance as he walks among their trudge and toil. He feels like his own ghost passing through them.

It's a steep climb into Leek, some seven or eight hundred feet high, on the edge of a gritstone escarpment he hears folk refer to as The Roaches, on the southern uplands of the Pennines. The air feels fresher here, but colder, and Amos is glad of the blanket. He enters the town just after lunch, a busy market day, noisy with cattle, sheep, pigs and geese crammed into pens too tiny for them. He passes a sign with the town's motto painted in Latin.

'*Arte favente nil desperandum.*'

'Our skill assisting us, we have no cause for despair,' he is told.

Above the motto is the town's insignia, which shows a double sunset. Intrigued, Amos asks a carter bringing in sacks of corn from the nearby Brindley Mill, named, he learns, for the engineer who built the Bridgewater Canal, who grew up here, as everyone he meets is keen to tell him, what it means. The carter is happy to talk. He shares some bread with Amos as he explains.

"In the days when there were still a sun to be risin' an' settin'," he says, somewhat ruefully chewing his crust, "you could stand in the graveyard of St Edward the Confessor – over yonder…" and he points to an old church at the top of the town, "an' look out across to Bosley Cloud – over yonder…" and he points in the opposite direction towards a hill, the highest among The Roaches, "an' the sun'd set twice – once behind the summit, then a second time from behind its northern slope. 'Twas a wonder to behold, but 'tis so long since I last saw 'im, I can't rightly remember just how 'twas…"

Amos tries to picture it. It reminds him of the patterns he would sometimes see in the kaleidoscope he had made as a boy with his adoptive father, which he and Agnes had shared from that time onwards, and which she had now put away out of sight since Jack ran away. He wonders what must be the scientific cause of it. His father would have told him had he been there, he thinks. He feels certain he would have known. Something to do with axial precession, the obliquity of the ecliptic, all of it caused by gravity, that inevitable force which pins Amos to the earth, to this path he has chosen for himself. He wonders whether his father might be proud of what he is trying to accomplish by this Blanket March. But he thinks not.

"We are a world unto ourselves," he hears his father say. "We are self-contained and self-governed. What need we to petition Parliament? We have our baker, our laundry, our farm. Our fire engine, night watchman, inspector of weights and measures, our overseer of roads, even our own physician. The soul must make surrender to God, Amos. Remember this. By means of an act of pure faith and faith alone. To make this surrender we must be quiet before God – quiet, Amos – making no effort to save ourselves. Our deeds cannot save us, only our faith. That is why we make a separation from the world and all its temptations."

But Amos still cannot accept this. We are responsible for our own actions, he believes. If we make mistakes, we must try to atone for them. That is what he is doing now by making this walk. He may be walking to London, but deep down, he knows, he is walking back to Agnes. At least that it what he hopes.

"They do say," continues the carter, breaking off a second piece of bread for Amos, "that 'twas from St Edward's graveyard that folk did first see the Great Heathen Army of The Danes appearing over the brow o' Bosley Cloud betwixt the two sunsets. Like the four horsemen of the Apocalypse, cloakin' theirselves in all the colours o' they twin suns. Conquest ridin' a white horse, War a red. Famine astride a black horse, and Plague the colour o' grey mist. The villagers hid inside the nave o' the Church o' St Edward the Confessor, and the Good Lord, 'E spared 'em, for the Great Heathen Army rode on by."

But still war comes, thinks, Amos, and famine, and plague. We can't bury our heads in the earth for ever and hope that somehow we will be spared, or leave it all to some external power, benevolent or otherwise. No. He is done with the Lot. We have to act. We have to risk the smoke and ruin and stand up for what is just, for the better lives we all of us want for our children. Surely that is not too much to hope for? He remembers his time in the School for Single Brethren back in

435

Fairfield, where he felt he was being prepared to take his place in the world, not shut himself away from it. He remembers the 'Stories of the Saints' Brother Swertner used to tell them, of how their suffering was endured in order to make the world a better place for those who followed them, so why in that case would he want to shun it? He remembers one particular story vividly, and it comes back to him now, as the bells from the Church of St Edward the Confessor ring the hour, quietly but determinedly. It is the story of St Pancras, a fourteen-year-old boy, who would not renounce his faith in the face of torture from the Emperor Diocletian. Fourteen – the same age as Jack when he ran away for a soldier. Whenever a church is named for St Pancras, Brother Swertner told the boys in the schoolroom in Fairfield, inscribed on the bell, however small and mean it may be, are the following words:

"*Quamvis sum parva*
Tamen audior ampla per arva…"

"*I may be small but I am heard over a wide distance…*"

By making this walk Amos hopes he will find his own voice, and that perhaps he may ne heard.

He leaves the carter then, for he still has fifteen more miles before he reaches his journey's end for the day, which will be in Ashbourne, still following the route of the Jacobite Rebellion, the Young Pretender.

It is five and a half hours hard walking before he reaches the base of Old Hill, from where there is a final steep climb into the town itself. Ashbourne sits at the cross-roads of five different coaching routes, converging from all points of the compass, and has long proved a challenge to even the most experienced of coach drivers. As a consequence, a new

Turnpike is being constructed on the road to Derby, the farthest point reached by Bonnie Prince Charlie on his march south towards London. When Amos arrives, although it is some hours since darkness fell, work is still going on by torchlight. He passes a chain gang of what he first assumes must be convicts labouring to dig the new highway. It is only as he hears them curse, when the blades of their shovel or axe strike solid rock, that he realises they are French. Prisoners-of-War from Napoleon's scattered and defeated army.

He slips past them in the shadows with a mixture of guilt and shame. From what he has read in the newspapers, Waterloo was a close run thing. It could easily have gone the way of the French. It all came down to weather and timing in the end. In which case, had things turned out differently, it could have been British lads digging roads in the fields of France, Jack among them. If he's been spared. But deep down Amos knows that can't be possible. Not now. Not after nearly two years. Unless, somehow, he is simply lost.

Weather and timing.

A cold wind picks up. Rain begins to fall, hard and stinging. Amos beds down for the night in a stable behind *The Green Man*. The straw is clean and dry. He is warmer than he has been since he left Elton. But he still covers himself with the blanket, which has become a kind of comfort or charm, a superstition, an extension of who he is. He closes his eyes and invites sleep to come to him. He hears the busy rustlings of others seeking shelter from the storm. As his eyes accustom themselves to the darkness, he makes out the unmistakeable shape of a female rat about to give birth to her litter just a few feet away from him. He watches transfixed. One by one they come, eight of them in all, pushing their way down the birth canal one after the other, some of them head first, some rump first. The mother uses her paws and teeth to help each one, pulling away the placenta and the birth sac, which later she will ingest, together with the umbilical cord, for they are rich in protein. First she will lick away the membranous film covering each pup to clear their airway and to oxygenate their blood. When the last pup has been safely delivered, and each is securely fastened onto one of the mother's nipples, Amos very gently pads the nest with fresh straw. She allows him to do so without fear or protest. The pups are blind. They will not open their eyes for fourteen days, and even then they will not be able to detect anything more than different gradations of shadow and light. For now they navigate by smell, by touch, but mostly by instinct. If they were somehow to stray any distance from the nest, or more specifically from their mother, they would not survive.

*

Jack wanders blindly across the battlefield, dazed and disorientated, his eyes stinging with the smoke rising from the piled corpses, through which he trips and stumbles. It is the worst kind of nightmare from which there is no waking.

He still carries his drum. Slung around his shoulder, it swings across his chest as he stumbles through the gore and carnage. He does not know what to do, where to go. He simply flails his arms in front of him, the mist and smoke clinging to him like ghosts in torment. He attacks them furiously with the drum sticks still clenched in his tiny fists. The wraiths separate and reform.

He reaches the base of the elm tree, takes rest beneath its indifferent canopy. A few persistent fingers of sunlight poke and jab him through their leaves. The rain has stopped. Rooks croak like witches. He surveys the desecrated orchard. Pigs still root and forage. But not for apples.

He looks down at the drum hanging round his neck, at the sticks he still clutches like a life raft, and slowly he begins to play. He delivers his full repertoire, his whole tattoo – from the Dutch *do dem tap toe*, played to call the soldiers back from their late night drinking sessions – the Reveille, the Call-to-Arms, the Rapid-Advance, the Open-Fire, the Charge-for-

Glory, the Retreat, the Lock-Step, and now the Slow-March, the Funeral-March, the Dead-March.

When he has finished, the air around him trembles, as if holding the memory of what he has played in tiny pockets, which the still rising, still swirling smoke and mist carries up with it high into the ether, where the echoes never quite fade, but mix and conjoin with all the other sounds of fury.

Something sharp and glinting catches his eye. On the other side of the hill, behind the elm, away from the charnel-house of slaughter just below him, a dagger of light strikes a small duck pond, which glitters like a mirror. Jack stumbles towards it. Far back in his mind he knows this water must be foul, but something even farther back impels him towards it. His cracked lips crave it. His empty stomach cramps for it.

But when he reaches its edge, what he sees there roots him to the spot. The shock of his own reflection. Every inch of him spattered in blood. His face, his neck, his hands. Dappled flecks of crimson, almost as if a child has been given his very first paint brush and has been studiously flicking it at this person standing there before the water to see what effect it might cause. Jack does not recognise himself. It is as if he is seeing somebody else who has taken his place. He falls to his knees and plunges his head beneath the scum of the pond, holding his breath for as long as he can, before resurfacing.

He comes up for air gasping. But when the water settles again, he sees not one, but two reflections of himself, one kneeling, the other standing, their faces haloed. Like two suns. The one that is standing begins to smile. It raises its right hand and jerkily waves it. The kneeling Jack waves back. Then stands. Then turns. He looks this *doppelganger* in the eye. He blinks. Counts to ten. Reopens his eyes. The *doppelganger* is still there. Jack reaches out a hand towards it. It too is wearing a drum about its neck. Just when Jack's fingers are within touching distance of it, it raps Jack's knuckles sharply with its stick. Then laughs. Delightedly. It makes Jack think of the way the river runs over stones at the weir on Elton Brook.

The other Jack starts to speak.

"Bonjour. Je suis Gaston. Moi aussi, un jeune tambour. Comme toi. Nous sommes camarades, non? On fait la paix. Comment tu t'appelles?"

The boy holds out his hand towards Jack, who takes it, examines it as if he can't fully comprehend what he's seeing or hearing. But once Gaston has begun to speak, there is no holding him back. The words tumble out of him like a torrent, when the Elton Brook is in full spate. No, thinks Jack, listening to the constant chatter dancing round him, not the brook, but a swallow when it skims across it, intoxicated by the banquet of insects it offers up to it. Not that Jack is offering anything at all by way of return. He says nothing. The power of speech is still locked deep inside him and the key is lost, or has been thrown away. But Gaston appears either not to notice or not to mind. He maintains a constant running commentary. He opens his beak and an unstoppable cascade of song pours out.

"Quel âge as-tu? J'ai quatorze ans. Où habites-tu? Moi, j'habite Lille. Je travaille dans les filatures de coton mais je ne l'aime pas. Un jour, Napoléon est venu dans notre ville. Nous avons besoin de plus d'armes, a-t-il dit, et nous avons besoin de plus de soldats pour les renvoyer. Je voulais être un soldat mais j'étais trop jeune. Mais tu peux être un batteur, me disent-ils, un tambour. J'étais exalté, mais avant que je puisse y aller, la Marine Nationale m'a pris pour un singe en poudre. J'étais à bord du Borée, un Téméraire combattant avec soixante-quatorze armes à feu. La Marine Britannique a bloqué le port de Toulon et on nous a ordonné de nous frayer un chemin. C'était terrible. Je courais à travers les entrailles du navire, transportant le poudre à canon des magazines aux emplacements pour armes à feu. Des incendies se sont déclarés partout. J'étais sûr que j'allais mourir. Nous avons perdu notre tête de mât, mais enfin nous sommes arrivés au port. Aussitôt, j'ai sauté à terre et j'ai couru pour ma vie. J'ai traversé toute la

France. Pendant plusieurs semaines j'ai marché. J'ai dormi dans des granges ou sous les étoiles. Finalement je suis rentré à Lille, mais mes deux parents étaient décédés. J'étais orphelin. Je vais au fort en ville. Avez-vous encore besoin d'un batteur? Un tambour? je leur ai demandé. Ils ont dit 'Oui!'. La semaine prochaine, j'ai suivi l'Armée du Nord du Comte d'Erlon jusqu'au château d'Hougoumont, chantant tout le chemin La Marseillaise."

He then proceeds to burst into song, at the top of his high, piping, still unbroken voice.

"Allons enfants de la Patrie
Le jour de gloire est arrivé
Contre nous de la tyrannie
L'étendard sanglant est levé
Entendez vous dans les campagnes
Mugir ces féroces soldats
Ils viennent jusque dans vos bras,
Egorger vos fils, vos compagnes…"

Gaston gaily prattles on in French uninterrupted for another hour, a mixture of storytelling, questions he knows will not be answered, and pointing things out along the way. A tree, a bird, a flower. Then he will continue with *La Marseillaise*, carrying on from where he left off before.

Jack has no idea what Gaston is singing, though he recognises the tune, nor of what he has been talking about. Somehow he believes it has been a story not unlike his own. Gaston's *joie de vivre* is somehow infectious and Jack finds he is quite happy to be swept along by it, to link arms with this new found companion, and run together side by side along a narrow, sunken, covered lane towards the village of Papelotte.

It is here, on the edge of the village, which is still smoking from where it has been put to the torch and looted, that the incident occurs.

441

Jack becomes aware of it first. The sound of muffled screams coming from the other side of a hedge where clumps of flattened cow parsley are just beginning to unfurl once more. He tries to quieten Gaston, make him aware that something's not quite right, but he's irrepressible and won't be stopped. They round a bend in the lane and stumble straight into the cause of those screams. A young girl has been hiding in one of the barns but the soldiers have smoked her out. Now they are taking turns with her, two and three at a time, covering her mouth with their rough hands so that her screams won't interfere with their pleasure. She manages to bite the fingers of one of them for which she is rewarded with a fist to the face that knocks her unconscious but does not prevent the men from carrying on.

It is only when he is almost on top of them does Gaston realise what is going on and finally stop singing, but not before some of the soldiers – all of them British – have taken up the chorus and are singing it back to him with their own mocking words.

"Bonaparty's been defeated
No more frogs' legs, no more snails
If we catch his frogs retreating
They won't live to tell the tale…"

Immediately Gaston's senses go into overdrive. In a single movement he whips out a knife from inside his tunic with one hand, wrenches the left arm of Jack tightly behind his back with the other, while holding the knife to his throat. It all happens so fast that Jack is too surprised to react.

"Pardon, mon ami," hisses Gaston into Jack's ear. *"Je le fais pour toi aussi bien que pour moi. Ça peut nous faire gagner un temps précieux."*

Gaston's instincts prove right. His actions have not only shocked and frightened Jack, but they have surprised the soldiers, who smirk uncomfortably at the sight of the two drummer boys. They don't honestly care whether Gaston slits the silent English boy's throat or not, but something stirs within them about needing to defend their own.

"I wouldn't do that if I were you, son," says one of them, a Corporal, buttoning up his trousers as he heaves himself away from the prostrate French girl, who he now kicks for good measure. "The way I see it is like this. Right now, you think, because you're threatening one of ours, we're somehow going to let you just walk away from here. Well, you may be right, but you may be not. If you do kill 'im, we'd be onto you so fast afterwards you wouldn't get five yards. Then we'd cut you into little bits that we'd feed to the crows. So I'd advise against it if I were you, my son. But what's the alternative? You just stand 'ere? You could do that if you like, but for how long? We could wait all day if you like. Couldn't we, lads?"

The other soldiers laugh, scenting sport. By now they have formed a circle around the two boys and are advancing slowly towards them. Gaston's eyes dart from side to side like a cornered fox. In a last ditch attempt to escape he throws the knife in the direction of the Corporal and dashes back towards the lane in the opposite direction. The Corporal easily cuffs the knife aside, while another of the soldiers brings down Gaston and carries him squirming back to the clearing in front of the barn, where he dumps him on the ground before the Corporal, who places a boot firmly between the boy's wriggling shoulder blades, pinning him like an insect to a board.

"I've got a better idea," he says. "We could do with a bit of sport, couldn't we, lads? A nice bit of cock fighting. We was hopin' to find some cockerels in this barn 'ere," he says, jerking his head over his shoulder, "but the only two we could find were such scrawny little things they scarcely merited the name, did they, lads?" He indicates a pair of bantams strung up with their necks wrung beside the barn door. "And then we got distracted, didn't we, lads?" He looks back towards the young girl who is just coming round and trying to crawl away. The Corporal shakes his head and wags his finger at her. "An' where d'you think *you're* goin, *Mademoiselle*? We ain't finished with you yet." The look he throws her stops her in her tracks. "But first things first." He hauls up Jack and Gaston by the respective scruffs of their necks, one in each hand, and regards them with a squint and a smile. Jack can feel the sour breath emanating from his crooked mouth. The blackened teeth inside look as though they've been filed and sharpened. "We got ourselves two new cocks now, so what we're gonna do is this. We're gonna 'ave ourselves a nice little fight. Drummer boy against drummer boy. Cock against cock. King George against Boney. Who's your money on, lads?"

A great shout goes up from the other soldiers as they all declare for their favourite.

"A fight to the death, boys," says the Corporal, "with a prize for the winner." He looks lasciviously back towards the young girl. "Whoever wins can warm 'er up for the rest of us."

Another guttural roar erupts from the troops, whose blood is well and truly up now, as the Corporal flings Gaston and Jack towards each other, so that they fall to the ground, wrestling as if in a lovers' embrace.

Jack understands what he is expected to do but he cannot bring himself to do it. He looks into Gaston's eyes and sees only himself, reflected back very small. But Gaston is wild now. He feels panic and terror. When *he* looks into Jack's eyes he sees nothing, a black void, which reminds him of his time as a powder monkey at the Battle of Toulon, ferrying the sacks of sulphur, charcoal and saltpeter back and forth between the magazine and the cannons, a boiling rage building up inside him, which if he lets go of for just one second, he will be blown to smithereens and lost. He places his hands around Jack's throat and starts to squeeze.

A loud cheer greets this first act of aggression and money furiously changes hands between the baying soldiers.

Jack instinctively raises his own hands towards Gaston's. He tries to prise the fingers from his neck. Already he is beginning to feel himself starting to slip away. He becomes aware of the hate in Gaston's face, the sheer effort of will twisting his features into knotted ropes of fury. He brings up his knee hard between Gaston's legs, who howls with the pain just long enough for his fingers to loosen a fraction around Jack's throat, so that Jack can release himself from their grip and fling Gaston onto his back, where he can sit astride him, pinning his arms beneath his knees, and begin to smash his fists into a face he no longer recognises.

But Gaston manages to free one of his hands, which he launches like an arrow straight for one of Jack's eyes, which he would most certainly have started to gouge had not Jack dodged to one side at the last moment, feeling instead his attacker's nails scoring deep into his cheek.

The soldiers are now in a frenzy, like a pack of wild dogs circling for the kill. But just when it seems as though they will be able to contain themselves no longer and leap into the cock pit themselves, a volley of gunshots cracks above their heads, silencing them in a heartbeat.

Jack and Gaston separate from each other, becoming themselves once more, their bodies trembling, appalled by what they have been capable of.

A small contingent of British outriders gallops into the clearing. At their head is a coldly furious Major-General Sir John Byng, who swoops down upon them like Moses coming from the mountain after he has found his chosen people worshipping the golden calf. He sees the frightened French girl, he sees the shaking drummer boys. He dispatches one of his Lieutenants to wrap them all in blankets. Then he turns towards the Corporal and his men.

"You are soldiers of the King, but today you have forfeited the right to the uniform. Where is your honour? Where is your discipline? We are members of the British Army, loyal to His

Majesty. We are magnanimous in defeat and generous in victory. Yesterday we won a great victory. Today you have shown yourselves no longer fit to wear the laurel. You bring shame upon your regiment, your country and yourselves. I trust that the punishment that awaits you on your return will afford you the opportunity to reflect upon what I have said and henceforth mend your ways. Take them to Ghent."

Like dogs with their tails between their legs they slink away to face whatever fate will befall them. Which, as like as not, will not be what Sir John would prefer. He suspects that once they are out on the open road, they will just melt into the air and make their own way back to England, that the soldiers he has dispatched to escort them will simply look the other way, for they will recognise those darker forces that lurk within all of us, he thinks. There but for the grace of God *et cetera*.

He watches them till they have disappeared from sight, then he approaches the two drummer boys.

"Go home," he says to them. "*Rentrez. Ce n'est pas un endroit pour vous.* This is no place for you." He wheels his enormous horse around and canters away in the opposite direction.

Jack and Gaston look at one another. They are still shaking. After several seconds, Jack makes a move towards his reflection in an attempted gesture of friendship. Startled by the sudden movement, Gaston bolts down the lane, into a thicket of trees and is gone. Jack will not see him again.

He stands staring at the spot where he vanished wondering what he should do. He feels a soft hand upon his shoulder. It is the French girl. She leads him by the hand back to the barn, where she takes a cloth, dips it in a bucket of water and begins to wipe the blood and dirt and tears from off his face. Eventually he stops trembling. After she has finished, she lays him down gently in some straw, covering him with the blanket given to her by Sir John's Lieutenant. By the time she has crept away to attend to her own wounds, he is already asleep.

8

17ᵗʰ March

'Johannes Kempe, together with your wife, family and a further eight hundred and eight divers weavers, fullers and other artisans engaged in the Cloth Trade, you are hereby banished forthwith from the regions of Brabant and Flanders by order of the Count Louis of Nevers, with the blessings of his benefactor, patron and suzerain Lord, King Philip VI of France, for your part in the recent uprising against their rightful dominion over the aforesaid Lands. You will not be permitted to return for a minimum of three years, or until such time as the Count deems you are no longer a threat to the security of his realm...'

Count Louis of Nevers
Anno Domini 1332

*

'To Johannes Kempe and friends, weavers of woollen cloths, His Majesty King Edward III, King of England, Lord of Ireland, and Rightful Heir to the Throne of France, doth extend by these letters patent permission to enter England in order to exercise and practise your trade, freely and without encumbrance, under His most gracious protection. To this end he commends you to his Consort and Regent, Queen Phillipa, who we believe is not unknown to you, having been born in the town of Valenciennes in the province of Hainault, who will greet you upon your arrival

on his behalf and escort you to the towns of Norwich, York
and Manchester, where you will receive a royal welcome...'

Edwardus Dei Gracia Rex
Anno Domini 1335

*

'Manchester is pre-eminent in all England in the
weaving of cloth, particularly in that process known locally
as 'frizzing', the raising of the nap, or 'cottoning'. The
climate there is especially conducive to the manufacturing of
these cottoned fabrics, because of the plenitude of rain, the
free-flowing rivers, and the humidity of the air, which doth
greatly enhance the control of the fibres. Additionally there
is an abundant supply of wood for building and burning
from the woods which surround the town...'

Jean Froissart, Queen's Chronicler
Anno Domini 1361

*

Back at Arley Hall, four miles south of Lymm in Cheshire and
some seventeen miles distant from Manchester, where Major-
General Sir John Byng is a guest of the Egerton-Warburtons in
their country seat with its fine Neoclassical facades, he allows
himself a quiet, contented smile of satisfaction as he reflects
upon the bizarre events at St Peter's Field just one week before.
A peaceful resolution with no recourse to unnecessary force. A
powder keg diffused. Though not yet extinguished, he fancies.
A far cry from Hougoumont. Though both of them farces in
their different ways. After the battle he had spent several
distressing days harrying the desperate hordes of Bonaparte's
deserting armies, frequently rooting them out from where

civilians had been hiding them, in barns, wells, even cess pits. Many of those had been wrapped in blankets, hunched round their pitiful shoulders…

He had been disappointed when Lord Sidmouth, the Home Secretary, posted him to the north after his return from Waterloo. It felt more like punishment than reward, there's no point denying it, and he felt the disappointment keenly. Had he not won famous victories at Vitoria and Nivelle? Had not his stubborn resistance at Roncesvalles, where, vastly outnumbered, he had held back the French for long enough to allow Wellington time to consolidate a sufficient number of troops to emerge victorious the following day at the Battle of the Pyrenees? Had he not driven a wedge between Napoleon's armies at Orthez, Toulouse and even more decisively at Quatre Bras? And finally had he not played a vital role in the defence of Hougoumont, planting the colour of the 31st Regiment of Foot there? So that the Prince Regent himself had kissed him on both cheeks and told him:

"You are now permitted to wear over the arms of the family of Byng, in bend sinister, a representation of the colour of the 31st Regiment of Foot, and the following crest of honourable augmentation, out of a mural crown an arm embowed, grasping the colour of the aforesaid Regiment and, pendant from the wrist by a ribbon, the gold cross presented to you by Our command, as a mark of Our royal approbation of your distinguished services."

And for that he had been banished – there's no other word for it, for that is how it felt to him – to these cultural barbarians in the north.

But Sir John has never been a man to shirk his duty. That is something that was drummed into him by his father, Sir Robert Byng, who had served as Governor of Barbados shortly before he died. Sir John has only hazy memories of his boyhood there, but enough to remind himself that riches can be found in the least promising of places, which has already begun to be proven since his posting as Commander of the Northern Forces of the British Army.

There has been unrest here in Manchester. Lord Sidmouth warned him he would be facing a foe just as much a threat to the safety and security of the realm as Bonaparte had been, in the not inconsiderable danger posed by the upsurge in Radicals to be found in the town, agitating most traitorously for what they deemed was necessary Reform, but what he, the Home Secretary, regarded as nothing short of insurgent Revolution. But Sir John, for his part, has found that to be a misrepresentation of the facts as he has observed them on the ground in the few short months he has been here so far. He believes the spinners and weavers to be suffering grievously and unjustly at the hands of their avaricious masters. Many of these lads served with him in France, under the command of that giant of a man, Captain Josiah Blacker, who had brought a whole contingent of Volunteers from the cotton mills of Lancashire to join him at Hougoumont. Giant of heart, as well as of stature, his fall in the battle had been a grievous blow from which many of his men suffered a near calamitous loss of morale as a consequence. It had taken all of Sir John's skills as a soldier and a leader of men to bring them back to themselves, so that they could fight in memory of their fallen hero's honour as much as their own.

He especially remembers a drummer boy, who was so grief-stricken at the loss that he could not bring himself to speak. He finds himself from time to time wondering what became of that poor little chap. A battlefield is no place for a boy...

And so, here at Manchester, when finding himself having to disperse what, under the strictest terms of the letter of the law, was an illegal assembly, he applied the same common touch. Firm but fair. That had been his father's motto when dealing with the occasional uprising of slaves in Barbados, whose cause he had had much sympathy with, and that would be his own watchword too. Firm but fair. So long as the Radicals committed no acts of violence, he saw no reason for them occasionally to gather in a public space to listen to some speeches and then go quietly home afterwards. He knows from experience, though, that it only takes a few hot-headed fellows, like that trio of agitators in St Peter's Field, to shift the mood from one of jolly festivity to something altogether uglier, and then he is left with no option but to act, and to act swiftly and decisively. Better a few banged heads than a riot on one's hands. Firm but fair. He must remember to emphasise this point the next time he meets the Boroughreeve and Magistrates – although he hopes that that will not be necessary for some time yet. Yesterday he purchased a fine brood mare at Macclesfield Fair. He has half a mind to breed from her in time for a colt to be entered in the Ebor Handicap at York in a couple of summers' time. If he is still banished to this northern wasteland then.

*

Jack follows in the footsteps of those early Flemish weavers. Not that he knows this. He remembers the Major-General mentioning Ghent, so that is where he aims for first. Not with any great purpose or haste. Only when he reaches a fork in the road and a fingerpost points in its direction does he remember that that is where he's making for. But he can't think why any more. Successive dark days are followed by even darker nights. Sometimes he walks through the night, sometimes he sleeps through the day. There is no pattern to it. He simply stumbles on. Mostly he avoids towns. The noise frightens him. The press of people confuses. They remind him of the Battle.

He follows the sunken, covered lanes which criss-cross the fields of Flanders. He can skirt round the edges of hamlets and villages without being seen. Though sometimes a small unit of soldiers rides through, causing him to hide. Climbing a tree, if one is close by, is usually the best way to avoid being seen. Each time he hears the horses' hooves approaching he wonders if it's the Corporal come back to catch him and force him into another cock pit. But it never is. He watches them ride by. They're British soldiers, rounding up French Prisoners-of-War.

When he gets to Ghent it is more crowded than anywhere he has ever been. The people speak in a mixture of languages, none of which he understands. He has to cross lots of bridges. He squeezes himself against the walls so that he doesn't get knocked down. One time a pack of stray dogs snap at his ankles. He finds if he bangs his drum very loudly when this happens they usually go away and leave him alone. As do the people, who look at him strangely.

He sees a ship anchored in the harbour. It's a twenty-two gun Laurel class frigate by the name of *HMS Daphne*. She is ferrying British troops back to England. His uniform of a drummer boy is enough for him to climb aboard unchallenged. There are so many people crowding the decks Jack worries they might sink. He wonders what he might do if that happens for he cannot swim.

It takes a whole day for the *Daphne* to sail to Norwich. Jack is swept ashore by the tide of people pushing and shoving in their anxiety to be back on English soil again. It doesn't seem that different to Jack from the lowlands of Holland, except that everyone now speaks English, albeit in a strange accent, which he finds just as impossible to understand as Dutch or French.

He has no idea which direction to take. He doesn't really care. He can't think where he's meant to be going, which town or village he's supposed to be trying to reach. He knows he is lost. He starts to walk in the hope he might find himself. But he strays deeper and deeper into the Fens, where he can no longer distinguish between water and land. He drifts with the tides that wash far inland before retreating back to the sea, tossing him up among the maze of mud flats and salt marshes like discarded jetsam. He wanders from shack to shanty among the Townlands. Car Dyke, Crowland, March and Soham. He never stays long anywhere, preferring to forage and scavenge alone,

452

down among the labyrinth of braided rivers, with just the other wading birds for company, knot and turnstone, corncrake and curlew, sanderling and snipe. He dives for cover from the gulls and skuas, fulmars and kittiwakes screaming overhead. He hears a bittern boom in the reed beds, comes face to face with one standing motionless for hours, seeing who will blink first, until they both become invisible. He survives on eels mostly, which are so plentiful that the locals use them as a kind of currency instead of money. He skins then roasts them over peat fires. He chews and swallows them, but he can't say he ever really tastes them. They keep him alive. Just.

He continues to track without knowing the course of the Flemish Weavers. He passes the cathedral in Ely, which rises up from the marsh mists like a great ship. Johannes Kempe and his family took communion there, but Jack steers a wide berth around it.

He follows an ancient causeway across Flag Fen, raised up by the Romans on gravel dug from the bog. At the Bronze Age fort of Must Farm he reaches an old medieval triangular bridge made of wood. Another fork in the road. The watery sun is blotted out by a dark, fast moving cloud. He looks up. It takes him a while to realise that the cloud is made up of thousands of migrating birds returning home. Fieldfare, redwing, brambling.

A memory pricks him.

He is standing with a man in a small thicket of trees beside a fast running brook. Slung between the branches of these trees are large nets. When Jack looks up they grid the sky. Like a weft of yarn when it has been threaded through the warp. The man, who Jack thinks might be his father, is trying to cut loose the nets before a large flock of birds is caught and trapped by it. He keeps anxiously looking over his shoulder as he frantically saws at the rope with his knife. Jack watches him helpless. The sound of the birds flying overhead reminds Jack of a shuttle dancing across a loom.

He stops where he stands. His eyes track the black cloud of

birds as they arrow north. He picks up his drum. He beats out a rapid tattoo and marches across the Fen in time to its rhythm as he follows the birds home.

*

By arresting the ringleaders of the Blanketeers Major-General Sir John Byng effectively cuts off the head of the snake. Then, by kettling the protesters along the route they would have chosen to take in any case, shepherding them into a *cul de sac* a mile out of Manchester, away from prying eyes, the whole affair is professionally managed with the minimum of fuss. The March simply peters out, while the reputation of the 7th Hussars is fully restored. Yes, he thinks, a job well done.

*

Amos wakes surprisingly refreshed. He experiences the rare sensation of feeling the sun on his face. It slants in through the slatted stable door in bars of light, making sharp delineations in the straw. He looks about him. The rat and her new born pups are nowhere to be seen. She must have carried them somewhere she thought would be safer.

He goes out into the yard. A few chickens scratch around in the dirt. He fills a bucket with water from the pump. It is icy cold and fresh. He splashes it freely over his face and arms. He feels himself coming alive, inch by inch, pore by pore. There is a scent in the air that is familiar to him but which he can't quite place. Then it comes to him. It is the first stirrings of spring.

He leaves *The Green Man* behind him and walks towards the summit of Old Hill, from where he can see the line of the Derbyshire hills. There is still a fine mist rising from the valley below. He fancies he can make out shapes emerging from it. He sees what appears to be a Queen and her Ladies-in-Waiting. They are arrayed as if for a Maying. Each has broken a branch of blackthorn and is carrying it before them, or wearing sprigs of the white flowers in their hair. They are bedecked in garments of Lincoln green. Marching towards them is a procession, a caravan of merchants and their families, dressed in the Flemish fashion. The man at the head of the train bears a bolt of cloth before him, of the same colour as that worn by the Queen and her attendants. He is assisted to unroll it by his wife, their child, and a young man. Behind them stands an older man, perhaps the merchant's father, with a separate bolt of cloth of a different shade, should the Queen wish to examine it. For the moment she appears content with the first that has been submitted to her, which she carefully scrutinises with an elegant finger. A group of local children, poorly dressed in rags but with clean hands and faces, kneel before their sovereign. One little girl, momentarily forgetful of her sister's crying beside her, ventures to make a face at a Flemish girl her own age riding on the back of a cart wearing wooden shoes. A small boy, standing apart on the steps of a Market Cross, is being admonished by his mother for not joining the others, but he is evidently too shy. Beside the Market Cross is a shop, where an older weaver, whose name is Jan van Brugge, for it is clearly stitched into his jacket, is seated under the open shutters behind his loom, next to his apprentice, who pretends to be working but who is really attempting to catch the eye of a young maiden standing nearby, who is smilingly avoiding his gaze. His master's daughter is trifling with a kitten, affecting to see no one, but hoping the Queen will notice her. Her hornbook, bag and apple lie neglected at her feet, while the cat warily watches the Queen's greyhound straining at his leash. Three archers, to the rear of the Queen's retinue, fire an arrow each up into the sky. Amos follows the course of these arrows till they disappear from sight. When he looks back down into the valley, the mist has lifted and, with it, the scene that had been playing out before him, which, like some insubstantial pageant, has faded...

He is about to set off on the road to Derby, the next stage in his journey south to London, when he notices a lone figure emerging from the cleared mist. At first he wonders if this is just another figment of his imaginings, but as he watches, the figure grows before him. A small black dot which straightens, slowly stretching to assume the form of a thin vertical line, shimmering and re-forming in the morning haze. Amos continues to watch as this attenuated line begins to thicken and grow. It is unmistakeable now, a sentient being, not a wraith from the past. It walks towards him in a disconcerting stutter. Knees bent, shoulders hunched, feet precariously balanced on tiptoe, eyes trained on the ground in front of him. A young man, rail thin, face weathered almost black, a tattered uniform upon his back, a small drum around his neck, upon which his hands play with two worn sticks a crazed staccato rhythm.

"Jack?" calls Amos in disbelief.

The boy does not answer.

"Jack!" cries Amos again, louder this time, with more conviction.

Still the boy makes no answer. He continues to rap his broken tattoo until he reaches Amos at the cross roads.

"Jack," whispers Amos. There is no doubting it now. "My son."

The boy registers no sign of recognition in his dead eyes. Amos lifts his hands towards his son's wrists and gently brings his drumming to a halt.

The dry, grating caw of a rook fills the silence, a broken nail scraping a kettle

Amos pulls Jack towards him, enfolds his skeletal body in his wide arms, inhales the whole smell of him. They stand like this a long time. Amos feels a slow juddering pass through him. He is not sure whether it is Jack's or his own shoulders that have begun to shake. He lets the judder grow until he is convulsed by it and he can no longer stop it even if he wanted to. He finds he doesn't want to.

He takes Jack's face into his hands, sees a glimmer of

recognition begin to dawn in those dead eyes, watches this grow and widen until it is as clear but fragile as the young sun breaking through the pall of cloud after two forgotten, frightened years.

Amos kisses his son's forehead.

"Let's go home," he says.

Wrapping his blanket around Jack's shoulders, he turns the way he has come, and together the two walk back to Manchester

*

Sir John pours himself a second cup of coffee.

"Yes," he repeats. "A job well done."

A view that is universally shared by the town's newspapers, even *The Manchester Observer*, who have been the self-proclaimed mouthpiece of the spinners and weavers ever since the Shude Hill Potato Riots a dozen years before.

The Manchester Observer

17th March 1817

A JOB WELL DONE

Here at *The Manchester Observer* we have not been shy to criticise the actions of the Magistrates when they have been faced by calls for Reform to address the genuine grievances suffered by the downtrodden labourers of Manchester, especially the Spinners and Weavers, who have seen their wages fall while prices soar, nor of the Military, who have often been invited by the aforementioned Authorities to suppress all attempts at legitimate protest by a starving populace with a ruthless and cruel efficiency.

Not so a week ago, when a joyful meeting in St Peter's Field of upwards of ten thousand souls, who had gathered to wish the Brave Blanketeers *Bon Voyage* before setting out on their intended March to London to make known the particularities of their plight to no less a personage than the Prince Regent himself, was peacefully dispersed without recourse to the rattling of sabres or the charging of Cavalry.

This was in no small measure down to the calm but decisive leadership shown by Major-General Sir John Byng, the recently-installed Commanding Officer of the 7th Hussars, who managed to keep a good order throughout the entire proceedings with an almost invisible but reassuring presence of well-drilled soldiers, who kept their swords sheathed and their powder dry.

This newspaper has been critical in the past of the 7th Hussars – and rightly so. When, after the final defeat of Napoleon, against all odds, at Waterloo, this company returned to be garrisoned here among us in Manchester, we welcomed them with open arms as heroes to be garlanded. But such was their behaviour in their first few months, with frequent complaints about their many lewd and drunken disorders, that we were forced to ask a series of critical questions.

"Are these so-called heroes unaware that they are now back in England? Or does the delirium produced by their unexpected victory at Waterloo still possess their faculties? Do they still suppose themselves in an occupied country?"

The answers we supposed to these questions were 'Yes, Yes and Yes', and we roundly condemned them for it. But the appointment of Sir John Byng as their Commanding Officer has remedied those faults at a stroke. He has restored a sense of discipline, a pride in their regiment and a respect towards their hosts, the good people of Manchester, and we applaud him for it. All of these qualities were much in evidence two days ago, when Sir John's calming presence ensured any tensions simmering at the meeting at St Peter's Field were quickly and quietly diffused.

We wish we could extend the same grateful plaudits to the Boroughreeve and Magistrates, who once again showed a complete insensitivity to the mood of the people they are elected to govern, by the wholly unnecessary and deeply provocative reading of the Riot Act, when Sir John Byng showed, by contrast, the effectiveness of a calmer, more considered and constrained approach.

If only they had shown similar restraint a few weeks previously, when instructing the 4th Dragoon Guards to break up the piteous sight of the striking Spinners & Weavers and their starving families making one last desperate plea to the mill and factory owners for a modest increase in their wages – a stance supported by this newspaper – from a miserable six shillings to just thirteen shillings a week, a figure still well below the national average. To be fair to the Magistrates, they conceded that the masters could well afford such an increase, even in these difficult times of failing harvests, but once the masters refused to yield, the Magistrates lent the full weight of their authority to an indiscriminate clearing of the strikers from outside the factory gates.

It is within the context of such harsh, unfeeling

and brutish tactics that events such as those witnessed on St Peter's Field earlier this week take place. It has not been the first and we cannot imagine it will be the last. But while cool heads, such as Sir John Byng's, prevail, we can take some comfort that legitimate demands for Reform – demands which may well be encouraged by the publishers of *The Manchester Observer* – will not be met with the kind of retaliatory clampdowns that would only serve to inflame, rather than to soothe, when emotions are running high. Parliament may, in its infinite wisdom, have temporarily suspended *habeas corpus*, but we are not living under martial law – yet. Nor shall we, we maintain, as long as the sage advice of Sir John Byng continues to be listened to.

So wither now the Blanketeers?

Having been rounded up in Longsight, with the remaining stragglers dissuaded from continuing in Stockport, this brave action can at best be described as a well-intentioned, if somewhat naïve, failure. Its proponents – Messrs Thomas Johnston, John Drummond and Samuel Bagguley – currently languish in the New Bailey Dungeon, where they are no doubt licking their wounds and contemplating their next move. We would urge them to be more patient, less hot-headed, in the future, and listen to the counsel of older, wiser, more experienced campaigners.

The advice from this newspaper to them and other leaders among the Reformers would be to remind them of Julius Caesar's maxim when attempting to invade Gaul – *divide et impera* – '*divide and conquer*'. This is what those loyal to the current iniquitous *status quo* are banking on, that the various factions within the Radical Movement will continue to squabble among themselves. If the champions of universal suffrage truly mean to pursue their calls for *'No Taxation Without Representation'* – an ambition shared by this newspaper – then they must put aside their differences and unite behind the common cause. *Utilitatem.*

Reading this article ahead of his weekly meeting with the other Magistrates, Sir Hugh Hornby-Birley breathes a pleasantly surprised sigh of relief and begins to enjoy his morning coffee much more than he has been expecting to. It is rare, if not unique, for that damned rag, *The Observer*, to come out in their favour.

"We've got away with it," he says when the meeting is convened. "More than that, our actions have been vindicated. I believe we are entitled to give ourselves a well-deserved pat on the back. Not only did we diffuse a potentially explosive situation speedily, but we did so without a single injury being reported. The crowds dispersed, if not happily, then at least unscathed. Cause for a celebratory glass of claret, what?"

His remarks are greeted with a resounding chorus of "Hear, hear" and the gentle rapping of hands upon the surface of the oak bench around which they are all seated – all except for one, that is. Matthew Oldham does not join in with this self-congratulatory table-thumping. Nor does he accept one of the generous measures of claret which are now being passed around.

"If I may add a wrinkle," he says. "While I, like everyone else, rejoice in the general approbation delivered upon us by that newspaper whose name shall never pass my lips, I remain concerned by the actions of Sir John Byng."

A collective astonishment greets this remark.

"But he saved the day," protests the Boroughreeve. "He is

the hero of the hour."

Matthew smiles thinly, an awkward, little-used expression, so that his mouth curves upward in a strained, almost disturbing manner, an effect confirmed by the lack of any corresponding warmth in his eyes, which remain icily cold and fixed upon Sir Hugh.

"He quite deliberately disobeyed your instructions. He undermined my reading of the Riot Act, and he chose to act in an altogether independent manner."

"But with considerable success," counters Sir Hugh.

"On this occasion," interrupts Matthew. "He was lucky. He might not be so again."

By now the rest of the Magistrates have paused, their glasses of claret halfway to their mouths. Their confidence evaporates like the steam still issuing from the Boroughreeve's coffee pot.

"What do you suggest?" asks Sir Hugh, glancing about him awkwardly.

"Nothing," says Matthew, picking up his claret just as everyone else is putting theirs down, "yet. We must ride this wave of popularity we are currently enjoying for as long as we can, let it run and run, like a bolt of cotton when it becomes so popular the public can't get enough of it, so we just keep manufacturing more and more lengths of it, till we have flooded the market. Then, we quietly put the old boy out to grass – with a generous pension and our heartfelt thanks…"

"We can't do that, Matthew, you know very well. Sir John is a General."

"*Major*-General," corrects Matthew smartly.

"Yes, yes, a technicality," continues Sir Hugh. "But he has command of the entire Northern Branch of the whole British Army, whose jurisdiction includes Manchester, an appointment bestowed upon him by no less a personage than the Home Secretary."

"He must be fifty if he's a day," retorts Matthew, with an

accompanying dismissive wave of his left hand, "with more than thirty years campaigning behind him, time enough for anyone to step down and pursue something quieter, something less…" Matthew searches for the word, "… contentious perhaps."

"I happen to know he's only forty-five, with *twenty* years' experience, not thirty," counters Sir Hugh testily, "of the most distinguished service imaginable, an unblemished record, with Lord knows how many medals and ribbons and accolades presented to him, who will not agree kindly to our telling him what to do."

Matthew is momentarily crestfallen. But not for long. A new thought occurs to him, as easily as turning a page in a book. "In which case we promote him still further. We thank him for his timely and decisive intervention with the Blanketeers and suggest, given his outstanding record *et cetera, et cetera*, that we desire him to assume a more advisory, more strategic role, and leave the more mundane, operational matters to those with their ears closer to the ground."

"An interesting suggestion," remarks Sir Hugh. "But aren't you again forgetting the Home Secretary? He may not wish to see his protégé so summarily sidelined."

"I don't believe we need worry about that," answers Matthew. "Sir John is a Government appointment – true – but as Commander of the entire Northern Region. Operational matters are entrusted to the likes of us to call upon his services *if* required."

The Boroughreeve strokes his chin thoughtfully. "I'm beginning to follow your drift," he says, pouring himself a second cup of coffee. "The General has a penchant for breeding racehorses, I understand, which he would much rather be spending his time upon, back on his country estate in Cheshire, than he would be in getting his hands dirty with our insubordinate spinners and weavers. I understand he was more than a little miffed when Lord Sidmouth gave him this posting, mistaking our bustling metropolis for some provincial little backwater."

"Excellent," continues Matthew, moving swiftly to his main theme. "So once we have flattered him and parked him safely back in Cheshire, I propose we create a new military unit, one that carries no baggage of history along with it, one that is answerable entirely to the Boroughreeve and his Magistrates – we might call it something along the lines of The Manchester Cavalry…"

"The Manchester *and Salford* Cavalry," interjects one of the Magistrates, all of whom are now hanging onto every syllable of what Matthew has to say.

"The Manchester and Salford *Yeomanry* Cavalry," suggests a second.

"Known as the *MYC*," adds a third.

"Yes," continues Matthew impatiently, "whatever…"

"But who will assume command of such a body?" asks Sir Hugh, regarding Matthew intently.

"My point precisely," continues Matthew. "In a twelve months' time, Sir Hugh," he says, placing an arm about the older man's shoulder, "your term of office as Boroughreeve will be approaching its end."

"Shame," cry the other Magistrates, once more resuming the rumination of their claret glasses."

"Yes, yes, quite so," says Matthew quickly, not wanting to lose the thread of his thought. "What better person, then, to take on the role as Commander of this new body of men, the MYC, to protect the interests of all loyal subjects resident within Manchester and Salford?"

The rapping of fists upon the table top which follows this rhetorical question is nothing short of thunderous.

Another individual reading the article in *The Manchester Observer* that morning with a certain degree of vindicated satisfaction is the former weaver and warehouseman, now the self-appointed leader of Lancashire's Radical Movement, Samuel Bamford, who pours himself a second cup of weak, diluted tea before heading out for work. He particularly enjoys reading the criticisms heaped upon the Unholy Trinity of Johnston, Drummond and Bagguley.

"Eh up," says Mima, hurrying in to clear away the dishes, "tha'll be late for work if tha' dun't get a shift on."

Samuel taps the newspaper with his finger and points to the passage describing the current incarceration in the New Bailey Prison of his three foes. His eyes assume a mischievous glint.

"Tha' should know better than to gloat, Samuel. Tha' weren't there that day, while *I* was. Those three din't do that much wrong, they were just in too much of an 'urry, that's all. I 'ate to think what they must've 'ad to endure at th' 'ands o' Joe Nadin an' 'is men."

The smile fades from Samuel's eyes at this thought and he involuntarily shivers.

"They'll be all reet, I expect," Mima continues. "They can't 'old 'em for long, there's been no charge issued against 'em. I worry more about poor Amos. Where is 'e? Has anyone 'eard? It were a reet brave thing 'e tried to do, an' now 'e's all but forgot. Why, 'e dun't e'en get a mention in t' newspaper. We've let him down an' no mistake, wi' all this in-fightin'. It's time to sing a better song, Samuel."

And with that she whisks away his unfinished second cup of tea from under his nose and leaves him to his thoughts.

Once again, he reflects, Mima is in the right of it. As she always is. Even when she forgives him when his affections stray towards another pretty lass at t' Mill. Especially then. They must somehow bury their differences and focus instead on what it is that unites them.

The next weekend, at a Combined Meeting of all the Hampden

Clubs of Manchester and her surrounding towns, held in the Independent Methodist School Room on Mosley Street, barely a stone's throw from St Peter's Field, Samuel proposes a private letter of support be sent to Messrs Johnston, Drummond and Bagguley care of the New Bailey, signed by all two hundred people present, demanding their immediate release, followed by a declaration of intent to find out what happened to Amos and make sure his wife has everything she needs. This is passed *nem con*. He then delivers the following heartfelt oration, which first he has run by Mima for approval, an approval she proudly gives, and which she demonstrates by promising to read out a copy of it to the meeting of the Female Reformers taking place at the same time in the Chapel on Great Bridgewater Street, behind *The Britons' Protection*.

"We need summat bigger, summat bolder, summat better," they say simultaneously. "Summat that brings t' people together, summat we can all stand behind, shoulder to shoulder, marching forward to a brighter future. Summat that will reverberate down the years. Summat that will bring about change, when everyone will have a voice, a voice that is listened to, a voice that is heard. We've 'ad our differences in t' past, I know, but we must try to overcome 'em and realise that together we're stronger precisely because of those differences. I look at this river of faces before me, flowing into t' town from all corners o' t' world an' my heart swells wi' pride. We're a magnet, here in Manchester, an' like a magnet, we can be strong. They say that opposites attract, an' I foresee a time when all those opposites that we see today – master an' servant, mill owner an' mill worker, rich an' poor, young an' old, men an' women, king an' commoner – can live an' work as one, forging summat that is greater than the sum of its parts. Out o' t' crucible o' conflict can flow t' river o' Reform."

*

Agnes sits in the cottage. It's been exactly a week since Amos left on his march to London. His fool's errand. She has not moved in that time. She has remained precisely where she now sits, her eyes fixed on the grassy lane behind, the way Jack will come if he returns. *When.* She has never given up hope that he will, but she has to correct herself more and more these days.

The loom sits quiet. She has not touched it since Amos left. A patina of dust has already begun to settle upon it. Like old bones.

Her attention is caught by a moth, which must have lain there undisturbed among the framed weft from when Amos last clicked his shuttle back and forth across it. It flutters now, around a candle she has lit as dusk has begun to fall. Its paper thin wings are a wonder, the way the light passes through them. She encloses a hand around the flame so that the moth won't get too close. Its agitated fluttering begins at last to calm and settle until it alights upon the backs of her fingers. It weighs no more than a breath. She lets it linger there, holding it nearer to her face so that she might examine it more closely. It is the colour of lichens and tree bark.

She becomes so lost in contemplation of it that it takes her some time to realise that a shadow has fallen across the loom. At first she mistakes this for the gradual onset of night but then she hears a sound from outside. A twig snapping, a leaf rustling, a slow exhalation of air, as if someone has been holding their breath for a long time.

She turns quickly round. The moth flies up and away from her, becoming lost in the shadow of a corner. Just for a moment she thinks she sees a shape at the wind-eye, but when she looks again there is nothing. She picks up the candle and heads towards the back of the cottage. And that is where she sees him, framed in the doorway, gazing in, as if looking for something he once had but can now no longer remember what it was.

She reaches out her arms towards him and he falls into her waiting embrace as naturally as a leaf from a tree. She is reminded of when she pulled Amos out of the waters of the Irk more than thirty years go. She clings to him now not wanting to let him slip from her grasp again. She sees Amos over Jack's shoulder, standing outside quietly watching this silent reunion. She feels the tension leave her body bone by bone, muscle by muscle, a caterpillar unfurling upon a branch. The moth dances around their three heads.

Cradle to Diamonds.

Diamonds to Candle.

Candle to Six-Pointed Star.

Six-Pointed Star to Bird's Nest.

Bird's Nest to Long Case Clock.

Long Case Clock to Kettle.

Kettle to Moth.

FOUR

1819

Weave A Gay Garland

in which many thousands gather on a great field
with sprigs of laurel in their hair
to listen to some speeches –
but are prevented from doing so
by the actions of a powerful few –
a lost baby is found –
and two brothers meet for the first time

9

2nd July – 14th August

"With Henry Hunt we'll go, my boys
With Henry Hunt we'll go
We'll mount the Cap o' Liberty
In spite o' Nady Joe…"

Two years pass.

The Unholy Trinity of Johnston, Drummond and Bagguley are
released from the New Bailey Prison without charge. They are
no longer deemed a threat to public order and it's easy to see
why. They emerge from the twilit months of their entombment
in the dungeon as shadows of their former selves, after
attracting the scrupulously close attention of Joe Nadin and his
henchmen. Hands have been smashed, fingernails extracted,
ribs cracked and bones broken. Lips are bruised and bloated,
teeth are absent. Cheeks are gaunt and hollow. Eyes wear a
haunted, hunted look.

Bamford, Fitton and Knight tread cautiously until they are
ready to proceed with that 'summat big' Samuel has promised
after the failure of the Blanketeers, and, although conditions
continue to worsen for the spinners and weavers, there are no
major incidents, only a rising tide of frustration and impatience
vehemently expressed in the fortnightly meetings of the
Hampden Clubs and Union Societies. Talk is all very well,
some members mutter darkly, but actions always speak louder.
For two years Samuel manages, just, to keep the lid on this
steaming kettle, somehow contriving to keep it simmering
without ever allowing it to boil over or dry. So that by the end
of 1818 the Home Secretary, Lord Sidmouth, is able to write in

his dairy: 'The threat of Combinations in Manchester is now nearly dissolved. The arrest of Johnston, Drummond and Bagguley, the admirable example shown by Major-General Sir John Byng, the restraint shown by the Civil Authorities, all have effected this most fortunate change. I look forward with happy anticipation to an even more peaceful 1819.'

Nadin continues to rule his fiefdom more or less unchecked, though he is nearly undone by what comes to be called the Hindley Affair. Two boys are given stolen property by a minion of Nadin named Joe Hindley to mind for a while but are then arrested on charges of felony. The Radicals pounce on this and make their concerns known through *The Manchester Observer*, which has by now become their unofficial mouthpiece. Hindley is dismissed but Nadin survives, as he does several other accusations of bribery, bullying and corruption. It is clear that something has to be done. A consensus grows that Manchester needs to have its own independent Corporation. Even the Magistrates reluctantly concede this. Sir Oswald Mosley offers to sell his manorial rights for ninety thousand pounds. And there is the rub. For who can be expected to come up with this vast sum? Not the interfering Radicals – the thought of handing power to them through this financial arrangement is intolerable to the Authorities – and anyway, comprising mainly spinners and weavers, they are simply too poor. The shopkeepers and mill-owners can afford it but are not prepared to stump up. And so the Magistrates, with feigned reluctance, retain overall control of the town, while Nadin emerges unscathed, to continue his reign of tyranny unopposed.

"It would appear," says Sir Edward Clayton, after being duly elected as the new Boroughreeve, "that Bishop William Paley, a long time friend of ours in Manchester, was in the right of it when he published his *Reasons for Contentment Addressed to the Labourers of England*, now such a popular tract it is to be found on our street corners everywhere. Does he not urge all of

472

us to accept our Lot with grace, to be patient, and trust in the goodness of the Lord? Likewise we urge all spinners and weavers who may feel discontented with their current situations to exercise the same patience. Loyalty will be rewarded. Reform will come. When the time is right. But if one must dwell on perceived inequalities, it should be remembered that Providence, against whom it is impious to complain, has contrived that while fortunes are only for the few, the rest of Mankind may well be better off without them, for the consequence of riches is the perplexity of choice. What joy is there in taking disproportionately from a large unmeasured fund? The peasant, whenever he goes abroad, finds a feast, whereas the epicure must be sumptuously entertained if he is to escape disappointment. 'Blessed are the poor for theirs is the Kingdom of Heaven'. 'Blessed are the meek for they shall inherit the earth'."

When the time is right.

"Perhaps," muses Samuel out loud to his ever loyal Mima lying beneath him after a particularly energetic bout of lovemaking, "that time is now."

"I'm still waiting," she says with an impish smile, "for that 'summat big' tha's been promising me."

A week later, at the inaugural meeting of the recently formed *Manchester Patriotic Union Society*, Samuel, along with the Reverend Harrison from Stockport, is one of the speakers. In the Chair is Joseph Johnson (not to be confused with *Johnston* of the Unholy Trinity). *Johnson*, a former brush manufacturer, is now the proprietor and editor of *The Manchester Observer*. Although set up as a local newspaper, a radical alternative to the Tory *Herald* and *Mercury*, it now has a national reach, selling more than four thousand copies weekly, attracting the attention of supporters and detractors alike in Liverpool, Leeds, York, Birmingham and, significantly, London, where one of its most avid readers is one Henry 'Orator' Hunt Esquire.

Henry Hunt, the son of Thomas Hunt, a gentleman farmer, is born in Upavon, on 6th November 1773. After ten years' education at the local grammar school, Henry joins his father in looking after the family estates. When his father dies in 1797, Hunt assumes ownership of three thousand acres in Wiltshire, as well as a large estate in Somerset. In 1800 he becomes embroiled in a dispute with Lord Bruce, a Colonel in the Wiltshire Yeomanry, over the killing of some pheasants. Lord Bruce takes Hunt to court over the matter. Hunt is found guilty and sentenced to six weeks imprisonment. It is during his court case that he starts to become interested in radical ideas, particularly the goal of universal adult suffrage, which he espouses as a cause. This brings him into further conflict with local landowners, and, in 1810, he moves to a new twenty thousand acre estate at Worth, near East Grinstead. While living there, he becomes even more active in politics. He is exactly the kind of charismatic figure the Radical cause has been looking for, a figure from *inside* the Establishment holding *anti*-Establishment views. He rapidly achieves a reputation as a magnificent orator and is constantly being asked to speak at public meetings where, with his Napoleonic curls and Byronic charm, he becomes something of a darling among the Female Reformers. In 1818 he is selected as the Radical candidate for the Westminster constituency. In his campaign he advocates annual Parliaments, universal suffrage, the secret ballot and the repeal of the Corn Laws. Although popular with the large crowds who attend his meetings, he is deeply distrusted by the majority of the electorate, and he wins only eighty-four votes. Nevertheless this setback only serves to heighten his reputation as a passionate advocate for Reform, and the demand for him to appear as a public speaker grows. He addresses rallies in Birmingham, Oxford, Nottingham and Stoke, as well as in London.

It is at one of these London meetings, at Smithfield, where

Samuel meets him, and the formulation of his bigger, bolder, better plan begins to take shape.

Joseph Johnson, that former brush manufacturer and now editor of *The Manchester Observer*, is just coming to the end of his opening address to the newly-formed *Manchester Patriotic Union Society*.

"The state of the district is truly dreadful," he concludes. "Trade is worthless. Life is almost at a standstill. Nothing but ruin and starvation stare folk in the face."

While this may be an accurate assessment of the current parlous situation, it is not what people have come to hear. People know this already. What they want is something positive, something to give them hope, something they can *do*.

Seizing his moment, Samuel takes to the floor.

"I'd like to tell thee a story," he begins. "About a man of whom tha' art all aware, but whom I 'ave 'ad t' pleasure an' t' honour to 'ave met. I speak o' that famed gentleman, Orator Hunt."

A ripple of interest spreads through the room. They are meeting in *The Spread Eagle Inn* on Long Millgate, which is packed to the rafters. Mrs Ellen Schofield, the Landlady, is doing a brisk trade, as she does most nights, for her Upstairs Room is a magnet for groups of all persuasion. Hers is a favourite watering hole for members of the MYC, as well as this new Reform Club. So long as they pay the hire charge and drink the ale, it matters not to her what they choose to debate while they are there, but even she has heard of Henry Hunt, and so she takes a little longer to refill the various pots and tankards while Samuel resumes his tale.

"The Orator is most gentlemanly in 'is manner an' attire," he continues, "six feet an' better in height, an' extremely well formed." A barely suppressed giggle from the females present tinkles like the ale being poured from Mrs Schofield's jug. "When I first met 'im, 'e were dressed in a blue-lapelled coat, light waistcoat an' kersey o' ribbed cloth wi' a short nap, an'

475

topped boots. 'E wore 'is own hair, which were in moderate quantity an' not a trace yet of grey. His lips were delicate, rather thin an' recedin'. His eyes were a blue tendin' to light grey – not dartin' or quick, but strong an' firm in their gaze, especially when 'e were excited in speakin', at which times they would stand out proud from beneath 'is refined eyebrows, an' if 'e worked 'isself furious, as 'e sometimes would, they became blood-streaked, an 'almost started from their sockets. His voice sounded like a church bell, while 'is gripped hand beat the air as if it meant to pulverise it. His whole manner gave token of an unstoppable flow of energy, a force o' Nature to be reckoned with. In short, friends, Mr Hunt is someone who convinces thee as much by 'is very presence as by t' power of 'is argument o' t' force an' rightfulness of 'is opinion. I propose, therefore, that we invite Orator Hunt to address a Public Meeting here in Manchester at 'is earliest convenience. His reputation will guarantee, I am certain of it, the most numerous meeting that ever took place in all of Great Britain."

To rapturous applause, accompanied by the drumming of feet so loud and rhythmical upon the wooden floor that customers in the Inn below might be forgiven that the Manchester Yeomanry Cavalry have already ridden in to break up the gathering, the proposal is unanimously passed, and Joseph Johnson, in his capacity as Secretary of *The Patriotic Union of Manchester*, is tasked with the issuing by letter of the formal invitation, a commission he is delighted to undertake.

When news arrives a few short weeks later that Hunt has accepted the invitation, the whole town is electrified, as if by a lightning storm. The Reformers fling open their windows to rejoice at the prospect, while the Magistrates batten down their hatches and bolt their doors. The 'summat big' promised by Bamford is coming. It is more than big. It threatens to be cataclysmic. For the next month Manchester is deluged with placards supporting both positions with equal force.

As midnight approaches, Mrs Schofield reluctantly calls

out, "Time, gentlemen, please."

*

The Manchester Observer

Monday 5th July 1819

OFFICIAL ANNOUNCEMENT OF PUBLIC MEETING

The Public are respectfully informed that a MEETING will be held here in Manchester on MONDAY 9th AUGUST 1819, on the ground known as St Peter's Field, behind St Peter's Church, to take into consideration the most speedy and effectual mode of obtaining Radical Reform in the Commons House of Parliament, being fully convinced that nothing less can remove the intolerable ills under which the People of this Country have so long, and do still, groan; and also to consider the propriety of the *Unrepresented Inhabitants of Manchester* electing a PERSON to represent them in Parliament; and of the adopting of a Bill thereto. Henry Hunt Esq. will be in the Chair.

Letter from the Office of Lord Sidmouth, Home Secretary, to the Manchester Magistrates

Thursday 15th July 1819

Sirs,

I have now to acquaint you that the Attorney- and Solicitor-General, Sir Robert Gifford and Sir John Singleton-Copley respectively, have jointly given their Opinion that the Election of a Member of Parliament without the King's Writ is

477

a High Misdemeanour, and that any parties engaged and acting therein may be a Conspiracy. As Home Secretary I express the hope therefore that if such an Election should be attempted in Manchester, measures must be taken for bringing the offenders to Justice. From the aforesaid Opinion of the highest Law Officers in the land it must also follow that any Meeting held for the purpose of such an Election is of itself an Unlawful Conspiracy.

But if the Meeting is not convened for the said Unlawful Purpose, the illegality will not commence until the purpose is developed and directly expressed (and of course after the crowd has been collected), when it must be a question of Prudence and Expediency to be decided by the Magistrates on the spot, whether they should proceed to disperse the persons thus assembled.

I am in no doubt that this matter will be judiciously decided upon by the Magistrates of Manchester.

Yours etc
pp Lord Sidmouth

The Manchester Herald

Friday 30th July 1819

OFFICIAL WARNING NOT TO ATTEND ILLEGAL MEETING

Whereas an earlier edition of The Manchester Observer (Monday 5th July) has stated that a PUBLIC MEETING is convened for MONDAY 9th AUGUST in the area known as St Peter's Field, behind St Peter's Church, WE, the UNDERSIGNED MAGISTRATES of the Town, acting for the Counties Palatine of Lancaster and Chester, do hereby caution All Persons to

ABSTAIN AT THEIR PERIL *from attending what is an* **ILLEGAL MEETING**.

Sir Edward Clayton, Boroughreeve
Reverends William Hay & Charles Ethelston
Messrs James Norris & Matthew Oldham

Letter to The Manchester Observer from Mr Henry Hunt

Monday 2nd August

Sirs,

Am I the only reader to be puzzled by the Manchester Magistrates' strained use of grammar in their recent injunction (published in The Manchester Herald of Friday last) cautioning 'All Persons to Abstain at their Peril' from attending the Meeting planned for a week today on St Peter's Field? My understanding of this warning is that the said Magistrates are exhorting all good citizens to go – or else! In which case I find myself for once in surprising agreement with the Civic Authorities.

Yours etc
H. Hunt Esq

Subsequent Letter from Lord Sidmouth to the Manchester Magistrates

Tuesday 3rd August

Sirs,

Having again sought the Opinion of the Attorney-General, I am minded to advise you that there is Great Difficulty in

479

pronouncing the Meeting scheduled for next Monday as Illegal <u>beforehand</u>, for the Radicals have not stated that they intend to elect a representative to Parliament, merely that they should like to <u>consider</u> it, which is of itself <u>not</u> illegal.

Yours etc
pp Lord Sidmouth

Letter to The Manchester Observer from The Manchester Patriotic Union Society

Wednesday 4th August

Sirs,

*Having consulted with our own counsel, Mr Harold Ranecock, we, the Committee Members of The Patriotic Union Society of Manchester, have considered deeply the warning given by the Magistrates last Friday concerning the proposed Public Meeting due to take place next Monday. Although we can see no cast iron legal reason why the Meeting should be prohibited, we have nevertheless, in the interests of safety, decided **not** to hold it. We therefore request the Boroughreeve to convene a further meeting at his earliest convenience.*

Yours etc
(Signatories enclosed)

The Manchester Observer

Thursday 5th August 1819

NEW DATE FOR PUBLIC MEETING

A   deposition   having   been   presented   to   the

Boroughreeve and Constables of Manchester, signed by more than Seven Hundred Inhabitants, requesting them to call a Public Meeting 'to consider the propriety of adopting the most LEGAL and EFFECTUAL means of obtaining a REFORM in the Commons House of Parliament', and they having declined to call such a meeting, or even to reply to the deposition at all, therefore We, the Undersigned Requisitionists, give NOTICE that a Public Meeting will be held, on the ground known as St Peter's Field, behind St Peter's Church, for the above-mentioned purpose on *the new date* of MONDAY 16th AUGUST at 12 o'clock midday. Henry Hunt Esq. will take the Chair.

(Note: The Signatures of Householders who have since come to the Office of The Observer have exceeded One Thousand, which, for want of time and room, we are compelled to omit, but which are available to view upon receipt of a written request).

*

Minutes of Meeting of Committee in Aid of the Civil Powers, Star Inn: Friday 6th August 1819

Present:

Sir Edward Clayton – *Boroughreeve* (Chair)

Magistrates: Reverend William Robert Hay, Mr James Norris, Mr Matthew Oldham, Reverend Charles Wickstead Ethelston

Joseph Nadin – *Deputy Constable*

Sir Hugh Hornby-Birley – *Commanding Officer, Manchester & Salford Yeomanry Cavalry*

Lieutenant Colonel Guy L'Estrange – *Deputy Acting Officer in Charge, 15th Hussars*

Mr Simon Hetherington – *Magistrates' Clerk*

Apologies:
Sir John Byng – *General, British Army Northern Division*

There being but one item on the Agenda – the matter of the Public Meeting now rescheduled to take place on Monday 16ᵗʰ August in St Peter's Field – there followed a full and frank discussion with many differing shades of opinion being expressed, but which all pursued the common thread of how best to maintain order during what many feared was an attempt by the Radicals to provoke Riot and Revolution.

HAY:
I hear that Hunt is already making his way to Manchester.

CLAYTON:
The Observer says it is because word of the postponement failed to reach him in time.

BIRLEY:
Or that the postponement is a ruse and the Radicals intend to catch us unawares with their mischief.

NADIN:
We'll be ready for them, never fear.

CLAYTON:
I am relieved to hear it.

HAY:
But what are we to do with Hunt once he is here? He will have a whole week in which to stir up the populace ahead of the meeting.

ETHELSTON:
I still maintain that we should declare the meeting unlawful.

HAY:

But that will only lead to further restlessness and disquiet.

NORRIS:

And besides, the advice from the Attorney-General is that the meeting itself is not unlawful. It only becomes so if they declare seditious intent once it is in progress.

HAY:

Which Hunt is bound to do as soon as he opens his mouth.

NADIN:

Whereupon we can arrest him at once.

BIRLEY:

Perhaps we could place him under House Arrest as soon as he arrives?

CLAYTON:

Where is he due to stay?

NADIN:

At Smedley Cottage.

HAY:

The home of Joseph Johnson?

NADIN:

The same.

HAY:

The proprietor of *The Observer*? Can you imagine what capital they will try to derive from that?

BIRLEY:

Then we should place a restraining order upon them too.

ALL: (*except Matthew, who continues to remain silent and watchful throughout*):

Hear, hear.

CLAYTON:

Gentlemen, we cannot impose upon the freedom of the press. That would be tantamount to breaking the very laws we are trying to uphold.

HAY:

Desperate times require desperate measures. If the Government sees fit to suspend *Habeas Corpus*, bridling one outspoken newspaper does not seem disproportionate.

CLAYTON:

No, but it will be perceived so. Better instead to flood those organs of the press that do support us – *The Herald, The Mercury, Bell's, Prescott's* – with material that reveals the Radicals' true intentions...

NORRIS:

... which is *not* to better the lot of the labouring man...

HAY:

... but to bring down His Majesty's Government.

ETHELSTON:

I hear rumours that Hunt will invoke the name of the Bastille to excite the people into storming the New Bailey.

NADIN:

Leave him to me, Gentlemen. We'll keep him on a tight

leash.

CLAYTON:

How will you do that?

NADIN:

I have my ways.

CLAYTON:

I take it you're referring to your spies? Infiltration?

NADIN:

If he just once steps outside the strictest boundary of the law, we'll come down on him with such a wrath that he'll wish he'd never come to Manchester.

BIRLEY:

I hear he regrets his decision already, finding our northern ways rather too uncultured for his liking.

NORRIS:

I have some sympathy with him on that score.

HAY:

Yes, yes. This is all very well. But we need some detailed plans in place before the 16th. There's talk of a hundred thousand people attending.

BIRLEY:

Nonsense. Typical Radical exaggeration. They'll be lucky if they get ten.

ETHELSTON:

They got that many for the Blanketeers. With Hunt confirmed to speak, there are bound to be many more.

NORRIS:
But not a hundred thousand.

ETHELSTON:
I agree. But we must prepare as if there will be.

CLAYTON:
Very well. What do you suggest?

BIRLEY:
We put forces at every toll-gate entrance to the town. Prevent the people from entering in the first place.

ETHELSTON:
What? And risk riots breaking out in many places simultaneously. No, gentlemen. Better to contain them in a single space.

CLAYTON:
Kettle them?

BIRLEY:
Precisely. It worked against the Blanketeers.

CLAYTON: (*to Lt Estrange*):
I assume Sir John will be attending?

L'ESTRANGE:
Actually he will not.

There is considerable alarm expressed on hearing this.

L'ESTRANGE:
You must realise, Gentlemen, that he is His Majesty's Commander for the whole of the Northern Region. He is

486

currently needed in York.

HAY:

But *we* need him *here*.

BIRLEY:

He has a horse running there, does he?

L'ESTRANGE:

I shall pretend not to have heard that remark, which casts a most unwarranted slight upon Sir John's integrity. He has sent me a letter, explaining his position, which he has asked me to read out to you all. And so, Gentlemen, with your permission...?

CLAYTON:

By all means.

L'ESTRANGE: (*reading*):

"Sirs,

You must forgive my brevity and curtness. I am suffering a most violent headache, no doubt brought on by the oppressiveness of the weather, but neither is it improved by the confusing contradiction in messages concerning the current situation in Manchester with which I am daily beleaguered. The Reverend Hay writes to tell me that my presence is most urgently needed, then on the same day he retracts this, but in such vague and confusing language that I am at a loss to know what is expected of me. 'Such was the aspect of things at the moment at which I applied to you,' he writes, 'but I am happy to report that the aforesaid aspect has materially altered, if recent reports which we have since received are to be believed, and in such a degree, we may now conclude that there is now no further need in applying to you in the same vein as in the first instance we felt it was our duty so to do…'

Matthew makes no attempt to conceal his amusement and contempt for his colleagues' shilly-shallying, while Lieutenant-Colonel L'Estrange continues to read from Sir John's Letter.

"I have the fullest confidence in all my officers commanding the troops in or around Manchester, so that should a serious disturbance occur I see no benefit from my additional personal presence. My attention in any case is being particularly exercised elsewhere – in Sheffield and in York – but should the situation change in Manchester, I stand ready with my regiment to come to your aid."

HAY:
Yes – well, I am sure I meant only for the best.

CLAYTON:
Do not trouble yourself, Reverend. The more pressing question is this: should we avail ourselves of Sir John's offer to come to our aid or not?

BIRLEY:
I think the General speaks plainly enough. His meaning is clear. He doesn't believe the situation warrants his being here in person –

NORRIS:
– a view shared by the Home Secretary…

ETHELSTON:
… and he has complete faith in his Deputy.

NORRIS:

> As do I.

CLAYTON:

> As do we all.

L'ESTRANGE:

> I thank you, Gentlemen. I await my orders.

CLAYTON:

> You may rest assured we shall get back to you with those at the earliest opportunity.

L'ESTRANGE:

> No time is too soon. The better we are prepared, the less likely we are to encounter trouble.

CLAYTON:

> At least not something we can't nip in the bud.

MATTHEW (*speaking for the first time*):

> Indeed. Thank you, Colonel. You may leave us.

Somewhat surprised at being so summarily dismissed, L'Estrange departs.

Matthew now takes the opportunity to articulate a plan that he has been formulating for the past several weeks.

MATTHEW:

> Now, Gentlemen, before we proceed to the details of operational planning, I wonder if I might crave your indulgence with some thoughts that have been running through my mind this past febrile fortnight.

CLAYTON:
By all means, Matthew. What is it?

MATTHEW:
Thank you. I don't believe we need minute this section of the meeting. So, Mr Hetherington, if you wouldn't mind leaving us for a few moments... We'll call you when we need you to continue.

Mr Hetherington withdraws. The others all wait and watch him as he gathers up his paper, pens and ink, then retires into the adjoining chamber. Then, as one, they all turn back towards Matthew, leaning in attentively.

MATTHEW:
I believe that what faces us is far more than the potential for insurrection, which has quite rightly been exercising our minds so far. I regard it as an opportunity. We have all heard reports of the Radicals exercising upon the moors outside the town. I expect that you have been as alarmed as I have been. Their apologists in *The Observer* will doubtless claim that this is a testament to their desire for discipline and order when it comes to their convergence upon St Peter's Field next week. Whereas *I* regard it as further evidence, if such were needed, of their true intention, which is nothing less than an attempted *coup d'etat*. They mean to march upon Manchester as an army – an army several thousand strong. The dandy Hunt has been brought here deliberately to stir them to insurrection by his lofty and preposterous rhetoric. What they are doing upon the moors with their drilling is nothing less than preparing for war. They are training soldiers, Gentlemen, but we shall be ready for them. Far from fearing the riot and disorder that may descend upon us next Monday, let us instead embrace it. In fact, let us go further. Let us be the catalyst for it. Let us

have our own forces drawn up in readiness – the 7th and 15th Hussars, the Cheshire Yeomanry Cavalry, our very own MYC, under the expert leadership of our friend and colleague, Sir Hugh Hornby-Birley, all marshalled and co-ordinated by you, Mr Nadin, with your Regular and Special Constables lining the streets in great numbers, while the soldiers are kept hidden from view in alleys and courtyards, out of general sight, until all the people are assembled at the Meeting Ground. Think of St Peter's Field as a great cauldron, heated by the sun at its zenith, the rising temperature increased by the compression of so great a number of individuals into a single, overcrowded space. Let us think of the Radicals arriving in the place as the basic ingredients one might put into this steaming cauldron, to be stirred and agitated by the inflaming of their passions. Let us kettle them there by exactly the route *we* decide for them, so that they believe they are leaping into this pot of their own accord, and, once there, let us keep them simmering for longer than they would wish, while they await the arrival of their hero Hunt, their demi-god, by parading him via a circuitous route from where he is lodged, so that by the time he arrives, he will be like the final ingredient to this teeming soup. Then we will add our own secret, special ingredient. We shall pour in the seasoning – a pinch of salt here, a grind of pepper there, a dusting of hot, keen, sharp mustard to finish – by which I mean the Cavalry, Gentlemen, mounted and proud, bayonets fixed, sabres gleaming in the sunlight, ready to give that all important last stir. The *pièce de résistance*. In short, I mean to crush these Radicals and Traitors once and for all, teach them a lesson they will never forget, from which they will never again dare to rise up for the kind of reform which *we* know, Gentlemen, will only heap ruin upon us all. Lunch, anyone?

*

491

For the last twenty years Billy has pounded the streets of Manchester delivering letters, packets and parcels right across the town. There's not an address he cannot find, not a street he has not walked down. He knows every short-cut, every cut-through, every cellar, every yard, as well as every new grand house that is being built to accommodate the dreams of merchants, bankers, managers and mill-owners, together with every factory, warehouse, forge and sweat-shop that services these dreams.

There is quite a team of postboys now criss-crossing the town, but Billy has been there the longest and the others all defer to him in terms of his knowledge. If ever a letter arrives with the barest of information scrawled across the envelope – *"Jilly, by the Market Cross"* – Billy is sure to be able to direct them to the correct lodgings.

He has watched the town grow year on year, with old buildings being torn down and new ones springing up in their place practically overnight, feeding off the ruins of their forebears like larvae hatching among the rotting carcasses of fallen trees. He remembers a time, when he was a boy, when there were still many trees in Manchester. Now there is hardly a one, not until he reaches the toll-gates which mark the entrances to the town from the north, south, east and west, beyond which open ground with hedges, lanes and orchards can still be found, between the neighbouring villages of Ardwick, Chorlton, Stretford and Cheetham, although this open ground is shrinking by the week. It will not be long, thinks Billy, before it is all one continuous municipality, an unbroken maggot sprawl, restlessly colonising, burrowing underground, before coming up gasping for air.

His thoughts have taken on this melancholy demeanour ever since his sister Lavinia died. He is haunted by the image of her frozen and preserved beneath a sheet of ice. His own sheets at night are soaked with sweat after yet more feverish dreams. And so he has thrown himself into his work, plunging deeper and deeper into the darkest corners and recesses of Manchester's continuous creep. Its buildings grow ever taller and its streets between them ever narrower. More and more they tunnel and twist, their tangled, unregulated spread choking the air, their myriad tentacles forcing their way up from beneath the earth, threatening to grip the unwary traveller round the ankle and suck him down, never to surface again.

But not Billy. He stays one step ahead of this many-headed hydra, still hoping he can find that golden apple of the sun that it guards so jealously. The apple was his once. His sister held it in her hands. She offered it out to all the hungry children who came to her school, thirsting for knowledge, for wisdom, those ornaments of grace which are everyone's birthright, only for it to be snatched from her, roughly, greedily, by those who wanted to keep it for themselves, locked away in scented, carpeted rooms, which none could walk upon but a privileged few.

Sometimes he thinks he sees it, glinting in a shard of splintered light, if the sun should ever poke a finger into those Stygian yards or cellars, only for it to be a mouldy core feasted upon and then forgotten by a wasp or beetle. Once he comes across it in a steaming dung heap by the stone steps leading up to The Exchange on Penniless Hill, but he is too late. By the time he reaches it, it is being devoured by an iridescent swarm of fly.

His mind turns to when he came across the body of Leigh Phillips, five years ago, his own collection, the brood he had spawned, feeding off him, until Billy had burst in, flung open the windows, so that the whole cloud of them appeared to block out the sun. Knowledge, like food, must be planted, watered, harvested, then shared, for the common good of all.

Billy is passing where Leigh had lived right now. Byrom Street. Close to where Billy's father Zachary had first worked as a surveyor, aligning his compass and rod, his level and rule, trying to gauge his place in the world.

But the office is long gone, metamorphosed a dozen times since then, now a solicitor's chambers, where Billy delivers several important-looking sealed letters. He wonders how many words it takes to capture the weight of what a person is worth, of what they might leave behind, that others may inherit from them.

What *he* had inherited from his father was an unbridled optimism that things would always get better, that somehow that was in the very nature of things.

Look, he would say to Billy when he was a small boy and he would take him with him when he went to survey a new site, where now there is just an empty space, an absence, soon a mighty building will grow towards the clouds, a church with a steeple, a mill with a tall chimney, or a row of houses for people to live in, the people who continue to flock towards us here in Manchester, the centre of the world.

Now, what Billy feels, surrounded by all these buildings so many of which his father laid the ground for, is that absence, the empty space where his heart used to be, where his sister was.

He has never married. Not *yet*, his sister Susannah still insists. But he knows he never shall. There's no space left any more for anyone else. And so he works. Six long days each week. From before the dawn until long after sunset. He tips up all his wages to Susannah, making sure that there is enough food on the table for his younger siblings. Lemuel, Ginny, Richard and Paul the twins, and Jemma. Susannah's husband, James, is a good man. He would never see them go short, but Billy wants them to stand on their own feet if they can. And mostly they do. Lemuel is a promising surveyor himself, following in their father's footsteps. He has risen quickly in Byrom's new office on King Street. Richard and Paul have jobs at Oldham's Felt Factory. They work hard. Their efforts are noticed, then rewarded. Now they are both foremen. One works the morning shift, the other the night. Their paths rarely cross.

But when they do, their talk right now is all about the Meeting at St Peter's Field that is scheduled for next Monday. They mean to miss work and attend. The whole work-force is intending to strike that day and so the factory will not be able to open. Mr Oldham will not be best pleased, but his attention will be on the Meeting too. As a Magistrate tasked with maintaining order. In any case he can't sack them all.

Billy pays little attention to what they are saying. He will not be going to the Meeting, he says. Not that he doesn't support what they are seeking. Reform is needed. He knows this. But even if it comes, it will not fill that emptiness deep in the heart of him, a core that moulders and festers, and anyway, there will always be letters that need delivering. Time and tide – and the post – wait for no one, he says.

He carries on walking down Byrom Street after delivering the sealed letters to the Solicitors. It is busier than usual. Mounted soldiers on horseback are mustering there. They appear to be practising some kind of drill. The street is narrow, cobbled, largely unseen from the Dean's Gate into which it eventually spills. They are members of the MYC, Billy realises. The Manchester & Salford Yeomanry Cavalry. An unruly lot. Billy often has cause to give them a wide berth as they drunkenly tear up and down Manchester's wider streets, not caring who gets in their way. They behave as if they own the town, that it is theirs to rampage through as they will. Rather than maintaining the peace, they largely appear to disrupt it, as far as Billy can make out. But today they seem different, more focused, more disciplined. They are repeating the same exercise over and over, forming in tight lines in the narrow street, marching the length of it in a controlled, co-ordinated walk, breaking as one into a unified trot, then a canter, finally a gallop, before reining to an impressive, thunderous halt.

Billy feels the ground tremble beneath him as he walks between them towards his next destination, where he always heads for whenever he is in this part of the town, the graveyard behind St John's Church, where his sister Lavinia is buried.

He normally has the place to himself, apart from a few crows tugging at the banquet of worms that are always to be found there, or a couple of grave diggers preparing a new resting place. But today there is someone else at his sister's grave. That is not entirely unusual. She captured the hearts of all of Manchester when she died, and many came to visit her here, but that was more than five years ago now, and so fewer come these days to pay their respects.

Billy wonders who this newcomer might be. It is a man. He has his back to Billy as he approaches. He is bent over something. From the other side of him there emanates the sound of a hammer chipping away at stone. Billy realises what must be happening but is puzzled nevertheless.

The man is a stonemason. He is fashioning some kind of monument for Lavinia's headstone. The family have not authorised this. Billy wonders how it can be happening. When he gets level with the man, he pauses. He had been intending to ask him just what he was doing, order him to clear off if need be, but the sight of what he is carving stops the words in his throat.

Instead he simply stays where he is and watches. He watches for many minutes, lulled by the rhythmic tapping of hammer upon, not stone he now realises, but brick. The tapping continues, its steady, sure rhythm echoed intermittently by the caws of the crows and the thwack of the gravediggers' spades upon the earth.

Billy waits until the mason finishes. He stands back from his creation, surveys it, much like Billy's father might have done over a piece of empty ground.

It takes Billy's breath away.

The cloud of brick dust created by the mason's work showers like ash and settles around them. Billy can feel it on his hands, his hair, his eyelashes, almost as if he has become a part of the composition, all three of them motionless in the

496

dusty air, himself, the mason and the figure that is emerging before them.

A young woman, fashioned out of local clay, a creamy, yellowish white.

She appears to be emerging out of a chrysalis, a moth shaking off the care and weight of years. The buds of wings are growing from her shoulders. Shards of skin lie at her feet, like flaked crystals of ice. Around her head is a garland. At first Billy assumes it is flowers but on closer inspection he realises they are not flowers but stars of light set within a wreath of laurel, an ornament of grace. Her eyes are turned upwards watching it descend, while her right hand is stretched outwards towards him. Curled in the fingers is a still unripe apple. Unripe but also unspoiled.

Billy turns towards the mason, who is already packing up his tools and preparing to leave. He carries a jute bag into which he places them. Picked out in letters tacked on in cotton running stitch is what Billy presumes must be his name. *J. Stone*. Billy recognises it. He has delivered letters to this man sometimes. He lives on Hanging Ditch beside the Jewish Tailors.

He is about to thank him but he has already gone. Billy thinks about following him but he is already late. He has more letters he must deliver. This past week there has been a steady stream between the Magistrates care of *The Star* Inn, where they appear to be permanently encamped, and the Home Office in London. The eyes of the nation are turned on Manchester right now, where the eyes of its citizens, like the statue of his sister before him, are gazing upwards, waiting for what will fall upon them.

*

Abner rubs his eyes. They are tired and sore. The whites even redder than usual. He has spent the previous night the same way he has spent every one of the last seven nights – glued to his Dollond & Aitcheson telescope, which has been trained onto the northern sky, specifically on the constellation of Perseus, with its characteristic diamond sword and the head of the Medusa, with its trail of stars like writhing snakes. August is an excellent month to observe Perseus – with his rescued wife Andromache to the west, her mother Cassiopeia to the north, Auriga, the Charioteer, to the east, and Aries and Taurus to the south – because of the spectacular meteor showers emanating from its centre, the Perseids, whose brightest star, Algol, is visible to the naked eye. Algol, the Gorgon, the Demon. Abner was excited to discover, when he first observed it through his telescope, that it is in fact not one, but two stars, duplicitously revolving one around the other, so that its luminosity is variable and cannot be trusted.

Abner has spent the entire night lost in the wonder of the meteors shooting out of Perseus, almost as if he has been cutting them down with his sword, scattering them to the four corners of the sky, showering the heavens with stardust, like blood spilled upon a battlefield.

Abner marvels in the knowledge that Ptolemy first watched this display, more than one and a half thousand years before, and after him the Babylonians, the Chinese, then Copernicus, Galileo, and now, with the aid of telescopes like the one he is looking through at this moment, it is available for anyone to lose themselves in its dance and sword play. As he has been doing this past week. These telescopes are now even being made right here in Manchester – he himself has been grinding ever more powerful lenses, a hobby he has only recently taken up – so that he imagines that there is an invisible but tangible thread, like the finest spun cotton, stretching all the way from where he stands, in the upstairs room in his house on Brazenose Street, to the heart of the Perseids themselves, bouncing back down to earth. It is as though Abner is observing them through the refraction of his finely crafted lenses in much the same way Perseus used his shield, as a reflecting mirror, so that he would not have to look the Gorgon directly in the eye and so be turned to stone. All eyes are now, it seems, trained on Manchester. Overhead the constellation spits and hisses its snakes of fire.

*

Benjamin & Rachel Halsinger cordially invite you to their home on Brazenose Street for the occasion of the Golden Wedding Anniversary of their parents Reuben & Leah, which also coincides with Reuben's 75th birthday.

Please note the rearranged date, which is now to be Monday 16th August at 12pm midday.

When the news reached Benjamin that the Meeting called by the various groups of Manchester Reformers for Monday 9th August had now been postponed until the following Monday, he could not help emitting an exasperated curse.

Eyn imglik iz far im veynik. One misfortune is too few for him.

As a rule Benjamin was the mildest and most patient of men, but arranging the party had been difficult enough in the first place, with invitations going out to Jewish communities across England. Why, even Count Rothschild himself had accepted.

'It has been more than eight years since I left Manchester for the fleshpots of London,' he has written, 'but I never forget my time there. Reuben has been a most loyal friend and I shall be delighted to attend.'

Then, when the news broke that the Reformers had persuaded the scoundrel Henry Hunt to address the discontented masses of Manchester on the very same day, Benjamin had had to hastily send out these amended invitations with the change of date, hoping for the best. Fortunately, such

499

was the universal good will in which his father was held that people were only too happy to accommodate the postponement and nearly all had replied to confirm that they would still be able to come on the new date of 16th. And now the Reformers had decided to postpone their own meeting to clash with all his newly-made plans.

Zol es im onkumn vos ikh vintsh im, he cursed again. May all I wish on them come true. K*hotsh a helft, khotsh halb, khotsh a tsent kheylik.* Well, at least half of it, perhaps a little…

They couldn't rearrange the party a second time, but at the very least he could write once more to everyone who was coming to warn them of the likely crowds that they would encounter in the town, and to make their arrangements accordingly. Their house would be open from ten in the morning if people preferred to arrive early. Most of the attenders lived in Manchester, or close by, a few of their friends having recently moved to the leafier suburbs of Ardwick, Chorlton, Burnage and Levenshulme, and so would be fully aware of the growing tension in the town ahead of the Meeting to be held on St Peter's Field, but those living further afield would need to be apprised of the situation.

It was not that Benjamin held anything against the Reformers. He had read their arguments in *The Manchester Observer* and he saw the sense in much of what they said. The fact that Manchester, despite being the fastest growing metropolis in England, with the highest population outside of London, still had no Member of Parliament and therefore no legitimate representation at Westminster, was nothing short of scandalous. But Benjamin had come to understand that this was a country distrustful of and resistant to change. Laudable though the aims of the Reformers were, their methods were surely guaranteed to entrench the views of the Establishment further against them. Unlike he and the rest of his people, they had not yet learned to play the longer game. Patience. Endurance. Dignity. These were the qualities he most admired, qualities embodied by his father Reuben, whom they would be rightly celebrating with this party. Which now, instead of being a cause for joy, would be tempered with a growing sense of foreboding. The arrival of Orator Hunt was a new piece being placed upon the chess board. A knight with moves that were bold and unpredictable. These were two words which caused Benjamin even further anxiety. He much preferred their antonyms. Cautious and foreseeable. These were how he liked to play his cards, not revealing his hand until it was absolutely necessary, and even then keeping any aces in reserve.

There was no arguing that the current administration of Manchester was archaic and in much need of modernising. Courts Leet and Boroughreeves were positively medieval. Yet while the *status quo* survived, they must be accommodated. Matthew Oldham remained one of his most valuable clients. He had only recently been requested by him to become the Executor of his Will, with Matthew having neither dependants nor family. "Nor likely to now," he had added while signing the meticulously prepared papers Benjamin had had drawn up for him. And so, although his heart sympathised with the Reformers, Benjamin's head directed him not to wear that heart upon his sleeve and, by so doing, alienate in any way the trust placed in him by Manchester's plutocracy, of which he liked to consider himself also a part. All he – and the rest of the *diaspora* could do – was to ensure that they treated their own workforces with decency and compassion, pay the going rate, not undercut the market, nor try to circumvent Sir Robert Peel's Factory Act.

This was something with which Pity, had she the words or the will, could well have concurred. She still worked as a seamstress with Jacob's Tailors, now run successfully by Lemon's son Philip, and her neat, careful, dextrous work had brought her to the attention not just of her supervisors, but the women of other local families, who would request her to sew or embroider individual items for special occasions – handkerchiefs, table-cloths, shawls – for which she received handsome financial reward. She would hand this over directly to Jem, who would nod, smile and put it away somewhere safe. Pity never thought to ask where. It was of no concern to her.

And so it was, with the rearranged date for the party fast approaching, that she was invited by Rachel to make a series of delicate lace plate settings. "Something in keeping with the happiness of the occasion," Rachel had said, "something to celebrate our arrival and establishment here in the town. Something local."

Pity nodded that she understood. Her thoughts went immediately to the shawl she had wrapped Matthew in as a baby, with its pattern of intertwining laurel leaves. She drew what she had in mind and showed it to Rachel, whose eyes lit up in a delighted smile.

"Perfect," she said. "Laurels are always awarded to the victors, are they not? And these bushes grow everywhere on the outskirts of the town."

*

In the days leading up to the 9th Billy is run ragged delivering letters between the Magistrates in Manchester and the Home Office in London, all of them 'Special Delivery' and all of them requiring signatures. In addition missives had been flying back and forth between the Reformers and Henry Hunt, but in this particular case to no avail. The final letter from Samuel Bamford to the Orator, informing him that the Public Meeting has had to be postponed by a week, fails to reach him in time, and so Billy is tasked with delivering directly into Mr Hunt's hands a telegram of apology from Mr Johnson of *The Observer* the moment he steps down from his carriage, which he does at precisely midday on Saturday 7th, having made the final leg of the journey from London that morning, when he set off from

502

Macclesfield immediately after breakfast.

To say that Mr Hunt is not best pleased would be an understatement. He flings the telegram crossly into the mud at his feet.

Billy, who experiences almost a physical pain when he sees such desecration of His Majesty's Royal Mail, hastily picks it up, smoothes away its creases and returns it to his breast pocket. "Mr Johnson said to say 'e will be along directly to escort you to 'is lodgings."

"Did he indeed? Well I'll be damned if he will. I intend to start back for London this very afternoon. You will kindly inform Mr Johnson so."

"Yes, sir." Billy touches his cap, not impressed by his dealings thus far with the legendary orator about whom he has heard so much talk, but nor can he vouch for the competence of the Reformers either, who, if they can find something to disagree about, they surely will. If one of them should chance to remark that the weather is set fair today – which it most certainly is – another will be bound to reply that a change for the worse is forecast – which Billy knows only too well to be accurate.

He is about to continue with his rounds when Mr Hunt suddenly pulls him towards him.

"Who is that?" he whispers most urgently into his ear, pointing to a flurry of gentlemen hurriedly approaching.

"Mr Johnson, sir. Thy apologetic host, together wi' Messrs Knight, Fitton an' Bamford."

No," hisses Hunt, "not them, I know who they are, but those other disreputable fellows following them."

Billy strains to see who Hunt might mean, not seeing anyone in particular among the always busy crowds thronging around *The Boar's Head*, the coaching inn upon the London Road and the main disembarkation point for passengers alighting there. But then he sees two men, lurking melodramatically behind a lamp post. One self-consciously chews a matchstick, while his companion feigns unconvincingly to be reading his newspaper. Billy recognises them at once.

"John Shawcross an' James Murray, sir," he says with unconcealed distaste.

"And they are…?"

"Spies o' Joe Nadin. An' Joe Nadin is…"

"I know who Joe Nadin is, Postman. His reputation stretches far beyond Manchester's town gates."

"Yes, sir."

Without pausing to greet the huffing and puffing Joseph Johnson, whose increasingly scarlet face betrays the growing extent of his embarrassment in arriving late to meet his most honoured guest, Hunt storms directly over to where Murray and Shawcross are still pretending disinterest towards him.

"I know who you are," he says at once. "Please do not insult my intelligence by bothering to deny it. Direct me at once towards the New Bailey Prison."

Shawcross – the inveterate chewer of matchsticks – is so astonished that his jaw drops open and his current matchstick tumbles to the ground. Murray, equally taken aback, drops a part of his newspaper. As he bends to retrieve it, he drops a different part of it. He repeats this pantomime several times until its entire contents have rearranged themselves in screwed up balls, which he unsuccessfully attempts to juggle.

"If you will just follow me," says Shawcross, adding, "I know it well," at the same time as Murray retorts with, "I don't know where you mean, sir, we're strangers in town," who then both look at each other in confusion, before Murray pelts Shawcross with what remains of his newspaper.

"Lead on, gentlemen," barks Hunt, prodding them both from behind.

Soon a small procession has formed – Shawcross, Murray and Hunt, hastily followed by an increasingly flustered Joseph Johnson, with an applauding Fitton, Knight and Bamford encouraging more of the crowd to accompany them. Billy too decides he will join the parade – he has letters to deliver to the prison after all – and by the time they are crossing the New Bailey Bridge almost two hundred people are thronging after the furiously striding Orator.

Johnson, who has by now caught up with Hunt, offered his most profuse apologies, which have been duly accepted, proceeds to explain to his guest the symbolic significance of where they are all now converging.

"Not only is this the site of the notorious dungeon, where Nady Joe carries out his most fearsome atrocities and tortures, it is the exact spot where Joseph Hanson was given a hero's welcome after completing his sentence for his wrongful arrest after the meeting at St George's Fields a decade ago." Hunt pricks up his ears at that. He has heard of Hanson – what Reformer worth his salt hasn't? – and the impulse he has so drastically acted on now begins to take a clearer shape.

When he reaches the prison steps, he marches to the top of them, hammers on the imposing front doors, then turns to face the large crowd which has followed him, increasing in size by the second, and prepares to address them directly. Framed by the prison's imposing Doric columns, he appears before them like an actor on a stage, a comparison with which he is more than comfortable.

He waits until the Boroughreeve appears, flanked by several of the Magistrates, as well as Nadin himself, who collectively gather on the steps in a semi-circle behind him, then speaks in a booming voice.

"Do you intend to arrest me, gentlemen? Is that why you send your lackeys to spy on me even before I have set foot in the town?" He points accusingly towards Shawcross and Murray, who try to make themselves anonymous but who are pushed forward none too surreptitiously by Messrs Fitton, Kinight and Bamford to a chorus of jeers from the crowd. Hunt continues unabated. "If so, on what charge?"

505

"I have here in my possession," replies the Boroughreeve, "a letter from Lord Sidmouth's office, which deals with this matter directly." He nervously brandishes a piece of paper above his head. Billy recognises it from one of the many such dispatches he has been delivering daily. "I shall read you the concluding paragraph. 'His Lordship thinks that if you find good ground for issuing a warrant it will be advisable not to forbear from doing so in the expectation of Mr Hunt giving you a better opportunity, unless some other reason for forbearance presents itself'."

There is a confused silence following this pronouncement. Nobody appears quite sure what has been meant by it.

"Well, sir," declares Hunt, "what have you decided? Are you going to arrest me or not?"

"I believe the Home Secretary's meaning is perfectly plain," stammers the Boroughreeve.

"Not to me, it isn't."

"Nor me, nor me, nor me!" come a chorus of cries from the crowd.

"We are considering the matter," says the Boroughreeve in a vain attempt to quell the growing agitation.

"Oh well," continues Hunt, his arms sweeping wide to take in the entire surroundings, "we can now all rest easy in our beds, knowing that the Civic Authorities are 'considering the matter'." He makes mocking speech marks with the first two fingers of each hand.

His remark, and its accompanying gesture, is greeted with uproarious laughter, which immediately dies down as Nadin steps threateningly forward.

Mr Clayton breathes a sigh of relief, but one that is short-lived. At that moment a commotion breaks out elsewhere on the Bridge where a Punch & Judy Show takes up the equivocating, indecisive theme of the day.

"Oh!" cries Mr Punch to an oncoming puppet Constable. "Ye *sinking* Manufacturers and Shopkeepers, is it the Starving

Labourers who have ruined you?"

"No!" cries the crowd as one.

"Or," continues Mr Punch, "is it Dear Provisions, High Rents and Crippling Taxes?"

"Yes!" they answer him.

"Come, come, Mr Punch," bumbles the Constable, "that's not the way of it at all."

"Oh yes it is."

"Oh no it isn't."

"What is it then?"

"Oh!" cautions the Constable. "Ye *thinking* Manufacturers and Shopkeepers, is it these Canting Reformers who will preserve you?"

"Shame!" cry the crowd.

"Or is it Kind Masters and Full Employment?" concludes the Constable.

"No," reply the crowd. "Never!"

The puppet Constable then proceeds to produce a truncheon, with which he threatens to belay Mr Punch, but Mr Punch is too quick for him. After a brief tug of war, Punch emerges triumphant, waving the stick in the air, which he now brings down hard upon the Constable's helmet.

"That's the way to do it!" he crows.

Hunt, although enjoying the spectacle, recognises a danger when he sees one and quickly uses his booming voice to bring the attention of the crowd back on him.

"We shall meet on Monday next, my friends, on the new date of the 16th August, and by our *steady, firm* and *temperate* deportment, we will convince our enemies that we have an *important* and *imperious public duty* to perform. The eyes of all England, nay, of all Europe, are fixed upon us, and every friend of real Reform and Rational Liberty is tremblingly alive to the result of our Meeting. Our Enemies will seek every opportunity, by means of their sanguinary agents, to excite a *Riot*, that they may have a pretence for the *spilling of our blood.* But we shall give them no such pretence. Come then, my friends, to the meeting next Monday, armed with *no other weapon* but that of a self-approving conscience, determined not to suffer yourselves to be irritated or excited by any means whatsoever to commit any breach of the public peace."

His words are greeted with thunderous cheers. The people drum their feet so loudly upon the New Bailey Bridge that for a brief moment there are fears it may give way. Hunt is applauded unceasingly as he makes his way through the crowds, which part before him like the Red Sea. He walks at such an accelerated pace that Joseph Johnson has great difficulty in keeping up with him. Eventually he manages to reach his side, and, while gulping for air, says to him, "If you will follow me, Mr Hunt. Once we have crossed the Bridge we must walk the length of the Dean's Gate, past The Exchange, towards my house, Smedley Cottage, on Shude Hill, which is at your disposal for the duration of your stay."

Hunt is about to respond with his re-stated intention of taking the first carriage back to London, when a bevy of young women reformers leap from the crowd to place kisses upon his cheek. With ever the eye for female pulchritude he decides that Manchester may yet have its diversions between now and the 16th August.

"Thank you, Mr Johnson," he says gallantly. "Pray lead me to your abode."

Watching the crowds enthusiastically following Hunt away from him, Mr Clayton, the Boroughreeve, turns lividly towards Nadin. "Continue to keep an eye on him. Now that he knows we're on to him, there's no need for discretion – which is just as well," he adds, throwing a withering glance in the direction of Shawcross and Murray. "I want daily reports."

"You shall have them," replies Nadin.

As soon as the Boroughreeve has retired back inside the imposing front entrance of the New Bailey Prison, Nadin slams his two spies hard against the wall. "I'm disappointed in you," he says, with threatening quietness, "very disappointed, and you know how I hate disappointment. Make sure I'm not disappointed again."

He releases his grip on their jackets and drops them both to the ground. Once he is out of their sight, they pick themselves up and dust themselves down like whimpering dogs.

"Does he mean what I think he means?" asks Shawcross.

"That depends what I think you think," replies Murray, and he silently draws his finger across the front of his throat.

As the square finally clears, an itinerant preacher, standing on a crate, attempts to speak to the empty air, listened to half-heartedly only by a parliament of otherwise occupied rooks, examining the contents of the heaped dung piles at the entrance to the Bridge.

"To all Reformers, at this critical juncture in our nation's history, I urge you to pay heed to the wisdom of the Lord. It is incumbent upon you most seriously to consider the consequences of the steps you take. Yet a little further and you will plunge the country into all the horrors of Civil Warfare. This is how they began in the French Revolution – they wanted nothing more but peaceable Reform and Liberty – *reasonable* Liberty. Instead they ended by sinking into Tyranny, more galling than that which they had first endured. *'If we hope for that we see not, then do we with patience wait for it, for the Lord is good unto them that wait for him'.*"

The rooks patiently continue to tug up the worms.

The preacher looks around at the deserted square. "I thank Heaven," he says, "above all mercies that I am born a Briton."

*

After the crowd has dispersed three gentlemen remain in the Square – not to listen to the itinerant preacher...

"A weak voice," remarks the first.

"Too thin," avers the second.

"Too reedy," declares the third.

"And his bearing is altogether too retiring," says the first.

"Too bashful," agrees the second.

"Too apologetic," concludes the third.

… but to listen to Mr Hunt.

"A fine carriage," admires the first.

"Such noble bearing," reflects the second.

"One might almost think him one of us," suggests the third, clapping his two fellows on the back for emphasis.

Mr Cooke, Mr Harvey and Mr Browne are all actors in Mr Macready's Company at the *Theatre Royale*, where they began ten years ago as walk-ons and have since progressed to taking leading roles. Unusually for actors they bear each other no ill will, for they do not regard the others as rivals, each of them having carved out their own particular niche in the roles they specialise in. Mr Cooke delights in playing villains. His Richard III is a perennial favourite – '*And thus I clothe my naked villainy*' – while Mr Browne has had such success with his Falstaff and Sir Toby Belch that he finds himself regularly inhabiting the roles in various taverns around the town, where the world is his oyster and discretion is not the better part of valour, and where he can usually be stood an extra quart of sack in return for a rendition of *Cast Away Care, He that Loves Sorrow* – '*Dost think because thou'rt virtuous there shall be no more cakes and ale?*' – and Mr Harvey has won many plaudits and renown for the gravitas and nobility of his Cassius or his Prospero. His gaze follows the departing back of Henry Hunt before he turns towards his companions, sweeping a theatrical arm across the empty square.

"*Men at some time are masters of their fates;*
The fault, dear Brutus, is not in the stars,
But in ourselves, that we are underlings…"

Mr Cooke and Mr Browne applaud their friend, who removes his hat with a deep bow.

"As you from crimes would pardon'd be
Let your indulgence set me free…"

"But some crimes are simply unpardonable," says Mr Cooke, indicating the itinerant preacher who continues to invoke the wrath of God upon the evil Reformers, none of whom are there to hear him.

"One should never play to an empty house," agrees Mr Browne.

"And nothing empties a house quicker than a sermon," expounds Mr Harvey.

Mr Cooke and Mr Browne acknowledge the truth of this remark with a laugh and a shake of the head.

"Preachers make poor players," sighs Mr Cooke.

"Who should indeed strut their hour upon the stage and then be heard no more," declares Mr Browne.

"There are exceptions," replies Mr Harvey.

"Name one," says Mr Browne.

"Yes," says Mr Cooke, "name one."

Mr Harvey knits his brow in an effort to call one to mind.

"Friar Francis in *Much Ado*," he says, more in hope than expectation.

"Anonymous," says Mr Browne dismissively.

"Never heard of him," underlines Mr Cooke.

"You cut me to the quick," cries Mr Harvey. "I gave the definitive portrayal of him in Oxford. '*For it so falls out that what we have we prize not to the worth whiles we enjoy it, but being lacked and lost, why then, we rack the value of it*'."

Mr Browne stifles a yawn. Mr Cooke puts his fingers in his ears.

"Very well," declares Mr Harvey undeterred, "what of Friar Laurence?"

"A meddler," declares Mr Cooke.

"A mischief," furthers Mr Browne.

But Mr Harvey is not to be suppressed. He immediately

plunges into character, adopting an overly pious voice.

*"The grey-eyed morn smiles on the frowning night
Chequering the eastern clouds with streaks of light..."*

Mr Browne and Mr Cooke try to silence him but he is too quick for them, evading the handkerchiefs they would stuff into his mouth.

*"These violent delights have violent ends
And in their triumph die, like fire and powder..."*

Mr Cooke and Mr Browne catch up with him and physically try to restrain him. They pin him to the ground but not before he can say one more line.

"Wisely and slow, they stumble that run fast..." rebuffs Mr Harvey, picking himself up and brushing himself down.

"Well," declares Mr Cooke, proffering a conciliatory hand to help Mr Harvey to his feet, *"an the fire of grace be not quite out of thee, now shalt thou be moved."*

Mr Browne beams upon his fellow actors. *"Give me a cup of sack to make my eyes look red, that it may be thought I have wept; for I must speak in passion,"* he says. *"The Bull's Head doth call, I warrant."*

"You are as a candle," says Mr Harvey, shaking his head with a smile, *"the better burnt out."*

"I must tell you friendly in your ear," replies Mr Browne, fully relishing his assumed role of the Merry Sir John once more, *"sell when you can, you are not for all markets..."*

They have barely ventured one link of a chain when Mr Harvey stops in his track, a new revelation dawning in his eyes.

"Wait, wait, wait. I have it. The Duke in *Measure for Measure* disguises himself as a Friar and thereby unmasks treachery and sedition."

The other two look at him, thunderstruck.

" '*Condemn the fault and not the actor of it*'," he adds, as if his meaning is self evident. Mr Cooke and Mr Browne continue to look baffled, but Mr Harvey is now on a roll and not to be downcast. "*The tempter or the tempted, who sins most?*"

Suddenly the penny drops with his hitherto exasperated audience.

"*Haste still pays haste,*" says an excited Mr Cooke.

"*And leisure answers leisure,*" adds a now smiling Mr Browne.

"*Like doth quit like,*" continues Mr Harvey before taking from his waistcoat pocket a penny, which he tosses into the air, catches in his right hand, then swiftly turns it over on the back of his left hand, which he covers again with his right, then slowly reveals the head of the king.

"*And measure still for measure,*" chorus all three before running the half mile towards the *Theatre Royale* in Fountain Street as if Hell was empty and all the devils were behind them, hot upon their heels.

Mr Macready is just sitting down to a late luncheon of pork chops when the three actors burst in on him. They all begin talking at once, and it takes him some time to be able to understand what they are saying. Eventually their meaning becomes clear. He rewards them with a broad smile.

"By Heaven you are in the right of it," he declares.

Mr Macready is no lover of Shakespeare. He is poor box office. The people prefer something lighter, a pretty romance, a witty comedy, but his actors adore him and are for ever pestering him to include at least one play by the Bard each season. Why, only last month Miss Appleby, still basking in the glow of her success as Ophelia for the special memorial performance in honour of the tragic and untimely death of Lavinia Robinson, which had galvanised the mood of the whole town, had asked him if they might present *Coriolanus* this year. She would, she informed him, as if bestowing upon him a most gracious favour, consider the role of Virgilia. "Not a large part," she had admitted, "but so affecting." *Coriolanus!* Macready had almost had an apoplexy right there on the spot. Nobody presents that play any more – and with good reason, for he's such a hateful character. Of course he knows what game she's playing. She means it as a tribute to her erstwhile mentor, the late Mr Whiteley. That old fool. Macready knows he shouldn't speak ill of the dead, but Whiteley belonged to an altogether different age. He failed to move with the times, that was his downfall. Who is the theatre for if not for the audiences? They pay their money and make their choice.

But before he could say any of this, Miss Appleby was already speaking to him.

"We are custodians of a heritage, are we not?" she was saying, deploying all of her characteristic traits, which audiences go wild for, that softly rising blush upon her pale cheeks, those disarming dimples, her maidenly bosom heaving with such passion.

He knows exactly what her game is, but nevertheless he finds her impossible to resist. She knows full well he will never agree to mounting *Coriolanus*, not even for her, but in its stead he will offer her another Shakespeare, and honour will be satisfied.

And now these three old hams have hit upon what could very well be the talk of the town, the sensation of the age, and he sees at once how he may kill three birds with one stone – present a rarely performed Shakespearean play to keep the traditionalists happy, appease the demands of Miss Appleby by offering her a role she can really get her teeth into and at the same time raise himself hopefully higher in her esteem, and provide his audiences with a night to remember.

"Capital," he says to his waiting trio. "You must join me for lunch so that we may discuss the idea further."

Like all actors, Mr Browne, Mr Cooke and Mr Harvey accept the invitation of something for free at once. "Cakes and ale," declares Mr Browne with relish. One never knows in this trade, they each acknowledge inwardly, where the next meal might come from.

"*Measure for Measure*," declares Macready. "Mr Cooke, you must play Angelo, one of the great hypocrites and villains."

Mr Cooke inclines his head modestly.

"Mr Browne, might you consider Lucio? A whoremongering, drunken rogue?"

"I shall play him to the manor born," he declares.

"And you, Mr Harvey, you of course must play the Duke. And I have a particular proposition to put to you regarding a new interpretation…"

Intrigued, Mr Harvey helps himself to a chop and listens with growing astonishment as Mr Macready outlines his bold idea.

*

Despite the success of his march upon the New Bailey Prison on the day he arrived, Hunt has been more or less under house arrest in the home of Joseph Johnson and his wife in Smedley Cottage ever since. Not that Joseph has placed any restriction upon his movements. Far from it. He has encouraged him to accompany him to all of his meetings as the days leading up to the meeting tick by. But every time that Hunt ventures outdoors, even if it is merely to accept the arrival of mail from the tireless Billy Robinson, he is mobbed at every turn. He cannot take a stroll, or ride out to Kersal Moor, or take coffee in one of the town's growing number of such establishments, without finding himself besieged on all sides. "God bless you, Mr Hunt!" is the cry that greets him. "Three cheers for the Orator!" is another. But "might I just have a word…?" is by far the most common salutation that falls upon him, or "would you do us the honour of coming to dine with us…?" It's not that he minds the attention – far from it, he feeds off it, it is his very life blood – but rather in a manner of *his* choosing, than in these freer, more spontaneous outpourings, which are beyond his control, and which threaten to bury him. The grandstand arenas of public meetings are his bailiwick, where he can rouse a crowd to passion and resolve, rather than the tittle-tattle of private *soirées* and supper parties, where he must, for the sake of form and politeness, refrain from talking politics, or talking about anything much at all. The trouble with the Reformers, he decides, is that they are all too earnest, and this opinion is confirmed for him by the procession of guests Joseph Johnson invites morning, noon and night to descend upon Smedley Cottage to pay their respects – Non-Conformists, Unitarians and Methodists all, most of whom abstain from the finer things in life, such as a bottle of good French claret. And when he can stand it no longer and decides – damn it – to poke his nose out of doors, that organ is at once overcome by the pungent cocktail of aromas that assail it from all sides. Smedley Cottage is situated just a few yards from where the Irk meets the Irwell, each river now little more than a stagnant sewer, and each contending with the other as to which might emit the foulest stench. And always, everywhere, loitering at a corner are Nadin's spies – Shawcross and Murray. At first Hunt will approach them directly, bid them a cheery "Good day, gentlemen", but the joke soon wears thin. They will be his conspicuous shadows for the duration of his stay and, like all shadows, they are silent, offering nothing in return by way of sport or banter, and so Hunt quickly comes to ignore them. Occasionally he will walk up to them as an evening draws to a close and say, "I am about to retire for the night, gentlemen. I suggest you do the same," but they merely smirk and stay exactly where they are, so that when he pulls back the curtains the next morning and looks down into the street below him, where already, by the time he rises, it will be thronging with carts and wagons laden with goods being brought to market, they will be standing in exactly the same spot they occupied the previous night. As the week proceeds, he no longer deigns to acknowledge them.

On the morning of his fifth day in Manchester, Billy delivers him two fresh invitations, both of which Joseph urges him to accept. The first is from a Mr Edward Holme, Vice President of the *Manchester Literary & Philosophy Society*, the much-loved *Lit & Phil*, of which even Hunt has heard, as well as a founder member of The Portico Library on Mosley Street. Mr Holme, together with a number of other wealthy Unitarian merchants and manufacturers, is proposing the formation of a Museum of Natural History for Manchester. Five years ago, upon the untimely death of Leigh Phillips, this consortium of businessmen and academics purchased his cabinets of insects, which will form the core of the proposed museum's collection. They have decided to launch an appeal for subscriptions from the public to raise sufficient funds for a building to house their exhibits. They have identified a site on Peter Street, not a hundred yards away from where Hunt will be delivering his oration the following Monday. Would he do them the honour, they ask him, of attending one of their regular monthly meetings?

Joseph urges him to accept. These men, he explains, represent Manchester's moral backbone. They are also wealthy, being physicians, academics, establishment figures as well radical in their views, many of them more enlightened factory owners.

"These are men of influence and capital," Joseph reminds his bored-looking guest. "They will lend our cause respectability", he stresses.

"Yes, yes, yes," concedes Hunt, putting aside the invitation while vigorously attacking his boiled egg which, as usual in Smedley Cottage, is too soft. "I'm sure you're right, but do I actually have to attend? Can't I say something along the lines that I am flattered to be asked but am acutely conscious that my attendance might attract too much attention which may detract from the seriousness of their purpose *et cetera, et cetera*…?"

"I suppose you can," sighs Joseph, inwardly acknowledging that there is some substance in what he knows Hunt is suggesting as a less than transparent excuse for wriggling out of something he would rather not do. His guest does not in fact do anything he does not wish to, he has observed, and will go to extraordinary lengths to avoid mixing with anyone who he does not think will be useful to his own agenda in the longer term. Ah well, if that is the price they must pay for having him address their meeting next Monday, then so be it. They are useful to each other in this respect and they both understand this. It is in the nature of the game they are playing, although for Joseph it is a less of a game, more of a cause. Yes, he has aspirations for *The Observer* as a newspaper, and personal ambitions for himself as its Editor, but he is passionate in his support for Reform. He sees the need for it every single day, in ever aspect of daily life for all who live and work in this town that is his home. Whereas Hunt, though no less passionate in his zeal for Reform, sees in the crusade his own role as nothing less than a Richard *Coeur du Lion*, with Manchester a necessary milestone on his quest to retake Jerusalem.

The second invitation, therefore, is one that pertains much more closely to his mission. It is from Mr Macready of the Theatre Royale.

To Great Britain's Most Celebrated Orator
From a Company of Poor Players Who Humbly Practise a Similar Occupation

Sir,

We would indeed be most honoured if you would bestow upon us the inestimable benefit of your attendance at our latest production of William Shakespeare's too oft-neglected masterpiece, 'Measure for Measure', which we are presenting Friday of this week, for One Night Only, in recognition of your most esteemed presence among us at these most interesting of times, the hottest days of the year, the dog days, when

Virgil cautions vintners to protect their vines when 'the Dog star cleaves the thirsty ground.'

Your most loyal and humble servant,
Charles Macready, Esq.

Hunt seizes upon this with alacrity.

"Now this is more to my liking," he says.

Joseph shakes his head. He is not a fan of Shakespeare, and he generally finds actors frivolous or self-seeking. His honoured guest, he has come to realise, is both, for he too is an actor. But he underestimates those other two typical qualities found in practitioners of that wandering profession. Rogues and vagabonds they may be, but they are also dreamers and frequently hard-nosed. Hunt is both of these.

"Why are you holding your meeting next week?" he asks, suddenly serious.

"Because the Civic Authorities insisted we postponed," replies Johnson, taken aback by this new tone in his guest's voice.

"No, no, no," he continues quickly. "I mean why in the first instance. What do you hope to achieve by it?"

"What we have stated so many times. Our due and rightful Representation in Parliament. Manchester needs an MP."

"Quite so. But why?"

"To give her poor beleaguered citizens a voice, where their grievances can be heard, and where their Lot can be improved."

"And you have requested this many times before?"

"We have."

"And your petitions have fallen on deaf ears?"

"They have. You know this. Why are you asking such obvious questions?"

"Let me ask you another obvious question then. What do you hope will be different this time?"

"That we will at last be listened to."

"And how do you hope to achieve this now, when all

previous attempts have failed? What is it you are doing that is different this time? "

Joseph pauses, too embarrassed to reply.

Hunt, recognising this, leaps in to ease his host's discomfort.

"Modesty forbids me from saying that the difference lies in my presence. I am not seeking flattery, Mr Johnson. But what is it that my presence guarantees?"

Joseph looks up, acutely aware of where this conversation is heading. The look in his eyes is of one who has been caught with his pants down.

"Your presence," he stammers, "will ensure greater numbers will attend."

"Precisely so," says Hunt, clapping Joseph on the back. "That's nothing to be ashamed of, is it? How many do you think will come? Fifty thousand?"

"Possibly more."

"Sixty – a hundred thousand?"

"If the weather holds, yes, I think so."

"And what is the current population in Manchester?"

"The last census put it at a hundred and twenty thousand. But if you add in those from the outlying towns – Stretford, Stockport, Ashton, Oldham, Royton, Middleton, Rochdale, Bury, Bolton – all of whom have pledged attendance, perhaps as high a figure as two hundred thousand, possibly a quarter of a million."

"Yes. And so if a hundred thousand souls do descend on St Peter's Field next Monday, that will amount to almost one in two of the entire population of South East Lancashire, will it not?"

"Yes, I suppose it will."

"No 'suppose' about it, Mr Johnson. It will. And that is not a number to be trifled with. That is not a voice to be silenced. That is a number, is it not…" He paused, making sure he had Joseph's complete attention before continuing. Here it comes, thought Joseph, the *coup de grace*. "A number that may vastly increase the readership of your newspaper, Mr Johnson?"

"That is not the principal consideration here, Mr Hunt."

"No? Well – not the principal, I grant you that, but a not insignificant corollary. Nor is it something to be ashamed of. Our cause needs oxygen, Mr Johnson. If my presence here contributes to greater numbers attending and rallying to the cause, and if then those new recruits desire to wish to be kept abreast of subsequent developments, which they can read about in your newspaper, and if all of that combined hastens the implementation of the reforms we are all of us seeking, then where's the harm? Publicity provides that oxygen. Mr Macready understands this, Mr Johnson. He sees my presence here in the town as an opportunity for attracting more audiences to his theatre. If, by attending, I grant him that wish, my appearance there, at a high profile, well-attended public event, reminds the people that I am here already in Manchester and gives you, Mr Johnson, along with all your rival publications, I might add, a legitimate reason for informing people of that fact, without explicitly appearing to do so, thereby avoiding any risk of censorship by the Civic Authorities. Pragmatism, Mr Johnson."

Joseph has to admit the legitimacy of his guest's argument. He himself could not have thought up such a ruse. Dreamers and pragmatists.

He decides to give Mr Macready's invitation a full page in the following day's edition of *The Observer.* Doubtless the other papers will follow suit the day after, if Macready has not already let slip his plans to their editors, knowing as he does, each of their preferred watering holes.

*

521

The Manchester Mercury

Thursday 12th August 1819

THE DOG DAYS ARE UPON US

The Dog Days are upon us and no mistake. The hottest, muggiest, most sultry days of summer. When temperatures rise and, with them, tempers also. The middle of August which we have long associated with heat and drought, storms and fever. When here in Manchester we must hold our noses even more tightly when we walk abroad, especially when in the vicinity of our once plentiful, now sluggish and stagnant rivers and brooks. When women are most wanton and men most feeble. When the bark of trees is blighted and the blood of dogs is boiled, so that they fester and go mad.

Older readers may remember the old rhyme which stated:

> *"Dog days bright and clear*
> *Indicate a most good year*
> *But when accompanied by rain*
> *We hope for better times in vain..."*

Perhaps our younger readers need reminding of the wisdom of this, especially this year, which is turning out to be the hottest in living memory. And so, if the old adage holds true, why all this huff and puff for Reform? Better times are just around the corner, says *The Manchester Mercury*, so our advice to our readers is to stay at home next Monday. Do not suffer yourselves to have to endure the heat of the day, when the sun is at its zenith, to listen to the puffed up, vainglorious rantings of a Notorious Orator, who is currently to be found residing in our town. We mention no names, but you will not have to *hunt* him down before you catch him.

The *Theatre Royale* has announced a Special Gala Performance in honour of this most Unwelcome Guest, who, we are told, is sure to put in an appearance. We are reminded of Homer's description of Achilles, marching into Troy to bring ruin and destruction upon their heads by plotting to murder their hero, Hector, by means most foul. We thought it might amuse our readers to be reminded of this, but then to wipe the smiles from off their faces, and view these Dog Days as a warning to all Respectable, Law-Abiding Citizens of Manchester to do everything in their power to deny this false Achilles who has come amongst us a voice, by refusing to attend both this Theatrical Performance and the Public Meeting arranged for Monday next. Let both events be damp squibs in these febrile times.

> *"Sirius rises late in the dark, liquid sky*
> *On summer nights, star of stars,*
> *Orion's Dog, they call it, brightest*
> *Of all, but an evil portent, bringing heat*
> *And fevers to suffering humanity.*
> *Achilles' shield gleamed like this as he came…"*

*

By the time Friday comes around – Friday 13th, observes Mr Harvey mischievously to his fellow thespians, while at the same time wilfully whistling and quoting from the Scottish play, he looks out upon the empty auditorium of the *Theatre Royale* before the doors are flung open to an excited public and mischievously declares:

> *"This castle hath a pleasant seat. The air*
> *Nimbly and sweetly recommends itself*
> *Unto our gentle senses."*

"Somebody's confident," remarks a still scantily-clad Miss Appleby, delaying the moment when she must don her nun's costume for Isabella for as long as she can.

"So should you all be," calls out Mr Macready, striding up the central aisle of the auditorium. "We have a hit upon our hands."

"A hit, a hit, a palpable hit," jokes Mr Browne, applying the finishing touches to his make-up for Lucio as a drunken sot.

"Break a leg, boys and girls," adds Macready, clapping his hands. "We open the house in five."

Joseph has arranged for an open-top barouche to convey Henry Hunt the less than half a mile from Smedley Cottage to the *Theatre Royale*. It is seven o'clock. The evening is still light, the temperature warm, so that the streets are lined with people cheering him every yard of the way. The theatre seats two thousand, but more than five times that number accompany his royal progress along High Street, across Market Street Lane, towards Marble Street, then down into Milk Street as far as York Street, where the theatre is situated at the junction with Fountain Street. Tickets for tonight's performance sold in under two hours. Many of those who follow Hunt's barouche will be joining him in the audience, but for many more the real performance is already taking place, here on the streets of Manchester, and will do so again once the curtain comes down later and he makes his return journey along the same route, where the crowds will still be waiting for him, the play itself being a mere *entr'acte*.

*

When Edward Holme, gentleman, scholar and President of the *Lit & Phil*, surveys the crowds teeming through Manchester, squeezing their way through the town's narrow streets as they follow Mr Hunt's barouche on his way to the theatre, he breathes a sigh of relief that his own invitation to the Orator has been declined. Every enterprise needs the oxygen of publicity but does not wish to be suffocated by it, as he surely would have been had Mr Hunt agreed to meet him this evening. He comes with too much excess baggage, which can sometimes prevent the other travellers from reaching their destination.

Instead he can now contemplate an altogether quieter occasion in his home on Peter Street, from where he can look out of his first floor drawing room window towards the vacant lot opposite, where he hopes his planned Museum of Natural History for Manchester will take root, providing he can raise sufficient capital.

Joining him this evening are two important potential benefactresses – the mother of the late Leigh Philips, whose Cabinet of Insects will form the cornerstone of the Museum's specimens, and the widow of Sir Ashton Lever, who has kindly offered to donate the entire catalogue of her late husband's vast collection.

"His *Holophusicon* may no longer be intact," she says with a wry expression on her face, "being scattered to the four corners of the globe, quite literally I might add, but I have here the Catalogue for the Complete Miscellany, all twenty-five thousand items of it. I don't mind admitting to you, Mr Holme, my husband's obsession bankrupted and finally killed him, and it has driven me at times to absolute distraction, but these papers represent a life's work. I hope they contain enough to pique the curiosity of serious scholars and academics for many years to come. If you can house them in your Museum, sir, I shall be only too glad to contribute a significant sum to your fund."

"Lady Ashton, your generosity overwhelms me. I am delighted to accept your gift of the Catalogue, which shall take pride of place in a room devoted exclusively to it."

Lady Ashton inclines her head to indicate her satisfaction with the arrangements.

"Legacy is so important, is it not, ladies? Without your son's Cabinet of Insects, Mrs Philips, we would have no actual exhibits for our Museum. We hope that once it becomes known that such a meticulously assembled and researched collection as his will form the centrepiece of the new institution we are proposing that other botanists and naturalists will feel emboldened to offer their own bequests to us."

"Thank you, Mr Holme," says Mrs Philips softly, wiping away a small tear from the corner of one eye. "You must forgive me. It still upsets me to remember how much all of this meant to him. He was only a boy when he first began collecting."

Edward turns to his nephew, sitting quietly in the corner, whose twelfth birthday it is today, who has also expressed an interest in *lepidoptera*. "Do you hear that, Giles? It's never too young to start."

"Yes, Uncle."

"Isn't that right, ladies?"

"I remember your son very well," says Lady Ashton, offering a handkerchief to Mrs Philips. "On the night of the Earthquake he was most anxious about the safety of his flies."

"With good reason," smiles Mrs Philips.

"Although neither of us smiled at the time, did we, dear?"

Mrs Philips shakes her head. Her eyes are welling up, threatening to overflow once more.

"He had three *vivaria*, Giles," continues Lady Ashton. "Do you know what they are?"

"I think so, Ma'am," he replies nervously. "I believe they are ventilated glass jars in which one may keep live specimens."

"Quite so," says Lady Ashton.

"I never cared for them," says Mrs Philips. "I was always afraid they might escape and spread throughout the house."

"Which is exactly what they did on the night of the Earthquake," laughs Lady Ashton, remembering.

"Ugh," shudders Mrs Philips. "Thank goodness he stuck to pinning what he collected on boards after that. Behind glass, under lock and key, in cabinets."

The two ladies share a smile. How the years have softened us, thinks Lady Ashton. *That evening I spent with you at your house was one of the dullest of my life. I couldn't wait to get away – until the Earthquake struck, that is. Then it became exhilarating. All of your son's flies angrily swarming around us. But now I find we have more in common than we did back then. We have both known sadness since. We have each lost a husband, and you a son. I find I like you better than I did. What does that say about us, I wonder? That we are still capable of change, no matter what stage of life we have reached? I hope so, for that is a most comforting thought.*

Edward fetches one of Leigh's mahogany cases with great reverence and places it carefully on a rosewood table in the centre of the room. He bids the two ladies and his nephew to come closer to examine its contents. He holds a lamp above it, so that they might see more clearly the small display of what at first sight look like six identical moths, but which on closer inspection reveal subtle distinctions between them.

"Well, Giles," says Edward, "what do you make of these?"

"I know this species," he says confidently. "*Biston betularia.*"

"The peppered moth, that's right."

"Of the phylum *arthropoda*," continues Giles. "They're quite common."

"Yes, yes – but look more closely. Have you ever seen any like these before?"

It takes Giles only a few seconds before he sees what his Uncle is driving at and his eyes nearly pop out of their sockets.

"But – but…"

"Yes?"

"Each one is subtly different from the one before it. Almost as if it has evolved." He looks back towards his Uncle, his expression a mixture of incredulity, tinged with fear and awe. "But that cannot be, can it?"

"This was your son's greatest discovery, Mrs Philips. He believed it was evidence of one species of moth transmuting into quite a different form."

"But that goes against everything it says in the Bible."

"It does, and it cost him his reputation in the end, for nobody would accept his claim."

"What do *you* think, Mr Holme?" asks Lady Ashton, examining the tiny creatures more closely.

"If I'm honest, I simply don't know. But isn't that where all new knowledge begins? By recognising something we don't know the answer to and then trying to find out what it is? That's what I want our Museum to do. To honour the past, with collections and catalogues like the ones you are both so generously donating, but using the information they contain to make new discoveries, to push back the frontiers of what we know and understand, to inspire the next generation, people like you, Giles, to contradict what we currently take as gospel and challenge us to look at the world with fresh eyes. To be a place for argument as well as wonder, a forum for debate and disagreement, an open, not a closed, book. A place of expanding, not shrinking knowledge. For the getting of wisdom. For does not the Bible that you speak of, Mrs Philips, also instruct us that 'wisdom is the principal thing'. Therefore if we get wisdom we may also get understanding, which shall 'bring to our head an ornament of grace'. A Museum for the Future as much as the Past."

"And Manchester seems exactly the right place for such an enterprise," says Lady Ashton, "for we are not afraid of embracing change here."

But some people are, thinks Edward, looking back out of his window at the crowds still thronging the streets below. There will be even more there in a couple of days' time, he thinks, when tens of thousands will gather on Monday in St

Peter's Field, which he can see directly if he turns his gaze to the right, all of them agitating for change, for tossing aside the *ancien regime* and all of its excess baggage along with it, like Mr Hunt and his admirers, or perhaps more like young Leigh Philips, whose flies, once they are set free from their bell jars, simply cannot be controlled and will swarm where they will. You can try to catch them again, he thinks, and force them back into their jar, or you can try instead to crush them, but they'll keep coming back, evolving into new iterations of themselves, the same but different, more adapted, more streamlined, more evolved.

*

Once inside the theatre Hunt is applauded all the way to his seat, where the eyes of the audience remain firmly fixed until a bell is rung and Mr Macready steps in front of the curtain, nervously clearing his throat. It takes him quite some while to attract everyone's attention away from Mr Hunt, who is extracting as much as he can from his moment in the limelight, even going so far as requesting his admirers to "listen to the most excellent Mr Macready".

"It is not our custom," explains the Actor Manager, "to introduce our performance with some kind of Prologue. We prefer as a rule to let our play speak for itself, and certainly I am a poor substitute for Mr Shakespeare. But tonight is a special occasion, a Gala Performance, for One Night Only, in honour of our Special Guest..." And here he pauses to indicate where Mr Hunt is sitting, encouraging him to stand from his seat and take another bow, which he is only too happy to oblige. The applause which follows lasts a full minute and a half. It sounds like a deep explosion rumbling from deep below the earth. Those in the audience who are old enough to remember recall the night of the Earthquake some forty-two years before, when Manchester tilted on its axis and was never quite the same again. It eventually subsides, allowing Mr

Macready to continue. "A Gala Performance, as I said, of a rarely performed play by our most noble Bard, but one, I submit to you most humbly, whose time has come. *Measure for Measure*. I believe I may be so bold as to presume that very few among you here this evening will have had the opportunity to see it before. I ask you to indulge me, therefore, Ladies and Gentlemen, by permitting me to set the scene. Our play is set in Vienna, a modern metropolis experiencing a profound moment of change. There is great wealth to be found there, but only in the hands of a few, at the expense of the many, who see little of the benefits of their labour. Corruption and squalor are rife. Manners are loose, morals looser. Presiding over this morass is a distant Duke, who realises that something must be done to bring about the necessary reform, but that he has not yet earned the right to be the man to do this. And so, when our play begins, he abdicates. He hands over the reins of power to his most able of Deputies, Angelo, a man who sees it as his own personal crusade to clean up the city streets and re-impose the law to the absolute letter. But as we shall see, he too is not a man without secrets of his own, with skeletons lurking in his cupboard. The Duke, meanwhile, disguises himself as a Friar and explores Vienna's less salubrious quarters where he can come and go undisturbed and unrecognised. Thank you, Ladies and Gentlemen. Our play now begins, not in fair Verona, but in less than fair Vienna, and is now the two hour traffic of our stage."

Mr Macready exits the stage to polite, intrigued applause before an expectant hush falls upon the audience, who do not have to wait long for the first big surprise of the evening. The curtain rises on a setting which is noticeably familiar and at once draws an audible gasp. A backdrop has been painted to depict a townscape of factory chimneys and cotton mills, the outlines of recognisable buildings peppered in between, The Exchange, The Infirmary, The House of Correction, The New Bailey Prison. The second surprise is that the actors are wearing modern dress. In recent years there has been a growing trend to stage the plays of Shakespeare in the periods when they are set – ancient Greece for *A Midsummer Night's Dream*, ancient Rome for *Julius Caesar* – with a growing emphasis on spectacle – horses and chariots, armies and shipwrecks. Mr Macready is of a generation of theatre managers responsible for this fashion. It's what the public wants, he has argued, to be diverted, bread and circuses. He knows full well that in Shakespeare's own time all of his plays were staged in the contemporary clothing of the day. All of his actors wore Elizabethan doublet and hose, over which a breastplate of armour might be attached, or a toga casually thrown. The point was clear. This play may be set in Athens, or Troy, or Verona, or Rome, but really its concern is here and now. The themes are timeless, universal. What better way then to emphasise their undying relevance than to stage them in such a way that underlines that point. And so, when Mr Cooke first appears as the Deputy, Angelo, to assume the reins of power, he wears the immediately recognisable garb of Joe Nadin. The inference could not be clearer. Mr Cooke, in the way he stands and moves, conjures up his bull-like demeanour, speaking in a way that is blunt, to the point, uncompromising and intimidating, even down to the false, bulbous, potato-shaped nose. This is a man not to be trifled with, to be feared, to steer a wide berth around.

Many of the play's speeches and lines sound fresh, new-minted, to accommodate the times through which the town is now living.

"Condemn the fault and not the actor of it?" sneers Angelo as Nadin when asked to show mercy, a quality he is incapable of showing, strained or otherwise.

"O, it is excellent," counters Miss Appleby as Isabella, *"to have a giant's strength, but it is tyrannous to use it like a giant."*

Isabella. What of Isabella? A nun who has renounced the

evils of society portrayed by Manchester's darling, Miss Appleby, who, since her rendition of Ophelia in memory of Lavinia Robinson, has assumed angelic status throughout the town. The fact that she is also blessed with a face that is fair, a figure that is shapely, hair that is lustrous and eyes that are sparkling has not hindered her success. Usually she is to be seen in roles which accentuate these natural advantages, often appearing beguilingly *déshabillée*, as Juliet, Cleopatra, Desdemona or Cressida, or disguised as a boy, as Viola, Rosalind, Imogen or *La Pucelle*, so that she may show off her finely turned legs. But here, as Isabel, she is clothed from head to toe in a nun's habit, with not even a wisp of hair to be seen falling upon her marble forehead. However, Macready has seen to it that her habit is white and snugly follows the contours of her breasts, waist and hips in a most arresting fashion. Hunt can be seen to lean noticeably forward in his seat whenever she takes the stage. Her every utterance is warmly applauded.

"*Truth is truth to th' end of reckoning…*"

Time and again the play speaks to the matter on everyone's lips, the upcoming meeting on St Peter's Field in less than three days' time, not three hundred yards away from where they now all sit.

"*The miserable hath no other medicine but only hope,*" laments Claudio, Isabella's brother, wrongly accused and languishing in prison, whose case she will take up with Angelo, who expresses the hypocrisy at the heart of the play. "*The tempter or the tempted – who sins most?*" But against all odds the oppressed must somehow find the courage to rise up to take what is rightfully theirs. "*Our doubts are traitors,*" muses Mr Browne as Lucio in the arms of Mistress Overdone, who bears an uncanny resemblance to Mrs Schofield of *The Spread Eagle Inn*, delighting all members of the audience no matter which side of the political divide their interests might lie. "*They make us lose the goods we oft might win by fearing the attempt.*" There are shouts of agreement from the Reformers at this remark, so that when Lucio is himself whisked off to prison by Angelo's soldiers, marching implacably in the reds and whites of the MYC, they can take not a little solace from Claudio's observation that "*if I must die, I will encounter darkness as a bride and hug her in my arms*".

But the biggest surprise of the night, Macready's ultimate *coup de théâtre*, comes near the end, when the Duke, having wandered through the play disguised as a Friar, throws off his monk's garb to reveal his true identity. He is dressed exactly like Henry Hunt. Down to the last detail. Jacket, waistcoat, shirt and cravat. Trousers, handkerchief, kid gloves and leather boots.

The theatre is in uproar.

There are cat calls and boos. There are whistles and cheers. Hats are thrown into the air. Feet are stamped upon the floor. Programmes are waved or torn into shreds. There is thunderous applause. The numbers of those in support of Hunt far outweigh those who are against. The play is brought to a halt for a full five minutes.

In the end Hunt is encouraged to stand in his seat, whether to acknowledge the support or to quell the noise is unclear, but then Mr Harvey, carried away on the tide of emotion, does something quite extraordinary. He steps off the stage. He walks directly to where Hunt is standing. He shakes him by the hand. Then he raises his arm aloft in triumph, the two of them as indistinguishable as twins, a double threat to those representatives of the Civic Authority who have attended tonight's performance under sufferance, or, as in Matthew's case, out of curiosity. Unlike his colleagues, he is not alarmed by what he sees. Rather, he is amused.

Eventually the furore subsides. Mr Harvey returns to the stage and Hunt resumes his seat. In the closing scene of the play The Duke, like a descending *deus ex machina*, rights the wrongs, punishes and forgives with measure for measure, and captures the mood of the times.

"*Virtue is bold*," he proclaims, "*and goodness never fearful*."

Then, in a final coda, he appeals directly to his audience.
"*My business in this state*
Hath made me a looker on here where I
Have seen corruption boil and bubble
Till it o'er run the stew. Laws for all faults
But faults so countenanced, that the strong statutes
Sound like the forfeits in a barber's shop,
As much in mock as mark..."

When the curtain at last comes down, after the actors have taken more than a dozen calls and the stage has been showered with a thousand fallen flowers, Miss Appleby allows herself a quiet moment alone. She looks up towards the flies and says a silent word of thanks to her one-time mentor, Mr Carlton Whiteley – may he rest in peace – who would have loved everything about this evening.

Buoyed by the euphoria Hunt does not head directly back to Smedley Cottage after the performance as originally planned. Instead he accepts the invitation of Mr Macready to "join the company in a small after show supper party they have arranged in his honour at *The Spread Eagle* – simple fare, plain but honest." Hunt regards Macready, his head bowed, hand placed upon his heart, with wry amusement. It would be churlish to refuse. And besides, he can never tire of being the centre of attention, especially when there are pretty ladies also present, which he is sure will be the case, after having witnessed their uninhibited displays as whores of Vienna, whom he now wanders freely and happily among in various states of undress backstage, where Mr Macready allows him to linger before taking him to meet Mr Harvey, who is waiting to greet him once more, his double, his twin, his likeness, his mirror.

Once at *The Spread Eagle*, the talk flows freely, the ale even more so. Hunt quizzes Harvey about a particular gesture he deployed which he found most affecting. Harvey, knowing precisely on what side his bread is buttered, describes an illustration he claims to have seen of Hunt addressing the crowds at a public meeting in Smithfield Market in London, a copy of which he has seen in *The Times*, on which he has based his interpretation. Hunt drinks all this in like nectar.

The only sour note in the evening comes at around eleven o'clock, when Hunt notices his two shadows glowering in a side bar. Shawcross and Murray. He invites them over to join them all for a drink. He enquires as to whether they saw the play. When they reveal that they did, he is anxious to know what they thought of it. When they reply that they found it hateful and repellent, he demands that they make an apology to "my good friends, the actors". When they refuse, he slaps one of them, Murray, hard across the cheek with one of his kid gloves, whereupon Murray launches himself directly upon Hunt. Shawcross vainly tries to pull his colleague away, just as Harvey attempts to extract his twin also from the fray, but their actions are too little, too late. Soon the whole tavern is in uproar, a brawl breaking out across the entire premises, with Radicals and Loyalists wading into each other with chairs, bottles, whatever comes readily to hand. Fortunately for Mrs Schofield a posse of Special Constables had been posted outside the door as soon as the crowds poured in from the *Theatre Royale*. They quickly step in to separate the combatants and eject them out into the streets. Perhaps influenced by the events of the play, they make no arrests, merely issue stern warnings for everyone to go quietly home. Hunt is whisked away by a beleaguered Joseph Johnson back to Smedley Cottage, and Shawcross and Murray take their chance to slip away, an action that does not go unnoticed, however, so that they are pursued by three or four young men whose thirst for blows has not yet been fully quenched.

Back inside *The Spread Eagle*, Mr Macready offers to reimburse Mrs Schofield for any damages, and the actors settle back into their comfortable rituals of drinking and anecdotes once again. This has been a night to remember. "Enough about me," they will say. "What did *you* think of my performance?"

*

Matthew leaves the theatre immediately the performance ends, not staying for the orgy of curtain calls which follow it, and is soon swallowed up by the crowds still thronging the streets outside. What struck him most forcibly in the play was how the portrayal of Angelo so closely resembled himself, rather than the more obvious figure of Nadin, who was understandably selected by the company for the target of their satire. Everyone in Manchester knows Nadin, while very few know *him*, apart from his immediate circle, which numbers very few individuals, and this is how he prefers it, how he has arranged matters.

Over the years he has cut an increasingly solitary figure, having few acquaintances and fewer friends. True, he has his business associates, who he cultivates through necessity, but who he always maintains a professional distance from, and there are the Magistrates, along with other members of the Civil Authority, who he sees rather too often for his liking, but these are, he accepts, unusual times. Some of those colleagues were present at the *Theatre Royale* this evening and Matthew could see their faces grow pale when the actor playing the Duke stepped off the stage to raise the arm of Hunt in supposed triumph. They worry that the tide of opinion may be turning irreversibly against them.

Well, thinks Matthew, that may or may not be so, but the Meeting scheduled for Monday will be significant one way or another, he is certain of this, but not in the way his fellow Magistrates fear it. No, he believes the Reformers have over-reached themselves, that Hunt is proving too much of a loose cannon, and that they are already regretting inviting him. This little charade this evening has only served to underline that the man is self-seeking, more interested in promoting himself than the cause of Radicalism. But if he does succeed in rousing the crowds to a riot on Monday, then he, Matthew, will be ready for him. The MYC are itching for a fight, and Matthew might just be inclined to give them what they want. What is it that the Bard said? '*Let slip the dogs of war and cry havoc*?' Let them do so indeed.

As he continues to make his way back to his empty house on Oldham Street, weaving in between the warp and weft of the crowds still shuttling back and forth across the town, he recalls a different quotation from the play he has witnessed this evening.

'O what may man within him hide
Though angel on the outward side…?'

He reaches his home, places the key inside the lock, turns the handle, steps inside, then closes it behind him immediately, shutting out the world. For a few moments he allows himself to savour the particular quality of silence and shadow that always greets him there. His feet echo loudly on the wooden floors as he takes the stairs to his study at the top and back of the house. He enters the even more sequestered hush of this small, private room, which none but he has visited. The only decision he has to make is which of the two curtained recesses he will reveal first – the portrait of Mercy and the caged bird, or the framed cotton shawl that belonged to Lavinia, the daughter of his beloved Fanny, all of whom deserted him.

*

Shawcross and Murray flee *The Spread Eagle* as if the hounds of hell themselves were after them. The bells of the Collegiate Church of St Mary, St Denys and St George toll a quarter to midnight. They run for two miles before they dare to stop to take a breather. They crouch in the shadows, straining to hear whether they are still being pursued. They hear nothing, apart from a pair of owls hooting back and forth above their heads, informing each other of the whereabouts of their quarry. Shawcross and Murray dare to hope that they do not mean *them*.

They have reached the southern edge of White Moss, an extensive stretch of wetland marshes, around whose perimeter lie the villages of Harpurhey, Moston and Blackley. Further to the north are to be found Chadderton, Middleton, Greengate and Alkrington. There are rumours that some of the creatures from Sir Ashton Lever's *Holophusicon* may have escaped from there some years before and begun to breed upon the Moss. Shawcross and Murray hear the distant boom of a bittern, and the hairs on the backs of their necks stand on end to attention.

As their nerves begin at last to settle, they hear another noise, distant, more rhythmic, getting nearer. The sound of a hundred men marching in step, to the beat of fife and drum. They hear voices issuing orders, then a great huzzah echoing from the silent, swampy ground. They see shadowy figures mustering on the marsh in the moonlight. Sirius, the Dog star, is so bright that it illuminates the entire Moss, as white as its name. It carves a clear pathway, glittering across the heath, into which pour the whole Chadderton contingent of Reformers, secretly exercising their drilling routines ahead of Monday's meeting. To Shawcross and Murray they resemble nothing less than a phantom army preparing for the fray.

In a panic they run, but they are not familiar with the ways of the Moss and they soon become stuck fast in its vice-like, slimy grip, sucking them down. The Drillers, hearing their shouts for help, rush to their aid and pull them out. But when they discover who it is they have rescued, two of the hated Nadin's men, their mood turns on a sixpence. Instead of trying to save them, now they want nothing more than to kill them. It is only through the swift and timely intervention of their leader, William Fitton, that they manage to escape – kicked and beaten unconscious, but alive still.

When Samuel Bamford learns from Fitton what has transpired, then reads a far more lurid and sensational account of it in *The Mercury* – "*Reformers Show Their True Colours, Two Special Constables Left For Dead*" – he is furious.

"This will eradicate from the minds of the Magistrates, and our opponents generally, whatever vestige of indulgence they might have hitherto retained for us."

Fitton is so shaken by the events that he decides he will not attend the Public Meeting to be held on Monday, the following day.

Sir Edward Clayton, the Boroughreeve, writes one last desperate letter to Lord Sidmouth.

'The Magistrates, Military and Civic Authorities of Manchester have been occupied nearly the whole day in concerting the necessary arrangements for the preservation of the peace tomorrow, and for the safety of the town in case Riot should ensue. As at present advised, we do not think to prevent the Meeting, yet all the latest accounts tend to show that the worst possible spirit pervades the country. I hope in my heart that peace may be preserved, but under all the possible circumstances it is scarcely credible to expect it. In short, in this respect, we find ourselves in a state of painful uncertainty.'

Not so Matthew, who spends a pleasant Sunday beating the bounds of the town.

Nor Lord Sidmouth, who departs for his favourite shooting resort of Broadstairs in Kent, not intending to return to London before the morning of Wednesday 19th at the earliest, *'for the purpose of receiving an account of what I am certain will be a peaceful demonstration in Manchester on the Monday'*.

*

Prescott's Weekly Journal

Saturday 11th August 1819

IS THIS THE TRUE FACE OF A REFORMER?

Orator Hunt in his Cups?

While Manchester steels itself for what some are claiming will be the Most Numerous Meeting Ever to Take Place in Great Britain, some of them hopefully, some of them fearfully, its Chief Protagonist, the infamous Henry 'Orator' Hunt, was last night to be found CAROUSING into the early hours at one of the town's less reputable taverns in the company of ROGUES and VAGABONDS, many of whom might easily have been mistaken for members of an even OLDER PROFESSION.

All of us want REFORM, but the majority of HONEST CITIZENS are prepared to wait, trusting in the WISDOM and JUSTICE of our CIVIC AUTHORITY, until the time is right. Change is always welcome provided that it is ushered in with MODERATION by people with CALMER HEADS, than that shown by Our Most UNWELCOME VISITOR.

Let us hope that the shame heaped upon him for his exploits at the *Theatre Royale*, where his presence almost sparked a RIOT, and at *The Spread Eagle Inn*, where his actions brought about a BRAWL, might induce him to go back to London and LEAVE US IN PEACE.

*

It would seem that Shawcross and Murray were not the only spies and informants operating that night. News of the attacks on the Constables on White Moss, together with more lurid accounts of Hunt's antics in *The Spread Eagle Inn*, made the front pages of all the newspapers apart from *The Observer*, relegating Mr Macready's theatrical triumph to less prominent positions, buried on the inside next to appeals for information regarding missing cats and dogs. Although *The Mercury* rather wittily placed its review of the production alongside its Obituary Column.

'Is This the Death of Theatre As We Know It?'

All self-righteously ask this same question, before answering it themselves with an unequivocal hope that this may indeed be the case.

"When actions in the auditorium eclipse those that are on the stage, it is surely time to acknowledge that the game is up. When actors debase the forces of Law and Order in their crude pantomime, they are sinking to new lows of Moral Depravity, and this newspaper calls on the Good People of Manchester to boycott all future performances at this disreputable Whore House that goes by the name of the *Theatre Royale*, delivering their own verdict, which will be a true 'Measure for Measure'."

Reading this in bed the following morning beside the delightfully tousled head of a still-sleeping Miss Appleby, Mr Macready licks his lips in gratification.

"All publicity is good publicity," he says aloud. "Even *bad* publicity."

"*Especially* bad publicity," murmurs a waking Miss Appleby.

A sentiment echoed by Hunt over breakfast with his host Joseph Johnson, who is wringing his hands with anxiety.

"*Prescott's* is in the right of it," declares Hunt.

Joseph looks up in alarm.

"Monday next shall indeed witness the most numerous meeting ever to take place in Great Britain. I'll stake my fee on it."

*

The Dog star is so bright that Abner can study it with the naked eye, even with sight as compromised as his. Not only is Sirius by far the brightest star in the night sky, at this time of the year, its heliacal rising enables him to see it briefly, but brilliantly, when it appears above the eastern horizon at dawn, just before sunrise.

He has also taken to studying it at night, through his Dollond & Aitcheson telescope, when he is not losing himself in the Perseids. Dominating the constellation of Canis Major, just below Orion, it pulses in a series of concentric rings which glitter so brightly that sometimes he fancies he sees a twin, a second star hiding in its shadow, but he knows he would require a telescope of much greater magnification than currently exists to verify this. It is rather like when looking in a mirror, which he has to do daily in order to place soothing drops in his tired and scarred eye tissue, he sees, as his vision blurs and clears then blurs again, a tiny fleck within the iris, a flaw, which somehow defines him, which he would never be without, and which has still to be explored.

10

16th August

"I was busy all morning," says Benjamin Halsinger, "up with the lark, helping prepare for the party to celebrate the golden wedding anniversary of my parents-in-law. It was all hands to the pump, let me tell you."

"I was up even earlier," says Rachel, his wife, "before dawn, seeing to the food. We had more than forty coming for lunch. Including Count Rothschild. The whole household was in a flurry.

"Fortunately he arrived early," adds Benjamin. "The crowds were already large, he told us. Any later and he might not have got through."

"I never left the house all day," says Rachel.

"*Baruch hashem*."

"Thank the Lord."

"Mercifully my nephew Giles had returned home the previous day," says Edward Holme, in his first floor lodgings on Peter Street.

"I would have been fearful for his safety if he'd been travelling on this day. All the roads into Manchester were crammed with people, I understand, trying to make their way in. It would have been impossible for anyone attempting to travel in the opposite direction. I was relieved to be alone. I looked down upon a surging sea of humanity below my window, so many I could not count them. As they seethed below they reminded me of the story related by Mrs Philips the other evening, when her son's collection of flies escaped during the Earthquake of almost half a century ago. They were impossible to distinguish one from another. But if one looked closely, as I found myself doing as the tide of people continued to flow past, I began to discern differences – in race, ethnicity and gender – all of them individual and unique within this teeming mass, and I began to picture them as dioramas for our Museum when we open it."

"The inmates were especially restless," says Dr John Ferriar, Senior Physician of The Manchester Royal Infirmary and Keeper of the Lunatic Asylum.

"Especially those in Bedlam. Maybe there's something in this nonsense about the dog days after all. Maybe the alignment of the stars produces a pattern in the temperature that affects the patients' humours. I prefer not to think so. Old wives' tales. They claim to be seeing ghosts, receiving visitations, having presentiments and forewarnings of disaster. Poppycock. These are nothing more than optical illusions, as I pointed out in my *Essay Towards a Theory of Apparitions*. And yet... My patients do appear to be especially sensitive when it comes to the anticipation of a calamitous event. They sense when a storm is imminent. They become excitable, agitated. They rattle the bars of their cells, they pace anxiously and obsessively up and down, they howl, they scream. This morning they began to do so just before sunrise, just as Sirius was clearly visible above the horizon."

"There was great fear in the Settlement," says Brother Pohlman.

"We held a vigil of silent prayer throughout the night," says Sister Caroline.

"I arranged for extra watchmen to guard the gates," says Brother John. "We had heard that contingents of people..."

"... numbering many thousands..." interrupts his wife.

"... would be passing by from Ashton. It were rumoured

544

they carried pikestaffs," says John. "It were a necessary precaution."

"I would have liked to have walked with them," says Brother Pohlman, "to listen to what Mr Hunt had to say, but the Elders would not have countenanced such a suggestion. I have already been reprimanded for taking too keen an interest in the matters of the world."

"We shall be safe here in Fairfield," says John. "We have each other an' we have the Lamb."

"I wonder if Amos an' Agnes'll be walking wi' 'em," thinks Caroline sadly. She does not give voice to these thoughts but keeps them locked away in her heart.

"A great evil is being visited upon the world," say the Elders, "which is why we shun it, removing ourselves to our own Eden, here by the waters of the Tame."

"Fairfield is a fortress," says John.

"Sometimes," thinks Caroline, "I think I might be Lot's wife, turned to a pillar o' salt as I looked back on what I left behind. No. Not salt. Stone."

"I was delivering His Majesty's mail," says Billy. "As I always do. Rain or shine. It's my duty. I were not going to let t' crowds prevent me. But I began even earlier than usual, so that they might impede me less."

"We decided we'd go to t' Meeting," says Agnes. "If Amos hadn't been on t' march o' the Blanketeers, we may never 'ave found Jack again. An' Jack seems so much better now. 'E still in't speaking, I'm not sure 'e ever will again, but 'e listens, 'e responds, 'e smiles. When Ham an' Shem come round to tell us they were going – with Samuel Bamford's Middleton contingent – we thought, why not?"

She unfurls a long, thin scarf.

"It'll be a day out," she continues. "It'll be good for us to do summat together, as a family. We'll put sprigs o' laurel in our hair. I'll make a picnic."

She pauses, remembering.

"The night before, we stayed up all night making a banner. Amos on 'is loom, me knitting t' words into t' scarf that we could attach later, Jack bangin' out a regular beat on 'is drum. The three of us in tune, in time, the different rhythms clicking an' clacking, rollin' an' clatterin' into a single, unified pulse."

"But soon t' crowds became so thick I could no longer make me way between 'em," continues Billy.

"I 'ad to keep looping back on meself, doublin' an' redoublin' me tracks, getting' nowhere. I ducked into a side street behind *The Britons' Protection*. A great roar rose up from inside. I poked me 'ead round t' door to see what it were. Members of t' MYC were tankin' 'emselves up. I din't like t' look, or t' sound of it."

"I was visiting my good friend, the Reverend James Norris, on Mount Street," says the Reverend Edmund Stanley, Vicar of Alderley Edge.

"I had no idea there was to be a Public Meeting. I arrived at Mount Street just as James did, accompanied by all the rest of the Magistrates, and a rather frightening looking fellow with a bull neck, who later I learned was Deputy Constable Nadin. They all appeared to be terribly worried. But I said to them, 'Look – there are so many women and children among their ranks. They are the guarantors of their peaceable intentions. You need have no fears'. But they looked at me witheringly as if I knew not of what I spoke."

"I finished t' rest o' me delivery as fast as I could," says Billy, "then 'eaded straight for t' Meeting Ground. I wanted to try an' find Richard an' Paul, me brothers, warn 'em to be careful. I were 'oping they 'adn't persuaded Susannah an' Ginny to go wi' 'em."

"I was looking forward to hearing Mr Hunt speak," says Ginny. "We watched him the other night on his way to the theatre. He looked so handsome. He saw us from his barouche. I swear he looked at me directly, and blew me a kiss."

"I was making my way back along the Dean's Gate," says Abner. "Or trying to."

He polishes his glasses vigorously.

"It was barely a hundred yards from Mr Dalton's house to our own on Brazenose Street, but it might have been a hundred miles, for the crowds were so numerous, and all of them coming towards me, that I simply couldn't make my way through."

"We were worried about Abner," says Rachel. "He was meant to have arrived hours ago."

"But he is so hapless," says Benjamin, not unkindly, "so unworldly."

"I had been helping Mr Dalton all night with his titration experiments," says Abner.

"He was slowly adding the solution of a known concentration – Sodium Hydroxide – into the known volume of another solution of unknown concentration, until the reaction reached a point of neutralisation. Typically this would be revealed by a colour change, from blue to red. He was also experimenting with precipitation titration, where a solid will form from the mixture of the two solutions and settle at the base of the tube, sometimes becoming so cloudy that it is not possible to measure or calculate the effects until it has completely cleared. A litmus test."

"I overheard the Boroughreeve confiding most anxiously with the Deputy Constable," says Reverend Stanley.

"Is it not possible for the Special Constables to issue the warrant for Hunt's arrest?" asks Sir Edward Clayton in the Upstairs Room on Mount Street, as he watches the enormous crowds in growing dismay.

"Never," says Joe Nadin, "not with the numbers we have currently on the streets. Not with ten times that number. Not with all the Special Constables in England."

"Can it not be executed without the intervention of military force?" asks Sir Edward a second time, breathing in as deeply as he can.

"It cannot," says Nadin, his face set hard as stone.

"Then you shall have military force," says Sir Edward. "We mustn't sacrifice the lives of the Constables."

"I had not been back to this part of Manchester for fifteen years," says Mercy Chant. "I never thought to again. When I walked away from Matthew after the end of my house arrest, it felt like stepping off a cliff. 'Leap and a net will appear,' my mother used to say back in Barbados, and I believed that when she said it. Less so in the years that followed. But as I walked away from Matthew, her words came back to me. I felt so free that I didn't think twice about it. I would not be going back to those dark days after Monsieur Talleyrand left for the last time. It was a giddying sensation. I leapt, opened up a parasol as I did so, shut my eyes and merely floated, oh so gently, back to the ground. When I opened them again, I found I was in Newton Heath. People on the streets were speaking French all around me. Quite freely and openly. It was only a matter of days before I found myself on the doorstep of Monsieur and Madame Robidoux again. They had moved there from Levenshulme after Talleyrand had returned to France, back to where the Huguenots had first arrived and settled in Manchester, to establish a new enclave of lace and language, poetry and protest, trying to hold onto that strain of idealism in the early days of the Revolution, after the storming of the Bastille, before it became tainted by Robespierre and the Terror, Napoleon and imperialism. I quickly resumed my old life with them and forgot all about Matthew. When we heard about the Meeting, we felt we had to go. Elijah Dixon had told us about it, and his wife Martha. Elijah had been one of the Blanketeers. But he was arrested in Stockport, then taken in irons to London for his part in it, imprisoned in Bridewell, then released without charge. 'Let's march to St Peter's Field together,' he said, and we were swept along by his fervour and enthusiasm."

"I make matches now," says Elijah, laughing grimly. "Lucifer matches. A bargain with the Devil."

"Nothing will happen," says Madame Robidoux, "*comme d'habitude*, you will see. There will be no storming of the New Bailey. It will be – how do you say? – a storm in a tea cup."

"I wondered if I might see Matthew there," says Mercy finally.

"But we shall wear the cap of liberty *toutefois, n'est-ce pas? Le bonnet rouge.*

"Strike it. Watch it spark and flare," says Elijah.

"I had finished knitting t' scarf," says Agnes, "wi' t' words to be stitched to t' banner."

"*Unity is Strength*," says Amos.

"I began to sing," says Agnes, "to t' rhythm o' t' loom an' drum. Jack were so 'appy 'e started to dance."

"The loom goes click and the loom goes clack
The shuttle flies forward and then flies back...

The yarn is made into cloth at last
The ends of the weft they are made quite fast..."

"I looked out of the window," says Mr Edward Holme, "and tried again to see if I could tell the people apart. I looked closer. I began to see even more individual differences, light and dark, as they passed from sun into shade and then back into the light again, men and women of all races, and children too."

He looks once more at the range of peppered moths collected by Leigh Philips, which he had been showing his nephew just a few days before.

"I have observed in nature," he says, "that hybrid varieties are generally stronger and suit most situations better. It is the phenomenon known as heterosis, wherein the progeny of diverse varieties of species, or crosses between species, exhibit greater mass, speed of development and fertility than both parents."

He returns to the window to watch this crowd of many colours. "A Cabinet of Curiosities," he says. "This gives me great hope."

"A time of great hope indeed," says Count Rothschild, on being invited to propose the toast to Reuben and Leah Halsinger.

"Change can be frightening," he continues. "Uncertainty always is. But we have learned to be patient over the years. Caution and risk. The eternal balancing act. When I was still living here in Manchester, on Brown Street, I went one evening to the Michaelmas Fair in Acresfield. You were there too, Benjamin, I remember, and Rachel. *La Funambola*, the great tightrope walker, gave her final performance. She walked on a wire slung between St Ann's Church and The Exchange. Those twin pillars of Religion and Commerce. So high up was she that you could not see the wire she walked upon, just her, putting one foot carefully in front of the other. It was as if she was walking on the very air itself. Such high risk. But such rich rewards when she reached the other side. We have been walking a similar wire for centuries. Sometimes we have fallen off. But so long as we have kept our faith and trusted in what we believed in, someone has come along to help us back up again. These are difficult times right now here in Manchester, and what happens here today may well affect the whole of England in the years to come. But we will be ready for whatever comes, for, like Reuben and Leah, we have built our house on strong foundations. To Reuben and Leah."

The shuttle flies forward and then flies back.

"A fortress."

"A cabinet of curiosities."

"A titration."

"The dog star rising."

"A tightrope."

"Then falling."

"A precipitation."

"Out of the shade, into the sun."

"A storm is coming."

"You need have no fears."

"*Baruch hashem*."

"A storm in a tea cup."

"He blew me a kiss."

"Stir the sediment until it clears."

"A mixing together."

"Unity is Strength."

"*Un bonnet rouge.*"

"A pillar of salt."

"Risk and reward."

"A rhythm, a pulse."

"A litmus test."

*

Pity says nothing.

She is up before all of them. She works through the night, stitching the lace place-mats, sewing each moth carefully upon its allotted leaf of laurel. She does not finish until dawn. She stretches her arms above her head, rubs her eyes, pushes back the chair she has been sitting in, and stands up. A young rat is investigating the ashes of yesterday's fire which have not yet been raked out in readiness for the one that will be built anew this morning for preparing the food for the feast. She watches it raise its nose curiously, scenting a change in the air.

Rachel comes into the kitchen. She is carrying her youngest child, Ephraim, who is still a baby. She stands beside Pity and picks up the last of the lace place-mats, which she holds up to the light, then looks back towards Pity and nods.

"Where did you learn how to do this?" she asks admiringly.

Pity shrugs. She doesn't know. It's just something she has picked up, along with the rest of her life.

Ephraim begins to skrike.

"Here," says Rachel. "Can you take him for a while?"

Pity hoists the baby onto her arm and cradles him against her shoulder. Rachel watches her curiously.

"Have you ever had a child?" she asks.

Pity looks away, then shakes her head.

Rachel shoos the rat away from the grate, towards the back door, through which she ushers it out into the street. A pale golden light is climbing the sky.

"It's going to be another hot day," says Rachel, then comes

back inside. She cleans out the grate and re-lays it for the fresh fire. She screws spills of paper on the top, which she lights with a Dixon match, then blows on it to make sure it will catch. When it does, she takes the now quiet Ephraim back from Pity.

"Are you going to the Meeting on St Peter's Field today?" asks Rachel.

Pity shrugs.

"You can," says Rachel, "if you'd like to. You can have the rest of the day off. You deserve it," she adds, looking towards the place-mats. She places Ephraim into his basket, while she begins to chop the meat. "We're not opening the shop today, and my husband says the banks are staying shut too, and the Exchange. The whole of Manchester's going to the Meeting, it seems. Except us." She continues to chop.

Pity joins her and starts to scrub and peel the potatoes.

Rachel places a hand upon her arm. "No," she says. "You've done enough already. Go home, while you still can, while the streets are still quiet. Get some sleep."

Pity nods. She wipes her hands on the front of her skirt, pauses briefly to crouch beside Ephraim and stroke him once beneath his chin, which is something he adores, then steps outside.

The Dog Star is glittering in the sky just above the horizon. She watches it fade with the rising of the sun as she makes her way back to Jem in their house on Hanging Ditch, who she knows will be waiting for her. She thinks she will go after all to this Meeting that everyone is talking about. Perhaps Jem will come with her? He will if she makes it plain to him that she wants him to. And she does want him to, she decides.

She sees the smoke rising from the chimney of the Halsingers' home on Brazenose Street as the fire takes hold. The light continues to grow in the eastern sky, turning unmistakeably from blue to red, the sun a blistering cap of liberty.

*

As Pity makes her way back home in the quiet, early-morning streets, all the churches in Manchester begin to toll the hour.

Six o'clock.

One Thomas Horrall, Assistant Surveyor of the Paving of the Town, is marshalling a team of scavengers – children mostly – to remove every stone, brick, piece of glass, metal, or any other possible missile, from St Peter's Field and the streets adjoining it. He does so upon the instructions of the Magistrates under the watchful eye of Matthew, who walks in the footsteps of the scavengers making sure that nothing is missed. Three hours later, when the Stockport contingent of marchers is the first to arrive, led by the Reverend Joseph Harrison, they will comment on the verdant smoothness of the ground, and thank the Civic Authorities for their thoughtfulness in accommodating the place so comfortably for the women and children to spread their picnics upon it.

"If a stone is thrown this day," remarks Matthew darkly to Nadin afterwards, gently massaging the pulse that flickers at the side of his temple, "it will only prove what we feared – that the crowds have come already armed and primed for mischief."

"Just let 'em try," answers Nadin, cracking the knuckles of his hands.

Having overseen the clearance of the ground, Matthew heads back to his Felt Factory on Oldham Street, which he reaches as the church bells chime a quarter to eight. The streets are starting to get busier now, but not, he notices, with people heading for their shift at his Works. He has recently moved over to continuous twenty-four hour production divided into three eight-hour shifts – eight in the morning until four in the afternoon, four in the afternoon until midnight, and then midnight until eight in the morning. The steam-powered looms are never switched off. They rumble permanently.

But not this morning.

554

An unearthly silence hangs over the town. He does not normally arrive himself at such an early hour. Not that he's a late riser. Far from it. But usually he has other things he prefers to do at this time. Like his paperwork as a Justice of the Peace. He keeps his records meticulously and he generally likes to be the first in his chamber at the Court Leet.

But not this morning.

This morning he'll be damned if he's not at the Factory in time for one shift to end and another to begin. Except that he knows there will be no such changeover on this day. He has – most generously in his view – informed his workforce that if they do decide, quite unlawfully, to withdraw their labour for the day, they will suffer no other punishment than the loss of a day's pay. They will not lose their jobs – although he is perfectly within his rights to sack them, he tells them. He makes certain that they all of them know this. He posts up notices both inside and outside the Factory for those who can read. He instructs his two foremen to make sure that everyone is made aware of his *largesse*, and he announces it personally himself. He even offers a bonus for anyone loyal enough to turn up for their shifts on this day. Not that he expects any of them to. A kind of madness has taken over the town – dog days indeed – with words like 'unity' and 'solidarity' being bandied about as if they were the litany for a new religion, which in a sense he supposes they are. He has grown quite accustomed to hearing these parroted genuflections being trotted out meaninglessly, much as one says 'Amen' at the end of the Lord's Prayer. 'Give us this day our daily bread.'

But not this morning.

St Peter's Field will be their cathedral today and Henry Hunt their preacher. The body and blood of Christ. Matthew emits a ball of phlegm as he turns into the Factory Yard and watches it sizzle on the hard baked earth. 'Forgive us our trespasses as we forgive those that trespass against us.'

But not this morning.

555

Waiting for him at the Factory Gates are Richard and Paul Robinson. Twins as alike as two peas in a pod. Matthew has never been able to tell them apart and nor has he needed to. He simply calls whichever one he sees "Robinson". They are his foremen. They still operate under the old twelve-hour stints, so that there is a smoothness of transition from one shift to the next, with one twin handing over to the other midway through. They are each good men, as far as Matthew is able to judge such matters. They maintain the looms in perfect working order, they ensure the Factory runs efficiently – and profitably – at all times, and they have never missed a day's work, either of them.

And not this morning.

They both greet him in unison as he reaches them.

"Good morning, Mr Oldham," they say.

"Is it?" snarls Matthew. "A good morning?"

"No, sir, it is not," says Richard. "Nobody turned up for t' midnight shift."

"And nobody this mornin'," adds Paul.

"As you can hear," says Richard unnecessarily, "we've 'ad to turn off t' looms"

Matthew says nothing. It is after all exactly as he was expecting. He looks at his two foremen, who wait patiently for him to issue their next instructions. Now he comes to look at them more closely, he can see that there is in fact a difference between them. One is slightly taller than the other. But which? And unless he were to see them again together, knowing this would still not help him identify which was which. He notes the way they finish each other's sentences, mirror each other's gestures. Do they share the same thoughts, he wonders? Do they feel incomplete by themselves? Only half a person? Or are they quite independent of one another? Do they want the same futures? Lust after the same women? (*Share* the same women perhaps? Stand in for one another?) Do they fight, quarrel, argue? Are they rivals? Or best friends? Do they ever want

556

what the other desires? Or do they only want each other to be happy? Do they feel separate, complete, fulfilled when by themselves, alone? Or unfinished, bereft, as if a part of them is missing? A limb, a sense of who they really are…?

Matthew thinks such thoughts often.

But not this morning.

This morning he merely turns to them and says, "Thank you. You may go. Consider today a holiday. I will pay you each a bonus for your inconvenience. And your loyalty."

"Yes, sir. Thank you, sir," they chorus back, each of them touching their hats as they hurry round the corner.

Once out of sight – and, they hope, out of earshot – they bite on their fists to prevent themselves laughing out loud.

"Come on, brother," says Richard. "Let's mek a day of it."

"Ay," says Paul. "Our Ginny's mekkin' a picnic."

They run together down the street.

Matthew looks around the vast cathedral of his Factory, with its silent looms as Stations to the Cross. The vast, single-storey weaving shed, with its cast-iron mules, unmoving and unpopulated, caught in the rays of a northern light streaming through the window at one end, dust devils dancing in each beam, like an altar, with the black boiler opposite, like a kind of giant font, which on most days will glow red with the heat of the steam.

But not this morning.

Matthew turns on his heels and strides purposefully towards *The Star Inn*, where the Civic Authorities have agreed they will convene, before relocating to the home of Reverend Norris on Mount Street, from where they will have a complete uninterrupted overview of the Meeting Ground, and from where they will be able to direct operations. Matthew feels lighter and clearer than he can ever remember, certain of purpose and relishing the day to come. He has no need of the extra fortification to his courage that the proprietor of *The Star Inn* will try to press upon him. He wants nothing to stand in the

557

way of what he feels his whole life has been leading him towards. Not even that still quiet voice that tries to make itself heard sometimes over all the other noise that's in his head.

Like a lost twin.

'Deliver us from evil.'

Evil. It is a word both sides of this political debate the whole of Manchester is engulfed in use to describe the actions of their opponents. Each accuses the other of committing it to further their own ends, along with other words – treachery, betrayal, tyranny, oppression – all of which fan the flames of their own holy purpose, for each claims to have God on their side.

Matthew wonders about this a lot, certain as he is in the rightfulness of his own cause and zealous in his pursuit of it. He is not a particularly religious man himself, not really. He attends church of course – appearances do matter and in any case attendance promotes all manner of business opportunities – but he frequently finds his mind wandering during the minister's sermons. He prefers the plainness of chapels to the marble and stained glass of churches. Their lack of adornment appeals to that streak of self-denial in him that he is quite happy to acknowledge. But Church equals Tory and Tory equals power. For the moment. He is all too aware that this might change. The Dissenters and Non-Conformists outnumber the Anglicans by two to one in Manchester, many of them mill and factory owners like Matthew. Like his father was. His adoptive father. He wonders whether the realisation that he was adopted, was not in fact who he thought he was, has led him to take the opposite positions in almost every aspect of his life to those held by his father. Is it *his* voice he hears buzzing away in the back of his brain so often like an insistent fly? No. He thinks not. His father was not a man to criticise. He was much more likely to say nothing at all, but let his silence articulate his disappointment. A silence that pervades in his house still today, which Matthew inhabits alone and does everything he can to avoid it being disturbed. More like a monk's cell than a home. Yes. He may not be especially devout but he can well imagine a life of abstinence, of self-flagellation, a practice he still indulges in, but not before a cross bearing a suffering Christ, but before the painting of Mercy and the caged bird, or the framed cotton shawl that was Lavinia's. Icon and relic.

What has made him who he is, he thinks? Nature? Nurture? Was Locke right, he wonders, when he spoke of a *tabula rasa*, a blank slate that we are all of us born with, free to shape and define who we become based on our own thoughts and experiences? Or are we the sum of all we inherit, the innate ideas Descartes insists we come into the world already born with? Matthew recognises the contradictions in these two positions which he exhibits in himself, favouring the independence of thought put forward by Locke's emphasis on empiricism, not just a blank slate waiting to be filled, but one that he can wipe clean whenever he chooses, yet at the same time clinging to the *status quo* of the Cartesian premise that all knowledge emanates from God, immutable and unchanging. To challenge that authority is to challenge God therefore, and so what the Radicals are calling for with their demands for change goes against nature, against the divine.

And yet...

Matthew recognises that he is playing both sides against the middle here for his own ends. Has he not personified in his own reinvention of himself since his father died Locke's *tabula rasa*? He has effectively wiped the slate clean many times in order to justify his own actions and desires. He takes solace from that other famous maxim of Descartes. *Cogito ergo sum.* I think, therefore I am. And his belief that nothing comes from nothing. *Ex nihilo nihil fit.*

But if not from nothing, from where? As he inflicts stroke after stroke of the whip upon his back, he asks himself that question over and over again.

But not this morning.

No. Today he feels an excitement he has not felt since he was nine years old and Fanny was taking him to see Mr Sadler's Balloon Flight. It is a kind of euphoria, an exaltation, a sense of rapture.

He is at one with himself.

Amos steps away from the loom. He hands the finished woven banner to Agnes, who starts at once to stitch the scarf on to it, with the words she has embroidered earlier. *Unity is Strength.* Are they a unit now, wonders Amos? Not complete. Never complete. Not without Daisy. But strong? Certainly stronger than they have been, since their midnight escape from the Settlement when the Lot decided against them. Their strength was so pure that night, so convinced were they of the rightness of what they were doing. But it has been tested many times since then. The years of wandering in the brickfields where they lost Daisy. The separation while he burrowed in the mines of Bradford, where he lost the Roman coin Agnes had given him in lieu of a wedding ring, the same coin given to her by her brother James, which they had found beside the Elton Brook, and who knew how it had first got there? Then the misery of Dimity Court, followed by the silent years when they thought Jack had been lost at Waterloo. And in a way a part of him was, thinks Amos, looking at him now, holding the kaleidoscope up to his eye, trying to catch the light of the Dog Star as it climbs above the eastern sky. Amos wonders what it is his son looks for there, in the ever-changing patterns of the glass crystals that he, Amos, had placed there himself when he first helped his adoptive father make it – John from whom he has been estranged these many years. How did his rescuer become his betrayer?

He looks across to where Agnes sits stitching. In her hurry to get it finished before Ham and Shem arrive to accompany them on their march to Manchester this morning, she pricks her finger on the needle and pauses to suck it. She catches Amos watching her and smiles. A happy, open smile. One he thought never to see again when Jack did not come home for so long. But which has never been far from her lips ever since he did. She looks at him now, as he stares deep into the kaleidoscope, and smiles again. She and Amos rarely look in it now. It has become Jack's entirely.

Jack has still not uttered a word since he came home two years ago. Who knows what horrors he endured at Waterloo that have locked him so deep inside himself? He dreams about these things, they are sure, for they hear him sometimes in the night, whimpering, like a dog. But these are the only sounds he ever makes. Not recognisable speech. Not even wordless sounds attempting explanation.

As Amos looks upon his son's moon-like face, what does he see? Traces of himself? Yes – and of Agnes too. But also someone decidedly other. The same ghost Amos has sometimes glimpsed when catching sight of his own reflection unexpectedly – in a pool of water, or a shard of glass – the impression of somebody else looking back at him. But then he will smear the glass, or stir the water with a stick, and the ghost will disappear, and he will see only himself.

Ham and Shem arrive as a red sun rises and the Dog Star fades from sight.

Jack puts down the kaleidoscope and looks up at his cousins, who have always been heroes to him, haloed by the sun's corona.

"Are you ready?" they say. "We need to be on t' road if we're to meet Sam Bamford's Middleton contingent at Heywood."

"We're ready," says Agnes, snapping the thread as she finishes the last stitch. She holds up the banner for her cousins to inspect.

"*Unity is Strength*," says Ham approvingly. "That about captures it."

"Come on, Jack-the-Lad," says Shem, ruffling Jack's hair. "We need a drummer boy to beat out a fast rhythm if we're to make it in time."

Jack, beaming, begins to play *The Assembly*, the beat that summons the soldiers to report to their rendezvous point, to muster behind their colours. Ham and Shem hoist the banner aloft between them. Amos and Agnes hold hands and march in step behind them. The sun continues to climb the sky.

By nine o'clock tens of thousands are converging on Manchester from all points of the compass.

The contingents from the high fells of Lancashire, led by the self-appointed 'Doctor' Healey, from Diggle, Delph, Denshaw and Dob Cross, from Rishworth, Ripponden, Slathwaite and Dovestone, from Quick Edge, Carrbrook, Wessenden and Winscar, come down from the moors, carrying black flags with the inscription *'Equal Representation or Death'* painted upon them in a stark white.

At Royton a large female section leads the way carrying banners of green and purple, topped with red caps of liberty.

At Oldham John Knight gives the signal for columns of marchers to swing in orderly fashion from off the Green where they have assembled to make their way to Manchester via Failsworth and Chadderton, picking up so many followers that by the time they reach St Peter's Field their contingent alone will be more than ten thousand strong.

And at Middleton Samuel Bamford waits until all the separate contingents from the outlying villages and hamlets of Back o' t' Brow, Barrowfield, Boarshaw and Birch, Alkrington, Bowlee, Blackley and Tongue, Hopwood, Heabers, Heatons and Higginshaw, have all arrived at the muster point beside the River Irk, which they will follow all the way in to Manchester. But before they set off he gathers them together for one last rallying call.

"Friends an' neighbours," he begins, "I have a few words to relate. You will march off this place quietly. Not to insult anyone but rather to take insult. I do not think there will be any disturbance. There is no fear, for this day is our own. Therefore before we set off on this great journey together, let us each cut a sprig of laurel from t' bushes growing so wild an' free along the river bank an' weave from them garlands o' victory to wear in our hair. An' then, in t' words o' Mr Hunt, whose speech at midday we are all so eager to hear for ourselves, joining wi' our brothers an' sisters from all around this great metropolis we call home, let us march towards it, armed only wi' our self-approving consciences."

A great shout goes up from the throng of many thousands listening to him, followed by the blowing of a fanfare on a bugle, after which they all begin to march south in tight military columns with order and discipline, high spirits and good humour.

At Heywood they are joined by several thousand more – men, women and children who have walked there in dozens of smaller, separate groups from Bolton and Bury, Walshaw and Whitefield, Shuttleworth and Stubbins, Tottington and Elton – Amos, Agnes, Ham, Shem and Jack among them. Jack falls in step, striking up the *Beat for Orders*. Samuel Bamford gives him a rousing cheer. Jack mistakes him for his old Captain, Josiah Blacker, and immediately quickens his pace, taking up the insistent beat of *The General*, which gives notice to all troops to be ready to march.

"By the left," booms Bamford, "to Victory!"

The laurel-garlanded army sets off as one.

"With Henry Hunt we'll go, my boys
With Henry Hunt we'll go
We'll mount the Cap o' Liberty
In spite o' Nady Joe…"

Someone else who has been up since first light is Colonel L'Estrange.

Like Matthew he has been watching Thomas Horrall clearing the Meeting Ground of all its stones and bricks and shards of glass to ensure a smooth and safe surface for the people to gather upon when they arrive – which they are already beginning to do.

Right now he is reading yet another letter that has arrived from Major-General Sir John Byng, delivered by Billy, who stands to one side as the Colonel studies its contents, in case there is a reply to be delivered or dispatched.

Sir, it says

I want you to know that I have the utmost faith in your capabilities. I delegate the supervision of the day to you entirely. You have my complete confidence that you will do a most thorough and professional job.

My one piece of advice to you would be to avoid at all cost the use of firearms should you find it necessary to disperse the crowd hastily – an action that I do not believe will be required in any case. The crowds will have come to listen to Mr Hunt deliver a speech, possibly to pass a series of resolutions, not to act upon these should any of them urge insurrection. I trust you to judge the mood of the day as it unfolds.

You should draw up your troops therefore as a necessary precaution, which I sincerely hope you have no cause to deploy except for the reasons of crowd control, ensuring an orderly arrival at and departure from the agreed Meeting Ground.

Let us hope that the fine weather we are promised will keep the people in a happy and a carefree temper, regarding the day more as a public holiday than a call to arms.

But should events turn unpleasant I am certain you will be
ready to do whatever is needed.

Yours etc
Sir John Byng, Major-General
Commander, Northern Division, British Armed Forces

"No reply," says L'Estrange to the waiting Billy, who touches the peak of his cap with his forefinger before continuing with his rounds.

The Colonel mentally goes over his plans for the umpteenth time.

Six hundred men from the Cavalry of the 15th Hussars are to be deployed in Lower Mosley Street. Another six hundred from the 31st Foot, his own regiment, veterans of Waterloo, are to be concealed in Brazenose Street, with a thousand men from the 88th Foot waiting in ambush in George Street. In spite of the Major-General's advice to avoid firearms, the Colonel has instructed Major Dyneley to have the Royal Horse Artillery primed and ready with their two six-pounder cannons on Great Bridgewater Street lying in wait if needed behind the line of Cavalry.

And then there are the four hundred troops from the MYC, the Manchester & Salford Yeomanry Cavalry, who, at the insistence of the Magistrates, particularly Matthew Oldham, who L'Estrange can see now, supervising the clearing of the Ground, are to be used as the vanguard of any operation, the first line of attack, a phrase the Colonel found most disagreeable. It is essential in his view, something he has learned from the Major-General, that the military should not be perceived as the aggressors if any confrontation should arise. The MYC are to muster in Byrom Street under the command of the former Boroughreeve Sir Hugh Hornby Birley, who has so far not revealed any willingness to conform to any overall plan the Colonel has tried to put forward, claiming that he, and he alone, has sole authority over the deployment of what were essentially amateur, untrained volunteers. In addition four hundred Special Constables under the command of Joe Nadin will assemble in St James's Square, over whom the Colonel has no jurisdiction whatsoever.

L'Estrange frowns. The Constables have been designated the role of lining the route that Hunt's barouche will take, to keep order in the surrounding streets, and to act as stewards lining the four sides of St Peter's Field once the Meeting gets under way. Hopefully their presence alone will be enough to deter any potential troublemakers among the more than sixty thousand people it is estimated might attend. But if any trouble does occur, L'Estrange will be ready for them.

The MYC are the fly in the ointment. He knows that he does not carry the weight to keep Birley in line as the Major-General could, despite Sir John's kind words to the contrary. His plan is to form a ring of steel around St Peter's Field with Cavalry detachments mounted on horseback armed with sabres. This will be the speediest and most efficient way of dispersing the crowds – but only if necessary, to quote from Sir John's letter. The Infantrymen behind will only be used if they have a serious riot on their hands, which the Colonel hopes to God will not be the case.

Standing to one side of him is a young Subaltern – Douglas Rich. He is nineteen years old. He joined the 31st Foot as a Drummer Boy when the regiment returned from Waterloo and has stayed on ever since, earning his stripes through hard work and devotion. L'Estrange saw promise in him, regarding him as something of a blue-eyed boy, and recently appointed him as his personal valet. He calls him over and Douglas is at his side in an instant.

"Yes, sir?"

"I want you to take this message to the Cheshire Yeomanry." He hastily scribbles a note, which he places into the Subaltern's hot and sticky hand. "They're currently awaiting orders on Sale Moor, five and a half miles to the south. Tell them to make their way here immediately, where they are to report to Lieutenant Jolliffe in St John Street and await further orders."

"Yes, sir."

"But first ride over to Byrom Street to let the Lieutenant know to expect them."

Douglas leaps onto his horse, untethers it from one of the railings beside St Peter's Field, and gallops away.

What L'Estrange does not say is that he has called the Cheshire Yeomanry up as a possible replacement for the MYC, whose readiness he doubts. The Lieutenant will know this without needing to be told. He is a man of perception and discretion and will know how to integrate them if necessary without Birley even being aware.

As soon as young Douglas has ridden away, L'Estrange decides he will do a final round of his troops and check they understand their instructions. He will begin with the MYC. He knows where he will find them. Not on Byrom Street, where the main body should be, nor in Pickford's Yard, off Portland Street, where their reserve should be, but in *The Britons' Protection*, where doubtless Sir Hugh Hornby Birley will be plying them with drink, either to provide them with the courage they might need for the day ahead, or to prove to them what a jolly fine fellow he is.

The ring of steel, thinks, Colonel L'Estrange as he rides towards them. The ring of steel.

On St Peter's Field, where the Stockport contingent led by the Reverend Joseph Harrison is now just arriving, boisterous and triumphant, taking up their places close to the hustings that are just being erected for when Mr Hunt will arrive later, various stallholders, fruit sellers and tinkers are setting up for what they expect will be an excellent day's business. A ballad singer is standing by a pole on which various songs and broadsheets are attached. He takes out a pair of spoons and begins to beat out a repetitive, mechanical rhythm on them, a rhythm that is soon taken up by the tinkers and stallholders using pots and pans, knives and forks, as the ballad singer starts to sing.

"Since cast iron is now all the rage
And scarce anything's now made without it
As I live in this cast iron age
I mean to say something about it..."

The Magistrates make their way from *The Star Inn* to the home of the Reverend Norris on Mount Street, from where they will be able to look out over the whole of St Peter's Field. They arrive just in time to see Lieutenant Douglas Rich galloping south, the rhythm of his horse's hooves matching that of the song being sung below their window.

"Here's cast iron coffins and carts
Cast iron bridges and boats
Corn factors with cast iron hearts
That I'd hang up in cast iron coats..."

With the exception of Matthew, who positively skips up the stairs to the upstairs room which will be their headquarters for the rest of the day, they all appear nervous and agitated.

"Everything in hand, Mr Nadin?" asks the Boroughreeve.

"Just as we planned it, Sir Edward," replies the Deputy Constable. "We'll be ready for 'em. You need have no worries on that score."

"But I do worry," says the Reverend Norris. "We are such easy targets up here."

At that moment there is a loud knocking on the front door below. Norris almost leaps from his skin at the sound but Matthew bounds down in a matter of just a few strides. He opens the door to find a rather perplexed vicar standing on the front step, vigorously polishing his spectacles.

"Good morning," he says. "Reverend Stanley of Alderley Edge. I am expected, I believe. Have I come at a bad time?"

"Not at all, Reverend," says Matthew with a mischievous glint in his eye. "I'm sure your presence is exactly the tonic for Mr Norris's somewhat shattered nerves."

"Edmund? Is that you?" calls an increasingly anxious Reverend Norris from upstairs. "Did you not get my letter? Today is not convenient at all, dear friend. Still, now that you're here, you'll have to take us as you find us, I fear."

Introductions are swiftly made. It is at once apparent that the Reverend Stanley has no idea of what is about to take place.

"You must be the only person in Lancashire that doesn't then," says Nadin, squeezing past him on the stairs. "Excuse me, Reverend, I have business to attend to."

"Report back in an hour," calls out the Boroughreeve.

Once outside Nadin commandeers one of the Special Constables' horses to make his way to Smedley Cottage to check on the progress of Henry Hunt. As he gallops along Mount Street towards Cross Street, and from there along the Dean's Gate towards The Exchange, whose marble halls are strangely silent this morning, the singers and stallholders on St Peter's Field continue their song.

"So great is the fashion of late, sirs
We have cast iron hammers and axes
And if we may judge by their weight, sirs
We soon shall have cast iron taxes…"

Nadin reaches Smedley Cottage, where, in contrast with the deserted steps of The Exchange on Penniless Hill, an enormous crowd is gathering, waiting to greet Hunt when he begins his own journey to the Meeting Ground later.

Nadin smiles. He knows his foe. Hunt will be busy at his

ablutions, dousing himself with lotions and perfumes, puffed up like a turkey cock, wanting to look his best for his adoring followers. How he loathes the man. He digs his iron spurs hard into the sides of his horse as he forces a way through the crowd, not caring who might get in his way.

> *"Tommy Whalebone has grown quite a blade*
> *So dextrous and clever his hand is*
> *Swears he now shall have excellent trade*
> *Making cast iron stays for the dandies…"*

Nadin marches up to the front door of Smedley Cottage and raps it hard with his riding crop.

"Open up in the name of the Court Leet," he bellows.

A harassed Joseph Johnson opens his door.

"I do not recognise the Court Leet as representing the people of this town," he says.

"It is subject to annual election," says Nadin dismissively, "as you well know."

"But who gets to vote in these elections?" asks Johnson.

"*You* do, I imagine?" sneers Nadin.

"But not the vast majority of people who will be attending to Mr Hunt today," rejoins Johnson. "Who speaks for them?"

"Not your Mr Hunt. He speaks only for himself."

"And that is yet another point on which we must disagree, Mr Nadin. Now what is it you want? You knocked – rather peremptorily if I may say so – and I answered."

"Is Hunt ready?"

"I have no idea. I am his host, not his keeper."

"Then be so good as to inform him that he must follow the prescribed way from here to St Peter's Field as indicated by my Special Constables, who will be lining the route to make sure there are no incursions by the crowd that may prevent him from reaching his desired destination."

"You are most attentive, Mr Nadin. I shall pass on your

instructions but I cannot guarantee he will follow them."

"It would be better for him if he did."

"Is that a threat?"

"A piece of advice. My concern is only for his safety."

"In that case I suggest you stand down your Constables. Mr Hunt's followers will see he safely gets through – you need have no worries about that."

"Ah, but I do worry, Mr Johnson. It's my job to worry. I worry about all kinds of things. Today I'm chiefly worried about the health and safety of all these crowds who are a-clamouring to listen to Mr Hunt."

"I'm touched by your concern, Mr Nadin."

"As long as we understand one another."

"Oh, I think we do. Good day to you."

"And a good day to you, Mr Johnson."

Nadin wheels his horse around and forces his way back through the crowds, which are growing larger and louder by the minute, not caring who his whip alights on as he lashes it this way then that, horse or human.

Joseph closes the door and leans his back against it, breathing heavily. That was close, he thinks. The truth is, he has no idea when they will be setting off. Hunt has been an age getting himself ready upstairs. There are a number of women present there with him, supposedly assisting him with the finer points of *la mode elégante*, but each time he has attempted to enter, he has glimpsed him more *déshabillé* than *habillé*. Joseph sighs. Privately Hunt has been a disappointment to him – he has been vain, demanding, self-serving – but in public he has been nothing short of electrifying. His appearance before the New Bailey Prison the day he arrived, then his triumphant progress to the *Theatre Royale* two nights ago, were miracles of seizing the moment, object lessons in how to turn potential disaster into triumphant victory, and he has no doubts that his speech at St Peter's Field will go down in history as a major turning point in the struggle for Reform, but right this minute

571

he wishes the day were over already and his guest returned to London.

"Iron bedsteads have long been in use
With cast iron they now pave our streets
Each tailor has a cast iron goose
And soon we'll have cast iron sheets

We have cast iron husbands and wives
Who scold with such cast iron tongues, sirs
As we live in such cast iron lives
That's an end to our cast iron song, sirs..."

When Billy sees the consternation on the Colonel's face as the first contingent from Stockport arrives on the ground; when he witnesses the way in which the young Subaltern rides out of the town as if the hounds of hell were pursuing him, and then when he chances upon members of the MYC, drunk and carousing outside *The Britons' Protection*, he senses only trouble ahead.

He decides to abandon the rest of his deliveries for the day and hurries back to Bridge Street, hoping to intercept his sisters, Ginny and Susannah, before they set off for the Meeting, as he knows they intend to. If they cannot be dissuaded from going, then at least he can accompany them and try to keep them safe. But when he reaches their home, they have already left. Frantically he looks up and down the street, vainly hoping that he might spot their retreating figures among the ever-increasing crowds, but they are nowhere to be seen. It seems that his brother, Lemuel, has had the same thought, for within seconds he arrives at their door hot and panting from having run the six hundred yards from Byrom Street, where he too has seen drunken members of the MYC making a nuisance of themselves.

"Let's make our way to St Peter's Field by different routes," suggests Lemuel. "I'll follow the route Hunt is meant to take, while you cut through Cross Street, Princess Street and Portland Street."

"There are a couple of wagons on the ground that have been set up for the hustings. Let's meet up as near to those as we can get."

"Agreed."

The two brothers depart, each of them weaving their way in and through the unstoppable surge of crowds like shuttles on a loom.

After two hours' hard marching Samuel Bamford gives the order for a short pause. Jack beats out a quick *Tap-too*, signifying the call to stand down and rest. He follows this with a rapid burst of *Peas Upon a Trencher*, which is the signal for light refreshment. Those among the contingent who formerly were soldiers explain the meaning of each new rhythm to everyone else and make a fuss of Jack, which pleases him greatly. When he is happy these days, he grins sheepishly, puts his head to one side, blushes and looks down. Agnes notices him doing this and alerts Amos to take notice. Amos nods and walks towards his wife, placing his arm around her waist. Neither can remember the last time they felt so happily carefree.

They sit with the others in the grass beside the Irk to eat some of their picnic. The river flows clear and freely here, still some miles upstream of where it has been polluted by the factory waste and effluent of Manchester. The sun climbs the sky and casts dappled reflections upon the water, where trout and perch swim plentifully. Dragon flies dance above them. Water boatmen skim the surface. Red poppies grow in profusion beside the track they have been walking along. Jack picks a handful of them and hands them to Agnes, who plaits them between the garlands of laurels the three of them all wear.

Samuel's wife, Mima, begins to sing the refrain Amos

recalls from before The March of the Blanketeers, when she had sung the same song upon Red Lumb. One by one others join her until the whole contingent is singing, thousands of voices soaring into the air.

"*So beat the drum slowly*
And play the fife lowly
Marching to victory as we go along
And lead us to Manchester
Where wounds no more fester
And free from arrest, sir
When we've righted each wrong…"

Jack plays the *Beat for Orders* while everyone gets back into their respective columns. At a signal from Samuel he switches back to *The Quick March*, and as one, by the left, they pick up the pace for Manchester.

At the same time, about five miles to the east, the Ashton contingent is passing through Fairfield.

In the week running up to the day of the Meeting, members of the Settlement have erected a wooden palisade around their borders to keep the marchers away from their land. Extra Watchmen have been employed for the day, who now patrol the palisade's length, interspersed with all of the Single Brethren, who stand with their backs turned to the road, so that they do not have to look upon those making their way to Manchester. Inside the Church the Single Sisters hold an unbroken vigil of prayer from dawn until dusk, asking God for a safe deliverance.

"We crave only to be left in peace," they murmur, "to do Your bidding here on Earth, in return for which we promise to be law-abiding citizens, loyal to His Majesty the King and his Officers."

But John and Caroline both prise open their eyes to peer

between their clenched fingers, seeing in the faces of the thousands marching past traces of their own lost children, of Agnes and Amos and Jack, such expressions of hope through their stream of tears.

Brother Pohlman, seeing these tears, mistakes them for fervour and is concerned. He understands the need for separation. Throughout their history the Moravians have always encountered persecution, mostly through fear and ignorance, and so it has been both necessary and natural to set themselves apart. " *'Consider the lilies of the field',* " the Elders remind them, " *'how they grow. They toil not, neither do they spin'.* " But everyone at Fairfield toils exceedingly hard, reflects Brother Pohlman. They also spin. They are not so very different from these poor souls who march past them now, desperate for a better life, a fairer one, which rewards them justly for their labour, which represents them in Parliament. "There but for the Grace of God," argue the Elders. But Brother Pohlman disagrees. They are not godless, these protesters. Most of them are Methodists, or Unitarians, with views not so very different from their own, in their rejection of icons and relics and graven images. He casts his eye upon Brother Swertner's picture of The Great Vine, so lovingly maintained by Brother John, with its yearly addition of new clusters taking root around the world. Why, then, this insistence on shunning, on turning one's back? Do we not live *in* this world also, he ponders? Do we not trade with it? Sell our goods to those not of our persuasion? Do we not take advantage of the latest innovations to give us a better yield of crop, produce more lengths of cloth? Where do we draw the line? The Lot. That is where. Brother Pohlman believes that the Lot has run its course, that it has become outmoded, is no longer in keeping with their present needs. Too many decisions taken by it recently have seemed arbitrary and cruel and self-defeating. Brother John and Sister Caroline have never been the same since the Lot decided against the marriage of Agnes and Amos. They have accepted it – if anything, it has made them even more ardent in their devotion of the Lamb, especially Brother John – but at what cost? Brother Pohlman sees the stoop in Sister Caroline's body grow more pronounced with each passing year. He sees the sadness in her eyes, hears the loneliness in her voice, even now, as she offers up her prayers for deliverance and salvation. "Only the Lord knows the truth," say the Elders. "That is why we submit to His will through the Lot." But Brother Pohlman is no longer convinced. Yes, he thinks. The Lord is our Father and we are His children. But like all parents there comes a time when He has to trust them, to let them go, to let them make their own mistakes and learn from them, to go out in to the world and be a part of it. He watches the marchers file past. The Lot has let them down. Not the Lot itself but how it is administered. Now they agitate for change, for a Lot in which they too can cast their vote, and then abide by its decision, knowing that at least their voice has been listened to, their vote has been counted. They were singing as they approached. John Bunyan's *To Be A Pilgrim*. '*Who would true valour seek? Let him come hither…*' But when they saw the members of the Settlement turn their backs upon them, they fell silent. They then took up a low, insistent hissing. It entered the minds and bodies of all who heard it and would not let them rest. Like a swarm of flies. Now, as the column finally marches past, the noise reminds Brother Pohlman of something altogether different. Not flies. But kettles. All of them simmering. It will not be long, he thinks, before they all come to the boil at once.

Count Rothschild is in full, unstoppable flow. He is talking about change and opportunity and a brighter future.

But Rachel is not listening. She is worrying about Abner. He should have been here hours ago. She hopes that her mother-in-law Leah has not noticed his absence. She thinks not. She is surrounded by all these people wishing her and Reuben such joy she is already beginning to look fatigued, a condition not helped by the Count's speech, which shows no sign of finishing any time soon.

He has just begun another of his anecdotes about the time he spent here in Manchester when he was younger. Rachel didn't know him then. She was just a young girl, barely past her own *bat mitzvah*, when Benjamin began to court her. She had no time for tales of the old country back then. But as she has grown older she has learned to think differently. She recognises the importance of telling stories. Telling stories helps us to define who we are, she realises. They provide us with a place in history, give us an anchor, something to feel tethered to, a past which informs our present and helps us to shape our future. A future she is determined will be better for her children, for Rebecca, for Naomi and finally for Ephraim, the son her husband always wanted but never complained about when his daughters were born before him, these daughters he dotes on, than it was for her parents and for Benjamin's parents, Reuben and Leah, whose life together they celebrate today, while all around them Manchester boils.

Manchester.

Her home now and her family's.

She feels as much a daughter of Manchester as she does of Israel, a country which exists only in the imagination, or the Talmud, which they have always tried to make manifest wherever they have settled during their wanderings.

And now they have alighted here.

In Manchester.

In a small enclave on Shude Hill, which is already expanding right across the town. A town that is clamouring for change.

Her ears are assailed by that clamour now, its rising full-throated roar threatening to drown out their esteemed guest's final words as he bids the assembled company to raise their glasses in a toast.

577

"To Reuben and Leah," concludes Count Rothschild.

"To Reuben and Leah," echo the assembled company.

Outside their window, in the streets below, Rachel hears what sounds like the shattering of glass as the water in the copper pots on the stove threatens to boil over. She recalls a time, when they first arrived here and she was still just a girl. She was playing with a ball, which she threw up high into the air, only to lose sight of it against the sun, to drop it, and have to scramble after it between the legs of another great crowd that was pressing all around her, until she came into a clearing, where there was another girl, also called Rachel – *R-a-ch-e-ll-e* – who had caught the ball and was holding it out towards her...

In the moment's silence that follows the toast as the crowds outside move away from below their window in pursuit of someone in a barouche who is waving his hat to all he passes, Rachel speaks aloud the thought that continues to ferment inside her.

"Where's Abner?" she says.

"Who knows?" says Benjamin, hurrying to his wife's side. "Away dreaming somewhere most probably. You know my brother, everyone? Always he has his eye glued to that telescope and his head up in the clouds."

Everyone laughs, seemingly unconcerned.

"Abner's a fine boy," says Leah.

"Not so much a boy any more," adds Benjamin. "He's a grown man now with two jobs."

"He'll always be a boy to me," says Leah. "I'm his grandmother."

"One in the bank – the best accountant we've ever had, such a gift he has for numbers. He can bend them entirely to his will."

"And the other...?" asks one of the relatives, visiting from Liverpool.

"Who knows?" shrugs Benjamin. "Something in the University, assisting the great John Dalton with his scientific

578

experiments."

"The two are not unrelated," says the Count, "for both require dreams to make them happen. We need our dreamers. Where would we be without them? That is what these people down below who muster in their thousands are doing. Following their dreams. And isn't that what *we* did, all of us, when we first chose to settle here? Reuben and Leah, you are doubly-blessed to have two such sons – the man of business…"

Here he points to Benjamin. "And the man of dreams…"

Here he spins around, spreading his arms out wide. "Wherever he is."

Everyone applauds. Benjamin tries to conceal the scowl that passes fleetingly across his face. He feels slighted by their guest of honour. As if these idle dreams of his irresponsible brother carry more weight somehow, more substance, than his own practical, measurable achievements, not only in the Bank, but in the town as a whole, where he is known, respected, can walk freely in the streets unmolested, even enter their holy of holies, the Exchange, and feel, if not exactly welcomed, then needed and recognised for his worth. It is why he feels a certain unease about today's Meeting on St Peter's Field and all this talk of change and insurrection. He will not be seen to take sides, however. He will wait to see how things fall out, then adapt accordingly. Plan for both eventualities then see which way the wind blows. Hasn't that always been their way?

But this shadow soon lifts from him. He is fond of his brother and he hates to see his wife upset.

"I shall send word to Mr Dalton to see if he is still there and ask him to join us directly."

"I don't advise that," says the Count, once again exerting his authority. "There is little chance of it getting through in all this crowd. I suspect that Abner realises this too and is waiting till the streets begin to quieten, which they are sure to once Mr Hunt has arrived at the Meeting Ground. The rest of Manchester will be deserted then, and Abner will be able to make his way home."

"And we shall be able to hear ourselves think," says Reuben, speaking for the first time.

"*Mazel tov*," they cry, raising their glasses once more.

"People often avoid making decisions," continues Reuben, looking closely at his son, "for fear of making a mistake."

Everyone murmurs their agreement.

"When in truth," he adds, "the failure to make decisions is the biggest mistake of all."

A sigh of recognition ripples around the room, accompanied by warm applause.

"*Shalom bayit*," he says.

"*Shalom bayit*," they answer.

Peace in the home.

Count Rothschild is right. Abner, seeing the crowds, has decided to stay a little longer with Mr Dalton.

"Well since you're here," says the great man, "we may as well put you to use."

Abner smiles. "What would you like me to do, sir?" he says.

"Fetch me a calibrated burette, a stand, two glass beakers, a conical flask and a pipette."

"At once, Mr Dalton."

The great man sits at a table in his laboratory. The curtains are closed, shutting out the brightness of the day. It is a scene his assistant, Abner, is well used to, the sequestered calm and shade of a temple, which is what this room represents to both of them, a tranquil retreat from the febrile atmosphere seething just below the window.

"Manchester is built on a bed of Permian red sandstone," says Dalton, preparing his quill pens and ledgers. "Take any sizeable rock or stone, break it open, and what do you find?"

Abner, taking the quills from his master, shrugs. He has no

idea. His eyes are turned more towards the skies than to what lies beneath his feet.

"Metals," continues Dalton. "Iron mostly – hence the pervasive ferrous colour. But also quartz. And sodium. Usually in the form of crystals. Hand me that jar, will you?"

He points to a shelf behind him, where there are rows of glass jars, each filled with different ground powders. Abner takes down the one Mr Dalton has indicated.

"Thank you. Today we shall delve into the mysteries of titration."

"Yes, sir."

"First we must prepare our equipment."

Without needing to be told further, Abner fetches the conical flask, the calibrated burette, the glass pipette, a gill of water. He empties a tea spoon of the ground powder from the jar he first reached down into the conical flask. Sodium Hydroxide. Into this he pours the gill of water and stirs, at the same time applying a fierce heat, using a coiled tubing device that mixes gas and air. It is highly volatile and Abner always quakes at the prospect of lighting it, but his master values it highly. "A gift," he tells him with a chuckle, "from Mr Faraday, a former pupil of mine."

Once the solution has become completely aqueous, with the powder dissolved into the water, Dalton instructs Abner to turn the tap at the foot of the calibrated burette a couple of notches in order to release just a few drops of the indicator that he has previously poured into it. Abner is forced to hold his nose each time he is asked to perform this most delicate of operations, for the indicator is a liquid dye obtained from the stag's horn orchil, a lichen found growing on some of the same rocks containing the sodium crystals. Once collected it is steeped for five weeks in urine and allowed to grow putrid. Then it is mixed with a concoction specially devised by Mr Dalton of lime from the Daub Holes combined with burnt snail-shells. This is then boiled down to produce a vivid purple colour.

Then, depending upon which solution is added to the mixture of the Sodium Hydroxide with the indicator – acid or alkali – the purple will change to either red or blue.

"Manchester is always on the cusp of change," Mr Dalton observes. "We plunder her natural resources – crystals, lichens, lime and water – and she continues to astonish us with her resilience. We separate the solution into its individual component parts to test out the various properties of each, to understand them better, and to discover which compounds are stronger, which more resistant to pressure, which of them survive and which decay, and we need this indicator," he adds, taking back the calibrated burette from Abner "to help us understand just how many drops we need to instigate the next change."

He releases the tap and watches as two drops are added to the crystals. Satisfied, he instructs Abner to add the chosen indicator. Hydrochloric Acid. Immediately the solution turns red.

Thomas Horrall, Assistant Surveyor of the Paving of the Town, having cleared St Peter's Field of all stones, bricks and glass, proceeds to take down all of the lamp posts in the adjoining Windmill Street.

"So that the Reformers," he reports to the Magistrates immediately afterwards, "may be destitute of every means of resistance." He spits with satisfaction.

"Resistance to what?" enquires an anxious Reverend Stanley.

"Nothing, Edmund," replies Norris hastily. "Just a figure of speech, that is all."

"Then it is a most curious one."

"And he is a most curious fellow," cuts in Matthew swiftly. "Would you care for some wine, Reverend?"

"No. Thank you. I believe you shall have no cause for

concern this day, Gentlemen. Many of those arriving have brought their wives and children with them. Surely they cannot be intending any mischief. Those children are the guarantors of their peaceable intentions, you may depend upon it."

Norris and Clayton exchange nervous glances.

"Are you sure you won't join us in a glass of wine, Reverend?" asks Matthew once more, as the bells in the tower of James Wyatt's neoclassical St Peter's Church on the edge of the Meeting Ground begin to chime midday.

"Oh well, if you insist."

"To peaceable intentions," toasts Matthew, raising his glass.

"To peaceable intentions."

"Well, Abner," says Dalton, holding up the conical flask that now contains the changed solution, "tell me what you see?"

"You're asking the wrong person, Mr Dalton."

"Perhaps, perhaps not. Neither of us has the most reliable of eyesights, do we? You with your astigmatism, me with my deuteranopia. I cannot tell red from green, while for you different objects become blurred."

"We make a good team, don't we?"

"I think it's misleading to place too much emphasis on the evidence of our senses. Things are what they are. We cannot change their fundamental properties by choosing to see them differently."

"What *can* we rely on then, sir?"

"The empirical collection of data, the carrying out of experiments again and again, testing out their results until there can be no room for error or misinterpretation. A proof is a wonderful thing, Abner. It is nothing less than a revelation from God, a truth He allows us to share not through blind faith, but through a clear and rigorous scientific method. *Novacula Occami*."

"Sir?"

"Ockam's Razor. A phrase not coined by William of Ockam himself, but by Libert Froidmont in his essay *On Christian Philosophy of the Soul*, which he dedicated to Monsieur Descartes."

"*Ceteris paribus.*"

"Exactly."

"All other things being equal."

"Often wrongly taken to state…"

"The simplest solution is most likely the right one?"

"Whereas in fact what Ockam stated was more subtle. That when presented with competing hypotheses that make the same predictions, one should select the solution which makes the fewest assumptions."

"The Law of Parsimony."

"*Non sunt multiplicanda entia sine necessitate.*"

"Entities are not to be multiplied without necessity."

"His thinking was not new. Ptolemy had said much the same thing before."

"We consider it a good principle to explain the phenomena by the simplest hypothesis possible."

"Whereas there may be an extremely large, possibly incomprehensible number of possible, more complex, more subtle, more complete alternatives."

"But…?"

"Ockam never intended his method to be used for deciding between hypotheses that make *different* predictions."

"So…?"

"Nor did he test out his method to cast doubt upon the existence of God."

"As Thomas Aquinas did."

"Quite so."

"With his *quinque viae*…"

"His five proofs…"

"… in the world we observe that things change."

"And whatever is changing is being changed by something

else."

"And if that by which it is changing is itself changed, then that too is being changed by yet another thing."

"And so on *ad infinitum*."

"Except that the chain has to stop somewhere. There has to be a cause which is not itself caused by anything further."

"And this everyone understands to be God."

"And Ockam agrees. It is futile to do with more things that which can be done with fewer."

Abner removes his spectacles, which he absent-mindedly cleans with the edge of a tablecloth, squinting at the lamp beside the titration equipment. "I'm not sure I like that notion," he says.

"Explain," demands Dalton, holding up the glass beaker to see if a precipitate has yet formed.

"It's too…" Abner struggles for the right term. "Black and white," he says eventually.

"Meaning?"

"There are so many more gradations of colour in between. So many possibilities."

"I agree," says Dalton. "That's why I can be both a scientist yet still believe in God. When I partake of the Eucharist, I celebrate the plurality of miracles."

"And how is that plurality possible?"

"I like to think it is simply because it pleases God."

"We don't have a sacrament in our religion, not in the way you do, but we understand the importance of the breaking of bread."

"Between enemies as well as friends."

"And the ability of things to change from one thing into another."

"Or at least give the semblance of doing so."

Abner pauses a few moments before speaking next.

"This last week," he says, "I have been studying the Dog Star, Sirius."

"Yes...?"

"I am convinced that it has a twin, a shadow."

"Can you prove it?"

"No, I can't. Though perhaps I could if I had a stronger telescope."

"Then you must have faith."

"But if it does, that would make it an altogether more interesting, more complex celestial body, don't you think?"

"Undoubtedly. A parallax invariably offers greater understanding."

"A parallax?"

"An alternation. The displacement in the apparent position of an object when viewed along two different lines of sight."

"Yes! Exactly so!"

"It offers a neat parallel, no, to our current political crisis?"

"I'm sorry, sir. I take no interest in such matters."

"Ah but you should. We are all made up of the same particles of matter. Reformers and Loyalists alike. Everybody claims to be in possession of the truth. The answer to all our problems. They each claim that if we follow *them*, and them alone, they will be able to deliver a better life for us all, rich or poor, young or old, Christian or Jew, but they differ fundamentally in precisely how they intend to achieve it – one side insists upon the *status quo*, the other advocates change, each have their prophets and both claim to have God on their side – yet despite their differences both deploy similar methods – the mustering of large forces to take to the field and take up arms against each other. But can they both be right? What would William of Ockam say? He was a nominalist, a philosopher who felt it was entirely possible to hold two different views simultaneously. That while entities are not to be multiplied without necessity, sometimes there *is* that necessity. Especially if choosing between hypotheses that make different predictions. Then it may well be necessary to acknowledge the possibility of far more complex and quite probably incomprehensible alternatives."

"So what do you suggest, sir?" asks Abner.

"That we continue with our experiment to mix Sodium Hydroxide with Hydrochloric Acid and see what colour the precipitate ultimately forms."

"Even if we cannot tell what that colour is?"

"Especially then."

The two men smile, master and pupil.

"And now I suggest you go, Mr Halsinger. It will be some hours before all of our layers have settled and formed, and didn't you say you had a party to attend?"

"Goodness, yes. I had quite forgot the time, sir."

"There's not many can say that on such a day as this. Away with you."

The bells in the Collegiate Church of St Mary, St Denys and St George echo those of St Peter's and toll the hour of midday. In its shadow Mr Jeremiah Smith, Headmaster of Manchester Grammar School, can see that the excitement and curiosity of the boys can be contained no longer.

All morning they have been trying to master the beginning of *Book IV* of Virgil's *Georgics,* but with diminishing success. The noise from the crowds outside their classroom window grows ever louder and more distracting.

> *"Next I'll speak about the celestial gift of honey from the air.*
> *First look for a site and position for your apiary,*
> *where no wind can enter since the winds prevent them*
> *carrying home their food, and where no sheep or butting kids*
> *leap about among the flowers, or wandering cattle brush*
> *the dew from the field, to wear away the growing grass…"*

587

Even Mr Smith finds himself becoming caught up in the mood of heightened excitement. Instead of admonishing the boys for their lack of attention, he hears himself recalling the time when he attended James Sadler's Balloon Flight in Haworth Gardens as a boy no older than *they* are now. He even attempts a joke or two, which the boys, exchanging puzzled and awkward glances between themselves, nevertheless laugh at politely.

"Let the bright-coloured lizard with scaly back, and the bee-eater
and other birds – Procne, the swallow, her breast marked
by her blood-stained hands – keep away from the rich hives:
since they all lay waste on every side, and while the bees are flying,
take them in their beaks, a sweet titbit for their pitiless chicks...."

Abner flings open the front door of Mr Dalton's house, his head still deep in their discussion. The plurality of miracles. He continues to turn the phrase over in his mind, paying no heed to where he is walking, oblivious of the press of people suddenly surging all around him. Out of nowhere, it seems, a Cavalry Officer bursts through the crowd at full gallop, scattering people indiscriminately, heedless of their care, as they leap and dive for cover.

Abner can feel the breath from the horse's mouth and nostrils hot upon his neck, see the sweat rising from its flanks, hear the thunder of its hooves upon the cobbles. But just as he seems destined to be trampled beneath its unstoppable charge, a hand grabs him by the shoulder and yanks him back just in time. Abner loses his balance and falls backwards into an alley where several others have taken refuge.

The hand, which has remained firmly clasped to Abner's jacket, now shakes him to check that he has not been hurt by the fall. Abner looks from the hand, along the arm, a slender, graceful arm, to where that arm reaches the shoulder, a pleasing, shapely shoulder, which is in turn attached to a long and swan-like neck, which, Abner can see, by dint of being in such close proximity to it, supports a most attractively-featured face, a woman's face.

"I beg your pardon," he stammers, attempting to extricate himself from her grip. "I believe I owe you my life."

The face, which formerly wore a look of grave concern, now smiles, then reddens, now looks once more concerned. A whole gallery of different impressions proceeds to pass across her face, like high clouds scudding across a summer sky, or the whole spectrum of watercolours blending together on a canvas to form the most perfect portrait, or the dazzling display of the *Perseids*, a meteor shower whose radiant is this young woman's smile.

Abner opens his mouth to speak but finds that no words are forthcoming and so he closes it again.

The young woman laughs. "Are you a goldfish?" she asks. "Shall I place you in a bowl and watch you swim around and around?"

Happily, thinks Abner, his head already dizzy from imagining it.

The young woman peers at him even more closely. She has never seen anyone with such pale, translucent skin before. His eyes are of such a light blue that she wonders if he has fallen from the sky. I have rescued an angel, she thinks.

"You must be more careful," she says. "There's never been a day like this in Manchester before."

"No," he says. Or should that be yes?

"What's your name?" she says.

"Abner."

"Abner?"

"Yes."

"And where do you live, Abner?"

"Oh – not far from here," he says, waving an arm airily.

"I think you'd better let me walk you home," she says. "You look as if you've had a bit of a shock."

"Yes," he says. "I think I must have."

"Let me take your arm," she says. "To keep you steady."

As the church bells strike the twelfth and final toll, Jeremiah Smith can contain himself no longer. He looks through the window and watches the crowds pass beneath. They are festive, in the highest of spirits, dressed in their Sunday best, waving flags and singing hymns. It seems a shame to keep the boys cooped up in the classroom when the town is enjoying a holiday. The danger that some of the newspapers have warned about is nowhere to be seen.

> *"But let there be clear springs nearby, and pools green with moss,*
> *and a little stream sliding through the grass,*
> *and let a fruit tree or a large wild olive shade the entrance,*
> *so that when the new leaders command the early swarms*
> *in their springtime, and the young enjoy freedom from the combs,*
> *a neighbouring bank may tempt them to leave the heat,*
> *and a tree in the way hold them in its sheltering leaves…"*

"*Lectio super*," he declares. Much to the astonishment of his pupils who cannot believe their ears, so that for a moment they sit like statues, turned to stone as if they have gazed upon the Gorgon, before Mr Smith repeats his invitation, only this time in English.

"Class dismissed."

As one, the boys scrape back their chairs and fly out of the room, early swarms heeding the advice of Virgil to look for a site and position for their apiary and seek the celestial gift of honey from the air.

Mr Smith watches them depart with fondness and affection, calling out the school motto to them as they leave.

"*Sapere aude*. Dare to be wise."

The Angel and the Radiant of the Perseids walk the few hundred yards back to Brazenose Street, oblivious of the crowds, oblivious even of the concealment of Colonel L'Estrange's 31st Foot skittering nervously close by. They make their way to the Upstairs Room of Abner's home just as all the assembled guests are toasting Reuben and Leah.

"*Shalom bayit*."

"*Shalom bayit*."

It is Rachel who spots them first.

"Abner," she cries. "You're here. We've been worried. What kept you?"

"I think we can all see the answer to that, Rachel," laughs Count Rothschild. "Some dreamer, hey?" he adds, turning to Benjamin.

"Well," says Rachel, "aren't you going to introduce us to your friend, Abner?"

Abner opens his mouth to speak but once again finds that words fail him.

"I'm Ginny," says the young woman brightly. "Ginny Robinson."

"She rescued me," says Abner, finding his voice at last.

Hot on the heels of Lieutenant Douglas Rich, the rider from hell whose fiery steed has thrust Abner and Ginny together, comes the whole of the Cheshire Yeomanry Cavalry, who form up in columns in St John Street, having taken the salute from

591

Lieutenant Jolliffe.

Colonel L'Estrange, who has ridden across from St Peter's Field to greet them, whispers in Jolliffe's ear.

"I only intend to deploy two units of the MYC if I can help it," he says. "Too many of them are already too far in their cups to serve any purpose. They're neither use nor ornament. But Sir Hugh Hornby Birley outranks me – or thinks he does, being a former Boroughreeve. He has the eyes and ears of the Magistrates so he'll ride roughshod over any orders I might care to give him, so I'm putting Rich here in charge of the Cheshires – they seem a good set of chaps, so he should be able to handle them, much more easily than the MYC who appear to take orders from nobody, not even Major Trafford, who appears to have lost their third unit somewhere between Portland Street and Mosley Street. You'll lead the second unit. Understood?"

"Yes, sir. I've already exercised them once this week, and I've got them corralled in Byrom Street as we speak, sir, well away from any Public Houses. They know what to do if called upon."

"Excellent. In that case I'll attach the Cheshires to you as well. Relay your orders directly to Rich, who's earned his spurs already today by getting them all here in such good order."

"Yes, sir."

Lieutenant Douglas Rich, the Subaltern who tore through the Dean's Gate not fifteen minutes before, is now back on his horse awaiting further orders.

"Good show, Rich," says L'Estrange as he rides past him. "Make sure the Cheshires are refreshed and ready within the hour. Take your lead from Lieutenant Jolliffe."

"Yes, sir."

The bells of the Church of St John join in the noonday pealing across the town, which follows the twelve strikes. The young Subaltern beams with pride, his days as a Drummer Boy long forgotten.

Twelve o'clock is also the hour that the Meeting is scheduled to start, but it is only now that the barouche to take Hunt to St Peter's Field arrives at Smedley Cottage. Why it is so late nobody can tell a by now extremely harassed and flustered Joseph Johnson. The crowds waiting excitedly for Hunt to appear have grown so large that they are threatening to spill inside to his front parlour. But even now Hunt fails to appear. There is a disagreement over who, in addition to Hunt, will address the rally once – if – they ever arrive there. Hunt is adamant that he and he alone will speak. Joseph feels that the leaders of the various Hampden Clubs will want to say a few words also. Especially Samuel Bamford. But Hunt will have none of it. While the dispute rages, the crowds grow ever more impatient and begin to hammer on the front door of Smedley Cottage, demanding to see the great man. It is at this moment that John Knight is summoned. Someone has spotted him at the head of the Oldham contingent, who have just arrived at Withy Grove and, hearing that Hunt's procession has not yet set off, decide to accompany it through the streets of Manchester. Knight goes upstairs and, after a heated exchange which can be heard all too clearly by all those assembled in Joseph's front parlour, the two men come downstairs shaking hands.

"It has been agreed," declares Knight, "that you, Joseph, as Chair of *The Manchester Patriotic Union*, shall move the Resolutions and Remonstrances, that I will second them…"

"And I shall be the only speaker," interjects Hunt.

"But what of Samuel?" asks Joseph. "He will be most disappointed."

"Then he must learn to live with it," concludes Hunt brusquely. "He may have the honour of leading the procession."

"But he is not yet here," says Joseph, looking around, as if in doing so he may conjure him out of the air.

"Then let the ladies of *The Manchester Female Reformers* lead us. They are far prettier than Samuel Bamford. Come. Let us depart at once."

The most direct route for the procession to take would have been down Shude Hill to Nicholas Street, but instead Hunt takes a much longer route, travelling an additional mile and a half along The Exchange and then down the length of the Dean's Gate until he reaches Peter Street. The crowds are enormous, pressing in upon the barouche on all sides, at times almost threatening to topple it. Nadin's Special Constables line the streets, clearing a path for the entourage to make its way safely to St Peter's Field, but only by the route they have determined for it.

John Knight and Joseph Johnson observe this with a frown.

It's as if, far from trying to stop this meeting, they want it to take place, thinks Joseph.

It's like they're kettling us, thinks Knight, recalling Major-General Byng's tactics on the day of the Blanketeers.

At precisely that moment, sixty-three miles to the north-east, the Major-General is arriving at York Racecourse with his prize black colt, bred from the filly he purchased at Macclesfield Horse Fair two summers before, which is entered for the Ebor Handicap, due to set off in a little over an hour's time.

Another who is remembering that day of the failed Blanket March is Elijah Dixon of Newton Heath. He has set off with several hundred Reformers to join up with the Ashton contingent who, having passed through Fairfield, have made their way as far as Miles Platting, which serves as the rendezvous point. Their ebullient good humour reminds him painfully of the optimism accompanying the Blanketeers when they set off for London two years before from the same

Meeting Ground of St Peter's Field where they are headed for now.

But today seems different somehow. The event is better organised. There are thousands more expected to attend. This time everybody is marching *towards* Manchester, instead of *away* from it. It speaks of a greater confidence in the Movement. Manchester has become the epicentre for Reform, the focus for political debate and action, perhaps indicating a power shift from the soft south to the industrial north. That is what he hears the intellectuals discussing all around him as he walks. He himself is not an intellectual. He is a labouring man, who's recently made good with his match factory. He thinks their talk is pie-in-the-sky. How can there be a power shift until Manchester has its own proper representation in Parliament? That's what today is all about. Elijah recognises this. The intellectuals have shown him, with their talk of wresting the power from the centre and redistributing it to the people, that the force of their argument is reaching new, more influential ears. This is what was missing two years ago, when wages kept falling and food prices kept rising, and they were quite literally starving.

The idea of a march to London wrapped only in a blanket was a powerful image, but it was not thought through and had little chance of success. As soon as they left St Peter's Field, albeit to cheers and songs, they simply faded away. The military were too clever for them, kettling them into a series of dead ends and *cul de sacs* until they were forced to surrender and skulk back home. A few carried on. One, he heard, even got as far as Derbyshire before he had to turn back.

He himself was rounded up outside his late father's mill at Houldsworth, just outside Stockport, arrested and transported in irons to London, where he was arraigned before Lord Sidmouth, accused of high treason, then forced to languish in Bridewell Prison for more than a year before being released without ever coming to trial. Then he'd been forced to make that walk, only in reverse, from London all the way back to Manchester, alone and unaided. It took him several weeks. During it, he had time to think. When he finally made it back home, he sold the mill, opened up a match factory, which immediately thrived. He became a friend and associate of Samuel Bamford. Together they continued to petition Parliament for the restoration of *habeas corpus*. When that failed, he lent his support to the decision to invite Orator Hunt to address the people of Manchester.

"We must strike a light," he said, "in people's hearts and minds. Then watch it spark and flare."

The intellectuals were thrilled by that notion and supported it unreservedly. They liked its poetry. "*Il faut craquer l'allumette*," they'd say. "*Puis le regarde étinceler.*"

There had always been a French enclave in Newton Heath. Ever since the Huguenots first arrived there two hundred and fifty years before. Fleeing persecution in their native land they found a welcome here in Manchester and quickly made it their home. Producing the highest quality lace and linen they soon carved themselves a niche in which politics and the arts flourished alongside manufacturing, adding yet another dissenting voice to Manchester's Non-Conformists. They supported the early aims of the Revolutionaries back in France but then despaired over their subsequent betrayal in the Reign of Terror. About Napoleon they were more equivocal and this uncertainty was mirrored in the way they began to be viewed with growing suspicion. Their trade began to suffer, as did their standing among parts of the local community, but their undying commitment to the cause of Reform, in solidarity with any group suffering from persecution at the hands of the authorities, as *they* had had to, meant that the doors of any Hampden Club, Benefit Society or Patriotic Union were always opened to them.

Monsieur and Madame Robidoux moved there from Levenshulme shortly after Talleyrand had left for the final time, leaving little behind him except broken dreams, unfulfilled promises and a district to the east of the village named after him. Sheltering him from his enemies, both in England and Europe, had proved costly for the Robidoux, and they felt the need to be once more part of the wider Huguenot family to recuperate. They continued to follow the fortunes of Charles Maurice de Talleyrand-Périgord from afar. Not for nothing was he nicknamed *L'Homme aux Cinq Têtes*, serving under five different régimes and changing sides as often as he changed his clothes. His most recent incarnation, much to the chagrin of the Robidoux, was to be the key agent in the restoration of the House of Bourbon after the final defeat of Napoleon. Although even now he was opposing the legislative rule of King Louis XVIII, leaving yet another possible escape route should the political climate change once more. In this he was aided and abetted by the notorious courtesan Catherine Worlée, whose long painted fingernails had stretched right across the Channel to drag him from the arms of the Robidoux's maid, Mercy, whom he cruelly abandoned.

Realpolitik. The art of diplomacy based more on considerations of practicality within the context of given circumstances, rather than on any explicit ideological, moral or ethical beliefs. Talleyrand was the master of this black art, had even coined the phrase while in Austria, or claimed he did, which, for him, amounted to the same thing, and Mercy was collateral damage. When she turned up unexpectedly out of the blue on the Robidoux doorstep some five years later, they felt it was the least they could do to give her a home, having introduced her to Talleyrand in the first place.

Mercy had not set out to find them. When she waltzed away from Matthew on the night of the Michaelmas Fair, after watching the last walk of *La Funambola* high in the air above the whole of Manchester, she thought little of where she was heading. She was singing the song her mother had taught her, back in Jamaica.

"Me know no law, me know no sin
Me's just what ever dem make me
Dis is de way dey bring me in
So God nor Devil take me…"

She walked till midnight when she found herself outside the Gate House to a rather grand house on the edge of Newton Heath, nestled at the confluence of the River Medlock and Shooter's Brook. A lit torch attached by an iron sconce to the outer wall threw a flickering light onto an elaborately-painted sign.

Culcheth Hall.

There were several coachman waiting in the driveway. Mercy could see more lights in the windows up at the Hall. Some people were starting to leave. She heard them speaking to one another in French. She thought she recognised one of the voices, a woman's, informing the driver that they had decided to make a night of it, and if he wanted to return home without them, that was fine, otherwise he would be welcome to bed down in one of the estate cottages. *"Ce que tu préfères…"*

"Oui, Madame."

"Merci, Jacques."

This was followed by a trill of laughter and a man's voice.

"Mon Dieu, Hélène, qu'est-ce qu'on s'abandonne…?"

Mercy stepped into the light.

"Monsieur et Madame Robidoux? Vous souvenez-vous de moi?"

"Mercy? Is that you? Can it possibly be? After all these years?"

"Oui, c'est moi."

"You must tell me everything that has happened. We looked for you everywhere, didn't we, Henri, after Talleyrand left? But we…"

"It's a long story. *J'ai… disparue.* I suppose I wanted to – needed to."

598

"I want to 'ear all about it, but first you are in luck."

"That's one word for it," put in Henri, lighting a cigar.

"Don't listen to 'im," said Hélène, playfully blowing out his *allumette*. "The young Lord who owns this 'ouse is promising us *une recitation*."

"Oh?"

"Of 'is latest *poèmes*. *Fugitive Pieces*, 'e calls them."

"I can respond to that," smiled Mercy.

"*Bien sûr*," said Hélène, linking her arm through her *protégée*.

Inside Culcheth Hall they listened to the seventeen-year-old George Gordon, Lord Byron, deliver with drunken, flamboyant dash a number of his most recently published juvenile verses. In their simple, unspoiled rhymes Mercy hears echoes of her own lost hopes, rekindled now by this chance re-encounter. Talleyrand forgotten, the caged bird set free.

"*Ye scenes of my childhood, whose loved recollection*
Embitters the present, compared with the past;
Where science first dawn'd on the powers of reflection,
And friendships were formed, too romantic to last;

But if, through the course of the years which await me,
Some new scene of pleasure should open to view,
I will say, while with rapture the thought shall elate me,
'Oh, such were the days that my infancy knew'."

Within weeks of their chance rediscovery of one another Mercy and Hélène accompany each other everywhere. Mercy is given a room in the house of Hélène and Henri, more a personal companion than a lady's maid, and she becomes part of the intellectual set of Newton Heath, which centres around the descendants of those first Huguenot settlers, but also includes many local Reformers and Radicals. It is here she meets Elijah Dixon, just fifteen years old and apprenticed to his father, Job, a textile manufacturer, who is also a Methodist lay-preacher and something of a firebrand, quite the opposite in temperament of his Biblical namesake, impatient for change.

The French, with their unquenchable appetite for endless debate – as opposed to direct action – infuriate him. It is Thomas Paine who brings them together. At meetings they quote from *The Rights of Man* and, as frequently, if not more so, than he does from scripture, he answers from *Common Sense*. The Father of the American Revolution acts as the Great Intermediary between them.

" *'The world is my country'*," begins Hélène, " *'all mankind are my brethren, and to do good is my religion'*."

" *'If there must be trouble'*," answers Job, " *'let it be in my day that my child may have peace'*."

" *'These are the times'*," throws in Mercy, " *'that try men's souls'*."

" *'The harder the conflict'*," comes back Elijah, " *'the more glorious the triumph'*."

Elijah and Mercy become firm friends. She is like an older sister to him. It's to her he first brings young Martha Dyson round, a young cotton worker he has met in his father's mill. For all of his egalitarian views, Job would prefer his son to set his sights higher than a factory maid. But Martha is so sweet-natured that it is not long before she wins him round. When he marries them at the Old Ebenezer Baptist Chapel two years later, there are tears in his eyes. And when he learns that Elijah has been arrested and transported to Bridewell for his part in the Blanketeers, he collapses, and it is Martha who nurses him. He recovers just long enough for him to see Elijah return but dies just days afterwards.

After this the mantle of leadership in the local Reform Club falls naturally upon Elijah and he wears it easily. He is much more radical in his views than Knight or Fitton, or even Samuel Bamford. When Elijah calls for universal suffrage, he includes votes for women in his demand and is a lone voice crying in the wilderness, but undeterred for all that, so that when he hears of Hunt's imminent arrival in Manchester, he asks Martha, Hélène and Mercy to lead the response from Newton Heath, taking both pride and pleasure in the happy resumption of their former debates.

"I make matches now," says Elijah, laughing grimly. "I leave the intellectual decisions to you, the three Graces – Charm, Beauty and Creativity. I make Lucifer matches. A bargain with the Devil."

"Nothing will happen," says Madame Robidoux, "*comme d'habitude*, you will see. There will be no storming of the New Bailey. It will be – how do you say? – a storm in a tea cup."

"I wonder if I might see Matthew there," says Mercy finally.

"But we shall wear the cap of liberty *toutefois, n'est-ce pas? Le bonnet rouge?*"

"Strike it. Watch it spark and flare," says Elijah.

The midday chimes also see the grand arrival of the last contingents of marchers arriving at St Peter's Field. 'Doctor' Healey's from Saddleworth, William Fitton's from Royton, John Knight's from Oldham, John Saxton's from Ashton, Elijah Dixon's from Newton Heath and finally, the largest of them all, Samuel Bamford's from Middleton, adding their considerable numbers to Joseph Harrison's from Stockport, who have been there nearly three hours already, together with tens of thousands more who have arrived as individuals, in smaller Chapel or family groups, so that not a blade of Thomas Horrall's freshly swept and cleared grass can now be seen.

Mr Edward Holme, observing this multitude from his upstairs window in Mount Street, opposite the site he hopes will house his dream of a Manchester Museum of Natural History, finds that he is deeply moved by the sight. He pores over the individual differences, light and dark as they pass before him from sun into shade and then back into the light again. A true Cabinet of Curiosities. A cloud of peppered moths fluttering and evolving before his eyes. He finds himself buoyed up by the emotion of the moment, his hopes borne aloft on the gentle breeze, which carries the sound of tens of thousands of voices singing as one, as the band of the Middleton contingent strikes up a lively rendering of *Rule Britannia.*

"When Britain first, at Heaven's command
Arose from out the azure main
This was the charter of the land
And guardian angels sang this strain..."

"What a sight," declares Samuel as the singing stops. Everywhere he looks are happy, smiling faces, enjoying a rare holiday from work, savouring the sun on their slowly unstiffening bodies, as if waking from a long winter.

Knight, who has hurried on ahead of Hunt's procession, greets his old friend.

"How many people are here, dost tha' reckon?" asks Samuel when he sees him.

"Sixty thousand at least," says Knight.

"I'd put it at more than a hundred."

"The Magistrates will say that it's less than twenty."

"Ay, well they would, wouldn't they?"

"And there'll be thousands more soon..."

"Those following Hunt?"

"There are so many of them that he's having a hard time making it through."

"Will he be much longer, dost tha' think?"

"Half an hour, perhaps a little more."

Samuel nods his head. "Perhaps we should let the people know?"

Knight puts a hand on Samuel's shoulder. "That's what I'm

here to tell thee."

Something in Knight's tone makes Samuel pause.

"It's been decided," says Knight. "Joseph will propose our Chair. I will second him. Then Mr Hunt will speak. Nobody else."

Samuel says nothing. He tries to take it in. Mima, his wife, who has overheard this exchange, flies to his defence.

"Why, that's a wicked suggestion, John. If it weren't for Samuel, Mr Hunt wouldn't be speakin' to us today. None of these good people," she sweeps her arm around the expanse of St Peter's Field, "would be here."

"I know," says Knight. "I'm sorry. Tha' can second Joseph instead of me, if tha'd like to, Samuel?"

Samuel shakes his head. "Nay, lad. I'll not be disturbin' th' arrangements now they've been set. It's the Orator they've come to listen to, not me"

"That's most selfless, Samuel."

"But I'll be damned if I don't say summat now, tell 'em 'e won't be long."

"Ay, lad," says Knight, clapping him on the back. "You do that."

Samuel mounts the hustings. A great roar goes up from the crowd, followed by an almost equally deafening silence as they wait to hear what he has to say.

"Friends," he booms, "Mr Hunt will soon be here. He is making his way along the Dean's Gate even as I speak an' will arrive shortly. You must not attempt to create any riot or disturbance until his arrival, but wait with patience and good humour. Thank you."

Samuel climbs down from the hustings to great applause, followed by the sounds of a peaceful crowd enjoying the sunshine as if at a carnival or fair.

The Magistrates, looking out from the balcony of Reverend Norris's house on Mount Street, look ashen.

"Did you hear that?" hisses the Boroughreeve. "His

meaning couldn't be clearer."

"I don't understand," says a puzzled Reverend Stanley.

"He means," sneers Nadin dismissively, "that they may do so *after* Hunt has arrived."

"Do what?" asks Stanley.

"Create a riot," explains Matthew coolly. "It is as we predicted, Sir Edward," he continues, directing his words to the Boroughreeve. "They've been drilling in secret, preparing most carefully for this moment. Their good order and discipline more resembles an army than a crowd enjoying a picnic."

"But we've been preparing for this too," says Nadin. He looks at Matthew, who nods decisively.

"Do what you have to," says the Boroughreeve, trembling as he speaks. "Law and order must be maintained."

Nadin leaves the room at once.

On St Peter's Field, Agnes, Amos and Jack are finishing the last of their picnic. Agnes is happier than she can remember. She looks around at the thousands of people all gathered together for this single purpose. The many flags and banners with their slogans of intent.

"Annual Parliaments."

"Universal Suffrage."

"Vote by Ballot."

"No to the Corn Laws."

"Success to the Female Reformers."

"Liberty, Equality, Fraternity."

"No Boroughmongering."

"No Taxation Without Representation."

"Liberty is the Birthright of All."

"Let us Die like Men and Not be Sold like Slaves."

"Labour is the Source of Wealth."

"Unite and Be Free."

And the one she and Amos had made.

"Unity is Strength."

As she looks around, her eyes alight upon the gang of Magistrates deep in conference upon a balcony directly opposite where she is standing. They remind her of a clattering of jackdaws tugging at a worm, and she laughs. How silly they look, she thinks, how puffed up and proud, their shiny heads jerking back and forth like tiny hammers. They occupy her attention a full minute while Amos is seeing to Jack, brushing some breadcrumbs from his drummer boy's jacket, which he has insisted on wearing today. He must be so hot in it, thinks Agnes, but he will not take it off.

She turns her attention back to the jackdaws. One of them, a thick-necked bullying type, struts back inside the house, while another steps forward to gaze out over the crowd pressed so tightly on the ground, almost as if they were a feast of worms all wriggling to be free, from which he might take his pick. She sees him now, full in the face for the first time, and reels back in shock. It is as if she has seen a ghost. Except that this figure is very much alive. He is pointing and signalling, as if directing soldiers in battle, from his position on the mountain top, looking down, directly at her, or so it seems, and she turns to Amos. The likeness is uncanny, but the demeanour could not be more different. She taps him on the shoulder to distract his attention momentarily from Jack and look for himself, to see if he too can recognise his own twin. But as he turns, the phantom on the balcony steps back into the shadow, so that his face can no longer be seen.

"What is it?" says Amos.

"Nothing," says Agnes, for in truth she is no longer sure of what she has seen, and then the moment passes.

A great cry goes up from the crowd. Hunt's barouche has been spotted turning into Peter Street and everyone rises to their feet, straining to see him approach. Jack immediately delivers a rapid burst of *The Preparative* on his drum, the signal to make ready for the battle to commence.

Pity, by chance, is standing not twenty feet away.

She sees, for the first time in nearly forty years, both her boys together.

Her boys.

That is how she likes to think of them, these twins she helped come into the world on the night of the Earthquake. Just look at them now – fully-grown and come into their own. She hasn't seen as much of Matthew since she found herself standing before him at the Bench, when he inadvertently gave her her name. From time to time she has observed him from afar, strolling confidently towards The Exchange, or coming down the steps outside the New Bailey Prison. And today, standing on the balcony surveying St Peter's Field as though it were his kingdom. But always alone. No queen stands beside him now. Or ever has, she thinks. She sees a man entirely self-sufficient. In need of no one else. Or so it seems. And there is still time for him to meet someone. He is not old after all. Younger than *she* is. And she feels no age at all.

But Amos she has not seen in three decades. Not since the day of the Balloon Flight, when he slipped the hand she held him by and fell into the Irwell. Where she was rescued by a small girl. *This* girl, perhaps, thinks Pity now, as she watches the way she looks at Amos, having caught the briefest of glances of Matthew and seen the unmistakeable likeness. But Amos misses him. Each of them, these two boys of hers, has no idea of the other's existence, nor of her role in how they came first to be born and then to be separated. Have they ever wondered, she thinks, whether a certain part of them is missing? Have they looked in a mirror perhaps and thought for a second that they might have been looking at somebody else? She remembers Septimus from her time in the Hulks, the Old Retainer, who had lost part of one arm, but how he used to feel a pain sometimes, an ache, where the limb had once been but was no more.

She turns her attention now to the one she assumes must be

their son. Jack. She hears the woman call him by this name. He bears a strong likeness for his father. He carries a drum that he never lets go of. He has a way of looking at the world as if someone might snatch it from him one day, and so he is going to hold onto it for dear life until they do. She sees at once that he does not speak. It is not that he can't, but that he has elected not to, or has been forced by weight of circumstance to keep his voice locked away, because if he once opens his mouth and lets it escape, he might scream and never stop, and then he might lose it for ever.

Like her.

But unlike her he speaks with his drum, which he now begins to play.

Pity steps back into the shadows.

Subaltern Douglas Rich watches the slow, stately procession of Hunt's barouche as it turns from the Dean's Gate into Peter Street with growing contempt. It reminds him of the accounts his father used to read to him of Roman Generals, or Emperors, marching into the Forum, soaking up the adulation of the fawning, adoring crowds. But Hunt is no Caesar. He is nothing but a vain popinjay in his ridiculous, extravagant clothes, flamboyantly waving his hat to the people, those blocks and stones and worse than senseless things, who throw down their flowers for him to walk upon.

What angers and sickens him more than anything is the number of Hunt's followers who wear ex-army uniforms, veterans of Waterloo who should know better, who now betray all that they fought for on that glorious day to prostrate themselves before this imposter, a glorious day that he, Douglas, wished he'd been old enough to participate in. But he had been too young, only a drummer boy with a regiment whose services were not called upon.

Above the clamour and tumult of the crowd, he fancies he

607

hears a drum beating out *The Preparative*. He scoffs. If it's a battle they want, he's more than ready for them. He only hopes that Lieutenant Jolliffe will not prove too conciliatory a commander, but teach these traitors the lesson they deserve.

Lieutenant Jolliffe watches Hunt's procession with extreme care. He waits patiently with the dismounted Cheshires in Byrom Street. He regards the Radicals passing along the Dean's Gate saluting their hero, but doing so with discipline and calm, so that their undoubted enthusiasm does not spill over into anything that might be interpreted as disorderly. He sees nothing to give him any cause for concern or alarm.

Lemuel and Billy find each other at the junction of Windmill Street and Mosley Street.

"Have you seen Ginny or Susannah?" asks Lemuel.

"Susannah, yes. Ginny, no. Susannah's wi' 'er husband, an' Richard an' Paul, who've not seen Ginny either, an' they would've, they say, for they've been 'ere since first thing this mornin', before all t' people began to arrive."

"What're you going to do?"

"Go back 'ome. See if she's there."

Lemuel nods. "In that case, I'll stay here. Just in case."

He watches Billy run back along Windmill Street. The whole of Manchester appears to have converged on St Peter's Field. The rest of the town is deserted. The mills and factories lie silent. The shops are shuttered. The Exchange has closed its doors. Sunlight slants down onto the narrow, cloistered streets, as if illuminating the nave of a church, in which motes of dust dance in the air. A rat scurries undisturbed in an empty square. Billy runs through the maze of back alleys, which he knows so well he could pass through them blindfold, across the New Bailey Bridge, past the unguarded prison, towards his house where he finds no one at home.

Lemuel climbs on a wall to get himself a better view of the crowds gathered on the Meeting Ground. With his surveyor's eye he calculates there must be eighty thousand souls pressed into the place. They are so tightly packed that not a blade of grass can be seen. If his estimate is correct, then from the whole of South-East Lancashire, upon which the event is drawing, one in two of the entire population must be present.

He imagines a time in the future when St Peter's Field will be paved over, when fine buildings will surround an enclosed square, in the centre of which will be a great stone Cenotaph to honour the dead of successive wars, where people will come to lay wreaths of laurel intermingled with blood red flowers.

At last Hunt arrives. The bells of St Peter's Church toll one o'clock.

The crowds on Mount Street are so thick that no way through can be found for his barouche. He is forced to dismount and walk the final quarter of a mile on foot. It takes him nearly forty minutes.

News of his arrival spreads through the Meeting Ground as rapidly as a semi-automatic spinning mule. The massed bands on the field begin to play *See The Conquering Hero Comes* from Handel's *Judas Maccabeus*.

> "*See the conquering hero comes*
> *Sound the trumpets, beat the drums*
> *Myrtle wreaths and laurel twine*
> *To deck the hero's brow divine…*"

The first thing Hunt does when he reaches the hustings is to ask for the angle that they are facing to be altered slightly. Although the day is sticky and hot, there is still the lightest of breezes. Hunt is concerned that this may carry his voice away from the crowd and so he requests this small but necessary realignment.

While several strong men nearby manhandle the cart around, Hunt notices a pregnant woman in a distressed and fainting state, who has been leaning against it and who now threatens to collapse. Ever the gallant towards the fairer sex, Hunt moves swiftly to her side to prevent her from falling. As soon as the hustings have been reconfigured, he arranges for a space to be set aside upon it where she may sit, away from the press of the crowd.

When all is ready, he takes up his position, joined by Joseph Harrison, John Knight and a Mr John Tyas, a journalist with *The Times* from London, who has travelled down especially for the event. Hunt, ever the publicist, approves Tyas his place on the hustings.

The first thing Tyas will write as Hunt readies himself to begin is that he is now present at the largest assembly ever to be seen, not only on Lancashire's, but on all of England's soil.

Beyond the perimeter of St Peter's Field and its adjoining streets, L'Estrange orders all troops very slowly to take up closer order.

From Mosely Street, Portland Street, Byrom Street and John Street, St James's Square, Pickford's Yard, Dickinson and George Streets, they silently advance.

The ring of steel is tightened.

Hunt thanks Johnson and Knight for their words of welcome, then begins. John Tyas, already writing his article for *The Times*, notes the time on his pocket watch. Twenty minutes before two.

"Good friends, sweet friends," says Hunt, "let me not stir you up to mutiny…"

*

Just before Hunt can continue, a last single trumpet note hangs in the air in a fading *diminuendo*, as the massed bands' rendition of *See The Conquering Hero Comes* reaches its finale. Hunt looks up, almost as if he imagines a bird hovering overhead, which has been responsible for producing such a sweet and harmonious sound.

Almost at once, another trumpet note joins it, so close in pitch that at first the listener might be forgiven for thinking it is perhaps an echo, returning from a distant point within this natural amphitheatre, but the effect is jarring, the difference between the two notes so infinitesimal, less than a semi-tone, as to set the teeth on edge. The discord between the two pierces the brain, like a hot needle being inserted into the ear. And where the first note is diminishing, the second is rising, in pitch and in volume, as it grows nearer and nearer in a deafening crescendo.

The source of this second note is a Captain Meagher, Bugler, who at this very instant is leading the charge of the MYC under the command of Sir Hugh Hornby Birley from Pickford's Yard.

What is intended as a controlled trot soon disintegrates into an undisciplined gallop, as if St Peter's Field is in fact a race course, such as might be found at Kersal Moor just across the Irwell, or much further afield in York, where Major-General Sir John Byng is watching his prize filly canter down to the start of The Ebor through the eye-piece of his telescope.

If he had been on the roof top of the tower of St Peter's Church, looking through that same telescope, he would have seen the catastrophe that was about to unfold.

Unfortunately Colonel L'Estrange does not have such a telescope. Nor does he have the advantage of an elevated position from which he might direct operations. Instead he hears only the sound of a hundred sets of horses' hooves galloping *pell mell* towards the Meeting Ground.

611

"I have given no such order," he says to Deputy Nadin standing beside him.

"No," says Nadin coolly. "But *I* have."

Within seconds L'Estrange has mounted his horse and instructed the 15th Hussars under *his* command and the Cheshires under Lieutenant Jolliffe's to follow him at once to the Field.

The sound of the twin trumpets has now given way to the timpani of hooves. The crowds feel the arrival of the MYC before they see them, rumbling from deep within the earth, as if it might split and crack beneath them.

With sabres drawn, their freshly sharpened blades glinting in the sunlight, still led on by the strident note of Captain Meagher's bugle, the Cavalry plunges headlong into the tightly packed crowds, who, temporarily blinded by the winking flashes of the raised swords, stand like startled rabbits corralled into the centre of a field before the wheat, the only place where they might hide, is cut down.

The people strive to get out of the way of the thudding hooves. But the very density of the crowd makes such evasive action impossible. Men and women fall backwards into the arms of other men and women. Children are dropped and trampled, scooped up, then dropped and trampled again. A concertina pattern develops with the people squeezing and separating, squeezing and separating, the only music emanating from them their screams of panic and terror.

A narrow way is cleared sufficient for the Special Constables to drag Hunt, Johnson, Knight and Tyas down from the hustings, place them under arrest and haul them off towards Mount Street, where they are locked in a room next to the Magistrates, who look out over the carnage that is unfolding before them with a mixture of fear and hysteria.

"The mob is attacking the Cavalry," cries Norris.

"Read them the Riot Act," commands Clayton.

Both Ethelston and Hay read it simultaneously. Neither is

heard.

The Reverend Stanley retires to a corner, where he tries to pour himself a glass of wine but his hands are shaking too violently. He sits on a chair, shuts his eyes and covers his ears.

Only Matthew remains outside, patrolling the balcony, waving his hat high above his head, as if it is some kind of signal.

From the corner of Windmill Street, Nadin returns the gesture.

Down on the ground the MYC have lost all semblance of control. They cut and slash indiscriminately. Now they have tasted blood, they want more. They delight in taunting their helpless victims.

"You want reform, do you? Then I'll reform you."

"You'll come again, will you?"

"Spare your lives? Damn your bloody lives."

"I'll show you who's the soldier today."

"This is for Waterloo."

Lieutenant Jolliffe arrives just as Birley is ordering another charge, which overthrows the hustings, crushing dozens of people who had been trying to take shelter behind them.

The crowd is trapped. There is no escape from the Field. Whichever way they turn their path is blocked by more soldiers, their sabres raised aloft, glistening in the sun, their blades now more red than silver, so that once more they concertina, trampling onto each other, as much as they are ridden over by the horses. One of the first to suffer such an injury is Elijah Dixon, who is kicked to the ground, before receiving a sabre slash to his arm. It is only Mercy's speed of thought and presence of mind that enables him to escape further calamity, as she rolls him beneath one of the carts of the hustings, where they can both take temporary shelter.

"Gentlemen," cries Lieutenant Jolliffe, "Gentlemen, for shame, forbear! The people cannot get away!"

At that moment he is knocked aside himself by Subaltern

613

Douglas Rich, who, with a wild gleam in his eye, charges into the fray.

Jolliffe has no option but to order the rest of the Cheshires onto the Field with clear instructions to disperse the people before any further harm befalls them. L'Estrange, arriving at the same time, follows suit with the 15th Hussars. Being the more professional soldiers, used to the mayhem and chaos of battle, they proceed to try and clear a swathe between the people in order to kettle them towards the various streets leading into the Field. They use the flats of their sabre blades to do this, rather than the edges, but no sooner have they managed to herd them one way than the MYC begin driving them back.

Amos, Agnes and Jack somehow manage to cling fast to one another. Amos has received a cut to the arm, just above the elbow, but it is not too deep and Agnes has torn a strip from off her skirt to form a tourniquet around it.

Just as she is tying this off, Jack escapes from her grip. He runs towards a tiny clearing which has just been made by Lieutenant Jolliffe. He stands in the centre of it, wheeling round in circles, with horses thundering all around him, rearing up on their hind legs, then crashing down again, their hooves thudding into whoever happens to be in their way, trampling and crushing them. He sees the various banners of the different contingents fluttering in the air above his head. Some are being torn down, some are being hurled as weapons. He hears the shouts of the soldiers and the cries of the dying. He is back at Waterloo, at the farm beside the Chateau d'Hougoumont, the noise and the chaos and the fear flooding back to him. He picks up his drum sticks and begins to beat the long roll of *The Alarm*, followed by the rapid repeats of *The Retreat*, before a last desperate attempt at a *Chamade*, calling for *A Parley* with the enemy.

Douglas Rich hears these calls rattling above the general clamour and din, and wheels his horse around in search of their source. He spies Jack in the centre of the clearing. He sees him in his blue drummer boy's jacket, his Waterloo uniform, and is filled with an uncontrollable rage and hatred. That this pathetic excuse for a soldier should have been allowed to serve His Majesty on the Field of Waterloo, to have witnessed Wellington's greatest triumph, and is now here, desecrating this holy ground with his cowardly calls for retreat, is too much for Douglas to bear. He steadies his horse, draws his sabre above his head and prepares to charge.

Jack hears Douglas approaching. He turns around and sees him accelerating towards him. Captain Meagher, pausing briefly in between his own personal slaughter count, raises his bugle to his lips and blows. The high discordant note once more pierces the air. Everyone seems to hear it and time slows to an agonising halt. Jack sees in Douglas's eyes the same hatred, the same instinct to survive, he had seen in Gaston's, when another set of soldiers had forced the two of them to fight to the death, before Major-General Byng rode to the rescue. He sees that same expression now on the Subaltern's face. He understands it and he forgives it. He opens his arms to embrace him as he gallops towards him. But this time Major-General Byng will not be riding to save him. Douglas raises his sabre high into the air. His face twists with loathing. The crowds part just long enough for Amos and Agnes to see him plunge his sword straight through their son's heart and out through his back. Above him, on the balcony, Amos catches sight of Matthew, who has mirrored the Subaltern's actions in full-throated triumph.

Jack's uniform undergoes a complete transformation, experiencing a litmus change, shifting from blue to red. The last turn of the kaleidoscope. The bugle note lingers then fades.

*

The bell in the tower of the Church of St Peter tolled two o'clock. The chimes echoed solitarily and long in the still, silent air. Just twenty minutes after Hunt had begun his address,

615

when the MYC had made its first charge, it was all over.

Samuel Bamford surveyed the scene in disbelief. His wife, Mima, her hair loose and falling about her face, raised a hand to remove the garland from her head, smearing her cheek with blood as she did so. Softly she began to sing with bitter mockery.

"I'll weave a gay garland with victory entwining
With murderous valour pot-valiant combining
I'll weave a gay garland with victory entwining
To crown the brave Yeomen of Peterloo Field

The field was now an open and almost deserted place. The sun beat down through a sultry and motionless air. The hustings remained, overthrown but intact, with a few broken and hewn flag-staves tottering but erect, and a pair of ripped and gashed banners drooping forlornly. Sprigs of laurel lay discarded where they had fallen. Strewn among them were bonnets and hats, shawls and shoes, together with other remnants of male and female dress, trampled, torn and bloodied.

"Bold Hunt spite of devils again will address you
The New Bailey Dungeon his mouth hath not sealed
While thraldom alone with her fetters caress you
Upheld by the Yeomen of Peterloo Field

Will Manchester still these foul Yeomanry nourish
Must asses and monkeys dominion still wield
And fools with their truncheons o'er Englishmen flourish
Who strove for their freedom on Peterloo Field..."

Those of the MYC who had remained – those not intent in harrying the poor souls who had desperately tried to make their escape among the adjoining streets – had dismounted. Some were easing their horses' girths, some adjusting their accoutrements, while some were wiping their sabres clean. Several mounds of human beings still remained where they had fallen, crushed and smothered. Some of these were still groaning, some with staring eyes were gasping for breath, while some would never breathe more. All was silent save these low sounds, and the occasional snorting of horses and the pawing of their hooves upon the ground.

> "*Yet their laurels are mingled with cypress and willow*
> *Killed, wounded and starving, Reformers must yield*
> *And Conscience the Yeoman disturbs on his pillow*
> *For shedding of blood upon Peterloo Field...*"

More women now joined with Mima to take up the song, turning to face the balcony from where the Magistrates had been directing operations.

> "*Our Town Legislators some medals should order*
> *The Yeomen to wear them, their safety to shield*
> *And on them inscribèd 'The Sons of Disorder'*
> *Who butchered Reformers on Peterloo Field...*"

But none were there. The doors and the windows were locked and bolted. The women drifted away. Only Mima remained.

> "*I'll weave a gay garland with victory entwining*
> *With murderous valour pot-valiant combining*
> *I'll weave a gay garland with victory entwining*
> *To crown the brave Yeomen of Peterloo Field...*"

Samuel lifted her from the ground and took her up in his arms, where she buried her face in his chest.

*

Just then a great cry rose up from the opposite corner of the Field, as if from a wild beast howling in pain.

Samuel looked across. It was Amos Lees. He was clutching his arm, which appeared to have been slashed by one of the soldier's sabres. But it was not this that had produced that deep-throated roar, which seemed to have been wrenched up out of the bowels of the earth, from the flames of hell itself.

He was pointing towards another part of the Field. Samuel followed the direction of his arm, which picked out Matthew Oldham. He was doing the grisly rounds of the bodies piled high beneath the balcony from where he had supervised the day's carnage. He heard Amos's cry and turned around. If he saw Amos, he did not register it. Instead he commandeered one of the horses that was quietly munching on some grass in a space between the rows of the wounded, hoisted himself up into the saddle and began to trot away in the direction of Mosley Street and his own home at the farthest end of it.

Agnes did nothing to stop her husband. She was too consumed with grief of her own to comprehend anything at all of what was happening, for Jack was dead.

He lay now in her arms, his eyes still open and staring, past Agnes and Amos, towards something only he appeared to see, as if a huge murmuration wheeled in a great black cloud, the birds having escaped from the nets and lures that had threatened to entrap them, to clip their wings and deny them flight, briefly blocking out the sun in one last defiant cry, that while some of their number might have perished, a great many more of them had survived, to live and fight another day, before swooping down on to every rooftop, ledge and chimney, every Church and Chapel, steeple, tower and weather vane, forge and factory, mill and mine, each crevice, nook and cranny, where they would hunker down and wait, ready to take wing once more, when their time had come at last.

In these final moments Agnes felt certain that Jack was about to say something. For the first time in more than two years. She watched his face contort with the pain of his wounds and the effort of trying to wrestle some long forgotten vestige of sound from his throat, which began to gargle horribly. She bent over him trying to catch whatever it was he was trying to say. Three times he tried unsuccessfully to twist his vocal chords into some form of recognisable shape and three times he failed. Finally a long, shuddering, wordless sound issued from his lips and emptied him. He was gone. What had he been trying to say to her? Not catching it, she knew, would haunt her for the rest of her life. It had sounded vaguely like a long drawn out, protracted "G-a-s-t-o-n…" – which meant nothing to her.

Heedless of the wound to his arm, Amos tore after Matthew. The pain in his heart was far greater than any sabre slash, and the sound as he roared this pain was so terrible that all who heard it would never forget it. It would continue to haunt them for years afterwards.

Among these was Pity, who heard from where she had been tending to one of the wounded, who was now being helped away. She lifted up her head, like a rat nosing the air, and scuttled off in pursuit of the sound.

Matthew's progress was perforce quite slow as he manoeuvred his way between those people who were still struggling to leave the Field. Amos caught up with him somewhere between *The Portico Library* and *The Assembly Rooms*, both of whose heavy neo-classical doors were locked and bolted. He reached up and grabbed Matthew's arm and tried to pull him from the horse. But Matthew was too quick for him and began to lash out at his attacker with his riding crop. Several of the blows cut across Amos's face but he scarcely felt them. He continued to cling on to Matthew's arm and would not let loose his grip. Matthew kicked the sides of his horse hard in an effort to quicken his pace, at the same time planting the heel of his right boot firmly into Amos's face. But still

Amos refused to yield.

Eventually he succeeded in dragging Matthew from his horse on the edge of the Daub Holes almost directly opposite the Lunatic Asylum. Inside, the inmates, already terrified and excited in equal measure by the events of the day, which they had heard from inside their cages, began to screech and howl like monkeys, leaping up at the bars of their windows to try and see what was happening just below them. Some of the older ones recalled a time when the earth had shaken before and began to sing, tapping a mechanical rhythm against the bars with metal spoons, cavorting like jerky marionettes.

"Still we sing bonny boys, bonny brave boys
Bedlam Boys are bonny
For we all go bare
And we live by the air
And we want nor drink nor money…"

But Amos and Matthew neither saw nor heard them. Instead their whole worlds diminished to only the space their two bodies took up as they rolled around and on top of each other like crazed and demented lovers, clasping, squeezing, biting, scratching, clenching, choking.

Neither man had ever fought another before but the instinct for survival overcame what reticence either might have had. Kill or be killed, that was the only choice that faced them. Attack, defend. Revoke, repel. Vengeance and vindication.

First one had the upper hand, then the other. One moment Matthew had Amos beneath him, his fingers tearing his hair, banging his head against a rock. The next Amos was on top, his hands round Matthew's throat, trying to drain the last drop of life from him, while Matthew's arms shot out in front of him, his fingers jabbing themselves unerringly into Amos's eye sockets as he tried to gouge them out. Amos brought his knee up sharply between Matthew's legs, who howled like a cat, hissing and spitting, but Amos followed up his advantage by grabbing Matthew's balls and squeezing them as hard as he could, but in so doing he loosened his grip on his throat, and Matthew seized the arm, the arm already wounded from the sabre slash, and jerked it behind his back. Amos felt something snap and he at once let go of Matthew's balls, who in the next second was up on his feet, one of which he thrust into Amos's face and tried to force him under the sucking clay of one of the Daub Holes. Amos could feel himself begin to suffocate. In a last desperate effort he wrapped his own legs around Matthew's and scissored him to the ground, allowing him to free himself from the Daub Hole's sickening grip.

The two of them now proceeded to roll over and over on top of one another, further out into the centre of the clay pits. From a distance they were now each completely indistinguishable from the other, covered in the grey lime and thick clay, which smeared their faces, clogged their mouths and noses, stuck fast their eyes and matted their hair.

Finally they rolled and fought themselves to a standstill, locked once more in their lovers' embrace. Their faces were almost touching, almost kissing. They each thrust out a hand to the mouth of the other, peeling back the lips in a hideous, deformed death mask.

Like two species of what had once been the same moth, one merging with the other.

They saw each other reflected back in identical pairs of eyes.

A sudden realisation dawned.

But it was too late.

The Daub Holes had started to suck them down. The more they fought, the more they sank. Their feet and legs disappeared first. As if the hands of another who had drowned there before were reaching up and pulling them down to join her.

Scylla and Charibdis.

Then their heads went under.

Last of all their hands, their fingers, interlaced like branches, almost delicately, waving like starfish.

Amos and Matthew.

Separated at birth, conjoined at death.

In the final moment Matthew heard, or thought he heard, a woman's voice, strung taut in the air in the heightened whinny of a horse, Mercy's voice, and she spoke to him over and over, "That's the thing about freedom, Matthew. It's like love. It must be unconditional. You can't place restrictions on it. You can't buy it, no matter how much money you have. You can't keep it in a cage or hidden behind a curtain. You've got to let it into the light, let it feel the air on its skin. You've got to trust it, Matthew, however fragile and precarious it may seem…"

While Amos saw, or thought he saw, three pieces of paper fluttering on the breeze, like birds returning after a long migration, trying to avoid the nets and traps strung between the trees that waited to entangle them. On one was written the word 'Aye', on the second the word 'Nay', while the third remained tantalizingly blank, for ever just beyond his reach.

Then both were gone.

Pity, who had witnessed all this from the other side of Lever's Row, watched in horror. The pit which had claimed them was the same one in which she and Septimus had buried their mother on the night of the Earthquake.

The Bedlam Boys broke out into a prolonged and manic shriek of applause.

*

The horse which Matthew had ridden away upon now bolted down Mosley Street, away from the Daub Holes, back towards St Peter's Field. Its nostrils flared with fear, its flanks steamed with sweat. It wickered and neighed, bucked and reared, and careered wildly from one side of the street to the other. It was terrified.

The MYC, still drunk from the wine they had imbibed all morning, the orgy of violence they had been inflicting upon anyone and everyone who happened to be in their way as they rampaged through the narrow streets surrounding the square, their brains addled by the stifling heat, spilled into Mosley Street. This particular troop, numbering no more than thirty, were led by the Bugler, Captain Meagher, who had spent the last quarter of an hour gleefully slashing and hacking off limbs. They spotted the riderless horse and saw another opportunity for sport. Some of them carried firearms – pistols and flintlocks – which they proceeded to fire at random above the horse's head. Like a chained beast with no escape it whirled around in a ring of panic. Its eyes rolled, its mouth foamed. Finally cornered, with all possible exit routes blocked, it reared up on its hind legs, then charged directly at Captain Meagher, who raised his pistol, took aim and prepared to fire.

Just at that moment, a great roar went up from an adjoining street. His attention was distracted and he wheeled away from the advancing horse just as it threatened to rear up once more and kick him from his saddle. The troops, responding to the shouts from close by, rode towards the source of the sound, Captain Meagher among them, so that the horse was suddenly alone. No longer harried by their taunts and gun shots it now turned face and proceeded to gallop back towards the Daub Holes.

Mercy, who was emerging from the Infirmary, where she had left the injured Elijah, was on the point of returning to St Peter's Field to see if there was any sign of Hélène. In the panic after Elijah had been struck, the two women had become separated. Satisfied that Elijah's wounds would soon be patched up – the sabre slash to his elbow had been partly mitigated by the thickness of his jacket, while the kick to the head had left him not as badly concussed as was first feared –

Mercy stepped onto Mosley Street right into the path of the oncoming horse.

Quickly realising that she could not escape it, she stood her ground. The horse reared up before her, its front hooves pawing the air, while it continued to shriek in terror. Still Mercy stood her ground. She did not flinch, she did not move, not a hair, not a muscle. She simply waited for the horse to calm itself. Which eventually it did. It lowered its hooves back to the ground. It ceased its frightened whinny. It shook its head from side to side, scraped the ground in front of it, snorted. Finally it slowly walked the remaining few paces towards Mercy, who held out her hand towards it. She stroked its muzzle and behind its ears. She allowed it to butt her gently, as it sought further attention and reassurance. She looked directly into its eyes, which were no longer rolling, and whispered to it softly. Then, interlacing her fingers between its mane, she mounted upon its back and began to walk back towards the near-deserted Meeting Ground.

She spotted Hélène at once. She was wandering in a daze. She had lost her shoes and she trailed her *bonnet rouge* loosely from her fingers. Her face was streaked with dirt and her blouse was spattered in other people's blood. But otherwise she seemed unhurt. Mercy raised a hand in greeting, not wanting to call too loudly, in case she spooked the horse once more. Hélène saw her approach, a silhouette against the sun, and raised her other arm to shield her eyes from the glare. When she realised it was Mercy she began to run towards her. Mercy held out a hand so that Hélène would wait. She drew alongside her and the two women looked at each other a long time in silence.

The horse waited patiently. If it possessed a memory of what had happened on this ground less than half an hour before, it showed no sense of doing so. Its heaving flanks had slowed and calmed.

Mercy stretched down her hand. Hélène reached up to take it. Mercy then pulled up her friend to join her astride the waiting horse, sitting behind her, with her arms looped around her waist. The distant shouts of those still escaping down the warren of Manchester's streets were growing fainter, their pursuers gradually letting them disperse. Mercy took one last look at the devastation surrounding her. Not so much a killing field now but a hospital. Those bodies which still lay there were being attended to by friends and strangers alike. They would survive this outrage. It may take some years yet, but their voices would be heard, their demands met.

Mercy kicked her heels into the sides of the white horse, turned it around, and together she and Hélène made their slow way back to Newton Heath, the words of their friend Elijah Dixon echoing round their head.

"Strike a match, then watch it spark and flare."

That match today had been cruelly extinguished. But they had others. One by one they would light them. Eventually one of them would take.

*

When the white horse first careered into Mosley Street, Pity retreated into a doorway and shrank into the farthest corner, while the inflamed MYC charged past her. She was reminded of her times as a child, when she would take refuge in the Hulks, where she could render herself almost invisible.

She had been only a child when she first helped Amos and Matthew into the world on the night of the Earthquake, and now she had witnessed their demise at another time when Manchester was rocked and riven. While the white horse raved and the members of the MYC taunted and terrorised it, Pity kept her eyes fixed on the particular Daub Hole where the two men had perished, where the clay and lime had sucked them down to join the bones of their mother, where now the woman whom she presumed was Amos's wife roared her pain. Pity knew she must help this poor woman somehow, but right now she was beyond reach.

Once the MYC had ridden off elsewhere in the town, Pity

crept from the doorway and tentatively approached the grieving woman. A gust of wind caused by the Cavalry stamping on the ground stirred a spiral of dust devils which rose and eddied into the air, carrying with it the remnants of one of the torn and tattered banners that had not half an hour before bedecked the Field. It danced defiantly on the breeze before coming to rest at Pity's feet. She stooped to pick it up. It was a simple piece of woven white cloth with embroidered letters stitched onto one side. Pity held it up to read, which was something she had learned to do in recent years, helped first by Jem and then by Rachel.

"*Unity is Strength.*"

Pity tiptoed towards the woman, who was now bending over the body of her son, who somehow she had dragged after her while trying to prevent her warring husband from attacking his murderous twin. She was rocking now, back and forth, endlessly keening. Pity stood behind her, looking down upon her. She placed the banner round her shoulders and held her until she grew still and quiet, then stepped away.

She thought back to that time, more than forty years before, when she had wrapped the baby Matthew in another piece of woven white cloth and left it on the doorstep of the house in Newton Lane, which she could have seen now if she had turned to look in that direction, but she didn't. She simply walked slowly away, allowing the woman her space, her quiet, her privacy, her dignity. She reached inside the tiny hessian purse she always wore around her neck, had done for as long as she could remember, and withdrew from it the two pieces of coloured glass she had found on the night of the Earthquake and had saved ever since. One red, the other green. She looked at them intently the entire length of Mosley Street as she walked back towards St Peter's Field. Each winked at her as she passed from sunlight to shadow, shadow to sunlight, the two colours indistinguishable, like the grass she stood upon, now stained with blood.

She walked through the debris of abandoned shoes and shawls, bonnets and caps, her feet kicking through the sprigs of laurel that had been worn around the heads of the marchers with such pride and hope. She stopped by the overturned, broken hustings and looked up towards the balcony from where she had seen Matthew excitedly directing the forces of the MYC. He had worn an expression upon his face that she remembered from when he was a small boy, tugging at the hand of the maid who looked after him, pointing skywards towards an untethered balloon, into whose fragile basket a cat was leaping.

She turned away and surveyed the scene of ruin before her. Once again she was reminded of her time in the Hulks, when buildings were constantly being thrown up, torn down, then yet more new ones would grow from the bones of the old. Manchester would rise again. She knew that. The ground would continue to shake and tilt, convulse and heave, and out of the chaos and tumult, a new order would flutter and evolve, a cloud of moths, which at first glance may look just like the old, but which, on closer examination, would all be subtly different, individual, unique, a mosaic, a kaleidoscope, which, although it might be shattered from time to time, could always be put back together in constantly changing configurations.

She slowly returned the two pieces of glass to the home-made hessian purse around her neck. She would keep them always. She would not forget her two lost boys.

A voice called her name and she turned. It was Jem. The look of relief on his face was palpable, the sun re-appearing after a cloud has briefly passed across it. He picked up a Cap of Liberty mounted on a broken pole and walked towards her.

She was just about to take his hand in hers when she heard a faint cry.

She stopped.
She turned.
She listened.

She heard it again, unmistakeable this time, coming from behind the fallen hustings.

She hurried round to the other side of it, and there lay the woman who had been pregnant, who Henry Hunt had helped climb onto the cart to protect her from the press of the crowds before he began his oration.

The woman had, not five minutes before, died.

But not before giving birth to her baby.

A girl, who now cried lustily, filling her lungs with Manchester air.

Pity picked her up. She held this bawling, mewling, scrunched up, angry face close to her own and smiled.

She turned to look at Jem who was regarding her curiously.

A strange palpitation began to tremble in her chest. She felt a surge of bile rise up in her throat. She opened her mouth. An odd bird-like squawk emitted from it. She tried again. This time, the unaccustomed vowels and consonants began to twist and contort in her larynx.

"I… will… not… give… you… up," she managed. "Not… this… time."

She held her high above her head and slowly circled her round. Orbiting the sun.

The baby cried louder and more determined and Pity joined in with her.

They were both of them finding their voice.

She looked around at the fallen garlands at her feet and stooped to pick one up. She turned to Jem and held out the child towards him, "Laurel," she said. "I…shall… call… her… Laurel."

11

28th August

The Manchester Observer

28th August 1819

THE FIELD OF PETERLOO

This is the Field of Peterloo

These are the poor Reformers
Who met on the state
Of affairs to debate
On the Field of Peterloo

These are the Butchers bloodthirsty and bold
Who cut, slash'd and maim'd
Young, defenceless and old
Who met on the state
Of affairs to debate
On the Field of Peterloo

This is Hurly Burly, a blustering knave
And foe to the Poor
Whom he'd gladly enslave
Who led on the Butchers bloodthirsty and bold
Who cut, slash'd and maim'd
Young, defenceless and old
Who met on the state
Of affairs to debate
On the Field of Peterloo

These are the Just-Asses gentle and mild
Who to keep the peace broke it
By lucre beguiled
And sent Hurly Burly, that blustering knave
The foe to the Poor
Whom he'd gladly enslave
To lead on the Butchers bloodthirsty and bold
Who cut, slash'd and maim'd
Young, defenceless and old
Who met on the state
Of affairs to debate

On the Field of Peterloo

*

Dr John Farrier, Senior Physician of the Manchester Infirmary, confided in his diary:

'The hospital is still over-run with the victims of what the newspapers are now referring to as 'The Peterloo Massacre'. Our nurses are rushed off their feet with treating the more than four hundred people who were injured, some slightly, but many egregiously, from the effects of having been slashed by sabers, or trampled upon by horses, or suffocated in the sheer crush of people attempting to escape, or a mixture of all of these.'

He remained especially concerned with the emotions of the inmates of the Lunatic Asylum, whose care he undertook most seriously. A week on from the events of 16th August they were still displaying signs of great distress.

'Maybe there is something in this nonsense about the Dog days after all,' he wrote.

'My patients do appear to be especially sensitive when it

comes to the anticipation of a calamitous event. They sense when a storm is imminent. They become excitable, agitated. They rattle the bars of their cells, they pace anxiously and obsessively up and down, they howl, they scream. On the morning of the massacre they began just before sunrise, just as Sirius was clearly visible above the horizon. They have barely stopped since..."

Daily he compiled a record book of those who had died, either on the day itself or subsequently in the Infirmary as a result of the injuries they incurred, as well as an ongoing record of those patients they were still continuing to treat, so that the newly set up Manchester Metropolitan Relief Committee had the relevant details for when they began to make charitable payments to some of the victims.

'John Baker, 3 Pump Street. This poor man was beaten by the Constables but his principal injury was overstrain due to carrying a certain William Taylor of Boardman's Lane off the Field, who was wounded and had lost so much blood.

Margaret Goodwin, 8 Bury Street, Salford. Trampled on by the horses. Her eyesight has been much injured. Cut at by Meagher. A widow with one child. Is much distressed.

Catherine Coleman, 40 Primrose Street. Three ribs displaced in the right side and trampled on. Totally disabled. Though condition may improve with time. Widow with three children.

Mary Jervis, 17 Longworth Street. Trampled on and crushed dreadfully. The calf of the leg has been taken off. In consequence the Doctor's Bill – unpaid – is four guineas.

William Butterworth, Stake Hill, Middleton. A dreadful sabre cut on the right arm between the shoulder, which was first false-healed for want of proper medical aid and is still in a bad state.

Billy Leigh, 23 Queen Street, off the Dean's Gate. 11 years old. Severely cut on the head. His mother is a poor woman with four children living in a cellar, whose husband no longer lives with her.

Elijah Dixon, Houldsworth Mill, Newton Heath. Sabre cut to the right elbow. Much bruising to whole body from having been trampled on. Bruising and swelling to the head from having been kicked by a horse. Should improve with time…'

In addition he kept a detailed log of all those who died – all, that is, he knew of. He wrote elsewhere that there were almost certainly others, whose details went unrecorded.

'John Ashton, Cowhill, Oldham. Sabred and trampled on by the crowd.

Thomas Buckley, Baretrees, Chadderton. Sabred and stabbed.

James Crompton, Barton. Trampled on by the Cavalry.

Mary Heyes, Rawlinson's Buildings, Oxford Road. Rode over by the Cavalry, her foot stripped of its flesh..

Sarah Jones, Silk Street. Multiple injuries sustained by being trampled upon by crowds.

Arthur O'Neill, Pigeon Street. Inwardly crushed.

Samuel Hall, Hulme. Sabred in the neck.

Martha Partington, Eccles. Thrown into a cellar and killed on the spot.

Joseph Ashworth, New Cross. Shot.

William Bradshaw, Lily Hill, Bury. Sabred and crushed.

Edmund Dawson, Saddleworth. Died of sabre wounds.

John Ashworth, Bull's Head, Manchester. Sabred and trampled. He was a Special Constable, cut down in the early panic by the MYC.

Joseph Whitworth, Hyde, near Stockport.. Killed by a musket ball to the head in Ancoats Street while fleeing the scene.

John Rhodes, Hopwood, near Middleton. Sabred on the

Field, by which he lost much blood. Also dreadfully crushed in the body. An inquest returned a verdict of death by natural causes.

William Fildes, Kennedy Street. Rode over by the Cavalary. Just two years old.

John James Lees, known as 'Jack', Elton. Sabred.'

*

Agnes stood at the back of the stone cottage in Elton that had once belonged to her Cousin Silas, to which she and Amos had first come after their midnight flight from Fairfield more than fifteen years before, and which she had known much earlier, when she and her mother had lived there, with her brother James, while her father was away, helping to build the Moravian Settlement at Fairfield.

Now she had returned. This time, alone. The loom still occupied much of the one downstairs room. She would never hear its rhythm again, its clickety-clack. Already in the past week since she had come back, she had fancied she'd heard it starting up once more, but it had only been the wind blowing through the warp and the weft. She would turn her head, and, for a moment, she would think she saw Amos still there, bent over whatever it was that he was weaving, and it was more than she could bear.

She would ask Ham or Shem to take it off her hands, to sell it. Despite the decline in the handloom weaving trade, there would still be those grateful for it. It had served them well, and Silas, and, before him, Edwin Stone, and it would see many more years yet, she was sure, even outlasting her most probably. But not in this cottage. It was someone else's turn now.

As for herself, she had no idea as yet what she would do next. But it would be something. She would not return to Fairfield. Of that she was certain. She could not leave Elton. Not when everything that mattered to her most was still here.

633

She stepped outside. A hard rain had begun to fall, slanting in from the hills to the north. In the distance all around her she could make out the forests of factory chimneys belching out their thick black smoke. A stone circle that was inexorably edging closer to her, stamping across the fields with each successive year.

Change was coming. Still not quickly enough for the likes of Ham and Shem, but it was coming nevertheless, and not just in Manchester, but across the whole country. Amos and Jack would not have perished for nothing. Of that she felt certain. It was her creed, her faith. The rain stung her arms and face. But it was a good pain, fierce and necessary, a reminder that life was hard, but that it would be endured.

She looked at the row of graves that stood in the ground at the back of the cottage. Silas, Meg, her brother James, Daisy, now her husband and son, Amos and Jack. Amos's body could not be there. That was feeding the earth back in the Daub Holes, just as Daisy's was feeding the brickfields of Colleyhurst, but she had dug a hole nevertheless, and into it she had placed the kaleidoscope he had made for her when they were both children. Each of these graves now carried a memento – James with his Roman coin, Jack with his drum, and with Amos, as well as the kaleidoscope, she had placed a ball of string.

Cat's cradle.
Cradle to Diamonds.
Diamonds to Candle.
Candle to Six-Pointed Star.
Six-Pointed Star to Bird's Nest.
Bird's Nest to Long Case Clock.
Long Case Clock to Kettle.
Kettle to Moth.
Moth to Soldier's Bed.

Agnes began to sing, the final verse to a litany that had followed her for much of her life, through all her lost years of wandering, first with her mother while her father was building the Settlement, then with Amos, when they roamed the wilderness of the brickfields, scavenged with the rats in the dark of Dimity Court, coming up for air at last back here in Elton, where now she stood, as the rain continued to fall, a lone survivor. But survive she would. She owed that much at least to the boy she pulled from the stinking waters of the River Irk, as recompense for her drowned brother, and her darling silent boy, whose eloquent drumbeats rose up from beneath her feet one last time to accompany her as she sang.

*"And though our son who marched to war
To Manchester has come back
There's nowt left for him here no more
Save the Cavalry's sabre attack
And as I sit by the fire at night
There's none to comfort me
To Heywood, Hooley, Heap and Hell
The Good Lord has delivered me…"*

*

In their lodgings on Hanging Ditch, above Philip Jacob's Tailors, Dressmakers & Milliners Shop, Pity was rocking Laurel against her shoulder. She walked towards the window at the back of their single room and looked out. Below Jem was working on a new brick sculpture. Or rather, he was amending an existing one. His first one. The handloom weaver built during a single furious, desperate, inspired night, as a homage to his father. He was fashioning a cap of liberty to place upon the figure's head as still he wove a piece of cloth that would never be finished.

Pity delicately took hold of one of Laurel's starfish fingers and pointed it towards where Jem was working through the night and smiled.

*

Benjamin and Rachel stood in the empty hallway of Matthew Oldham's now shut-up house. As executors to his estate their task was to make an inventory of all his goods and possessions and dispose of them as they saw fit. Such were the unambiguous terms of the will, which had been entrusted by Matthew to Benjamin several months before.

Matthew had no children and there were no named beneficiaries. Benjamin had already put up the Felt Factory for sale, and there had been a steady stream of enquiries, including one from a Mr Laurence Peel and another from the Brothers William and Daniel Grant. Benjamin had little doubt that it would soon be sold and that work would continue there much as it had before.

As far as the house and all its effects were concerned, that was a more delicate matter and explained why Benjamin had brought his wife Rachel with him to inspect the contents. Once it had been decided what should be done with these, then the house could be put on the open market. It would make a fine family residence, as it once had been, if not for the last twenty years.

The long-case clock still ticked in the hall, though somewhat slowly. It would not be long before it came to a complete stop. As time itself seemed to have done, or so it appeared to Rachel as she wandered through its unloved suite of rooms. She was remembering the weeks she spent here fifteen years before when she had been commissioned to paint the portrait of Mercy looking up in rapture towards the bird singing for freedom in its unlocked cage. She had not set foot inside since. Now, as she went from room to room, she conjured up those times again and wondered whatever became of Mercy. They had become close during those cooped-up, sunless sittings. When they had finished, she found she missed the intimacies of those confessional conversations, and nothing had ever quite replaced them since.

While Benjamin scrupulously listed every item, room by room, Rachel drifted more freely. She climbed the stairs to the upper storey. She opened a door at the end of the landing and stepped inside. The curtains were drawn and the room was stuffy, as if windows had not been opened for many years. It smelled of disappointment. Disappointment and longing. Longing and secrets. She flung back the curtains, almost choking with the dust as she touched them. A cloud of moths flew out of them, dispersing themselves about the room. With difficulty she forced open the sash window to let in some much needed air. She breathed deeply, then exhaled, as if letting all those secrets that had been stored here escape, along with some of the moths, which fluttered about her head.

Once she was sure she was completely free of them, she turned around. The sight which greeted her made her gasp involuntarily.

"What is it?" called Benjamin, hurrying up the stairs.

When he entered he found Rachel standing before the two recesses either side of the fireplace, her hand drawn up to her mouth.

"Look," she whispered.

It took a few seconds for Benjamin's eyes to adjust to the still sequestered light here at the back of the house. A rat poked desultorily among the cold ashes in the grate. Benjamin peered through the dust which continued to hang suspended in the air. To his left hung the portrait of Mercy. The beauty of the painting quite took his breath away. To the right was the framed white cotton shawl, which had once belonged to Lavinia. Rachel, not knowing its provenance, was studying it minutely.

She spoke in a low, hushed voice.

"It's exquisite," she said. "Look at the workmanship, the detail."

Benjamin, who was still studying the portrait his wife had painted, could only summon up a barely audible, hoarsely croaked, "Yes."

"Moths caught among the laurel."

Dragging himself reluctantly away from the painting, Benjamin joined Rachel and saw at once to what she was referring. It was indeed remarkable. He privately wondered who it might have once belonged to and how it had come to be in Matthew's possession. Clearly it must have been extremely special to him for it to have been given such pride of place.

"May we keep these?" said Rachel suddenly.

"I don't see why not," said Benjamin, looking at his wife and smiling. "The painting deserves to be looked at and admired, instead of being shut away like this."

"And the cotton cloth will make the perfect prayer shawl for Ephraim when he's older," said Rachel.

"Yes," agreed Benjamin. "You are in the right of it. As always."

She leant her head against her husband's shoulder and smiled contentedly to herself. "We could use the place-mats Pity made for your parents' anniversary again. They're a perfect match."

"Yes," said Benjamin again, marvelling at his good fortune.

"Now that we have a son," she said, "as well as two lovely daughters, I feel we are complete."

Benjamin kissed the top of her hair. "So do I," he said.

They stood for several minutes longer, lost in each other and their thoughts, the long journey across half a continent that had brought them to this place.

Eventually Benjamin turned to Rachel and said, "Let's find something to wrap these two frames in, then return home. I've listed everything else in the house. Let it be sold and dispersed and consigned to the past, along with all the other unhappy memories locked up in here."

They stepped outside and began the short walk back to their

home on Brazenose Street. The weather had broken. A light rain had started to fall. Such a welcome change after the stifling, oppressive heat of the last few weeks. Rachel turned up her face to receive the gentle drops upon her cheeks. A soft breeze lifted the veil she wore from off her hair. She let it lie around her shoulders a few moments before covering her head once more. The dog days were over. Who knew what tomorrow would bring?

Rachel linked her arm through her husband's as they strode together along Lever's Row, past the Daub Holes, down Mosley Street, as far as the now clean and swept St Peter's Field. A lamplighter was walking just ahead of them. The gas lamps hissed and sputtered into life like amber flowers, around which moths began to gather and dance. Benjamin remembered the evening when Leigh Philips looked down upon the dark and treacherous streets below the first floor window of Heywood's Bank, and the idea came to him to bequeath his money to the building of The Gas Works, which now rose up behind St Mary's Parsonage, not two hundred yards from where Benjamin and Rachel lived with their son and two daughters. Beneath one of these now lit lamps a small child was playing with a ball, throwing it against the iron post in a complicated game of catch. She was singing a rhyme to herself quietly and solemnly as she did so.

"Keep the kettle boiling
Miss a beat you're out…"

Just as they approached her, she dropped the ball, which rolled towards Rachel, stopping at her feet. Rachel bent low to pick it up. She stretched out her hand towards the little girl, who nervously walked towards her.

"Here you are," said Rachel, remembering the little French girl who gave her back her own ball when she first came to Manchester, along with Benjamin and the rest of the fourteen

639

families, more than thirty years ago. The child nervously crept towards her, carefully took the ball from Rachel's palm, holding it closely to her as if it were a bird's egg that she might break, then darted back into a still dark, unlit alley, where the gas lamps' amber flowers were yet to bloom, but which would do in time. Rachel knew this. Just as she knew the silent, solemn girl would, who she had just returned the ball to. Things would be passed on, passed down.

She rejoined her husband. Together they turned right into Mount Street, empty now save for a small column of rats, who marched determinedly ahead of them, then left into Brazenose Street, just before the Dean's Gate, where their home waited patiently for them. Someone was lighting a candle. She watched it being carried up the stairs to the room at the top of the house. Abner was encouraging his friend Ginny Robinson to take her first look through his Dollond & Aitcheson telescope, through which she would see Venus, the evening star, rising.

The future might be hidden from them, but it was not without its fragile hope.

Epilogue

1918

in which a vote is finally cast

Manchester Guardian

Monday 16th December 1918

99 YEAR OLD WOMAN VOTES IN HISTORIC COUPON ELECTION

Saturday saw the first General Election in Britain since the signing of the Armistice to end The Great War barely a month ago.

This was an historic election for many reasons, not just because it follows so swiftly on the heels of the terrible losses inflicted upon the nation by the conflict with Germany, but also because this has been the first election since the introduction of the 1918 *Representation of the People Act*, which sees the vote extended not only to all men over the age of 21 years, but to all women too who are over the age of 30 and are property owners.

Not enough, say many of those who campaigned so passionately and so long for female suffrage, women such as Millicent Fawcett, who continue to demand for nothing less than the same rights as men with all women over the age of 21 being granted the vote, regardless of their property owning status.

But a start, say those, like Manchester's own Emmeline Pankhurst, who first spearheaded the movement which came to be known as *Votes for*

Women, when she founded the *Women's Social & Political Union* right here in Manchester in 1903.

Saturday's election saw the first of those women cast their votes in a British General Election, following their decades-long campaign, a campaign consistently supported by this newspaper and championed by its editor, Mr C.P. Scott.

Among those casting their vote was 99-year-old Miss Laurel Stone.

Miss Stone was born on 16th August 1819, on the day of the infamous Peterloo Massacre itself, an event many claim to have set this country on a steady and continuous path towards Reform, first by providing the people of Manchester with representation at Westminster, next by extending the franchise to include a wider cross-section of the male populace, and now resulting in the current situation which allows Miss Stone to vote herself for the very first time.

The events of Peterloo continue to divide opinion today. The crowds who gathered there that fateful day did so in the belief that their needs could be better served if there was a Member of Parliament for Manchester, who could speak for them in the House of Commons. The Civic Authorities at the time feared the actions of a 'mob', seeing echoes in their demands of those who had stormed the Bastille in Paris and overthrown the French monarchy, and so sent in the troops to disperse them with disastrous effects. The number of casualties suffered that day is still disputed and the true figure may never be known. But it is now generally accepted that at least 17 people were killed and more than 400 people injured, from a crowd the size of which varies in estimates between 30,000 and 150,000 – the figure claimed by this newspaper's predecessor, *The Manchester Observer*.

Much blame at the time was attached to Major-General Sir John Byng, a veteran of Waterloo, who was conspicuously absent on that day. Some even said he was more interested in watching his prize filly race in the Ebor Handicap in York than attend a political rally in Manchester. But Sir John always pointed out that as General in charge of the Northern Division of the entire British Army, he was needed in many places at once. He stood ready to come to the aid of the Magistrates in Manchester, he maintained, but was not invited. We may never be able satisfactorily to clarify these opposing accounts but what cannot be disputed is that, when the Reform Bill was finally passed by Parliament in 1832, through which Manchester was finally able to acquire her first MP, of all the former military commanders who were then sitting in the House of Commons, only Sir John voted in favour.

There are scholars today, however, who continue to cast doubt upon the importance of Peterloo in our nation's march towards greater democratic representation, stating that, contrary to popular myth, the events of 16th August 1819 had no wider historical significance and did not change Britain beyond feeding a tendentious account of left-wing historians of Britain's tradition of successful radical protest. Such a view, they argue, is to throw together wholly disconnected movements – such as Peterloo – to form a misleading narrative that takes a single isolated outrage out of context and blows it out of all proportion.

Here at this newspaper we state here and now, for the record, that we dismiss this view entirely. Moreover we would argue that Manchester has always been at the vanguard of important political, social and economic reform, and that, without the terrible events of what was undoubtedly an 'outrage', though one which was in no way 'isolated', Miss Laurel Stone would not have been eligible to take part in the Election two days ago when just 99 years young.

Thousands of cheering crowds lined the streets of Manchester leading to the Town Hall in Albert Square, where Miss Stone, along with the rest of the first-time women voters resident in Manchester converged to cast their vote – barely a stone's throw from St Peter's Square, just around the corner, scene of the notorious massacre, and where Miss Stone herself was born.

Among the dignitaries waiting to greet Miss Stone as she arrived to cast her vote was the Manchester suffragist Hannah Mitchell, ever a hugely popular figure here, who broke away from Mrs Pankhurst's WSPU when she refused to support the latter's White Feather Movement during The Great War, preferring instead to continue her efforts to work towards a lasting peace as a Co-Founder of *The Women's International League*. Her arrival on the steps of the Town Hall provided cause for an even louder cheer from the waiting crowds.

Standing on the steps beside Mrs Mitchell was her protégée, Miss Esther Blundell, a miner's daughter from Gorton, who is not yet able to cast a vote herself, being neither 30 years old, nor a property owner.

When asked for her views by this newspaper, Miss Blundell remarked:

"I hope the Government will take heart from the success of this election, in the way that those women who are eligible to vote have exercised their right to do so peacefully and enthusiastically, and that they will now extend the franchise to include all of us, affording us the same rights as our fathers and husbands, brothers and sons, regardless of the eventual outcome of this election."

That result will not be known until the turn of the year, for votes will not begin to be counted until after 28th December, after the tallies cast by our soldiers and officers still serving overseas have been given time to arrive. Whoever emerges victorious from this historic 'Khaki' Election, as some have called it, or the 'Coupon' Election, as it has been nicknamed by others, following the decision by David Lloyd-George, the current Prime Minister, to send out his letters of endorsement to those candidates who had supported the Coalition during the time of War – an opportunist ploy which this newspaper condemns, but which, it fears, will be a successful one.

But let us not end this report of such an historic and joyous occasion on a sour or divisive note. Let us leave instead the last word to the oldest female voter in Britain, Miss Laurel Stone.

"I was given my name – Laurel – by my adoptive mother, the woman who found me just after I had been born, in the aftermath of Peterloo. I was lying among the garlands of laurel leaves that had been worn by the people attending the meeting that day to request a voice in Parliament, many of whom died. Including my birth mother. Thanks to the courage of women like both my mothers, who were there that day and who were not afraid to speak out, that voice is being heard today. When I cast my vote in a few minutes time, I'll be doing so, not only for me, but for them, and for everyone before me, as well as all of those who will come after me."

Laurel continues in:
Volume 3: Victrix
(Ornaments of Grace, Book 8)

Dramatis Personae

CAPITALS = Main Characters; **Bold** = Significant Characters;
Plain = Characters (who appear once or twice only)

Joseph Hanson, former Lt Colonel, Salford & Stockport Rifles
Joe Nadin, Deputy Constable of Manchester
MATTHEW OLDHAM, a Magistrate
Mr William Starkie, former Boroughreeve
AMOS LEES, an itinerant labourer
AGNES LEES, Amos's wife
Cousin Silas, a handloom weaver
Cousin Meg, Silas's wife
Ham, Silas's son
Shem, Ham's younger brother
John James 'JACK' LEES, Amos & Agnes's son
Daisy Lees, Jack's sister
John Lees, Agnes's father
Caroline Lees, John's wife
Adam, a miner, later a spinner, Amos's friend
Samuel Bamford, a Reformer
Dr Healey, a Reformer
John Knight, a Reformer
William Fitton, a Reformer
Joseph Johnson, Editor of The Manchester Observer
Mr Hanson Senior, Lt. Col Hanson's father
Lt, later Major Trafford, 4th Dragoon Guards
Charging Cavalry Officer
Sir Ashton Lever, a collector
Lord Grey de Wilton, Heaton House
Sir John Edensor Heathcote, Earl of Stafford
Mr Matthew Fletcher, investor
John Fletcher, Matthew's son
Mr Peter Drinkwater, mill owner
John Drinkwater, Peter's son

Mr Thomas Hatfield, of Bolton
Mr Walter Hatfield, Thomas's brother
Mr Nathaniel Heywood, cousin of the Hatfields
Mr Thomas Butterworth Bayley, of Salford
Mr Robert Andrews, of Rivington
Mr Marsden McNiven, of Pilkington
Mr Wareing, of Manchester
Rev Dauntsey, of Richmond
Mr Justice Goose, King's Bench
Mr Cockell, Attorney-General, Lancaster
Mr Park, Common Pleas
Mr Topping, Counsel for the Crown
Mr Wardley, King's Bench
Mr Yeats, Counsel for the Crown
Mr Litchfield, Solicitor to the Treasury
Mr Raine, Counsel for Defence
Mr Williams, Deputy Counsel
Mr Littledale, Deputy Counsel
Mr Ambrose, Solicitor for Mr Raine
William Fitzherbert Brockholes, Foreman of Jury
Mr Richardson, Reader of Indictment
Corporal Wrighton, 4th Dragoon Guards
Constable Bickerson, a witness
Clerk of the Court
Thomas Appleby, calico printer
John Carey, schoolmaster
William Gaskill, book keeper
James Moss, Special Constable
John Sneddon, groom
George Bluntson, Excise Officer
Edward Shepley, clock & watch maker
C.B. Stennett, property holder
John Carr, tax collector
Charles Satterthwaite, visiting businessman
Joseph Oliver, commercial traveller
Robert Norris, Manchester resident
John Speerit, market porter

James Brocklehurst, cotton spinner
John Brierley, upholsterer
Alexander Patterson, publican
Mrs Hanson, Lt. Col Hanson's mother
Carlton Whiteley, actor-manager
Mr Macready, Theatre Royale
Miss Appleby, an actress
Frances 'Fanny' Cox, later Robinson
LAVINIA ROBINSON, Fanny's daughter
Harriet, a pupil of Lavinia's
Zachary Robinson, Lavinia's father
Susannah Bentley, Lavinia's married sister
Billy Robinson, a postman, Lavinia's brother
Lemuel Robinson, Billy's younger brother
Richard & Paul Robinson, twins
Ginny Robinson, Lavinia's younger sister
Jemma Robinson, youngest of the siblings
Robin Holroyd, Lavinia's fiancé, an accoucheur
MERCY CHANT, companion to Hélène Robidoux
James Bentley, Susannah's husband
Charles, a waiter at The White Bear
Ragamuffin, a note-deliverer
ABNER HALSINGER, Benjamin's brother, a dreamer
PITY, a seamstress, Jem's 'wife'
Jem Stone, a mason
Percy Goodier, a miller
Nathaniel Milne, coroner
Mr Ainsworth, a surgeon
Mr Jupp, undertaker
Mr Gittings, Mr Jupp's partner
Rev John Clowes, Vicar of St John's
Young Woman at Theatre Royale
Brother Pohlman, Minister at Fairfield
John Dalton, a scientist
Capt Josiah Blacker, 30th Regiment of Foot
Thomas Johnston, Reformer
John Drummond, Reformer

Samuel Baguley, Reformer
Lord Sidmouth, Home Secretary
Rev Joseph Harrison, Stockport contingent
Jemima 'Mima' Bamford, Samuel's wife
Major-General Sir John Byng, 3rd Hanoverian Brigade, later
Commander of Northern Forces of British Army
Sir Hugh Hornby-Birley, former Boroughreeve, later C/O of
MYC
Minister's Wife, Congleton
Gaston, French drummer boy
French Girl in Barn
English Corporal after Waterloo
Sir Edward Clayton, Boroughreeve 1819
Henry Hunt, an Orator
Ellen Schofield, landlady of The Spread Eagle Inn
Rev William Hay, Magistrate
Mr James Norris, Magistrate
Rev Charles Wickstead Ethelston, Magistrate
Simon Hetherington, Clerk to the Court Leet
Lt Col Guy L'Estrange, Byng's Deputy, 15th Hussars
John Shawcross, a spy
James Murray, a spy
Mr Cooke, an actor
Mr Harvey, an actor
Mr Browne, an actor
Edward Holme, President Manchester Lit & Phil
Mrs Philips, John's widow, Leigh's mother
Lady Ashton, Sir Ashton Lever's widow
Giles, Edward Holme's nephew
Benjamin Halsinger, Heywood's Bank
Rachel Halsinger, Benjamin's wife
Reuben Halsinger, Benjamin's father
Leah Halsinger, Benjamin's father
Dr John Ferriar, Manchester Infirmary
Rev Edmund Stanley, Alderley Edge
Elijah Dixon, a blanketeer
Hélène Robidoux, a Huguenot

Thomas Horrall, Assistant Surveyor of Paving of the Town
Subaltern Douglas Rich, 31st Foot
Count Rothschild
Rachelle, a French girl
Jeremiah Smith, Headmaster Manchester Grammar School
John Tyas, The Times
Capt Meagher, a bugler with the MYC
Lauren Stone, a baby, later a voter
Little girl with ball
Hannah Mitchell, a suffragist
Esther Blundell, a miner's daughter

The following are mentioned by name:

[Manchester Spinners & Weavers, St George's Fields]
[Residents, Angel Meadow]
[Shopkeepers, St George's Lane]
[4th Dragoon Guards]
[Dwellers in Dimity Court]
[Ham's wife]
[Ham's two children]
[Shem's wife]
[Mill Workers, Ramsbottom]
[Edwin Stone, handloom weaver]
[Henry Stone, Edwin's son]
[Ulysses]
[Penelope]
[Circe]
[Calypso]
[Grave robbers]
[Miners at Charlotte seam]
[Scylla]
[Charibdis]
[Cronos]
[Drinkers at The Crown & Kettle]
[King George III]
[Queen Charlotte]
[Moravians at Fairfield]
[Children in House of Correction]

[The Firebrands, extreme radicals]
[Napoleon Bonaparte]
[William Pitt, the Younger]
[John Cartwright, Reformer]
[John Thacker Saxton, Reformer]
[Laurence Peel, factory owner]
[Nathaniel Philips, factory owner]
[Jonathan Haworth, factory owner]]
[William Yates, publican then factory owner]
[William & Daniel Grant, factory owners]
[Andrew Oldham, Matthew's late father]
[Special Constables, St George's Field]
[Cavalry Officers, St George's Field]
[John Raffald, former publican of The Bull's Head]
[Capswick Shawe, current landlord of The Bull's Head]
[James Brindley, canal engineer]
[Lord Francis Egerton, 3rd Earl of Bridgewater]
[Robert Peel, mill owner & politician]
[Hugh Henshall, engineer]
[Skipper of coal barge on River Irwell]
[Barge passengers]
[Crew of the Sarah Lansdale, an ice breaker]
[James Lees, Agnes's dead brother]
[Soldiers escorting Joseph Hanson]
[Messrs Sergeant & Milne, assistants to Mr Cockell]
[John Harrison, juror]
[Edmund Leigh, juror]
[Robert Lightollers, juror]
[James Orrell, juror]
[John Hodson, juror]
[John Jackson, juror]
[John Adams, juror]
[George Grundy, juror]
[John Whittle. Juror]
[William Tarbuck, juror]
[Joseph Armstrong, juror]
[Magistrates at St George's Fields]
[Members of Public Gallery, Lancaster Assizes]
[Soldiers at Castlesteads]
[Constable, Lancaster Assizes]
[Traders, shopkeepers, Castle Hill]

[Lord Mansfield, former Solicitor General]
[Sir John Scott, Lord High Chancellor]
[Anonymous Baronet]
[Mr Francis Astley, ex-Military Officer, Dukinfield]*
[Mr William Nabb, gentleman]*
[Mr Joseph Kershaw, gentleman]*
[Mr William Shaw, gentleman]*
[Mr John Whitehead, calico dyer]*
[Mr Edward Rushton, wine merchant]*
[Mr Gavin Hamilton, surgeon]*
[Mr Richard Hancock, cotton merchant]*
[Mr Thomas Millington, cotton merchant]*
[Mr William Cowdrey, printer]*
[* all presenters of affidavits in support of Joseph Harrison]
[Supporters, well-wishers of Joseph Hanson outside New Bailey Prison]
[William Shakespeare]
[Thespis]
[Schoolchildren from Miss Robinson's Academy]
[Charles Wesley]
[Edward Byrom, surveyor]
[Sarah Willatt, former postmistress]
[Eli Cross, a felon]
[Lady Visitors from Penal Reform Society]
[William Hogarth]
[The Graham Children, daughters of the Apothecary to George II]
[John Hoppner, artist]
[The Sackville Children, daughters of 3rd Duke of Dorset]
[Sarah Moulton, aka 'Pinkie', 11 yrs old]
[Smokey, a cat]
[James Sadler, balloonist]
[Crowds at Whitsuntide Fair, Acresfield]
[Dr Charles White, founder of Manchester Infirmary]
[Maypole Dancers]
[Still-born baby, Dimity Court]
[Merchants outside The Exchange]
[Robin Hood]
[Maid Marion]
[Robin Goodfellow]
[Woman giving birth in Angel Meadow]
[Mrs Inchbald, a playwright]

[Mr Davis, an actor]
[Attenders at The Assembly Rooms]
[Estate Workers, Worsley]
[Bird Trappers]
[Diners, The White Bear]
Manager, The White Bear]
[Diana, a huntress]
[Daphne, pursued by Apollo]
[Pedestrians, New Bailey Bridge]
[Philip Jacob, tailor]
[Dwellers in the Hulks]
[The Old Retainer]
[The Great Usurper]
[Mrs Jacob, Philip's wife]
[Chimney sweep]
[Special Constables, searching for missing persons]
[Thomas Hardman, Boroughreeve 1813]
[Roger Touchin, Chief Constable]
[Attenders at Inquest, The Star Inn]
[Mourners, St John's Church]
[Stone throwers, Bridge Street]
[Board of Trustees, Manchester Infirmary]
[Special Constable, Court Leet]
[Audience at Theatre Royale for Miss Appleby]
[Young Blade, who assists Carlton]
[Brother Christian Gottfried Clemens, former Fairfield Minister]
[Brother John Swertner, former Fairfield Minister]
[Joost Kam, Moravian missionary to Spice Islands]
[Joseph Kam, Joost's father, Dutch wigmaker]
[William Cobbett, writer]
[Potter's Parlour Planners, reformers]
[Moravian Settlers in Barbados & Russia]
[Elders at Fairfield]
[Manchester Anti-Slavery Committee]
[Galileo Galilei]
[Christian Horrebow, Danish astronomer]
[Drummer Boy, Castlesteads Fort]
[Henry Blacker, a giant]
[Toby the Sapient Pig]
[Duke of Cumberland]
[Thomas Spence, a Radical]

[Manchester Female Reformers]
[Members of Union Societies, Hampden Clubs]
[Alice Kitchen, female reformer]
[Susanna Saxton, female reformer]
[Sara Fitton, female reformer]
[Attenders at rally on Red Lumb]
[Soldiers of 30th Regiment of Foot]
[Duke of Wellington]
[Marshall Ney]
[General Blücher]
[King Edward III]
[Queen Philippa of Hainault]
[Flemish Weavers]
[Blanketeers]
[Crowds at St Peter's Field 1817]
[Soldiers at Hougoumont]
[Bonnie Prince Charlie]
[Jacobite Army]
[Prince Regent]
[John Bradshaw, Attorney-General during Civil War]
[King Charles I]
[Richard Perceval, a Puritan weaver]
[Thomas Tyldesley, a Royalist]
[Oliver Cromwell]
[King Charles II]
[Men & Women at Knyperley, Black Bull, Chatterley Whitfield pits]
[Edward the Confessor]
[Carter in Leek]
[Danish Army, Bosley Chand]
[Four Horsemen of the Apocalypse]
[St Pancras]
[Diocletian]
[French prisoners-of-war]
[Count of Erlon]
[French Naval Ratings]
[Powder Monkeys]
[English Soldiers post-Waterloo]
[Outriders under Major Byng]
[Johannes Kemp, a Flemish weaver]
[Kemp's family]
[Count Louis of Nevers]

[Jean Froissart, Queen Philippa's Chronicler]
[Sir Robert Byng, John's father, Governor of Barbados]
[Horse traders at Macclesfield Fair]
[Crowds at quayside in Ghent]
[Sailors on board HMS Daphne]
[Fen dwellers]
[Vision of Maying, Ashbourne]
[Jan van Brugge, a weaver]
[Ragged children]
[Queen's attendants]
[Little girl making a face]
[Flemish girl with clogs]
[Brugge's apprentice]
[Young maiden with kitten]
[Three archers]
[7th Hussars, Manchester]
[Julius Caesar]
[Joe Hindley, Nadin's assistant]
[Sir Oswald Mosley, Lord of Manor of Manchester]
[Bishop John Paley, Panglossian apologist]
[Henry Hunt's father]
[Lord Bruce, Colonel Wiltshire Yeomanry]
[People leaving flowers at grave]
[Crowds at London Rd Mail Coach]
[Crowds outside New Bailey Prison]
[Mr Punch]
[Puppet Constable]
[Hell-fire preacher by prison]
[Well wishers of Hunt at Smedley Cottage]
[Theatregoers for Measure for Measure]
[Crowds lining Mosley Street]
[Drinkers in The Spread Eagle]
Drillers on White Moss, Harpurhey]
[La Funambola]
[Ephraim, Benjamin & Rachel's baby son]
[Stockport contingent, St Peter's Field
[Oldham contingent, St Peter's Field]
[Middleton contingent, St Peter's Field]
[Ashton contingent, St Peter's Field]
[Lancashire contingent, St Peter's Field]
[Local crowds on St Peter's Field]

[Major Dyneley, Royal Horse Artillery]
[Cheshire Regiment, Sale Moor]
[Ballad Singer, St Peter's Field]
[William of Ockam]
[Thomas Aquinas]
[Schoolboys, Manchester Grammar School]
[Virgil]
[Charles Maurice de Talleyrand-Perigord, Machiavellian ambassador]
[Monsieur Robidoux, Hélène's husband]
[Catherine Worlée, Talleyrand's mistress, later wife]
[King Louis XVIII]
[Jacques, Robidoux's groom]
[Guests at Culcheth Hall]
[George Gordon, Lord Byron]
[Marsha Dyson, later wife to Elijah Dixon]
[Thomas Paine]
[Mr Dixon, Elijah's father]
[Massed Bands, St Peter's Field]
[George Frederick Handel]
[Manchester Yeomanry Cavalry, aka MYC]
[Lunatics at the Daub Holes]
[White horse on Mosley Street]
[John Baker, wounded at Peterloo]
Margaret Goodwin, wounded at Peterloo]
[Catherine Coleman, wounded at Peterloo]
[Mary Jervis, wounded at Peterloo]
[William Butterworth, wounded at Peterloo]
[Billy Leigh, wounded at Peterloo]
[John Ashton, died at Peterloo]
[Thomas Buckley, died at Peterloo]
[James Compton, died at Peterloo]
[Mary Heys, died at Peterloo]
[Sarah Jones, died at Peterloo]
[Arthur O'Neill, died at Peterloo]
[Martha Partington, died at Peterloo]
[Joseph Ashworth, died at Peterloo]
[William Bradshaw, died at Peterloo]
[Edmund Dawson, died at Peterloo]
[Thomas Ashworth, died at Peterloo]
[William Fildes, died at Peterloo, 2 yrs old]
[Lamplighter]

[Column of rats]
[Women Voters, 1918]
[Millicent Fawcett, suffragist]
[Emmeline Pankhurst, founder of WSPU]
[C.P. Scott, Editor of The Manchester Guardian]
[Former Military Commanders, later MPs, 1832]
[Cheering crowds, Albert Square 1918]
[Women's International League]
[Overseas Soldiers 1918]
[David Lloyd George, Prime Minister 1918]
[Election candidates, former supporters of Wartime Coalition]

Acknowledgements
(for *Ornaments of Grace* as a whole)

Writing is usually considered to be a solitary practice, but I have always found the act of creativity to be a collaborative one, and that has again been true for me in putting together the sequence of novels which comprise *Ornaments of Grace*. I have been fortunate to have been supported by so many people along the way, and I would like to take this opportunity of thanking them all, with apologies for any I may have unwittingly omitted.

First of all I would like to thank Ian Hopkinson, Larysa Bolton, Tony Lees and other staff members of Manchester's Central Reference Library, who could not have been more helpful and encouraging. That is where the original spark for the novels was lit and it has been such a treasure trove of fascinating information ever since. I would like to thank Jane Parry, the Neighbourhood Engagement & Delivery Officer for the Archives & Local History Dept of Manchester Library Services for her support in enabling me to use individual reproductions of the remarkable Manchester Murals by Ford Madox Brown, which can be viewed in the Great Hall of Manchester Town Hall. They are exceptional images and I recommend you going to see them if you are ever in the vicinity. I would also like to thank the staff of other libraries and museums in Manchester, namely the John Rylands Library, Manchester University Library, the Manchester Museum, the People's History Museum and also Salford's Working Class Movement Library, where Lynette Cawthra was especially helpful, as was Aude Nguyen Duc at The Manchester Literary & Philosophical Society, the much-loved Lit& Phil, the first and oldest such society anywhere in the world, 238 years young and still going strong.

In addition to these wonderful institutions, I have many individuals to thank also. Barbara Derbyshire from the Moravian Settlement in Fairfield has been particularly patient and generous with her time in telling me so much of the community's inspiring history. No less inspiring has been Lauren Murphy, founder of the Bradford Pit Project, which is a most moving collection of anecdotes, memories, reminiscences, artefacts and original art works dedicated to the lives of people connected with Bradford Colliery. You can find out more about their work at: www.bradfordpit.com. Martin Gittins freely shared some of his encyclopaedic knowledge of the part the River Irwell has played in Manchester's story, for which I have been especially grateful.

I should also like to thank John and Anne Horne for insights into historical medical practice; their daughter, Ella, for inducting me into the mysteries of chemical titration, which, if I have subsequently got it wrong, is my fault not hers; Tony Smith for his deep first hand understanding of spinning and weaving; Sarah Lawrie for inducting me so enthusiastically into the Manchester music scene of the 1980s, which happened just after I left the city so I missed it; Sylvia Tiffin for her previous research into Manchester's lost theatres, and Brian Hesketh for his specialist knowledge in a range of such diverse topics as hot air balloons, how to make a crystal radio set, old maps, the intricacies of a police constable's notebook and preparing reports for a coroner's inquest.

Throughout this intensive period of writing and research, I have been greatly buoyed up by the keen support and interest of many friends, most notably Theresa Beattie, Laïla Diallo, Viv Gordon, Phil King, Rowena Price, Gavin Stride, Chris Waters, and Irene Willis. Thank you to you all. In addition, Sue & Rob Yockney have been extraordinarily helpful in more ways than I can mention. Their advice on so many matters, both artistic and practical, has been beyond measure.

A number of individuals have very kindly – and bravely – offered to read early drafts of the novels: Bill Bailey, Rachel Burn, Lucy Cash, Chris & Julie Phillips. Their responses have been positive, constructive, illuminating and encouraging, particularly when highlighting those passages which needed closer attention from me, which I have tried my best to address. Thank you.

I would also like to pay a special tribute to my friend Andrew Pastor, who has endured months and months of fortnightly coffee sessions during which he has listened so keenly and with such forbearance to the various difficulties I may have been experiencing at the time. He invariably came up with the perfect comment or idea, which then enabled me to see more clearly a way out of whatever tangle I happened to have found myself in. He also suggested several avenues of further research I might undertake to navigate towards the next bend in one of the three rivers, all of which have been just what were needed. These books could not have finally seen the light of day without his irreplaceable input.

Finally I would like to thank my wife, Amanda, for her endless patience, encouragement and love. These books are dedicated to her and to our son, Tim.

Biography

Chris grew up in Manchester and currently lives in West Dorset, after brief periods in Nottinghamshire, Devon and Brighton. Over the years he has managed to reinvent himself several times – from florist's delivery van driver to Punch & Judy man, drama teacher, theatre director, community arts co-ordinator, creative producer, to his recent role as writer and dramaturg for choreographers and dance companies.

Between 2003 and 2009 Chris was Director of Dance and Theatre for *Take Art*, the arts development agency for Somerset, and between 2009 and 2013 he enjoyed two stints as Creative Producer with South East Dance leading on their Associate Artists programme, followed by a year similarly supporting South Asian dance artists for *Akademi* in London. From 2011 to 2017 he was Creative Producer for the Bonnie Bird Choreography Fund.

Chris has worked for many years as a writer and theatre director, most notably with New Perspectives in Nottinghamshire and Farnham Maltings in Surrey under the artistic direction of Gavin Stride, with whom Chris has been a frequent collaborator.

Directing credits include: three Community Plays for the Colway Theatre Trust – *The Western Women* (co-director with Ann Jellicoe), *Crackling Angels* (co-director with Jon Oram), and *The King's Shilling*; for New Perspectives – *It's A Wonderful Life* (co-director with Gavin Stride), *The Railway Children* (both adapted by Mary Elliott Nelson); for Farnham Maltings – *The Titfield Thunderbolt, Miracle on 34th Street* and *How To Build A Rocket* (all co-directed with Gavin Stride); for Oxfordshire Touring Theatre Company – *Bowled A Googly* by Kevin Dyer; for Flax 303 – *The Rain Has Voices* by Shiona Morton, and for Strike A Light *I Am Joan* and *Prescribed*, both written by Viv Gordon and co-directed with Tom Roden, and *The Book of Jo* as dramaturg.

Theatre writing credits include: *Firestarter, Trying To Get Back Home, Heroes* – a trilogy of plays for young people in partnership with Nottinghamshire & Northamptonshire Fire Services; *You Are Harry Kipper & I Claim My Five Pounds, It's Not Just The Jewels, Bogus* and *One of Us* (the last co-written with Gavin Stride) all for New Perspectives; *The Birdman* for Blunderbus; for Farnham Maltings *How To Build A Rocket* (as assistant to Gavin Stride), and *Time to Remember* (an outdoor commemoration of the centenary of the first ever Two Minutes Silence); *When King Gogo Met The Chameleon* and *Africarmen* for Tavaziva Dance, and most recently *All the Ghosts Walk with Us* (conceived and performed with Laïla Diallo and Phil King) for ICIA, Bath University and Bristol Old Vic Ferment Festival, (2016-17); *Posting to Iraq* (performed by Sarah Lawrie with music by Tom Johnson for the inaugural Women & War Festival in London 2016), and *Tree House* (with music by Sarah Moody, which toured southern England in autumn 2016). In 2018 Chris was commissioned to write the text for *In Our Time*, a film to celebrate the 40th Anniversary of the opening of The Brewhouse Theatre in Taunton, Somerset.

Between 2016 and 2019 Chris collaborated with fellow poet Chris Waters and Jazz saxophonist Rob Yockney to develop two touring programmes of poetry, music, photography and film: *Home Movies* and *Que Pasa?*

Chris regularly works with choreographers and dance artists, offering dramaturgical support and business advice. These have included among others: Alex Whitley, All Play, Ankur Bahl, Antonia Grove, Anusha Subramanyam, Archana Ballal, Ballet Boyz, Ben Duke, Ben Wright, Charlie Morrissey,

Crystal Zillwood, Darkin Ensemble, Divya Kasturi, Dog Kennel Hill, f.a.b. the detonators, Fionn Barr Factory, Heather Walrond, Hetain Patel, Influx, Jane Mason, Joan Clevillé, Kali Chandrasegaram, Kamala Devam, Karla Shacklock, Khavita Kaur, Laïla Diallo, Lîla Dance, Lisa May Thomas, Liz Lea, Lost Dog, Lucy Cash, Luke Brown, Marisa Zanotti, Mark Bruce, Mean Feet Dance, Nicola Conibère, Niki McCretton, Nilima Devi, Pretty Good Girl, Probe, Rachael Mossom, Richard Chappell, Rosemary Lee, Sadhana Dance, Seeta Patel, Shane Shambhu, Shobana Jeyasingh, Showmi Das, State of Emergency, Stop Gap, Subathra Subramaniam, Tavaziva Dance, Tom Sapsford, Theo Clinkard, Urja Desai Thakore, Vidya Thirunarayan, Viv Gordon, Yael Flexer, Yorke Dance Project (including the Cohan Collective) and Zoielogic.

Chris is married to Amanda Fogg, a former dance practitioner working principally with people with Parkinson's.

Printed in Poland
by Amazon Fulfillment
Poland Sp. z o.o., Wrocław

61090357R00392